RUBĨCON

*The Love Story of
Emily Dickinson's Brother,
Austin, and Mabel Todd,
the Woman Who Saved
Emily's Poetry*

A NOVEL BY

CANDACE
RIDINGTON

ARLINGTON PRESS

Birmingham, Alabama

PUBLISHED BY ARLINGTON PRESS
2225 Arlington Avenue, Suite A, Birmingham, Alabama
e-mail address: jxcunnif@ix.netcom.com

FIRST EDITION

DESIGNED BY ROBIN MCDONALD

LIBRARY OF CONGRESS CATALOGING-IN-PUBLICATION DATA

Ridington, Candace, 1941-
    Rubicon : the love story of Emily Dickinson's brother, Austin, and
Mabel Todd, the woman who saved Emily's poetry : a novel / by
Candace Ridington, — 1st ed.
        p.   cm.
    Includes bibliographical references.
    ISBN 0-9656773-1-1
    1. Dickinson, Austin, d. 1895—Fiction. 2. Todd, Mabel Loomis,
1856-1932—Fiction. 3. Dickinson, Emily, 1830-1886—Fiction.
I. Title.
PS3568.I35845R83 1997   97-6883
813'.54—dc21   CIP

Printed in the United States of America

Acknowledgments

I DEDICATE THIS BOOK TO THE MEMORY OF MY parents, Bill and Edie Ridington, who gave me my love of reading and writing, a gift which has given me joy all my life.

I also thank Bobby Frese for encouraging me and for directing me to June Cunniff, my agent and consultant, who has supported me without hesitation from the very start in my quest to be published. For this support, I will always be grateful.

My husband, Jack Lebowitz, has also taken such an active interest in *Rubicon* that a friend once remarked it was in a sense his book, too. Indeed, he bailed me out during the dark hours of computer failure and the hasty trips to Kinko's, and listened to my litany of woes during the long process of bringing this book to fruition.

In addition, I thank my book designer, Robin McDonald, and those who read the manuscript in its earliest stages: my siblings, Robin Ridington (and his wife Jillian), Jean Goldfine, and Joy Boyce; and Debbie Burrell, Eleanor Heginbotham, and Annie McDade. I also thank the New Jersey Fairview Lake friends who read the book in a more finished stage, along with members of the recorder-playing group and the Unitarian Church of Birmingham.

In a way, I owe the existence of this book to Polly Longsworth, whose own non-fiction book about the lovers, *Austin and Mabel*, first fired my imagination. Without Polly's book, I couldn't have written *Rubicon*. In addition, Polly read my manuscript at the eleventh hour and made invaluable corrections and suggestions. Thus, I thank her unequivocally for her scholarship, her hard work and her kindness. I recommend her book to my readers, who will find it in my List of Works Consulted.

Preface

WHEN I READ POLLY LONGSWORTH'S BOOK, *Austin and Mabel: The Amherst Affair and the Love Letters of Austin Dickinson and Mabel Loomis Todd*, I was captivated immediately by the power of this unwavering love affair and the way it defied convention. The mutual attraction of Austin Dickinson and Mabel Todd was fascinating enough by itself, set in quiet and conservative Amherst in the 1880's. But knowing that Emily Dickinson, brilliant and reclusive poet, knew about the affair, made me think about her in a new light, see her from a different angle. Understanding the need for love both in herself and others, she condoned the affair, despite the pain and dissension it brought to her family.

I also realized that if Mabel Todd had not fallen in love with Austin, she would not have spent tedious hours upon hours preparing Emily's poems for publication at Lavinia Dickinson's frantic request. Thanks to Mabel Todd, we now have as many of the poems we do and in the form we do.

Neither Emily nor her sister Lavinia ever married, and thus left no heirs. Although Austin and Susan Dickinson had children, only one survived to marry, and she, Martha Dickinson, left no heirs. Since Mabel's daughter, Millicent, had no children either, no one was left to tell the story of this extraordinary love. Austin and Mabel often wished someone would tell their story—explain its necessity, its truth, its pain. This is what I have tried to do in *Rubicon*.

NOTE—For convenience I have used the Thomas H. Johnson edition of Dickinson's poetry rather than the manuscript versions which Mabel Todd would have seen.

A Great Hope Fell

Less than a year after Austin Dickinson's death, everyone in Amherst, Massachusetts, knew that Lavinia Dickinson, Emily Dickinson's sister, had filed a Complaint that May of 1896 against Mabel Todd and her husband David Todd concerning the strip of meadow land, claiming Mabel had tricked her into signing over the deed. Everyone also knew the Todds had countersued, which surprised no one. But most villagers knew well that far more lay at issue than the ownership of a mere strip of meadow land fifty-three feet wide which had belonged to Austin Dickinson, and they burned with pent up curiosity, indignation, and downright glee to see whose suit would win. They took ferocious sides, too, though the suit didn't come to trial until March 1st, 1898, and they would hold those ferocious sides generations later.

"Susan Dickinson didn't even go to the court house," some people said. "Yet she's behind it all, you can be sure. What a perfect way for her to get back at Mabel Todd. Poor old Lavinia—Susan must have put her up to it, scared her into taking back her promise to Austin, and in turn to Mabel, about the land. But surely that land should belong to the Todds, considering that Mabel brought out Emily's poems and letters practically single-handedly—to say nothing of how close the three of them—Mabel, Austin, and Lavinia—were."

But others sided with Susan. "Just imagine what she's been through all these years," they said. "The shame and embarrassment of it all. Mabel Todd and Austin Dickinson, under *our* very noses, too. And all those years, Lavinia letting those two meet in her house...The very least Mrs. Dickinson deserves is that land—to save her and her children's dignity, if nothing else. Mabel Todd took enough. Can't she keep her hands off the land, at least? No wonder Susan Dickinson didn't go to the court house."

Susan's grown children, Ned and Martha, represented the family at the trial. "Mattie looked so *grim*," said Frank Jameson. But Lavinia, sitting in front of them in her worn blue flannel dress, her strange yellow shoes, and her long mourning veil, attracted the most attention. On the stand, her inconsistent answers and cunningly naive demeanor baffled, amused, and irritated both the judge and spectators. "But what she said, that's perjury, isn't it?" Mary Stearns whispered to Mabel at the noon recess. But Mabel, still dressed in mourning for Austin, ("Was that really necessary, her wearing black in front of everyone?" Professor Emerson said later to Professor Crowell?) was too stunned at the turn of events against her even to nod.

Lavinia claimed, under oath, that she hadn't understood when she signed her name on "this little piece paper" after Austin's death that it was a deed to the strip of meadow land running along the east side of the Todds' house, the Dell. She denied ever inspecting the land late one December night in 1895, though David Todd took the stand later and swore that he saw her do so from an east window of his own house.

Anyone observing both Mabel Todd's displeasure during Lavinia's testimony and Lavinia's eyes, so carefully averted from Mabel's, would have trouble believing how close the two women had been until this dispute. "In and out of each other's parlors, day and night they were," Maggie Maher, the Dickinson's Irish servant, would say, "drinking tea and conferring over those poems and letters of Miss Emily's. Oh, how Lavinia used to tell Mrs. Todd to copy faster, faster, no matter how tired she was. And of course they both doted on Mr. Austin Dickinson."

Mabel Todd, slim in her stylish dark dress and black hat topped with two white bird wings, contradicted Lavinia's testimony consistently, looking at Judge Hopkins from time to time with those brown luminous eyes of hers, though she claimed not to know how much she and her husband had paid for the house lot, part of the Dickinson meadow land deeded to them by Austin Dickinson in 1886. She claimed she deserved compensation for the long hours of labor she spent, and was still spending, in editing Emily Dickinson's poems and letters. In return, she had earned only $200 in royalties. From her seat, Lavinia sniffed and muttered, "But ask her what she gets paid for the lectures she gives about my sister for anyone on earth who asks! Who does she think she is, Emily's sister?"

When all testimonial evidence had been gathered and recorded, Ned Dickinson offered his arm to his Aunt Lavinia, who groped with arthritic hands to drape her veil over her face, and escorted her out, his sister following behind, looking straight ahead, her chin high.

Later, Mary Stearns asked Mabel, "Just how is Ned these days, really? The same old problems? He looks so frail, poor soul, for someone in his thirties."

"I wouldn't know," answered Mabel. "Not anymore. But I hold no malice for Ned Dickinson."

Mabel and David Todd never expected to lose their suit. Thus, the final decree, a scant month later, April 15th, 1898, shocked and embittered them both. But it was not even a victory for the victors, for Ned Dickinson died two and a half weeks after the decree, and Lavinia sold the strip of meadow land soon afterwards. Later, after the Todds tried to vindicate their name by appealing to the Supreme Court of Massachusetts, they lost again. That was why Mabel closed the trunk full of Emily Dickinson's poems and put it away in storage—that, and because she was exhausted. Besides, Austin was dead and nothing else in her life could ever mean so much as her love for him.

PART ONE

THE
TRANSIT
OF
VENUS

1881-1883

CHAPTER 1

August, September 1881

∾

ON AUGUST 31ST, 1881, THE *AMHERST Record* announced Professor David Todd's appointment to Amherst College's astronomy department, as well as his wife's name, the same day he and Mabel arrived on the train from Washington, D.C., and checked into the Amherst House, the best hotel in town.

"Well, that answers my question," said Sue Dickinson that afternoon to her husband as she tossed down the newspaper. "David Todd *is* married. You weren't sure before. We'll call on them when they find rooms and get settled, but not before. I wonder what kind of people they are."

"They are young, President Seelye says, still in their twenties," said Austin Dickinson, reaching out to catch their youngest son, six-year-old Gilbert, in his sprint across the piazza, as they called the side porch of their Italianate home, the Evergreens. Caught in his flight past the high-backed wicker chairs where his parents sat, partly shielded by thick hanging vines from the late afternoon light, Gilbert struggled playfully. "They'll no doubt find us old," said Austin.

"Let me go!" laughed Gilbert, as his father tousled the light hair and then released him, watching him leap down to the grass and tear toward the back of the house.

"I think we should put a lamp post at the front gate, Austin," said Sue. "It's entirely too dark on Main Street. We certainly do enough entertaining to warrant it, don't you think?"

He did not answer.

Sue rose rather heavily in her blue skirts, replaced a few pins in the tight bun of her still dark hair, and said, "We'll cultivate them—the young Todds—if we like them. I'm sure they'll need some cultivating if they're so young and from Washington. The South is backwards, even the capital. Oh, I hope they'll be people we can enjoy."

She looked over at Austin, quiet in his wicker chair. "It's not often you sit here with me of an afternoon, is it?"

She went into the house to check with Mary, their servant, about a light supper, leaving Austin gazing up Main Street from his chair. Piano music drifted across the piazza from their daughter Mattie's practicing inside. Another sonatina. Austin didn't sit still for long, but rose slowly, and pulling absently at his thick side whiskers, walked down the porch steps to examine his property. The lilacs he'd transplanted that spring seemed to be doing well, but the hydrangea would need pruning next season, and the Japanese maple looked dry. He walked slowly toward the front of his land where it met Main Street. Across the street from his house, the church, First Church, whose construction he had helped supervise in the '60's, looked especially warm and beautiful in the waning sun, and he considered walking over its land instead and then down to the Dickinson meadow which he had inherited from his father. But he changed his mind, and strolled across his own property to where it met his father's next door, and examined some of the trees and shrubbery around the Homestead as well, where his mother and two sisters still lived.

Gilbert emerged from the back of the Evergreens with a cat in his arms. "Walk over to Aunt Emily's and Aunt Vinnie's with me, Gib," Austin called to him. "That cat needs to go back to Aunt Vinnie anyway."

"Aunt Emily played a game with me after lunch today, Papa."

"She did? And what was it?" Austin stopped to examine a mushroom ring by an oak near the path between the two houses.

"It was 'Blow the dandelions and make a wish.'"

"Did you tell her what you wished?"

"Yes, I wished that we would all go to Sugar Loaf Mountain again for a picnic. Can we ?"

"Yes, I think we can go again this year, Gib, maybe even twice."

Gilbert gave a little jump, and the cat sprang to freedom, heading off toward the barn back of the Homestead. Gilbert ran ahead also to the Homestead's back door and into the kitchen, where he found his Aunt Vinnie peeling tomatoes and shrugging her shoulders to make her shawl stay up, and their Irish household helper, Maggie, salting a thick chicken soup.

"Gib, there you are again!" said Vinnie, "I think you must be our best and most frequent visitor! Why don't you persuade your Papa to visit more often?"

But as soon as she had spoken, Austin entered the kitchen too, with his heavy step. "Good Lord, it's about time you came over here. Where have you been these days?" she said, while Maggie called out in her Irish brogue, "And what a busy man you've been of late, eh?"

"Is everything all right?" Austin asked, while prowling around the kitchen looking for tidbits to eat. "Where's Emily? Upstairs with Mother?"

"No, she's out in the garden picking some flowers. Didn't you see her? She'll be back any minute. Maggie, does the soup have enough potatoes, do you think?"

"Oh, and sure it has, Miss Vinnie, plenty of potatoes."

A gentle step at the door made Austin turn around. "Austin!" said Emily, standing by the door with flowers in one hand, reaching for Gilbert with the other. "Oh, I'm glad you came over. I haven't seen you at all for a week or more, at least. Have you abandoned us?"

"Mama shouted at him this morning," announced Gilbert, looking almost relieved to have come out with such a bold statement.

"Why did she do that, Gib ?" asked Emily.

"I don't know." He tucked his head into the crook of his Aunt Emily's arm and then turned to make a funny face up at her, which she returned. "Can we eat supper here, Papa?"

"No, we're going to have supper at home very soon." He directed his comment to his sisters: "Mattie's having some friends over for whist tonight. It's her first official whist party."

"She's getting to be an expert, isn't she, Austin," said Vinnie. "I can't abide that fool game. I'd rather sweep the shutters than sit around playing whist! I've no patience for it."

"Well, don't tell Mattie that, Vinnie," said Emily, "She's becoming quite the young lady these days at fifteen, and having her friends over means a lot to her." She kept her arm around Gilbert, and the two of them walked in tandem to the kitchen table where she laid down her flowers. "What does Ned have planned for this evening, Austin?"

"I hope he'll turn up for refreshments later, but he'll probably hide out with his friends as long as he can. He still tries to avoid Mattie's parties. He's been better the past few weeks, though. No night episodes for some time now, and I think maybe he's got more color in his face. What do you think?"

"Maybe he does, now that you mention it. Oh, I hope he's stronger," said Emily.

"What's an episode, Papa?" said Gilbert, holding the flowers as his Aunt Emily cut their stems off. "Is that when he yells at night?"

"He doesn't really yell, are you sure you heard him yell?" asked Austin.

"Yup, I'm sure."

Austin caught Emily's eye for a second, then told his son, "Well, sometimes Ned doesn't sleep well, but it's nothing to worry about, and you shouldn't ask him about it."

There was a brief silence as Emily continued to cut stems and hand the flowers to Gilbert, while Maggie gave one last stir to the chicken soup and began to collect her belongings. "I'll be off now," she said. "We'll finish putting the peaches up tomorrow."

"Thanks, Maggie," said Emily. "We'll manage without you. Say hello to your sister and Tom for us."

"Did you get your tomatoes, Maggie?" asked Vinnie. Her shawl had fallen to the floor behind the table where a calico cat now sat on it to wash its paws.

"I've got them here in my basket, right safe and sound. Now Gilbert, mind you don't eat too many sweets tonight, you hear me? I'll see you ladies tomorrow morning sharp."

"We must go too, Gib," said Austin, "after I run up and see how your grandmother is."

"She's asleep," said Vinnie. "She ate early and then dozed off. But do come tomorrow, it'd do her good to see you."

"And you're still managing to lift her without too much trouble, between the two of you?"

"I'm strong, Austin, I'm strong," said Vinnie, giving a little hoot.

"Will you be meeting the new faculty this week?" asked Emily, reaching around Lavinia to grasp a stoneware pitcher for the flowers. "You always say President Seelye expects you to meet newcomers almost as soon as he does himself, since you're treasurer and practically second in command at the College."

"Well, soon. The new astronomy and math professor is settling in right now at the Amherst House. David Todd. I hope he and his wife adjust to life here. They just came from Washington, and they may find Amherst a little primitive at first—only Sue thinks we may find them a little backwards. She wants to give them plenty of time to settle in before we call on them."

"They won't find you and Sue in the least bit primitive," said Vinnie. "Or at least, not Sue. I'm not so sure about you, brother Austin," and she laughed her raspy laugh. "Of course, if they meet Emily and me, they'll be frightened and shocked to death. Maybe you'd better warn them, Austin, about the two Mansion bats!"

"Speak for yourself, Vin!" said Emily. "Besides, I won't even meet them."

"No, but you'll eye them from your window and behind doors, you know you will, too!"

"If that's spying, Aunt Emily, we can spy together," said Gilbert, "I love to play spy."

"Come on, let's go, Gib, time for supper." Austin gave his son a little push in the direction of the back door.

"Will you come again tomorrow? And say hello to Mattie and Ned for us?" said Emily.

"Yes, and I'll bring you some more vegetables from the garden. What do you need?"

"Well, no more cucumbers for me, thank you," said Vinnie, "I don't intend to sit in church and belch another Sunday!"

"Good heavens, cucumbers," said Austin, "that's what we have the most of, except for squash and tomatoes."

"Well, I just know I can't look another cucumber in the face."

Emily broke in. "Not even for pickling? Come on, Austin, bring us some more, despite her grumblings, and whatever else you have. That meadow garden grows the best vegetables around."

"All right, look for me tomorrow. And I'll try to stay longer. I miss being here, it's just that I'm far too busy." But his last words were cut off by the sound of the door being opened and solidly closed.

True to her word, Sue Dickinson postponed the official Dickinson call on the Todds, but by September 20th, she began to make her plans. At 9 a.m., as she sat down to her desk with a calendar, the church bells of Amherst began to toll.

On College Hill, old Professor Tyler removed his spectacles and said to his recitation students, "You must know what this signifies: President Garfield has finally passed away. We will have a moment of silence."

Hearing the bells from his office, Julius Seelye, president of Amherst College, bowed his head in renewed grief as he remembered his wife, who had died in March.

On Pleasant Street, slender young Mabel Todd stood perfectly still before the mirror a moment, her arms frozen in place above her head as she pinned an indigo feathered hat on her shining hair. Could bells be the way this small New

England town announced a fire? No, more likely some special church service. The townspeople struck her as being excessively preoccupied with religion. She would ask David at midday dinner about the bells. She pinned the hat to her head and leaned close to the mirror to peer at her own bright eyes.

In the Homestead on Main Street, Maggie Maher called out to Vinnie in the dining room, "God's saints, do you think the president has finally died of his gunshot wounds, poor suffering soul? Mr. Dickinson said he'd have the bells rung."

Before Vinnie could answer, Emily came out of her room to the upstairs hallway railing and leaned over. "Vinnie?"

"Don't be frightened, Emily, it must be President Garfield. Only the president."

"Only the president?" said Emily. And then to herself, "Only death, Vinnie, only death." Instead of returning to her own room, she went down the hall to her mother's room to see if the bells had frightened her.

CHAPTER 2

September 29, 1881

MABEL TODD, SITTING TALL IN THE parlor of her boarding house on Pleasant Street, viewed her two callers with a critical eye. Did the conversation have to be so serious? She sighed inwardly, pushed back one of the loose curls around her face, and continued with the subject at hand.

"And are your favorite writers the same ones you teach to your students, Professor Chickering?" she asked.

"Some of them, certainly," he answered, turning toward her. "We read the metaphysical poets, including Donne and, of course, Shakespeare. I try to keep abreast of our American writers, but we don't always study those writers in class. Mr. Thoreau is a case in point. We do not read his works as a matter of course, but we do read Emerson's essays and poems."

"My father met and walked with Mr. Thoreau," said Mabel.

"Indeed?" said Mr. Elwell, the Todds' other visitor. "Did you know that Mr. Emerson lectured here some years ago? Back in the late '50's, I believe. He stayed at the Dickinson home—the Austin Dickinson home, I mean, the Evergreens."

"In the late '50's? I was only a toddler then," said Mabel. "But tell me, do either of you read Mr. Whitman's poetry?"

"No, I do not," said Professor Chickering, emphasizing the "not." Mr. Elwell was silent. After an uncomfortable pause, Professor Chickering cleared his throat and added, "I am in accord with *The Nation's* reviewer, Mr. Higginson, I believe it was, who finds Mr. Whitman's poetry without style or decency. I hope you will not trouble yourself to read *Leaves of Grass*."

Mabel smiled and ignored Professor Chickering's obvious wish to change the subject. "If someone tells me not to read something, then I am very likely to read it," she said. "I'm not convinced yet that I should follow this Mr. Higginson's judgment without seeing for myself."

The room was quiet for a moment. "Will anyone have more hot chocolate?" asked Mabel, including her husband David in her glance.

"Maybe just a little," Professor Chickering murmured, but he was interrupted by steps on the porch and two sharp raps on the front door.

Exchanging a smile with his wife, David walked into the entrance hall, where the others could hear him open the door and exclaim, "Mr. Dickinson, we are so glad you have come. And Mrs. Dickinson. It's a pleasure to meet you." A deep voice answered his, joined by a woman's strong voice, followed by steps in the hallway which made the floor tremble gently. Then those in the parlor heard shuffling on the floor matting as the guests handed over their capes and cane.

In a moment, the new arrivals emerged into the sitting room with David Todd, as the gentlemen rose. "I am sure you know Mr. Chickering and Mr. Elwell," began David, "but..."

"We know everyone here but your wife," said Austin, who stood behind Sue Dickinson, his thick reddish hair oddly disarranged at the back of his head. "Mrs. Todd, may I present my wife, Susan Dickinson, and I am Austin Dickinson."

Sue, her tightly combed hair supporting a large bun, stepped forward, her eyes solidly on Mabel, the only unknown quantity in the room. Her querying eyes quickly turned smiling, as their hands met in a lady-like touch and Mabel pointed her toward the best chair. Handshakes or bows were exchanged all around then, after which Mr. Chickering and Mr. Elwell insisted it was time for them to leave, and once again, David returned to the entrance hall to retrieve their wraps and canes.

Sue Dickinson settled herself in the chair opposite the pumpkin-colored chocolate pot with much rustling of dark silk skirts and a solidly upright posture, while she looked openly around the room. "You did well to find these rooms, Mrs. Todd, but I imagine you'll be looking for something more permanent soon?"

"A Mrs. Robison may have something larger for us on Prospect Street," said Mabel, seating herself so that Austin could sit as well. "We need a room for our little daughter, Millicent. She's in Washington now with her grandmother."

"How old is your daughter?" asked Sue.

"She's about a year and a half old now. She was born in February of 1880."

"I look forward to seeing her. Such a sweet age!"

"May I offer you some hot chocolate?"

"No, I think not, since I indulged at a tea party earlier today, but thank you all the same. I'm just so glad to meet you finally, and to find out how you and your husband are getting on here."

"Mr. Dickinson?" Mabel turned to him. "Chocolate?"

"I would love a cup, if it's no trouble," said Austin, who was trying to unrumple the rug he had disturbed with his boots.

"Certainly."

Sue gave Mabel a conspiratorial smile as she watched her husband iron out the last wrinkles below his feet, not knowing he was being observed. "We are delighted you are here, Mrs. Todd," she said, "and want to show you around. I don't think you'll miss Washington a bit, there's just so much going on here in town. And I don't mind saying that our own household is the center of much activity. We look forward to having you and your husband visit us."

Mabel looked up, pleased, from the low burning candle which kept the chocolate warm, the unusual prominence of her eyes set off by the cream shawl she wore against her teal blue dress. "I would love it. Did you hear, David?" she said as her husband returned. "You were right, Mr. and Mrs. Dickinson are the center of the Amherst social scene. I don't mind telling you, Mrs. Dickinson, that I am a very social person. Of course, we will keep many of our ties with Washington life, but I fully expect to find life in Amherst more fun than I ever imagined."

"I might have an idea of what you did expect," said Sue, turning in her chair to take in a painting behind her, then facing the room once again. "Austin, she's handing you your cup, mind. I come from Geneva society originally, Geneva New York, of course, where I still often visit, but I well remember thinking Amherst was the end of the earth. Austin and I have done all we can to keep up the social standards here, and I think we've been quite successful. Proper entertainment is important in a village, and we've also played host to some noteworthy visitors."

Mabel turned to Austin Dickinson, who drank from his cup with an absent look, both feet flat on the floor. "You were born and raised here, is that right?" she asked.

"Yes, I've lived here all my life, except for school, of course."

"Harvard," said Sue, "Harvard Law School."

"The Boston area is wonderful," said Mabel. "And to think how close we are by train. I couldn't get over it on our trip here. Do you go to Boston often?"

"I go fairly often," said Austin, "mostly for the College's business. But also for concerts. I'm sure you'll visit there often, Mr. Todd, for the Harvard observatory."

"I hope so," said David, "but right now, I'm interested in Amherst College building its own new observatory. I haven't spoken recently to President Seelye about it, but he had seemed almost definite about funds a few months back. The hope of supervising a new observatory had a lot to do with my coming here, I can tell you! What do you think the chances are?"

"I'm optimistic," said Austin, "but I haven't talked to President Seelye either about it for a while. He seems to be moving a little slowly on those funds, but it depends on the donor's decision, of course. Let's hope for the best."

"David's already making plans for the Transit of Venus in December of 1882," said Mabel. "Now *that's* looking ahead!"

"What on earth is a transit of Venus?" asked Sue.

David Todd uncrossed his legs and leaned forward, raising his voice. "You don't know what a transit is? It's a rare event, believe me, for Venus. The last one was in 1874, and after this one, there won't be another one until the twenty-first century."

"Eighteen seventy-four. That was the year my father died," said Austin to the group in general.

"I was here then as a student," said David.

"As a student here at Amherst College? I didn't know that," said Sue. "Then you know the area after all. Well, tell us what a transit is then, Mr. Todd."

"A transit is when you can see the shadow of Venus pass across the sun like a tiny black dot. It's amazing—this tiny spot across the huge face of the hot sun. And in broad daylight."

"But I thought you said transits were so rare," said Sue. "If the last one was only in 1874, they don't seem so rare to me."

"But they occur only in pairs. One pair in a century." He stood up in his excitement about the subject. "If one occurs in June, the other will be in December. But separated by years. That's the case now."

Sue nodded politely, but looked confused.

"Tell her why they are important, David," said Mabel, smiling at Austin, who had turned to watch Mabel as she listened.

"They're important because we can measure more accurately the distance from Venus, or whatever planet it is, from earth. And then we can better figure the size of the solar system and the sun's distance from earth."

There was a pause while they all took in that information. Then Austin said, "I guess I can understand a little better why you want to go all the way to California to look at such a thing."

"California?" exclaimed Sue. "Good heavens."

"Yes," said Mabel, "the Transit will be much clearer from that vantage point. And David, don't forget to tell them about how you can study Venus's atmosphere."

"Well," said Sue, "all I know is that the goddess of love must have a warm atmosphere, but I hope you scientists don't measure it to death."

David laughed. "Venus must be smiling on me, because the first time I observed her fiery transit, I was a single man. Now I return to the scene of my first transit a married man." He smiled across at Mabel who leaned briefly over Austin to touch David's outstretched hand.

Sue smiled briefly. "Good luck, Mr. Todd, with your Transit of Venus . Who knows what we'll all be doing then in, what did you say, December of 1882?"

"December 6th, to be exact," said David, sitting down again. "A little over a year from now. You all may not know what you'll be doing, but I certainly expect to be in California."

"Are you musical, Mrs. Todd?" asked Sue, tired of astronomy.

"Very. I studied piano a year at the New England Conservatory of Music, and I enjoy singing. I was hoping I could join a choir here..."

"Then do come visit us as soon as possible. We have a splendid piano, and my daughter, Martha, can play duets with you. She's fifteen now, and doing nicely with her studies. Oh yes, I welcome musical people."

"My sisters have a Chickering piano too, you must come play for them and my mother sometime," added Austin. "Mother isn't well but she loves to hear piano music."

"Yes," added Sue, "she's confined to her bedroom now—a stroke she suffered some years back, and her daughters must take complete care of her. But she listens when Mattie plays the piano for her, and she loves to have letters read to her. And the newspaper, of course. Emily's best at that, with all her editorializing."

"Emily's the older of my two sisters," explained Austin. "Lavinia's the other. You'll meet Lavinia soon, I'm sure, but Emily doesn't get out."

"Is she an invalid too, Emily?" asked Mabel.

"Oh no, not at all, she just likes to stay at home."

"She's quite brilliant, she reads constantly, and writes, too," added Sue. "And she's devoted to her mother. Well, they both are. But it's rather a pity they don't both get out more and mingle with people. Now as for me, I love to be with people. Do you, Mrs. Todd?"

David let out his breath in a laugh and slapped his knee. "I can answer that for you easily enough, she's always looking for new people to meet, aren't you

Mabs? Never sits still, and always analyzing the people she does meet. Oh...I don't mean that she's going to analyze you!"

"Oh, go ahead and analyze, it's all right with me," said Sue. "In fact, it makes a nice change for me—Austin here never says anything much about anybody. Too quiet, that's what he is. A family characteristic. Except for Lavinia, of course. Being too quiet is certainly not *her* problem!"

Mabel leaned back and folded her arms defensively across the bodice of her dress. "Of course I like to meet new people, David, it's fun."

Sue gestured with her head toward Austin. "*He's* not so anxious to meet new people or do new things. He's something of a homebody."

Austin didn't respond, but set his cup carefully down in its saucer. There was a brief pause during which Mabel's eyes met David's for a second, then returned to Sue's face.

"At any rate, Mrs. Dickinson," took up Mabel, "I'd be happy if you could introduce me to your friends and advise me on joining activities here in Amherst. I know I'm going to love it here. I do already. In fact, just seeing the Pelham hills and hearing the crickets and cicadas and looking at the wildflowers when I take my walks have made me love this place."

Austin turned fully toward her at that, and she could see that his eyes were dark blue. "You like the countryside? You have walked here already?"

"Certainly."

"I think I like nothing better than to walk or to take the carriage far into the countryside looking for plants and trees. I can show you whole fields of wildflowers if you're interested, and trees well worth transplanting to grow on our college campus. Fossils as well. Have you been to Sunderland yet? That's a lovely ride."

"No, we haven't. Why don't we all go soon before the snow flies?"

"A good idea," he said soberly, still turned on the sofa to half face her. "A good idea. My son Gilbert begs to go on a picnic. And when the weather gets cold—have you ever been to a sugaring off party, Mrs. Todd?"

"You mean to gather maple syrup? No, I haven't. But David has, in the days when he was a student here, isn't that right, David?"

"Oh yes, plenty of times. Lots of fun. Only in those days, I didn't have my steady girl to sit under the carriage blankets with, eh Mabel?"

"Well," said Sue rather loudly, "if you want to spoon at your age...!"

But David only laughed heartily and loudly, leaning forward to include them all in his laughter.

"Austin," said Sue, "it is a little late and we've been on the run today. I think we should start off now. Mattie will wonder where we are."

"Yes, I suppose you're right." He folded his embroidered napkin and stood after Sue rose, turning first to Mabel. "Thank you for your hospitality, Mrs. Todd. We hope to be seeing a lot of you and Mr. Todd."

"Will you call on us soon?" asked Sue.

"We'd love to."

"Then we will plan to be at home this week. What about the day after to-morrow? No, make it October 3rd, that's four days from now."

"Yes, yes," said Mabel, "I think that would be fine. Evening?"

"Evening is fine."

"I might not be free that evening, Sue," said Austin.

"They should come in any case; I want to get up a musical evening. We'll have a wonderful time, and Mattie will be excited when I tell her."

"I can't wait to meet her, and did you say you have other children too?"

"Yes, two more. Maybe you can catch Gilbert before he goes to bed. He's our youngest, six years old. Ned's our oldest. He'll be twenty-one in June."

In the foyer, they said their goodbyes, and the Dickinsons stepped out into the tranquil September evening for their nearly wordless walk back to the Evergreens on Main Street. But behind them in the parlor of their little boarding house, Mabel gave David's bearded cheek a kiss and danced a dainty minuet around him in her excitement at having met Amherst's most important people.

"Only four days from now, David, and we'll visit this famous Evergreens everyone talks about and I'll get to show what a good singer and pianist I am. I'll bowl them over, you just wait!"

She whisked up Austin's napkin to make herself a miniature bull's cape, which she shook in her husband's path, until he caught her, and, one hand on her breast, pushed her up the stairway to bed.

CHAPTER 3

October 3, 1881

Autumn in Amherst, Mabel, don't you love it?" said David as they strode energetically toward the Evergreens on the evening of October 3rd. "Now admit that we did the right thing in leaving Washington."

She refused to answer his challenge, but gave him a full smile as they approached the corner of Main and Pleasant Street. "But David, don't you think Susan Dickinson is remarkable looking? I mean she has a kind of presence. She somehow takes charge of things once she's in the room."

They turned the corner onto Main Street and walked past shops.

"Is that where Mr. Dickinson's law office is, across the street?" asked Mabel.

"Yes, in the Palmer Block. You talk about presence, I think he's the one with presence. You should see him at college. Some of the younger faculty are afraid of him, the way he comes out with his opinion in that rough way."

"Some of the younger faculty? But you're certainly not afraid of him!"

"Of course not. I like him. He can be a bit abrupt all right, but a strong personality appeals to me."

"So you like Mrs. Dickinson too?"

"She's all right, but I can't see myself flirting with her, even if she were closer to my age."

"Why do you always bring the question of flirtation into things? Even the thought of you flirting with someone of Mrs. Dickinson's age and social stature is ridiculous. You haven't heard me talking about flirting with Mr. Dickinson, have you?"

"No, that isn't it, I just mean a woman should be..."

"Prettier than Mrs. Dickinson is?" said Mabel. "Is that what you mean?"

He squeezed her arm. "Oh, forget it, I don't know what I mean, except that you are the prettiest woman I've ever met." He stopped and looked at her. "Have you done something special with your hair?"

"I managed to make my curls turn under perfectly around my face. Have you noticed how most women in this town have such severe hairdos?"

David started walking again. "We're almost there now. It's that huge Italianate house. Look, is that a cupola on top?"

But Mabel was distracted. "Oh, look at the church in the shadows over there across the street. So charming."

"Watch your step, it's dark right here by the trees." David held her arm more tightly. "But look how the house is lit up, almost like a party. I thought you said we were the only ones coming."

"We are—I think. Unless the sisters are coming from next door. Their house looks so dark though. I don't see any light downstairs, and only those dim ones upstairs. What a grand house; I'd like to go inside it someday."

They paused. "Well," said David, "we have to go up all those stairs to the front door. Did you ever see such a big front door?"

"Very impressive for a small town."

As they approached the immense front door, it opened and a thin young man stepped out hurriedly until he saw them. "Oh, sorry, I thought I'd just slip out for a while. But you can go on in. No, that's not right, I'll see you in." He turned, flustered, until Mabel reached out and slipped her gloved hand neatly around his arm. "Are you the Dickinson son I've heard about? You must be, you look just like your parents!"

"Well, I'm Ned," he said, rooted to the step in front of the door, looking down into Mabel's smiling eyes.

"I didn't know you were so handsome. I think people have been keeping a secret from us! I'm Mabel Todd and this is my husband, David. Please call me Mabel, none of this Mrs. Todd formality for me! I hope you will show us in before you run away, but are you sure you have to run away at all?"

"I might be able to come right back...It wasn't anything important, just meeting some fellows, you know, at the college."

"You're a college student? What year are you, Ned?"

"I'm starting my last year. I'll graduate in June." He stood behind Mabel now and gestured for her to enter, while at the same time, the household servant, Mary, appeared in the hall to take their coats and closed the door gently behind them, leaving Ned outside. But he opened the door again and stuck his head into the hallway. "I'll come back later," he called.

"See that you do," said Mabel, smiling and waving her fingers in his direction. But he advanced into the hallway while Mary bustled about the visitors.

"Good evening, Mr. and Mrs. Todd. Mrs. Dickinson is just coming," said

Mary. "Make yourselves at home." She led them into the carpeted parlor where they could see a brightly burning fire and walls crowded with paintings and etchings. A bowl of apples sat on one low table, while on another was a small basket of dried leaves and grasses beside a pile of knitting, some books, and someone's spectacles.

"It's beautiful here," exclaimed Mabel to Ned. "Your mother has exquisite taste. And here she comes."

Sue swept through the doors from the back of the house and came toward them with outstretched arms. "Do come in, I'm sorry I wasn't here to greet you. Did Mary take care of you properly? Ned, what are you doing here? I thought you'd left."

"I'll just be going, but I've decided to come back early after all. So I'll see you later. Just thought I'd tell you."

"Mattie, our company is here," called Sue. "Come in and sit down." A moment later, Mattie appeared quietly in the room, her posture as straight as if she had practiced carrying a book on her head, her gray dress and white collar in perfect order, but her eyes curious. She went at once to the Todds and curtsied.

"So this is Mattie. I can hardly wait to play some music with you," said Mabel. "I've been looking forward to it all week. Sit by me and tell me all about yourself." Mabel sat on the love seat Sue gestured toward, patting the place next to her.

"Mr. Todd, sit over here by me," said Sue. "I regret that Mr. Dickinson could not be here tonight, due to a town meeting and a legal appointment. But we will carry on without him. We're used to his busy schedule."

"I think your clock needs winding," said David abruptly as he sat beside her and glanced at a wooden clock whose hands both pointed to twelve.

"Oh, don't pay any attention to that broken clock. It stopped working two weeks ago and nobody has done a thing about it."

"I can probably fix it," said David, bending to turn the clock around for a closer look. It's a hobby of mine. I fix all sorts of things."

"You do? I would hate to impose on you—but Austin isn't clever that way. And besides, he's run ragged by all the responsibilities he has in this town. Maybe someday though you could just take a little look..."

"Oh, I'll take a look right now, if you don't mind. At least I can see how long it might take to fix it. Do you have some old newspaper?"

"Well, if you're sure it's all right..." She arose to fetch yesterday's *Republican* from a basket on the floor. Soon David was busy inspecting the innards of the clock, while Sue moved to join Mabel and her daughter.

"I'll be attending Miss Porter's school in Framingham next year," Mattie was announcing, "and I'll miss Mother a lot, but all the girls I know of who went there just adored it. And of course I can come home and visit."

"You've heard of Miss Porter's, naturally, Mrs. Todd?" asked Sue. "Some of the finest young women in the country graduate from there."

"Certainly I've heard of it. Mattie can be proud to attend next year."

"She's a serious girl, our Mattie. Rather like her namesake, my sister, Martha Gilbert. But Ned and Gilbert and I call her Mopsy for fun, don't we? So Mopsy, why don't you play the piano for us?"

Without complaint or hesitation, Mattie went to the piano and played a Chopin mazurka by memory. And when they applauded that, she went on to play a song, " Memories of you, dear."

At its conclusion, Mabel was on her feet. "I'll sing that one if you'll play it again."

"Yes, please. Let's do all three verses."

Mabel stood behind Mattie at the piano while Sue leaned back, smiling, to listen, and David tinkered, oblivious, with the clock. Mabel's soprano voice rose strong and without hesitation, and carried through all three verses, even when Mattie played some wrong notes and fumbled to correct them. But they made a good team, and at the end, Mabel caressed Mattie's shoulders, laughing with pleasure. Any remnants of Sue's formality were also broken, as she said animatedly, "You are very talented, Mrs. Todd. May I call you Mabel though? I hope you feel free to call me Sue."

"Please do call me Mabel, and I would be honored to call you Sue. What wonderful evenings we have ahead of us!"

"Let's play some duets, Mrs. Todd," said Mattie, "I like this book with Mozart and Beethoven arrangements. Do you want to try?"

"Certainly, let's!"

"Mrs. Dickinson," spoke up David. "Do you have any small dish or cup I could lay some of these parts in?"

"Goodness, I almost forgot about you! Yes, I'll get you something. And call me Sue if you'd like, just as I've told your wife. Mabel, keep playing, I'll go tell Mary we'll have some hot cider soon, if you would care for some."

"I would love it."

"Good. Play away then." The music rang out along with Mabel and Mattie's laughter, and when Ned returned, breathless, barely an hour later, he displaced his sister by the piano so he could stand near Mabel Todd.

CHAPTER 4

October 1881

MRS. JAMESON, LIVING OPPOSITE THE Evergreens, was quite taken with the gas lamp post which Sue and Austin Dickinson installed at their front gate in mid-October, for it lighted both sides of the street as well as the Dickinson's sidewalk and front entrance. Now Mariette Jameson and her husband, John, needn't fear stumbling in the dark on winter evenings, or summer evenings either, for that matter. Mr. Jameson began to look forward to the bright glow as he walked home on dark winter afternoons from the post office where he was postmaster, and Mrs. Jameson enjoyed catching a better view of the frequent guests who went in and out of the Dickinson's Italianate front door.

The wife of the new astronomy and mathematics professor, Mabel Todd, began to be a frequent daytime visitor that fall of 1881, but she also visited with her husband in the evenings, sometimes with other guests, sometimes just the two of them. Mrs. Jameson enjoyed looking at Mabel's smart clothes which she wore well, her figure being trim and her posture so fine. She had asked her husband, "How old do you suppose Mabel Todd is? She certainly looks young." But Mr. Jameson had no idea and didn't feel like guessing, so Mrs. Jameson asked Susan Dickinson herself one afternoon when they were both outside.

"She's twenty-five, she told me so just the other day," said Sue. "But our being almost thirty years older than she doesn't enter into things. Oh, I suppose she may find Austin rather old-fashioned and stodgy, but if so, she doesn't show it. Anyway, it's me she comes to visit chiefly. And Mattie next. Mabel and I have so much in common, that what with Mattie's musical interests, we keep ourselves wonderfully busy. She's simply charming. And isn't her husband handsome?"

Mrs. Jameson found herself secretly amused at the merry social chase Sue Dickinson led her husband. Not that he didn't want to carry out any social obligations. He, like his father Edward Dickinson before him, hosted with pride the many college ceremonies such as graduation teas, faculty socials and trustee dinners, and kept important people like Judge Lord of Salem or Samuel Bowles of Springfield overnight. No, it was the other sorts of events which amused Mrs. Jameson. The whist parties, the choir and drama dinners, the elegant late afternoon teas where every member of the family appeared in what Mrs. Jameson privately called their "haughty clothes". She couldn't quite imagine that Austin enjoyed those events, since his usual serious demeanor turned quite somber, even stiff, when he stepped outside to greet Sue's laughing, lively guests with his sad face. At least she thought it was sad, especially since he sometimes left his own house during such parties and walked up to the College and back all by himself as though he needed to be alone.

But this splendid new gas light! It was exciting and modern, but it spelled Austin's doom if he disliked Susan's parties, because although she didn't count them, it struck Mrs. Jameson that after Mabel Todd came, Sue Dickinson gave more parties than ever before. It also struck her, not long after the gas light had been installed, that Austin was more than somber and reserved when she chatted with him on the street—that he was actively unhappy. Of course, his mother was an invalid and he and his sisters were at that age when people have to look at the future critically. And no one ever expected a Dickinson to be jolly or light-hearted or easy to get along with. One had only to remember Edward Dickinson, Austin's father, to know that. But Mrs. Jameson wondered sometimes whether things were not well between Austin and Sue, and for that, she pitied them both, for her own simple family life satisfied her.

Thinking of family life reminded her that it was time to send Frank another letter at Johns Hopkins where he was teaching history. He loved to hear College news, since he had graduated from Amherst College, and of course he appreciated bits of Dickinson news since he had spent some years living just across the street from the Evergreens. Pen in hand, Mrs. Jameson settled down at the table to tell Frank all about the splendid new lamp post which shed such light on the Dickinson family.

CHAPTER 5

February, March 1882

Aunt Emily? I'm here," called Ned at the bottom of the stairs one late, overcast February afternoon of the new year, 1882.

Emily came to the upstairs hallway from her mother's bedroom, an apron over her white dress and a towel in her hand. "Good, Ned. Come up and see your grandmother for a minute. She's awake."

Ned came upstairs still in his overcoat. "How is she?" he asked, lowering his voice a bit.

"A little better. She ate well and I read the paper to her. She knew you'd be stopping by this evening and wants to see you."

They entered Mrs. Dickinson's room where one lamp burned low on the bureau, leaving the bed in shadows. As Emily leaned over her mother's bed, a pencil slipped out from behind her ear. "Oh, I've been looking for that pencil," she exclaimed, and slipped it into her dress pocket. "Mother, Neddie is here."

Ned stepped to the bed awkwardly and pressed a cool hand on his grandmother's tiny lifeless one. "It's cold outside, Grandmother," he said. "My mother sent you some soup for tomorrow night."

Mrs. Dickinson's eyes crinkled shut in a brief effort to speak, then opened in a smile while her lips pursed together and she made an "m" sound.

"What's she saying?" Ned asked Emily, straightening up.

"Mattie?" Emily asked her mother. "Are you wondering how Mattie is?"

Her mother nodded wearily.

"Mattie is fine, Grandmother," said Ned. "She's going to play the piano to-night for Mrs. Todd. We're going to practice waltz steps too."

But the old lady's eyes stared vacantly into the shadows of the room now, closing more and more often, and Emily took one pillow from behind her head so she lay arranged for sleep. "Mother, I'm going downstairs to chat with Ned before he goes back home. I'll leave the lamps low for a while. You'll be all right, won't you?"

"You look tired, Aunt Emily," Ned said, as he watched her gather up some scraps of paper from the bureau and tuck them into her dress pocket, along with the pencil. "Is there anything I can do right now?"

"Would you mind just carrying down your grandmother's chamber pot? You can empty it on your way home. I do feel awfully tired tonight, and Vinnie's rather weary too, I think."

Ned fetched the chamber pot and they both made their way downstairs.

The front rooms were dark in the late afternoon gloom, but a small fire burned in the library.

"Now what did your mother send?" Emily asked Ned as soon as they reached the kitchen.

"Chicken soup and scalloped potatoes."

Lavinia emerged from the pantry wearing a checked apron over her dress and a long soiled scarf around her neck. Several strands of her hair had come loose from the pins. "Sue sent soup and potatoes?" she asked. "Who made it, Sue or Mary? Sue doesn't have time to cook, with all her socializing."

"Well, Mother made it all this time," said Ned.

"See, Vin, you always expect the worst," laughed Emily. "Sit down Neddie, you can stay a little while, can't you? I want to write a short note to Sue, so if you can wait, I'll write it now." She sat at the kitchen table with a piece of paper.

"For the Lord's sake, Ned, don't sit down until you move that chamber pot from this kitchen!" said Lavinia.

"Oh, sorry, I forgot!" Ned went outside and returned in a few moments.

"Emily," said Lavinia, "I don't know why you bother to write another note to Sue—she didn't answer the last one and she probably won't answer this one."

"She did answer, Vinnie, Mattie brought over a note last week while you were napping. She asked me a question, so I'm answering it now."

Lavinia sat down opposite Emily. "What question, what did she ask you?"

"Oh, nothing important, Vinnie."

Lavinia stared at Emily's moving pencil for a moment, then picked up one of the three cats under the table and stroked it while she turned her attention to Ned. "Well," she said, "what's going on at your house tonight? More music and games with Mabel Todd? Seems to me you're always telling us she's coming or going. She's going to take years off Sue, if you ask me. Might do us all some good, as a matter of fact. I'd ask to meet her, but your mother hasn't been over here for so long that I'd faint if she walked in the door with Mabel Todd."

"Mabel Todd is so much fun," said Ned. "She's full of enthusiasm for every-thing—music, charades, dancing—I'm practically her age, you know. She likes to see me just as much as Mother and Mattie. Maybe more."

"But she has a baby girl, Neddie," said Lavinia. "She has responsibilities."

"I know," said Ned. "But that doesn't mean she can't have a good time with us. Besides, her parents keep the baby half the time."

"That strikes me as rather strange. And where is Mr. Todd during all this dancing and carrying on?" asked Lavinia. "Or where is poor Austin, for that matter? Huddling in the library?"

Emily looked up briefly from her paper and laughed. "Dear Austin," she said.

"Mr. Todd comes some of the time," said Ned, "but he's busy at the observa-tory most evenings. Mrs. Todd is lonely. At least I think so. It's lucky she has us to keep her company. Father even joins us sometimes, at least for the charades and cider. He likes the Todds. I'm glad they moved to Amherst. Now we don't have to be so serious all the time."

Emily looked up from her note. "I'm glad too if the Todds make you happy. Why don't you go over one evening, Vin, and see for yourself?"

"Certainly not," said Lavinia. "I have no desire to sit in the parlor and watch people dance. Sometimes Sue's need for activity amazes me—what's wrong with quiet evenings at home, I ask you?"

"Not a thing, Lavinia, not a thing," said Emily. "Ned, here's the note for your mother. And tell Mattie to come over soon. I'd like to see her."

Ned took the note from his aunt and fished his gloves from his overcoat pocket. "I have to shave and eat some supper before Mrs. Todd comes," he told them. "See you soon." He buttoned his coat and let himself out.

"That boy has a crush, doesn't he?" said Emily to Lavinia.

"Oh please, will you let me tease him?" said Lavinia.

Next door at Sue and Austin Dickinson's, the waltzing began in the hallway for the second time that week, with Mattie playing the piano for Mabel and Ned.

"But the steps I learned in Washington don't fit what you do here," Mabel had laughed to Ned the evening before, when they had danced briefly and spontaneously to a tune Mattie had produced while Sue looked on. "Teach me, Ned, you must teach me!"

And so he had for a while, joyously, with his arm around Mabel's waist, his hair damp against his forehead, until Austin had come home and they all settled down with cups of hot cider and little cakes. But tonight was another night, and Ned waited impatiently for his earliest opportunity to lead Mabel again. He didn't have to wait long.

"Ned," Mabel called to him after singing only two or three songs by the piano with Mattie, "Did you say you'd teach me the waltz again?"

He was on his feet instantly.

"You don't mind, do you, Sue?" Mabel asked, even as she stood up. Sue smiled and settled comfortably into her chair. "You go on, I'm delighted," she said. "Let Ned teach you out in the hallway where the rugs won't catch you up."

"Tell me when you're ready," called Mattie from the piano, as Mabel took Ned's hand and drew him from the room. There was a silence and then some giggles from Mabel, followed by a rustling of her skirts and some laughter from Ned. Then Ned called out, "Ready, Mattie. Play!"

Sue reached into her sewing basket and pulled out a small embroidery hoop, smiling at the sound of steps, turns, and laughter from the hall. Working contentedly, she called out to them now and again. "How is he doing, Mabel? Will he be ready for the fraternity ball?" And later, "Ned, you could ask Alice to dance now at her next party. You see how easy it is to dance with a lady."

But Mattie began to tire. "I don't want to play anymore," she called finally. "I'm tired of all these waltzes." She closed the piano lid, but the noises in the hallway of swishing skirts and toe turns on the floor continued. Then more laughter, a "whoops!", and finally a little scream as one of them banged into the wall.

"Come on," called Mattie, a little petulantly. At that, the two emerged, hand in hand and half bent with laughter.

"You two!" said Sue observing them fondly. "Well, is that all the dancing for this evening then?"

"I guess it is, if our accompanist has given up," said Mabel, leading Ned by the hand to Mattie's chair. "Thanks, Mattie, you were perfect." She dropped Ned's hand and sank down onto the loveseat. Ned squeezed in beside her after a moment's hesitation, and the small talk came to a halt. In the ensuing silence, the front door opened with a sudden thrust, making Mabel lurch slightly in surprise. Heavy footsteps crossed the hall and Austin stepped part way into the parlor, still wearing his black coat and the wide-brimmed hat that hid part of his face, leaving in relief only his prominent auburn side whiskers and and the outline of his nose.

"Austin, are you tracking mud in here?" Sue said sharply, looking up from her embroidery.

He returned to the hallway, wiped his feet, and reappeared without his coat and hat. "Good evening, Mrs. Todd," he said. "Where's David?"

"At the observatory," she answered.

"Well, maybe I'll see him tomorrow. I wanted to talk to him about something."

"Mabel doesn't want to hear about school matters now," said Sue. "Please excuse his manners, Mabel. He works too hard, he loses track of things."

"I'm sorry, I didn't intend to be rude." Austin sat down solemnly until Mabel caught his eye and smiled. He smiled back, and Sue arose, satisfied. "It's time for refreshments then, now that we're all here. Austin, look at Ned's healthy glow. Can you tell he's been dancing? You don't know what you've missed."

Lavinia threw back her head and clapped her hands in delight one March morning. "Ned has such a crush on Mabel Todd, Maggie."

"He has taken to visiting her at her boarding house," said Maggie, dusting inside the cover of another book in the library where she and Lavinia sat companionably. "Pass me that cloth, please."

Lavinia handed over the three-volume set and picked up another book to dust herself.

"You're sure of it?" asked Lavinia.

"Sure I'm sure. Tessie has seen it herself. She's been maid to Mrs. Todd's landlady long before the Todds ever came to board there and she don't tell fibs. She said Ned comes in the mornings after Mrs. Todd finishes her piano playing —she practices faithful-like every day—and stays a-chatting for as long as she'll have him. Tessie said he laughs like you never heard him laugh before, too."

Lavinia laughed herself and called out in the direction of the conservatory, "Emily, can you hear me?"

"Just barely, Vin," came the reply.

"Maggie says Tess told her that Ned visits Mabel Todd practically every day, all by himself, over at the boarding house. Isn't he a sly devil?"

No reply came from the conservatory, and Lavinia called out again: "Emily?"

In a moment, Emily came into the dining room with a pot of hyacinths in one hand and a trowel in the other. "I heard most of it, but it's too hard to shout from in there. What's all the fuss about?"

"Well, I think it's funny, our shy little Ned, combing his hair as never before and brushing his suits with a whisk broom three times a day. That's what Mary next door told Maggie."

"Mrs. Dickinson isn't worried about it," said Maggie, "but Mr. Dickinson thinks Ned skips lectures sometimes when he visits Mrs. Todd. Mary told me Mr. Dickinson spoke to him about it the other night—asked him not to go so often."

Emily held up the hyacinths. "Aren't they perfect? Smell them!" She held them under Maggie's nose and then Lavinia's.

"You're sending them off to someone, are you, Miss Emily?" said Maggie.

"Yes, as a matter of fact, I'm making up a box and sending it to Mabel Todd. She's been such a lively friend for Sue and Austin—I want to welcome her back to Amherst. She'll be returning from Washington tomorrow, so I thought I'd have them sent over in the morning." Emily smelled the hyacinths herself, leaned forward to wrinkle her nose at the smell of musty books, and returned to the conservatory.

"Mabel is going right back to Washington in a few days with her husband," Lavinia called after her. "Are you warm enough in there, Emily? Put a shawl around you if you're the least bit cold."

Lowering her voice, Maggie said to Lavinia, "She seems frail to me. She should eat more."

"Well, Maggie, I do what I can," sighed Lavinia. "She doesn't have a big appetite these days, that's all." She looked at the pile of books, and picking up a cloth with a sigh, said, "Look at all we have left to do. I'm tired. Maggie, what do you think of Mabel Todd?"

Maggie pursed her lips and shook her head a little as she eyed a half-dusted book cover. "I have to admit, Miss Lavinia, I think she's leading Ned Dickinson on a bit. I mean, after all, she's a married lady and he's so shy. I don't think it's quite proper, visiting a married lady in her parlor of a morning, or riding out the road on horseback together, neither."

"They ride together?" asked Lavinia.

"That they do. In the carriage or on horses—Sarah Warner's husband saw them from his farm sitting under a tree resting while Ned lay back and had a smoke. If you ask me, that's not proper. I don't wonder Mr. Dickinson is disturbed."

"I don't know, Maggie," said Lavinia, unsure. "But maybe she is good for him. He needs bringing out of himself. That's why Sue lets it go on, no doubt."

"No doubt," said Maggie, "but that don't make it right."

Emily came to the dining room again with more flowers. "Oh, Emily," said Lavinia, "heliotropes? Your special favorites! Heliotropes for Mabel Todd. She really must be someone important then!"

Emily smiled. "I like to hear her voice outside from the pavement, and she walks with conviction. She brightens our little corner of Main Street, so I'm giving her a reward: my conservatory flowers. Don't you think she'll fall in love with them?"

"That she will, Miss Emily," said Maggie, just as our Ned has fallen in love with her."

CHAPTER 6

March 1882

Miss Emily Dickinson sent them, David, just look! And with a lovely note. That makes my second note from her, and now flowers. Imagine, such beautiful flowers in March. She tends them in her conservatory, Sue told me. These are hyacinths, and these are heliotropes, but what are the yellow ones? I've never seen any like them."

"Don't ask me what they are. Come on, shouldn't we do some more packing for Washington? Wednesday is only three days from now."

"Yes, I suppose we should. Thank heavens we left Millicent with my parents; I couldn't face packing all her things. I must answer this attention from Austin's sister though. Her notes are so unusual and special; my note has to be special too."

"Well, paint her something in watercolor then," said David, going over to open their trunk.

"A wonderful idea," said Mabel, following him. "Oh, I love mysterious and interesting people. Maybe she'll be fascinated by me too, and we can meet soon."

"I hope so, but it won't be for a while if you stay any length of time with me in Washington. I'll be at least a month and a half at the Nautical Almanac Office, maybe more. But you won't miss Amherst that much, will you?"

"You know, David, I'd have never believed it a year ago, but I'm torn between both places. I have such a wonderful time while I'm in Washington that I can't imagine being back in Amherst, but when I return, I fall in love with everything here too. Being in Sue Dickinson's circle puts a different light on village life. Not to mention all the college activities and the sleigh rides this winter."

"Yes, with all those young students to sled with! You hardly gave me a chance!"

"I notice you found some pretty partners yourself, David/husband/lover."

"Are you going to flirt again in Washington as outrageously as you did the last time we were there? Especially with Mr. Eliot? Are you?"

"Oh David, it's only a game, you know that. Besides, you like it, don't you? Tell me it's true." She circled him, smiling.

"If it's only a game, and if it makes you all the more exciting, then I like it some. And if you like it..."

"It's only a game. You know I'm really innocent. And don't point too strong a finger at me, after the Polly Worthington episode. Her husband was watching you very closely while we played cards."

"And you were too, then?"

"Only a little. Let's change the subject. Have you written again to Dr. Newcomb about the Transit of Venus expedition?"

"Yes, I let him know how hard I was pushing for it. As soon as I arrive in Washington, I'll talk with him about the chances of bringing it off. It all depends on whether the funds come through. I'm counting on your coming with me to California. We can leave Millicent with your parents again."

"I suppose I'll come, but I'd rather stay in Washington, if I didn't know how much I'd miss you. I *could* stay in Amherst, of course, but things might be tedious here for that long without you, and besides, it's so cold here by December. All that snow and ice for months and months..."

"Please come with me, lover. I'll be busy, but I won't be working all the time."

Mabel took some shoes from the trunk. "Let's wait and see how likely this trip is before we discuss it in detail. But I hope the money comes through, for your sake, David. And surely the college will release you from classes?"

"Austin assures me it can be worked out, though I admit, President Seelye isn't keen on it. I'm glad I've got Austin on my side, because I'm not sure I trust Julius Seelye. I tell you, Mabs, our getting to know the Dickinsons so well has been the best thing that could have happened. They can do a lot for us."

"They already have. And Sue is such an impressive person. I think she truly understands me, and wants to bring out the best in me. I like her above anyone in Amherst." She held up a Hudson Bay blanket. "Do you think we should take a couple of these along this time?"

"Might as well. If you like Sue best of anyone in Amherst, I like Austin the best by far."

"That's good. I'm glad you can talk to him. I like him too, but he is rather odd, and sometimes I can't figure out what his mood is—whether he's annoyed about something or just thinking. He hardly ever smiles."

"True, but I find his very oddness appealing. He's different, anyway, and everyone respects him. Even those who think he's a snob."

"People call him a snob?"

"Oh yes, but they don't single out Austin alone. It goes for the whole family."

"How ridiculous, David, they're just jealous. You know, I think if I ever had a terrible problem, I'd get advice from Austin, even though right now I have trouble talking to him. And yet, he reminds me a little of my father, and I don't have any trouble talking to *him*. They must be about the same age, and they both seem—well, wise, although my father couldn't be considered odd the way Austin is."

"I think I'd go to him too if I had a serious problem. And yet I get the feeling that his own children might not ask him for advice. Have you noticed how distant they act around him? The way they look away from him? Ned and Mattie, I mean, not Gilbert. I could tell right away that Austin and Gilbert were close."

"Who wouldn't be close to Gilbert? " said Mabel, "He's a darling boy. But yes, I've noticed a distance with the others. Mattie is warm enough with me, but stiff around him. But she is at an awkward age."

"Could be, but then there's Ned. Has Sue ever said anything to you about Ned? "

"What do you mean?" asked Mabel.

"I mean, to explain why he seems a little slow, or kind of...well, not always altogether following things."

"No, she never said anything, except that he isn't taking a full course load at the College. I don't think there's any special problem. He's excellent with horses, have you noticed? And he can be loads of fun."

"Of course *you* think he can be fun, he has a crush on you. We're back where we started this conversation."

"Oh David, he's only twenty, let him have his crush on a more experienced woman. It's good for him."

"Just don't set him up for a big fall. He seems a bit simple-minded to me. I'm sorry, but that's the way I see it, you needn't look at me that way."

"Well, you'd better be patient, because he's coming on the train with us as far as Palmer. He's planned a visit with this Jenkins family they all talk so much about, and he asked me which train we were taking."

"Who are these Jenkins people again?"

"Jonathan Jenkins used to be minister of the First Church, you know, across from the Evergreens, and he and his wife were friendly with the whole family. They have children, and they live in Pittsfield now."

"Well, Ned's all right. I just get a little tired of his hanging around and staring at you, that's all. You'll have to control him better."

"Let's forget about Dickinsons for a while and get packed," said Mabel. "Are you taking many books from Walker Hall for the work in Washington?"

"No, and I'll leave most of my paperwork there in the office rather than try to drag things back and forth."

"I can't wait to have more space, David. I feel so cramped in this boarding house. Do you think it'll be a long time before we can have a house of our own?" She stacked three hat boxes into the corner.

"I hope not, but it won't be as fast as you want it."

"I miss the barn studio you made for me in the Rock Creek house. It was a perfect place to paint.." She sighed. "What do you suppose supper will be tonight? Hash browns and eggs again?"

"I don't know,"said David, "but I could do with a thick pork chop."

"I wonder if Millicent misses us a lot," Mabel said. "I don't want her to be a clinging child. Being with Mother and Grandmother so much should help prevent that problem from developing. I don't know, David, I'm not cut out to be a devoted mother. I hope Millicent can survive me."

"Oh, she'll do fine. Let's just remember what her arrival taught us about your safe and unsafe times, that's all."

"A lesson I'll never forget," said Mabel, rolling her eyes. She began to pack her clothes in earnest for their departure from Amherst.

CHAPTER 7

March 1882

IF COLLEGE VACATION HADN'T BEGUN, SURELY someone would have seen the flames burst from Walker Hall before 10:30 that night of March 29th, 1882. Of course, no one would ever know if the disaster could have been prevented, least of all Austin Dickinson, who cursed the fates that he had stayed overnight in Boston on Wednesday.

In Washington, D.C., Mabel and David Todd were sleepily discussing new clothes for Millicent even as the flames ate into David's books: the ones stacked neatly on his desk, those on the shelves, and last, the books he had left casually scattered on the floor a few days before.

William Esty, professor of mathematics, sat up wide awake the minute he heard the fire bells, and prayed that nothing at the College was on fire. But the direction of the racket and bustle convinced him that the fire was, indeed, either on the campus or near the Common. And though his wife tried to persuade him not to get up, he got dressed anyway and walked in a kind of daze until he discovered the worst: Walker Hall aflame, the place where he kept much of his most valued work and where his classes had always been held.

Sue Dickinson would write to the Todds later to let them know that some of David's work had been preserved in the vaults of Walker Hall, along with William Esty's calculations and old Dr. Hitchcock's mineral collection, the one Austin and Emily loved so much. Dr. Hitchcock's son, Ned, whom everyone called "old Doc," rejoiced Thursday morning with Austin over those minerals as though the Hitchcock family itself had sprung, Phoenix-like, from the vault.

Austin's father, Edward Dickinson, treasurer of Amherst College before his son, had dedicated Walker Hall in 1868, and Austin himself had helped supervise its construction. But by some oversight, the building was insured for only half its value. So when Austin poked around the rubble later, his very pores filled with that unmistakable malignant burnt smell, he tried to stave off thoughts of his dead father's pride in this building, a landmark both of them had assumed would endure into the next century. Of course they would have to rebuild, and as fast as possible. So many of the science and math classroom and offices had been located here—the college would suffer without Walker Hall.

The other college officials who had toured the ruins with Austin that morning had departed, leaving him alone, a solitary figure in black, scraping the bricks and beams with a walking stick and expelling steamy breaths. His law office schedule was full and his college appointment diary teemed with meetings, so that a half hour ago, he had had a sensation of tightness in his chest and the impression that he was almost running from job to job. Yet suddenly, he had no idea what he would do next, either today, tomorrow, or the next day. A kind of blankness settled over him. He might have called it a lethargy, except that it gave way to an odd, rising sense of panic. He'd felt small panics before, but never as often as in the last six months.

A group of boys ran toward the acrid ruin shouting, slowing up when they saw him there. "Watch out, boys, don't cross over the ropes. It's dangerous," he called. He turned and stared again into the heart of the rubble: bricks, beams, twisted pipe, desks, papers and books. A leather case caught his eye lodged partway under a bookshelf. He picked his way over to dislodge it, and saw that it had escaped the flames entirely and showed only a few water spots. Turning it over, he found the owner's name stamped in gold letters: David Todd. Good, he would keep the case for young David Todd and write to him tonight, or let Sue tell Mabel what had been salvaged from the fire. He bent to pick up the case, and as he did so, he was startled by a vivid picture of Mabel which flashed across his mind's eye: Mabel singing in their parlor on one of the many occasions she had visited that winter, singing with raised chin and far-seeing eyes, but stopping to dissolve in laughter and dimples when Mattie played a wrong chord just at a crucial spot. He suffered a strong, unexplained feeling of loss, as though he might have known her well but would never see her again, along with a sensation that he somehow had known her well but had lost her. The feeling confused him. He was reminded of what Emily used to tell him during her visits home from Holyoke Female Seminary: "I know how much you all mean to me now, and once I leave here, I'm afraid I'll never see you again!"

At least the sense of panic was easing. Dullness and depression he was more familiar with these days. He brushed the case off and tucked it under his arm gingerly, but already, the malevolent burnt odor had penetrated his hands. The boys milled about at a distance now, telling stories about the fire, pointing here and there. One of them threw a stone at the ruins. Austin decided to leave David Todd's case in his own office on the way home and had begun walking slowly in that direction, when he had an idea. Why not write to the Todds himself? Sue had probably already written her letter to Mabel telling her about the fire, but there was no reason why he shouldn't write his own version. And of course, he could mention the leather case. In fact, he could reassure David that Walker Hall would be rebuilt as soon as possible; that he, as treasurer, would see to that. He began to walk faster. He could address the letter to both of them, with a special greeting for Mrs. Todd. For Mabel.

He was old enough to be her father—perhaps she would be reassured to hear from him about rebuilding plans, for surely, some bad luck had followed David to Amherst, starting with President Seeyle's reluctance to approve the Transit of Venus expedition, and now, the destruction of David's office, classrooms, and books by this fire.

When he reached his office in the Palmer Block, he began to hum a somber favorite hymn, and although no one he passed thought he was smiling, it seemed to him that he was.

CHAPTER 8

March 1882

THERE'S NO NEED TO RAISE YOUR VOICE," SAID
Sue, backing away from Austin's chair in the library. "Why can't you answer
me properly yes or no? You will go with us to Geneva or you won't. It's not an
outlandish question."

"I'm sorry, but I should think you'd know I'm far too busy to make the trip
now," said Austin, looking at her over a folder of papers, "and especially in
March. There's no telling what kind of weather we might have. I'd rather stay at
home."

"You always prefer to stay at home, the more so the older you get. Please
don't cultivate Emily's oddities on that score, that's all I beg of you."

"That's unfair. I travel to Boston and Northampton all the time—it's natural
I would want to stay home and rest when I'm not working. Besides, there's so
much to be done about this fire right now, you know that. Most of the responsibilities fall on me."

"You certainly spent enough time going over the ruins this afternoon," Sue
said. She went into the hallway, then turned and approached him again. "What
about the musicale this evening at Seeyle's house? We're going, aren't we?"

Austin sighed. "I suppose so."

"There it is, a perfect example of your unenthusiastic attitude. Mattie told
me she doesn't dare ask you how you liked something for fear your answer will
spoil her fun. Why can't you think about liking something instead of disliking
it before you've done it or heard it? I try to tolerate your scepticism but it's hard
sometimes."

She made an elaborate show of smoothing the pleats on one of the curtains
in the library. Finally, stepping back and glancing quickly at Austin, she said,
"Mrs. Parsons made an interesting remark the other day when I was visiting her
in Northampton. She said—she said I'd changed so, from the days when we
first met and our children were young."

"Oh?"

"Don't you wonder what she meant?"

"Did she tell you?"

"Yes, she did, as nicely as she could. She wondered why I wasn't so lively as I used to be—that's what it boiled down to. She says I'm subdued."

Austin did not respond.

"Do you think I'm subdued?" she persisted.

"No, certainly not."

"Well, I feel subdued much of the time."

"I don't know what she means by the word 'subdued' anyway," said Austin.

"But I've always liked thinking of myself as lively and stimulating," said Sue. "Remember how the Bowles would come over here and we'd laugh so and play music and make up games? That's how I like to think of myself—the way I was with Samuel Bowles and the other guests we used to entertain. Now I see I've been fooling myself for some years. I've become more like you."

There was silence between them and finally, Austin's tired sigh. "I thought we had seen the last of this discussion," he said in a barely audible voice. "I remember we used to have it after some of those parties when Samuel Bowles was here. But I thought you had agreed to accept me as I am and that I had agreed to accept you as you are. Didn't we find agreement after all?"

"Yes, I suppose we did. But to have Mrs. Parsons make such a remark—it made me think about things again."

"I wish you wouldn't think about it," said Austin. "The most honest thing I can tell you is that I can't change to please you any more than I already have over the years, and I doubt you can either. I think we've both done our best and there the matter must rest."

"It all seems so final," said Sue. "Is that the way marriages are supposed to be, final like that?"

"I suppose so," said Austin. "But no point in dwelling on it or on Mrs. Parsons's remark. I need to finish reviewing this brief now—I'm in court day after to-morrow."

"Go ahead, I won't bother you anymore."

"It's all right, it's all right," said Austin, looking down at his papers again.

"Well, not quite," said Sue, and left the room swiftly.

CHAPTER 9

June 1882

MILLICENT, BE STILL!" SAID MABEL AS THE train pulled in. She handed the two-year-old a bit roughly to Grandma Wilder, Millicent's great-grandmother, who had accompanied Mabel back to Amherst that June, since David had been detained in Washington. But Millicent began to whimper and hold her arms out to her mother. Mabel ignored the fretting, holding on to the back of the seat as she adjusted her hat with its azure feather, smoothed out her azure skirt, and gathered their bags together.

"You sit still, Grandma, and I'll see if Ned has come to meet us. Susan said he might." She craned her head to look as the train came to a final halt, jerking her backward and then forward. "I don't see him, but wait here, I'll take a look."

In a minute she was back, flustered. "I don't see him or anyone else I know to help us, for that matter." Millicent's whimpers rose into wails. "Oh bother, Millicent, will you be quiet?" She helped Grandma Wilder to her feet and they advanced slowly down the corridor to take the porter's arm and make their way onto the platform.

The clean bracing New England air hit her at the same time that she heard Ned's shout, "I'm here, I'm here!" as he came running from the street toward the depot in an awkward gambol, waving his hat.

She turned all smiles. "Why Ned Dickinson, aren't you sweet to meet us! You really didn't have to, but now that you have, I'm so glad." As he reached the platform, she held out both hands which he took shyly with a broad, self-conscious grin.

"Our man is coming round with the carriage; I'll take care of everything," he said, shifting his feet and casting glances down Main Street toward his house. "At least I told him to hitch up the horse. Where is he?"

"Oh, he'll be here, don't worry. You have met my grandmother? Grandmother, this is Ned Dickinson, Sue's son, you remember?" Ned bowed. At that moment, Millicent struggled once again to grab for her mother, but Mabel refused to take her.

"How are graduation plans going, Ned?" she asked, advancing with him slowly down the platform toward the street.

"I'm planning a big party on the 19th of June at my house. I hope you'll come. There'll be dancing, and I know you can't resist that. Mother will give you all the details. Oh, here comes the carriage."

It emerged from Austin Dickinson's drive and made its way toward the depot, a short ride. "I can see why your mother is so proud of that carriage, Ned. It looks quite royal, doesn't it?" She took his arm.

He leaned close to her for an instant. "Yes, it does. I'm a good driver, too, but I'll sit with you in back today and make sure you are comfortable."

"Mabel," came Grandma Wilder's voice from up the platform, "I think you must take Millicent now, she's not settling down until she gets you."

"Well, I can't, please just wait," Mabel called back, and continued to hold Ned's arm, putting her other hand over his arm as well. "Do you mean I'll get to dance with you and your friends at this party? Mr. Todd probably won't be back, you know. Scandalous!"

Ned smiled in delight and confusion but didn't answer. Instead, he walked her to the carriage which by now was pulling up near them. "I'll get your bags."

As soon as he left to gather the bags and hand them to the driver, Mabel turned and took Millicent. The whimpering and crying stopped, but Mabel's eyes were distracted. "Grandma, you didn't forget your gloves, did you? Oh, for heaven's sake! I'll ask the porter to run and look for us."

Ned came dashing back. "Gloves? I'll get them. Where were you sitting?" He hurried in his uneven gait to the train, returning in a few minutes with the forgotten pair of gloves.

Eventually all was ready, and they climbed into the Dickinson's carriage as the afternoon shadows lengthened. "I forgot to ask you something," said Ned. "Mother wants to know if you can all stay for supper."

"How sweet your mother is. But we can't, especially with Millicent so cranky."

Grandma Wilder spoke up. "I'd just as soon stay at home, Mabel, but why don't you go over once we get Millie settled down. She's ready for an early supper anyway, and then maybe she'll sleep. I wouldn't mind a nap too. "

"Oh, are you sure, Grandma? Really sure?"

"Yes, you just go ahead whatever hour they want you. We'll be fine."

"Well, Ned, tell your mother 'yes' then."

"I'll send the carriage back for you."

"No, too much bother. But if you want to walk over for me... It's going to be such a lovely evening—just look at the sky—and I'm so glad to be back, away from that damp and noisy Washington."

"I'll be there then. We all missed you."

"I missed your family a lot, but especially you."

And at that, Ned boldly slipped his arm behind Mabel along the leather seat, and they set off for the boarding house past the Dickinson meadow, the young green leaves, the lilies and fading peonies, and the orderly fences of Amherst.

When Ned and Mabel arrived at the Evergreens for supper, Mattie, who had spotted them earlier from the piazza just as the gas lamp began to glow, opened the front door and ran outside to hug Mabel. "I've been practicing the piano," she announced, "and I'm all ready to play for you tonight. Was Washington exciting? Did you go to any balls?"

"Oh, Washington was quite exciting, Mattie, and I did, in fact, go to two balls. But I missed Amherst, especially our times together here at your house. Dickinson society is as good as any society for me!" Arm in arm, Mattie and Mabel entered the house, Ned behind them.

"Welcome home, Toddy! How we missed you!" said Sue, advancing from the parlor with outstretched arms.

"I missed you too!" said Mabel, and the two embraced.

"We simply loved your letters," said Sue. "Ned began to ask every afternoon, 'Did Mrs. Todd write today?' Tell me, is everyone quite well in your family?"

"Quite well. David hopes to return soon and tackle all the mess of Walker Hall. I must say, I dread seeing it, at the same time as I'm fascinated by the way a solid building like that can be turned into a blackened shell within a few hours."

"Awful, dreadful. Austin's been in a perfect fuddle over it. He's late tonight again—he's probably forgotten we might have company. I told him I'd ask you to supper if you felt up to it."

"That's all right, I understand how busy he must be," said Mabel.

"Ned, if he doesn't come home in fifteen minutes, you'll have to run over to the office. If he's not there, we'll just eat without him. Will you take Mabel's wraps?"

Ned returned to the hallway with Mabel's things while the others settled down in the parlor, Sue in a chair and Mabel on the little loveseat where she and Ned had sat after their waltzing, while a delicious aroma of baked chicken wafted through the house. "Mama, can I play something for Mrs. Todd before supper?" asked Mattie.

"Of course, dear, that would be lovely." Mattie ran toward the piano while Sue leaned toward Mabel. "She really has been working hard. You've been such a good influence on her. She's delighted that you're back. Is that a new dress from Washington? Such a beautiful azure color."

"Yes, it's new, but I added the embroidery myself," said Mabel.

"A sonatina. By Clementi," announced Mattie loudly, adjusting her skirts and moving the music into place. "And I know some of it from memory, but by no means all, so I'll keep the music in front of me."

"Of course," said Mabel. "That's to be expected."

Mattie began to play, ignoring the sound of the two back doors closing as someone entered the house. She stumbled only once or twice, and at one point, she looked up at someone or something Mabel couldn't see, her back being to the doorway, but continued playing smoothly. When the dried flowers in the basket by Mabel trembled slightly and the air felt heavier behind her, she realized someone had walked up and stood near her, Ned probably, anxious to be close. But Mabel was fully absorbed in the music, as usually happened when she listened or played and sang herself. Her own months at the New England Conservatory came back to her vividly. Mattie's playing showed talent and delicacy, and deserved careful teaching.

When the sonatina ended and she and Sue clapped, Mabel glanced behind her to see not Ned, who was nowhere in sight, but his father, Austin. He was almost leaning over her, but his head was turned toward the window where he looked out with a distant, absorbed gaze, as though he had remembered something and was thinking deeply. The end of the sonatina and Mabel's glance caught him off guard, and he now looked at her directly, focusing his eyes on her in surprise. Ready to tease him, she started to say, "What on earth are you thinking about?" when something made her stop, and all she said, unplanned, was "Sit with me." Without a word, he sat beside her and looked toward Mattie, as though they were in a formal concert hall.

"Austin, what took you so long?" said Sue. "I was about to send Ned for you. In fact, he may have already left."

"I'm right here, " said Ned from the hallway. "I couldn't leave our beautiful guest."

Sue rolled her eyes and laughed for Mabel's benefit, but Mabel didn't seem to have heard Ned's comment, and rose quietly to look over Mattie's music.

Austin and Sue sat in silence, Sue fondly watching her daughter, Austin staring at the rug. But when he stood up and began to leave the room, Mabel turned quickly. "Are you leaving? I forgot to thank you for writing to me in Washington."

"Did you write to Mabel and David? You might have told me," Sue said turning to her husband. "I could have included your letter with mine. What on earth did you have to say?"

Mabel left the piano and rejoined them. "It was about the fire and David's losses. And that satchel of his which miraculously survived. Do you have it for us, Mr. Dickinson?"

"I told you," said Sue, "if you call me Sue, you must certainly call him Austin. He doesn't mind. He just looks fierce." She laughed heartily.

"The case is safe and sound in my office, but I'll bring it here to the house where you may find it," said Austin. "Or if you need it sooner, I can even get it now." He half rose from his seat.

"Oh, don't be silly, there's no rush. Why don't I just stop by your office in the next few days when I'm on Main Street doing errands anyway, and pick it up?"

"If that doesn't inconvenience you..."

"It would be a pleasure. Just keep it there, I'll be by."

"Your husband has certainly suffered some losses in the fire. Let me tell you again in person how sorry I am. It's hard luck for a young professor, but I'll do everything I can to ease his problems and support him, both now and when he returns."

"You are very kind to watch over us this way," said Mabel sitting on a footstool in front of him. "I don't know what we would have done had not you and Sue been so hospitable to us. We think we are very lucky, David and I."

"Think nothing of it," said Sue. "We are only too glad. Now Mattie, Ned, entertain Mrs. Todd while I make sure everything is on the table for dinner."

Ned joined his father on the settee, Mabel remained on the footstool, her azure skirts trailing gracefully on the floor, while Mattie sat in a chair apart from the three and watched them, smiling with pleasure.

CHAPTER 10

June 1882

Mabel Todd, ignoring the threat of rain, left Kelly's tailor shop, passed Arthur Bardwell's clock and watch repair, and headed for Adams Apothecary on the corner of Phoenix Row by the Common. But instead of entering it, she postponed buying the cough drops in favor of a visit to Austin Dickinson's office in Palmer's Block. She had told him she would come any day to pick up David's leather case. "If it doesn't inconvenience you..." were his exact words, but she felt he would be glad to see her. And of course, it didn't inconvenience her—she found that she wanted to drop by, very much. Oddly, it was the first thing she had thought about when she had awakened that morning, lying stretched out in the bed which seemed so empty while David was gone.

Austin's heavy, serious presence, his sober eyes, the remote air he affected with most people but dropped so disarmingly with her—all these things had begun to appeal to her, to linger sweetly in her mind. It struck her that he was wise. As wise as her father. Someone to learn from. And yet, Sue laughed at him often, leaving him alone in his own circle of thought.

But he had been so kind to David, and towards her, he behaved with an air of tenuous solicitation, as though he were afraid she would rebuff his efforts. Underneath that gruff exterior lay a tender interior, she felt sure. Anyone who took such an interest in planting trees and shrubs—who carefully planned long rides into the woods to look for just the perfect specimens, despite his busy schedule—well, there had to be more there than met the eye. "I don't like to trust anyone with an oak," he had said solemnly. David said Austin had been responsible for planning and clearing out the Amherst Common, the very Common she was crossing right now.

She glanced upward at the windows nearest her and was startled to see a man's figure looking down at the street in thought, pulling his sideburns, his shoulders hunched forward. His eyes were unseeing until he turned his head to catch her in his vision, when in sudden recognition, he straightened up, raised his hand to her and turned quickly to leave the room and descend the stairs.

That it was, indeed, Austin Dickinson, unnerved her for a moment, so dark and almost foreboding had he looked, thinking himself unobserved. It crossed her mind that his was a brooding, unpleasant temperament after all, or that something had lately gone wrong in his life. But before she could pursue her thoughts, his boots sounded on the stairs, and he stood above her, smiling.

"I'm so glad you've come. Please, step inside to see my office and visit while you are here. I have no clients right now."

"If you are sure I'm not disturbing you. I musn't stay long in any case—it looks like rain, and I'd rather not be caught out in it without my umbrella."

He advanced ahead of her on the creaking stairs, looking back as she, ascending behind him, inhaled the woody smell of varnish and pencils so typical in village offices. His door was ajar, but the painted letters struck her eye: William A. Dickinson: Attorney-at-Law. Inside his office on his desk, she could clearly see David's leather case, looking both familiar and unfamiliar at the same time.

He stood back to let her enter the room and then pulled out a chair for her in front of his desk, while he stood awkwardly a moment, then sat behind the desk in his large leather-backed chair. "You have been doing errands, I see. Have you many more to do?"

"No, this is the last and then I'm off for our rooms. Though I must say, I will be glad when we find a house of our own. Living in rooms has become tiresome."

"I'm sure it has. You can visit us at the Evergreens as often as you like, you know, even though it's not the same thing as having your own home. But that will come in time."

"I miss having a place to paint," said Mabel, pulling off her gloves and laying down her parcels. "In Washington, David fixed up a little studio for me behind the house where I could spread out my things. I spent many a pleasant hour in that studio."

"I hope you can arrange something similar here too. Will your father and mother visit you here, do you think?"

"Oh yes, and soon I hope. I'd like you to meet them, especially my father."

Footsteps sounded on the stairs, and Austin rose to open the door. Mabel could hear his low voice outside and that of a younger person, an errand boy. In a moment, he returned with a delivery, a sheaf of papers which he laid on the desk before he turned to her again, poised to resume his seat but yet not doing so. Instead, he straightened up and walked around the desk, where he pulled out a smaller chair and sat near Mabel. She smiled and caught his eye. "Don't want you to think I'm playing your lawyer," he said, returning her smile.

Her eyes went to David's case on the desk, but before she could ask about it, Austin came out with, "I find your artwork, your paintings, attractive."

Puzzled, she looked into his face. "You do? And where on earth did you see any of my paintings?"

"Emily showed me the painted flowers you sent her in March. Right before the fire in Walker Hall, I believe. The wildflowers."

She laughed in pleasant surprise. "How nice of her to show you." She turned to face him more directly. "How nice of you to remember."

He gazed thoughtfully at the desktop.

"I guess you know then that Emily sent me some flowers? I was so touched and pleased—imagine, getting such beautiful hyacinths and heliotropes in the midst of a Massachusetts March! She has quite a way with growing things, Sue tells me."

"Yes, she does," said Austin. "She'll probably send you other gifts. She likes you."

"She does?" Mabel smiled. "I'm so glad, though I don't know why she would like me, she hasn't even met me!"

"But she's heard all about you from us."

"From you and Sue?"

"I meant from Vinnie and me."

"Oh." There was a pause while each considered those words.

Mabel changed the subject. "Ned tells me he is having a graduation/birthday party soon. Twenty-one at last."

"Oh that, yes," said Austin. "I leave all such parties and the planning for them to Sue and the children. In fact, I probably won't even be there—I have to be in Boston, but I may return late that evening. They plan it for June 19th, I believe."

"Well, they have invited me and I intend to come. I'm sorry you won't be there too."

He stood up and reached for David's case. "Here you are. Look how miraculously it survived the fire." He placed it into her outstretched hands and watched her examine it, running her fingers over it and even smelling it, as he himself had done, fascinated by the pervasive, sharp burnt smell.

"Amazing," she said. "Just amazing. He will be glad to have it. We both thank you. Surely you cleaned it up?..."

"Yes, it needed cleaning, but not so much as you might expect. It was a pleasure." He remained standing, as though he were going to say something else, but since he did not speak after all, she stood too.

"Thank you very much. I must go now, before it rains," and she reached for her parcels, looking out the window as she did so.

"You needn't go yet," he began, but walked over to the window to look out. "It may be raining. Please, wait here while I run downstairs to see." He went directly down to the street while she stood waiting, her gaze taking in the array of papers on his desk, the diploma and the drab walls. It was a plain office, austere and business-like, made even more so by this cloudy day. She moved to the window and observed Austin below, a dark figure looking up into the sky, his hands outstretched, soberly testing the heavens. It was raining. She could see it now, see how he was squinting. She went to the office door and prepared to descend, but he stopped her by returning rapidly himself.

"It's raining. If you must go, I'll walk you home with my umbrella." He reached the top of the stairs and she backed into the office as he advanced. She did not protest. It was all settled, she would walk home with Austin Dickinson.

CHAPTER 11

July 1882

"PICNIC DAYS, OH, PICNIC DAYS!" SHOUTED Gilbert, whirling in a circle until Mattie caught him, both of them laughing.

"You may sit wherever you like," Sue Dickinson told her friend, Emily Fowler Ford, who stood by the carriage in the Evergreens drive. "You are the guest of honor as long as you stay in Amherst. It's so good to have you back again."

"How kind you are!" said Mrs. Ford. "The way everyone is spoiling me, I won't want to return to Brooklyn, and Gordon won't want to let me go for so long, either!" She went around to the other side of the stage. "I prefer to sit inside in the middle, if it's all right with you."

"Good. I'll sit with you. Who else wants to sit here? Mabel? Mattie, do you and Gilbert want to sit outside in front with your father?"

Before Mattie could answer, Austin spoke up from his position by the horses. "I told Mabel she ought to sit in front again for a change. She can try the reins if she'd like. Mattie doesn't like to sit in front."

Mabel, wearing a soft white dress with a deep collar and a wide brimmed straw hat with a pastel blue ribbon, advanced without hesitation toward the front, while Mattie obediently unfolded her parasol and climbed in back, after which Austin assisted Mrs. Ford and Sue into the carriage. Gilbert scrambled up on his own, chattering away to no one in particular, while Austin turned to Mabel with two outstretched hands, which she grasped firmly while she stepped onto the board and into the leather seat next to Gilbert, her dimples showing as she smiled at the view from this position. She turned around and called to Sue, "You don't know how I've looked forward to this, ever since the first time you took me to Sunderland Park."

"Maybe you'll find another four-leaf clover," called Mattie.

"Find me one, find me one, Mrs. Todd!" cried Gilbert.

"Oh, I know I will. I find them easily. I hardly think anything of it anymore."

She turned, laughing, toward Austin, who stood prepared to step into the carriage himself. With a leap, he made his move, rocking the carriage and turning to smile at her about the four-leaf clovers.

"Well, Sue, are we all ready?" he said, looking back. "Ned has already left with Brad Hitchcock and the rest. Is the food all packed?"

"Yes, yes, everything. You put in the badminton set?"

"Yes."

"Well then, let's go. I must say, you look almost jolly, Austin. And just look at the sky, Mrs. Ford."

"It could hardly be more blue," she replied. I love July days like this. They remind me of wonderful times when we were children here. I wish your Emily would come along with us. We used to enjoy many a blue sky when we were young girls together."

With a click to the horses and a pleased glance at Gilbert and Mabel next to him, Austin set them moving out of the drive into the sun and down Main Street, out toward the Sunderland road.

"I wish I could see Emily while I'm here," said Mrs. Ford behind them. "I can hardly believe she'll flatly refuse to see me, girlhood friends as we were in the old days. We do write from time to time."

Sue laughed. "Don't make any bets on it. She's been reclusive for so long that I can hardly remember the days when we went places together. Of course, we still write notes back and forth. But somehow, that household has never been the same since Mr. Dickinson died. You never know what's going on."

"Really? What do you mean, Sue?"

"Well, for instance, one day I went over there and found Emily in the arms of…"

"Sue, don't tell that story again," said Austin quietly but sternly, turning to look back. "I refuse to hear it. It's not true or fair to my sisters. Excuse me, Mrs. Ford, I didn't mean to upset you."

"I'm surprised he could hear me from up there," Sue whispered to Mrs. Ford.

Mabel looked toward Austin's impassive face, intrigued. His tone had quieted Sue. It had quieted everyone, in fact, but left Mabel more curious than ever about this sister whom she had never met. No one talked for a few minutes. Then, in the silence, Gilbert said, "Aunt Emily made the bread in our picnic basket, Mrs. Todd."

"Oh, good, Gilbert," said Mabel. "I can't wait to have a piece."

Conversation restored, the ladies and Mattie chatted in back while Austin pointed out various sights to Mabel: family cemeteries, a barn struck by lightning two years ago, abandoned farms, and trees, especially trees. Their conversation ranged from hymn singing and ministers to apple butter and funny-cake. And when they weren't talking, Gilbert entertained them with tales from school.

While his son chattered, Austin observed Mabel, both when she caught his eye and when she did not, but simply sat in profile to him with her curved straw hat, her dimples, and her gentle young woman's figure in the soft folds of the white dress. He observed her when he was at home too, in his mind's eye, and sometimes saw her face before he slept at night. She seemed to enjoy his company more and more now that David was so often away—though he saw that she enjoyed Ned's company too. He hadn't wanted to join in Sue's constant round of parties and soirees, until in mid-June, he discovered he enjoyed the events if Mabel and David Todd were there. Mabel's lively conversation and her interest in nearly everything attracted Sue as much as they did him, it was clear. Sometimes, it seemed as though the whole family fought one another for Mabel's undivided attention. Mattie had thrown a small tantrum one week when her piano lesson was cancelled in favor of a country drive organized by her mother with Mrs. Todd. But the battle for Mabel was an invigorating one, and everyone emerged a winner at one moment or another.

The dappled sunshine formed patterns on their heads as they rode under branching trees and then out into clear stretches again. When the carriage wheels hit particularly large bumps in the road, the silverware and dishes in the picnic basket rattled loudly, and Gilbert begged for more bumps and turns even as he held on to his father's arm on one side and Mabel's on the other. Passing Turner's pond, they could all clearly hear the "glumph" of frogs and see turtles on the bank, and by old man Stone's meadow, Austin stopped the carriage so they could watch a kestrel swoop and wheel, and hear its high "klee". They passed martin houses on some farms, and were chased by dogs at others, causing Gilbert to bark back until his mother stopped him.

With a sigh of pure contentment, Mabel finally leaned back and gazed straight up into the sky through the trees, her hands behind her head for a moment. Austin glanced at her with a strange shiver of recognition and something like envy. Had he ever felt that way too, long ago, contented with the moment, or did he only think he had? Didn't he wish he could stare at the sky and smile for no reason at all? But maybe that was what he was doing right now, as he glanced again at Mabel's upturned face and her soft form, all laid out in front of him to see. He looked quickly away, both excited and strangely afraid.

"Austin?" called Sue from behind. "Let's try to set up under the largest picnic grove. There are fewer yellow jackets there than the one we used last time. Did you bring the horseshoes?"

"I helped put them in, Mama," said Gilbert. He began to bounce in his seat a little as they approached the familiar streets of Sunderland and then headed toward the picnic grove where other families were also picnicking. I see Ned, I see Ned! " he shouted as they got closer. Indeed, Ned and his friends Brad Hitchcock and William Clark were waving from beside their little carriage and unloading old rugs to sit on, along with some canvas chairs.

"There, you see Mrs. Ford, we're going to have a wonderful time. Can Brooklyn better this for entertainment?" asked Sue.

They drove to their chosen spot and stopped while Ned ran over to Mabel's side of the carriage and extended his hand as he greeted her. "I've saved a special chair just for you."

Austin, who had also started over to Mabel's side, turned to answer his wife's call to aid Mrs. Ford, who was gathering her skirts about her in preparation for stepping down.

"Thank you, Austin," she said, extending a gloved hand and a tenuous foot. He supported her arm carefully, but not without a look in Mabel's direction just in time to see her jump down from the carriage, Ned's eager hands on her waist. They began to stroll around the picnic grove chatting animatedly, while Austin escorted both Sue and Mrs. Ford to their chosen spot under the trees and returned to the carriage with Gilbert and Mattie for baskets, rugs, wraps, chairs, and games. "Let's take a long walk," said Ned returning with Mabel.

"A short walk," pleaded Gilbert. "I'm hungry."

"No, a long one," said Ned firmly with a smile at Mabel.

Sue settled it. "We'll walk over to the little orchard and then back by the stream. A half hour or so. By then we'll be hungry and we can start setting out the food. Is that all right with you, Mrs. Ford?"

"Certainly. I'd love to see the little orchard grove again. I remember picking apples there on fall days. But mind, I don't walk very fast nowadays."

"Well, neither do we. Just let the young ones go on ahead, as fast as they please, and you and Austin and I will take our time. Austin? You weren't trying to follow Mabel and Ned and Brad were you? Don't be silly!"

"No, I'm just watching Gilbert. I guess he can run ahead with them."

He watched Gilbert scamper off and join the little bevy around Mabel, who seemed to be in the middle of telling some story or another, since she gestured lavishly from time to time, and Brad and Ned broke out into laughs.

"She's wonderful for Ned," said Sue to Mrs. Ford, looking at Mabel ahead of them. "He's much less quiet than he used to be, and more outgoing, more confident, I think. She draws him out. Don't you think so, Austin?"

"Yes, I believe she does."

"She works like a magic charm on him," continued Sue.

"And where did you say she is from?" asked Mrs. Ford.

"Most recently from Washington, D.C. She and her husband started out their married life there, but they've only been married a few years."

"And where is her husband?" asked Emily.

"In Washington again. He's there half the time, it seems. President Seelye is becoming a little testy about it. But Mr. Todd has obligations at the Nautical Almanac Office. He used to do astronomical work there."

"It's lucky she has no children yet, or she couldn't be off on picnics so easily."

"Oh, but she does, she has a little girl, Millicent," said Sue. "She's about two years old, and she often stays with the grandparents in Washington. But she's in Amherst now, along with the grandparents. Loomis is their name. I haven't met them yet, but Mabel promises to bring them around soon."

"How odd," said Mrs. Ford. "Somehow I wouldn't have thought she had a child."

As they spoke, Mabel turned back for an instant. "Lower your voice, she'll hear you," said Austin. But Mabel only smiled and waved, and turned to accept a dandelion from Ned, a gray-headed one which she blew.

"She's lively and she's fun," continued Sue. "We've all enjoyed having her and her husband David around."

"Austin," asked Mrs. Ford, "do you think your sister, Emily I mean of course, will receive me sometime soon if I visit with Vinnie at the Homestead? Maybe if I write her a special note?"

"I'm almost positive not," said Austin, "but you can ask Vin what she thinks when she drops by the house tonight. Of course, Vin will see you with pleasure any time you want. If anyone could persuade Emily to visit, it would be Lavinia."

"Oh, I hope so. I love her letters, and she has always held a special place in my heart. I haven't forgotten our school days and the talks we used to have. Oh, the funny games we used to make up. Emily was always so terribly clever."

"The best you can do is try," said Austin. "But if she refuses to see you, don't take her refusal to heart. She turns almost everyone down. It's just her way, and there's nothing else to be said about it. She prefers quiet times with family members or writing by herself. I think she's written quite a bit by now."

"Do you see her often, Sue?"

"It may seem hard to believe, Mrs. Ford, but I don't see her these days. She leaves it to me to go over there rather than the other way around. But we do write notes back and forth often. Of course, she's wonderful with my children. And she still shows me some of the poems she writes, but we don't see eye to eye anymore on some things."

"Is her hair still that lovely auburn?"

"It has hardly changed a bit," said Austin.

"Does Mabel Todd know her?"

"Not at all, and you know, I have to laugh," said Sue. "She is absolutely dying of curiosity about Emily. She keeps asking us questions about her, as though she's some mysterious ghost in the attic. She's so frustrated that she can't see Emily face to face. Well, she's met her match I think."

They had reached the orchard and Austin had his eyes on the trees, stopping to examine the condition of some of them. Ahead, Mabel tossed an apple at Ned, who caught it and threw it back, making her scream in surprise and duck. Gilbert ran back to join his parents. "Will we eat soon? I'm hungry, Momma."

The picnic hampers and linens lay in disarray. One tablecloth had been left outstretched in the sun to dry, lemonade having been spilled over a large portion of it, and most of the glasses were still unpacked for those who remained thirsty. Gilbert continued to practice badminton by himself, while Ned and his friends played a foursome.

"Last chance for coconut cake," called Sue. "Mrs. Ford, you'll have these last few crumbs, won't you?"

"Oh no, you have them, I couldn't."

The two settled down in their striped canvas chairs, chatting about schools in Brooklyn and about the teachers at Amherst Academy.

Mabel had played horsehoes with Ned and his friends, but when they finished and decided on a badminton game, she had returned to help Sue with the picnic provisions. But since the conversation between Sue and Mrs. Ford did not interest her, she had wandered off by herself to enjoy the waning sun, the pungent fresh air, and a particularly beautiful little meadow she spotted a way off where cows grazed.

Austin had walked into a harness shop in Sunderland village, and returning, saw Mabel set off alone. Without hesitation, he followed her, and when he drew close enough, he called out, "May I walk with you?"

"It's you," she said. "Of course you may. This balmy afternoon is too beautiful to waste sitting in a chair, and I'm tired of games. I need a little time to enjoy the quiet. Do you too?"

He caught up with her, striding by her side. "Yes, I do. To tell you the truth, I tire when I am with groups for too long. Too much chatter."

She glanced at him. "You are a quiet person, aren't you? I've noticed that. I myself like both to chatter and to be still too. I hope my chattering doesn't annoy you!"

"Never," he assured her. "I wouldn't call your way of talking chatter, anyway. It's talking with something to tell."

"You're very kind to say so." She pointed. "I'm heading toward that meadow over there. It just looks so peaceful, especially after all the games and noise. I decided to let it be the memory of Sunderland I would see in my mind tonight before I sleep."

He was quiet as they walked on together. After a few minutes, she said, "This is a good time for me to thank you and your wife for all your kindness toward David and me. I know we would have been lonely if it weren't for your family."

Austin inclined his head. "We are glad to welcome you here. Sometimes life in a village like Amherst can become too much the same thing every day, so having new faces here pleases us too."

He walked on, and then, taking a breath and glancing sideways at her, added, "Especially faces like yours."

Mabel smiled, looking towards him just as his glance returned to the way in front of him. But her attention was quickly distracted. "Wait!" she said, and kneeling down, pulled a four-leaf clover from the grass in front of his boot. "There. The third one today, what do you think of that, Austin Dickinson?"

He pulled his sober gaze from his boots, looked at the clover she held before him, and smiled a sudden broad smile to meet hers, crinkling the corners of his eyes and transforming his face for her. She continued to hold the clover out toward him, so he took it from her fingers, and after they began to walk again, fished his wallet from his pocket, pressed the clover in a folded calling card, slipped it inside, and put the wallet back. She observed this curiously, glancing at him briefly but without comment. They had reached the old fence dividing them from the meadow, and there they stood, leaning on the wooden rails in the setting sun and taking in the scene: the cows, the bells, the crickets and cicadas, the bees and clover, and the redwings, swallows and martins.

After a pause, Mabel said simply, "I love it." They stood quietly, sharing their enjoyment. A few cows walked up to the fence and thrust their faces toward Austin and Mabel, their muzzles soft and curious. Then with little snorts, they turned and joined the other cows moving toward the end of the meadow by now, rounded up by the farmer's boy for milking. The sound of their clanking bells grew dimmer and dimmer. In their wake, the cicadas' song emerged, barely audible before, but growing stronger and more persistent as the afternoon wound down toward evening.

"It's a strange thing," said Mabel looking to the horizon, "but David doesn't even hear the different bird calls, sometimes not even when I point them out to him. He says they all sound alike. And he certainly doesn't make much of crickets. I call them crickets, but I suppose they're really cicadas. Of course anyone can hear crickets, physically hear them. But—well, how should I say it so that it doesn't sound odd? I find the sound of crickets so comforting. And yet sad at the same time. Why should that be so, that the sound of crickets should make one feel sad?"

Austin shifted his weight and recrossed his arms on the fence railings. "Because of autumn," he said. "The end of things. But mostly, they make me feel happy. They remind me of childhood evenings at home, for some reason. I don't know why. And of the long walks I have taken in the country, just looking at beautiful things—trees, plants, rushing water. Or my walks over our own meadow."

"You mean the land across from Emily and Lavinia's house? Where you said you kept a garden?" asked Mabel.

"Yes. It's a beautiful lot." He was silent a moment, then added, "But if the sound of the crickets ever makes me sad, it's only because sometimes the past is more pleasant to think of than the present."

"Is it?" she asked.

"I shouldn't have said that, I didn't think it out," he said huskily, looking straight ahead. "Sometimes it just seems that way."

They stood quietly and listened together. The glow of the sun began to reflect on their skin and clothes, and they squinted. Austin shielded his eyes for a moment, but Mabel continued to look toward the pink and orange clouds with pleasure.

"Don't stare at the sun," he warned. They turned to face each other. "I would like to be buried where the crickets sang their loudest, that's how much I like their song," he said without preamble, and suddenly, after a long moment when they looked directly into each other's eyes, their hands reached out and touched, then clasped without fear or awkwardness. But as soon as they released their hands, the strangeness of the moment, of the gesture, came over them, and they began to walk back in silence, each full of thoughts, each aware of a new pulse, a shared recognition.

They came within sight of the picnic grove having exchanged no words, but when the others could be seen in the distance bustling about, they slowed their steps and turned to each other again. Mabel smiled first, and Austin followed with a brief smile which hardly touched his eyes. "Thank you for the walk and for talking with me," he said. They returned to the others, who had hardly noticed their absence, except for Ned, who spotted Mabel from afar and loped up, waving an arm and calling, "I won four games of badminton and I'm hardly even tired!" And except for Mattie, who seeing Mabel, asked, "Did you find any more four-leaf clovers?"

"No," answered Mabel, "not a one."

"Goodnight, Mother," called Mattie on her way upstairs to bed.

"Goodnight Mattie dear," answered Sue. "Sleep well!"

"Goodnight, Father," Mattie added. But Austin, deep in thought and trailing behind his wife on the way to their downstairs bedroom, did not hear her.

"It was a fine picnic, don't you think?" Sue asked as she stood unpinning her hair. "Look, a dandelion Gib put in my braid." As Austin didn't answer, but sat to remove his boots, still deep in thought, she raised her voice. "Well, wasn't it, wasn't it a good picnic? Good heavens, Austin, are you listening?"

"Yes, yes, it was a fine picnic. I was just thinking about something. Gib has sunburn on his arms and face again. Did you give him any salve?"

"Yes, I did. Your nose is red too, have you noticed?"

"My nose?" He touched it. "It does feel a little sore, come to think of it. I didn't stay in the shade as much as you did. Or carry a parasol, of course."

"No, you went walking, walking. I'm not surprised you got sunburned.

When you walk off alone like that, you forget about the sun. Next time, take someone with you and wear your widest brimmed hat. Don't always go off alone. You are such a solitary character."

He made no comment, but sat remembering Mabel in white by his side, both of them awash in the orange glow of the sun.

Sue stepped into the little room adjoinng their bedroom to finish undressing and emerged in her gown, plaiting her hair into a single loose braid. In turn, he found his night clothes and finished changing in the adjoining room as well. The evening was warm, and when he returned, he opened another window, letting in the July night breezes and the sound of night owls and bob whites. He leaned out for a moment and breathed deeply. He felt both heavy and light at the same time, happy and sad.

Sue had pulled back the quilts and was in bed, but instead of curling up for sleep, she seemed in a mood to chat.

"Do you think your sister will unbend enough to see Emily Ford?"

"I doubt it, frankly."

"Oh, I do wish she realized how peculiar she has become."

"Just let it go, Sue," said Austin from the window. "There's nothing wrong with not being like everyone else. You know that, as close as you've been to her. You have to accept her as she is."

"Of course I have to accept her, what do you think I've been doing all these years? I love her, despite the emotional demands she's always made on me. And about what I said happened next door that day—she was embracing him, I know what I saw."

"Maybe he was embracing her. Anyway, I don't see why she can't embrace Otis Lord, they are friends.

"Maybe more than friends, Austin."

"It might seem strange. But who are we to question it? And besides, it was probably an innocent embrace."

He remained at the window.

Sue dropped the subject. "Are you coming?"

He moved away from the window, turned down the gas, and got into bed.

There was a rustle of bedclothes and then silence, until Sue spoke up again, clearing her throat as she began. "Austin, I...Well, I want you to know that I've noticed your respect for my...wishes...in the past months. And I appreciate it. Your forebearance with me..."

He was uncomfortably silent, lying on his back.

"It's all right for you to lie close to me if you want to. I don't mind that... Are you listening?"

"Yes, I'm listening."

"Well, I don't mind. In fact, I would like you to stay close sometimes, even if we don't... It's very hard for me to say this."

There was a silence again, but in a moment, he turned to face her awkwardly. She made the first move, sliding toward him until he circled his arm under her neck and around her shoulder. She lay loosely in his embrace, while they listened to the soft sound of their breathing and the rustling mattress. The silence between them was strained, and she did not lay her feet, cold with poor circulation, against his to warm them.

"Ned seemed fine today, didn't you think?" she asked finally.

"Yes, he did. Maybe the epilepsy attacks are really dwindling now. I hope so."

"I think Mabel Todd's flirting with him is just what he needs. In fact, I've encouraged it. It's all perfectly timed, what with David Todd being away so much. She misses him and she's full of high spirits, that's all."

"You really think she's intentionally flirting with Ned? He's only a college boy, after all, and she's a married woman."

"But a young married woman, a very young married woman." Seeing him turn his head toward her, she laughed. "Oh, Austin, it's only a harmless game. They are very close in age, after all. We are old enough to be her parents, you know."

"No, hardly," he protested.

"Of course we are, Austin, Eben Loomis is exactly your age! Mabel told me so."

He had no answer to that. Then, "And you don't think Ned will take it too seriously?

"No, he won't get hurt, he'll just have fun and learn how to get along with girls his own age. I'd like to see him marry one of these days not too long from now."

"Well, yes, I would too, naturally. But his epileptic attacks worry me so."

"Don't let's talk about them tonight, please. I have enough on my mind. And if I don't want to dwell on them, think how Ned would feel if we told him. His confidence in himself could be completely undermined! Better he not know, since he doesn't remember them anyway." She adjusted her braid to one side. "Oh, I set up the photography appointment with Mr. Lovell for Saturday. We're doing the picnic pose we all agreed on. It was Mabel's and my idea."

He shifted his weight slightly. "Move your head a little, my hand is going to sleep."

"Well, your hand is pulling on my hair." She raised her head and he removed his arm, massaging his hand a little as he did so.

"Time for sleep?" she asked

"I think so."

"But I like her so much, Mabel Todd," continued Sue, as she turned away to prepare for sleep, "and I like cultivating her. She has a lot to learn, but I enjoy teaching her. She thinks she is more sophisticated than she is, having lived in both Boston and Washington D.C., but she'll learn." She yawned. "But how young she and David are. Were we ever that young?"

Austin had turned on his back again.

"And will you continue to cultivate the Todds with me?"

"I will," he said, and turned away from her.

CHAPTER 12

July 1882

Shh, your grandma will hear you," said David, rubbing his chin on Mabel's shoulder.

"Then stop, Davey! Besides, I'm only giggling," and Mabel giggled the more as David bit her ear and reached his arm around to fondle her through her night gown. "It's just so nice to have you back home. Soooo nice...No, we can't, we have to get up, last night was enough. Davey! Grandma will hear us, you make the bed shake too much."

"Then it's your turn," said David. "I'll bring you alone and you can be as quiet as you want." She kept her back turned, but as his fondling became more insistent, she turned toward him, and within a minute, was breathless with climax, David breathing noisily with her. She lay pressed close to him, catching her breath, ready to rise again. When she was satisfied again, she whispered in his ear, "You?"

"No, I just enjoyed watching you this time."

"I love you, David."

"I love you too. Stay here, I'll see if Grandma has water heating for your bath."

"Today's the day Sue Dickinson arranged for us to sit for a picnic photograph with John Lovell," said Mabel. "You'll pose with us, won't you?"

"Yes, why not? It will make up for not being at the Sunderland picnic you talked so much about. Besides, I have to talk with Mr. Lovell some more about the Transit of Venus trip. I hope I can persuade him to come with me. If I receive funds for Lick Observatory, that is. You'll love California, Mabel." He threw the covers off and put his feet on the floor.

"I will?" she said. "I've come to like it here pretty well."

"Oh, come on now, there's no comparison between a sunny winter in California and a frozen one here! Wait 'til you see the flowers in the West. They grow all year round!" He stood up.

"I hope *all* the Dickinsons will be there for the sitting. But Ned said maybe his father wouldn't be there."

"You'd better watch out for that Ned, Mabs, he's really got a crush on you. I think he's sorry I'm back in Amherst. When I met him on the street coming up from the train, he sounded almost cool when he said hello, and sort of looked me over, as though he wondered what rights I had around here. But maybe that was just the Dickinson frost. I've decided that we're lucky to be on the right side of Austin and Sue. Phew, they can freeze people out when they want to! I saw Sue stare some woman down in the post office." He found his slippers, used the chamber pot, and put on a dressing gown.

"Well, I'm getting to know Austin a little better," said Mabel, sitting up in bed, "and I think that gruffness hides a sweet soul underneath. He can say gentle nice things when he's alone with people. At least he has to me."

"And he's been nothing but nice to me," said David, "though why he's taken us up so fast, I don't quite know." He lit the little stove and set the kettle of water on top, then went into the adjoining chamber for the tin tub. Returning and opening the door to the hall, he said, "I'll get more water, you snuggle up until I come back." In a moment, Mabel heard him talking to her Grandma Wilder on the stairs, and then Millicent's babbling. Next, Mabel could hear Millicent's little hands moving over the bedroom door as she balanced herself on her chubby legs and said "Mama? Mama?"

"Mabel, shall I bring Millie in?" said David from the stairs.

"No, she can wait until I'm bathed and I see her downstairs. I want some peace and quiet in here before my bath."

Millicent's whimpers could be heard next, as David swept her up from the bedroom door and carried her downstairs. Alone, Mabel lay back in the bed and stretched luxuriously, thinking about the crickets in Sunderland, the colors of the setting sun, the rough feel of the fence she and Austin had leaned upon, and above all, the touch of his large warm hands. She imagined those hands holding a pen and writing her a letter which had traveled safely all the way to Washington with her name on it. She imagined him forming the letters themselves of her name—"Mrs. Todd"—the proper formal way, yet full of feeling, the way she read it, as though he had touched her physically, somehow. He had trouble calling her "Mabel," even though Sue had suggested they use their Christian names, and avoided the problem by referring to her through his children whenever possible—"Mattie, would you ask Mrs. Todd if she needs help with the basket?" Or, "Gilbert, show Mrs. Todd the woodchuck hole you found." She suspected now that he was attracted to her. But what struck her this morning with clarity was that she herself was attracted to him. Strongly so. Playful attractions to men in Washington and to young men here, like Ned, delighted her, made her even more amorous with David and he with her. But her growing awareness of Austin as a force almost, to be met and studied, met and touched, took her by surprise. Discovering slowly that the profile he presented to the world was not the one he lived by had sparked her attraction to him. She had thought the Dickinsons had everything: social position, respect in the community, material posessions, self-assurance, and fine children. But she could see now that imperfections aplenty lurked behind the family face the Dickinsons presented to Amherst. For some reason, Ned was not mentally or physically strong, Mattie was wary of her father, several villagers had hinted at resentments toward Sue and her fine ways, Austin's mother was an invalid and his sisters eccentric, and above all, Austin was troubled, somehow unhappy. At first, she had thought his somber manner was just his way. But she had seen by now, and more than once, his whole face change, utterly change into warmth and trust, and two of those times, he had been looking at her. The other times, he had been playing with Gilbert or looking at the hills and trees from his seat in the carriage. And the look on his face as they had impulsively clasped hands in Sunderland a few days before—that look and those somber eyes came to her as she woke in the morning, and followed her descent into sleep after she turned from David and curled into her pillow. She found herself wondering if her father would like Austin Dickinson. She would write a letter to him, describing the whole Dickinson family in more detail than she had so far given.

David made his way along the hall to their room and set down the hot water while he opened the door. "Are you ready for your bath?" He carried the water to the tub and began to pour.

"All ready." She stood up, removing her nightgown and making her way to the tub, shivering a little despite the warm July weather.

David bustled about her, fetching the soap and sponge and readying her towel, then finally sitting on the bed to watch her.

"You're beautiful," he said, "And I'm your lover husband."

She smiled, luxuriating in his attention and the warm water as she soaped and rinsed. There was a silence, except for the sound of water splashing, Mabel humming a tune, and Millicent and Mabel's grandmother talking below.

"You missed a spot, let me rinse the soap off right there, under your arm," David said, going to her. She sat still while he rinsed carefully, not stepping back until he had checked her sides and shoulders and kissed both nipples lightly. Then he was all abustle readying the towel to dry her and holding it for her to step into.

"Oh, David, if people knew how you pampered me!" she laughed.

"I love to pamper you and I always will," he said.

"But let me finish drying now myself, I'm getting chilly and I'm hungry."

He stepped back. "All right. What do I wear for this photograph?"

"Picnic clothes, of course, what else?"

"What are you wearing?"

"The white dress."

"Ah, good. My favorite. And which hat?"

"The big straw one."

She moved toward the wardrobe and began to take out her clothes. Everyone loved the white dress, and the large brimmed straw hat she had bought in Washington set off her face well. If Austin Dickinson sat for this photograph along with everyone else, she would have, in a sense, a tangible record of their private moment to match the record in her heart.

At breakfast, she held Millicent in her lap to make up for not letting her come into the bedroom, but paid for that indulgence by having to pry herself from the child when it was time to leave and give Mattie Dickinson her piano lesson. "Come to Gran," crooned Grandmother Wilder, and led Millicent off to her toys and pictures so that Mabel could leave. David had already gone to work in the observatory, so Mabel set off alone for the Evergreens, hoping Austin would be there in his study as he had been last week during the piano lesson.

She stopped at John and Candida Musante's food stand on South Pleasant Street to buy some hot peanuts, waiting her turn behind a group of hungry little boys counting their pennies noisily. "Mrs. Todd, good morning!" said Mrs. Musante, emerging from the shop to help her husband dip peanuts from the roaster, her dark Italian eyes smiling. "You are hungry, yes?"

"Yes, but these are for the Dickinson children," said Mabel.

"Oh, very nice, Mrs. Todd. They love the peanuts, the children. Especially the little one. What is his name?"

"Gilbert. He's sweet, isn't he?"

She accepted the hot bag of peanuts, paid, and was crossing the street when the dark familiar figure met her eyes, moving in her direction with an inevitability which arrested all her attention. He held his hand up for an instant, and they advanced toward one another, ignoring the carriages raising dust in the street around them and the other pedestrians.

"You're going to the house?" he asked as soon as they met, without any preliminary greeting, peering close at her eyes to read any expression there.

"Yes," she answered softly. "You'll be back?"

"I can't," he said. "Some building and grounds problem at the College. I need to organize some repairs. I'll try to come back soon, but I don't know..."

"Try," she said. "You're wanted in the photograph."

A cautious smile transformed his sober face.

From across the street came a warm greeting. "Good morning, Mr. Dickinson, Mrs. Todd."

"Mrs. Stearns, how are you?" replied Austin, turning to bow to the smiling woman who approached them. "I haven't seen you since you took cold last week. You are free of it now?"

"Absolutely. The further I advance into my middle years, shall we say, the faster I seem to recover from these things."

"You have met Mrs. Todd, haven't you?" asked Austin. "I think you two might have much in common."

"Yes indeed, we met at the sewing club. It's nice to see you again, Mrs. Todd. You haven't dropped in at The Convent yet. I meant for you to take my invitation seriously and see our little school." She laughed. "I think you need visual proof that it's not really a convent, just a school for girls."

"I'd love to, Mrs. Stearns," said Mabel. "Would Monday afternoon be convenient, since you ask?"

"Certainly. And we'll talk more about the possibility of your giving the girls art lessons. Why don't you bring some of your watercolor studies along? Mr. Dickinson, are you walking toward the College?"

"Yes. Can I do something for you there?"

"No, it's just that I'm going that way too. Shall we all walk together, if we can match his stride?" she said laughing.

"You go ahead," said Mabel, "I'm going another way."

"Then I hope I see you later today, Mrs. Todd," Austin said turning formally to Mabel.

"Yes," added Mrs. Stearns. "Nice to have met you again so soon; I was thinking about you. Until Monday, then. Shall we say about 11 in the morning?"

"Just right," said Mabel. "I hope to see you later too, Mr. Dickinson."

At 3 p.m., the members of the picnic party assembled in John Lovell's studio on Main Street, minus Austin Dickinson.

"But he might be here yet, don't you think?" Mabel asked Ned.

"Not a chance, not when he's busy running things at the College."

"Which is all the time," said David Todd. "Amherst College couldn't run without Austin."

"Well," pursued Mabel, "he should be here for this photograph. He's the only one absent from the picnic group."

Sue Dickinson spoke up. "It doesn't matter, there will be plenty of other picnics. And anyway, we've all learned not to count on Homestead Dickinsons showing up for things. Especially photographs. Can you imagine Aunt Vinnie and Aunt Emily sitting for a group photograph?" She laughed, looking at Mattie and Ned. "Mr. Lovell?" she asked, "Do you need any more props?"

John Lovell, bustling about the studio arranging the backdrop, stopped and looked at the items on the floor—the picnic hamper, the bottles, tennis rackets, and a fan or two—and shook his head. "No, that looks fine. Why don't you start arranging those items here," and he indicated an imaginary line. "The gentlemen will sit on the floor in front, and the ladies will sit or stand in the back."

"What about me, shall I sit with the gentlemen?" called out Gilbert anxiously.

"Sit with me, sweet elf," said Sue, clasping him to her as she sank onto a camp stool. "And here, let me fix your collar."

"Mrs. Todd, I suggest you stand in the back. Yes, there, away from the painted fireplace. And Mrs. Dickinson, you may as well take that stool and sit next to her with Gilbert. Mattie, you may sit by the prop fireplace. And don't burn yourself."

Mattie smiled and sat on a stool with a tennis racket in her lap and a large fan in her hand. She adjusted her straw hat carefully so that her hair showed.

"Mr. Todd, you may kneel or stoop if you wish, in front of Miss Dickinson, and Ned, you stay on that end too, only in front, and you may lean on your elbow."

David put on his straw hat, smoothed his beard and moustache, and winked at Mattie, while everyone else found their final positions. At last, all was ready.

"Everyone, keep absolutely still. You remember how long this takes." Mr. Lovell prepared to go under his black cloth. With further instruction and posing, the first photograph was taken. Then a second, a third and a fourth to be sure they all came out. After the last photograph, someone applauded, and the group, yawning and stretching, broke up.

"Everyone for tea at our house," announced Sue Dickinson, whereupon Ned rushed over to Mabel, opened the door for her, and took her arm with a smile in mock courtly style. David trailed patiently behind as they all sauntered down the street toward the Evergreens, where Sue served up a fine tea on the piazza and everyone enjoyed the soft summer afternoon, despite the absence of the master of the house.

CHAPTER 13

September 10, 1882

I DON'T FEEL LIKE WALKING," SAID SUE TO
Austin and Mabel. "You two go on if you want, and stop in next door for a few
minutes, but come back soon for tea. Mattie has made gingerbread after Emily's
recipe."

"I want you to meet my sister, Lavinia, and to see the house," said Austin as
soon as he led Mabel down the front steps of the Evergreens and out the gate
toward the Homestead. "Today is the day."

"Now? Are you sure it's all right? Do they expect me?"

"Yes, I slipped next door and asked them while you and Sue were talking.
They want you to play and sing for them." He stopped and turned to look
down at her. "And I want them to know you," he said, "very much."

She met his gaze head on, as serious as he was. "And I want to know them."
She laid her gloved hand on his wrist, and he quickly turned his palm over to
make her hand rest in his. At the same time, he quickly glanced up toward the
windows of his father's house, the Homestead, before he withdrew his hand.

"Can we walk a minute before we go in?" asked Mabel. "I want to think
about what to play. And will I meet your other sister, Emily? Or your mother?"

"No, neither one. Mother doesn't like company, confined to her bed as she
is ever since her illness. She's quite weak, and prefers to see just us, her children. Emily rarely likes to meet company either, as Sue told you. It's just her
way. But she is glad you are coming, I can promise you that. She's undoubtedly
seen you from the windows when you didn't know you were being looked at."
His voice became husky. "Just as I have seen you." Mabel closed her eyes tight
for a moment.

They walked past the Homestead, then crossed of one accord to the Dickinson
meadow. "This is my favorite part of the village," said Mabel, "your beautiful
meadow land."

"It's my favorite, too. Look, there's Gilbert and his friends working on their stick castle. It's their most recent project, Camelot, they tell me, in case you can't guess." Mabel laughed, and they walked toward Gilbert and his two friends busy constructing castle ramparts.

Gilbert glanced up and saw them coming. "Papa, come look. We're working on a bridge. Now don't step on anything."

"No, Gib, we'll watch out for Camelot."

He and Mabel stood a moment and watched the boys kneeling in the grass, adding sticks carefully to the little world they were creating, and then walked on through the meadow, the last grasshoppers of the season flying up at their feet, the last crickets chirping unseen. "I could see you living here in a little house," said Austin. "Then you could look at the meadow the minute you woke up." Mabel let her bonnet fall by its ribbons around her neck and smiled as they continued around the meadow and up toward the little railroad depot before their turn back to the Homestead. "Do you know what you will play now?" he asked her after a silence.

"Yes, I do. I'm rehearsing it in my mind. Something light but maybe a little melancholy to start with. Not a hymn though! I'll save that for tonight at the church. I hope you're going to come."

"I'll be there."

They approached the Homestead now, and Mabel found herself glancing at the windows as Austin had done. "Which room is Emily's?" she asked.

"The one in front, upstairs on the left. One of her windows looks out toward the Evergreens."

Mabel's gaze rested on the second story windows for a moment. Then she adjusted her collar and cuffs as they ascended the steps in front of the gate and walked inside the property which sat above the street, separated from the carriages and the people who walked below.

Austin rapped once loudly and then opened the door, stepping back to let Mabel pass in front of him. "Vinnie? We're here," he called. "Mrs. Todd is here."

Lavinia Dickinson emerged immediately from the parlor where she had been standing by the window. The green shawl, stained at the edges, slipped from one shoulder as she reached out her hand. "Mrs. Todd, I am so glad to meet you." She inspected Mabel's face and figure openly as she spoke. "You are lovely— I didn't know your hair was so curly around your face. Why didn't you bring her before, Austin? I was getting tired of waiting."

"Miss Dickinson, I think it's about time I met you too," said Mabel. "Your brother has spoken of you so many times that I decided Amherst would not be worth anything until I had met you!"

"Come, sit down here," said Lavinia, bustling with excitement as she indicated a chair and began and arranging pillows. "Oh, your hat and things, I forgot!" she exclaimed, and reached for Mabel's hat and gloves, which Austin ended up taking from Lavinia. "Our Maggie has typhoid," explained Lavinia, "or she'd be here to take your things. Oh, poor Maggie."

"How terrible. Has she reached a crisis?"

"We think so, but nothing is sure. Emily writes to her to keep her cheerful. You certainly have a small waist!"

"Why, thank you! How is your mother today?" asked Mabel.

"Somewhat stronger than yesterday. That's why we decided today would be a good day to bring you over. Mother is anxious to hear you make some music. The days are so tiresome for her, and Austin says you sing beautifully. But will you take tea first?"

Austin, who had sat next to Mabel, stood up. "We can't, Vin, Susan expects us for tea over there. I'll bring her back soon for tea another day." He crossed to the fireplace. "What happened to that fire? It's almost out and it's cold in here."

"Well, I can't do everything, with Maggie sick. Besides, I knew you'd fix it," said Lavinia.

Austin took the fire tongs, added another log, rearranged the one already there, and tucked in some kindling. In a moment, the flames blazed forth.

Upstairs, the floorboards creaked. "I'll run up and make sure Mother and Emily know we're here," said Austin, and disappeared into the hallway where he took the back stairs.

"They know we're here all right," said Vinnie bluntly. "The pair of them are sitting up there, all prepared to enjoy your company from afar. Two blackbirds on a fence. This is the highlight of their day."

"And Miss Dickinson won't come down to see me?" asked Mabel.

"Oh, heavens, no, I hope you're not counting on that, Mabel Todd. She'll probably listen to you from the stairs. I suppose I shouldn't tell you that, you might be squeamish about people's little oddities. When will I meet your husband?" Lavinia said all in a rush.

Mabel smiled at Lavinia's bluntness. "Whenever you want. Just invite him."

"Well, I've seen him over there—" she gestured with her thumb toward the Evergreens—"and he looks like a nice man. I like his beard and that straw hat he wore in August. And Austin likes him, so you may as well bring him over soon and not wait." She stood. "Here's our piano." Her shawl had fallen to the floor.

Suppressing a smile, Mabel picked up the shawl for Lavinia and then went immediately to the instrument, for her eyes had found it the minute she stepped into the front parlor. At the same time, she heard Austin's steps returning. But as he entered the room, Lavinia jumped up."Wait, wait, the Hills's dog must be worrying Buffy again in the garden, I'm almost sure I heard something!" She rushed to the hallway and out the back, a wispy-haired plump spectre, calling over her shoulder toward the stairs, "Now Emily, don't be cross, it's Buffy. Just wait a minute, wait a minute now."

Austin crossed solemnly to face Mabel where she sat at the piano bench, but she was laughing. Covering her eyes for a moment, she looked up to say, "I'm sorry, but is she always like this?"

In an instant, Austin's face was transformed into a smile too. But before he could say anything, Mabel continued with, "And does she have a crush on David, do you suppose? She likes his straw hat and his beard!"

"Well, well, my sister Lavinia," he said, looking at the rug and shaking his head. "She is entertaining, isn't she?"

Mabel lowered her voice. "Oh, I like her, don't misunderstand me. She just makes me laugh. She's fun. I like the unexpected."

Silence fell on the parlor as they waited for Lavinia, both mindful of being alone, yet of being listened to at the same time by the unseen pair above them.

Mabel began to look through some music in the cabinet next to her, while Austin walked slowly to stand behind her. They waited, acutely aware of each other's physical presence. Finally, Austin said, "You must come visit here often. Everyone will welcome you. And..."

Mabel waited for him to go on, but he did not. She prompted him after a moment. "And?"

"And I...Can I say that...Mrs. Todd, I am very much afraid of offending you at this moment."

"I said you should call me Mabel. Unless I am offending you in suggest-ing —"

"No, no. But I find the turn of events lately so unexpected. So pleasant...I meant that ..." and he actually stuttered for a moment.

She turned and faced him. All was quiet. His shoulders relaxed, he took a deep shaky breath, and simply held out both hands. She placed hers in his, and he took a breath again. When he spoke, his voice was almost a whisper.

"Being alone with you here at home—it has made me want to talk with you in ways I can't to anyone else. The more I see you, the more I think of to tell you. I want you to know that I have enjoyed your company very much, and I feel sad because I know I cannot expect to enjoy it as much as I hope to. But for a moment, here in this quiet room with you alone, I can imagine other quiet times with you like this. And if I have said inappropriate things, I know you will not condemn me. Maybe laugh at me, but with understanding, I hope. You are so young, and I am just a sad man, old enough to be your father. But somehow, I have thought we have things to give each other."

"Laugh at you? Oh, never!" Mabel whispered back. "Don't you know that the first time I looked into your blue eyes, I knew I could trust you? Trust you forever!"

He stared at her, caressing her knuckles with his strong thumbs, his expression fixed and serious. "You can trust me. Fully. And I can trust you too, I feel sure. Mabel, I've felt happy for the first time since you came. Maybe there is hope for me."

"Hope for you? But what is making you so unhappy? Tell me, what is making you sad?"

He dropped her hands, and hunching his shoulders, began to pace a few steps, when they heard Lavinia returning from the back. Mabel turned quietly around to face the piano squarely, while Austin sat down on the settee.

Lavinia's footsteps came through the front hallway and then into the parlor, as she brushed cat hair from the front of her dress. "Buffy has been naughty. It wasn't that cursed dog after all, she had a half dead bird. I took it away from her and gave it its final rest in the waste pile. Now Austin, don't you dare mention that bird to Emily. Play now, Mabel. Oh, pardon me, I should say 'please'. I'll sit down here in the best chair and listen. It's about time we had some music around here."

Mabel played "Never Weather Beaten Sail" through in its entirety, before singing three verses in her clear, pleasing soprano. At first, she looked only at Lavinia or the music, but finally she stole glances at Austin as she sang the chorus lines. He stared at the floor, deep in concentration, never raising his eyes.

When Mabel finished, Lavinia clapped and exclaimed, "You sound beautiful! Just beautiful! Did Austin say you will sing in church tonight?"

"Yes. Just a short "Amen" arrangement. Something I used to sing in Washington."

"Well, maybe I'll have to come then, if Mother continues as well as she has this week. Austin, did you know she sang so well?"

"I told you, she has sung with Sue and Mattie next door lots of times. Yes, I knew she sang so well."

"Sing something else. Or play something else. Whatever you like," said Lavinia. "Oh, Mrs. Todd, you are so talented."

"What do you think your sister and mother would like to hear?"

"I think they'd like a hymn, don't you, Austin, since they never go to church?"

"A hymn would be fine," confirmed Austin. "Do you know "Come Thou Almighty King"? That used to be one of Jonathan Jenkins' favorites—he was our minister at First Church for years."

"Where is your hymn book?" said Mabel.

Lavinia came over to the music cabinet and found the book, riffling through pages until she found the place. "Here," she said, placing it on the piano, "And play it loudly."

Mabel played the hymn through first before she began to sing. After the first verse, Lavinia sang along with her warbling notes, and at the third verse, Austin stood next to his sister at the piano and added his voice. At that, all three sang ever louder, Lavinia looking up at Austin and laughing some of the words instead of singing them. After the sixth and last verse, all three laughed, Lavinia the loudest, as she reached for her brother's arm and shook it affectionately.

"Oh Lord, what fun, Austin! Why don't we do this more often?" Still laughing, she went out into the hallway and called toward the stairs, "Emily, did you hear that?" Returning to the parlor, she added, "Stars, how could she miss it? What would Sue say if she could have heard you bellowing away just now, Austin? Oh let's sing and laugh more often. It reminds me of when we were young."

Mabel now began playing a Bach prelude, softly enough so that Lavinia could continue talking. Austin had returned to a chair, his smile faded, vaguely listening as Lavinia chattered to him about Maggie's health, the apple trees, and Henry Hills's horse. Mabel went on to play the matching fugue, when there was a knock on the ceiling above the hallway.

"Mother or Emily wants something. You go, Austin, I'll stay with Mrs. Todd."

Austin rose and went straight upstairs. In about five minutes, he could be heard descending the stairs and walking to the back of the house. Shortly, he reappeared, carrying a tray with two ruby colored wine glasses and a folded piece of paper beside them. "Thanks from your listeners," he said. "And the tray and its contents from Emily." He set down the tray. "Come sit over here," he said to Mabel. When she sat on the sofa, he handed her the piece of paper first. "She wrote this especially for you." He watched as she unfolded the paper, while Lavinia leaned over to see the words.

Elysium is as far as to
The very nearest Room
If in that Room a Friend await
Felicity or Doom—

What fortitude the soul contains
That it can so endure
The accent of a coming Foot—
The opening of a Door—

"She wrote this for me? While I was playing?" exclaimed Mabel, and read the poem aloud.

"My sister is very, very clever," said Lavinia. "She writes beautiful poems and sends them to people, but only to people she likes."

"She told me," said Austin, "to tell you to come here often. She enjoyed your playing and singing, and wishes she could sing the way you do."

"Does she play the piano?" asked Mabel.

"She used to play well, didn't she, Austin?'" said Lavinia, turning toward him. "But in her own Emily way. Remember those strange unearthly melodies she used to make up?"

Austin smiled. "Yes, I do. How very long ago that was..."

"Yes, odd eerie melodies she made up on the spot. They used to give me delicious gooseflesh. But Father didn't like them. 'Why can't you just play what's in your music?' he used to ask her. Austin, give Mrs. Todd some sherry."

"I forgot." He stood and handed her a glass, taking the other himself.

"You don't want any?" Mabel asked Lavinia.

"Me? No, don't much like it. Go ahead, drink it up."

Mabel turned to Austin. "To your health," she said.

"To yours," he answered.

"And yours too, Miss Dickinson," said Mabel.

"Aren't we a cozy trio?" Lavinia said in return, looking with satisfaction from Austin to Mabel. "I'm glad you're starting to visit us here more often, Austin." She turned to Mabel. "For so long, it seems, we hardly ever saw him. He works too hard. College, college, always college. And if it wasn't that or the law office, it was entertaining. And now parties for Mattie."

"Yes, tomorrow, Mattie is having a whist party," said Mabel.

"Well, don't you get caught up in Sue's whirlwind, Mrs. Todd. And may I say right now, I am so glad you have turned out to be an agreeable person, because if you hadn't, I would be sick indeed of hearing your name every day. Everyone next door is raving about you."

Mabel smiled and prepared to answer when there was a knock at the back door. "Now who on earth could that be?" said Lavinia, going out into the hallway. In a minute, she returned from the back of the house. "It was Mary, next door, Austin. Sue sent her to summon you and Mrs. Todd home for tea."

Austin glanced at the parlor clock, checked it with his own pocket watch, and rose. "I'll get your things," he said to Mabel.

"How should I thank your sister for the poem and the wine?" she asked.

"I'll convey your thanks," said Lavinia. "But she knows already, she knows."

Austin placed Mabel's cloak around her shoulders and handed over her gloves. "I'll write to her," said Mabel. "Luckily I can thank you in person right now for inviting me and letting me play your piano. I enjoyed it so much."

"Come again soon. I'll nag at my brother to bring you over in a few days."

Austin opened the heavy front door, and they both stood on the steps a moment and breathed in the fresh air.

"It's going to rain tomorrow," said Lavinia. "You won't want to be out in the floods. Sometimes this street flows like a muddy old river."

"We don't mind, we'll cross the rivers if we meet up with them," said Austin. "Are you ready for the Evergreens now, Mabel?"

"Ready," she answered, and they descended to the path between the houses this time, rather than take to the open street.

September 10, 1882

~

JOHN," SAID MARIETTE JAMESON TO HER husband that same Sunday evening over supper, "I saw Austin Dickinson and Mrs. Todd on yet another walk this afternoon. Just the two of them."

"Now don't go imagining things," said John. "Those Todds and Dickinsons spend so much time together in all combinations. Saturday, you said you watched David Todd and his wife and Austin all walking together. And another time, it was Sue, Austin, and Mabel."

"I know, I know. It's just that Mabel Todd affects such a flirtatious air. She's always...I don't know...bouncy, you might say. Talks too much. Has to be the center of attention."

"Oh well..." John Jameson forked up a large helping of boiled beef and potatoes.

"It's not that I don't like Susan Dickinson either, but I do get impatient with her when she's bent on cultivating someone or other. She overdoes it, as though she wants the whole town to see what she and her chosen prize are up to. It can't be just a carriage ride. No, it has to be the fancy carriage with that driver of theirs. And it can't just be a stroll to church. No, it has to be a costume parade!"

John listened patiently. Although he was tired, he enjoyed hearing the latest news of the Dickinson houses across the street. Certainly there had been more news than usual as Mattie began to have parties of her own and Ned brought home college friends. But mostly, the Todds figured in Mariette's stories, for the two couples were spending more and more time together, and besides, any newcomers to Amherst attracted attention and study.

"Do you wish we went walking with them too?" John asked. "Are you jealous?"

"No," she exclaimed vehemently, "of course not. But I don't think it's proper Susan Dickinson should drag her dignified husband into all those goings on.

She's making him look like a fool. There he is, so serious in that red wig of his, with Mabel Todd laughing like a hoot owl on one side and Susan strutting along on the other. Why must he wear that silly thing on his head, anyway, just because he lost some hair when he had malaria? Of course, even worse than walking out with Susan and Mabel is walking out alone with that Mabel. They stood in front of the Homestead talking for a moment today, very close, too. Then they headed for the meadow and ended up back at the Homestead."

"Is there any more bread?" John asked.

Mariette went to slice some on the cutting board.

"You don't really think there is anything improper going on, do you?" John said, buttering a slice of bread. "I'll grant that Mabel Todd acts flirtatious and forward sometimes, but in my opinion, she acts that way mostly with Ned. And I don't think that's anything more than a game."

"A game, yes, but with poor Ned? The boy is something of a fool. I sometimes wonder if he'll ever grow up. John, you should have seen the bit of writing he showed me one day when I was over there. Mattie can write ten times better, and she's three years younger than he is. It's a good thing he's not in college under the regular program."

"Maybe you're right," he acknowledged. "Maybe Mrs. Todd shouldn't lead him on any chases. But if you want my opinion, a little of her games with Austin wouldn't hurt anything. He wants loosening up, does Austin Dickinson."

"John, no. How can you say that woman should flirt with poor Austin? It's immoral, you know it is."

But John only laughed. "I might need a little of Mabel Todd too if I were married to Sue Dickinson. Sometimes she right scares me!"

At that, Mariette laughed too, rising to take her plate away. "Oh, I shouldn't laugh. But sometimes Susan Dickinson is funny, even though she doesn't know it. She thinks she is so important. Come to think of it, Austin does too. Think he is important, I mean." She reached over for John's plate. "But then of course, he is important."

"He does, and he is," said John, and they laughed together. But just as suddenly, they stopped.

"He's hard to figure out, so somber and gruff and kind, all at the same time," said Mariette, and John nodded. "I think he's a sad man, that's my view," she continued. "What are the Dickinsons living up to, the whole lot of them, do you suppose?"

"Well, don't they say Austin's father was much the same way?"

"Oh, they say he was far more serious," said Mariette.

John shook his head. "Too much work and worry will kill that man. And Emily, lord, she's likely to die from solitude."

"Which leaves Lavinia," said Mariette.

"It would take a lot to kill that one," said John, but then grinned and added, "Oh, I like that crazy Lavinia."

"Well, so do I, some of the time. If she's not too moody. But you have to admit, things are changing over there since the Todds came to town. And I can't quite put my finger on how Austin's family is changing, but it is."

"It all started with that gas light over there," said John. "Before, you didn't see so much, that's all." He chuckled. "Now you see everyone in the spotlight, that's your trouble!"

"Oh, you," she said.

"Yes," he persisted, "you have a front row seat. Good thing it looks like rain tomorrow. You need a rest from looking."

She sniffed indignantly, then smiled, and brought out two dishes of egg custard. "All right, let's forget about Dickinsons for a while. We need the rain anyway."

CHAPTER 15

September 11, 1882

For years afterward, autumn rain always reminded Mattie Dickinson of that strange evening, September 11th, 1882, the evening of her whist party. Looking back, she was to realize that the clandestine events of that evening geared into motion all the other events which changed her family's life irrevocably. Much later, when she read her Aunt Emily's lines about the slant of light oppressing "like the heft of cathedral tunes," she recognized the feeling born in her that rainy September evening of whist.

Not that Mattie stopped adoring Mrs. Todd precisely then. Not at all. The adoration ended some time later. But looking back, she recognized the impact—the malignant power—of the evening on her life, to say nothing of Ned's, and, above all, her mother's life.

It had rained most of the day, threatening to put a damper on her spirits, but her mother had cheered her up. "Don't let the rain bother you, Mopsy. Look, the fire is bright and we have hot punch. And won't Mrs. Todd keep things lively!"

It was true. Mrs. Todd had been keeping things lively for some time, whether her husband accompanied her or not. Mattie couldn't remember when the William Austin Dickinson family had done so much together, all focused around Mrs. Todd's bright lively eyes, her quick step, and her rapid conversation. Ned and Gilbert gathered around her, but it was their father who amazed them all. He began to come home earlier from the law office if he knew she was visiting, and even lingered in the house while Mattie took her afternoon piano lesson with Mrs. Todd, instead of visiting his mother next door or the Hills family. Lately, he had begun to take walks alone with Mrs. Todd, and not just when he fetched her from the boarding house either. He even joined the family regularly on the piazza while summer weather lasted, and spun out conversation when Sue herself tired of talking and began to yawn, and Mr. Todd reminded Mabel that he would be up late at the observatory the next night.

Sue laughed when Ned asked to fetch Mrs. Todd that evening of the whist party, even though he knew his father was counting on going himself. "Two boys quarreling over who will fetch Mrs. Todd?" Sue had said. "That's a strange pickle. But let your father go tonight, Ned, I don't want you out in the rain anymore today. Stay here in case some of the others come early."

So Austin went out into the rain with his largest umbrella, leaving Mattie and her mother to make sure the whist tables were set up and the refreshments ready. Since David Todd wasn't coming, they had asked Mrs. Todd to come early rather than sit alone in the boarding house. The other guests wouldn't arrive for an hour or so.

Ned sat rather glumly by the fire which his father had laid carefully before he left and read the newspaper while Gilbert played on the floor with toy soldiers, his fair head brooding over his regiments. The parlor was silent, so much so that Ned found himself listening to the clock ticking. He had been especially pleased to learn that Mabel Todd's husband would not be coming; even in rainy weather, he often found work to do in the observatory. But Ned was also confused to find himself irritated that his father was spending so much time with them all during Mrs. Todd's visits. He used to wish his father spent more time with them because fewer open tensions surfaced between his parents when his father worked less hard. But now, he found his father's presence intrusive. Ned had always envied the fellows who knew how to flirt with the most sought after girls in Amherst and South Hadley; and now, to have Mrs. Todd listening to his every word, teasing him playfully, laughing in his direction—well, he did not intend to give the pleasure up lightly.

He rattled the newspaper, looking for interesting local news. "I thought they would be back by now," said his mother after a while from the hallway. "Well, good, I'm not quite ready. Gilbert, don't forget that you must go to bed half way through the first set of games."

Gilbert nodded from his position on the matting before the fire, deeply absorbed in his soldiers.

Mattie entered the hallway from the dining room. "The table looks fine, Mother, there's nothing more to do there. I want to be near the door when Mrs. Todd arrives." She smoothed her dress.

"Yes, dearie, there's nothing else to do here that Mary can't do. Why don't you play a bit? They certainly should be here any minute." She returned to the back of the house.

Mattie sat at the piano, but instead of playing, she fluffed her petticoats, checked to see that her stockings were straight, and finally, stood to look in the little hallway mirror. Mrs. Todd always looked so pretty, so neat and fresh. Mattie loved the bright colors she wore, as well as the cool white dress she had chosen for the picnic. Her mother liked best the dress with the panels Mrs. Todd had painted herself along the collar and cuffs. No one else in Amherst would think of wearing such a dress, and certainly not of painting something on it—and that made Mattie and her mother like it all the more. In fact, the more criticism her mother heard about Mrs. Todd's colorful clothing, the more she stood up for her, and Mattie felt defensive in the same way. Mrs. Todd was theirs, in a sense, she thought, their discovery and their prize. It was they who as leading citizens should present her to the town, and defend her too, if necessary.

Mattie was impatient to see Mrs. Todd; she had much to tell her. But she would have to make sure her father didn't monopolize Mrs. Todd's attention, as he had in the last few days. Ned's prancing around her was one thing. That was a game, she thought, and silly as it was, Mattie didn't mind it, for it never detracted from the warmth Mrs. Todd directed towards her, or from that special lively smile she sent Mattie's way so many times of an evening. She was special to Mrs. Todd, she knew it. But she had begun to feel uncomfortable with her father's unaccustomed smiles and even his stares when Mrs. Todd was around. Mattie was startled the first time she had seen her father staring at Mrs. Todd when he thought no one was looking. That had occurred one early evening on the piazza about two weeks ago. She had been sitting sideways on the steps so quietly under the hanging vines that her father must have forgotten about her, but she felt she ought to save Mrs. Todd further embarrassment by making some noise or saying something. She contented herself by asking Mrs. Todd when they could next look through the observatory telescope, and Mrs. Todd answered promptly, but her father continued to keep his eyes on her as she spoke, and with an intensity that she believed Mrs. Todd herself noticed.

It was that sort of moment Mattie wanted to prevent tonight. And to do so, she herself would be lively, all smiles, and the center of attention. After all, it was her whist party, complete with invitations and favors. It would be, she hoped, the best whist party she had given yet.

But where were they? She wandered around, straightening the little card tables and checking the favor baskets. She looked at her teeth in the hall mirror. "I think I hear them," said Ned from the other room.

"I don't hear anything," said Mattie, but she stood still and listened. Could that be the sound of voices and steps by the door? She waited. It might be. She moved to stand by the door, ready to open it. But there was no other sound, and no one came.

"Is she here?" asked Ned.

"I don't know. Maybe they met someone out there." She peered through the long windows into the rain, but couldn't see well enough to decide. "Oh bother, I'll throw on my cape and open the door," she called to Ned, running to the back hallway to find her hooded cape and toss it around her loosely. It wasn't raining very hard. She opened the door and stood on the front step, following the glow their gas lamp cast over the lawn, steps, and street. No one. Wait. There, walking slowly away from their house and towards Aunt Emily's house, were two figures so close together under one umbrella that she couldn't tell at first who they were. But in a rush of comprehension, like the bits of glass in a kaleidoscope, the figures lined up into identities. The inner figure was Mrs. Todd's. Mattie recognized the cloak as it passed through the light shed by their gas lamp and into the gloom beyond. The other figure she knew without a doubt was her father's. But it was their pose, their attitude, which clicked into recognition as audibly as though she'd turned the rattling kaleidoscope. While Mattie watched, her father shifted the umbrella from one hand to the other, revealing his profile for an instant as he reached for Mrs. Todd's hand. They stood quietly, hand in hand for a few moments. And then, under their single umbrella, her father wound his arm tightly around Mrs. Todd's waist, as they moved, their heads bent together, into the darkness.

Mattie shrank against the front door in confusion. Anger followed. Then fear. She slipped through the door which she had never entirely closed, and walked to the back hallway, taking off her cloak.

"Well," called Ned, "did you see them?"

Before she could decide what to answer, her mother came into the hallway. "Everything is really ready now. Where on earth can they be?"

"Mopsy," repeated Ned, "did you see them?"

"No, I didn't see anyone," she said. "We'll just have to wait some more."

She wandered over to the card tables, straightening a chair here, a place card there, trying to collect her thoughts, to put some meaning to the tableau she had just observed. What could her father and Mrs. Todd have been talking about which caused them to clasp hands, caused him to put his arm around her waist? Why would they walk so close, leaning on each other almost, when such behavior was highly improper? Could it be that Mrs. Todd had some sort of problem which she had confided to her father? Something of a legal nature?

Or was she ill? She didn't look ill. Perhaps it was the other way around: maybe her father was ill. Maybe he had already told Mattie's mother, and now wanted to confide in someone else. But that didn't make sense, either. No one in their house was ill, unless you considered Ned, and his illness wasn't acute. And anyway, it was a secret. Ned's attacks, whatever they were, came mostly in the night when Mattie couldn't help but hear them, but neither of her parents wished to talk about them, for Mattie had asked before. Come to think of it, maybe that was it, then. Maybe her father was upset about Ned and was confiding in Mabel. She glanced cautiously at Ned who turned the pages of the newspaper by the fire.

But nothing would explain the need for her father to put his arm around Mrs. Todd. Nothing. Except...except things she had heard of in novels and scandals people had gossiped about in the village. Things that happened to someone else or to imaginary people. Such things did not apply to their family, so she would have to wait and find out where the real explanation lay. Eventually, the truth would come out, although in the meantime, waiting for it would be difficult. But she would wait. She would have to be patient, even though she might feel angry and uneasy. She would wait.

"Mopsy, who is escorting Sarah tonight?" asked her mother.

"She's coming with her brother, don't you remember? He'll make up one table with Ned, Sarah, and Ann. And James and Robert will make up a first round table with Mrs. Todd and me."

"I thought I was going to make up a table with Mrs. Todd," said Ned. "We were partners one other time, and we won. Why can't we be partners again?"

"Yes, Mopsy," said Sue, "they could be partners for the first round and then switch later."

"Well, all right, I don't care." Mattie stood over Gilbert, looking down at his soldier brigade. She ruffled his soft hair. "Some day you'll know how to play whist, Gib."

"I'll be a good player," he said amiably. "Maybe next year when I'm grown."

"Father won't be playing, will he?" Mattie asked her mother.

"Oh, heavens, I can't predict what he'll be doing this evening. He always claims he hates games, but he did have a go at it the other week when we all practiced with Mrs. Todd."

A log on the fire slipped. "Time for Austin to check on that fire," said Sue absently. No sooner had she spoken than the front door rattled and opened, and they could hear the quiet voices of Austin and Mabel Todd.

"Austin?" called Sue, getting up and going into the hallway. "What did he do, Mrs. Todd, leave you waiting on your doorstep while he did errands?"

Mabel and Sue clasped hands in greeting, while Austin helped Mabel off with her cloak. "No, are we late?" said Mabel. "I'm sorry, it must be my fault. I kept him waiting in our parlor while I looked for my gloves. And then of course, the rain..." She turned briefly to the hall mirror to straighten her hair, mussed by her hood, and then to check the top of her shoes for mud. Seeing none, she turned too quickly and nearly bumped into Austin who had walked behind her. "Oh, sorry," they both said at once, and for an instant, looked into each other's eyes, then away. Mabel quickly put a hand to her cheeks, as though she were warm, prompting Sue, who was laughing at their bumpy encounter, to say, "You've certainly got good circulation, to have pink cheeks in all this dreary rain! But come in, my dear, Mattie and Ned are waiting for you."

In short order, the whist party began, even though most of the other guests had not yet arrived. But when they did arrive, they played many laughing hands of whist, switching partners twice and allowing some players to rest for a while, looking at the stereoscopic set or writing in Mattie's guest autograph book. The refreshments were a rousing success, and two people requested recipes, Issie for the punch and Mabel Todd for the coconut cake. Mattie played the piano both alone and with Mrs. Todd, and when Ned asked Mrs. Todd to sing, she did so, without hesitation. That was when Austin rejoined the group, having gone to his study during the second whist hand. While Mrs. Todd sang, Mattie half thought what she had seen earlier had been a dream—it seemed impossible that her somber father sitting quietly in their parlor could ever have held this woman he hardly knew close to his side.

When the last game had been played, the last favors opened, and finally, the wraps brought out by Mary for Ned and the other young men to help the ladies with, Mattie began to dread hearing her father offer to walk Mrs. Todd home. But just when she felt she could not bear to see them go out into the night alone, a loud knock sounded at the front door. "It's probably David," called out Mabel. And indeed, David Todd strode in, ready to see his wife safely home.

"Goodnight, goodnight," people called to each other, and set out into the damp foggy air. The rain had stopped, but moisture dripped from the trees, and the glow around the gas light was fuzzy.

Mabel and David were the last to leave. "We'll miss you all so much while we are in Washington," said Mabel. "I wish we didn't have to go, especially just now." Her glance swept Austin's face. "We'll be there by supper time tomorrow evening, unbelievable as it seems. I hope you'll write to us."

"Oh, I will, I will," said Sue. "We'll miss you too, so very much. I don't know how we'll pass the time."

"Well, Ned," said Mabel, "Save a dance for me. And Mattie, let's plan what new pieces we can work on when I return. There won't be much for me to do without the wonderful Dickinson family."

"Don't work too hard, Mr. Todd, at the Nautical Almanac Office," laughed Sue.

"I won't mind anything," he replied, "just as long as my trip to California comes through for the Transit of Venus. If I can observe that transit, I'll be happy."

And then, with handshakes and more goodbyes, the Todds were off, and the heavy door of the Evergreens closed behind them, leaving the Dickinson family alone to clean up remains of their party.

CHAPTER   16

September 1882

~

OF COURSE SUE DICKINSON COULD HAVE
had no way of knowing that those few minutes her husband had shared with
Mabel Todd under the umbrella the evening of the whist party had changed
her life and that of her family irrevocably. There was no reason for her to wonder what Austin might have talked about to their lively new friend, young
enough to be their daughter. And so, in fact, she did not imagine the scene at all
or notice anything different about Austin the next day, or even in the next weeks.

But for Austin, everything had changed. He was a new man in a new world.
For he had risked everything that evening to tell Mabel clearly, despite his
shaking hands and voice, that he loved her, seriously and with all his heart, and
when in reply she lifted her face to his under the dripping umbrella, he risked
everything again to kiss her as tremulously as he had ever kissed anyone before.

They had made a crossing together. There would be no going back now.
The Sunday after the whist party, in his familiar pew at First Church, Austin
bowed his head in prayer with everyone else, but he heard the word "Rubicon,
Rubicon" with every beat of his heart, and was conscious of the word he had
printed like a glowing talisman in his journal. Mabel had called that rainy
evening of the whist party in September their "going by the gate" until he told
her the word "Rubicon" stayed in his head. "Rubicon," after Julius Caesar's irrevo-
cable crossing of the Rubicon River into Italy, defying the Roman Senate and
marching closer toward rule of the Roman Empire.

In Washington, not long after the whist party, Mabel woke before Sunday
morning daylight, tremulous with joy at the question she suddenly wanted to
ask her father: Was the divinity of Christ, which she had always doubted, to be
believed after all? Remembrance of Austin's large, strong hands and low reas-
suring voice turned her thoughts to her father and whatever answer he might
give. But asking the question of her father seemed more important than the

answer. David breathed gently in his sleep, and just as gently, she turned to nestle her cheek against his back and return to slumber.

Emily Dickinson also awoke with a question, but she often went to sleep with it as well, and the question was familiar to her: "Is immortality true?" She was to ask it later, after Philip Lord rallied from an illness, of Reverend Washington Gladden. The Reverend was to reply in a letter that it was true. Indeed, he said, it was "the only reality." Emily made a futile effort to take comfort in his words as she and Lavinia lifted their frail mother from the bed to her chair, where she sat quietly, holding whatever her daughters put into her faltering hands—a letter, a ball of yarn, an empty cup.

"Rubicon," thought Austin again and again. It was their word now, no longer Caesar's. They had crossed their Rubicon. He would have no more need of religion.

CHAPTER 17

November 1882

Not knowing whether he would get funds to observe the December Transit of Venus in California made David Todd exceptionally edgy. He snapped at Millicent for talking at supper, and when she cried at the tone of his voice, he snapped at her even more. Once when Mabel lay in bed and marveled for the tenth time over Sue Dickinson's perfect soirees, he told her to think about other things for a change. About his problems, for instance, and how he might feel if he couldn't go to James Lick Observatory. And if he were able to go, how she should forewarn her parents about taking Millicent while they lived in California.

Because Mabel's interest in the impending transit waned with every day, David's students learned more about the events to come on December 6th than some of them cared to know. But all of them could appreciate the rarity of this, the second in a pair of transits for the century, since pairs of transits take place at average intervals of one and one fifth century apart.

"There will be no transits of Venus in the twentieth century," David told them. "Because we can learn so much during a transit about the distance of Venus from the earth and in turn, the size of the solar system and the sun's mean distance from earth, we need to run all the studies we can during the short time that Venus crosses the sun's disk. That's what I intend to do. But ah, what a beautiful sight it will be, tiny dark Venus against the huge sun."

Mabel seemed more and more preoccupied with Amherst life and engagements with the Dickinsons, the theatrical group, the choir, the fraternity balls, and her growing friendship with Mary Stearns, who wanted Mabel to give her school girls art lessons. Then in early November, they moved to Mrs. Robisons's boarding house, and Mabel busied herself settling in there. David, on the other hand, spent more and more time at the College, having fallen behind in his work after their long trips to Washington. She did not mind his working hard though, since there was so much else to occupy her—including Austin Dickinson, whose company they both enjoyed so much.

In fact, it was during an autumn ride in Austin's carriage when the three of them had driven into the country that Mabel let David know she no longer wanted to go to California. Austin had asked him, "How long will you be gone then, all told?", and just as David began to say, "Three months..." Mabel spoke up. "David will be away three long months. You can see why that's too long for me. I think I'll be staying right here, David. Can you get along without me?"

David had been hurt and angry at first. But by the time they reached home and could talk it over alone, he saw her reasoning. It was true, there wouldn't be much for her to do while he was working with the photographic equipment. In addition, he didn't know exactly what the living arrangements would be, and he could see why she resented giving up her activities in Amherst for such uncertainty. Still, he tried to persuade her anyway, and she consented to think it over, but he could tell her mind was virtually made up.

So David, pacing the floor, was hoping against hope when she arrived home the evening of November 7th, flushed by a brisk carriage ride with Austin, unaware of his big news. "I've received the funds!" he told her at the door. "The trip is on. I'm to leave for California in three days. November 10th."

She embraced him before she took off her gloves and cloak. But when he asked her once again, "And you won't change your mind?" she released him and began to take off her gloves, turning away. "David, you know I can't, not at this point. November 10th, you say? My birthday!"

And so it was settled. The rush to speak with President Seelye, to pack, and to make plans with John Lovell, who would accompany David as photographer, occupied every minute. By the time he found himself on the train heading out of Amherst, watching Massachusetts spin away in autumn ambers behind him, he realized he would miss Mabel and Millicent. Very much, in fact. For a moment, the thought of being away so long made him uneasy. But he managed to distract himself and to attend to John Lovell's conversation.

"We'll be gone only three months," John was saying, "but I imagine we'll be surprised at how many things will change in Amherst during that time." David could only nod in agreement.

CHAPTER   18

November 14, 1882

ATER ELDERLY MRS. DICKINSON GASPED
and fell back lifeless in her chair at the Homestead Tuesday morning, November 14th, Vinnie tore along the path between the houses to tell Austin next door. Sue sent Mary to get the doctor, even though they knew it was too late, and on her way back, Mary told Mrs. Jameson across the street, who went right over to the Homestead, her apron still around her neck, the waist strings flying.

Mariette Jameson found Maggie in charge by then, and Austin upstairs with Emily paying last respects to their mother. Lavinia paced the hallway below, passing a crumpled handkerchief from one hand to the other, but stopped long enough to allow Mrs. Jameson to press her hand briefly before resuming her pacing in the library instead.

There wasn't much for a neighbor to do in the house, except to offer condolences and warmth, and to plan an afternoon's baking of supper dishes to be brought over later. Mrs. Jameson had been almost afraid to see Lavinia's grief, but now that she had studied her strained face, she found it easier to look at Austin when he descended the stairs wearily. As she expected, very little emotion registered on his face. She would never know what ravages Emily's face showed, upstairs alone; but she was glad that the Dickinson clan ministered to each other in their own inscrutable way, for anyone else remained an outsider at a time like this—and other times too, as far as that went.

Sue Dickinson came in from next door just as Austin reached the bottom of the stairs. "How is Emily?" she asked him, not seeing Lavinia in the library. "Holding on," he said briefly. "Have you told the children?"

"Yes. I'll keep Gib home from school, of course."

Austin saw Mariette Jameson then. "Thank you for coming over," he said.

"But what can I do, how can I help?" she asked.

"I have a telegram to send to Reverend Jenkins. We'd like him to do the service on Thursday if he can. But I can send Mary with the message."

"No, please, let me. I'll go right now."

She followed him into the library where he sat down and composed a message while Lavinia stood with her back to the windows and watched him, still turning the handkerchief over and over and pressing it occasionally to her cheeks and eyes. And so of course, Mrs. Jameson never saw Emily, never even heard her step. But her heart went out to the gentle soul who had sent her so many warm letters and who remained upstairs silently absorbing the truth of what it felt like to be in the world without parents.

"Father says Aunt Emily's lying down," said Ned, entering the dim back parlor of his house, the Evergreens, the day of his grandmother's funeral. "But she'll be all right. Mrs. Jameson thought Aunt Lavinia had been bolstering Aunt Emily up the last two days, but I think it was the other way around."

Her question about Emily answered, Mabel turned forward on the piano stool again and resumed her soft playing—a Chopin nocturne—while from the back of the house could be faintly heard the sounds of Sue and Mary Moynihan rattling dishes and silverware for that evening's funeral supper. The chill of the graveyard where they had buried Mrs. Dickinson that day had left them all trying to overcome a sense of slow motion. The Jenkins and Austin were still visiting next door at the Homestead, while a few guests awaiting their carriage sat talking quietly in the library at the Evergreens.

Ned walked restlessly about in his mourning suit and stiff collar, touching his moustache from time to time before he stood behind Mabel. "Let's sit together and talk."

Mabel stood immediately and extended her hand, which he held. They sat side by side before the glowing fire which cast shadows in the wintry room, shadows over the books, the plants, and Austin's carefully chosen paintings.

"I'm glad you're here," he said.

For answer, she squeezed his hand before gently trying to disengage it, but Ned locked his thumb over her palm. They sat quietly until Ned said, "None of us really knew my grandmother. She never said very much to us. I suppose I didn't even think much about her—she was just there. But now that she's gone—"

"Now you are thinking about her?" prompted Mabel.

"I'm thinking about her and Grandfather, both, out there in that freezing ground. It's hard sometimes to believe in the Resurrection and the afterlife. Do you? Do you ever doubt it all?"

"No human can ever answer the questions of life and death, Ned, or be sure about anything. If you didn't doubt, you'd be a fool. Yes, of course I have questions and doubts. But I believe God has not created us in vain. As long as I believe that, I don't need to know more. I leave it up to God and go on living."

"But oh, that cold ground out there in the cemetery, and us here, warm inside, but for how short a time!"

"That isn't the way to think about it, Ned. We are living now, and that's what's important. Even though your grandmother doesn't breathe anymore next door, you are breathing now. We are meant to enjoy life. I've always believed that."

"You make me feel better," said Ned, turning toward her. "I don't know who else I could talk to but you." He sat forward in his seat so that he could better face her, and looking into her eyes, slipped one arm around her. After a moment, Mabel reached her free arm around him and pulled him toward her for a quiet embrace. But he trembled palpably against her, and breathing heavily and rapidly, turned his hot face into her neck. Then with a soft cry, he leaned back and sought her lips awkwardly until she steadied him and directed the kiss, his very first, ending it for him as well so that he lay once more against her neck, his chest heaving.

"That was a surprise, wasn't it?" she said softly over his shoulder. "We should sit apart now though. Anyone who came in here would not understand."

Ned sat up but kissed her hand before moving apart from her. "Do you remember the four-leaf clovers you found at Sunderland that day of the picnic?" he whispered. "I still have the one you gave me."

"That's sweet," she said, her hands smoothing her hair while she glanced behind her. Ned also glanced behind them, then leaned closer toward her again, but she held him away and stood up. "Where can your father and Mr. and Mrs. Jenkins be all this time? Still over at the other house?"

"Yes," said Ned, "but I'm glad we had this time alone."

"Of course, and we'll talk again." But Mabel had begun walking toward the doorway while she spoke. "I wonder how long they'll all be? Do you think your father is taking cold? He's been coughing lately."

Before Ned could answer, Sue approached from the kitchen. "I'm sorry to leave you alone for so long but I just wanted to be sure things were in order for supper. Austin should be along soon with Clara Turner and the others, and I hope Lavinia will eat something with us. She probably won't want to leave Emily though. Emily's going to be despondent and probably ill for some time, considering all the attention she lavished on her mother. Well, they both did." She tidied the pins in her stiff bun and brushed her skirts briefly. "Ned, I want you to seat Mrs. Todd and me at supper. Your father will seat Mrs. Jenkins and Vinnie, if she comes."

"I hope she does," said Mabel. "She needs to get out of that house."

"Indeed she does," said Sue. "Well, this is one event your husband might be glad to have missed. It must be strange, having David so far away in California. And missing your twenty-sixth birthday last week too."

"Oh, I miss him, every day, but he's so busy out there I'd be completely forgotten. Only three weeks to the Transit, that's all!"

Sue looked at the fire to see how it was burning. "He's lucky to be busy out there instead of in Amherst attending funerals. We've had too many of them around here lately. It was only a month ago that Mary Stearns's daughter died. You never met Ethel, but she was a sweet child. And to lose her at seventeen... unbearable. It will be a sorry Thanksgiving for them. I can't imagine how Mary keeps her composure and strength. She's a marvelous woman."

Mabel moved further from Ned. "I couldn't agree with you more. I've been enjoying her company a great deal. Please let me help with the table now. Why don't I finish setting out dishes since Mary is still busy with the roast, and you can go next door or sit down and rest."

"Well, I don't want to go next door, but I think I'll collect the photographs I've saved to show Sarah Jenkins. She likes to keep up with the children's activities. Mr. Lovell finished the latest before he left, but none of them are in the albums yet."

As Sue went upstairs in search of the photographs and Mabel crossed into the dining room, the back door opened and slammed shut. Mabel advanced toward the sound, then paused. Ned watched her at a distance from within the doorway of the shadowy front parlor. She waited, listening, and hearing Austin's voice, advanced again. The floors shook a little as he strode forward, pushed open the remaining doors which separated him from Mabel, and stood facing her across the dining room.

"Austin," she breathed in a low voice.

"Oh God," he murmured, and she crossed to him, quickly unpinning a piece of paper from her dress and pressing it into his hand. He put it into his pocket without looking at it. Only then did she remember Ned in the other room.

"It's that poem of Emily's you let me see," she said a little too loudly. "Does your aunt write poems for you, Ned?" she called over her shoulder.

Austin had turned to face in his son's direction across the darkened hallway, but he could not see Ned. Then they heard his step as he appeared in the hallway to answer the question. "Of course she does," he said curtly, retreating immediately to the parlor, leaving Austin and Mabel standing rigid in place, like chess players.

Austin spoke softly again. "I came over to see if everything was all right. The Jenkins are having a good visit with Vin, but she's not up to having supper over here, so it'll be just Jonathan and Sarah Jenkins and Clara Turner. Where's Sue?"

"Upstairs looking for photographs to show the Jenkins. I'm so glad I've met the Jenkins at last. They are just as sweet as you said!"

"I knew you'd like them," said Austin. "The service was good, wasn't it? John gave Father's too, in '74, before they left our church and moved to Pittsfield."

"Yes. But how about you? I feel as though I've hardly seen you. Did you have a good rest last night?" Mabel whispered, looking critically at his eyes.

"No, I didn't sleep well, but I'll be all right."

"Sit down," she said, "I'm just finishing up the table."

"No, I must run back and bring the Jenkins over here. Vinnie was going on about the cats when I left, so I need to rescue poor Sarah. She used to get the giggles when Vinnie did her cat litany." He glanced across the hallway, and not seeing Ned, reached to squeeze her hand briefly. "It's Emily I'm concerned about, but right now she's best off with Vin. Emily's taking it very hard. And yet, Mabel, we none of us knew our mother very well. That makes grief all the more painful. How few people we end up really knowing."

For answer, Mabel stepped forward, closing the gap between them, and gripped both his wrists tightly, only to drop them again when she heard Sue returning in rustling skirts and calling, "Austin, I wish someone would keep things in order around here, I can't find those photographs anywhere. It's your turn to rummage in boxes and shelves."

The rooms had become perceptibly darker. "It's time to light the other lamps," said Austin. "We'll worry about the photographs later. It's so dark in here no one will want to come visit. Let's make this look like a home."

From the parlor, Ned called in a monotone, "There'll be snow tomorrow. I know it. There always is after a winter funeral."

But Austin had already turned his back on Ned and Sue and had begun to light the dining room lamps, starting with the center one nearest Mabel, casting her first into chiaroscuro tones, then into muted colors as he lighted lamps at each corner of the room. Mabel stayed where she was by the table while Ned left the parlor to peer in at her from the shadows and Sue smiled at her, patting Ned's arm. At the same time, Austin himself stood back to take in the whole effect of a room with Mabel in it, to smile his somber smile at Mabel, and to leave for the other house where the Jenkins and Clara Turner waited for supper.

CHAPTER 19

November 1882

~

THEIR DANCING TOGETHER, HIS AND MABEL'S, would have ended even if his grandmother had not died in November. Ned finally faced the truth during the long hours he sifted over and over the events of that fall and early December. That he had at first missed all the signs of his father's infatuation with Mabel Todd bothered him less than the fact that he himself must have been only a diversion for her after all, an amusing game. All along, she must have held her father's hands the same way she had his, peered into her father's eyes so closely that he had felt her breath on his face as Ned so tremulously had. He had not seen and recognized the evidence until it materialized unmistakably one afternoon before his eyes like one of John Lovell's photographs coming to life in the developing fluid.

He had spotted the family carriage in a grove of trees far down the lane a week after his grandmother's funeral when he and his friend Brad had set off collecting rocks for geology class. Brad had wandered down a gully leaving Ned alone, where he had stood still at first, looking for his father, since he could see the carriage was empty. But the scene which met his eyes after a few angling steps toward the carriage rooted his feet and froze his eyes. He struggled for a few seconds to make sense of the picture: his father, hatless, sat on their carriage rug with his arm around Mabel Todd, who leaned heavily against him and who held his father's free hand against her cheek. That both of them should look so familiar and yet so alien at the same time confused his thinking until he blinked and shook his head.

He had turned then and walked quickly away, the scene still emblazoned in his mind. He could see Brad some distance off, kneeling by the pond now. Hastening toward him, Ned pointed toward the road. "Let's head back and stop by the stream instead. We'll find much better specimens there."

So his father had not seen him, and Ned had been left with the kind of secret he had never dreamed he would carry. It did not cross his mind to tell Mattie or his mother until after the second incident in their own home a few days later when from the stairs, he witnessed Mabel Todd pass something to his father in the hallway, something so small that he could not see it as it went from her tight palm to his fingers and then into his pocket. He remained on the stairs until the hallway was empty, then hurried down and out the back door where he walked for over an hour in the late afternoon November wind, his hands and his heart stiff with cold and with ever-growing hostility toward his father.

When he returned, he had made a decision: he would alert his mother. He would not tell her everything he had seen, only enough to open her eyes to the treachery in front of her, enough to set her into action to protect the family. Maybe it wasn't too late to salvage the integrity of the family—he didn't know. But it was, of course, too late to salvage the joy and pride he had felt in thinking that Mabel Todd, resplendent Mabel Todd with her dark eyes and the lithe figure he wanted to touch all over, found him manly and appealing. He wondered whether he would ever feel that pride and joy again—and feared he would not. It amazed even Ned that this bottomless fear loomed over the acrid fury which knotted his chest when he thought of his father enjoying what could have been his.

December 5, 1882

∼

YES, MATTIE, TOMORROW IS THE TRANSIT OF Venus and Mrs. Todd still plans to take some of us to the observatory if the weather is fair. It's all settled."

Sue Dickinson swept into the parlor where Mattie was just putting down the piano lid and told her, "Go see if Gilbert is still playing in the meadow, and bring him back. I can't think why he likes it so much over there, even in winter."

Ned moved aimlessly from window to window while his sister found her cloak, gloves and hat, and set out for the meadow. His mother meanwhile was engaged in collecting the week's newspapers, conferring with Mary over whether enough chestnuts remained for that evening, straightening up the piano music, and fussing with the hall mat.

"It's Mr. Todd's big day tomorrow, isn't it, Mother?" said Ned. "I wish I could take photographs like Mr. Lovell and go along to California too just to observe a transit of some planet or another. Besides, I have a few things to discuss with Mr. Todd." He fiddled with the ends of an asparagus fern. "And not about astronomy, either."

"What do you mean by that funny tone, 'and not about astronomy,'" said his mother, smiling at him. Without giving him time to answer, she went on. "But Ned, you have more to chat about with Mrs. Todd than Mr. Todd. Your father and I have thoroughly enjoyed her, but you're clearly the best person to keep her company, as close to her age as you are."

She shook out a table cloth. "Here, hold these ends. No, I think Mrs. Todd brings out the best in you, and I'm glad you can be her escort and spare your father, since he has such a busy schedule. Besides, he's not naturally sociable, but you can be different if you try, like Mattie and me. Certainly you don't want to end up like your Aunt Emily."

Ned held the ends of the tablecloth while she straightened her side of the cloth and then met him to collect all four corners. "But I don't plan to be around tonight when Mrs. Todd comes over," he said, "and I'll tell you why. I'm not sure whether she has as fine a character as I thought."

"You're bothered by her flirtacious manner, aren't you? But it's just her way. Her husband isn't worried by it. I do think it's possible she's trying a little too hard to attain the sort of social position she wants, but that's not surprising. And Mr. Todd can be a rather crude person. He's not from the same social class as we are, and it shows. But we like them and can help them along. After all, why do you think your father and I have invited her and her husband to so many soirees and events as we have?"

Ned had turned to the windows facing the piazza and was staring through the thick vines which shielded the house and kept it dim. Drawing the ends of a drapery tassle from one hand to another, he spoke more loudly than before. "I don't trust her, Mother, and you shouldn't either. It's things I've seen lately, things that you ought to know about. Especially you."

Sue had been half way out of the room, but she stopped now and turned. "Things? What things? What do you mean?"

"Did you know Father goes on walks with her? And carriage rides too?"

"Yes, I do, and even though it might embarrass you, we can humor Mrs. Todd's youthful selfishness once in a while, I expect. She enjoys monopolizing your father's attention on those walks to impress other people. She feels important being seen with your father."

"But they walk alone sometimes, Mother, and in the country where they can't expect to see anyone in particular."

"I doubt that, Ned, I very much doubt that. She may be a flirtatious woman, but it seems to me that she has given a great deal of attention to *you*." She sank into a chair and began to roll up loose yarn. "I think I'll have Gilbert eat early tonight again and the rest of us will have a later supper."

Ned began to speak but he mumbled, and his mother said sharply, "What, Ned? Speak up!"

"Friday afternoon, on the road to South Hadley, I saw Father and Mabel Todd together in our carriage. Remember, I told you I walked with Brad as far as the old pond? Well, I saw them from there, from the lane."

"And you didn't say anything to them?" asked Sue.

"No."

"Well, you should have. No need to keep things mysterious, Ned. If you saw your father, you should have said something."

Ned looked out the window across the street towards the church. "They were talking, they didn't, they didn't want...," Ned began in a low voice until Sue interrupted him.

"What, they were talking and what?" asked Sue. "Couldn't you call out to your own father as he went by?"

"They weren't going by right then. They were stopped."

"Stopped?"

"They had stopped part way up the lane to the pond and were talking about something. I don't know what it was, but I didn't want to interrupt."

Sue was rolling yarn faster as he spoke, and finishing one ball, reached into the basket for more. Finding none, she rummaged for some mending instead. For a moment, neither spoke. Then she began, "Did you...," and stopped. Starting again, she said, "What made you decide to tell me about this now?"

"I don't know," Ned said. "But I don't like the way Mabel Todd spends so much time with Father—sticks to him."

"Sticks to him, that's putting it rather strongly, Neddie."

He didn't argue her point, but said instead, "Mattie and I think that you and Father ought to spend more time together. That makes me all the more angry with the way Mabel Todd takes up Father's time. Besides, I thought Mrs. Todd was more my friend—and Mattie's, of course."

Sue suddenly shook her mending and said in a harsh voice, "Why doesn't that husband of hers spend more time with her? *Stupid* man, running off to California for weeks on end. What's wrong with him. What's wrong with *her*? I thought she was your friend too." She arose. "Don't misunderstand though, Ned. What you saw has no great importance. Don't read things into it. But you were right to tell me, and I think I should let Mabel know how I feel."

"Don't tell her I said anything to you!"

"I won't. But she'll know I'm displeased with her, don't worry, and that should take care of it. If she's trying to lead your father around like an old dog, well... But it won't go on." She paused. "I think I hear Gilbert and Mattie. Quickly, before they come in—in light of what you've told me, I think it's better that you not spend time alone with Mrs. Todd anymore."

"Not spend time with her?" said Ned instantly, turning from the window. "But we've got lots of things planned to do, including a play rehearsal. And she's coming for supper tonight, isn't she?"

"Well, I can't help that, I invited her three nights ago. But in the future, you just finish up whatever you must do with her and be gracious about it, but after that, stay away a while. I see I was wrong in viewing her teasing as healthy fun.

Maybe it's partly my fault, to have let it go on so long. Just do as I say."

"I'm hungry, Mother, what can I eat?" Gilbert rushed into the room followed by Mattie, both of them aglow from the December afternoon air.

"Go see what tidbits Mary has for you, but you're going to eat early tonight. We're having company for supper."

"I hope it's not Mrs. Todd again, Mama. She talks too much! Hey, look what I found." He pulled some stones from his pocket to show Ned.

"Very nice, Gib, what kind do you think they are?"

"Dunno, we'll ask Papa!"

From the kitchen, Mary could be heard opening the back door and greeting Austin Dickinson. His low voice answered her louder country one. Then came his footsteps, slow and heavy, crossing the kitchen, pausing by the dining room door and stopping. Ned had already advanced to the stairs and had begun climbing. Sue had frozen, her mending in mid air. Mattie stood where she was in the hallway holding her cloak, but turned half way around to watch her mother. Gilbert, however, rushed toward the kitchen shouting, "Papa, Papa, I found special rocks and stones!" When Austin emerged into the dining room, through which he could see his wife and daughter as rigid as statues, he lifted Gilbert onto his back, the light hair soft against the thick coarse auburn wig.

"Why are you back so soon? Didn't you meet all your appointments?" said Sue. "Or are you overly eager to play host to Mrs. Todd tonight?"

Mattie shrank into her chair and scuffed at a corner of the rug with her boot. Gilbert only continued to clasp his father's neck and call out as though his mother hadn't spoken. "Where do snakes go in the winter, Papa? Davy says he wants a pet snake in the spring. Can I have one too?"

"They go underground, Gib, like hibernating bears. They would freeze if they tried to live above ground."

"But it's so cold underground! Why don't they freeze there? I wouldn't want a house under the ground, would you?"

"I know it seems colder under the ground, but it really isn't, it's warmer. And if you dug to the center of the earth with your shovel, you'd find that it was very very hot there! Gib, I've got to put you down now. Ready?"

"Yup."

"Then heave ho, here we go, ready or not!" He swung Gilbert over his head and down to the floor. "Oh my poor back, it's harder every week to swing you over my head. I must be too old for this now, what do you think Gib?"

"For that, and for a lot of things besides, Austin. I want to speak to you," said Sue. "Go next door, Mattie, and see if Aunt Emily wants you to do any errands for her tomorrow. Then you and Gilbert can visit with Aunt Vinnie or Emily for a short while before supper. They both need cheering up."

Even as Mattie stood up and took Gilbert's hand, she could hear her mother's voice begin to rise from the library where her parents had retreated. When Mattie reached the back door, her mother's voice was even more audible, more shrill, as she shouted outright at Austin.

In the kitchen, Mary ruffled Gib's hair. "A bite of gingerbread?"

"I'm not hungry," he said politely, and followed Mattie sedately out the door, but once he reached the path between the two houses, he began to skip a little, and finally, to sing, "We're going to see Aunt Emily, Aunt Emily, Aunt Emily, we're going to see Aunt Emily, yes, we, ARE!"

When Mabel Todd's landlady, Mrs. Robison, answered the bell a few hours later that evening, she saw both Mr. and Mrs. Dickinson on the porch to fetch Mabel, instead of just Austin Dickinson as usual. And Mabel, running down the stairs and emerging into the hallway, was visibly taken aback as she saw the two of them waiting grimly for her. But she rallied as quickly as possible, and reached first for Sue Dickinson's hand, looking away from Austin's face after a quick but penetrating look at his eyes. "How nice of you both to come," she began, but Sue's hand repelled hers by its very rigidness, and Mabel withdrew her own to pass Austin her cloak as a lady should, no matter what the situation. Austin held it gingerly for her as she turned and slipped her arms into it.

The Amherst streets lay quiet under a cloudy sky. A few students strolled off in the opposite direction, probably on their way to dine with a faculty member or at one of the boarding houses.

"What do you hear from David?" said Austin at last.

"Nothing since the end of last week, but he promised to give me a full account of the transit. I hope the California skies are clearer than ours promise to be. The Almanac says we'll have clouds all day tomorrow, and so far, that report looks right." She turned to Sue. "You do still want to observe whatever we can of the transit tomorrow at College, don't you?"

"Is Mary Stearns coming too?" was Sue's reply.

"Yes, along with Mariette Jameson and Ellen Mather."

"I'll come along then."

No one spoke further. A strained silence fell upon them, relieved by the hooting of two owls calling back and forth a few streets over. That sound was overtaken by a horse and carriage proceeding up Main Street. "George Montague," said Austin. They paused to exchange waves and "good evenings" with George, after which Austin allowed his hand to touch Mabel's waist since Sue had walked slightly ahead for a moment. They had reached the Evergreens now, and again, Sue quickened her step, allowing Austin to touch Mabel gently once more as they proceeded up the steps and into the house where Mattie greeted them and Gilbert called out from the kitchen, "Papa's back, Mary, I hear them!"

"Where's Ned?" Mabel asked Mattie.

"Gone to dinner with some college fellows and then to pay some calls—on some girls I think. You won't see him tonight."

"Well, I'll miss him then. But this way, you and I can spend more time playing the piano if you like."

"Oh yes, let's. I've been practicing pretty hard, but the girls from school don't play duets very well. Can we work in the Classical Greats duet book?"

"Of course." Austin waited to take her cloak. "Thank you," she said to him. And then in Sue's direction as they advanced into the parlor, "You are so kind to take me in while David is away. I hardly have an appetite at Mrs. Robison's." She hovered in the middle of the room, uncertain about which seat to choose, although she hadn't been asked to sit at all yet. Austin left the room to put away the cloaks while Sue spoke pointedly to Mattie about her lessons, ignoring Mabel who continued to stand awkwardly for a moment, but then drew herself up and stood before the fire.

Mary came in from the kitchen. "Some sherry, Mrs. Todd?"

"Yes, thank you, Mary, sherry would be lovely. I enjoyed what you served here last week. Sue, was that the Amontillado?"

"Yes," said Sue coldly and briefly, and turned to ask Mary if the potatoes would be done within a half hour. A brief discussion ended with Sue heading back toward the kitchen with Mary, leaving Mattie and Mabel alone.

"Sit down, Mrs. Todd, here by the fire."

"Thanks, Mattie. Your hair looks lovely by the firelight. Did you wash it today?"

"No, yesterday afternoon. Mary helped me dry it. She always thinks I'll take cold! She worries almost as much as my aunts."

"Well, you look beautiful. The blue velvet bow brightens your dress."

Mattie smiled and became more talkative, ignoring her father as he came in to stand scrutinizing the fire. While they talked, he took the poker, studied the fire further, and then reached in to dislodge one smaller log slightly, enabling him to move a larger one with the fire tongs. Thus adjusted, the fire burned brighter while he studied it until he seemed satisfied.

Mary returned with sherry and Sue followed her, a sweep of rustling skirts. "Austin, must you poke at that fire constantly?"

He turned and sat on a chair far from Mabel. "You know," he said, " even now, nine months later, the flames sometimes make me think of Walker Hall burning down. That's a fire I'll never forget. David won't either. He's just lucky his most important papers and calculations were spared. But to be without his other papers, and, of course, his office...It can't be easy."

"It hasn't been," said Mabel. "But the excitement over the Transit of Venus has distracted him for a while. He has looked forward to this for so long that I hope he isn't disappointed."

"Imagine," said Austin. "Even while we are speaking here in the dark evening, Venus is turning through all that emptiness, about to cross the face of the sun itself. Fire on fire, if we can believe what they tell us about Venus's surface." He turned to stare again into the domestic flames.

"And while those gigantic celestial bodies shift around out there, we don't notice a thing—unless we are astronomers of course," said Mabel. "Though don't you think that once you know some astronomical event is happening, you almost think you sense it? I do, anyway. Or maybe I just like to imagine I do."

"I feel that way about eclipses, always," said Austin.

"And full moons, Father?" Mattie asked.

But Austin was no longer paying attention, for Gilbert had peeked around the corner giggling and hurried over to his father's chair holding a wooden wagon with one missing wheel. "Fix it, Papa," he said, producing the missing wheel from his pocket.

There was quiet as Austin fiddled with the wagon and Gilbert hung on his chair watching. A log shifted slightly, the clock ticked, the vines outside rustled in the breeze, and far above, Venus moved inevitably toward the sun.

CHAPTER 21

December 6, 1882

~

IN THE DAYLIGHT OF DECEMBER 6TH, 1882, the sun, Venus, and earth began to line up in space, just as astronomers had predicted years before. These events within the solar system proceeded inevitably. Like the workings of a monstrous timepiece, all moving parts advanced toward this alignment, and would move through it and on to other alignments. No one alignment was more imporant than another, unless viewed from a selected human perspective.

In California, atop the James Lick Observatory, near where James Lick's body would one day be buried, the experts waited, instruments at the ready, for Venus to creep toward the sun and begin to cross it, a tiny black dot against the monstrous and gaseous globe.

The weather was mild, the clouds almost nonexistent, and members of the team took photographs and collected data for more than five hours. This was only the fifth transit in human history ever to be observed, and no other could be observed until the year 2004. The team remained busy.

In Amherst, the day was not clear, and by the time Mabel led a little group of four—Mariette Jameson, Mary Stearns, Ellen Mather, and Susan Dickinson— to the observatory telescope, nothing of the transit could be seen, no image was reflected. Events nevertheless took place behind earth's obscuring clouds, hard as they were to imagine. But the ladies enjoyed looking about the curved wooden dome of the observatory, asking questions about the equipment, and staring at the great gazing telescope pointed toward the sun. And then it was time for tea.

Later that afternoon, David sent a telegram to Mabel: "Splendid day. Splendid success." The message crackled in her pocket that evening at dusk under the trees on the Mill Road when Austin pressed her tightly, tightly, in his arms and told her what he had already said in letters: "I love you. I love you!"

The Transit of Venus had passed, unobserved, over the heads of everyone in Amherst, and the earth now bowed toward night, accepting the flowing darkness from the east, in Massachusetts, to the west, in California, where David Todd closed his eyes, exultant from his day's observations.

CHAPTER 22

January 1883

WHAT IN GOD'S NAME WAS WRONG WITH
Sue tonight?" said David, recently returned from California. They stood on the pavement outside the Evergreens after an evening visit. "The way she treated you—such rudeness! I saw a whole new side of her I didn't know existed!"

Mabel gripped David's arm as she skidded on a patch of ice.

"Mabs? You must be angry..."

"Angry?" said Mabel through gritted teeth. "I'm furious! Absolutely furious!" She began to cry.

"Don't cry, just tell me what's going on! I leave you and Sue intimate friends when I set off for California, and return this week to find her attacking you in her elegant parlor like a barbarian. Did you quarrel while I was gone? You never said anything about it."

"No, no," said Mabel in a querulous tone. "She's become terribly jealous of me because I am so popular now. I'm displacing her in the village, don't you see? That's all it is. I'm young and talented, and I've threatened her little world. People ask about me and my talents now, not her. She can't take it."

"Then what did she mean when she made that remark about college boys— that you would always enjoy eligible boys in Amherst, year after year, or something like that? Did that have to do with you and Ned?"

"Probably it did." Mabel blew her nose. "And yet she wanted me to take Ned under my wing, and now see how she acts!"

"You did go rather far with Ned, you must admit. I felt a little jealous myself."

"Did you?" Mabel smiled. "Well, I'm letting him down as gently as possible."

They stepped onto the front porch of their boarding house.

"And why has Austin taken to staring at you so much?" said David, opening the door. "He didn't do that before I left. Is he infatuated with you too, like Ned?"

"Shh," whispered Mabel. "Suppose Mrs. Robison is around?"

"She's long since in bed."

They removed their wraps and ascended the stairs to get ready for bed.

"But he did stare at you a lot, you have to admit it," said David upstairs in their room. "I think he felt embarrassed for you, but he didn't do much to help."

"He was embarrassed."

"But you exchanged looks with him too from time to time. Don't think I didn't notice. Maybe Sue noticed too. She could be jealous of you that way, have you thought about it?" He shook his head. "If we can expect to be surrounded by rude or morose or reclusive Dickinsons every week, I don't know if we can weather this village life after all. Have you figured out why Austin's older sister stays inside all the time, by the way?"

"Austin says she is shy and thoughtful and simply prefers to stay at home. But she's always writing letters to people, and Austin certainly keeps in touch with her—he visits over there with both Lavinia and Emily nowadays, though apparently he didn't used to so much. Lavinia told me that Emily said he visited 'as rarely as Gabriel' a year ago. But now, the three of them sit over there in the kitchen and chat. In my opinion, Austin is trying to escape Sue—they don't get along. Two different temperaments."

"How do you know they don't get along?"

"Austin has told me things—not a lot, but enough to make it clear he's not happy with her."

"He's told you things of such a personal nature? I can't believe it. He doesn't seem the type."

"Well, he has. He trusts me, and he needs someone to confide in, apparently. I'm glad he feels he can. I like him very much."

"What does he say is the problem with him and Sue?"

"He says she has an unpredictable temperament and is apt to go into an absolute diatribe about something trivial and then the next moment, play the part of the gracious hostess. And she has no tenderness—or softness—I forget which word he used. Doesn't that sound to you as though they don't have any physical life?"

"But they're old anyway, they probably have lost interest in that sort of thing," said David. "Austin is fifty-three, isn't he?"

"David! I'm surprised at you! Is that what you think will happen to us when we're that age, that we'll not have fun in bed anymore?"

"I guess I can't imagine being that old."

"But I don't think you can imagine losing interest in bed, either, so don't be so smug, my dear husband. I think Austin would be a wonderful lover if he had married the right woman, and I'm sure he thinks about love more than you might imagine. Oh no, don't write off Austin Dickinson when it comes to passion."

"All right, all right," said David smiling. "But don't give me the same story about Lavinia Dickinson."

"Certainly not, but that reminds me, Lavinia likes you, David. She asks about you all the time."

"Well, I like her too, even though she's a strange bird. That laugh she has when she tells a story—I get her talking just so I can hear it. Were you there when she was telling about Mrs. Jameson across the street—how curious she is to find out what's going on in both Dickinson houses?"

"No, I must have been playing the piano."

"She imitated Mrs. Jameson at great length—it was hilarious! I've only met the woman a couple of times, but I think I'll burst out laughing when I see her. She imitates President Seelye too—which around here is like imitating God."

"Lavinia has always done wicked imitations," said Mabel. "Austin told me so. Better watch out—she'll do us next."

"She probably already has. I wonder if Emily watches us from the windows and imitates us after we leave?"

"I don't think she's that sort of person," said Mabel. "It's just an impression I have. You know, it's my goal to meet Emily one of these days. I don't see why I can't manage it—I usually get what I want if I try hard enough."

"Then you'd better mend your fences with Sue Dickinson," said David. "I doubt she's used to games that involve flirting with people's husbands or wives."

"You mean the kind of games you teased me about last night? The way that Effie or whatever her name was took such a fancy to you out there in California?"

"Maybe. Come here. I think games are fun sometimes, don't you? They stimulate the imagination. I don't mind if Austin likes you, and you shouldn't be jealous if I made eyes at someone in California. It didn't mean anything, and I know your games with Ned or Austin don't mean anything either." He embraced her. "It's still your auspicious time, isn't it?" he asked softly, nuzzling her neck. "We're safe?"

She kissed him. "I told you, we timed your return carefully so we could be free. Mmmm, very free. It's the perfect time of the month. And having Millicent with my parents, what could be better? We can have a wonderful time every day for a while."

"Then let's forget about Dickinsons and Effies. I want to make love to you tonight and watch you take your bath tomorrow and pamper you like—like I don't know what. Just show me again how much you missed me, the way you did last night."

For answer, Mabel smiled into her mirror, sat on the bed, and pulled David towards her. "And we won't even turn down the lamp," was the last thing she said.

February 1883

David found the valentine Mabel had made him under his plate at noon dinner. "So that's what you've been working on the past few days," he said, looking at the figures she had painted in watercolors and then framed with lacy white paper cut in the shape of a heart. "Did you send one to Millicent too?"

"Of course. I made four. One for you, one for Millie, one for Mattie, and one for Austin."

"You made one for Austin? After you and Sue have been at relative peace you make her husband a valentine? Why did you bother to clear the air with her if you intended to wave a red valentine in her face?"

"She'll never see it. I just thought Austin deserved a kind thought from me."

"What about me? Maybe I don't like the idea of my wife sending a valentine to another man."

"But it's Austin. It's not just anybody, it's Austin. We both think so much of him, you know that. You'd better get used to my watching out for Austin, because I think he needs my attention. It's the least we can do for him, after all he's done for us, you especially. He puts in a good word for you with President Seelye whenever he can."

"Well, you don't have to throw yourself at him," said David, pushing his valentine aside.

"I haven't thrown myself at him! I've done no more than you did in California with that Effie…"

"I wish you wouldn't bring her up every time we discuss Austin. You made me feel guilty at first, but now I think you just make Effie an excuse for you to do whatever you want."

Mabel reached across the table. "All right, I'm sorry. You're right. Here, give me your hand."

David grudgingly extended his hand. "You won't talk about him so much?"

"All right, I'll try not to, but I must go on talking *with* him. You have to know that and try to accept it. Austin and I have developed a special relationship that I can't lie about—it's too important. We talk about so many things he's had bottled up all these years that it would be criminal of me to abandon him now."

David withdrew his hand. "Abandon? Isn't that rather dramatic?"

"Come on, David," Mabel said. "This doesn't affect *our* relationship at all. Don't be silly. You are my husband and my lover and nothing will ever change that."

"I have to go back to the College," said David, pushing back his chair. "But I'm going to think about all of this and we'll talk it over again. Only not tonight. I have to set up some measurements at the observatory this evening and I'll probably come in late."

"I'll be waiting for you."

"Will you be bored alone?"

"No, I'm going to Lavinia's for a while. I've been invited."

"Good. Yes, visit with Lavinia. She'll keep you amused."

But Lavinia did not amuse Mabel that evening, for she withdrew according to prior arrangement after Austin closed the Homestead dining room doors and gathered Mabel slowly, gently into his arms with a renewed certainty that his life was beginning all over again.

March 1883

M R. LOVELL TELLS ME YOU SO OBLIGINGLY dropped in on him while he took photographs of Mabel the other day," said Sue emerging from behind her dressing screen in her nightgown. "I was mortified! I hardly knew how to answer to the fact that my husband wanted to sit and stare at a woman young enough to be his daughter, and in front of a village tradesman everyone knows."

Austin silently turned back the quilt and got into bed, lying with his back to Sue. The March wind whistled in gusts against the hemlock trees outside the window.

"Well, aren't you going to say anything? I refuse to stand here and do all the talking."

Austin's voice came muffled against his pillow. "Yes, I stopped in at John's. I don't have anything else to say."

"I told you I wouldn't stand for it, your following that woman around and embarrassing us all. I meant it, too. I simply won't stand for it. I can make life so miserable for her that she'll cut you dead if you so much as look at her. I can make her wish she had never come to Amherst. She's already had a chance to feel how I run hot and cold, and you saw what she did—come running to me to make amends because she couldn't stand the atmosphere."

Austin propped himself up against his pillows while Sue gathered a blanket around her and sat shivering in the rocking chair. "I've told you Mabel and I share mutual interests," he said. "I haven't tried to deceive you about that anymore." He rubbed the whiskers on his chin and took a deep breath. "So I suppose it's the best policy not to deceive you about my feelings for her, either."

Sue gave a little cry and pulled the blanket ends tightly under her chin. "What? What do you mean, feelings for her? Don't tell me things like that! I won't be able to stand it!"

"I'm sorry. But you'll have to stand it. I didn't plan it and I didn't go looking for it, but I've found something in her too deep to pass off lightly—and she feels the same way. It's not one-sided. I know you think it is, but it isn't. She thinks I'm a person to consider seriously. She understands that I have feelings."

Sue began to shiver violently, talking through chattering teeth. "You're my husband, the man I counted on to be moral and honorable and decent. What you're talking about is immoral. Wrong. Do you mean you don't love me and the children anymore, is that it? I can't believe it! Do you mean you wish you could leave us, is that the sort of thing you have in mind? Are you going to ruin our lives? Because I won't let you! I won't!"

Austin raised his voice. "I don't mean anything like that, I haven't made any plans, nothing like that! I'm just telling you, I feel something for her that I've never felt before and that I wish you and I had felt from the start. But we didn't. And we never will."

Sue was crying now. "No, no, maybe we can. I know I never enjoyed the parts of marriage you wanted me to, but I've tried to make up for that in many ways, you know I have. I've given you a perfect home and been hostess to so many interesting people, and I've raised the children. You know I've done that single-handedly almost. You never had much time for them."

"Yes, you have, I don't deny that, and of course I have feelings for you, but there's always been so much missing between us. I'm not talking just about those certain parts of marriage you never really enjoyed. I was looking for more— more sharing, more respect of sensitivities. When those things never came, I decided I could live without them, but I've changed now. I don't think I can live without them, not anymore."

"But why haven't you discussed this with me lately?"

"We had those talks the first few years we were married, you know we did. They never went anywhere. I haven't seen any hope for change ever since. And your temper always gave me pause. I prefer withdrawal to fighting."

"You're like Emily—you say you don't want to fight but you provoke fights all the same by your very intensity. Emily used to drain me when we were young. And you do too, in your way." She wiped her eyes with a handkerchief and blew her nose loudly. "I could hate you," she said with a sob.

"We're in a fix," said Austin. "But we can't solve anything tonight, and maybe never. Let's try to get some sleep and go on with our lives until we can find some resolution. Nothing is going to happen now, we're together in our home with our children. Gilbert is our bright spot—one look at his face and the future always looks brighter."

Sue got up from the chair, and dragging her blanket listlessly along with her, shuffled to bed, letting the blanket fall to the floor as she lay down facing Austin.

"Turn down the lamp?" he asked.

She did as he asked, then lay down again. In a moment, during which they both listened to the other breathe, she moved over against him. He put his arm around her and patted her elbow lightly. In a voice thick with the tears she had shed before, she said, "Don't ever say there is no hope for change. Maybe I am glad you told me what you did, because now I can do something to make things better. We both need to do some changing and some talking. You say we discussed things back in the early years, but did we? You always cut things short once you met opposition."

"That's not true."

"Never mind. Will you promise me not to see her for a while? That could make all the difference."

Austin didn't answer.

"Austin? It's important."

"I don't think I can."

"Please, please, promise me. Try not to see her for a while. Oh, please!"

"Then I'll try," he said, but knew as he turned heavily away that he had deceived Sue once again.

CHAPTER 25

March, April 1883

ARIETTE JAMESON WASN'T SURPRISED
when Mabel Todd took the train to Washington, D.C. in mid-March loaded
with enough trunks and bags to prove she would stay a long time. "People are
beginning to gossip," she told John, "but the most obvious thing is the way Sue
Dickinson snubs her. How embarrassing for everyone!"

David Todd remained in Amherst with a full load of classes, and could be
seen often, strolling on Main Street or across campus in animated, friendly
conversation with Austin Dickinson. "But see what good friends they are," John
told Mariette. "Your theory doesn't make sense in the face of it."

At the end of March, when spring vacation began at the college, David Todd
left too, and joined his wife and daughter in Washington. His exit was followed
by Sue's and Mattie's when they took the train to New York for more than a
week of theater, music, and entertainment with friends. The Evergreens settled
into quiet except for Gilbert's playful voice and running footsteps. When Austin was at home, Ned usually went out; the two of them shared only the care of
Gilbert, whose games, laughter and questions never failed to make them smile.
It was Austin's special pleasure to read to Gilbert every evening before bed.

One bright warm afternoon of early April when the first crocuses began to
bloom, John Lovell stopped by Austin's office. "David told me to bring you
these photographs of his wife you've been waiting for. He said you'd want to
pick one and then send the rest on to them in Washington." He eyed Austin
curiously.

"Oh, yes, thank you. We discussed the idea but I'd forgotten about it. I hope
I can get to it—you see all the matters needing my attention on this desk."

But as soon as John left, Austin closed his office door and spread the photographs out, brooding over them: Mabel in the white dress whose texture he
knew so well, Mabel in dark blue, smiling at something in the distance and

holding a nosegay of sunflowers, Mabel holding her picnic straw hat and star-ing thoughtfully into the camera and his eyes. He looked at all of them over and over again, finally picking one for his own. He would have to keep it here in the office, he supposed. No matter. He would be able to recall every detail wher-ever he was.

The sound of footsteps on the wooden stairs outside set him to gathering up the photographs in absurd haste. When the knock sounded at the door half a minute later, Mr. Hampton, a new client, found Austin perusing a folder of briefs on a full but orderly desk.

The letters traveled thick and fast between Amherst and Washington. Mabel addressed hers to Lavinia at her post office box where Austin picked them up on his way to collect the rest of Lavinia's mail as usual. "Her letters will come to your box," he had told Lavinia, and Emily too. "I wanted you to know. We've always been honest with each other and I want to be honest with you now about this. Yes, Mabel and I are writing, because we have found something in each other worth pursuing. I'll tell you more when the time is right. But I'm so glad you like her."

"Of course we like her," said Lavinia. "I think it's horrible that she has to hide in Washington because Sue makes life so miserable for her here! I wrote her myself and told her so. You don't mind if Emily and I correspond with her too, do you?"

"I'm pleased. Then you won't mind, Vin, addressing some of my envelopes to her so they don't arrive in my hand? It's not that David minds, you under-stand, but her parents..."

In mid-April, Mabel, having pondered ways to appease Sue, sent her a box of flowering arbutus from Washington. But day after day went by with no thanks, no acknowledgment of the flowers, which by then, Austin had rescued from Sue's neglect and planted in the meadow.

"She's impossible!" Mabel fumed to her bewildered mother.

"I just don't understand what this is all about, dear."

But finally, a long envelope, postmarked Amherst and addressed in Sue's handwriting, arrived. Mabel took it upstairs to her room, knowing, as she slit it open with a knife, that it was the wrong shape for a letter. Inside she found only dollar bills and a half sheet of paper scrawled with the lines, "For Mattie's piano lessons."

When Mabel emerged for afternoon coffee an hour later, her eyes were red. "Was it something in the mail?" her grandmother asked, holding Millicent on her lap.

"Nothing worth talking about," said Mabel. "Just signs of village provinciality. How glad I am to be in Washington right now."

But she could hardly wait to return despite Sue's hostility, and pressed her cache of letters close to her chest, amazed at the ever-growing strength of her love for Austin. She often found herself thinking about God without her usual scepticism, and during the church services which she attended with her parents, she thought joyfully about Austin. On long walks with her father, when he carried Millicent and they strolled around Rock Creek Park, she tried to tell him a little about the Dickinson sisters and their brother, but she broke off, fearing her voice would give away her special interest in Austin. "No matter," said her father. "We'll meet them all when we visit in Amherst."

But she missed David too with a sharp sexual longing—for he had visited Washington only once. Again, they planned their reunion in Amherst around what they called her "auspicious" time—her safe time. Despite the presence of Mabel's grandmother, Grandma Wilder, Mabel and David fell into each other's arms the first May night of her return to Amherst with a passion which left them dewy with sweat and then playful as children.

"The way you licked my ear!" said Mabel, kicking off the sheet. "And behind my knee? Where did you discover that delightful maneuver?"

"I developed a good imagination while you were gone," said David, leaning over to smooth the place where her buttocks met the top of her legs.

"Just so you didn't get the idea from anyone else."

"You should talk. You can't fool me with all this blather about Austin being your spiritual friend. I think you want to know him in quite a different way."

"Suppose I do?"

"Aha, now you're being honest."

"You like that?"

"Of course. Then I can be honest too if the occasion arises."

"What do you mean, 'if the occasion arises'? I don't want any occasion to arise."

"Well, if you can imagine what it would be like with someone else, why can't I? It's only fair. And it's interesting."

"But I love you. You're all I want."

"Wait a minute, what's going on? Then the rest is just so much talk?"

"Yes, just so much talk."

"Listen, Mabs, make me a promise. If you ever really think about an experimentation—you know, a time with someone else—will you promise to discuss it with me first? Will you promise to be open with me and not hide anything?"

"I will, David. I will. And you'll make the same promise?"

"Yes."

They held each other then, and David's body almost immediately relaxed into sleep, but Mabel lay awake until she heard the clock strike two. David's willingness to discuss an affair outside marriage had shocked her—but had also opened the doors at last to the aching question she and Austin saw coming closer and closer into the foreground: could they consummate their love, which was certainly as much physical as spiritual? Only now, the question seemed to have changed. Now, it was only a matter of when, when could they have each other completely? She would tell Austin at the earliest opportunity that something had changed. A barrier had fallen at a feather's touch. And though no one else had heard the reverberation of its fall, she seemed to hear it all night and the first thing next morning when she awoke to the sunshine that poured from the Amherst sky into her room and over her husband and herself under their amber and white quilt.

CHAPTER 26

June-September 1883

THE SPRING AND SUMMER DAYS OF 1883 WERE full with activities requiring Austin's attention: plans for the reconstruction of Walker Hall and a new gymnasium; court sessions in Northampton; and preparations for the annual Dickinson family reunion in August when literally hundreds of Dickinsons flocked to Amherst. "Oh, that reunion," Emily told him. "Such puffery!"

Mabel spent two weeks at the New Hampshire coast in June, and in August, Austin accompanied his family to their summer vacation lodgings in Shutesbury. August the first was Gilbert's birthday. "I've always wanted to be eight years old!" he shouted when he woke up that morning. After a picnic celebration featuring chocolate cake and gifts, family and friends played croquet and badminton, followed by turns in the hammock under the two oak trees at the edge of the meadow where crickets sang. Austin, returning in happy solitude to Amherst that night in preparation for a court case, thought joyfully about Mabel.

Sue relaxed her guard, seeing that her husband was preoccupied with campus business and his law practice. David took pleasure in the fact that Mabel appeared to see less of Austin alone, and that they often invited David to accompany them in relaxed walks or carriage rides when the three of them talked amicably together, Mabel smiling between them.

In early September, Judge Otis Philip Lord of Salem arrived in Amherst, accompanied by his niece, Miss Abbie Farley. Much to her annoyance, her uncle set off to visit the Homestead alone before she had finished settling into her room at the Amherst Hotel. "I had thought we would visit Sue first," she grumbled to herself before the mirror. "The less he sees of Emily Dickinson, the better."

But Judge Lord's note to Emily had confirmed the plans a few days before: "I shall look forward to our meeting as soon as I arrive. And as you said, Lavinia knows to leave us alone for a time, bless her heart."

Thus Lavinia never knew, because she wasn't there and because Emily never told her, that Philip Otis Lord of Salem, aged seventy-one, concluded his visit to the Homestead by tenderly embracing and kissing Emily before opening the heavy front door and stepping carefully outside into the warm September sunshine. He studied the path between the Dickinson houses. To appease Abbie, he would accompany her on a proper visit to the Evergreens later. He did not mind soothing Abbie's feathers, but she would soon have to learn not to view his attachment to Emily Dickinson as a threat to her inheritance from him or as an insult to the memory of her aunt, Judge Lord's deceased wife. After all, why shouldn't he remarry? It was, in fact, his intention. But so far, he had met resistance from Emily, even though she had made it clear to him in letters that she loved him. He could see why she would not want to leave her home and family, and she had been worrying lately about her health as well, though she liked to make a joke of it: "Jumbo Lord," she had said again in person, referring to the weight she had gained by recent fluid retention. "That would be my name!" He worried about his own health, too. But if time was short, all the more reason to consider marriage, he told her.

Before he left Amherst, he had visited Emily again and had made a total of three calls on the Austin Dickinsons. Lavinia, however, did not come next door to dine with them as she had on his other visits, and although Sue was as gracious and attentive a hostess as ever, she seemed somewhat subdued, as did the children, except for Gilbert, who practiced telling riddles to the group at large and asked the judge if he'd ever seen Indians in Salem.

As he saw Judge Lord off from the hotel four days later, after Abbie had stepped into the hack, Austin asked him, "How did you find Emily?"

"As wonderful as ever, though I could see her mother's death has been difficult for her. I care for Emily very much, and hope that she and I share a special understanding. I hope you don't mind my saying so."

"Certainly not. I expect you cheered her up. She has been somewhat low in spirit the past months, and Vinnie and I think she lacks her usual energy."

"Uncle Phil?" called Abbie from within the station hack.

"Just coming. Well, Austin, I will be keeping in touch with her by the mail, and Abbie corresponds regularly with Sue, so we will all keep abreast of each other's activities, I trust. Thanks once again for your hospitality."

With a wave he stepped into the carriage and was off for the station, leaving Austin in front of the hotel, his hat in hand, a figure so somber that Mrs. Jameson, heading across the Common in his direction, changed course to avoid saying hello to him.

CHAPTER 27

September 28-October 5, 1883

~

Mariette Jameson had not known Gilbert was so ill when she told Maggie to find out if Lavinia would like a visit that late September afternoon. But it all turned out for the best, because Lavinia, it became clear, wanted to talk, and Mrs. Jameson certainly wanted to listen. Heavens knows, the already eccentric Lavinia needed the conversation of someone less eccentric than her own family members. The way Emily worded her letters was a case in point: they were clever and interesting, but Mrs. Jameson couldn't always understand them.

So Mrs. Jameson spent a little more than an hour in Lavinia's parlor learning about life in the Dickinson households. Gilbert's illness was naturally foremost on Lavinia's mind. It seemed he had become ill suddenly the day before and worsened during the night so that his parents didn't sleep for attending to him. He was delirious, Lavinia said, and absolutely burning up with fever. "I told Lavinia not to worry, he is young and strong," she said to her husband later that night at home, "but quite frankly, I have my doubts."

Lavinia told her that Emily was worried sick and hadn't slept herself. The subject of Emily had led Mrs. Jameson to ask about Judge Lord's visit earlier in the month. "After all, John," she told her husband, "he's an important man, he sat on the Supreme Court of Masschussetts until a year ago, and when I see an important man visit across the street, I want to know all about it. I think he comes to visit Emily, rather than Lavinia, I really do. After all, you've seen all those letters Emily has addressed to him come through your post office."

But her husband was skeptical. "He comes to visit the Evergreen Dickinsons. They are the important people to him."

Mrs. Jameson was disappointed not to worm much out of Lavinia. Her questions about the Judge's recent visits seemed to evaporate into the air, for all Lavinia responded to them. But the fact remained, no important judge could have much to say to Miss Lavinia Dickinson and her cats. And yet, it was hard to imagine Emily coming downstairs and talking with Judge Lord, either. So the question remained a mystery.

John Jameson tended to taciturnity, but even he had begun to ask about the rumors surrounding Austin Dickinson and Mabel Todd. "Everyone knows Mabel and Susan are barely speaking," he had said. "I've seen it myself. But I don't waste my tears over the Dickinsons; they bring so much trouble on themselves, that's my opinion, the way they think they're better than everyone else."

But of course, Mrs. Jameson could hardly ask Lavinia about those rumors. Instead, she feigned surprise that Mabel Todd had been out of town all summer, and was rewarded with Lavinia's quick answer of "She came back today, she's here. I'm glad, too."

"And now won't we have a circus to watch," Mrs. Jameson thought to herself with anticipation. But the visit was interrupted by Mary next door, still in her apron, who had come in the back and tapped on the hallway door for Lavinia. "Mrs. Dickinson is up now, and wonders if you want to come sit with little Gib a while. Mr. Dickinson says to tell Emily to come over later if she's up to it—she had said she might."

Mrs. Jameson got right up and prepared to go home, wishing now that she had something on hand to bring over to the Evergreens. Perhaps some custard? Or maybe a soup would be better. She wished she could be around if Emily chose to come down those stairs and walk next door in her white dress. Imagine, if she met Emily Dickinson face to face after all this time! And so she left by the front door as Mary went out the back, and hurried across the street where she could continue to keep an eye on both Dickinson households, where it struck her that smouldering troubles threatened to break into fire.

There was a hailstorm the night Mabel returned to Amherst from her long weeks in New Hampshire. It woke Mabel's grandmother and it woke Mabel too, but she snuggled into her pillow next to David with a soft sigh, happy to savor more dreams about her impending reunion with Austin. She did not know that at the Evergreens, Austin bent anxiously over Gilbert's bed to feel his hot forehead once more while Sue held the child as he tossed fitfully and whimpered. "He's burning up," said Austin as the hail drummed on the roof. "I'll get more cool cloths."

Next door, the hail woke Emily, who went to the window to watch the silver stones bounce off the ground and off the black branches outside her window. Dimly from the west window, she saw lights burning at the Evergreens. "Ned? Or did Gib's fever go up since yesterday?" she wondered, and returned quietly to bed so as not to wake Lavinia.

The next morning, Lavinia sent Mabel a note with flowers explaining Gilbert's illness and thus Austin's absence. All Mabel could do then was wait and worry and gaze at the Pelham hills which never looked more peaceful. She snapped at Millicent for crying at the supper table and shook her head rudely when her grandmother offered her the newspaper.

"Who are you more worried about," David asked her crossly in bed that night, "Austin or Gilbert? All you talk about is poor Austin."

Mabel turned her back on him, jerking the quilt over her shoulder so that David's shoulder and side lay suddenly exposed to the chilly night air.

The next morning he was more patient despite her grim silence and stiff shoulders at the breakfast table. "Go for a walk," he told her. "After all, Sue isn't around, she's with Gilbert. She won't bother you now."

So Mabel walked up to the College and made a brief circuit around the grounds in hopes that Austin might be out and about. But she met scarcely anyone she knew except Professor Emerson, who tipped his hat to her with cold eyes. On the way home, however, she met Mariette Jameson near the Common, a basket on one arm.

"I just returned from New Hampshire," Mabel told her without preliminaries. "How is Gilbert Dickinson? You're right across the street, what do you know?"

"I think he's somewhat improved," Mariette told her, studying Mabel's face and figure curiously as she spoke. "Lavinia is hopeful."

"What good news!" Mabel told her, backing away, already on her way to Main Street. Mariette ran her eyes freely now over the agile figure in the fawn skirt with black trim and matching black hat. Then shaking her head slightly to herself, she shifted her basket to the other arm and made her way slowly toward Main Street too, walking sedately as a lady should. But she could understand why a gentleman might be intrigued with Mabel Todd. Those unusual button eyes, almost like an animal's, and that lively air—and she was even more attractive seen close up than at a distance. She had a disconcerting way of looking sharply at a person at first, as though she could read his nature that way. Mariette herself found that trait unattractive, but perhaps men who cared less for convention than others might be intrigued.

It was not until two days later that Lavinia herself brought Mabel up to date in the Homestead parlor. "Typhoid fever. That's what it is. He's getting worse by the hour, not better as we had thought a few days ago. The poor child is delirious and suffering so from thirst and fever. I've never seen Austin so upset. Well, we're all frantic. I wonder you can't hear Emily pacing the floor upstairs."

"Does Austin get any sleep at all?" said Mabel. "How long can he stand this pressure? Oh, if only I could do something.!"

"Emily says she's praying even though she doesn't believe in prayer," said Lavinia, pacing herself. "So why don't you pray? I am. Oh, I am."

"Oh yes, at least I can do that," said Mabel. "Yes, Austin will have all my prayers."

Susan Dickinson did not attend the funeral or the graveside rites for her son, Gilbert. She lay in her bed far from the stuffy "watch" room where Gilbert had died and tried, as hard as she had ever tried in her life, not to think, not about anything at all. The cloying taste of sherry remained on her lips, her stomach ached, and her feet and hands lay cold, inert. Mrs. Jameson hovered about the house somewhere, in the parlor probably, fussing with the fire, or maybe in the kitchen, checking with Maggie on the foods neighbors had brought for supper. A supper Sue would not eat. She hoped Mrs. Jameson would not feel compelled to tiptoe in once again and look at her laid out under the quilts. A tiresome woman. Too anxious to help for her own good.

Austin, she knew, would not tiptoe in and look at her. He would probably sleep in the other house next door again tonight, as he had last night. She had encouraged him to, in fact. They had not wanted to look at each other ever since the end—the end when Gib drew his last shallow breath and left them, standing together by the bed, stranded and separated at that moment from all the world and each other as well.

Vinnie would attend to Austin and Emily, just as she had when their father had died. The three of them ministered to each other in their silent ways, Austin, Emily, and Lavinia, holding each other up in the Homestead, isolated from everyone else. Who would attend to her? But she must remember not to think. A question formed in her mind, despite herself. Something she must ask Mrs. Jameson to find out for her. Did *she* attend the funeral? Did *she* stand there, all safe and sound with her David by her side, and pretend to share the Dickinson family grief for Gib? Maybe tomorrow she would feel up to asking Mrs. Jameson—and up to enduring the answer. She had to know.

Voices. Family, guests, returning to the house to sit by the fire together and dispel the oncoming darkness. She could hear Maggie bustling from the kitchen to help Mrs. Jameson receive people. After a while, someone paused outside her door. "Mattie?" Sue called. But no one answered, and in a short time, she fell asleep.

Early that evening, Mrs. Stearns called at Mabel and David's rooms, as Mabel had asked her to. Mabel drew her in, hand over hand almost, and helped her off with her cloak. She looked critically at Mabel, then remarked, "You and I look equally exhausted. What an awful day. Where is Mr. Todd?"

"At the observatory. Sit down. You'll have something to drink?"

"Impossible. I had supper at the Dickinsons. Food from the whole village, it seemed to me. Mary and Maggie served it up in style."

"Did Sue appear?"

"She did not. She stayed in bed, and the poor children don't quite know what to do with themselves. I've asked Mattie to take a walk with me tomorrow, join our art lessons and tea tomorrow afternoon, but I wasn't sure what to do for Ned. Do you have any suggestions? He's lost, utterly lost. They all are right now."

Mabel ignored her question. "Did Austin look sick? Did he manage to talk and carry on?"

"He managed to carry on, but no one who saw him today could say he looked well. He looked terrible. Depressed as ever anyone could be. Taking his arm was like taking a stone's—he could hardly respond for fear of losing grip on his emotions."

Mabel bent her head down and pressed a fist into her palm. "Oh no, no."

"Don't worry, I'm going to keep an eye on him. How many times he's taken me on carriage rides when I was feeling sad, how many gentle talks we've had. No, I'll not forget him. I'll be keeping a keen eye on Austin Dickinson. It's Sue I'm more worried about. She's harder to reach, despite what people say about the Dickinson family reserve. I find the Gilbert family reserve much harder to break."

"Did Austin leave any message for me?" asked Mabel.

"Any message? No, what do you mean?"

"Just any word, anything. I didn't have anything particular in mind."

"You and he get along well, don't you," said Mrs. Stearns.

"We are good friends, yes. David and Austin and I, we are all close friends. I think we have been good for Austin. To be truthful, we've sensed some sort of unhappiness there between him and Sue. They hardly talk to each other, have you noticed? Surely you must have. She's given to sending him all sorts of little cutting remarks."

"Some of us have noticed, yes. But I hate to talk about the family..."

Mabel looked annoyed. "I don't mean to dabble in idle gossip."

"No, no, I realize you don't. And I didn't mean to sound sharp."

There was a neutral silence. Then Mrs. Stearns returned to Mabel's question. "Well, he didn't leave any message, but I am sure he is thinking about you and David. Right now, of course, he's going to stay close to Emily and Lavinia. Or maybe Lavinia will minister to them both. Emily was particularly close to Gilbert, did you know?"

"I sensed so from some things Austin said. And Lavinia showed me some verses she wrote for him."

"The night Gilbert died," continued Mrs. Stearns, passing her hand over her forehead wearily, "Emily actually went into the Evergreens to the sick room. It's hard to imagine, but she hadn't been in that house for about fifteen years, Mattie told me."

"Fifteen years!"

"That's what Mattie said."

"But why on earth...?" gasped Mabel. "I know she prefers not to go out, but I had no idea she hadn't visited her own brother's house all these years."

"I'm not sure of all the reasons, but I suspect some of them have to do with Sue. Whatever problems Austin and Sue have together seem to affect the whole family somehow. Maybe she is half afraid of Sue! I know Lavinia is."

"Afraid?"

"It seems so. But so much of that seems like village gossip, Mabel, I feel uncomfortable adding to it."

"Tell me then about Emily's going next door when Gilbert was dying."

"Maggie took her over. In fact, Maggie told me this much, so I know it's true. She led her to Gilbert's sick room—I think Emily wanted to comfort him somehow, hold his hand, but he was so sick and so near the end by then that there wasn't much she could do but stand back and give Sue and Austin and Dr.

Cooper room. All the disinfectants they had been using filled the room and the hallway, and sensitive thing that she is, she became sick herself. She stayed on until three in the morning though, when Maggie led her home where she vomited and took to her bed with a violent headache. She's not well to begin with, poor Emily, so she should never have tried to see Gilbert through. But it almost makes me weep to think how she tried anyway." And suddenly, Mary Stearns began to cry quietly, thinking of her own lost children and the hours of their deaths.

Mabel was on her feet instantly, and half knelt by Mary's side. "I'm so sorry, so sorry, I don't know why I made you go on and on about it. I just didn't think, oh please, forgive me."

But Mrs. Stearns was already composing herself. "I assure you, my dear, Gilbert's death would have reminded me of my own children's without your doing a thing." She reached for Mabel's hand, and the two embraced briefly.

"You can see I feel even closer to the Dickinsons now because of what they have suffered, but I must confess, I feel especially close to Austin. He's been very kind to me, ever since I moved here. As busy as he is, he's always ready for a leisurely carriage ride to look at the hills or for a quiet talk. He's been a great comfort to me. If I asked him, he'd even take me sledding! You should have seen him and Lavinia one time, whizzing over the snow, laughing like children." She smiled, remembering.

"He doesn't laugh often," said Mabel, "but when he does..."

"Yes," echoed Mrs. Stearns, smiling. "When he does...!"

She put her hands on either side of her chair. "My dear, I'm exhausted and I ought to be back at the school. The Convent girls are in good hands, but I'd still like to read with them as usual before bed, and have our little refreshment hour. You're welcome to come, if you'd like. Sometime, I'd like to talk more with you about giving art lessons unless you're too busy with Mattie's piano lessons and your singing."

"Oh, but I'm not giving Mattie lessons anymore," said Mabel with a wry smile. "Sue asked me to stop, and engaged Elizabeth Scarrit instead."

"Why would she do that?"

"She's angry because she thinks I've trespassed on her social monopoly in this town. I'm too popular, that's all. I can't help it if people, including her own family members, make a fuss over me."

Mrs. Stearns' eyes expressed a hint of amusement, but she said nothing.

Mabel went on, "But I am interested in giving your girls art lessons, and I'd like to show you more of my work, too. I'll be keeping most of it in Walker Hall. David is fixing up a little studio for me there, did I tell you? It will be finished by the end of November."

"How wonderful. I look forward to seeing it." Mrs. Stearns stood up.

"Please let me see you home," said Mabel, and I'll return by way of the observatory. Maybe David would like some company."

"Oh, that's not necessary, really."

"No," said Mabel, "I want to, and I need the walk. I wish we had Austin here to see us home, but we'll have to do without him tonight, won't we?"

And setting out into the evening air, they linked arms and strolled the quiet streets, both consoled by their mutual admiration for the man who was suffering as he had never suffered before.

CHAPTER 28

November 1883

THE TRIO SET OUT IN THE CARRIAGE FOR A drive on the Northampton Road one brisk November morning, Austin and David on either side of Mabel. Their departure did not go unnoticed. Professor Clark Seelye waved at Austin, glad to see him without that vacant look he'd had in his eyes ever since Gilbert's death. "Have a nice ride," he called out. Charles Garman, reclusive and eccentric professor of philosophy, looked up at the carriage as he plodded across the path near the observatory, but continued walking toward the post office, one of his two overcoats flapping open and revealing several scarves underneath.

"You're so lucky, David," said Mabel. "You've seen Austin nearly every day and I've hardly had a glance at him until last week. He's looking a little better, don't you think? Oh Austin, I missed you so much! I'm so glad we're all together again."

Austin put his arm around Mabel and pressed her shoulder, leaving his hand there for a while but saying nothing.

"I wish we could be with you for Thanksgiving dinner," she said, leaning against him.

"I doubt you'd enjoy it," he said. "I wish we could just forget about Thanksgiving at the Evergreens. It's too painful."

"Of course it is," said Mabel. "I understand. That's why I wish I could be with you. I want to see you through it."

"I'll think about you both, my special friends," said Austin. "Well, Mattie will want to see some of her old school mates, I'm sure, and if Ned has anyone in, we'll have a busy household. I hope we do. It helps us all stop thinking, at least a little bit." He turned to catch Mabel's eye. "I hope we can have another ride or a walk tomorrow if the weather continues good. After that, we'll have to wait until after Thanksgiving." And suddenly, his right hand was nudging her left elbow. Moving her hand back toward his, she found the note between his fingers quickly, and closed it in the palm of her glove to read as soon as she could.

They were passing some lush meadows, bordered by farmers' fields and woods, and now and again, a pond.

"When I can't stop myself from thinking," said Austin without apparent emotion, "I have only the one thought, the one fact, that haunts me. I know it will never end, the pain and more pain for him, for Gilbert." He shook his head. "No, I don't have anything to be thankful for this Thanksgiving."

As Mabel was studying his profile and planning some answer, David took the lead, surprising them both. "I'm not surprised to hear you say that. If it had been Millicent..." He cleared his throat. "Look here, Austin. I don't usually say things like this, but I think you ought to know something, and that's how much I respect you and care about you. Both Mabel and I do, of course, but you've done so much for me in so many ways. I'd never have been able to stay away from the college so long for the Transit expedition if it hadn't been for you. And you spoke up for me when it came to giving me more office rooms in Walker Hall. There's not a faculty meeting goes by that I don't feel glad I know you. So in turn, I care about you and what happens to you. We grieve for Gilbert with you."

Austin smiled faintly.

"And," continued David, "although it may sound strange, you can be thankful this year for something you didn't have before—Mabel's respect and love for you. She'll stand by you through everything, just as she's stood by me. Having Mabel on your side isn't something to take lightly."

Mabel glanced at Austin's face, not sure how he had received David's speech, not sure how she herself should interpret it. But Austin's face bore a definite smile now, and she in turn smiled at him and at David on her other side.

"I won't forget what you said," Austin answered.

"Thank you, David, that was sweet," said Mabel.

"David and I need to return to work right after we look over the Walker Hall rooms with you," said Austin, "so shall we turn around at the sycamore grove before Hadley?"

"Well, if we must," said Mabel. "I wish we didn't have to."

She managed to open the crumpled, urgent note and to read it in Walker hall when David left the new rooms to look for a letter to show Austin. Austin's note read: "Can't bear separation any longer. Carriage ride tomorrow at noon? Usual spot? Let me know in any way. Need you!"

She held it in her palm when David returned from the hallway, picking his way around the packing boxes and wood shavings. "No, I can't find the letter," David told Austin. "It must be at home. I'll bring it to you later, because I want your opinion about the way President Seelye worded it. I think he's stalling on our observatory by trying to push my interest into Smith College's plan for one instead."

"I'll look at it tomorrow then, preferably before the faculty meeting. Well, are you still pleased with the rooms? Will they make good studio space for you, Mabel ?"

Slipping the note into her dress pocket, Mabel answered him with telling eyes. "Oh, yes, just perfect. Your plans couldn't have been better. If you were to see me tomorrow, you'd no doubt hear how much more cleaning up I'll have done by then."

So it was arranged, as best as they could arrange anything these days: a ride at noon into the country along the Sunderland Road, away from everyone, just the two of them. And for once, their plans came about without a hitch. After Austin turned down the lane of an abandoned farm house and stopped under three great elm trees, he took Mabel in his arms with a groan and kissed with a need which overpowered them both. They did not talk, but pressed into each other with all the longing that weeks of thinking, suffering, dreaming, and imagining had bequeathed them. Breathing, even panting, as loudly as he, she half lay below him, finally, while his lips and fingers caressed her nipples through the cloth which he cried with frustration to remove. Pressing against her in the cramped awkward space allotted them, their clothing only exciting their passion, his movements became insistently rhythmical, at the same time as he gasped, "No, not now, when? Please, please!" when suddenly, they both found their peak in strange, surprised unison.

In the silence, a red- tailed hawk cried out above several times just before Austin began to cry gently, calling Gilbert's name. Mabel held him tightly, running her hands over his neck, his back, his ears, soothing him with a soft protection David could never evoke in her, in a way David would never require, tears finally running down her own face.

The cramped space forced them to sit up, still holding each other, while all the emotions of the previous weeks rose at last, released for the other to see. They didn't speak for a few moments, but just held each other while tears from Austin's eyes fell, drop by quiet drop, on Mabel's shoulder. When he moved to look her full in the face, he had but one tremulous sentence: "I love you."

Her response was immediate. "I love you too, oh, how much! I thank God for how much!"

"Is there a God? I think for me, there is only you. Only you, now that my boy has left me." He bent his head with tears again.

"My darling, I've wanted to comfort you all these terrible weeks! Knowing you needed me and I couldn't help you—" she cradled his face tenderly. "It was like having the moon blot out the stars. One of David's occultations. The familiar stars are blotted out, and there is nothing to do but wait until the moon releases them. Oh, I love you! Can we be together now, can we see each other again soon? I can't stand it without you!"

He raised his head and searched in his pockets for a handkerchief.

"You're wet," she smiled gently, "and not just your eyes." Seeing his embarrassed look, she seized his hand and held it gently to her cheek. "It's a first for us. It's another landmark. And it must be just the start of our fullest love. We must have each other completely now. We must not wait any longer."

They sat silently in the carriage for a moment, hearing all the little sounds around them—the creaking of the leather, the gentle snorting of the horse, a catbird in a nearby bush, and the rustle of a squirrel in the fallen leaves . Austin pulled Mabel's cloak around her again, but held her with his hands underneath the cloak, nearest the warmth and contours of her body.

Unexpectedly, he laughed. "What is it?" she asked.

"It's all so new. I'm fifty-four years old, and I've never felt such wonder before. Never such sensations. Such joy." He held his head in his hands briefly. "I don't know what to make of it," he said, his voice muffled. But when he raised his head, he was smiling.

"But tell me why, Austin. Because you didn't love her? Or she didn't love you? Why?"

Maybe both. I don't know. I can't talk about it now. I don't want to think about it. I just want to think about being with you." He touched the curls around her face. "You have amazing eyes—so bright. I noticed them the day I met you."

"And I noticed your bright blue eyes that day you visited the boarding house last year, remember? When I handed you your cup, I noticed those eyes of yours. And then you rumpled the rug," she laughed.

He laughed too, but resumed a serious expression immediately, looking down at his hands.

"What is it?" Mabel asked.

"David."

"What about him?"

He looked up. "What about him? How can you ask that?"

"I'm sorry, I don't mean to be flippant. But we can go ahead despite David."

"You don't love him?"

She squirmed a bit. "No, it's not that. I do love him. But I love you too. Besides, I love you differently than I love him. Oh Austin, love has many sides!"

"But," Austin persisted, "what if he finds out? What would he do? And besides, I'm his friend. I care about David, very much."

"Well, I've been Sue's friend, haven't I?"

"Yes, but not anymore, and because she knows of our feelings. Sue already guesses that we have made commitments to each other. David is more of an innocent."

"Is he? Not exactly. He knows I care for you..." she said.

Austin interrupted. "But he doesn't know the truth of it."

"Well," she said, snuggling close to him, "he does have some idea..." She held his hand to her breast gently. "He knows I am thinking of you as a lover— and he certainly knows I respect and care for you. But not how deeply, how very utterly seriously."

"But you can't tell him what we intend—we do intend it now, don't we—to stand on the other side of that veil, that veil of deepest intimacy? Mabel!" He began to kiss her again, deeply.

"When, when?" she said, moving against him.

"Let it be at the Homestead. And soon," he said without hesitation, as though he had thought it out before.

"The Homestead? Right next door to Sue?"

"But where else?" he asked her. "It will be quiet and safe there, and besides, it's home. Home to me."

"And your sisters?"

"They know I care for you. They don't realize how very much, but they are glad for whatever joy I can find in life these days. Certainly you know they like you."

Mabel smiled. "I hope so. I have enjoyed the flowers and notes Emily has sent me, and Lavinia has been a delight."

"Well, you can see they are tolerant of us. I'll explain to them that we need to be alone together for a while to talk. They won't ask questions. Where Sue is concerned, they don't ask questions—and they know things are unhappy between Sue and me."

"And David, I'll talk honestly to David," said Mabel thoughtfully.

"Oh no, please don't talk to David, I fear that would be the end of us!" Austin said passionately.

"It won't be, believe me," she reassured him. But he was still afraid, shaking his head. "All right, maybe I won't," she consented. "Don't worry about it. I'll do the right thing." Seeing his worried face, she repeated, "I'll do the right thing. Everything will work out."

"I must have you. Completely have you, my beloved and loved one. You will let me know when your best time is? Your safe time?"

"It will be in two weeks."

"Then we will plan for that time. I'll make arrangements."

They moved apart, almost shakily, thinking of what was to come. "We must get back," Austin said. "Who knows how many people noticed us leave."

"But I don't care now," said Mabel. "It's all decided. After our going by the gate that rainy evening, we knew this would happen, didn't we? Our Rubicon..."

"But not until I lost my boy did I know I couldn't live without you. I love you and Gilbert more than any two beings on earth."

They turned and held each other one last time, then arranged their clothing and set off on the chilly road to Amherst.

After she put Millicent to bed and her grandmother had retired after nodding over her sewing, Mabel prepared to ask David the question outright, the question she had rolled over in her mind ever since the Transit of Venus. "Do you still think about making love to her, that Mrs. Lowry who took such a fancy to you in Washington last spring?"

"Fannie Lowry? No, that was all talk!"

"I don't believe you, David. I think you want to see what it's like, to have someone else, like we talked about before."

"To really do it?" He whistled. "Talk about trouble...!"

They were in their bedroom now, getting ready for bed. Mabel unbuttoned her shoes. "But you let me spend so much time with Austin. I don't think I'd want you to spend that much time with someone else."

David took off his collar. "Well, I know, it's strange. But Austin is different. And of course, he's so much older than I am. It would be different if he were my age. And anyway, you're not serious about Austin. Are you?" He turned to look at her as he unbuttoned his shirt.

"No, I'm not serious. But I am attracted to him, you know that, and he needs me in a way. He needs both of us."

"He does need us, you're right. It's as though he just ran to us—if a Dickinson would do such a thing."

"He's running away from Sue, that's what," said Mabel. "He's miserable, no one knows how much. Even you don't."

David placed his trousers in the press. "Why did you ask me about Fannie Lowry first? What does she have to do with it? Are you saying that if I wanted her, you could have Austin?"

"No, no," said Mabel, "It's not like that." There was a pause. She pulled her nightgown over her head, then took a deep breath as she tied the ribbons at the bodice. "I think we should be honest with each other, as we always have been. And the truth is, David, I think Austin wants me—you know, wants me—during this terrible period in his life. So I'm telling you about it, even though it's crazy. And that's why I wanted to know if you'd thought more about that Effie out in California, or Fannie."

"Well, all right," said David, turning down the quilt, "I have thought about it, but not as though it could ever happen. I didn't think you'd want that! Would you?"

Mabel helped him turn down the quilt from her side. "No. But it wouldn't be fair if I wanted Austin and you didn't want someone too."

David got in bed but propped his pillow against the headboard and sat up. "You're really thinking about this, aren't you? To do it, to actually be intimate with Austin Dickinson? That pillar of Amherst? He wants you, then, does he? He's capable of feeling so strongly about you? He'd risk his reputation for you? Good God!" And he laughed but without humor, shaking his head and raising his voice. "What would people say if they knew we were having this conversation!"

"Shhh!" said Mabel, "Grandma will hear you."

At that thought, they both stopped and listened, then caught each other's eyes and laughed in spite of themselves. "Come here, Mabs," said David, reaching for her and holding her close. "Do you love me?"

"Always and ever, David. You're my lover/husband."

"Then go ahead and at least think about doing what will make Austin happy. It'll be just a kind of game. And will you tell me about it?"

"Yes."

Her quick response took him back a little. "You think he really wants you then, in that way?"

"He does, David, he does. He wants me to meet him at his sisters' house. It might be soon. It has to be the right time for me, you know that."

His hand stopped stroking her back. "Then I will make love to someone too. Don't think that because Fannie is out of reach, there won't be someone else. You thought because she was so far away that I wouldn't get my turn. But I can."

"I know, there could be someone else," Mabel said, but her eyes were closed and relaxed. She had won her point, and she could not imagine any willing partner for David in Amherst or any other nearby New England village.

"It isn't fair though," David resumed. "Austin. Our best friend."

"Your friend too. He thinks so much of you. This won't change anything between us, David. He cares about you very much."

"And I care about him. Can you believe it, Mabs, we've captured the most important man in Amherst? Of all the people around here, he's chosen us. Us!"

"Austin will take care of us," murmured Mabel sleepily, and was already nearly asleep while David leaned over to blow out the bedside candle on her side. He felt excited in a strange unfathomable way, like the times when he was a teenager, discovering his body. He rolled against Mabel, but she sighed and floated into sleep. So he made himself come, as he had when he was a teenager, thinking he would be able to sleep well afterward. But instead, he lay awake, trying not to wake Mabel with his turning and shifting on the noisy mattress. Confused images drifted through his mind—images of Austin pointing out new offices on the blueprint for Walker Hall, except the head bent low over the plans was little Gilbert's, not Austin's. A picture of Sue, dressed in black and holding their Millicent, drifted across his mind, followed by a view of the Dickinson meadow covered with stiff black stalks, as though it had been burned, and he himself, David, walking over the burnt grasses and lifting his boots to gaze at the soot covering their soles.

He heard the clock downstairs strike 2:30. After that, he lost track of time and space, and wandered at last into a deep sleep.

CHAPTER 29

December 13, 1883

A SMILE INCHED ACROSS EMILY DICKINSON'S lips as she left the kitchen and heard her sister Lavinia singing loudly on the stairs, shaking her dust cloth: "Oh God, our help in ages past, our hope for years to come!"

The old hymn sounded out ever more clangorously as Vinnie worked her way down the stairs, until Emily's mouth opened in a generous smile.

"Who are you imitating, Vin, or is that wail supposed to be just you?"

"Mostly just me, if you please, with a touch of Mrs. Jameson thrown in." She flicked at the banister with her dust cloth and opened the dining room doors. "Time to clean in here."

"But Maggie did all that just a few days ago; you don't need to do it over again. I prefer pestilence to all this fuss."

"So you tell me all the time."

"You don't think Austin cares, do you? He's glad to be in a house less perfect than his own."

"Well, I like to keep things nice for Mabel. Of course, David wouldn't care. He told me he starts wiping his feet on the grass all the way up the steps to Sue's parlor. Oh, I slapped my knee I laughed so hard."

"When is Austin bringing her here?"

"Between 7 and 8, he said. I promised him they would be no trouble to us with their wanting to be alone. You're upstairs most evenings anyway, but maybe this evening, we could spend a little time together going over which sheets need mending, and even starting to work on some of them. You don't have to write tonight, do you?"

"No, I will surprise you and save time for housewifery! Just don't reward me with singing!"

But that remark set Lavinia off again, and the hymn lines came thundering out once more as the two laughed. Vinnie stopped after the first two lines though, and leaned by the window in the dining room looking out. "That's the first time we've laughed since Gilbert."

"I know, I thought of it just as you started to sing again when I felt a laugh coming on. It makes me feel in a maze. But I suppose we need to laugh, you know. Look at how we've worried about Austin. Yet even he's coming back to life again, thanks to her. I am forced to wonder if we should, too."

"I know we *should*, but I don't feel much life in me half the time. She helps though. What is it about Mabel?"

Emily pushed aside a plant on the deep window sill and sat stiffly, half sideways, looking toward Main Street and the bare meadow beyond.

"Do you feel all right, Emily? You look tired again."

"At fifty-three, I am allowed to feel tired now and again, so never mind. No, the question remains about Mabel. This has been a keystone year, has it not? Gib's passing has harrowed our hearts forever. If we will never be the same again, think of Austin! What is left for him now? He will gather to him what new comfort we suspect is waiting for him, or else give up. You saw it before I did, when he told you about her letters coming to your post office box. But I see it now, and more."

"And Sue, what about Sue?"

"There is nothing we can do for Sue that we haven't already done. We must try to continue as we have for her and know her mostly through the children. But Vinnie, don't cower so when she storms over you. I hate to see that."

"You are a fine one to talk, you upstairs all the time writing letters instead of meeting her and everyone else in the flesh!"

Emily smiled sheepishly and slid off the window sill. "All right, all right. Time to take the bread out of the pans. Don't clean yourself to death in here, the president isn't visiting, you know. And don't ask which president. I don't mean the president of Amherst College this time, I mean THE president!"

She walked into the hallway and turned toward the kitchen in the back of the house, calling as she did so, "Beef soup and bread for an early supper?"

"Yes, fine, I'll be in soon to help you. Austin may arrive early and eat with us."

Lights were visible now in the homes on Main Street, and from the back of her house, Emily could see the glow of lamps in the Evergreens' windows, too. Mattie might be playing the piano or visiting with a friend by the fire. Her mother had retired early to nurse her grief along with the cold she had been unable to shake since Gilbert's death. No telling where Ned was; his whereabouts were unpredictable these days. As for Austin, he was most often any-where but at home. Those in his law office could depend on seeing him regu-larly, as could almost anyone on the Amherst College campus, from President Seelye to David Todd. But the frail and bereaved inhabitants of the Evergreens rarely saw Austin Dickinson, nor did they wish to. He was unwelcome there, a barely tolerated presence, at the same time that he was received as a king by David and Mabel Todd. He was unaware that Millicent Todd, not yet four years old, feared and hated his heavy steps, his bushy auburn hair, and his stern demeanor, and always would.

A dark figure followed the path between the two houses and arrived at Emily's back door. Austin had arrived for supper, just as Lavinia had predicted. His tread, his voice, brightened Emily's face as she stepped back from the door to let him in while the cats retreated from the blast of cold winter air.

"Some more peach preserves for you." He handed her the glass jar, quickly shrugging his coat off and hanging it on a peg by the door. He peered closely at her for a moment, then paced around the kitchen. "You look tired, is Vin taking good care of you?"

"I think it's you who look tired. Are you hungry?"

"No. Yes. Oh, I'll just have a little something. I can't seem to get much of an appetite back."

"We have some nice beef soup and hot bread for you, just right for a frail appetite. Is Sue...is she...settled in?"

"She's been going to bed about 8 o'clock every night, but tonight, she went even earlier with this cold. We hardly ever see each other." He pulled up a chair and sat hunched forward, his elbows on the table. "You're not upset about tonight, are you?"

Emily was quick. "No, absolutely not." She sat down too, but leaned back so that he couldn't see her face.

"I mean, you aren't too upset with all that's...developed? You understand it? You see it truly? It was inevitable, you know." He lowered his elbows and showed his lined face. "It's hard for me to talk about. Especially since we haven't talked much in this family for so long. But I have to know, because I've in-volved you and Vin. It's time you understood how little has held Sue and me together. But in Mabel, I've found what I've wanted all these years. I feel as though she's saved me—I think I would have killed myself after Gib died if it weren't for her. You can tell Vin that, but she probably knows it already. Where is she?"

"Oh, still fussing with cleaning, you know her!"

"Have I embarrassed you too much?"

"No."

"I want to ask you—are you still writing so often to Otis Lord?"

She looked away, the abrupt question taking her by surprise. "Yes, why?"

"I just wondered. Does he plan another visit soon?"

"I doubt it."

The kitchen door opened and Lavinia bustled in. "Supper time, supper time, Austin. But first the cats must eat. Come here, Buskin, here Charlotte, time for dinner. Where's Snappers?" The house cats meowed and prowled around her feet. The outside cats had already been fed.

Austin stood up. "Is the green quilt still in Mother's chest upstairs?"

"Yes," said Lavinia, "just where it always was. Do you need it for the other house? I'll get it for you later."

"No, don't bother, I'll get it now myself."

"Is he ready for supper?" asked Vinnie as they listened to his steps upstairs.

"As ready as he'll ever be. Let's put things on, we need to clean up early tonight. Is Maggie coming back tomorrow ?"

"I think so. Her cousin is much better. I told her there was no hurry. But I must say, it'll be nice to have someone to start up the kitchen fire again. I wonder, will he find that quilt by himself?"

"Give him a few minutes. He's slow but he gets there. Besides, maybe he wants to be alone a few minutes."

Lavinia sounded amazed. "Do you think so? Well, all right. I don't know why he needs that quilt now anyway."

Emily didn't respond, and the two fell into silence as they brought bread and winter vegetables from the pantry to fill out the meal, added silverware to the table, and filled the glasses with water from a storage jug.

After a while, they heard Austin's footsteps descending by the front stairs, then disappearing into the dining room. A moment later, he called from the hallway, "I'm going to lay the fire in the dining room. Go ahead and eat if you want to."

Lavinia stuck her head outside the kitchen door into the cold hallway. "Why don't you wait? Lay it later, why don't you?"

There was no answer, only the sound of the fireplace grate being moved and of logs hitting each other.

Lavinia closed the door of the warm kitchen. She stood still in front of it, staring ahead. "Emily, I'm afraid."

"What, dear, what's wrong?"

"I feel very strange. I feel like something awful is going to happen here." She bowed her head and rubbed her hands together agitatedly. "This house sometimes feels horrible to me. So empty and sad. Austin out there lighting a fire all by himself and Mother and Father gone..." Her voice was quavering.

Emily crossed to her and rubbed her arms gently. "It's all right, Vinnie, nothing is different tonight and nothing is going to happen. It's not like you to be so upset. Isn't it you who usually comforts me? Tonight will be a good night because Austin has found some happiness. It's not what we expected, but it turns out to be right. Can you see it that way?"

Lavinia raised her head with some measure of calm, and Emily stepped back, reluctant for Austin to enter and see their fear. But when nearly twenty minutes had passed and he hadn't returned, they seated themselves at their usual places and began to eat slowly, saving part of their meal to eat with him whenever he joined them.

They next heard his footsteps upstairs again. "Washing off soot?" said Lavinia. "He could do that down here, I don't mind." She got up to see if the water on the stove was hot. "Let's not wash the dishes yet, surely he's going to eat something."

But when he reappeared, they could see his thoughts were elsewhere. His sleeves were still rolled up from having worked over the fireplace and then washed. His eyebrows lay damp from scrubbing, and his whiskers showed evidence of trimming. His sisters examined him, then looked down, embarrassed. "What will you eat, Austin?" said Emily.

"A little of that bread and some soup. I'll get it." He lifted the heavy kettle lid to ladle out some warm soup while Lavinia buttered a thick slice of bread. But he stood to eat, looking around the room with unseeing eyes, while his sisters began to collect dishes and put food back in the pantry. In five minutes, he had finished and rolled his sleeves down again. No one had spoken a word. Once again he went to the dining room, checked the fire which was now burning low but steadily, climbed the stairs, and shortly returned to the kitchen carrying waste water to empty outside.

His sisters had finished cleaning up and Vinnie was drying her hands, while Emily had already gone upstairs through the back passage. "We're going to sort and mend sheets. Don't let the cats out of the kitchen."

"I wouldn't worry, Lavinia, they love the warmth in here. I'm about to go fetch Mabel. Do you need anything before I go?"

"No."

"Do you think Emily is a little better lately or not?"

"A little, but she tires so easily, and she looks puffy to me, don't you think so?"

"I do. I wish she would let a doctor look at her."

"When horses fly. I think she's in pain sometimes but maybe it's caused by worry. Or maybe she should drink more water. Or less water, I don't know, I can't get her to do anything much about it. Tell Mabel, maybe she'll have a suggestion."

"I will. I'm glad that you're looking better lately. Mabel remarked on that the other day."

"Did she?" Lavinia looked pleased. "That's because you and David take good care of me. You bring us food and he fixes everything around this foolish old house."

"He's a good man, David Todd. But I must go now." He reached for his coat on the peg. "I'll see you in the morning." And pulse leaping, he left through the back door and strode along the side of the house out to Main Street, dark and hushed, on this winter evening of his love's consummation.

That same evening, David Todd walked from one end of Amherst College to the other, his head bowed against the dark cold, hardly aware that he had forgotten his gloves. After another circuit past College Hall, he entered the observatory and prowled around his desk, shifting papers without looking at them, glancing upward toward the telescope looming above him whose mechanisms brought him much pleasure, more than the stars and planets themselves by far. He stopped pacing for a few moments and looked upward steadily, expressionless. Then a smile shaped his lips and disappeared before it could establish itself. He paced again, aware that the time would pass slowly for him until he felt ready to go home again that evening. For he and Mabel had discussed what would take place that night at the Homestead.

In the Evergreens, Sue Dickinson slept on her back, her mouth wide open, breathing noisily and heavily. Earlier that evening she had prayed for the strength to go on with her life, and as she drifted toward unconsciousness, she felt God had rewarded her with this sleep, a bountiful respite from the pain she could hardly bear. But it was her fate to awaken only a few hours later and to lie there, numb from the accumulated grief, tensions, and quarrels of the last months. She did not light the lamps or attempt to arise. Instead, she lay rigid against the chill of the room and of her heart itself, and hardly noticed or cared when later, she heard the back door open and Austin's footsteps moving toward the downstairs bedroom.

Much later in the Homestead next door, the lamp in Emily Dickinson's bedroom still glowed, along with the fire in her little Franklin stove. She had finished working on the letters she had begun several evenings before—a letter to Mrs. Mather and one to Otis Lord. Thinking both of him and of Austin and Mabel below, she wrote:

> *Morning is due to all—*
> *To some—the Night—*
> *To an imperial few—*
> *The Auroral light.*

She was happy if love was saving her brother's soul, but she did not look easily on the future of that love. Lavinia was right to feel afraid—the Dickinsons in both houses walked more warily day by day, eyeing each other askance, whether with love or hostility. Gilbert's passing had opened the way to chaos. No one in either house would ever be the same again.

Austin lay in bed next door in the "watch" bedroom, the one he often took Ned to after one of his night seizures and the room where Gilbert had died. It was warm there, close to the kitchen, and lately Austin slept there to maintain a distance from Sue. With arms above his head against the brass bars, he meditated deeply, passionately, feeling almost more alive than he could remember. The intensity of this experience—this joining of his physical self to hers—made him wonder if he had discovered something no one else knew about. If people experienced such profound happiness, wouldn't they appear radiant, ebullient, laughing aloud in the streets? Or did people know these feelings so well that they grew easily casual? Maybe he himself had been the uninitiated. All these years with Sue—all the fumbled half-hearted moments, the accommodations to eclipse of feeling—he would never have to face them again. They were over, as of tonight, though they had virtually been over ever since he met Mabel, and certainly since Gib had died.

No makeshift bower could ever have turned out so beautifully, he mused, reviewing their time in the dining room, re-seeing it in his slow, vivid mind's eye. The cold outside, the warmth within, the tightly closed sets of doors, the quilts he lay ready and the pillows he had stashed away earlier, and above all, the knowledge that no one would disturb them. David knew exactly what was planned for that room and gave permission. Lavinia and Emily knew as much as they allowed themselves to know, and gave permission. And Sue seemed to have given up the fight. She barely figured in events anymore, for the magnetic power of Mabel skewed everything toward her own powerful field. Sometimes he saw his whole family snapping toward her, like hapless iron filings, along with others in town, even those who followed her progress in the street with their eyes as they sat indoors by lace curtains or geranium plants.

Though they had held each other before on carriage rides almost as lovers do, they had never seen each other's bodies bare before, never lain with each other before, and never joined together before, free and uninhibited. He had written to her earlier about the veil they stood before, poised to lift.

And now, they stood on the other side of that veil. He could hardly believe his happiness, hardly knew how to acknowledge it. His gratitude poured out of him until he couldn't lie still, but sat up, then sank to his knees by the bed to pray, but cried instead. Tears poured from his eyes as he saw pictures in his mind, scenes from this evening mixed with scenes from his imagination: Mabel lying below him, bringing her lips to his, then Gilbert, alive and well, riding his velocipede up and down the street. Then the three of them, he, Gilbert, and Mabel, walking hand and hand in the autumn meadow covered with hay-stacks and buzzing with insects in a waning afternoon sun. He felt he could die tomorrow, yet he wanted to live forever. He wasn't sure he believed in God, yet he wondered if he had had a religious experience. When his chest stopped shaking, he climbed into bed again wishing he could somehow share his feel-ings with Emily, who seemed so alone lately. He remembered the new private code with Mabel: they had consummated their love at nine that evening. Thus every day they would stop and think of one another, wherever they were, at nine, and again in the mornings at ten and the evenings at five. Thinking he would never fall asleep, he awoke six hours later to the sounds of crows outside and familiar household noises inside. And remembered his new life all over again.

PART TWO

INTO DEGREELESS NOON

1884-1886

CHAPTER 30

February 1884

Pussy Cat, Pussy Cat, talk to me, no one else does," said Lavinia, sweeping a fat sandy-colored cat into her arms and standing by the kitchen window to look out over the snow toward the barn and over the hillside in the direction of the graveyard beyond.

"Lavinia Dickinson, I talk to you and you know it." Maggie took dry clothes from the drying rack and folded them deftly. "And Austin's here nearly every day now to visit or even to take you for sleigh rides."

"Yes, Pussy Cat, your mama had a sleigh ride last week, imagine!" Lavinia held the cat's face to her cheek. "But I have a right to complain today, Maggie. It's February 28th. You forgot to wish me a happy birthday. And so did Emily."

"Oh, happy birthday, Miss Lavinia, I should have said something. I got caught up in morning chores. But don't blame poor Miss Emily, I doubt she's even half dressed yet. She must have had a bad night, or else she was writing especially late. She looks so puffy and tired these days—she worries me."

"She worries me too, Maggie," said Lavinia, putting down the cat. "I always try to be patient with all that writing and thinking she does. She *is* the thinker in this family, more than Austin. That's my decided opinion, you know. Even Father let her stay up late to write. Do you suppose that's why she's sick, from thinking too much?"

The kitchen door opened and Emily herself stepped quietly in. "Happy birthday, Lavinia! And no, sitting up late writing has not made me sick. Maggie, how's your back this morning?"

"Oh, Emily, you scared me, don't *do* that, creeping through doors that way!" said Lavinia, who had nearly bumped into Maggie and the drying rack.

"She didn't scare me," fibbed Maggie.

"But how is your back?" persisted Emily.

"Oh, much better, thank you. My sister-in-law gave me a nice massage yesterday evening after I got home, and then I had a hot bath and went straight to bed. Watch out, Miss Emily, don't get ashes on your white dress. I'm just about to empty the ash bucket."

"I suppose you ate breakfast long ago, Vinnie?"

"Of course. Especially today. Time starts to fly when you realize you are really fifty-one. It gives me the horrors to realize that it is already 1884. Or 1880 anything."

"The old, old sophistries of June," said Emily, as Maggie pushed her gently toward a chair at the kitchen table. "You can't catch time. Just some bread and tea this morning, my Irish Maggie, but you know I can get it myself."

"Nonsense, let me do it."

"Lavinia, will you go to the post office today or will Austin go for you? I'm sure cousins Fanny and Loo will send you a birthday letter, and Aunt Katie, of course. And maybe there'll be something for me."

"I'll let Austin go. There's probably a letter from Mabel for him anyway, even though she'll be calling here today. But calling in honor of me, you understand, not Austin, for a change!"

"Will you give her some of the birthday cake I made for you yesterday?"

"Yes, along with some Ceylon tea. But I won't eat any cake, I'll wait to have it with you tonight."

"Oh Vinnie, don't worry, have two slices, one this afternoon and one tonight! A career of butter!"

A shuffling and stamping outside the back door followed by a quick knock revealed Ned. "Didn't have time to run, eh, Aunt Emily?"

"I must have known it was only you, mustn't I? A cup of the richest East, Neddie?"

"Don't think so, just came with the book review you asked Mother for last week." He handed it over, pulling off his hat and sitting at the same time. "Happy birthday, Aunt Vinnie. How old are you, did you say?"

"Thirty," said Lavinia, while Maggie tapped him playfully on the head with a wooden spoon.

"What are you doing today then? Anything special?" Ned asked.

"Mabel Todd is coming this afternoon, and maybe Mr. Todd will drop by later."

"Oh yes, Amherst's leading lady," he muttered, turning toward the window. Emily studied his face quickly, then overlooked his comment. "Anything special going on at the College?" she asked

"I'm going to sit in on some lectures today. Then some of the fellows and I will brew up coffee in Mrs. Hall's boarding house and sit around talking.

"I imagine you'll smoke some of those foul little cigars you like so much, won't you?" said Emily, taking a cup of tea from Maggie's strong hands.

"I just might. Nothing like a smoke for a young college graduate. It's one of the gentlemanly arts, you could say."

"Well," said Lavinia, "keep those poisonous clouds of smoke out of this house, Neddie. What's that other parcel you have?"

"Oh, that's a photograph of Mattie. Mother thought you might like to see it." He passed it to Emily who unwrapped it. "Oh, Vinnie, look at this. She looks—well, ethereal!"

"Mattie, ethereal? Huh, you've got her all wrong, Aunt Emily," said Ned.

"But just look at that expression, Vinnie", said Emily. "Don't you think she looks almost like an actress? What literary character could she play, I wonder?"

"Here, Maggie, you look while I get some spectacles," said Lavinia, who walked with her heavy tread into the sitting room.

"Oh, saints, look at that dress, will ye," breathed Maggie, bending over the photograph in Emily's hand. "Them sleeves and that bodice—would that be the material she and Susan picked out in Boston?"

"Must be," said Ned, fiddling with a teaspoon. "I can't keep track."

"But it's the latest style, isn't it, with them high stuffed shoulders and the draggin' lace below the elbow. Wouldn't my sister-in-law love to wear something like this though?"

"Mr. Lovell does a fine job of photographing. I'm having mine done next—when Mother gives me a good hair cut, that is," said Ned.

"Now I'm ready," said Lavinia, hustling in with spectacles in her hand. "It's a pity we don't see Mattie in the flesh more often, but there you are. Nothing to be done. She's getting too stuck up, don't you agree Emily?"

"Settle down and look at the picture, Vin, Mattie is going through a stage." She handed the photograph over. Lavinia arranged the spectacles laboriously over her ears and adjusted herself in the chair before picking up the photograph. A long silence followed as she peered at it, first squinting, then opening her eyes wide, then holding the picture out to nearly arms' length. Just as Maggie gave up waiting and turned back to the stove, Lavinia chortled boisterously. "She looks like she's just got the news she's going to bear the Lord Jesus in her womb!"

Maggie's hands came down hard on the stove plate. "Oh Miss Lavinia, you blaspheme our Lord, you ought to be ashamed of yourself! And don't you two snicker either," she said to Emily, whose shoulders shook, and to Ned, who held his hand over his mouth.

"Oh Maggie, I thought you were used to Lavinia's attempts to shock us," said Emily.

"I'm sorry, but people shouldn't say certain things. Mr. Austin would never say such a thing," continued Maggie, still outraged.

"Oh, wouldn't he though?" said Lavinia. "Remember, Emily, the things you and Austin used to say when we were young and 'the ancient people' were away? How you used to shock me then! I used to think the Lord would cut you down with his mighty sword."

"You see, Maggie, he never did cut us down now, did he," Emily reassured Maggie. "Oh, Ned, what a lively house it was then, with those pegs on the wall behind you just *filled* with hats and coats. And we'd get up the best maple sugaring parties you can imagine. That's when Aunt Lavinia did some of her courting, you know."

"Don't look so surprised, Ned, I had my beaux, handsome ones too," Lavinia assured him.

Ned tried to cover his incredulous expression, and looked carefully at Emily to read her face. She was nodding.

"You're thinking of Joseph Lyman, aren't you, Emily?" The sisters looked at each other with complete understanding.

"Joseph Lyman, yes. The one you used to read with in the big chair, with your hair let down."

Lavinia shrieked with laughter. "Oh go on, how do you know that anyway! Were you hiding in the fireplace, you nosey goose?"

"I won't tell Ned how I know such things. But I don't see you denying it, either."

More laughter from Lavinia, while it was Maggie's turn to be privately incredulous. "Does he live near Amherst, this Joseph Lyman, I've never heard of any Lymans."

"No, Maggie," said Lavinia.

"He died a long time ago," said Emily. "In '72 I think it was. He went South for a while and then met his wife. He left her with six children."

"You liked him, didn't you, Em?" said Lavinia.

"Yes, I did, because I could talk to him better than I could to most of the other young men who came in and out of this house back then. He understood me. He didn't say 'What, what did ye say?' like half the others."

Lavinia began to imitate their voices. "What, what, what did ye say?"

The two laughed together.

"Besides, he was a good writer, wasn't he Vin?"

"Yes, he was. But on the stuck up side, you must admit. A little like our beloved but ethereal Mattie?"

"Well," said Emily, "you must admit your contacts with him were different from mine; we talked about books and..."

"And THOUGHT," said Lavinia, "that's what you always end up talking about. Honestly, Emily, be glad Maggie and I are here to give THOUGHT a holiday."

"I must go to that lecture," said Ned. "Do you want to keep the photograph a while?"

"Yes, may I, Neddie?" asked Emily. "Your father can return it after I've written a note to Sue and Mattie. I'd like to look at it some more from my writing desk upstairs."

"That's fine. I'll let Mother know. See you in church, Aunt Lavinia, if I don't see you before then. Goodbye Maggie, Aunt Emily."

"Goodbye, Neddie, thanks for coming over."

He retrieved his coat and let himself out, jostling a cat or two as he went. Maggie threw on a shawl and followed him out to discard the ashes.

"Well, Emily, what are your plans for today?" asked Lavinia.

"I'm going to make you chicken and dumplings tonight. And Maggie and I will do the lamp filling today since it's your birthday. You can catch up on the newspapers before Mabel comes."

"I know it's not worth saying, but I wish you'd meet her..." began Lavinia.

"Did you finish with yesterday's *Springfield Republican*?"

"All right, just ignore me. I knew I was wasting my breath. But Emily, she asks about you all the time. I think you should meet her not just because *she* is fascinated with *you*—it's that you'd enjoy talking with her about writing and books. She's so different from everybody else in Amherst— so independent and lively. She's traveled more than anyone I can think of around here, except David Todd, of course, or Helen Jackson. And did you know she even has her card filled up at the college dances? The students love her. Oh, I can imagine what Mother and Father would have thought of her, but even they would have admired her spirit, don't you think?"

"I doubt they would have, Vinnie. But I have no intention of talking about books with her. I like her mostly because of Austin, if you want to know the truth. Of course it pains me to face up to the fact that Austin has had to turn to her in the first place. But if she has saved him, I must be glad. And if she cares for his welfare, then I must care for hers, just as you do. That's why we agreed to open our doors to their meetings here, isn't it? And now, did you finish yesterday's *Republican* or not?"

At 3:30 that afternoon, Mabel Todd climbed briskly up the Homestead steps despite the remnants of snow, and raised the heavy door knocker. She wore a smart feathered dark blue hat which matched her coat, and a muff, while a quilted drawstring bag containing a jar of spiced apples from last summer hung heavily from one wrist. Her nose was red from the cold and her eyes seemed ever more prominent and luminous in the February New England air.

Maggie answered the door but Lavinia was close behind. "Come in, Mrs. Todd, may I take your coat?" Maggie began, while Mabel finished wiping her feet on the outside shoe cleaner.

"Yes, thank you, Maggie, how's your back?"

"Ever so much better, my sister-in-law gave me a good massage and set me up fine, almost like new."

"Mr. Todd had to do the same for me right after we moved to town and I made the mistake of carrying boxes one afternoon. Lavinia! So good to see you. These spiced apples are for you and Emily. And one other thing since it's your birthday." She drew out a small piece of wrapped paper from her muff and extended it to Lavinia.

"Come into the parlor and I'll unwrap it. There now, hand your things to Maggie."

Inside the dim front parlor, both of them seated, Lavinia unwrapped a bookmark painted with wildflowers and four-leaf clovers. "Oh, Mabel, you painted this, didn't you? Just for me? How beautiful! Emily will enjoy it, too."

"How is she today? Austin said she had seemed so tired all last week."

"She seems more lively now. She baked a lot yesterday, almost like old times. In fact, you are going to eat some of her cake today."

"Oh good! David thinks she bakes the best cake in town."

"And how is your dear David? Did you tell him the dining room clock is broken?"

"I certainly did. He'll try to stop over in a few days to take a look at it."

"Oh, I had hoped he could come sooner. So many things break down around here. Maybe I should drop by late tonight and remind him."

"No, don't do that, Lavinia. He'll probably go to sleep very early tonight. He's been working especially hard this week to replace some of the drawings he lost in the Walker Hall fire, and he's a bit discouraged. So much has turned out to be irreplaceable after all."

"Well, how important could those drawings be?"

"Very important, trust me. But he's more discouraged that President Seelye is dragging his feet on financial planning for a new observatory."

"But what's wrong with the Octagon? I like that old place. It's a campus landmark, and it looks all right to me."

"Its telescope isn't big enough, that's what's wrong," said Mabel firmly. "Its equipment is outdated. Look, Lavinia, let's talk about something else. I hear David talk about observatories and telescopes every day."

"You ought to have Austin look into this matter of a new observatory. He could take care of it. Ask him, he'll see that it's done right."

"As a matter of fact, I already have. But it's a more complicated issue than you think, I'm sorry to say."

"Well, let's find Maggie and have some tea and cake. My birthday cake."

"Perfect! And there's no hope of Emily joining us?"

Lavinia was already on her way out of the room. "No, no," she called over her shoulder as she disappeared into the hallway. "Maggie, oh Maggie, let's put the kettle on, Mrs. Todd will have some tea now." In a few minutes she returned with a newspaper under one arm and a cat under the other.

"A reader sent a poem to the letter section in last week's paper. Did you see this one, here?" and she tapped the relevant column. "It's called "Ode to Death."

"Yes, I read it last night. I don't like it. Do you?"

"Well, I wasn't sure. I thought maybe I did but I wanted to see what you thought. After all, they did print it. Emily could have something of hers printed if this woman could, don't you thnk? In fact, she *did* have some of her poems printed a long time ago."

"I imagine she could, too, but I've seen so few of her poems. Does she write many? A notebook full?"

"Oh goodness, I don't know. I never thought to count the ones she's showed me over the years. There must be a lot, probably enough to make up a book—not that she'd want to, mind. But sometimes I wish she would, because her poems would surely be better than some of these famous people's you hear about. Ralph Emerson is considered to be absolutely great, but I find his poems boring. Thoreau's too. Wait! I'll read you one of Emily's poems. I have it right here because I asked her to read out the lines for me the other day to send to our cousins. It's a good thing I copied it and not Emily—you'd never be able to read her handwriting—although Emily says mine is awful!"

Lavinia went into the library and returned with a piece of paper. "This is it, the one about the spider. Oh, I do so like this one. It almost makes me tolerate spiders. Emily won't destroy their webs or them, you know. We have to disagree about that. Here, you read it out for me, I like to hear your voice."

Mabel took the paper and read the poem in a strong clear voice:

> The Spider holds a Silver Ball
> In unperceived hands—
> And dancing softly to Himself
> His Yarn of Pearl—unwinds—
>
> He plies from Nought to Nought—
> In unsubstantial Trade—
> Supplants our Tapestries with His—
> In half the period—
>
> An Hour to rear supreme
> His Continents of Light—
> Then dangle from the Housewife's Broom—
> His Boundaries—forgot—

"How wonderful and different," said Mabel, smiling.

"Didn't I say?" Lavinia answered. "Fannie and Loo will like it too. They don't like poems that are too serious. But Emily writes so many serious poems. Especially ones about religious doubt. I tease her about that. I think the only reason she ever used to go to church was to find loopholes in the sermons. There's that poem about gestures from the pulpit—how was it..." She stood up, bent over in thought. "No, I can't recall anything but a few lines, but you must hear it. Wait, I'm going upstairs to ask Emily unless she's napping."

When she left the room, Mabel read the poem about the spider again, and then tiptoed into the hallway, listening to the murmured voices upstairs. She strained to distinguish Emily's voice, but couldn't. When Lavinia still had not returned, she tiptoed into the library and looked at the books until she heard a door open upstairs, and hurried back to her place in the parlor.

"Emily found me a copy I think you can make out," called Lavinia, still descending the stairs and waving a paper. Read it as nicely as you read the other one."

She handed Mabel a sheet of paper covered with pencilled lines. Again, Mabel read aloud:

> This World is not Conclusion.
> A Species stands beyond—
> Invisible, as Music—
> But positive, as Sound—
> It beckons and it baffles—
> Philosophy—don't know—
> And through a Riddle, at the last—
> Sagacity, must go—
> To guess it, puzzles scholars—
> To gain it, Men have borne
> Contempt of Generations
> And Crucifixion, shown—
> Faith slips—and laughs, and rallies—
> Blushes, if any see—
> Plucks at a twig of Evidence—
> And asks a Vane, the way—
> Much Gesture, from the Pulpit—
> Strong Hallelujahs roll—
> Narcotics cannot still the Tooth
> That nibbles at the soul—

"How I love this one, Lavinia. Will you tell her for me?"

"Of course. Do you see what I mean now, about these other poets? They aren't nearly as good! And then there's that awful man, William Whitman."

"His name is Walt Whitman. But he's not awful. Have you read his poems?"

"Of course not!" She lowered her voice. "They are indecent."

"Now there you are wrong. They are beautiful poems. I admit they are unconventional, but they celebrate—that's the word Whitman uses—they celebrate life and love and humanity. What could be wrong with that?"

"But Reverend Jenkins used to say those poems were indecent. Are you sure we are talking about the same person? Maybe there is a different Whitman—a William Whitman like I said."

"No, we're talking about the same person. People don't like him because he writes about the real human body. But I don't see anything wrong with that."

"Mabel!" Lavinia looked upset. "Have you told Austin what you think of this poet?"

"Well, I have. And he's promised to read some of Whitman's poems, especially the most controversial ones, but he's always too busy. How I wish that man would slow down! Everybody in this town expects him to do something for them. It's like he's being picked apart!"

"That's why he needs you, Mabel," said Lavinia, lowering her voice. "You are the only one who doesn't pick him apart. And Sue is ..." She stood up and approached Mabel, who also leaned forward to hear. "Sue is crazy. Well, so unpredictable, I mean." She stood back to see the effect of her words.

"What has she done now?" Mabel had also lowered her voice.

"She threw some of his clothes out the window last evening. Mary Moynihan told Maggie this morning and Maggie told me. But that's nothing. Maggie claims she waved the butcher knife at Austin not so very long ago..."

"Was that because of me?"

Lavinia did not answer, but continued, "And she can be so cool to Emily at times. To me too, but I think I can take it better than Emily. No, with Sue you never know what to expect."

"But since Gilbert died, I hardly ever see her, though come to think of it, she did ride over to the College in the carriage a few days ago. I was at my studio painting and saw her from the window."

"How do you like your studio?"

"Oh it's wonderful!" Mabel raised her voice again. "I've had so much fun painting there. Imagine, a studio all for me! I can thank Austin for that, too. Who could imagine that Walker Hall was a pile of charred wood two years ago, when now it's all new and better than before."

A rattle of dishes in the hall and a heavy step announced Maggie bearing the tea tray, a dish towel slung over her shoulder.

"Put it on that table by Mrs. Todd, Maggie, she'll pour. I hate to pour."

"Gladly," said Mabel. "I love to serve tea." She busied herself with the plates and cups while Maggie poked the fire and then looked out the windows, her hands on her solid hips. Suddenly she peered intently down the street in the direction of the village. "Is that David Todd headed this way?" she asked.

"David? What would he be doing here now?" said Mabel, putting down the cake plates and standing to look out the window. "Where?"

"Coming by the church now."

David walked fast, slipping slightly on a patch of ice as he crossed the street at a broad angle between First Congregational Church and the Homestead. Once across the street, he headed straight for the Homestead.

"I'll let him in, Mrs. Todd," said Maggie, but Mabel followed her to the door. David Todd stood on the porch wiping his feet thoroughly, one after the other, before he bustled in and announced, without greeting anyone, "Mabel! Plans for the Smith College observatory are definite. I'll be in charge, isn't it wonderful? Come on, shall we drive to Northampton right now, just to take another look? Is Austin's carriage free?"

"Wait, slow down, David. It's wonderful, and I knew it would happen, but we don't have to rush over there right now. Come in and sit. You've had a long day, you can show me another time."

"Can you fix the dining room clock then?" called Lavinia from the front parlor. Mabel rolled her eyes. "Come on, David," she continued, "Lavinia and I were just about to have some tea. Sit with us now, and let Maggie close the front door. You're letting in all that cold air."

"Well, I wiped my feet, anyway. Is Austin coming?"

"No, I imagine he's at his office, unless you saw him at the college."

"Soon be our anniversary, you know." He entered the front parlor and went to Lavinia's chair. "Five years on March 5th. March 5th will be our fifth wedding anniversary."

"Congratulations Mr. David Todd, and would you please put another log on the fire?" said Lavinia.

"Yes I will, seeing as how Austin's not here. Please don't ever ask me to poke the fire or anything while Austin is here."

"Good Lord, said Lavinia. "Don't worry, I never will."

He piled another log on the fire and stood back to survey its effect. "I stopped by the post office on my way here and found a letter from your mother," he told Mabel. "She says Millicent is so excited about learning to read that she sleeps with her story books under the pillow. And her grandpa taught her to call herself 'a capital girl', since she lives in Washington so much."

Mabel, serving tea, chuckled along with Lavinia. "You see, David, she's doing just fine with Mother and Father and Grandma in Washington. It's good for her to be away like this."

"But don't you miss her terribly?" asked Lavinia, reaching for her tea cup. "Such an adorable little thing."

"Of course Mabel and I miss her," said David, "but her grandparents dote on her, and we both are so busy, that the arrangement works out perfectly."

"Yes, we both are so busy," echoed Mabel. "Did she receive her birthday parcel, David, do you know?"

"Your mother said the second one hadn't arrived yet, but the first came on February 5th."

"February is Millicent's birthday too? Bless her heart," said Lavinia, "you should have told me and I'd have sent her something."

"She doesn't need to be spoiled any more than she is," said Mabel. "Now David, are you going to run along and mend Mrs. Robison's window before it gets too dark? You promised you would..."

"I'll do it tomorrow. Can't I be near my little wife for a while? Where's the clock that needs attention, Lavinia?"

"In the dining room on some newspaper. Maggie took the back off already. Maggie!" Lavinia called out in a shrill voice, but David interrupted her.

"I'll go find it. I think I left a few of my tools in the dining room, too." He crossed the hallway to enter the dining room by way of the library, past the dark shelves of Edward Dickinson's leather-bound volumes. Then his footsteps could be heard in the distant dining room, where Maggie joined him.

"Will you play for Emily and me today, Mabel?" asked Lavinia.

Mabel glanced upward at the ceiling in the direction of what she knew to be Emily's room. "Certainly, it's always a pleasure to play. She's not napping?"

"I doubt it. Just a minute, let me see." Lavinia pulled the old shawl, covered with cat hair, closer around her as she heaved to her feet and started into the hallway and up the stairs. When she reached the upstairs hallway, Mabel tiptoed into the downstairs hallway and peered carefully upward. She could hear muffled voices and then a soft tread, followed by Lavinia's heavy steps returning to the hallway. Swiftly, Mabel ducked into the front parlor and walked straight through to the piano in the back parlor. When Lavinia returned, breathing rather heavily, Mabel was seated on the stool turning over some of the music books.

"She wasn't asleep and she would love to hear you play. She wonders if you liked her cake."

"Tell her yes, yes, for me. Almost as much as her poems."

"Well, you play now for us. I'll just sit over here, not *too* close, you know."

Mabel sat straight and raised her hands above the piano. "I think you'll like this Chopin Mazurka; I know it by heart now." After closing her eyes briefly, she began to play. The melody rang out soulfully, with effective rubato, but before the first repeat, David entered the parlor talking to Lavinia, as though she had been in the same room with him. "...and this is the mechanism on most striking clocks of the '20's, always gives a problem, but I can fix it."

"David! " said Mabel. "I'm trying to play. Can't you wait a minute to discuss clock mechanisms with Lavinia?"

Lavinia stood up and followed David out of the room. "You start again, Mabel," she called over her shoulder. "It was just lovely. Play it for Emily. I want to see what David has done with that damned old clock. Oh, I do apologize, Mabel, I shouldn't have said 'damned.'"

Mabel shook her head in frustration, fluffed her skirts, and began again. This time, she finished the mazurka without incident, and after leaning out to peer into the front parlor, half hoping that Emily would be listening there in rapt attention, she played a Clementi sonatina from a bound collection of sonatinas she found on the little music shelf. After that, while Lavinia swept into the room again, she returned to Chopin, playing his Valse Brillante in A minor, more attracted to somber and romantic moods. The fire hissed, the light drained faster from the sky, and even David left the disassembled clock to sit near his wife in the dusky room, watching her while she played. The last piece, Chopin's yearning, somber Prelude No. 4 in E minor, had drawn yet two more unseen contemplative listeners: Emily, her head bent in repose by the upstairs hallway railing, and Austin, his body reclined against the hall side of the kitchen door from which he had entered a few moments before.

When the prelude ended, its last note barely audible to those outside the room, Austin took a deep breath, and then exhaling, made his way toward the front of the house, his face aflush with the brisk outside air and with excitement, until he heard David's voice. He stopped, stood impassive a moment, then continued toward the voices. Entering the parlor, he found Mabel still at the piano while David and Lavinia sat quietly nearby. But his entrance galvinized the tableau. Mabel gave an involuntary gasp. David said "Austin?" and then stared at Mabel instead. And Lavinia looked at them all before standing up and saying, "Dear Austin, I hope you have come to eat supper with us."

"No, I only came by for a few minutes to see how you all were." As Mabel arose and came to meet him, he stepped heavily forward and stretched out both arms at the same time to grasp Mabel's hand, and on the other side, David's. Both of them quickened under his enveloping touch, looking even younger beside his fifty-four years.

"Well, I'm off to the kitchen," said Lavinia, "but you forgot something, Austin."

"Was I supposed to bring something?"

"Oh, Austin! Now look, I always remember your birthdays, I don't see why you can't remember mine. Sometimes this family of mine, I don't know..." She started for the kitchen.

Austin permitted himself a smile in Mabel's direction and a shrug, then dropping both her hands and David's, followed Lavinia for a moment. "I remembered. Only teasing, Vin, only teasing. Go look in the kitchen. You'll find something there."

"Oh, will I?" She was off, dropping her shawl as she went. Austin retrieved it, then rejoined Mabel and David for some quiet conversation until Mabel interrupted. "We must go, David, Mrs. Robison likes to have supper on time. Go tell Vinnie about the status of that sick clock, or she'll be after you later on, and then we must walk home."

David looked closely at both of them, close and long enough to let them be distinctly conscious of his look, but then did as Mabel told him and went to find Lavinia. The second he left the room, Mabel and Austin stood and clasped each other tight. After a quick glance around, he kissed her long and hard, then cradled one breast in his hand. "When, when will our next meeting be?" he whispered, "I must talk with you."

"My darling, I have a note all ready for you again," she said, unpinning a small, densely folded piece of paper from her bodice. "I love you, is everything all right? We can't talk now." And she breathed out "Ahh" as he again touched her breast.

"What about at the Walker Hall studio next week?" he asked. "Maybe after the town meeting. I could come to you in the afternoon there. Would that work?"

"Probably. Let's count on it unless you let me know differently. Meanwhile..."

They separated hastily as they both heard David and Lavinia approaching.

"Is Maggie coming with our coats, Lavinia?" said Mabel.

"Here I am, Mrs. Todd, you wrap up now. There's a snowstorm coming, I do believe. Can't you feel it in the air? It's so heavy-like."

A few minutes later, anyone passing by on foot or in a carriage would have seen two slender young people walking briskly along, swinging their arms and chatting busily, oblivious to the village's darkness and aware only of the invigorating air and the open twilight sky above them.

CHAPTER 31

March 1884

~

Snow sheathed the Connecticut Valley and its drowsing villages redolent of wood smoke. The country roads barely showed the black of wagon ruts, while the streets of Belchertown, Shutesbury, Sunderland, Amherst and their like, lay crisscrossed by black and white under a late night March sky. The cold damp air hung heavily over the cemetery, where Gilbert's gravestone spelled his name above the snow, and just as heavily at the high end of Main Street, where the railroad depot resembled a white gingerbread house and the railroad tracks ran hidden into the darkness.

Few lamps burned in Amherst at 11:30. Few lights showed anywhere, though along Railroad Street and Irish Hill, steamed windows revealed weary men and women still completing chores, and at the Montague's, George's cough forced him to light the way to the cabinet where he kept a mixture guaranteed to soothe the throat.

A dim light also showed from the Homestead's second story and spilled narrowly under Emily's bedroom door into the hallway. A letter lay on her writing table, the latest from Judge Otis Lord. Beloved Salem. What to write to him this week, this night? She picked up his letter, at the same time absent-mindedly fingering the latest scrap of paper in her nightgown pocket, like the pockets she herself sewed on nearly every gown or dress she wore. Glancing at the scrap of paper, she lowered the hand holding the judge's letter, while she studied the lines she had written in the kitchen that afternoon by the brassy reflections from the snow outside...

Back from the Cordial Grave I drag thee
He shall not take thy Hand
Nor....

She moved to her dark-wood sleigh bed to work on the lines, but in a moment, set them aside for the letter. Otis had seemed so frail ever since his stroke almost two years ago, that she sometimes felt as if she were holding her breath for him. Austin said she worried too much, since, he pointed out, Otis managed to visit them all from Salem, staying at the Amherst House a week at a time and inadvertently provoking Lavinia into outbursts of laughter and quips at the supper table after he had gone. She found his very appearance an incentive to comedy: the high stiff collar, the eyes so heavy-lidded that you could hardly see his eyelashes, the large nose, and his demeanor, ponderous and slow to those who didn't know him well.

> *My Lovely Salem:*
> *Second of March and the Crow, and Snow high as the Spire—*

Emily bent her head to the letter, hoping his niece would not read this one as she had the last when she cleaned her uncle's desk, despite his request that she leave that job to him. He had found his niece in the act of reading it, in fact, or he might never have known. How many others had she read, Miss Abbie Farley? A Dickinson would never read another Dickinson's mail—unless that Dickinson were a jealous Sue Dickinson, alert to the correspondence between Austin and Mabel. Emily hoped Austin destroyed the letters Mabel sent him in Vinnie's post box, for if he didn't, he was courting a violent outburst from Sue. But well Emily understood the delight in writing, getting, and saving letters. Sometimes she felt her letter writing scarcely left her enough time for her primary occupation, composing poetry. And yet how priceless those letters and the art of composing them were. Letters received, all sealed and sacred, were like treasure chests with no keys. Their delight shone forth when the recipient picked the lock behind closed doors.

She smiled to recall the lines of her poem about letters:

> *The Way I read a Letter's—this*
> *'Tis first—I lock the Door—*
> *And push it with my fingers—next—*
> *For Transport it be sure—*
>
> *And then I go the furthest off*
> *To counteract a knock—*

Then draw my little Letter forth
And slowly pick the lock—

She went to the window facing Austin's house, being careful not to let her gown come too close to the Franklin stove at her feet. No light showed next door, though it was hard to tell through the thick evergreen branches. Sometime soon she and Austin needed to have a long sit-down talk. The two of them might both leave many letters behind them one day. What would happen to those letters, left in some box, some pile somewhere, unlabeled, unexplained? When should one burn private letters? When one no longer had any use for them? But that time would be death's time, for the letters in her boxes and trunks were part of her, her workshop and personal showcase combined, along with the rough drafts and finished products she saved.

Certainly Austin had thought hard about whatever letters he kept. Had Mabel? She was an intriguing creature, this young, bright-eyed Mabel who had bounced into the Dickinsons' lives and so utterly changed them all. She spoke her opinion on nearly every issue and at nearly every opportunity, but in the end, Emily wasn't sure how to read her, with her air of self-importance and her enjoyment of risk. Reading her correctly was no trivial matter, for Austin's happiness was at stake. Of course, Lavinia was sold over, no question there. She talked about Mabel and her oddly bustling husband every day. "Emily, what do you think, Mabel's father knew Henry Thoreau! What a quality family the Loomises are. David's going to make a name for himself. Just give him some time."

And Austin? It was as though he had started his inner life all over again. He let Emily know of this rebirth in ways Lavinia never saw: by his low, almost worshipping tone of voice when he took Emily aside to tell her that Mabel would be visiting the Homestead, or by the soft look in his eyes when he had just left Mabel from a carriage ride and returned far past supper time, having come to the Homestead first to compose himself before he went home to Sue. He often paced around the kitchen a bit, or sought out Emily in the conservatory and paced a little there, talking mostly about trivia but looking as if he wanted to talk about far more. Once, he made an awkward little speech, thanking her for letting him and Mabel meet, undisturbed, in the Homestead.

There had been a time years ago when Emily would have sharply, achingly understood what Austin must now feel for Mabel. That incandescence would never return. But loving her Salem quietly as she did, and being cared for in return, she found herself sympathetic to Austin—and loved him all the more for his confusion, his fallibility, the sad wreckage of his marriage. What kind of happy ending could he and Mabel find? They whirled about, a cursed duo, in her thoughts. No, Mabel had churned up more than she bargained for when she decided to love Austin, and Emily would reserve total commitment to her as long as Sue struggled in her dark and lonely dilemma. Whatever pain Sue had caused any of them, whatever darkness lay in hers and Austin's marriage, she remained a beloved sister-in-law and literary advisor, mother to a much-loved niece and nephew (she ground her fingers in her palm at the very thought of blonde Gilbert lying in the cemetery), and a wife to Austin. Presider of the Evergreens along with Austin.

Mattie and Ned had been hurt beyond repair, Emily feared, by the wrecked marriage. For that reason, they deserved her undivided and steadfast love, even though at times, both of their behaviors proved unattractive. The picture of plain shy Ned trying to keep pace with his mother's pretensions and strutting to church with cane and beaver hat, holding his head high like his pompous sister, pained her. What, in heaven's name, must be going on in their young heads as they struggled to deal with the dark and ugly corners at home? She would be there for them though, with all her heart.

"My lovely Salem..." What to tell him this March night, his health failing at the opening of his eighth decade, hers precarious as well. She felt slow, sick, more often than she cared Vinnie and Austin to know. What if...? But there was much to be done, much to write and much to love. If her Otis had really wished her to come to Salem—to marry him, it must be said—his thinking had been no more mistaken than hers that curveting spring before. They would not talk of marriage again. Meanwhile, he must stay healthy. The strained look she sometimes saw in both his and Austin's eyes frightened her, for it resembled that look of her father's in the weeks before he died. "Back from the Cordial Grave I drag thee..."

A tree outside her window dumped snow on the ground with a satisfying thud. Emily's eyes crinkled in a smile as she remembered the latest cat episode to tell Otis. Yesterday, she had emptied a dustpan full of bread crumbs and suet out the kitchen door, not noticing the tabby cat standing there, until he meowed angrily and stalked away with crumbs clinging to his tail and back. She would enclose another comical newspaper clipping to make him laugh. Poor Sue had little sympathy with laughter these days, unlike earlier times when her house was full of lively guests, including Samuel Bowles, with whom she enjoyed much banter. Despite the misunderstanding, Emily and Otis still smiled guiltily over the day Sue had marched into the Homestead parlor unannounced and found the two of them holding on to each other with laughter over something Vinnie, who stood by smirking, had just done. "Really, Emily!" Sue had said after a horrified glance at them, and had sailed out the front door without looking back. Later, Austin told them Sue lectured him about the need for Dickinson decorum. If only they could all have more carefree moments these days.

Drawing her shawl around her and returning to cover herself in the bed now, Emily settled back in earnest to finish her letter and prepare for sleep. She was tired after all. But when Amherst wrote to Salem, the night passed more smoothly than other nights.

Most of the little houses on Irish Hill were dark now, and icicles hanging from their roofs would not drip for a long time. On the corner of Main and Dickinson Streets, retired railroad conductor, William Hastings, nestled his cheek, scarred from the Palmer train accident, deep into the pillow and breathed heavily, dreaming of missed connections and lost tickets. In the darkness of John Musante's nut, fruit, and candy shop on South Pleasant Street, resident mice crept out to devour stray peanuts, scampering over the tightly closed peanut roaster Candida Musante would fill for her husband early tomorrow morning.

And under the snow protecting the Dickinson meadow, safe in the soil, lay the thousands of field cricket eggs which would hatch in the spring and emerge to fill yet another season with their spectral song.

CHAPTER 32

March 1884

HOW CAN YOU SAY SUCH A CRUEL THING?
How? You astound me," said Austin Dickinson rising wearily to his feet, even
though he had just sat down.

Sue testily shook the *Springfield Republican* with its obituary of Judge Lord.
"Well for heavens' sake, of course I didn't mean I was *glad*. But it was bound to
happen, and now she can stop dwelling on him as she was. What a mismatch
they were, admit it."

"I don't admit it, they made each other happy. Why have you always made
such a fuss and bother about it?"

"Oh, it's too ridiculous to discuss, just forget it. Let me finish the paper."

She snapped it free of wrinkles and began to read again. Austin sat down
and looked at the fire. There was quiet for a few minutes, while from outside,
the sounds of harness bells and horses' hooves broke the evening silence on
Main Street.

But Austin passed his hand over his aching forehead and stood again, as
though the conversation had not been interrupted. "I left her in tears, do you
realize that?"

"Oh, Austin, enough!"

"No, how often have you seen her cry, tell me that?" His face contorted. "Go
on, you know when the last time was as well as I do."

Sue slammed the newspaper down on her lap and inclined her head.

"For Gilbert," he said, the last syllable caught up by a kind of swallow. "And
yet you can sit there so callously and make light of her pain." His voice rose in
tone and volume. "How can you do that?" He paced away from the fire and
into the shadows of the room.

Sue sat slumped in her chair. The newspaper fell to the floor as she moved
to rummage for a handkerchief, crying out, "You are hurting me! You love to

hurt me, don't you? You drive in every nail you can so that I'm a laughing stock not only in my town but my own house. I can't say anything anymore, can I? Nothing about Emily or Vinnie or your parents, or even my darling boy," and with that, the tears burst through. "*She* ruined it all, she ruined all our lives."

Austin held his hands over his eyes. "*She* is not what this quarrel is about. This is about Emily and the way you belittled her. I can't bear it anymore, that's all, I can't sit there and see her pain and then come home to hear you make light of her life while you casually read that obituary. I'm going out for a while. I'm sorry, I need to cool down."

"All right, go out! Run away! But don't you dare go to the Todds' rooms, oh don't you dare!" she shouted after him as he went to retrieve his coat from the back of the house. In a moment, the impact of the door closing confirmed that he was gone. She would not see him until morning, for he slept now in the little room downstairs. Bending down for the newspaper, she began to smooth it out, then with a sudden cry, crumpled it and tore bits from the wrinkled ball she had made of it.

Austin walked around the back of the house past the old well and onto Main Street, still wrapping his scarf around his neck and pulling on his gloves. He wasn't sure where he was going at this hour of the evening, 7:30. Past Mrs. Robison's just for a glimpse of Mabel's windows? Or maybe the observatory? It looked like it would be a fairly clear night; maybe he could stop to see if David was there. Austin passed John Lovell's photography studio, and having passed his own offices, turned left toward the Common and across to the college campus where he strode even more rapidly, a somber figure in the night. The observatory, or the Octagon, as the older residents called it, looked dark, but he approached it anyway and tried the door. Locked. Probably just as well, he was in no state to talk to David anyway. On to Mrs. Robison's then? No, not a good idea. He would have to walk out Pleasant Street to calm his mind and then return home, hoping Sue would have gone to bed. But the lights at The Convent, Mrs. Stearns's school for girls, attracted him. If the girls were finished with study and reading hour, maybe Mary Stearns would enjoy his company for a short time. He enjoyed talking to her, always had, and now, Mabel saw Mary more frequently than he, since she had begun giving art lessons to the girls.

He stepped onto the porch of what had been the President's house for years until Dr. Stearns's death in 1876. Since Julius Seelye had no interest in living in the house, Mrs. Stearns, widow of Dr. Stearns's son William, had moved in to start her girls' school, The Convent, making a tremendous success of her endeavor.

He knocked. When no one came, he rang the bell, for he heard voices within. In a minute, two girls answered the door politely. "Come in, Mr. Dickinson, would you like to see Madame Stearns?"

"If I may...Is she about?"

"Austin, do come in," called Mary Stearns from the parlor where she stood with an opened book in her hand. "Is everything all right?"

"Yes, I apologize for barging in without warning. I was at the College and just thought I'd drop in before I went home. Should I come another time?"

"Oh no, you came just in time for some hot chocolate. We have finished our sewing and reading hour. Do sit down. Girls, won't you take Mr. Dickinson's coat?"

He sat near the fire, distracted for a moment by the way it was built; the logs could do with some shifting, but he would let that pass. "What do you hear from Annie," he asked. "Is her health improving in Florida?"

"I hope she's a little better. Alfred said in his last letter that the weather in Florida couldn't help but improve her lungs, and as cold and damp as it's been here this winter, I'm relieved they are both there. Of course I miss them terribly. No matter how many children I had, I would still miss each one for their special qualities. But at least the two of them are together."

"I know you do miss them. Vinnie tries to keep up with your news, and both she and Emily talk about you often."

"And how is Emily?"

"Not very well, she's prone to weak spells more often these days. Losing so many friends lately hasn't helped her. You heard about Judge Lord?"

She indicated the paper by her side. "Yes indeed, a sad thing. I know you all saw him frequently. I saw him briefly the last time he came to Amherst. He looked rather well, I thought. I will be writing to Emily tomorrow. Did you know I've saved the letters she sent me? The one she wrote after my Ethel died was the shortest I received but the best. I've never forgotten it: 'Affection wants you to know it is here. Demand it to the utmost.'" She smiled "And how is Susan?"

"She is well, thank you."

"Ah, here comes Sarah with our chocolate. Sarah, did you heat the chocolate pot thoroughly first with hot water?"

"Yes, M'am. And the cups, too."

"Good girl. I'll pour for my guest. You can pour for the others in the second parlor."

Austin had begun to relax. The tension slowly left his head as he leaned back, a cup warming his hands, listening to the pop of the fire, the soft talk of gentle girls' voices, and the clinking of delicate china. At Mrs. Stearns', he forgot about the constant call of duty—the board meetings, the trustees meetings, town meetings, financial reports, and most of all, domestic unrest. There was always something new and interesting to discuss with her: yet another story from her days in India, an anecdote about her girls, or even a brief piano recital by one of her promising students. And now that Mabel gave art lessons there twice a week, they had Mabel to talk about as well. Mrs. Stearns asked no questions, made no judgments, but Austin thought she sensed something of the truth about his and Mabel's relationship. Why she accepted it better than many in the village, despite her conventional religious and moral views, Austin had no idea, but being in a warm and lovely room with a woman whose conversation and placid temperament engaged him when he visited unannounced gave him more pleasure than he could say these days. The tensions in his life had accelerated at a frightening pace. He noticed with some alarm that his heart often seemed to skip a beat, just when he least expected it—during a budget meeting, in church, or on the train to Boston. He might wake at 4 o'clock one morning paralyzed with fear about his life, brimming with radiant gratitude the next. But he felt calm now. He would visit The Convent more often. Besides, it was one more place where Mabel had spent some happy hours.

"And Mrs. Todd's lessons, are they going well?" he asked.

"Beautifully. Come tomorrow and the girls will show you their work. They've been painting still life compositions in watercolor this week. She brought them a nice array of dried gourd, pumpkin, and various grasses."

"She does beautiful flowers too, and butterflies. Have you seen those?"

"Yes, she has showed me much of her work. You look tired, Austin. Mabel says you've been working too hard."

"She said that?"

"Yes, indeed she did."

He finished off his hot chocolate and looked into the cup, unseeing, for an instant. "Well, between the law office and the college and the church, I suppose I have been over busy. So much to do..."

"Can't you take a day off once in a while? Then Susan could see more of you too." She looked pointedly away from his face and into the fire as she said this.

"She doesn't...I'm not sure that..." He cut himself off and glanced quickly at her and then away. "I'm not very good company these days since Gilbert died."

There was a pause. She poured him the remains of the chocolate pot, settled back in her chair, and said, "It will get better I think. Try to believe that."

"Please forgive me, I never should have said that. After what you've been through...your Ethel..."

"No, no, it's all right."

He continued, "...but I guess I knew you would at least understand. When you lost your young Willie and then Ethel, I didn't really grasp your suffering. I do now. But the terrible thing is, I can't talk about it with Sue. We hardly even mention it, yet we are both equally—what's the right word—injured. And it doesn't get any better either. Often, I think it gets worse. Is that usual?" He managed a direct look into her face.

Her expression of concern turned quickly into a beautiful smile. "You will feel better, I trust you will. These loved ones of ours are gone from this world and we will always miss them, but I firmly believe they are happy with God now. In fact, I rejoice that they are." She smiled again, so directly into his eyes that he almost looked away, embarrassed, even though he felt her pure concern console him.

"And Sue?"

"You will both have to try patience, I think, and remember Job's story."

He could not imagine his Gilbert with God, much as he wished to, nor would he ever offer that picture to Sue, even if he thought it would help her. The idea that any god could have deliberately taken Gilbert from him was too alien and too much of an affront for him to entertain for anyone's sake, not Sue's, not Mary Stearns'. And Mabel would never expect him to accept such an idea.

Still, Mary's warmth and good faith had consoled him tonight, and he felt calmer, ready to return to the Evergreens.

"I must leave, Mary. You have comforted me. I hope I didn't upset your evening."

"Oh, Austin, how could you ever do that? Come as often as you like."

They both rose as she called one of the girls to bring his coat. At the door she pressed him arm, and he stepped out into the night, glad David Todd hadn't been at the observatory after all. He thought he could sleep now, but he hoped Sue was upstairs so he could go silently to bed.

CHAPTER 33

March 1884

M AY I COME IN?" AUSTIN KNOCKED gently on Emily's door upstairs one early evening in March a week after Judge Lord's death.

She let him in immediately with a smile, although her watery eyes convinced him she had been crying earlier.

"Mabel sends you this note," he said, handing her an envelope which she tucked into her pocket without reading.

"Thank her for me. I'm going to enjoy it later." She sat down by her table near the Franklin stove while Austin pulled out the other chair.

"Are you all right?" he asked.

"I hope not," she answered with a faint smile. "If I went through all this pain and still said I was all right, then I wouldn't be all right at all."

He smiled back, and they both looked at the fire.

"When had you last written to him?" he asked after a few moments.

"Sunday, a little over a week before he died. He managed to reply. It was strange, the way he ended that last note. 'A caller comes,' he said."

"You think he knew...?"

"Maybe."

"Do you realize," Austin said, "that for the past two years, when his health was so poor, the only place he traveled to was Amherst?"

"Yes." She inclined her head.

"It was because of you. Am I right?"

"I think so."

"I have been happy for you in your friendship with him. I never told him so, but I can tell you. You have it to remember now. With pride."

Emily nodded, but said nothing. A single tear escaped her eye, and Austin looked away, embarrassed, unable to say more. He changed the subject. "Do you need anything from the shops? The apothecary?"

"No, I still have more of the medicine Dr. Cooper prescribed, and Vin can always send Maggie, anyway. You have enough to do, Austin. How are Sue and the children?"

"Mattie still writes from Miss Porter's regularly. In fact, Sue told me to bring her latest letter to show you, but I forgot it. I'll bring it next time. Sue still hardly goes anywhere, you know. She prefers to stay inside. I'm the opposite. I can hardly bear to be in my own house."

"Oh, Austin," Emily said quietly. "Is there no hope of change?"

"None!" There was no doubt in his tone. "None. Especially not now. If I felt like living at all after we lost Gib, it was only because of Mabel. She has pulled me back from death and handed me over to life. I'm not exaggerating. And I can't return to what I was before. I am willing to tolerate the gossip that has already begun and to make the necessary sacrifices. Knowing her is that important. That...overwhelming."

"Necessary sacrifices?"

"Oh, I can't tell you what I mean by that because I don't know myself. And I don't know how all this will end. But I have to go on with it. I could never give her up unless she asked me to. And she won't."

Emily flexed her feet toward the fire a moment, but said nothing.

Austin went on. "I know all this must be disturbing you and Vinnie, and I don't blame you if you feel upset. There's so much I find hard to talk about..."

"That's all right, you don't have to talk about anything."

"But you must wonder about things. About how I feel, about David and what he thinks..."

"Vinnie and I stand behind you," interrupted Emily. "We feel much pain about you and Sue—but we felt that before you met Mabel. You let us know in many ways that you and Sue weren't getting along. But about the children—do they have any idea...?"

"Yes, they have. But what can I do about it? Maybe they are the sacrifices I mentioned before..."

"I hope not," she said. "Oh, I hope not. Not your children, Austin."

"Mattie and I have never been close though. She's always given herself over to Sue—directed all her stories and concerns to Sue. Now, she looks away when I enter a room. And as for Ned, he's jealous, on top of everything else. He thought he was in love with Mabel and here I am. His own father."

"But you don't think you can really be with her, do you? Give up Sue and your home for her? You don't think that?" she asked in a soft voice.

For answer, he sighed a long sigh and bent his head, closing his eyes. Then, rubbing his forehead, he said in a barely audible voice, "I don't know, I don't know." Abruptly, he stood up.

Emily looked at him in alarm. "I've scared you off! I was too blunt! Don't go."

"It's all right," he said, "but you did hit on the truth that drives me wild. There's no solution to anything, none at all." He paced in the small space by her bed.

"Does there have to be a solution?" Emily asked. "Could it be that knowing she is your friend in the world might bring you joy in itself? There are joys and truths in my mind that have kept me singing for years. There are people I have loved with my mind who never failed to sustain me. Knowing they were in this breathing world with me, their thoughts on me, was enough."

"No, that is not enough for me," he said, still pacing. "That is not enough. So there may be no solution for me. For us. I can't talk about it anymore. I wish you could understand how she makes me feel. It's inexpressible, Em."

"I believe you, then."

"One of these days, I want to share some of her letters with you. I've had some special ones—some so beautiful I could never destroy them."

"You *have* kept them. Be careful."

"I've kept copies of them in my own hand and burned the originals."

Emily shook her head sadly. A horse trotted by in the street and some tree branches rattled in the wind. "Be careful," she repeated.

"If Father were alive... Oh, I am glad he didn't have to see this," said Austin. "He would never understand, of course. That goes without saying. And yet, I have never once felt I was behaving immorally. In my heart, I have felt the utter rightness of this. The only wrong I have felt is the wrong of our not having found each other before, so we wouldn't have to hurt anyone. We are meant for each other. I believe that, and so does she." He stood by the door. "And you and Vinnie stand behind me? You don't think I am an immoral person?"

"We stand behind you and understand you. We grieve for you though, and Sue too."

"That's all I need to hear. That you understand me." He looked at his watch. "I came here to comfort you, and ended up asking you to comfort me."

"It's all right. We both have comforted each other."

"I'll drop by again tomorrow. Anything you need from downstairs?"

"No, nothing."

"Don't forget to read Mabel's note. I think she's still half convinced that you'll say you want to meet her, even though I've tried to explain…" He paused. "You wouldn't change your mind, would you?"

"No," Emily said simply.

"Good night then. Mind your shawl doesn't drag too close to the coals now."

"All right. Goodnight. And try not to think too hard right now."

He let himself out while she listened to his footsteps on the stairs, and later, heard the back door latch click and knew he was crossing the path to the Evergreens. Laying Mabel's note on her table for later, she retrieved some lines she had been working on during the past few weeks:

> Which question shall I clutch—
> What answer wrest from thee
> Before thou dost exude away
> In the recallless sea?

She read the lines several times and then gazed quietly at the fire.

Summer to Fall 1884

By MAY OF 1884, DAVID AND MABEL FELT sure they would soon be able to leave Mrs. Robison's rooms and take possession of the Lessey house. Old Mrs. Lessey lay unconscious much of the time now, and her children had promised to let the Todds rent the house, Oaklawn, after their mother died. It stood, white-columned and stately, only two properties away from the Homestead and the Evergreens.

"Furniture!" said Mabel to David. "How will we ever fill the house? I'll have to fetch our things from Mother in Washington. Oh, David, I'll have the piano shipped up! Imagine, being able to play whenever I want!"

"Well, you'd better go soon," said David, looking up from his eclipse figures, pencil in hand. "Who knows how long it will take all that stuff to arrive here?"

"I'll go this week then, why not? And bring Millicent and Grandma back here with me. But first, I should check with Austin."

"I'll tell him where you went, if you don't see him."

"David, don't be silly. Of course I have to tell him myself."

"But you won't be in Washington for long. Can't you go away for a short time without a fuss?"

"No." She arose to find her purse and cloak. "I'll send a telegram to my parents. Right now."

When she met Austin's carriage later that day near Hutchinson's Hedge on North Street by prearrangement, she had been thinking about their letters. "They are safe, my beloved," Austin said, kissing her ears and neck as soon as they were far enough down the road. "No one would ever think to look in Vinnie's post box but Vinnie. Anything addressed to her is safe."

"But afterwards? Eventually, you'll misplace one. Someone will find them before you burn them. You are burning them, aren't you?"

"Yes, most of them."

"All of them, you must burn all of them. Immediately. You musn't relax your guard at home, at the office, at the college. Nowhere. With me, it's different. David isn't inquisitive, and besides, he doesn't mind the way Sue does."

Austin couldn't help but groan in agreement.

"In fact, while I am away this time, I don't think I should write to you at all. You can write to me, but I'll have to restrain myself, hard as it is." She lay against his chest. "Let's try it, at least. It won't be for long."

But after Mabel left, the plan seemed intolerable to Austin, whose love for Mabel astounded him more every day, and when one noon he watched David reading a letter he had fetched from the post office, undoubtedly one from Mabel, he was overcome with jealousy, loneliness and frustration.

"Never again," he told her when they held each other at last at the Homestead, after weeks of abstinence. "We will risk earthquakes and volcanoes for our letters." They whispered, taking more care than usual not to be heard, in deference to Emily's mourning for Judge Lord. Emily had suffered some physical collapses as well, and more than once, Lavinia had summoned Austin urgently when her sister had a "bad turn."

The move to the Lessey House came in June. With more furniture acquired on indefinite loan and a new servant as well, Mabel found herself in full social swing at last. Parties, dinners—these she could give when she chose now. And upstairs, a spare room was set aside to be hers and Austin's, their retreat whenever it was safe. Meanwhile, Sue and Mabel rarely met in the streets or at social events, and when they did, each wore a thin veil of chilly politeness at best, barely disguised dislike at worst.

"I have it all," Mabel wrote in her journal. "Everything I want." She told David the same thing. "My loving husband," she said to him one evening. "You please me so. Aren't I lucky? I have you to love in our special wonderful ways, and I have Austin's friendship too, which you allow me because we both admire him so. And I am becoming a leading lady in Amherst. Have you noticed how Mrs. Cutler has imitated the new curtains I put up in the spring? And so many people ask me for advice about music and art. I think I've quite brought the cosmopolitan world to this village."

"Well, I am lucky too," David said, putting down the newspaper. "I have made one heart beat a little faster in Northampton."

"In Northampton? What do you mean?" Mabel asked, suddenly alert.

"Never you mind all the details. There is just someone in Professor Laity's boarding house who finds me interesting. Someone who is brave enough to let me know."

"David, I'm surprised at you! She sounds like a common sort of person. Did she make the first move?"

"It's hard to say," said David cagily.

"Then she must be inexpressibly common, that's all I can say. I don't think you should pursue this any further."

He leaned over to touch her arm. "That's not fair, Mabel. Don't act silly. I don't stop you from seeing Austin. I probably should have long ago, but I didn't only because I knew you loved me. And because he's so much older than you. He can't keep your interest long, can he? Who has the real manhood around here, eh?"

She ignored most of his comment except the part about age. "How old is this person, anyway? Some child? Barely old enough to know what it's all about?"

He smiled. "I'm not talking about her anymore. But it's about time you knew how it felt, having you talk about Austin all the time."

"If you want to find someone, consider Caro Andrews."

"Caro? Your worldly cousin?" said David, laughing.

"Better than some common creature. Caro likes you, David."

"She'd like anyone better than her drunken husband."

"She is on the chubby side, of course..." said Mabel.

"I think a chubby woman might be a nice change for me," David teased. "Too bad Boston is so far away."

Mabel stood up and walked to the window, tapping her foot and looking out with unseeing eyes into the darkness. "If I see Austin less, will you drop this woman in Northampton? If there is such a woman."

"Why should I?"

"I told you, I think she sounds common. Beneath us."

"You have no idea what she is like. You're unreasonably jealous. But I'm glad you are. Does this mean we can consider stopping our games? Stopping before it's too late?"

She didn't answer.

"Mabel?" he said softly. "Maybe we should."

Her eyes were distant.

"It's not too late, we still have control," he went on, still softly.

She went to him then, and they held each other quietly, listening to the clock ticking and the night sounds of their new house. David's shoulders began to relax as he imagined having Mabel all to himself again. So he was surprised when at last, she pulled away from him, and straightening up, said, "I love you. But it's too late to stop now. Let's not talk about it anymore tonight." Turning down the last gas lamps and lighting a candle, she began to ascend the polished stairs to bed ahead of him.

Looking back years later, those Edenic, ecstatic summer months of 1884 stood inviolate in Mabel's memory. Never was her lovemaking with Austin more fulfilling, never was the Amherst summer more sweet and aromatic so as to make her throw back her head and cry out. Never did she feel so inexpressibly and alertly alive. When she and Austin met on formal social occasions, each was hard put to control the pure joy that burst between them, and just the sight of Austin's figure in a distance was enough to transform Mabel's vision of the day. Sitting across from each other at faculty tea parties, they struggled to maintain neutral faces, while picturing privately this expanse of shoulder, that flutter of the eyelids, and that husky cry, "You bring me God!"

David continued to spend time nearly each week in Northampton working on Smith College's observatory, and sometimes visited Washington's Naval Observatory, while Sue languished, defeated by the death of Gilbert and the widening gap between her and Austin. So there was only Grandma Wilder, who spent long periods of time with them, to deceive at close range. But Mabel, at twenty-eight, was too young and reckless to cover all her tracks. Still, she regretted nothing, and her life with David remained sexually fulfilling as well.

In the fall, Mabel persuaded her mother to visit their fine new house in time for a lavish party. "Seventy-five guests?" gasped Molly Loomis, "How can you possibly manage so many?"

"Phebe is marvelous, Mother, you can't imagine. And Maggie and Mary from the Dickinson houses will help out that evening. You'll see."

Mabel decorated the house with orange leaves, bright yellow daisies, partridge vines, and pumpkins. Two loads of extra ice arrived to cool the dishes of chicken salad garnished with parsley, pitchers of sparkling punch lined the cellar cooler, and pans of chocolate cake stood moist and ready for dessert. The supper party was such a success, one to outshine any party that Susan Dickinson could ever give, that Mabel thought nothing could spoil her pleasure afterward as she basked in its glow. But her mother sent up the first alarm.

"There's something I simply must discuss with you, Mabel, must warn you about, much as I hate to," said Molly Loomis as she and her daughter sat peeling apples on the back porch one early afternoon. Millicent played at their feet with a doll buggy and her favorite doll.

"What is it, Mother?"

"Your grandmother feels you may be causing unnecessary gossip in your dealings with Mr. Dickinson. She thinks you see too much of him, just the two of you alone together. And before you protest, let me say that I know it's innocent, but people will misinterpret, given half a chance."

"Why couldn't Grandma tell me this herself," said Mabel hotly. "I don't like being talked about in my own house."

"I knew you'd be annoyed; that's why I hated to bring it up. But I decided I had to. Decorum is important everywhere, my dear, but especially in a small town like this. What will people think? You can't go on carriage rides with a man not your husband, and expect no one to notice."

"Oh, Mother, there's nothing wrong with it. You're making too much fuss. Why do you mind if David doesn't?" She handed a piece of apple to Millicent.

"Then he *should* mind, that's all I can say. Your grandmother has been disturbed. To tell you the truth, she wonders if you aren't a bit smitten with Austin Dickinson. I told her not to be silly, but she is worried." Mrs. Loomis looked at her daughter's face critically to gauge her reaction.

"I'm not smitten with him. What a word, 'smitten'. Goodness." She paused and looked down at the apple in her hand. "I do admire him, very much, and he admires me. He's told me so. We have many common interests and he complements David. David doesn't care about nature and ideas and..."

But her mother cut her off. "Mabel, this is more serious than I thought. You are indeed courting gossip by spending so much time with this man. What does his wife think? Have you thought of that? And you may be wrong about what David thinks."

Mabel stood up, trying to control her anger. "You've got it all wrong, Mother. All wrong. And I do know what David thinks. He knows Mr. Dickinson needs me right now. He lost his son last year, as I told you, and he's turned to me."

"To you Mabel? Where is his minister? Where is his family? He has no business turning to you for any comfort. What kind of a man is he?"

Millicent had stopped munching her piece of apple and watched her mother and grandmother cautiously.

"He's as true a man as I've ever met, that's what he is. He's pure and noble and fine, and I'm proud he cares for me."

"So you admit it, then," said her mother, standing while apple peelings fell. "He cares for you? Be careful, Mabel, you may be in grave danger. He may care for you in ways you didn't intend. He may even have impure thoughts."

Mabel did not know how to answer that. "I think your father should be here with us for a while," her mother continued. "Maybe he can help. I tell you, Mabel, I can't sit by and watch you endanger your reputation. I'm going to write to him immediately. He can spare time for something as important as this."

Mabel, shaking her hands as though flicking off water, stood. "Come on, Millie, let's take a walk with your buggy." Her mother was left standing on the porch surrounded by apple peelings, just as Grandmother Wilder appeared on the porch from within, anxious to hear the outcome of the discussion.

Mrs. Loomis did not let the subject drop. True to her word, she summoned Eben Loomis to Amherst to stay several weeks, where, somewhat bewildered, he sat discussing astronomy with David after supper, talked with his daughter about religion, and took long walks alone. It wasn't until he had been there a week that he met Austin Dickinson for anything more than a polite greeting. Tea at Oaklawn one afternoon found Mr. Loomis the object of severe glances from his wife on the one hand, and proud smiles on the other from Mabel as she introduced Austin to him. He liked Austin right off, couldn't see what the fuss was about, and resolved to avoid as much conflict as he could. He had no desire to quarrel with Mabel, and indeed, never had. With a little luck, he reasoned, he'd be back home in Washington in his office leaving Mabel to go on with her life at enough distance to allow Molly Loomis to relax her suspicions. He was more interested in David's work than Mabel's social life, and asked to hear about the transit data.

"Haven't written it up yet," said David in answer to Mr. Loomis's question.

"Haven't written it up? But you must!" said Mr. Loomis, shocked at David's carelessness. "What does Mr. Newcomb say?"

"He can wait," countered David. "I need to clear away other work first."

Mr. Loomis took long walks with Mabel to find the special trees and streams she had enjoyed, and reminisced about the walk he once took with Walt Whitman in Washington. He also walked with little Millicent who chattered busily, one hand in his, the other pointing at birds, flowers, and dogs. Sometimes she returned on his shoulder, and once, the two of them came racing down Main Street at a gallop to beat the rain, while Sue Dickinson, unseen, looked out the window at them, her eyes sad and drawn against the dark of her mourning clothes.

And so although Eben Loomis enjoyed his visit, he knew his wife found him a pale ambassador indeed. He hoped in vain that the delicate matter at issue could be laid to rest, but she insisted, a few months later, that he write Mabel a stern letter, one he regretted from the moment he sent it. Mrs. Loomis thought such a letter would force Mabel to take their concerns seriously. But they were to discover dramatically later on that they had only begun to grasp the seriousness of the situation.

Luckily, Grandmother Wilder did not observe events at Oaklawn during Caro and John Andrews' visit in the spring of 1885. The couple, Mabel's cousin once removed and her husband, bustled into Amherst from Boston full of talk about parties, concerts, art exhibitions, and all the modern conveniences of city life. They stayed only a week, but early in the visit, Caro let David know in many ways that she would accept whatever attentions he cared to give her. In fact, her hearty laugh, her casual attitude toward money, her talk about society people, and her frank pleasure in drinking just a little too much wine, captivated both Mabel and David, who managed to overlook John's querulous manner and his dislike of books.

While John napped upstairs one afternoon and Mabel sang at choir rehearsal, David kissed Caro full on the lips, received her open-mouthed kiss in return, and made plans to escape with her to the observatory the following evening while the others joined a whist party. Supper was a jolly affair as the Andrews described their impending European trip and begged Mabel to join them.

"To Europe? How could we ever afford such a thing? Anyway, David can't leave work and run off."

"But *you* could, it's not so expensive as you think. You can economize in so many ways," said Caro, John echoing her, his mouth full of roast beef.

"I've always wanted to go," said Mabel. "Imagine, David, Europe!"

"I don't know, Mabs, we'd have to think carefully. I did get my raise though, and you could borrow some money from your parents..."

"Only if they approve of me these days," broke in Mabel quickly, raising her eyebrows. "They think I'm some kind of heathen," she told John and Caro. "I don't behave properly enough for them these days. What nonsense."

"There's proper and there's proper," said Caro, "and I for one am glad you aren't like some of the matrons around this town, for Lord's sake. How dreadfully dull they are. I've never seen so much black crepe in my life! And so judgmental! But think about it, Mabel. What fun we could have, the three of us." She looked moon-eyed at David. "I wish you could come, David, I do, I do. Three months gadding about, seeing the sights, eating marvelous food..."

"Three months? Is that how long you plan to stay?" asked Mabel, taken back.

David looked at Caro. "She doesn't want to leave Austin. He's her mentor, you might say. Ha!"

"Oh David, hush, " said Mabel. "We'll discuss it later tonight. But I'm serious."

So was everyone. For Mabel, the trip meant a chance to satisfy her long-standing curiosity about Europe. For the Andrews, her company meant a pleasant diversion from each other. And for David, the prospect of Austin and Mabel being apart for three months meant there might be some hope that the affair would end sooner than he had presumed.

Phebe, sitting in the kitchen, heard Caro propose the toast loudly: "To interesting prospects ahead," while the others, laughing, raised their glasses and chimed in, "Hear hear!"

CHAPTER   35

May, June 1885

Austin had to stop his reading aloud
one evening in May because Mabel and David were laughing so hard. Between
chuckles, David repeated the words: "To be or not to be; that is the bare
bodkin..."

"He is so clever, Samuel Clemens," said Austin, smiling to see them laugh.
"This book is five times better than *Tom Sawyer*."

"I'm glad we decided to read each installment together," said David. "You
read so well, Austin."

"Like the north breeze," said Mabel, "all excitement and push!"

A log fell in the fireplace and Austin arose, still smiling, to lift it back with
the fire tongs. He returned to his chair, and the three of them sat peacefully
gazing into the fire, Mabel with the magazine in her lap and her feet on a stool,
Austin next to her in his favorite chair, and David half reclining on the hearth
rug in front of them.

"Comfortable?" Mabel asked Austin fondly, reaching over to touch his hand.

" More than comfortable even. Happy to be in this warm room with my two
best friends reading a good story in front of a well built fire."

David leaned his head backwards from his position on the floor to laugh up
at Austin. "Of course it's well built, you built it, by God!"

For a few minutes, no one spoke. Then Austin broke the silence. "I wish it
could always be like this. Like a home. People who care for each other spending time quietly together. No disagreements. No tensions."

"Who said there are no disagreements or tensions?" remarked David. "That's
a bit extreme!"

"Shhh!" said Mabel, waving her hand in his direction. "Yes, Austin, you and
David must take care of each other while I am gone."

"I've come to dread June," Austin returned. "Nothing will be right until you
are back from Europe. Besides, I've come to love this house and this parlor and

this fireplace. I hate the prospect that you'll have to move again in the fall."

But David wasn't concerned. "The Lincoln house suits me," he said. "As long as we have to rent, that is. The only way to stay in one place is to have our own house. To build one, even."

"But we talked about that, didn't we, Mabel?" said Austin, turning to her. "About using the meadow land and building a cottage for you. For us. I don't think it's a far-fetched idea. And it would be ours, built to our standards."

"You'd help us design it?" asked David. "Because if you did that, I could do much of the actual building."

Mabel leaned forward and the magazine slid to the floor. "This could be the answer to our problems," she said excitedly. "Our own house, designed to our specifications, and on the best land in Amherst—Dickinson land!" She stood up and touched the back of Austin's neck.

"You're forgetting money again, Mabs," said David.

"We can work something out," she insisted. "Don't give up before we've started."

David sat up, cross-legged. "It would be fun to plan, wouldn't it?" he said to Austin. "We could work it out together. Where in the meadow, exactly?"

"I'll show you tomorrow," said Austin. "I know exactly where it could be. We can walk over the land."

"Oh, how well I know that meadow," said Mabel. "We've walked there a hundred times—that perfect meadow with its crickets and hay and bees. How fine it would be to wake up there, to get out of bed and see the meadow first thing in the morning. But oh, Austin!" She looked stricken, her hand over her mouth. "Why are we even thinking about such a scheme. Are we crazy enough to imagine Sue would allow it?"

"Slowly, slowly," said David. "We're going too fast. I'll look at the meadow, but Mabel and I need to have some serious financial discussions."

"David," said Mabel, "you didn't hear what I said about Sue. The basic obstacle, you know. Let's not get too excited." She returned to her chair, David moved so that he rested his back against her knees, and Austin pulled his armchair closer to Mabel's. They all watched the fire again.

"I won't be able to sleep tonight for thinking about Europe, and now a house of our own," said Mabel. "Let's finish our reading. Maybe it will calm me down, and then you must go home and sleep, Austin, you look exhausted, dear."

Austin retrieved chapter twenty-one of *Huckleberry Finn*, "An Arkansas Difficulty," and resumed reading, while Mabel and David leaned close to enjoy every word.

~

The *Pavonia* sailed from Boston for Ireland on June 6th, 1885. As the steam horns sounded the departure and the tug boat crews turned on their engines, the kisses Mabel blew down to David grew more agitated and excited.

"Wave, Caro, wave! Does he see us? Oh, thank goodness Austin didn't come to the pier! I couldn't have stood it."

And so at last, the ship drew away from the pier, the seagulls swarmed around it fore and aft, the wind caught at the passengers' hats, and everyone felt the rise and fall of the sea under their feet.

Austin's farewell letter lay safely in Mabel's purse, proof of his love, as if she needed any. So when John seized Caro and Mabel by the elbows saying, "It's too windy and cold on deck, let's go to the salon and look out there," they followed him eagerly below and watched Boston recede at a breathtaking rate while they sipped tea and John raised his mug of foaming beer to his lips.

Ever increasing miles away in Amherst, Austin, fresh from the train, took out his watch on the piazza and began thinking with special concentration about Mabel, even though it wasn't quite 5 o'clock. Tomorrow was Sunday. It would be twelve long Sundays before she returned. He had wanted to be with her with no land in sight—"like going to heaven," she had written him in her last special letter. That was another letter he sometimes felt like showing Emily. He had already picked an earlier one to show her one day, when he felt ready himself. She would understand, she would know just how he felt.

While he thought about Mabel, imagining her activities, her surroundings, and her own concentration on him, she was standing in her state room showing Caro her new hats. It was the first 5 o'clock time she forgot. But at 9, while Austin prepared for bed in Amherst, she remembered, and lifted her head to the stars at the railing for a moment, ignoring the chatter of the couples around her.

Austin had wandered about the Evergreens straightening up his desk, mending a broken chair, and reading the newspaper. A south wind blew through the sunlight, gently riffling the tree leaves. He pruned some of the shrubbery half-heartedly, then gave it up and walked over to the Homestead where he found Emily and Lavinia about to have tea. He made desultory conversation there, then still restless, walked around the Oaklawn property. The sunlight had disappeared, leaving a darkness which intensified his growing depression, his sense of unease as he looked toward the blank windows of rooms where he and Mabel had known such joy only short days before. He stood still. Suddenly his steps became purposeful. He turned and strode briskly toward the cemetery. It was time to be with Gilbert at the grave.

The heading of the obituary still rolled around in his head, unbidden: "Death of a Promising Boy." But Austin held back his tears and stood quietly by the grave until the hour he waited for arrived: 5 o'clock. Only then did he give way and weep quietly, feeling Gilbert and Mabel by his side.

CHAPTER 36

June 1885

YOU WORK ON COLLECTING MABEL'S DRESSES, I'll work on my own wardrobe," David told Austin as they stood amid the packing boxes in the Todds' bedroom at Oaklawn. The Irish lace curtains Mabel had picked in Boston rippled gently into the room on the breeze from the open windows.

"David sat on a trunk and looked around the clutter. "By God, I'll never rent a house again on a single year's lease. Not worth it. I didn't think they'd sell the house so soon, much less expect us to be out so fast."

"I didn't either, but the fraternity has had its eye on this place for some years now, ever since Mrs. Lessey became ill." He walked toward the larger wardrobe. "This one?"

"Yes," said David. "I guess it's a good thing Mabel isn't here after all. She wouldn't like all this confusion, or living in college rooms." He stood up and opened the trunk he had been sitting on. "Can you believe they've been gone over a week now? Docked in England by now, your Mabel and my Caro, so to speak?"

Austin, his back to David, had just opened the wardrobe door, revealing Mabel's best dresses, each one a resonance, a reiteration of her. Hearing David's words and seeing the living dresses, in all their textures and colors, nearly doubled him over in sweet pain. He couldn't answer, but stood looking and breathing, the dresses standing before him, Mabel after Mabel. He let a few minutes pass before he dared touch them.

"You've heard from her?" David asked, from the other side of the room now.

"Yes."

"She told me she might send some letters for you under cover of mine as well. I'll hand over whatever I get for you."

"Thanks."

"I got one from Caro too." Austin didn't answer. There was a pause. Then David added, "I miss her, too, along with Mabel. She's a good woman. Not compared to Mabel, of course."

Austin went to the windows and gazed over the expanse of grass. "Ours is an unusual situation, isn't it, my friend?" he remarked, finally. "Our special secret. Our strange secret. Not for Amherst's ears." He laid several of Mabel's dresses on the bed in preparation for carrying them to storage at the Homestead.

David did not answer.

"You still agree that we should take most of the pictures and the good small furniture, along with the dresses of course, to the Homestead?" said Austin. "They'll be much safer there in the attic where it's bound to be dry."

"Yes, that's fine," said David. "Everything else will be safe in the gymnasium. Don't know if I can lug these paving stones over there though."

"Paving stones?" Austin joined David to look, puzzled, into two large boxes of heavy slate paving stones behind the bedroom door. "What are these for?"

"Oh, I don't know, just thought they might come in handy sometimes for the observatory, either here or at Smith."

"But how did you get them up here then?"

"I moved them one by one from the Stearns' house garden."

"From Mary Stearns' place? You mean The Convent? You took them?" Austin bent to look closely at the stones. "But you must not have told her. She thinks they've been stolen. She's been quite baffled by the whole thing." He looked up at David inquiringly.

"She doesn't need them," said David, shrugging. "I didn't think she'd even miss them. They're nice, don't you think?"

"But we must return them," said Austin. "Let's load them up in the wheelbarrow as soon as we can. They belong around the sundial, didn't you know?" He stood looking closely at David for a moment, while David, unconcerned, pulled his clothes from his wardrobe and tossed them on the bed.

"You'll return them?" Austin persisted.

"Well, if you say so. I suppose I don't really need them right now."

Austin stood in thought a moment longer, looking at the paving stones and then at David, whose back was turned. Puzzled, he returned to Mabel's wardrobe. "How are the plans for the Smith Observatory coming?" he asked.

"Virtually finished. I'm still going over the supply budget, and there's been a temporary snag with the telescope manufacturers, but I hope we can settle that. I also had my article accepted in a German journal."

"Which article?" asked Austin, laying another dress on the bed.

"The one on a trans-Neptune planet. That's the article Mabel proofed right before she left."

"You really believe there's yet another planet out there beyond Neptune?"

"I certainly think so. Something has to account for the behavior of Neptune's orbit. But whatever it is, it must be very far out."

Austin tentatively lifted the pile of dresses from the bed. "That's enough," he said. "I'll take this pile over to the Homestead and come right back."

"Yes, go on. If I'm not here, I'll be headed to the gymnasium."

Austin hoisted the dresses into his arms, walked sideways through the door and down the stairs, and soon found himself outside and alone in the back of the house, where he bent his cheek reverently to the silks and muslins, while he inhaled their odor and smoothed them with his fingers.

"Mabel," he whispered. "My Mabel. Gift of my God."

From the window, David, catching sight of the colorful dresses, stopped to watch Austin in his moment of reverie. When Austin raised his head and began to walk toward the Homestead, David remained by the window thinking. His face remained expressionless. He stood that way for five minutes, then aroused himself and turned to kneel by the boxes of paving stones. He stood one on end, still thinking, and then, letting it fall, began to remove more clothes from his wardrobe for storage in the next few months.

Across the street from the Homestead, Mariette Jameson had been dusting upstairs when some movement caught her eye. "What in heavens' name is in those bushes?" she said aloud. Stooping to look out the window, she saw Austin laboring across the Homestead lawn behind a huge pile of dresses. "Now what is he up to?" she said to herself, dust cloth in hand, as she watched him pass through the garden and head for the back door. "Not Lavinia's clothes, surely, from the look of them. Nor Sue's either, to judge from the colors."

But suddenly she understood. "*Her* clothes." Had the man no pride? Even now, she could hardly believe that Main Street, Amherst, might have adultery on its hands, a situation where someone they all knew and had known for years could be breaking a commandment in his heart and mind, might even be contemplating actually joining his body..." Her mind refused to take the picture further. She would pursue that another time. For now, she remained by the window to see what else might catch her eye. Suppose Sue happened along? Did she have any idea her husband was carrying another woman's clothes across the lawns for all to see?

Mariette Jameson returned to her dusting, working now on the picture frames flanking the bureau top. Nothing had been the same on Main Street ever since little Gilbert Dickinson had died in October, 1883. She had been observing it all from her own front door without even trying: Susan Dickinson stalking about in black, Mattie playing ever more the role of social debutante whenever she returned from Miss Porter's boarding school, Ned looking more and more glum and confused, and Austin, in his serious Dickinson way, pursuing Mrs. Todd. Or more likely, Mrs. Todd pursuing him. They were selfish creatures in the end, the Evergreen Dickinsons. Such a strange lot! Lived mostly to please themselves, though Austin was a kindly soul underneath that rough exterior. Simply misled by immoral people like Mabel Todd.

Mariette Jameson had to say it now—that Mabel Todd was immoral, through and through. And most unattractive, too, with that way she had of sizing up people while they were talking and then looking around as though she wanted someone new to talk to. How anyone could praise her protruding eyes was more than Mariette could imagine. She found them almost repellent, and now that she had met Mabel's father, it was clear where those eyes came from.

Poor Sue Dickinson. Couldn't even attend evening church in peace because Mabel sang in the choir now. Someone said Mabel had studied music at the New England Conservatory, and she *did* have a nice voice. Well, Sue still attended early Sunday morning services with Ned and Mattie, whenever Mattie was home from school, but evenings she devoted to her crazy charity scheme: bringing Sunday school to the poor folks of Logtown over in east Amherst. John always said, "Well, what's wrong with that?" but Mariette said it was showy charity. Not from the heart. Sue Dickinson didn't seem like a heart person.

John was big-hearted though. Here he had lost his postmaster's position due to the 1883 civil service reform, and he hardly complained. Always gave everyone the benefit of the doubt. Lavinia carried on more than any of them when she came over in March one day. "Civil service is a damned lie," she shouted before she had even understood the situation. Because John was so big-hearted and liked Lavinia besides, he hadn't told anyone but Mariette what he discovered about the mail. Lavinia's mail. "Letters for Miss Lavinia nearly every day, have been coming for months, lots of them in Austin's handwriting. Now why would he write to his own sister? It used to puzzle me. And now that Mabel Todd is in Europe, some of those envelopes in his handwriting are postmarked England and Ireland, while others are in someone else's handwriting. Mabel Todd's. You can figure it out for yourself."

Yes, the trouble on Main Street would all come to a head one of these days. Mariette lifted the little glass figurines a friend had sent from Venice and dusted them carefully, sitting on the bed, until movement from across the street caught her eye again and she stood. Austin was leaving the house empty-handed for the Lessey House, no doubt, and another load of Mabel's dresses. Poor Miss Emily, with her failing health, enduring all this confusion. Dr. Bigelow seemed seriously concerned. They all were, the whole family. Emily's "turns" came more and more frequently, yet she still found time to send over flowers and charming little notes. She managed to keep apart from all the confusion. A mystery she was, but a sweet one. Everyone liked Miss Emily, even if they had never met her. And she, Mariette, had not, but she'd been only a floor away, so to speak, had heard Emily's voice, and of course she'd seen Emily at a distance in the garden at dusk or in the late afternoon. A small gentle figure in white. Mariette liked her instinctively, and would have been jealous had Mabel Todd met her. But even Mabel Todd hadn't been so privileged.

Austin disappeared from view, but shortly afterward, David Todd came from Oaklawn by way of the street rather than the lawns, pushing a big wheelbarrow loaded with what looked like masculine clothing, his own no doubt. Off he went, headed up Main Street. Now and again he stopped to rest and to wipe his face with a handkerchief. He had reached First Church when Sue Dickinson opened her Italianate front door and stepped out, a dark figure in mourning clothes. Commencement day wasn't far off—she and Austin undoubtedly had many errands to do before then. Soon the town would fill up with visitors and the college would hold its last dances. Mrs. Todd would miss those, and Mattie Dickinson wouldn't be sorry. Rumor had it that when the Chi Psi boys asked Mabel Todd to matronize their dance in February, Sue prevented Mattie from attending—even from leaving Miss Porter's at all that week, despite the fact that Mattie had been counting on it.

Sue Dickinson looked down the street toward the railway depot and then down, where she saw David Todd and his wheelbarrow. He was mopping his brow again. She watched and waited until he picked up the handles and began to push his load. When he was nearly to the Common, she walked slowly down her front steps and made her way toward the shops of Main Street.

Mariette Jameson leaned far out of her window to shake the dust rag. Her work in the bedroom was finished and it was time she did some errands in the shops herself, so she did not see Austin the second time he crossed the lawn, his arms so full of Mabel's dresses, their silks and muslins and trimmings covering his body, that unless you knew, you'd have to look twice to be sure it was indeed Austin Dickinson.

CHAPTER 37

June 1885

By mid June, Austin and David had managed to empty many of the Lessey House rooms. Each time Austin carried a box of Mabel's artwork into the Homestead, Lavinia called for Emily. "Come here, Em, more things to look at."

The oils pleased them especially. Austin set everything in the dining room where they could look them over together: the wood panels and screens painted with delicate flowers and grasses, and the smaller canvasses featuring birds and ferns. There was also a box of painted china teacups.

"No wonder she's giving art lessons at The Convent," said Emily to Austin. "I'm so glad she doesn't paint the usual roses and robins like everyone else. These grasses are more special than any roses. Like her Indian pipes."

Austin began opening a box to show them the teacups. "Look," he said, "aren't these fine?"

By the window, Lavinia cradled a tiny saucer in her hand. "Lovely. Austin, when you next write, tell her I miss her. Things are so dull around here now."

"Aren't you going to write to her yourself?"

"Yes, but I want you to tell her anyway. Emily, will you be writing to her?"

"Of course," said Emily, who had sat down in front of a panel.

"Do you feel all right?" asked Lavinia.

"Just the usual tiredness," said Emily. "Austin, this is your busiest time of year, so you need to take care. Commencement always tires you out so. It did Father too, remember? Lavinia, did Maggie wrap up the cake for Mattie and Issie to take back to school?"

"Yes, it's all ready in the kitchen."

"Good," said Emily. "Austin, don't forget to take the cake along with you today for Mattie. When is Miss Porter's finished for the summer?"

"July 12th."

"Good. I want to see her again soon. The days go by too quickly. And tell Ned to come over more often, will you? I'm not going to be here forever."

"Emily!" said Lavinia. "Don't say that!"

"You mean to tell me you plan to be here forever?" said Emily. "Tell me your secret."

"Oh, don't tease," said Lavinia. "You know what I mean."

"I'm sorry. I didn't mean to."

Austin placed a teacup in Emily's hand. "Look," he said simply. And then, "Sometimes I wish I had gone with her."

"Gone with her? To Europe? Well, you couldn't do that, Austin," said Lavinia. "You wouldn't leave us alone, would you?"

But Emily, handing the cup back to Austin, looked at him carefully. "Have you ever imagined living somewhere else, really, Austin?" she asked.

He wrapped the cup in newspaper and fitted it back into the box. Just when Emily thought he wouldn't answer, he said, "Only in the vaguest of ways. Where would I go? If I...if I...married her, I'd have to go far. And that would mean leaving you and so much else I love in Amherst. Impossible."

The idea of legal marriage to Mabel had struck him suddenly and with a rush of conflicting emotions, emotions both his sisters felt as well. They all three sat startled for a moment. Marriage to Mabel meant divorce. Divorce from Sue. Divorce in their family. No one they knew had ever been divorced— the idea was unimaginable. Even hearing the word pronounced repulsed them all. And marriage to Mabel assumed that David was not in the picture. But David was in the picture. Most definitely. Austin's good friend, David.

No one said anything for a while. The enormity of their brother's love for this Mabel Todd had become clear with the word "marriage," and both sisters had to absorb that enormity, that force. But Lavinia couldn't remain quiet for long. "I don't like this conversation," she said, "I'm afraid. You promise not to leave, Austin? You wouldn't?"

"No, of course I won't leave. I should never have said what I did." He got wearily to his feet and folded up the three-leafed wood panel. "I'll always be right here, right next door. Don't think any more about it." He carried the panel out of the dining room for storage in the attic.

"Austin," called Lavinia after him, her composure quickly restored, "It's too hot to store that in the attic. The paint will melt. Store it in Mother's room."

"All right," he called over his shoulder.

"Did you ever imagine Austin so foolish as to think of leaving Amherst?"

said Lavinia to Emily. "What a thought! Father would put his foot down to that, wouldn't he?" she laughed.

But Emily didn't smile. "I think I'll take a little nap," she said.

"Yes, yes, Emily, take a little nap, you'll feel better. Here, I'll fetch a shawl and you lie right on the parlor sofa."

The house became quiet as Emily settled herself in the darkened back parlor, Lavinia read the newspaper in the front parlor, and Austin placed Mabel's art work in his mother's room, covering the panels carefully with sheets. When he finished, he returned to Oaklawn for another load, walking more slowly than before. Like Emily, he felt tired. Ned had wakened him again the night before with a seizure. A rather bad one, in fact, during which he had bumped his head on the floor and bitten his cheek. Sue had emerged from her bedroom during the whole seizure instead of cowering in her room as she usually did, and had stood outside the closed door while Austin settled Ned down again for the night. When it was all over and Austin emerged, he found her standing with her head against the wall in as defeated a pose as he'd ever seen her take. But he could not respond, and only began descending the stairs, saying briefly, "He's sleeping now. Go back to bed."

Who would look after Ned when he, Austin, was gone? He'd been feeling old these days of Mabel's absence, deprived of her vitality and push. He was sharply aware that Emily looked tired and ill, she only a year younger than he, and that Lavinia's step was slow. Maybe a nap after dinner would revive him, and then in the evening, he might enjoy a chat with David in his rooms at the Amherst House. David seemed to need Austin's daily presence these days. He seemed insecure, both professionally and emotionally—emotionally in part because he had been suffering from delicate and painful medical symptoms which he had, at last, confided in detail to Austin—scalding and frequent urination, accompanied by shooting pains. It was an unmentionable disease he had been worried about for several weeks, alone in his agony. And thus, Austin had learned about Caro Andrews and at least one other woman he had been intimate with.

"But did you tell anyone else about this problem?" asked Austin reluctantly and with distaste. "Shouldn't you tell Caro, at least?"

"I can't, I can't," groaned David. "It's too awful. I can't bear Mabel to know. It could affect us all, you realize."

And then the full implications had dawned on Austin, who in his naivete had never realized how he, Mabel, David, and the newcomer, Caro, were all intimately related. He had felt as though he were in some sort of play, maybe one by that Norwegian, Ibsen, who wrote such shocking drama.

"But you must see a doctor," he'd told David. And seeing David's face, "Not one in Amherst. Why not Boston? You'd be anonymous enough there."

"Let me wait a while," David had insisted. "It's probably only an ordinary bladder infection. You're feeling all right, aren't you? So with Caro and Mabel away, we're all in a good position to figure things out."

And there things stood for the moment. But David and Austin felt closer than ever before with their intimate secret, their personal lives depending on each other. Austin knew he was living with an intensity he'd never known or imagined before.

CHAPTER 38

Summer to September 1885

ABOVE ALL, IT WAS THE SUMMER OF LETTERS.
Letters voyaging back and forth over the ocean, wedged into bags on the swaying wooden floors of ocean liners which made their way past schools of whales and bent into prevailing winds. Austin sometimes thought he lived for nothing else but those letters, along with the sweet memories he saved up to think about before he fell asleep.

He told her what flowers bloomed in July along their favorite roads—the orange daisies, wild roses, buttercups, elder, and mullein. In August, he told her about Emily's snow white cape jasmine, and above all, about the crickets, "those weird creatures from the border land" who helped bring them together. "My sweet wife," he called her. He felt married, the more so during their separation.

Mabel wrote him that a tree in the Heidelberg castle grounds bore their initials now, and that no scenery in Switzerland could comfort her like the Pelham hills, the Sunderland meadows, and Sugarloaf Mountain.

Emily wrote to Mabel twice, signing herself "America" on one occasion, and telling her to "touch Shakespeare for me."

But letters brought tension, too. Mabel never forgot the venom of her mother's letter, twelve pages of criticism, anger, and pain stemming from her perception of the relationship between her daughter and Mr. Austin Dickinson. And David's purposely unsealed and lascivious letters to Caro, included with his letters to Mabel, aroused her angry jealousy, even as she included her own letters to Austin in the same envelope as those to David. But Austin and David read their letters together companionably, courteously scanning the headings before handing the letters over to each other as they sat in David's rooms or relaxed in wicker chairs on the Evergreens piazza while Sue was away in Maine. They depended on one another, needed one another in a village which understood neither them nor their unorthodox passions.

By September, David's private illness had disappeared, its course pointing to nothing more serious than a bladder infection, and despite some wariness on all their parts, for Austin had confided its nature to Mabel, all three began at last to focus daily on Mabel's return and the longed-for reunions in Boston. Who should meet her first at the dock? Who should first catch sight of her waving hand and her lively eyes? Who should be the first one to open the door of a room for her at the Parker House Hotel, and lie, famished, in her arms?

Mabel was almost sick with pleasure when David undressed her and made love to her at the Parker House Hotel in Boston, September 13th, the day she docked. But it was Austin who, lying above her two days later, after David had returned to Amherst, made her cry in happy relief, the frustrations of their long separation over.

"I love you. Oh my king, how I love you!" she said through her tears.

"You are God to me," he answered. "And heaven and all of pure nature rolled into one. I love to live now, because of you."

When he moved to lie beside her while they listened, relaxed, to the sounds in the street outside, she said, "I want to do what we all three talked about, and build ourselves a house on the meadow property where you could visit freely. I want you away from her."

"It would be heaven, living with you, if only I could," he said.

"We could call it the Dell, what do you think?" said Mabel.

"The Dell, yes. Our private house."

Mabel lay back and laughed up at the ceiling. "It's wicked, utterly wicked." But her expression turned serious. "Not really. Hold me."

He did, while they both closed their eyes again in joyous amazement that they lay together at last after the long summer months apart.

"You never wrote the letter I asked you to?" asked Mabel shortly, running her fingers up and down Austin's arm.

He didn't answer for a moment. Then he said, "Not yet."

"Is it so hard?" Mabel persisted. "So hard to write out what she is, how little of a wife, just so people might understand us, if it ever comes to that?"

"But it won't ever come to that, my love. And who would read the letter?"

"Well, I don't know," said Mabel with a trace of impatience, "but it would protect me from people. From lies and gossip. It's torture for me, the way some Amherst matrons give me their terrible looks. I get it much more than you do."

"Would you keep the letter somewhere safe, if I wrote it?" he asked, moving the arm she had been stroking behind his head.

"Certainly," she said.

"I wouldn't want the children to see it," he added, looking at the ceiling.

"They wouldn't see it. I'd just feel better if I had such a letter. As proof of our pure love. And as proof that I didn't destroy your marriage, that it was already destroyed when I moved to Amherst."

"I understand, sweet," Austin said, turning on his side to face her once more. "I'll try to write it. It's hard though."

"Well try, that's all I ask you," said Mabel, and kissed him gently. "And know that I love you."

He reached for her and they kissed each other long and hard. "If I could make love to you again right now, I would," he said. "I wish I could."

"Tomorrow morning," she said, smiling. "Tomorrow morning."

CHAPTER 39

Fall 1885

JUST AS MABEL CRIED OUT TO AUSTIN, "Oh more, faster," in a hoarse whisper, they both heard David on the front porch rattling the door knob. They froze for an instant. Then, "I can't stop," breathed Austin, and they moved together again. "He'll stay downstairs", whispered Mabel, "of course he knows you're here," and they closed their ears and eyes against all but each other and their pleasure.

David, returning earlier from the observatory than he had told them, stood still in the hallway and listened. He turned to hang his hat on the rack, still listening, then paced a few steps, glancing upstairs as he did so. The fire had gone out in the parlor grate—no point in sitting there, unless Austin and Mabel had intended to return downstairs later. No, of course not. It was too late for that. Clearly, Austin intended to slip out quietly into the darkness when no one would see him. But David wanted to see him. He had tried to catch up with him at the college several times yesterday and today to discuss funds for the observatory, but to no avail. Austin was too busy. Everyone wanted to see him, to claim his time. Well, it was time David Todd had his share too.

He climbed the stairs quietly but deliberately and headed straight to the spare bedroom door. There he stood still and listened without shame to what he had once inadvertently heard before. Mabel's low breathings, the rustle of the mattress, some muffled words from Austin and her reply, and finally, his long groan. Then more muffled words, much shifting on the mattress, and finally quiet. David knocked softly. The quiet intensified. All three became statues for a moment, concentrations of stone. Then David whispered, "It's me, Mabel."

The bedclothes rustled, and in a moment, someone, Mabel of course, padded to the door and opened it. Tousled, she held her dressing gown around her in the gloom as though David had never seen her without it before, and her eyebrows were furrowed. "David, what's going on?" She closed the door partly behind her.

"I tried to reach Austin yesterday and today, and he was always too busy. So I need to see him now. I don't care what you say." He pushed open the door, revealing Austin's shadowy form propped up against the pillows, shaggy and disheveled, his look as unsure as Mabel's in the light from the hallway.

David advanced into the room and stood at the foot of the bed. "Has President Seelye still not said anything to you about funds for the observatory? I'm tired of being put off, I tell you."

"David, really..." began Mabel, but David cut her off.

"Oh, I don't blame *you*, Austin, not at all. You're practically my only hope. No one else around here will talk to me about it. Why? That's what I'd like to know." He sat down on the rocker by the wardrobe and calmly contemplated Austin, who struggled to compose himself, looking back and forth between David and Mabel for a cue to his behavior. His clothes lay rumpled on the clothes stand across the room, and his bare chest left him feeling exposed, unable even to begin taking part in this strange conversation.

"Here, dear," and Mabel handed him a large knitted shawl which he wrapped around his shoulders. She lit a candle and pulled up a stool but left the lamps unlit so that she and David sat on either side of the bed in undulating shadows, Austin a bulky presence between them.

"You'll help me, won't you, Austin?" asked David plaintively. "I was promised a new observatory and I want it. Plus a fine new refracting telescope. I don't know how much longer I can wait."

Austin sat in the shadows, the multicolored shawl looking incongruously feminine against the folds of his neck and his whiskers, and stared at David, unable to speak. Finding no help from Mabel, who was rubbing her temples, he said finally, "Well, David, you certainly have my full attention now." The two men peered at each other until David started to laugh, a low chuckle at first, then heartier guffaws.

"You could say that, yes, I have your attention all right, Mr. Austin Dickinson." He leaned back in the rocker. "Oh, my God, how funny it is." He leaned his head back to laugh more.

Austin sat rigid, still unsure how to take David's entrance and this display of laughter. But when David leaned forward in the rocker again and asked, "Well, what does President Seelye really think about my requests?" Austin looked over at Mabel and smiled faintly in relief.

"He thinks you have to help more in raising funds—in finding a donor. So far, there just isn't anyone. You need to widen your reputation outside Amherst, and then maybe someone will come forward."

Mabel stood and put her stool in the corner. "I'll be next door," she said to both of them. "Goodnight." She blew a quiet kiss to Austin who raised his hand, and then lit another candle from the one already burning, carrying it to the hallway. David and Austin resumed their conversation.

"But I think I have something of a reputation outside Amherst," said David. "Whose idea was it to use the electric telegraph during solar eclipses? Who published the tables of Jupiter's satellites? And yet along with everything else, I'm so busy teaching for the college and writing that I hardly have time for myself. But does President Seelye care? He continues to ask more of me."

"What about your upcoming eclipse expedition plans?" returned Austin. "They arouse interest, and generate articles easily. Have you thought more about them?"

"Yes, of course I have. Japan is the place for the next solar eclipse in the summer of 1887. I'd like to go. I've already talked about it with Professor Pickering at Harvard."

"What are his thoughts?" asked Austin.

"He wants us to climb to Mount Fuji-San and..."

"Mount Fuji?" interrupted Austin, incredulous.

"Yes, Fuji, to see if the summit is a feasible place to establish an astronomical and meteorological station."

"Well," said Austin, still somewhat mystified, "plan for it then. And tell President Seelye now, if you haven't already. In fact, have you had a private conference with him lately?"

"No, I haven't. I sometimes get the impression he's putting me off. Is he?"

"It's possible. But be persistent."

"Will you put in a word for me, Austin?"

"Of course, yes. Anything I can do, David, I will. I want to see a new observatory here too."

"Well," said David in a suddenly business-like tone, "that's that. Time for bed." He slapped the arms of his chair and stood up. "You'd better hustle out of here. How's the family?"

"Fine, everyone is fine," said Austin, eyeing his clothes.

"Good," said David, "I'll leave you then. Thanks for your attention." He went to the door, opened it, and then turned back, saying with no change in tone, "Just remember that she still loves me. You know that, don't you?"

"I do."

"All right, then, see you tomorrow at faculty meeting. Goodnight." He closed the door as Austin got out of bed, dressed, and descended the back stairs with only one quick glance backwards at David and Mabel's bedroom door.

When Austin and Mabel met soon afterward for a chilly carriage ride late in the afternoon, Mabel burst out with "It was bound to happen, wasn't it?" before she had scarcely settled her skirts and cloak about her.

Austin flicked the reins. "Did he come home early on purpose?"

"I think he did, yes. He wanted it—to see us together that way."

"Why is it," Austin began, "that something which ought to be so wrong seems so right with us. With all of us, I mean." He reached for her hand. "I don't have to tell you that it's right between us. But when I imagine what the outside world would think of us three, up in that room together talking...and then I realize that I myself would have found the situation unimaginable not long ago..." He left the sentence unfinished. "But how long do you think David was standing outside the door that night?"

"Don't think about it, it doesn't matter," said Mabel.

"But do you think he *did* hear us, really hear us," persisted Austin. "Before, I mean."

"To be honest with you," said Mabel casually, "yes, he did hear us. He told me so right after you left."

Austin shook his head in wonderment, looking ahead at the road, the reins relaxed in his lap. "He's a strange man."

"I adore you. My king, my husband. I can hardly wait to hold you in my arms," said Mabel. "Let's stop by the old barn behind the ash grove for a while. I must hold you. I don't care how cold it is."

And so, twenty minutes later, they sat alone together in each other's arms. David Todd would not visit them here.

After a while, Mabel said something , but her voice was indistinct against his chest.

"What?" he asked, leaning back.

"You never wrote out the reasons why you and Sue are incompatible, did you?"

Austin closed his eyes. "I can't, I just can't. You'll have to understand."

Mabel didn't answer but turned her face into his chest again.

"Just remember," he said, "we love each other, wholly and completely, and in God's eyes. We are one. We are married in God's eyes, and nothing can take that from us."

"And you will be a husband in name only to Sue? Isn't that how it has been?"

"You know it has," Austin returned, running his fingers around the crevices of her ears.

"And you will never know her as a true husband again. Promise."

"You know I won't. So don't ask me to promise."

Mabel was silent at that. She had never offered to make such a promise herself.

"I wish we could live somewhere else, don't you?" she said.

"I wish we could. But we can't."

"But where would you go, if you left Amherst?" Mabel asked.

"I don't know...the Midwest? Some of the Dickinsons have done well there. But not my grandfather. Leaving Amherst was his ruination."

"We'd miss Amherst, you know we would. And Sunderland, and the Pelham hills and the November snow on the trees, and our special carriage rides."

"Like this."

"Like this," he said.

They said no more for a while, but held each other quietly. When a cold wind blew up, swishing in the evergreen branches, Austin held her tighter, but said, "We must go. I'm expected for a late supper. Mary Stearns is coming."

"I wish I could come."

"I do too, my love. I do too."

Mabel smoothed her hair and picked up her hat from the seat beside her. "Mary knows already, I think. Or strongly suspects, don't you think?"

"Yes, I do. Dear soul, I think she accepts us, too. Don't ask me why."

"Because she's sweet and kind and misses her own husband. She sees we are as happy as she once was. And she's glad for us."

"Maybe so," said Austin. "Button up your coat, that wind is strong." But he turned to her and buttoned her coat himself as he would a child's, giving her a kiss on the nose after the top button, which she accepted with closed eyes. So what she said next took him by surprise. "I wish we could have a child together."

He said nothing, the idea was so novel and confusing. She had opened her eyes and looked at him now. "Then we'd be really married, forever. Our love would go on and on."

He moved the corners of his lips into a half smile. "A lovely thought." But he turned from her to dismiss the idea and clicked to the horse. Mabel also looked straight ahead and arranged herself for the ride back to Amherst.

CHAPTER 40

Fall and Winter 1885
to Spring 1886

O
N NOVEMBER 6TH, WHILE THE FAMILY WAS
at dinner, robbers broke into the Evergreens, stealing a hundred dollars' worth
of jewelry, along with Ned's pocket-book and the money in it.

"What does it matter?" said Sue sarcastically to Austin later as they viewed
the disarray upstairs with Ned. "This house has been robbed already. And its
master is still missing."

Since both the Hills' houses had also been robbed the night before, Vinnie
took to sleeping with a stout walking stick by her bed and a heavy flowerpot.
But Emily laughed the whole thing off. "Is it quite safe to leave the Golden
Rule out over night?" she wrote to Ned when he was sick with a bad cold later
on that month.

"Aunt Emily is weakening, isn't she, Father, really weakening," said Ned
one Monday morning a few weeks later when Sue busied herself upstairs with
the dressmaker and Austin prepared to take the train for Boston. "She didn't
come downstairs either time I visited last week."

"She's very sick. We should spend as much time with her as we can."

"I know I will," said Ned. He took his hat from the hat stand, looking
quickly at his father in the mirror as he spoke. "I expect Mrs. Todd to realize
you have other pressing demands on your time right now."

Austin met his son's eyes in the mirror. "You think I haven't spent enough
time with Aunt Emily? You know that isn't true, Ned."

Ned ducked his head awkwardly. "All right, maybe not."

"Let's try not to criticize each other," said Austin. "I've been worried about
Aunt Emily for some time now. She still won't let the doctor see her, and I
don't think the prescriptions he leaves do much good. And Aunt Vinnie needs
help with Aunt Emily more than she cares to admit. That's why she likes

company to lift her spirits right now. You know how Mrs. Todd cheers Aunt Vinnie up—she's been a great help, so I hate to hear you criticize her."

"I wasn't going to."

"It's all right."

Ned opened the front door, and on his way out, said quickly over his shoulder, "At least I don't hate her anymore, in case you want to know." And was gone.

Austin stood quietly a moment in front of the little mirror, not really seeing himself. Then he focused his eyes, took his coat from the hook, and walked outside too, but the sight of Maggie's waving hand as she rushed from the Homestead next door stopped him.

"It's Miss Emily again," Maggie said as soon as she came closer, a hand on her heaving chest. "Miss Lavinia sent me to catch you before you went too far. We could hardly lift her from her chair back to bed...she looks something terrible!..."

But Austin was already striding along the path between the two properties, Maggie following behind him. He reached the rear door and made his way for the back stairs, calling, "I'm here" as he went.

Lavinia met him in the upstairs hall. "Oh thank heavens, Austin, I didn't know if you were going to Mabel's before you went to Boston or not, but luckily Maggie tried next door first." She lowered her voice. "She's had trouble getting her breath all morning, and she was up half the night for the potty. She's exhausted, but she can't breathe right lying down."

They both went quietly into Emily's room where she lay propped up by two pillows, her chest rising and falling swiftly. Austin stood by the side of the bed and took a good look at her face. "She looks worse," he whispered.

Emily stirred and opened her eyes. Seeing Austin, she held out her hand and smiled faintly. "Back from Boston already?"

"No, Em, he didn't go yet," said Lavinia, "and he's not going to, either. He's going to stay and help me take care of you."

Emily continued to smile, but closed her eyes. "I can't even read these days."

"We'll read to you," said Lavinia.

"Do your eyes hurt?" asked Austin.

"Yes," she said, "but I'm used to that from the old days. It must be the same old problem."

"We'll ask Dr. Bigelow. Is your breathing better now?" asked Austin.

"A little." But her chest rose and fell rapidly with shallow breaths. After a pause, she said, her eyes still closed, "I never sowed a seed unless it was perennial."

"What?" asked Lavinia.

But Emily didn't answer. "She's half out of her head," said Lavinia. "Oh Austin, what shall we do, what shall we do?"

"I'll stay with you today. We'll talk to Dr. Bigelow, of course. I'll let Sue know I'm not going to Boston, and Maggie can run over and tell Mabel." He looked down at Emily again. "Did she eat anything?"

"Just a few sips of tea. But she gave up when her breathing got so bad."

"She must eat as soon as she's able. Try broth and toasted bread."

Lavinia caught Austin's eye and gestured toward the door, indicating she wanted to talk. They both stepped out in the hall. "Oh, Austin," she said, "Why isn't Sue here? Is this the way it must end? I'll hate her forever, I tell you, I will!" she said, shaking her fists.

"Calm down, Vinnie. Of course Sue cares. She doesn't like to come here because of Mabel."

"But look what I found on her bedside table." Lavinia slipped back quickly into Emily's room and returned with a small piece of paper, torn on the top. "A rough draft, I suppose, but it has Sue's name on it..." She handed the scrap of paper to Austin, who read it with a strange, painful curiosity.

"...Emerging from an Abyss, and reentering it—that is life, is it not, Dear? The tie between us is very fine, but a hair never dissolves."

"You don't know if she sent a finished copy?" he asked.

"No, I don't know but I doubt it. I'll ask Maggie if she carried over any notes lately. But you can see she wants to reopen old ties with Sue. And if Sue got this and didn't answer..." She shook her head in frustration.

Austin made no other comment, but as he went downstairs to give Maggie a message for Mabel, part of the phrase stayed in his head: "The tie between us is very fine..." Both he and Emily remained bound to Sue by fine, tenacious ties. Ties which could not, would not, dissolve themselves. They bound the mind. And what about the heart? He would not tell Mabel about this note.

Although Austin spent as much time as he could with Emily, pressing legal business kept him away one early December day when she worsened. There was nothing to do but send across the street for Mrs. Jameson to help Lavinia. She arrived, all sympathy and strength, with a pot of soup and an apron over her arm, ready to support Lavinia while Maggie labored over laundry and baking.

"And you're sure you don't want me to help upstairs?" she asked Lavinia for the second time.

"Yes, I'm sure. I'll tend to all that."

And that was that. So of course she never saw Emily until afterward. In that way, Mariette Jameson was to realize, she treasured a memory Mrs. Todd never could.

And so the days passed. By Christmas, Emily had improved enough for Lavinia to receive Mabel's leisurely visits on several occasions. But most of that winter, the curtains stayed drawn at the Homestead, the blinds down. Maggie and Lavinia grew used to the continued murmur of Emily's and Austin's voices. They talked in Emily's room, in front of the dining room fire, or by the kitchen stove, and though their voices stayed low and serious much of the time, laughter also made its way into their conversations. When Lavinia heard that, she would rush in to stand over them. "What, what, tell me!" she would ask. Even if she didn't understand the reference, she went away smiling, flourishing her dust rag or settling back in her chair, opening the newspaper.

In the late winter of 1885, Austin found Emily occasionally in the conservatory starting seeds, even though the room's chill demanded that she bundle up in wool shawls. She started her heliotropes, a special favorite, in March. "You'll look at them for me when they bloom, if I'm not here?"

"You'll look at them with me," said Austin, watching her water them.

"But look at them for me," she persisted, her back towards him.

"Of course," he said.

After a silence, she added, "Otis Lord's favorites, heliotropes." She turned to smile at him. "I hope they still are, wherever he is."

Austin smiled soberly back at her.

"I was lucky to know him. I wanted you to be sure of it—that knowing him —made me taller than I am." She smiled again.

"Some people do that for each other," Austin said.

"And you look tall these days," Emily said. She turned back to her seeds. "But how frightening it's been."

"Just accept me, whatever happens," said Austin, "There's no answer to be had anyway. I live day by day—in pure joy and pure torment."

Emily sighed. "And is there nothing that can ever change how you and Sue feel...that can remedy...I don't even know how to ask the question. The same thing happens when I try to write to Sue these days."

"No, nothing can ever change anything that way. I can never go back on what I started. Never. Only, it was started *for* me. I didn't plan it, no one did. If only Sue and I could go our separate ways now..." He rubbed his eyebrows and looked at her. "Two tired old Dickinsons. Do you sometimes think we are two of a kind?"

"Often," she said.

And so Lavinia found them, Emily looking out the windows at the lawn she knew would soon be green, and Austin close by. She tiptoed out and joined Maggie in the kitchen. "Worn out, both of them," she reported, and lifted a cat away from the cooling custard, then peered at the rising bread dough. "Staying like two polar bears in that icebox conservatory. I'll give Austin twenty more minutes to wake up and take Emily out of there."

Another cold evening in March when the wind gusted through the evergreen trees, Austin sat with Emily upstairs in her room talking about Professor Edward Tuckerman's death three days before. "How is Sarah Tuckerman today, do you know?" Emily asked him.

"As gracious as always," said Austin. "Just like herself. Two of the nephews were with her when Sue and I called on her this afternoon."

"Things won't be the same without our Professor Tuckerman," said Emily. "I imagine you couldn't even count all the walks you took with him. Or that Father did." The wind beat against the windows in a sudden gust. " 'Dying whets the grasp' I told Sarah last October when she went to her cousin's funeral."

"What did you mean by that?" asked Austin, looking at the glowing coals.

"I meant it makes us want to hold on to the living even more. I told her October was a mighty month—" she glanced at his face—"because of Gilbert, of course. But I couldn't predict which month would be mighty for her. Now she knows. It's March."

Austin continued to gaze at the coals.

"You saw the plaque Mabel painted for me?" asked Emily, indicating the painted thistle on her cherry bureau.

"Yes, I saw it in progress. She loved your thank you note and the hyacinth you sent, but all this reminds me—she wants to know the source of the quotation in the note about figs and thistles. She had several guesses. Shakespeare, the Bible, or George Eliot, since she knows you love her so much."

Emily laughed. "Well, now I'm shocked. I thought she had a better scriptural education than that! And you too, Austin! Don't you recognize the verses? 'Do men gather grapes of thorn, or figs of thistles?' It's Matthew 7, verse 16."

"So it is," said Austin. "I'll tell her tomorrow. How pleasant it is to be able to chat with you about Mabel. I don't know what I'd do without you and Vin, supporting me the way you have. Supporting us."

"Good," said Emily, gently rocking in her chair. "Tell me about plans for the new house. Your Queen Anne style Dell house. Do the Todds own the lot officially now? Lavinia said the deed hadn't been signed yet."

"Well, it may as well be official. We can all trust each other, I hope. Anyway, the land will be a gift. I can't take their money. But we'll make up a bill of sale anyway."

"But Sue will have to sign that along with you..."

"I think she will." And seeing Emily's slight frown, he added, "I know, it might be a problem, but I think she will. It will all work out."

"I hope so," said Emily. "But just remember, poor old Harriet Merrill might have said the same thing when she willed over all her property and money to that young doctor who befriended her. And that case is still dragging on, as you well know, since you and your Mr. Cooper are representing her family. Things don't always work out the way you hope they will, even within your own family—that's all I'm saying."

Austin brushed some ashes off the rug with his foot. "There won't be any lawsuits in our family. Don't worry. I'm more concerned right now that David not neglect his duties at the College. He missed another faculty meeting, apparently, even after he was reprimanded."

"Is he absent-minded?" asked Emily.

"No, it's not that. He just does what he wants to. Once he has a notion, there's no moving him from it. I defend him whenever I can, but sometimes it's a challenge. Did you know he never wrote up his data from the Transit of Venus?"

"He didn't? Why not?"

"I hate to say it, but a combination of laziness and stubbornness, I think."

"Not good." But Emily was smiling. "Somehow that strikes me as funny. Lavinia makes such a fuss over David Todd—he's never lazy when it comes to doing all the little chores she asks him to do."

"He's kind that way, isn't he?" agreed Austin, shifting his outstretched legs. "But sometimes I feel I have to protect Mabel from his childish ways. I've stood up for him many a time. I hope he doesn't know that Sue has taken to calling him 'the little man' to anyone she meets."

"Oh dear," said Emily.

"But Mabel calls *her*—well, never mind. I shouldn't talk about it."

"'The Great Black Mogul,' or 'the old Scratch.' Oh, don't be embarrassed, I know all about it. Mabel told Lavinia one day when they both threw caution to the winds and laughed like two girls. I could hear them from up here. Maybe their giggling did them good. But it made me feel odd, Mabel calling Sue that."

"Really?" said Austin smiling. "To you, she fronts on the Gulf Stream, isn't that what you used to say once in a while when Sue frusrated you?"

Emily smiled, but said, "Our Sue, our lost, confused Susan."

"She's jealous of you, in a way—of your cleverness—" said Austin. "And she resents the way you keep to yourself, I know she does. But she doesn't realize how hurtful she can be." He shrugged. "She can't undo things now."

"I'm sure I demanded too much of her, especially when we were younger," said Emily. "All those letters I demanded she answer...No, I hold no grudges." Seeing her brother look at her, she added, "No, none at all."

"Not even about her letters to Abbie Farley? About you and Otis Lord?"

"Abbie is only his niece. She held no power over him. No one could say that this Daisy and her Judge Lord couldn't make up their own minds."

Neither said a word more until Austin arose to leave.

One bright April Sunday, Mabel brought six-year-old Millicent with her to the Homestead so she could see the barn. Emily managed to catch a glimpse from the upstairs windows of her dark bangs and white pinafore as she walked with her mother, stooping to grab at the hens along the way to the barn and to call out, "Kitty-cats, Mama!" Smiling, Emily watched them for a few minutes, while Maggie and Lavinia stood at the back steps and watched as well.

Inside the barn, Stephen, the Dickinsons' hired hand, held Millicent up to the horse, showed her the hens' nests, and finally, lifted her, rung by rung, up the ladder to the hay loft, where he let her run and jump, tossing hay in handfuls around her head. Mabel came into the house, leaving her daughter in Stephen's capable hands, and Emily could just catch her voice below, inquiring about her health: "Has Emily been down today?"

She hoped Mabel would play something lively on the piano. Some Scarlatti, perhaps. Or Mozart's "Rondo alla Turca." She could hear the music from her bed if she left the door open—and she knew it was time to rest again in bed. Even the walk around the upstairs hallway had seriously tired her. She hoped

Lavinia would remember to tell Mabel that the dramatic version of the book *Called Back*—the title always attracted her—would be playing on April 15th, the day before Austin's birthday, at the Springfield Opera House. She had greatly enjoyed the original novel version which Mabel had lent her some time ago.

Below, Mabel began to play the piano—a Bach gigue. Emily lay on her side, her head propped on the backs of her folded hands to keep her ear off the pillow so she could hear, and enjoyed the music.

CHAPTER 41

May 1886

Ⅰ N THE END, MAY TURNED OUT TO BE EMILY Dickinson's "mighty month." Saturday, May 15th. Yet almost to the end, despite her increasing weakness, her letters, notes, and flowers to friends and neighbors continued. In the last week of April, Lavinia walked over to the Jamesons with a basket of rare geraniums from Emily with a note. And there were other letters into May.

On the evening of May 2nd after Vinnie read her the newspaper's report of David Todd's search for a trans-Neptunian planet, Emily sat up longer than usual, intrigued. "Another planet, Vinnie? Oh, I wish they would find it soon. Just think of it turning about somewhere out there in space."

But by May 13th, anyone who asked about Emily learned that she probably would not recover.

"Well?" asked Sue from one end of the Evergreens hallway.

"Unconscious since around 10 this morning," said Austin from the other end of the hallway. "Dr. Bigelow is there now."

"Have some dinner then."

"I'm not hungry."

"Some tea before you go back?"

They stood looking at each other in the hallway, tired, off their usual guard.

"This is the end, you know," said Austin.

"I know. I've been thinking about her all morning. Remembering when we were young…" Sue's lips trembled into what might have been mistaken for a crooked smile, until it turned upside down as she fought off tears, looking helplessly at Austin.

He stared at her, at a loss. Then, the picture of Emily's bedside note to Sue in his mind, he crossed the hall to her, and putting his hands on her arms, let her rest her head lightly on his shoulder.

"That you two loved each other so," he struggled. "It matters so much to me."

She didn't answer, and when her shoulders shook gently, they both knew her emotions included more than Emily. He put his arms around her with feeling for a moment, and then they stood back from each other.

"I want to help with her clothes and all that, when it's time," she said. "Vinnie will let me, won't she?"

"Yes."

"And I've been thinking—I'd like to prepare the write-up for the newspaper myself. No one in town knows her as we do—of course—and I want to do it."

Austin smiled—the first time in days. And nodded.

"I have lost a dear friend," wrote Mariette Jameson to her son Frank a few days after the funeral. She realized she did indeed consider Emily a dear friend, even though she had never met her in life. But she had heard about her ever since she and John had moved to Amherst, had listened to her footsteps on the second floor while she chatted with her sister below, and now, she had sat with Lavinia during the final moments, and had been invited, actually invited, to come see Emily laid out in death.

"Emily's seen you up close many times," said Lavinia, "if you count seeing your picture along with seeing you across the street. So it's only fair now that you should see her—she cared about you. Our Emily is so beautiful."

And she was. Even if she hadn't been dressed all in white and lying in a white casket, her face would have looked spiritual. Mrs. Jameson was surprised at how much Emily favored her brother Austin rather than Lavinia, although all of them had auburn hair. He asked them so kindly, Austin did, if John would be one of the honorary pallbearers, along with the likes of President Seelye and Dr. Hitchcock, if you please. It was strange to look face to face at Austin Dickinson and remember that afternoon she observed him carrying Mabel Todd's clothes across the lawn. He seemed like two people, or maybe three, in her mind: one official and polite, another gruff and withdrawn, and another one—well, lost.

The beauty of the service on May 19th, the sunny afternoon of the funeral, would have distracted anyone from jealousies and pettiness. In fact, she and John decided this was probably the most beautiful funeral service they had ever attended, and others agreed. How perfectly suited to Emily it was, with Mr. Jenkins, the minister she and Austin particularly loved, over from Pittsfield, and Colonel Higginson Mariette had heard about over from Cambridge to read a selection from Emily Brontë. Apparently Emily had corresponded with Mr. Higginson over the years—they discussed her poetry, according to Lavinia. Naturally Maggie Maher came and wept quietly into her handkerchief. Finally, the family's Irish hired hands received the casket from the honorary pallbearers and led a simple procession out the back door and across the fields to the cemetery.

After the graveside service, which Lavinia couldn't bear to attend, Sue Dickinson took Austin's arm and off they went, Austin looking dark and bent and sadder than sad. Mabel Todd took David's arm and set off after a suitable interval, looking at the ground through her veil. She looked terrible, as though she had lost a best friend. But Mariette Jameson knew for a fact that Mabel Todd had never seen Emily either, until she was dead. No doubt about it, the notes which had passed across to the Jameson household from Emily were little treasures, little jewels, and she would be sure to keep them over the years in her gilded letter box.

One last thing surprised her—Lavinia's comment in the house about those two heliotropes she had placed into Emily's hand. "To take to Judge Lord," Lavinia had said, or words to that effect. Saturday had not been the time to discuss it, but she would be sure to ask Lavinia about that comment later. Mariette Jameson dipped her pen into the ink and resumed her letter to Frank.

PART THREE

FURTHER IN SUMMER

1886-1889

CHAPTER 42

June 1886

IN JUNE, NOT LONG AFTER EMILY'S FUNERAL,
Mabel's mother and grandmother arrived in town for a nine day visit, tying
Mabel, querulous and restless, to the house. Austin, too, spent more time
at home than usual, sitting longer at the dinner table, smoking a cigar on
the piazza, Mattie and Sue in wicker chairs nearby, while Ned read the paper
on the steps. Austin discovered that Sue was collecting and arranging all
her old letters and notes from Emily. "For a scrapbook?" he had asked her in
the library.

"No, not a scrapbook. I'm not sure what. But they ought to be collected and
saved, don't you think? She always wrote so brilliantly."

"Well, yes. I think Mattie and Ned would want them saved too."

He doubted the letters and poems were valuable in any sense beyond their
family, but seeing Sue take the trouble to collect them, to sit reading them in
the late afternoon sun, affected him strangely. He wished Emily could know.
He was still amazed at how many poems she had written and saved upstairs in
her room—hundreds of them. Lavinia, who discovered them, said they could
hardly be counted. "Why didn't she tell us about all these, Austin?" she had
said from the top of the stairs, holding a sheaf of papers in her hand. "I can't
burn these. But I *am* going to burn some of the letters."

In the end, Austin had joined Lavinia in Emily's chilly room, sorting rapidly through the piles of letters. It was he who found the packet of letters to
Judge Lord, rough drafts with corrections and scratch-outs. A glance at them
was enough to convince him: "We'll keep these. May I take them to read
through later?"

"I suppose she wouldn't mind," Lavinia had said. "Read them and
burn them."

But he had read them carefully and then locked them in his office safe along with the letters from Mabel he had copied. Someday he would show them to Mabel too, but right now, he preferred to keep them to himself.

Though he longed for Mabel in every way, this period of enforced separation came as a needed rest. A rest not only from the sadness and tension of the latest death in the family, but also from the physical strain of trying to steal time to be with Mabel, from the awful logistics of when and where. She had to please her mother and dispel her suspicions now—that was her job. It was his job to bandage some of the gaping raw wounds between him and his family. It was also time for legal chores: Emily's will, of course, and any changes her death meant for their father's legacy to them. And then there was still the matter of the meadow, the land for the Dell house he and David and Mabel were designing so excitedly. They were all three aching to begin construction.

Austin owned the land. But he had long ago told David and Mabel that he would give them the land. It was the only way—David couldn't afford to buy it. After all, it wasn't so much, only eighty-six square rods. Besides, he wanted to do this for Mabel more than almost anything. It would be their house, in a way, planned for their private needs, including an outside stairway to the second story. She could not be Mrs. Dickinson in the eyes of the world, but in their own hearts, she was. He viewed her as his real wife, and she called him "her king," "her master."

But the land: Sue would have to know about the deed purporting to sell it to the Todds. He prayed that he could convince her to accept the plan.

One evening, Mrs. Loomis set her daughter's nerves particularly on edge. After a series of "Why don't you do this or try that" questions, Mabel was ready to join Phebe in the kitchen rather than stay a minute longer in the parlor. When they all retired early and David tried to take advantage of Austin's sustained absence by taking her in his arms, she pushed him rudely away. She and David had not made love for over a month and she was in no mood to start now.

In the Evergreens that same night, Austin had followed Sue upstairs wtih a mallet to loosen two windows, stuck shut since winter. Looking about him at the familiar room—the russet quilted bedspread from Sue's family, his own Bible by his side of the bed, the candlesticks his parents had given them— he felt himself in a strange emotional limbo. He had avoided this room often since Gilbert's death, yet tonight, he wanted to linger. He began to tap the windows gently with the mallet, and when they still would not budge, he inserted a lever and tapped some more around the edges, first high, then low, dropping finally to his knees. Instead of busying herself with folding blankets or clothes, Sue sat quietly nearby on the cedar chest. There was a silence for a while, except for his tapping and shaking of each window. Then she asked, "How is Maggie?"

He leaned back. "Still in shock, I think, but strong. After all, she's supporting Lavinia almost completely. I don't know what we'd do without her."

The chest creaked as Sue shifted her position. "Ned told me today that he just can't believe he won't get another note from Emily. I think he feels it more than Mattie does right now."

Austin resumed work on the windows, succeeding in loosening one at last and sliding it up and down. "Aha. Some fresh air." He went on to the other window. Behind him, he heard Sue's rustling skirts as she crossed to her bureau, then returned. In a moment, the other window was also free to move. When he turned around, he discovered that she had taken the pins from her hair and was brushing it as she always did before bed, even though she had made no move to change into night clothes. The image of Mabel came suddenly, vividly, before him, then the plans for the Dell house and all they entailed. Confused, he stood and faced Sue across the room.

She sat on the chest looking at him a moment, then arose and started to speak, but instead, went to him, and with one final hesitation, put her arms around him. He held her awkwardly, both of them unused to anything but recriminations or trivial speech between them. When neither spoke, he held her closer, discovering that his heart was beating faster the longer he stood with her. Yet the possibility of desiring her frightened him.

"Stay up here tonight," she said in a low voice. "Can you?"

There seemed to be no choice. "All right," he answered.

Having made the decision, they separated, more awkward than before.

"Use your summer night shirt," she said, "no need to go downstairs."

He felt glad that Mattie had returned to Miss Porter's in Connecticut, and that Ned had gone to bed early.

After they had both undressed, Sue behind the screen, he turned out the little oil lamp in a kind of daze, and let her take the lead, for he had no idea what either of them wanted or expected, and no idea what he was capable of. To his surprise, she lined her body quickly against the length of his, pressing closely into him, and when he responded by kissing her, she lay atop him, urging him on to sex, whether from genuine physical desire or a mechanical effort to regain his interest in her, he didn't know, but as before, his actions did not result from choice. She urged him to enter her although he found her dry, but he reached a climax quickly, to his surprise and mild disgust. They lay together, not speaking, until she rearranged her nightdress, indicating she did not want to be touched further. This brief time together had been different from their last couplings several years ago, in that it carried with it immense, unspoken emotions and tensions, but it would change nothing. Austin knew that, and he hoped Sue did too.

He kissed her cheek. "Shall we turn for sleep?" he asked.

"Yes. Sleep well." She turned over, arranging her pillows. "It's nice to have you here," she said shortly, in a muffled voice.

In reply, he put his hand on her shoulder, realizing as he did so that tomorrow would be the ideal time to discuss with her his reasons for making the transfer of land to the Todds—putting the best face on the matter, of course. She had always thought Edward Dickinson's meadow land superfluous—surely she wouldn't refuse now and risk blasting this rare mood of reconciliation. So he needn't feel guilty on Mabel's account after all—this unplanned encounter couldn't have been more propitious. He fell into a restful sleep.

Two mornings later, Mabel received Austin's note: "The land is yours."

CHAPTER 43

July 1886

THE DICKINSON FAMILY SAT AT THEIR USUAL
picnic table atop Mt. Sugarloaf and passed around the familiar blue cups and
plates to be filled with home grown sliced tomatoes, pickled beets, deviled
eggs, baked chicken and ham, bread, lemonade, and cake. Ned and Mattie
stole occasional glances at their father, who hadn't accompanied them on a
picnic or walk the whole summer.

"My blister hurts, Dolly," complained Mattie to her mother, whom she had
taken to calling 'Dolly.' She reached down to loosen her shoe.

"I'll make a little bandage for it after we eat," said Austin.

"No," said Mattie huffily, cutting a piece of tomato. "Never mind."

"Let him look at it later, Mattie, don't be silly," said Sue. "Here, Austin, keep
the biggest piece of chicken. You look so pale. I think the trip to Ashfield tired
you out, but we're all so glad you went with us."

"I can't wait to settle in at Ashfield," said Mattie. "It's just about the best
place in the Berkshires, and this will be the best vacation ever. Mrs. Monroe
says she and her friends are glad we're staying at the hotel. She says we set the
right atmosphere."

"And so we do, Mattie. You can look forward to meeting some suitable and
lively young men, I expect."

Mattie smiled and began to eat heartily.

"You'll find time to come see us there, won't you?" Sue asked Austin.

Mattie and Ned glanced at him to see his response. To their surprise, he
said, "Yes, I think I can manage a short visit."

Ned caught Mattie's eye for a second before they both looked away. Then
Mattie looked hard at her father with lowered head. It was easier to be hostile
to him when he paid no attention to them, to wound him with little cutting
remarks. But lately, now that Mabel Todd was away, he'd stayed home more

often, when he wasn't at the law office or the college, of course. More significant, he'd come on several family outings like this one, and taken them on quiet evening carriage rides. Mattie didn't know how to react—his presence didn't relieve her hostility toward him, only made it harder to express. Nothing could take away her shame and embarrassment at being the daughter of a man who had broken his marriage vows. Worse, being the daughter of a man who thoughtlessly let everyone in town know he'd broken his marriage vows. Anyone could see Mrs. Todd stepping smartly out Spring Street to meet his carriage along the road, headed in the same direction out of town. Anyone at the college could see her father stop at Mrs. Todd's Walker Hall studio several times a week, or walk the back way to whichever house the Todds were renting that year. And soon, the Todds would live right on some of the Dickinson meadow land, the land she and Gib had played on so happily when they were children. As far as Mattie was concerned, the land might as well be burnt. She had no interest in it anymore, now that her father and Mrs. Todd had infected it with their plans and their presence. Once, coming home from a late tea at her friend Mary's, Mattie had discovered her father and Mrs. Todd on the Evergreens piazza relaxing in the wicker chairs as though Dolly was in Africa, instead of Geneva for a few days. Mattie had already stepped on the lawn before she saw them, but she didn't approach or greet them. Instead, she strode past the well to the back of the house and went straight to her room.

The first dream came after that—the dream that the Evergreens was on fire. She had wakened in a sweat, her heart racing. But the second dream, although similar to the first, left her strangely calm and—how did she think of it?— hard, like two rocks chunked together. There had been no third dream so far, but during the day, she sometimes imagined their house either on fire or black in ruins. She would never tell Mother—Dolly. Or Ned.

"Has Vin shown you the box of Emily's poems yet?" Austin asked Sue.

"She lugged over the box, yes, but I didn't have time to look, really," said Sue. "I was in the middle of organizing the Sunday School schedule. But so many poems! Oh, she was quite put out with me when I wouldn't stop everything and look. So impatient, that Vinnie."

"Were there any letters?" asked Austin.

"I told you, I didn't look. But I doubt it. Vinnie burned several bundles."

"Yes," said Austin, "she did. And now she regrets it."

"Typical of her," returned Sue. "Anyway, Lavinia wants me to go over the poems and get them 'printed,' as she puts it. Just like that. She doesn't understand that it isn't that easy. You don't just send things in and see them back in print. There'd be months of work just sorting and transcribing them. Where would I find the time to do all that with a busy household to run? She doesn't know what she's asking."

"Well, that's partly true," said Austin. "Vin probably has an inflated idea of what the poems are worth, too. She's naive in the ways of the world."

"Well there, Austin, you said it, not I," said Sue, pouring lemonade into his glass. "And there's something else." Her voice softened. "It pains me to look at some of those lovely poems I know so well. It may take me a while. She'll probably ask you to look at the box next. Will you?"

"I'll take a look when I have time, but I think we ought not to raise her hopes—much as I respect Emily's efforts, of course. She wrote beautifully. But her poems aren't the kind of thing most people want to read. I think we should organize them for the family though, don't you?"

"I do," said Ned suddenly and clearly. "I've saved everything she ever sent me. I'll never throw a scrap away, it's all precious to me."

"That's nice, Neddie," said Sue. "Mopsy, do you have Aunt Emily's letters?"

"Yes," was Mattie's only answer. Then, "And do you have the poems I wrote, Mama?"

"Of course I do, Mopsy. What a question! Your poems are simply lovely. I'd never throw them away."

Some other picnickers waved, the Taylors of Leverett, and the conversation rested while the two families exchanged pleasantries. But Austin was thinking of Mabel, somewhere in the Midwest now. The Library Association meetings David had gone for had ended, and now they were touring, since Mabel loved travel for its own sake. But she had told him that she had come to enjoy it for another reason: it distracted her from the tensions of their double life in Amherst. Sometimes, she told him, she came home from seeing him in public, when they could only nod politely, and wept upstairs on her bed. The gossip, though it infuriated her, she could stand. But the tension and agony of seeing him in the street or at social engagements and passing him by without a word, nearly killed her. Still, there was nothing they could do but live for the hours when they escaped to privacy.

Those moments crept closer and closer, as Sue, Ned, and Mattie readied themselves for a vacation in Ashfield—the long-awaited Berkshire retreat—leaving "the coast clear," as Austin and Mabel put it, for their love to range a little inside its prison walls. Austin planned to sit with Mabel on his own piazza in the late evening—even to take her inside and to cherish the sight of her beloved face in the lamp light of his own parlor, as though she were his wife in the eyes of the world.

Imagining Mabel sitting in his parlor, he with his arms around her, gave him such joy that when Sue said, "Austin, shall we take a ride to Leverett in a few days to visit the Taylors?" he smiled and said, "Certainly, yes."

CHAPTER 44

August 1886

"OH, OH," MOANED MABEL GENTLY, DROPPING the pincushion quickly on the Evergreens parlor rug. She squeezed her finger and sucked the blood. Austin, sitting close to her on the sofa, put his arm around her and smiled into her eyes mischievously.

"Why do you look at me that way?" she asked, smiling and half frowning at the same time. "The needle went in deep."

"I'm sorry," he said, "but the noise you made reminded me of other times you make that noise."

She laughed. "Oh that, yes," and kissed him quickly.

Still in a mischievous mood, Austin said, "This will teach you not to use Sue's needles. They're extra sharp."

Mabel laughed again. Then putting her embroidery down and leaning against him, she said, "My darling, how perfect these days have been. If we could only be like this always—open and free together this way. I wish they weren't coming back from Ashfield so soon."

"It can't be helped," said Austin. "But we have this to remember, don't we?"

"I know, and I will. Did you say they will arrive Thursday?"

"Yes, I think so."

"When? If it's evening, at least we'll have something left of Thursday."

"Well," said Austin, shifting his arm from around her shoulders, "I promised I'd go over a day earlier to help them manage things."

She sat looking straight ahead, silently. Then, "No, you didn't!" she said, looking straight at him. "You don't mean to tell me you're going to Ashfield yet a third time? After two unnecessary visits, a third? Tell me you don't mean it!"

"Well, they do need someone to help. Ned isn't very strong these days."

"But Austin," said Mabel, her voice rising, "I still can't believe it. Why should you cater to her? Why do you let her make you do things?"

They had moved away from each other on the sofa. His voice was low. "But she didn't make me do it, it really seemed best."

"Why do you call them 'your encumbrances' then, yet jump up whenever they need something?"

"Mabel, we know how things are, and we have to accept them." There was silence a moment. Then he added, in a low voice, "I'm not trying to be quarrelsome, but *you* call them 'my encumbrances'..."

"Austin!" Mabel broke in. "I won't argue. But don't go, please don't go. She's trying to control you, but we belong to each other now. Why tease her by doing what she asks? Besides, we have so little time together."

"It's as hard for me as it is for you; I'm torn two ways. Don't question this."

"I'll try not to, but right now it's late and I think I should go home."

The silence between them rang ominous now as she arose, and he could only follow, gathering her cloak and lowering the lamp, but in slow motion. That they had nothing else to say seemed grossly unnatural. They had never disagreed before, never even had a cross word before, not in four years of loving each other. The swiftness of the disagreement rendered them suddenly helpless in its rush and power.

But neither of them said a word, and there was nothing to do but walk silently to the piazza door. There, Austin paused. "All right, I won't go," he said. "I'm not happy about it, but I'd rather not see you so upset." He opened the door and repeated, "I won't go, but you've made a mistake in this." With a nightmarish sense of unreality, he gestured for her to step out so he could close the door behind them.

They walked across the lawn and out toward the street in an eerie silence they had never known between them. Neither had spoken by the time they reached Lincoln house, where a light showed that David had returned and was already upstairs.

At the door, Mabel turned and brushed Austin's cheek lightly with her lips, barely touching him, then went swiftly inside. He returned home with only one backward glance in time to see her light come on in the hallway and then disappear as she climbed the stairs. He remembered the night months ago when he had taken refuge in Mrs. Stearns's parlor. He wished he could go there again, but of course he could not, not at this hour. He would have to try to sleep, even though he didn't see how he could, thinking not only of this disagreement but also of the telegram he would have to send Sue explaining why he would not come help them travel home after all. He would be caught between two angers now. Back at his own porch, he longed for Emily's calming presence. It struck him that his life would never again be a placid one—if indeed it ever had been. He could expect turbulence and pain from now on to balance the moments of joy that made everything worth while. A phrase from one of his letters to Mabel struck him now: "Love has may ways." This quarrel belonged to some of those many ways. He stood and looked out at the night, a growing ache in his chest, then closed the door and went to bed.

Mabel's letter reached Austin the next morning at his office, carried there by Lavinia, who said, as she handed it to him, glancing at his assistant, Mr. Cooper, "Important. Couldn't wait, she said."

"Cooper, finish up with Mrs. Vineland's insurance claims, and I'll go over them with you in a few minutes. Vin, where are you headed?"

"Over to Cutler's market."

"I'll walk with you." He accompanied her to the sidewalk, where he asked her immediately, "Did she say anything?"

"Say anything? No. She just told me to bring you the note and that it was important."

"Well Vin, I'm going to stroll over to the meadow for a while. Take a break."

"Of course, go ahead and read your note. That's what you're going to do, isn't it?" She waved her hand at him, dismissing him. "Goodbye."

As soon as Austin reached his own land, he opened Mabel's note, walking toward the tract he had recently deeded over to the Todds for the new house. Reading only a few sentences caused him to look skyward, a sigh of release escaping his chest as the sweet thoughts came tumbling in: "She's sorry and she loves me. She loves me and she defers to me. And I love her more than ever."

There was more. She was miserable, penitent, full of a sense of failure. She had not, she said, lived up to his "nobility." He read it all, then leaned against an apple tree and read it all again, after which he stood quietly for a while. He felt as if he were falling in love all over again. When they sat alone together, how he would tell her what he felt! How, if anyone had bestowed nobility or grandeur or a sense of religion, it had been her. How he saw the reason for living through her intensity, and God through her sweet soul. Emily might have rejoiced with him today.

CHAPTER 45

December 1886

AFTER ALL HER TROUBLE, *THE CENTURY* DID not publish the poem Sue Dickinson sent them, one of Emily's poems about the wind. It had been a bother to type-write the poem and get it off, but Sue had done so, with considerable disruption to her busy schedule. Lavinia had hounded her until she had used Austin's machine and made nearly a day of it. Well, Lavinia would have be be satisfied now. Anyone in his right mind could see just by glancing at the box full of poems that even the *thought* of copying all of them was hopeless. Even if she felt up to it, Sue doubted she could handle the project—but she decidedly did *not* feel up to it, with grief added to grief.

She closed her writing desk and gathered some letters together for mailing. Sifting from time to time through the poems Lavinia had brought had reminded her of the old Emily and the girlhood confidences they used to exchange—the talks they had about marriage and religion, Amherst and Austin, death and poetry. She had recognized many of the poems of course. But that Emily had managed to write so many more astounded her. Taking care of her mother had been a full-time occupation for Emily, yet the poems poured forth in all handwritings, decade after decade, presumably. Too bad public sentiment probably wasn't ready for the creatively irregular stanzas and peculiar rhymes she and Emily had often discussed, along with the idiosyncratic themes. Emily questioned religious faith too closely, in Sue's view. Religion was a subject Sue herself treated with proper respect, and had brought up her children to do the same. But still, overlooking all that, the poems impressed her, and she had read quite a few to her friends over afternoon tea.

But no, Lavinia's idea that all of the poems should be read, recopied, and sent somewhere for publication, was naive and downright irritating, considering that she expected Sue to do it, as though she had nothing else to do. In this one thing, Austin agreed with her.

She heard a thud at the back door. In a minute, Austin appeared.

"Must you slam that door so hard?" she said when he appeared in the doorway. "I didn't expect you home for noon dinner—Mary's off today you know."

"I know. I just came to pick up the letters I forgot and to check on the construction," said Austin, walking toward the library.

"It's a never-ceasing wonder to me that you get any other work done, what with all the time you've put in on that house. *Must* everything be done in such a rush?" She followed him part way toward the library. "Well?"

Austin returned from the library with a few letters in his hand. "They have to vacate Lincoln house in January. In fact, they will have to move in even if the new house isn't finished."

Sue sniffed. "It's their problem. Why must we all upset our schedules?"

"We don't all have to upset our schedules. I don't see how it affects you."

"What affects you affects me," Sue returned hotly, "and if you go running off in all directions, the household suffers."

"But would you like to be told you have to move to an unfinished house in the middle of winter?" said Austin. "It looks as if it will come to that."

"How dare you ask me to consider *them*? Her? When I have to cross the street to avoid her, or sit embarrassed at sewing club and supper club and half the other places I go to try to enjoy myself? No, I will *not* consider them."

"Please," said Austin, wincing, and was gone.

He found David in front of the Dell, as they had all three decided to call it, looking up at the red brick chimney. They stood outside together for a few moments in the cold air, their breath clouds appearing and disappearing as they talked about the brick work and the shingles. The house rose before them, utopian dream of their mutual trust, Mabel, David, and Austin. Their painstaking, unflinching creation.

David smiled at Austin. "I think you'll be pleased with the crown molding in the dining room. It's all in place now, ready for painting. Did you see it?"

Stepping onto the muddy ramps, they entered the house and went to inspect the dining room walls and ceilings, picking their way around sawhorses and wood ends. "She'll paint her friezes around this room?" asked Austin.

"In the parlors and the entrance hall. She wants to start as soon as we move. But do you think we can move this month with so much left to be finished?"

Austin thought for a minute. "Probably, if we can finish off the kitchen—and I think we can—and the bedroom. The plumbing and heating are under control."

"But there's not even a chance we'll progress with the second floor rooms," countered David. "I don't see how it's possible. The partitions aren't up and we'd freeze even if they were."

"But the attic studio is virtually finished, and that other room up there too," said Austin, walking over to inspect a window sill. "Could you hold out on the attic floor until the second floor rooms are finished?"

"It's an idea," said David. "Phebe and Mabel would have to run up and down stairs a lot, but it might work. Come to think of it"—he winked without smiling—"are you prepared to run up and down stairs yourself, and in the dark too?"

Austin did not answer, but soberly continued his inspection of the dining room walls, conscious that David was looking at him. Getting no reply, David finally said, "Ha!" and stepped noisily into the hallway. He looked at the stairs, which lacked banisters, and began walking up. Austin continued his inspection of the dining room and one parlor, and then followed David. At the landing, he met David emerging from what was to be Millicent's room. "I like the way the trees shade the outside stairs to the second floor," Austin told him.

"Handy, too, wouldn't you say? We don't need prying eyes," answered David. "By the way, Mabel says Mrs. Emerson snubbed her royally yesterday. Those things hurt her more than she likes to admit. But what can we do about it?"

"Keep a stiff upper lip, that's all I can counsel," said Austin. "We're committed to each other, aren't we? We support each other?"

"Of course."

"Then we put up with small minds as graciously as possible. Let's not even think about it. Look at this beautiful house! Our retreat, our haven. It may be a cold winter, but here we can be together in peace. Nothing else matters."

Austin ascended the last flight of stairs to the top floor. Here eventually would be his and Mabel's private room, on the same floor as Mabel's studio. He longed for it to be finished.

David followed him and stood looking out over the trees. "Your rooftop seems so near," he remarked.

"It is near," said Austin shortly. He pulled his scarf closer around him as the wind swept through a window. "Millicent is such a funny child," he remarked after a moment.

"Oh?" said David. "Well, I guess she is. She's very afraid of you, I know that."

"Afraid of me?"

"She won't even stay on the walk in front of your house. She crosses the street. Madame Stearns couldn't get her to deliver a parcel to the Homestead without continued coaxing. When Mabel asked her about it, Millie finally told her that she was afraid to walk too close to your house. Silly girl. She should be getting over these things by her first year in school."

"If you go to Japan, she'll stay in Washington with her grandparents?"

"Yes. But I hope there's no doubt about my going—*our* going—even though Mabel says she can't decide what she's going to do."

Austin leaned on a window sill. "You are so much more traveled than I'll ever be. 'Once in Amherst, always in Amherst.' That pretty much describes me and my sisters. Boston is about the end of our range."

"But Mabel says you're thinking of going west in the fall with John Sanford. That so?" said David glancing over at Austin.

"Possibly. John is keen on it, anyway. If we go, we'd come back by way of the South. Louisiana, Alabama."

David whistled. "Back woods country, eh? Crocodiles, snakes, and mosquitoes, who knows what! I think I prefer Japan, from some of the stories I hear about the South."

Austin rubbed his hands together and pulled his gloves back on. "I don't think they have crocodiles in Alabama or Louisiana. Alligators maybe."

"What's the difference?" said David puffing the chilly damp air through his lips. "Anyway, I'm cold. Let's check out the fireplaces and get back to the College. I've got a class in thirty minutes."

They went down the outside stairs. "What's all this I hear about publishing Emily's poetry?" asked David on the way down.

"Publishing Emily's poetry?" asked Austin. "I don't hear much about it. Who's been talking to you?"

"Lavinia."

"Oh, Vinnie. She does have it on her mind. I hate to think about it, because it means just one more quarrel between her and Sue. Sue has the poems at our house right now."

"Have you read the poems?" asked David.

"You don't realize how many there are. Hundreds. I don't think anyone could read them all." Austin reached the front door first and they entered the front parlor to examine the fireplace. Austin stood inside the brick work and peered up into the darkness.

"Hastings does a good job, doesn't he?" said David.

"Yes he does."

"But back to Lavinia—she's trying to get Mabel to work over Emily's poems. I wish she'd lay off, if you don't mind my saying so. Mabel's planning to do a lot of writing for me this year. I don't want her distracted by other projects."

"Well, Vinnie might have mentioned having Mabel look at the poems," said Austin, "but I don't think she's very serious. She just wants them back from Sue, that's my impression. I wouldn't worry about it. Look, this fireplace is as well done as the other one in the dining room, even down to the color of the bricks."

"I can't wait to see a fire in it," said David. "But I must go to class now."

"I'll walk up with you," said Austin. Both men, stepping onto the porch and then across the lawn, looked back with obvious pride and pleasure at the house behind them before turning toward Amherst College and an afternoon of work.

CHAPTER 46

January 1887

MARY STEARNS NEARLY SLIPPED ON THE ICE patches as she made her way up the outside stairs of Mabel's new home, the Dell. At the top finally, holding on for dear life, she transferred the bag she carried to her other hand and knocked at the door. When there was no answer, she peered into the dim hallway and knocked again. But Mabel, wearing a painting smock, was already emerging from her studio a floor above, brushing curls back from her forehead with the back of her hand and waving with a paint brush in the other hand. Millicent, aged seven, also wearing a painting smock, followed her mother.

"Mary Stearns, how lovely to see you, do come in," said Mabel opening the door. "At first I wasn't sure if I heard a knock or not, what with the carpenters' racket below and this cold I have. My ears have been full for two days!"

"I saw your David yesterday before he left for Northampton, and he told me you'd both had colds," said Mary Stearns, "so I thought I ought to drop by. And how are you, Miss Millicent? Quite well, I trust?"

"Good afternoon, Madame Stearns," said Millicent, curtseying.

"Do you mind perching in the studio?" asked Mabel. "The mess is far worse than I ever imagined, but the studio is really fairly comfortable." They both jumped as the carpenters below dropped a piece of planking.

"My dear, how do you ever put up with it?" asked Mary.

"With difficulty, I assure you," said Mabel. "Please sit in the new rocking chair we had delivered from Boston."

Mary Stearns kept her coat on. "I brought you some beef barley soup," she said. "It's hearty and rich, just what you and David need these days to keep up your strength." She patted the bag beside her.

"Oh, lovely! You always know just what people need."

"It's nothing. Now, do tell me how things are going," said Mary.

"Well," said Mabel, "we have had to put up with a lot, but we know how special it's all going to be soon, and having a hand in the decoration has been fun for me. I'm painting oil friezes on the parlor wall right now. It may take me ages, but I think I can do the entrance hall as well. Would you like to see them?"

"Yes indeed."

But remember though, it's a bit dangerous down there. Of course, the stairs are in place, but they aren't finished off, and the banisters aren't all in place yet. So walk carefully, promise? Millicent, you stay here by the fire."

They descended slowly, Mabel pointing out changes along the way. "The mantels," she said, gesturing when they reached the first floor. "We picked them out in Boston. I'm so pleased with them."

"He has good taste too, like yours," said Mary.

"Well," said Mabel, "we disagreed at first. He thought something plainer might suit better, but he changed his mind."

"It's good that David is a compromising person," said Mary.

"Oh yes, he's willing to defer to Austin's taste," answered Mabel.

Mary Stearns looked puzzled, while Mabel went on. "But Austin can't imagine now why he thought something so plain would suit a Queen Anne style house." She stopped, realizing what she had inadvertently revealed about Austin's role in decision-making about the new house, and whom Mary Stearns had assumed they were discussing. There was a pause, during which neither woman chose to comment on the misunderstanding.

Mabel waved to a painter working on the library shelves, cautioned her guest to gather her skirts above the floor, and they advanced to the parlor.

"There!" said Mabel simply, gesturing.

An elegant floral frieze wound its way along one full side of the parlor wall, the end corner still gleaming wet with paint. Mary stood amazed.

"You did all this in just the past few weeks? I can't believe it. How lovely and original!. You really are clever!" As Mabel stood back proudly, Mary Stearns examined the frieze with careful attention to detail.

"After the parlor," said Mabel, "there's the entrance hall to go. But oh, won't it be worth it? If only I had more uninterrupted time to work on this project. It seems I have more to do every week. There's Millicent, of course, and the work I do to help David—writing up articles and things like that—and piano lessons, art lessons, choir practice—a regular whirl of activity. Some projects never seem to get finished. Lavinia wanted me to copy some of Emily Dickinson's poems, and I *did* copy a few, but that task turns out to be impossible. I can't do everything. And did you know about the expedition to Japan?"

"Austin mentioned it briefly some time ago. David's eclipse expedition?"

"Yes, in June," said Mabel. Then, "Watch out for that bucket! Your skirt will get dirty. Let's go back upstairs and I'll tell you about it."

Upstairs, Millicent ran out to the hallway when she heard them approaching. "Can I use a new blue on my canvass, Mama?" she asked.

"If it's a blue I've already mixed," said Mabel going to her palette. "Yes, there's some of this cobalt left." She reached for Millicent's palette, placing a glob of paint there. Mary Stearns had seated herself and was gazing about the room with its piles of books, papers, newspapers, and artwork.

"Are you going with David to Japan for the solar eclipse?" she asked.

"I think so," said Mabel.

"Just imagine, seeing Japan! It's been closed to the West for so long. And what about you, Miss Millie? Are you going?"

"No, M'am, I always stay with my grandmother and my great-grandmother when my mother and father travel. That's in Washington, D.C. I have a room there with violets on the wallpaper."

"Good," said Mary Stearns. "Your grandparents will take good care of you."

"But my plans aren't definite," broke in Mabel. "I may go, but I'm not sure. It could be such a long and tiring trip, and there's so much to do here. I might be quite exhausted by June, and ready to enjoy the house."

"I see your point," returned Mary, "and I know you will make the right decision. Keep in mind though that this trip won't be like any other. An eclipse in Japan! Think of gardens, bonsai trees, that oriental courtliness, and everything being so entirely new and different. And there won't be the poverty and dirt of India which I had to put up with when my husband and I lived there."

"You're probably right, and I'll probably go. David needs me, I know. But I have to be sure before I give him a definite answer."

"Is he staying over in Northampton tonight?"

"Yes, two nights, in fact, to confer on some problems with the Smith observatory."

"Come to supper tonight with us, then, why don't you? I'd love your company, and so would the girls. You'd like to come too, wouldn't you, Millicent? Do you like apple dumplings?"

"Sometimes," said Millicent, to which Mabel said, "You know you like apple dumplings."

Mary Stearns laughed. "You'll come then? Around five or five-thirty?"

"We'd love to," said Mabel.

"By the way, did David ever get a sundial?"

"A sundial?" returned Mabel, puzzled.

"Yes. He came by the garden one afternoon a week ago—things have never looked the same since someone took the rocks around the sundial—and asked if I was willing to part with it. I'm not, but I'm sure he can easily find one somewhere."

"He didn't mention it to me," said Mabel, "but whether he wants it for our new house or the college, I can't say. I hope you didn't mind that he asked for yours! My husband is quite unpredictable."

"No, his request didn't bother me. I just wondered if you were wanting one for your new garden, that's all. Well, until supper time then."

"Thanks for the soup and your company. I wish I had more friends like you, Mary."

"How dear of you to say so, and now, I'm off. Goodbye Millicent."

Mabel stood by the door for a few moments watching Mary's departure. Then there were only the icicles to watch dripping from the nearby trees, and finally the familiar roofs, including Austin's over the meadow and across the street.

At supper that evening, Sue Dickinson asked Austin to return the picture book of India she had borrowed from Mary Stearns for her Sunday School class. Austin finished his rice pudding and pushed back his chair.

"Where is it?"

"In the front parlor, on the round table."

Austin set out into the cold icy streets with slow steps, but finding Mabel seated before the fire with Mary Stearns at The Convent transfigured his day in a split second and revived his tired heart like a May morning. Warmth flashed between them and included the smiling Mary, who rose to hold out her hands to Austin, while Mabel, in her fawn dress and sage shawl, had only to look at him to convey her feelings.

"Ah, the book I lent Susan," said Mary, while Austin tried to focus his attention on his hostess. "Did her Sunday school class enjoy it?"

"I am sure they did," said Austin. "And she thanks you."

"You'll sit down for a few minutes and have something warm to drink?"

"I'll just sit and chat for a while, if I may." Seeing no chair near Mabel, he sat across the room from her with his back to the closed dining room doors.

"Mabel and Millicent have taken supper with us, and the younger girls are showing her their dolls before she has to return. I think Millie had a good time, don't you, Mabel?"

"Oh yes, and she discovered she liked apple dumplings after all. She can be quite a finicky eater, or have you already discovered that here?"

"She's rarely finicky. A dear little girl," said Mary Stearns. "I think it's her shyness I'd like to see changed. Or maybe I should say her fears. She seems to fear so much, don't you find?"

"What has she seemed afraid of, in particular?" asked Mabel.

"Lots of things. Let's see...The fire engine bells, for one. And the cats. And getting sick. Of course, many children fear all those, but I find her overly concerned that you might leave her, somehow. She's mentioned that fear several times."

"She is a rather clinging child," began Mabel, but stopped talking when the dining room doors opened a crack and one of the older girls entered with Millicent, who held a china doll dressed in velveteen and advanced toward Mabel, not looking at anyone else until she reached her mother.

"See this doll, Mama?" said Millicent, holding it out. "Her name is Amanda and she has teeth, look. And see her eyes?" Mabel leaned forward to see, admiring the doll, and reached for it, but Millicent would not release it.

At that moment, Austin stood to reposition one chair leg that had slipped from the rug. Millicent turned at the noise. Seeing him, she put the doll in Mabel's lap and stood completely behind her mother's chair in the corner, looking down at her buttoned shoes.

"Millicent, what are you doing?" asked Mary Stearns, while annoyance showed in Mabel's eyes.

"Come here," said Mabel. "Come take care of Amanda. Why do you give her to me?"

Millicent didn't answer, but scuffed her feet. "Millicent?" persisted Mabel.

"You take care of the baby," was all Millicent could be heard to say at last. With a sigh and a glance at Austin, who had sat down quietly, Mabel laid the doll aside and said, "We must go home, Mary. I need my rest to fight off this cold. Thank you for a lovely supper, and we'll talk more about those poems." She looked at Austin. "Emily's poems, I mean."

"We loved having you," said Mary. "Austin, may I ask you to escort Mrs.

Todd home?" After helping Mabel wrap Millicent's warm cloak and hat around her, she stepped back and observed how quickly Austin saw Mabel to the door, and how Mabel smiled under her eyes at him showing those dimples of hers. At the door as they stepped out, Mary added, "I am glad you arrived when you did, Austin. I didn't want to send Mabel off alone." With that, she closed the door softly behind them.

CHAPTER 47

Winter 1887

~

ARY STEARNS WOULD HAVE BEEN SURprised had she known that scarcely two hours later, Mabel lay in the dark alone crying, her journal beside her. Parting from Austin that night tore her with special cruelty: with David away, they found themselves so close to a different sort of freedom, yet so far. Austin could not spend the evening with her, let alone the night. Thus when they might have lain together and guarded each other's sleep, heard each other's descent into repose, they had instead to lie apart, frigid in their frustrations. How could anything ever change? Except for those rare, special nights at the Parker House Hotel in Boston, and a few occasions when both Sue and David were away at the same time, there remained no freedom to anticipate, no joy in the simple openness of daily trivial closeness that couples sanctified by society enjoy. When she thought for the hundredth time that she couldn't even smile and touch Austin's hand at any Amherst gathering—any tea, any lecture, any party—even had to act as though she barely knew him—her tears flowed afresh down her cheeks to her chin and the top of her nightgown. Her right ear had begun to ache and she suspected she had a fever. For the first time, it occurred to her to wonder seriously whether falling in love with Austin had blighted her life. And now this trip to Japan in June would take away their summer, just when life in the Dell would at last be comfortable. Should she go with David to Japan? Being utterly apart from Austin would be torture, as she had learned from her trip to Europe, although she *had* enjoyed it in the end, there was no denying. On the other hand, remaining in Amherst, near Austin but unable to love him freely, would be worse torture. Yet with David away for so long, she and Austin could seize some free moments, for surely, Sue would vacation in the summer as she always did with Ned and Mattie. But *would* she this year, if she knew Mabel were alone without David?

And there remained the question of gossip, ever growing malicious talk and ugly snubs which she bore the brunt of more than Austin. Some women haughtily turned their heads when Mabel entered a room or passed them on the street, but not before giving her cold, penetrating glances to make her feel the full force of the snub. Going to Japan would take her away from all that. Mabel held her aching ear. She would go then. She would go, even though it meant endless terrible weeks without Austin and his love-giving, strong body. The tears flowed again, but this time, with more of a calm resignation, and after a last reach for her handkerchief, she fell asleep.

The winter wore on. The Dell lay cold and damp except for the third floor which Mabel and David struggled to make comfortable despite the clutter and their colds and sore throats. In addition, mid-winter marked the beginning of David's suffering from what turned out to be kidney stones, a condition which confined him to his bed during the weeks he wished to be most active. For a while, the trip to Japan seemed in jeopardy, and Mabel began to think she ought not to go anyway. It would be simpler to stay at home, and each tiny hint of the spring to come, each gust of moist aromatic air, reinforced her feeling. But David began to recover just in time to organize the expedition, and in May, when blossoms hung on the Common trees, he took the morning train to Washington for ten days to make the final plans.

"Don't tell me you can't make up your mind," were his parting words. "I can't take 'no' for an answer." Then in a sudden pleading change of voice, "Please?"

The train hadn't been gone an hour before Austin slipped into the Dell by the outside stairs and pushed open the door without knocking to embrace Mabel in the hallway where she ran to meet him, almost whimpering with joy. They walked to the bedroom with their arms still around each other and fell down together, holding each other close the length of their bodies.

"Ten days," Austin murmured.

"Ten days," Mabel repeated, her voice muffled against his shoulder. "I wish you would tie me to you so I could never leave."

Austin tightened his arms around her, but in a moment, she moved and sat up. "I can't decide, I can't decide!" she exclaimed in exasperation, holding her face in her hands. "I wish the whole idea of Japan had never come up! I wish there were no such thing as eclipses! Oh, darling!" She half laughed and cried at her own predicament. "And you're trying so hard not to sway my mind, aren't you?" she added, turning and looking down at him.

He gazed solemnly back at her, reaching up to stroke her neck with the back of his fingers. "I adore you," was all he would say. But he looked worn out.

"You look so tired. Is she asking you to supervise papering another room? Not another room right after your study! She's punishing you for the Dell."

Austin looked tiredly up at her. "Let's not talk about it now."

"I'm sorry I brought it up again," said Mabel. "We'll just enjoy our time together. By the way, Vinnie was here yesterday still up in arms over the party your Power gave on the 15th."

"You're calling Sue my 'Power'?" said Austin. "Well, I wish she had never done it, held a party on the anniversary of Emily's death. I told her it was unsuitable, but she went ahead and made plans before I could say anything more."

"Don't you think she *enjoys* irritating poor Vinnie?" asked Mabel.

"Of course she does. Oh, the very thought of Sue's parties and of Sue's quarrels gives me a headache," he said, closing his eyes.

"Turn over," said Mabel. "You must relax." She helped him ease his arms from his jacket, opened his collar, and when he lay on his stomach, began to loosen his shoes and socks, then her own shoes. When her feet were free, she quickly unbuttoned her skirt and petticoat and straddled his hips so as to massage his shoulders and back with long heavy touches. He groaned softly. "You like it?" she asked, leaning down to nip his ear gently. For answer, he groaned again. They were silent then, as she continued to knead and loosen his muscles, and when she finished that, she massaged his neck, his head, and his chin, running her hand underneath his face, and finally, running her fingers around the crevices of each ear. When she finished and moved by his side, he continued to breathe slowly and evenly, and in a moment, she could tell he had fallen asleep. Smiling at him tenderly, she pulled the quilt over them both, curled up by his side, and lay quietly until little dreams began to weave their way into her consciousness so that she knew she too was falling asleep. They slept on together, in happy enjoyment of this rare chance to be together at home in broad daylight and in a soft bed.

Outside around them, the daily life of Amherst village went on. Sue Dickinson had gone to Springfield to buy dress material, but Mary, her servant, beat the rugs in back of the house. Ned worked at his part time job at the college library. Lavinia sat at the kitchen table talking to herself about Sue's refusal to help with Emily's poems, and trying to figure, how to get the box of poems back into her own possession. Mrs. Jameson across the street sat at her desk writing to her son, Frank. Mary Stearns listened to her girls recite their Latin lessons in her school, The Convent. David Todd's mathematics students sat together preparing for a test which another professor would proctor in his absence. And David Todd himself stared out of the train window with unseeing eyes, preoccupied with his plans for recording by photoheliograph a larger-scale impression of the solar corona at totality than had ever before been seen.

CHAPTER 48

Winter 1887

"NOT ANOTHER NOTE," SAID SUE DICKINSON, taking the scrap of paper from Ned one afternoon. "How long has this been lying around?"

"Since yesterday evening. I thought you had seen it."

Sue sighed and unfolded the paper, squinting at it for a moment. Then in exasperation, she tossed the paper onto a table. "Why doesn't Lavinia ever wear her glasses when she writes? I can't read a word of that miserable scrawl."

Ned retrieved the note. "I'll translate. 'Dear Sue,'" he read, stumbling from time to time with the ill-formed letters. "'As I told you, I have decided to collect the box of poems and keep them in my possession. I don't know what their future is, but I want them now. So I'll send Maggie over tomorrow morning for them, Lavinia. P.S. You put everything back, didn't you? P.P.S. I might come over myself.'"

Ned looked up. "Well, that's clear enough, once you decipher it. She or Maggie will probably be along soon."

"Well, I'll be glad to get them out of the way, I suppose. I don't have time to read them now. Still, I don't see why she can't leave them with me. Doesn't she trust me? Go tell Stephen to get the carriage ready, would you Neddie? I have calls to make."

Ned obediently left by the back door, tripping over some loose bricks on his way to the barn. His balance hadn't been good lately. He'd tell Stephen to fix them. Faithful Stephen spent hours taking care of their fine carriage, polishing the brass fixtures, cleaning mud off the wheels, and buffing the leather seats. The Dickinson carriage was without a doubt the finest in town, and the whole family took great pride in it and in the fact that people turned their heads to stare when they rode by. Mrs. Todd envied them their carriage; he would have known that even if he hadn't heard her husband tell Austin so, laughing heartily as he spoke. Mr. Todd would never own such a carriage, but he did not care.

Before he could get to Stephen in the barn, he heard his Aunt Lavinia's voice and looked up to see her coming along the path between their houses with the ungainly stomp and stride she had developed over the last few years. One end of a yellow shawl beneath her wool cloak dragged on the ground, and a pine cone had attached itself to the tassles. Pieces of her coarse hair had come undone from the pins, and her nose was red. "Give me your handkerchief, Neddie," she called, and reached out her hand as she came closer.

Ned went to meet her with his handkerchief, which she took wordlessly and used immediately to mop her nose, crumpling it in her fist afterwards.

"Did you come for Aunt Emily's poem box?"

"Yes, Neddie. I can't rest until I have it. I hope it's ready." Lavinia stopped to mop her nose again and to eye her nephew critically. "Well?"

"Well what?" asked Ned.

"Do you think it's ready for me?"

"Yes, I'm sure it is."

"Sweet boy, you look pale. Have you not shaken that cold yet?"

"Not entirely, Aunt Vinnie. I've not been very strong lately."

They entered by the same door Ned had recently used, and so came onto Sue from behind as she walked through the back hallway.

"Lavinia!" said Sue. "How did you get here? I'm just going out."

"Well," said Lavinia, standing back a few feet, "I just came to get that box of poems. Ned brought my note over, didn't he?"

"I don't know, I forgot about it," said Sue, adjusting her hair. "I'm in the middle of something right now, couldn't you let me know more exactly when you're about to rush over here? It would be easier on all of us."

"Well, I can't always plan the exact minute." But seeing Sue's imperious mood, she said, "I'm sorry if I caught you in the middle of something, but just give me that box and I'll run along."

But Sue had turned to the front hallway to collect her cloak and gloves. "Is Stephen ready?" she asked Ned.

"I doubt it, Mother, I didn't even get to him yet. Why don't you give Aunt Vinnie the box now? I'll go tell Stephen we're almost ready."

Sue sighed. "Lavinia, I will have to ask you to come back another time. I don't know where the poems are right now, and I'm not about to start looking now."

But Ned had started quietly for the parlor where he could clearly see the box by Sue's chair. "Here they are, Mother, let me just give them to her."

"Oh, take them, then, take them, for goodness' sake," said Sue. "I don't have time for them. If I stopped everything and tried to read them all, I'd disappoint a great many people in town who depend on me."

When Lavinia began to drag the box to the back door, Sue did not return her "goodbye," nor did Lavinia linger long enough to hear it even if it had been uttered. She tried clumsily to maneuver the box out the door, and then once outside, let Ned carry one corner while she carried the other. Together they hobbled back to the Homestead, she a crone-like figure and both of them panting. Struggling into the warm kitchen, they dropped the box triumphantly.

"Now go, Neddie, go!" said Lavinia, kneeling by box. "I want to be alone." Thus no one was there to see it, but the smile that swept over her face crinkled her eyes and dimpled her cheeks so that for a second, she looked almost young. It was time to put her next plan into action: to beg, absolutely beg, Mabel Todd's help.

Emily's poems had come home.

CHAPTER 49

August 20, 1887

∼

THE SUN HAD SET, A FIERY ORANGE, ON ECLIPSE day in Japan. In his tent on the castle ruins outside Shirakawa, David Todd rolled over toward Mabel and groaned in his sleep. His hands fumbled, still in slumber, for tripod screws; his thumb and forefingers tightened moving metal parts; his eye squinted into lens apertures floating before him. Instruments to measure the eclipse seemed to crowd around him, and he groaned again. His fingers quieted their spasmodic movements for a few minutes and his mind slipped into a merciful blankness. But then, dreaming again, he saw that everyone stood watching the sky—a sky that resembled a negative photographic plate so that the faces showed dark against a luridly light sky. Mr. and Mrs. Hitchcock, Mr. Holland, and Miss King of the eclipse party had gathered in a circle, their hair showing white against their dark faces as they stared up at the sky along with others, people he hadn't known would be there. President Seelye stood looking gruffly upward, shading his eyes with one hand. Wisps of Austin Dickinson's glowing hair blew in the wind as he too anxiously scanned the incandescent sky for the dark sun. "Mr. Dickinson is not staring at the sun, is he?" someone called out. But there was no sun.

The wind increased, and lightning flickered on the strange horizon. A rumble of thunder made David turn his head from side to side on the pillow, and then a sudden bolt jerked him awake in the darkness—darkness so deep he smiled in relief thinking that eclipse totality had been achieved after all, and he could begin to photograph. But feeling the bedding under him and seeing Mabel's shadowy form beside him brought the wash of ashen, leaden reality over him.

"David? You're dreaming," Mabel said, leaning toward him under the mosquito netting. "Did you think it was another earthquake? One of the night porters dropped a heavy box outside."

"Oh," he said in a flat voice, "I hoped I'd never wake again," and remembered how earlier that day clouds had obscured the sun from early afternoon on, dispersing only just after the moon and sun moved apart, spent, from their intimate alignment, the alignment he had traveled all the way to Japan to witness.

"My poor David," said Mabel, drawing close to him. "You held your head so high today. What I would have done to have pushed those clouds away."

"It wasn't a total waste, at least," he said. "The preliminary work went according to plan, and I don't think any moisture got on the plates."

"Or any of those little bugs this time?" asked Mabel.

"I think most plates will be clean. We can start writing up the data tomorrow before we get too involved with the Fuji expedition."

"I know we can," Mabel said tenderly. "You sleep."

Although David turned away from her, he couldn't stop himself from adding, "But why, why those clouds after a morning of perfect clarity? Why, just at the crucial moment?" He groaned but descended into sleep despite the noise of porters and servants outside which seemed to continue most of the night.

Cursing the fleas which plagued them wherever they slept, Mabel lay on her back, sleepless in her pain for David's disappointment. But after fifteen minutes of wakefulness, she found relaxation by picturing the Sunderland picnic grove awash with green and gold, the rough fence which she and Austin had leaned on to view the sunset and each other, and around them, the air alive with portent. When the next porter called greetings to another outside, she was breathing deeply, safe in her own world of sleep.

Only the most devout pilgrims to Fuji-San's summit linger at the tenth station or at the merciless and windy crater rim. A glance 500 feet down to the crater's bottom and its pool of green snow-water induces a shudder and a longing for ferns and flowers, birds and streams, rice fields and bamboo. The most devout wait for sunrise, deposit their coins, make their prayers, and descend quickly through the leaden air and ravished landscape.

The Todd party of six planned to stay at the summit four or five days, but after one night in the freezing thin air, everyone descended, albeit in different stages. Mabel came in the first group, her head pounding, and David descended later on when the effects of mountain sickness began to take hold.

Ten stations await climbers on Fuji-San, ten poor relief huts where the traveler may sit and pant or contemplate what lies above and below. Though the first station stands in fern and foliage, the climber emerges from the trees to see miles of fire-baked lava in the sun. By the sixth station, above which women or foreigners had been banned until 1868, the climber's shoes are filled with volcanic dust, and the pulse races to above 140. The wind is relentless, and one clings to sharp lava rocks to keep from being blown off the mountain. There is no path. If a mist descends, the eye strains for discarded straw pilgrim sandals to point the way up; the ear longs for the tinkle of pilgrim bells. Those who sleep on the summit hear a constant hail of fine lava against their hut roof and endure a leaden heaviness of limb, a lethargy which threatens the will power.

Yet despite all obstacles, David labored through the night on his mission to discover whether an observatory atop Fuji-San would be feasible. By dawn, he had observed through his telescope not only stars in all directions, but also the moon and Saturn with its ring system. He performed the tests he had planned, and by sunrise, began to observe the sun and the changes in its optical qualities.The party was a strange sight, its members wind-blown and covered with dust. Some were staggering from holding the telescope steady in the relentless gale, while others, after a few hours of sunrise, were sunburned and beginning to peel. The mountain held no supernatural terrors for them, no mystical demons, only its rigorous physical demands. They had a job to be done, and they bustled under the stars to do it.

David did not miss Mabel when she withdrew to one of the huts and settled herself under a pile of comforters to write an Amherst-bound letter, one which would travel further to reach Austin than any letter before it.

CHAPTER 50

November 1887

❧

OH, POOR BUMBLEBEE, I FORGOT YOUR dish," said Lavinia, eyeing the black and orange cat who stalked back and forth in front of the other six cats and their dishes. "Maggie, before you leave, could you get his dish and fill it? Poor baby." She watched as Maggie sighed and walked heavily to the pantry, returning with a dish which she filled with food scraps.

"What about you, do you have enough to eat now, Miss Vinnie?" asked Maggie, grunting a bit as she set the dish on the floor for Bumblebee.

"Oh yes, don't worry about me, it's those poor cats we need to worry about." Lavinia cut herself a slice of bread and returned to her baked beans, scraping the gravy with her spoon. "You run along, Maggie, you've done enough work for one day. Austin said he would look in on me tonight."

"Then I'll see you tomorrow," said Maggie, as she hastened out, thrusting her arms into her coat and pulling it around her broad figure.

The kitchen fell silent enough for Lavinia to hear the tiny mouthing noises made by her dining cats. She leaned back in satisfaction and watched them, all seven of them, in between bites of her own food. Now and again, she spilled pieces of carrot or meat from the dish onto the floor or her lap, but she didn't notice. Occasionally, she called directions or encouragements to the cats: "Biscuit, you're doing well. But no more squirrels in the house, please. Lady Bug, you need to eat more if you're eating for another family. Bumblebee, keep your nose out of Biscuit's dish."

The cats licked their paws and shook their heads, some ambling about under the kitchen table, others sniffing over empty dishes. Lavinia finished her meal, and having scraped up every trace of gravy with her bread, leaned back in her chair and sighed. "Oh my, oh my, now what next?" she muttered to herself. "Must get the wheels in motion. She can't be all that busy, not to help me." Running her tongue around her mouth, she searched for stray pieces of food. A cat arching its body against her chair leg drew her attention. "George? Where is everybody? Why do they all go away? And where's Austin? God forbid something should happen to Austin."

She pushed her chair back from the table and stood slowly, still muttering to herself. "Well, if I could go over and get him, I would, yes I would. But who wants to enter that lion's den?" She made clucking noises, then laughed out loud. "A lion's den, that's what it is. Oh, what would Emily say?"

Shaking her head, she gathered up her dishes and began to put away left-over food. When Austin arrived a few minutes later, he found her singing hymns to herself as she straightened up the kitchen.

"In a good mood, Vinnie?" he asked, stepping around two cats.

"No, not particularly," she answered, and laughed.

"I've got some things to discuss with you—fairly important."

"What about? Is Neddie all right?"

"Yes, Ned's fine." He pulled out a kitchen chair and sat down. "It's about my will. I've completed it, and I want to go over a few things in it with you."

"Oh, Austin, your will? I don't want to talk about such things! You're all right, aren't you?" She pressed her hand to her chest where she kneaded her fingers.

"I'm fine, Vin, but a will is a will. It's something that has to be taken care of, and the only way to take care of it is to talk about it. Just listen to what I have to say, that's all. I need you to help me. To do some things for me."

Lavinia checked the water in the tea kettle on the stove. It was still hot though she would let the fire go out now. "Chamomile?"

"Fine," said Austin. "And remember," he continued, "it's always wise to put things in order before one goes on a long trip. It's just good sense."

"Oh, Austin, I wish you weren't going out there, out to the West. It's not safe at all. Why must you accompany Mr. Sanford?"

"Well, I must admit, sometimes I wonder why I planned this trip. Amherst never looked more beautiful than right now. But seeing the country will be new and—and..." he groped for the right word..."educational. After all, I never go anywhere."

"That's not true, Austin, you go to Boston all the time. And Salem, and Pittsfield, and..."

"All New England, all New England. Those trips don't count. I've turned out to be provincial, have you ever thought of that? A provincial lawyer."

Lavinia smiled. "Do you remember one of Emily's phrases, 'to see New Englandly?' I like that, don't you? 'To see New Englandly.'"

Austin accepted his tea and smiled too. "Well said," he agreed.

There was a silence while Lavinia sat down and wiped away some spilled tea under Austin's saucer. Then Austin cleared his throat and spoke. "I want to leave some things to Mabel," he said. "Things I want her to have after I'm not here." He kept his eyes on his cup. "After all, she's so much younger than either of us...you understand what I mean. You have your share of the Homestead, of course."

Lavinia accepted this, but asked, "What things then? And what about Sue?"

"Naturally I'll leave Sue the bulk of the property. But there are other things I want Mabel to have."

"Sue will kill you!" said Lavinia, staring straight at him. "You can't leave things to Mabel. And tell me, what things?"

"A few stocks and bonds, a few paintings—but—" And here he paused, took a breath, and looked back at her—"my share of the Homestead and the rest of the meadow land."

"What?" Lavinia stared at him, incredulous. "Your share of Father's land?"

Austin hastened to explain. "I'll leave it to you in the will, but Vinnie, you don't need it, after all. You have the Homestead here to live in, and no need for the meadow land. They may as well have it. Besides, she loves that land. Mabel's young, she'll outlive us both, and David doesn't provide for her as well as I could wish. I don't know what his future is. He seems more and more unstable these days. So I'll leave my share of land to you, but I'm asking you—" He paused—"I'm asking you to be sure she gets it in reality. All you'd have to do is sign it over to her. You care for Mabel, you'd do that for us both, wouldn't you? For her and for me?"

Lavinia sat thinking. In a moment, she said, "Well, you may be crazy but you're also smart, because to leave all that openly to Mabel in your will would get you killed dead twice over!" She chortled, striking her fist on the table. Then she sat thinking again. "The meadow land to Mabel. To Mabel Todd." She thought some more. Then finally she looked up and said simply, "I can't think of anyone who would enjoy it more. Who deserves it more."

Austin kept his eyes on the table, but he breathed faster. "I thank you for saying that," he said in a moment. "I don't know what I would do without your support, Vin."

"Well, we like Mabel," said Lavinia. "I mean, Emily and I. We discussed her, of course. You know Emily liked her too. I think she would approve of your plan. I often ask myself what Emily would think. She had such sense, did Emily."

"Yes, she did," nodded Austin, still looking into his cup.

"I want Mabel to get Emily's poems published," said Lavinia. "I've been begging her to help. Just begging her. And she *has* copied out some, but she says she doesn't have the time to concentrate on it. Can't you help me persuade her, Austin?"

Austin, who had reached for his briefcase, looked up. "I wish you'd see that trying to copy out those poems isn't worth the time it would take. There's no one but the family who would ever want to read all that. Mabel's right, she doesn't have the time or energy for such a task. You can see how busy she is."

Lavinia's face fell. "Why won't anyone listen to me?" she said, half standing.

"Sit down," said Austin. "We can talk about it more another time. I didn't mean to be so gruff. But right now, will you look over these? This matter must be settled before I go on my trip." He pulled out a folder, passing it over to Lavinia.

Sitting down again, Lavinia squinted at the folder. "Can hardly read it."

"Aren't you using those glasses anymore? I'll get them, where are they?"

"Don't bother, I hate those things. She squinted at the pages for a few minutes. Then, "Where does it say anything about this land?"

"On the third page. Here, let me show you." Austin took the sheaf and flipped to the third page, where he found the passage and began to read. But she stopped him after a minute. "I can't understand that legal talk. I'm sure everything is all right. If you say it's all right, it must be."

"But I want to go over it more carefully with you so that you are sure you undersand it," said Austin.

"All right, but later, not tonight, I'm tired."

"But you understand," Austin persisted, "that you will be responsible for signing over my share of father's estate to Mabel, should anything happen to me?"

"Yes, yes, I understand. Neddie can help me," said Lavinia.

"But he might not be able to, don't count on Ned," said Austin. "In the first place, his health is so delicate. But more important, if and when Sue gets wind of this, she'll fight you about it, and she'll enlist Ned on her side. He's already caught in the middle. He's not strong enough to handle the strain, and besides, it needs a lawyer. Mr. Hills can help you."

"Fine," said Lavinia, "but I plan to die before you, so all this is just so much talk."

Austin ignored this comment and continued. "I'm thinking of leaving at least one painting, maybe two, for Mabel. She loves the oil landscape of Dresden by Pulian and the engraving of the lions at Persepolis. If I specified which ones in writing later, would you see that she gets them for me?"

"How am I supposed to take them from under Sue's nose, tell me that, pray do!" countered Lavinia.

"We'll work something out," said Austin lamely.

"*We* will? *We* will? I thought you weren't going to be here!" Lavinia cackled.

"No, really, be serious," said Austin.

"All right, I'll do whatever you say. You can count on me, don't worry. I care about Mabel Todd, and David too, you know I do. It's living next door to Sue that's the problem. Do you know I'm afraid to set foot over there these days?"

"I know you are," said Austin soberly. "Even if it weren't for her jealousy— you know—even if it weren't for what I admit I've done to cause her anger, Sue has become so—so—unpredictable. But she has always had a temper. I found that out within six months of our marriage."

One of the cats jumped on the table. "Emily knew about that temper," said Lavinia.

"Well, I tried to live with it," said Austin, gazing at the cat without seeing it. "I might still be trying to live with it if it weren't for Mabel. It's so hard for me to talk about, but it's important that you know. She's saved me in many ways. No one could know how bad I'd been feeling. I couldn't tell anyone. And I want Mabel to know how I feel about her, always, even after I'm gone. I wish somehow we could be together. Live somewhere else, I don't know."

"I don't see how," said Lavinia bluntly. "Don't be silly." And then all in a rush, "People are saying terrible things about you. Do you know how much? Don't you feel strange in church sometimes? When the Parish Committee votes to censure someone, I sometimes wonder if they'll decide to censure you." She laughed nervously and glanced at Austin who had bent his somber face to contemplate his joined palms. He stirred in his chair and rubbed his forehead.

"I feel married to her, Vin, can you imagine such a thing? I do, and she feels married to me. Our feelings for each other are not wrong. What's wrong is that I ever married Sue."

Lavinia studied him intently, saying nothing. Finally, she said, "You have two marriages then. I have none."

"Do you regret not...?" asked Austin, looking up.

"No, not really. Being with Emily and taking care of her made me happy.

No, Emily and I agreed many times, we had no regrets. But it's so lonely without her, I can tell you that."

"I'll take care of you," said Austin.

"And I'll take care of you," returned Lavinia.

Austin pushed back his chair and rose wearily. "I feel better, having told you about the will. Not better about anything else, though." He put the will into its envelope. "Shall I bring Mabel over tomorrow for a visit?"

Lavinia remained seated. "Yes, bring her over. I haven't seen much of her since she and David returned from Japan. David's a dear, I could hardly stand it when they were gone so long this summer. And how Millicent has grown over the summer while they were gone!"

"Has she? I didn't notice much difference."

"You don't pay attention. Millie grew a lot! Such a cute little thing with those thick straight bangs over her dark eyes. I wish Emily could see her now."

"Anything you want me to do now?" asked Austin.

"Oh, could you light the upstairs hall lamps, and the one in my bedroom before you go? I hate to go up there before the lamps are lit."

Austin went upstairs, pausing a moment in the doorway of Emily's room, then lighting the lamps for Lavinia and returning downstairs.

"I'll tell Ned to drop by often. With him and David and Maggie to do chores for you while I'm gone, you'll be fine." He reached the door. "Thanks for helping about the will."

"Oh, it's all right Austin, it's all right. We two have to stick together."

"Goodnight."

He left Lavinia in the silence of her kitchen where she locked the door after him and chose two cats to take upstairs. But once in her room, she did not undress for bed. Chilly though it was, she pulled up a stool and bent over the box of Emily's poems. So many pieces of paper lay there she never knew which sheaf to pull out first. But every day, she pulled out some and pieced through the lines, though even she had trouble deciphering the handwriting. "Your calligraphy, Emily!" she used to tell her. "Mother never could read you."

Where was the one about the birds coming back; Vin hoped she had remembered to set that one aside to read again. Ah, there it was.

These are the days when Birds come back—
A very few—a Bird or two—
To take a backward look.

She looked up, collecting her thoughts. This was the poem about autumn, Indian summer. She wanted to be sure it got published. Maybe if Austin saw this one... She read the rest of the poem to herself, then set it aside, and reached in for another poem.

> *Tis so much joy! 'Tis so much joy*
> *If I should fail, what poverty!*
> *And yet, as poor as I,*
> *Have ventured all upon a throw!*
> *Have gained! Yes! Hesitated so—*
> *This side the Victory!*
>
> *Life is but Life! And Death, but Death!*
> *Bliss is, but Bliss, and Breath but Breath!*
> *And if indeed I fail,*
> *At least, to know the worst, is sweet!*
> *Defeat means nothing but Defeat,*
> *No drearier, can befall!*
>
> *And if I gain! Oh Gun at Sea!*
> *Oh Bells, that in the Steeples be!*
> *At first, repeat it slow!*
> *For Heaven is a different thing,*
> *Conjectured, and waked sudden in-*
> *And might extinguish me!*

"This side the victory!" Lavinia began to rummage through the box with shaking hands. But in a moment, she stopped, and sitting back on her stool, stared into space, her eyes unfocused as she formulated her strategy. She sat that way a good five minutes, and then muttering, "That's it, I'll make it work this time," she bent over the box again and shuffled through the pieces of paper, pausing longest over the bundles fastened together with sewing thread. She shivered as she worked, and at one point, pulled a comforter from the bed to wrap around her, so that she sat hunched over, a fantastic figure swaddled in greens and blacks.

In two hours, she had finished. Carrying a sheaf of some twenty poems, she shuffled into the hallway, the comforter still wrapped around her, and peered out the window facing Main Street. She stood there thinking a moment and then muttered, "Good, good. Hurry, let's go."

Draping the comforter over the banister, she descended the stairs heavily, dropping hairpins as she went and clutching the railing with arthritic fingers. Downstairs, she fetched a bag into which she dropped the poems, and then drew her cloak around her. Another hairpin fell from her chignon, causing her hair to hang askew, but although she patted the back of her head briefly, she ignored the damage and unbolted the front door. A few steps across the street found her by the meadow, where she stopped for a moment and said aloud, "Father's meadow?" But she moved on to her destination, the Dell. She walked under the trees, picking her way carefully across the grass, to the back of the house where lights showed dimly behind curtains in the back parlor.

"It's me, Mabel, it's me!" she called at the back door. "I have to tell you something," and she rattled the door knob impatiently.

In a minute, Mabel appeared at the door, a pen in her hand. "Is everything all right?" she asked. "Did anything happen?" She drew Lavinia in to the warm cozy parlor where a fire crackled.

"Yes, plenty happened, plenty," said Lavinia. "Austin's going away and no one is doing a thing about these poems, and now's he's made a will, and I can't sit idle any longer. You've got to help me, Mabel. The time has come. Just look!" She fumbled for the poems in her bag, thrusting them at Mabel.

"Calm down, Vinnie," said Mabel, laying her pen carefully on a table covered with lined writing paper. "Sit quietly now, and show me what you have there."

Lavinia allowed herself to be led to a chair, but she continued to hold the sheaf of poems in front of her, waving them slightly. "This side the victory! That's what she said, and that's what convinced me never ever to give up. These will convince you, too!"

"What do you have there, Lavinia, what are you talking about?" Mabel took the papers from Lavinia's hand and unfolded one. "Ah, Emily's poems. I should have known." She sank into a chair, still holding the unread papers. "You don't have to convince me that they're beautiful, you know I think that..."

"Do you, though? How many have you read? There are hundreds of them, each so wonderful. I haven't even read them all!"

Mabel sighed. "That's just the point, Vinnie, I couldn't possibly read and recopy all these, even if they were written out legibly. I simply haven't the time. What about my painting and music classes? And then there's choir practice. And I have writing aspirations of my own, you know." She gestured toward the table. "I'm writing a long story right now. 'Stars and Gardens' I'm calling it. David needs me to edit his work, too."

"You don't hear me," said Lavinia, struggling clumsily to her feet. "These poems are for the world. I believe that, yes, I do. And you will too, if you will only read these. Just read them, please, please, read them." She stood before Mabel. "I'll start. I'll read these aloud to you, right now." She reached for the unfolded poem in Mabel's right hand.

"Of all the Sounds despatched abroad," she read, "There's not a Charge to me/Like that old measure in the Boughs—That phraseless Melody/The Wind does—."

Mabel leaned back in her chair and listened in spite of herself and in spite of Lavinia's quivering, rough voice which stumbled often.

"...—working like a Hand,/Whose fingers Comb the sky—Then quiver down—with tufts of Tune—Permitted Gods, and me—"

"Tufts of tune," repeated Mabel. "Unique. Go on."

> *Inheritance, it is, to us—*
> *Beyond the Art to Earn—*
> *Beyond the trait to take away*
> *By robber, since the Gain*
> *Is gotten not of fingers—*
> *And inner than the Bone—*
> *Hid golden, for the whole of Days,*
> *And even in the Urn,*
> *I cannot vouch the merry Dust*
> *Do not arise and play*
> *In some odd fashion of its own,*
> *Some quainter Holiday,*
> *When winds go round and round in Bands—*
> *And thrum upon the door*
> *And Birds take places, overhead,*
> *To bear them Orchestra.*
> *I crave Him grace of Summer Boughs,*
> *If such an Outcast be—*
> *Who never heard that fleshless Chant—*
> *Rise—solemn—on the Tree,*

As if some caravan of sound
Off Deserts, in the Sky,
Had parted Rank,
Then knit, and swept—
In Seamless Company—

Mabel held out her hand. "Let me see that." She spent some time reading the poem again. "All right," she said shortly, "read me another."

Lavinia began to read "I never saw a Moor", and finished its eight lines. Mabel sat up and held out her hand. "Give them to me, I'll look them over in the morning."

"No, now," said Lavinia. And added, "Oh, please!" as she saw Mabel's look of impatience.

Mabel stood up and added some small pieces of wood to the fire, then sat down. "Does Austin know you're here?" she asked, suddenly.

"No, of course not. He went home long ago, poor dear. He was so tired. He came over with his will." Lavinia glanced sideways at Mabel to see if this produced any reaction. It did not, for Mabel had settled back in her chair and was already squinting over another poem.

"Good Lord, her handwriting! I'd forgotten how difficult it was to read. What's this word, do you suppose?"

Lavinia moved to a large hassock by Mabel's chair and squinted. "Ocean, I think," she said.

There was quiet as Mabel read on. Sometimes she frowned, sometimes she smiled, and often she muttered lines aloud to test them out. "She had her own way of rhyming, didn't she?" she said at one point. And later, she breathed, "Oh, what a word for it, what a word."

At last, when Lavinia had moved back into a chair and dozed off, Mabel looked up and rubbed her forehead wearily. She thought quietly, staring into the dark corners of the room, listening to the night sounds, and glancing toward the fire occasionally, and finally, the clock. Lavinia continued to doze until the sound of David returning from the observatory woke her. She sat up, rubbing her eyes, while he stood looking at the two of them.

"What a nocturnal visitor you are, Miss Vinnie!" he said. "I never know who I'll find here," and he caught Mabel's eye.

Lavinia gathered her shawl about her and stood up, disheveled but triumphant. "Oh, David, she's going to help me now. She can't help it!"

At David's mystified look, she added, "Emily's poems, Emily's poems!"

David looked at Mabel. "Mabel?" he said.

Mabel looked quietly at him. "It's true," she said. "I'll have to. Just look at these. I can hear her voice speaking right to me. Lavinia is right. They are every bit as wonderful as she said." Before she could say more, Lavinia grabbed her hand and kissed it. Mabel smiled wearily. "Oh, Lavinia, go home and go to bed. We're all exhausted."

"You won't regret it, you won't regret it," said Lavinia. "Oh Susan, if you only knew! And the meadow land besides..." She rubbed her hands in glee.

"I'll walk you over," said David, who hadn't yet taken off his coat. "Come on, we've all done a good day's work, haven't we?"

After they left, Mabel sat with the poems still in her lap. She fingered a few of them, looking off again into space, then shuffled idly through them, pulling out one in particular. She was reading it when David returned.

"Lavinia is half crazy, you know that?" he said as soon as he had locked the door. "Sitting around in our parlor at midnight when practically everyone else is in bed. And you're crazy too. How do you imagine you'll have time to copy out all those poems, and even if you could, who would take them, who would publish them? I thought we'd been over all this for the last time."

"I'm tired, David. We'll talk about it in the morning." Mabel arose and began to put away her writing materials. While David broke up the remnants of the fire, she straightened up a few more things and went upstairs without another word. After she left, David reached up to extinguish the lamps, but a poem caught his eye. He stood and read it:

> *I shall know why—when time is over—*
> *And I have ceased to wonder why—*
> *Christ will explain each separate anguish*
> *In the fair schoolroom of the sky—*

> *He will tell me what "Peter" promised—*
> *And I—for wonder at his woe—*
> *I shall forget the drop of Anguish*
> *That scalds me now—that scalds me now!*

Suddenly, his sleepy, good-humored mood changed to one of leaden anxiety, nameless malaise. Something about the idea of scalding anguish reached his heart. For a moment, everything around him seemed meaningless—his beautiful new house, his work, even the sky itself which he studied with such precision. He and Mabel were living on the edge of some abyss; their experiments were dangerous after all, malignant. He looked at the poem again, with its odd handwriting, and wondered about the strange reclusive woman who wrote it. What had she been thinking of when she wrote this poem? He shook his head, and seeing Mabel's familiar lap rug over her chair, felt some of the menace vanish, but a deep sadness replaced it, and he felt his eyes water with tears. Lighting a candle, he extinguished the lamp and made his way upstairs to bed.

November 24, 1887

❦

Birmingham, Alabama, was by far the noisiest, roughest, dirtiest city Austin and John Sanford passed through on their trip west that November of 1887. But it seemed to them that all the cities—Wichita, St. Louis, New Orleans, Vicksburg—were noisy, rough, and dirty. John Sanford endured the confusion better than Austin, who grew increasingly disoriented and headachy, and who came to rely more and more completely on his traveling companion's directions and suggestions. By the time the train reached Union Depot in Birmingham, John almost had to remind Austin to collect his bags and prepare to disembark. The station platform teemed with swaggering, boisterous men in muddy boots and overalls or work-stained trousers. Spittle covered the walkways, over which ran stray dogs and small bands of children, apparently unattended by any adult. Cinders and smoke filled the air, making Austin cough as he and John passed through the station waiting room and out onto the street. Someone in Vicksburg had recommended the Florence Hotel, a four story building finished only three years before, and after a short but tiring walk past saloons like Gus Dugger's on First Avenue North and 21st. Street, and past any number of mules, drunken men, and women who called from windows, they located the Florence. They were lucky to find an unengaged room there, the proprietor told them as they signed in; there had been no available rooms the night before.

The hotel's standards were better than those in Vicksburg's supposed best establishment—Austin had written Sue that the window sills there looked as though they'd been used for chopping blocks. But they had hoped for better.

"And tomorrow is Thanksgiving," said Austin ruefully to John. "We could be in Amherst in our clean homes on our own land in sight of our precious church and friends."

"Only a week more," said John. "Cheer up. We'll retire early."

The next morning found Austin in the hotel lobby, still tired from a restless night's sleep interrupted by fights and shouts in the street. In his exhaustion, he had not written to Mabel the night before, so he took out paper and pen now while he waited for his breakfast. John slept on in their room. Thinking about Mabel both cheered and saddened him, now that he had learned one thing: he could never leave Amherst and settle somewhere in the Midwest, as he had vaguely imagined doing. In fact, he could not imagine living anywhere else in the world but Amherst, even with Mabel. He was a man caught in a vise. No wonder his head had ached nearly the whole trip, and his chest so often felt tight. It seemed there was both everything to give thanks for this day—he would soon see Mabel—and nothing.

"Well?" Mabel asked, hurrying down the stairs from her work room to answer Lavinia's knocking. "How is he today? Any better?"

"Still exhausted," said Lavinia bustling in. "He looks every bit his age. Should never have gone off to the West, riding this train and that, and staying in filthy rooming houses. No wonder he's taking on a cold. Now how many poems did you copy off today, can I see?" She extended one hand.

"Wait," said Mabel. "Didn't you bring a note?"

"Well, when I went next door I thought *she* was out—and she was, but she came back with Mattie for something they had forgotten and was quite put out to see me. So he couldn't hand me anything, but from the look in his eyes, I think he had something ready for you."

Mabel released an exasperated sigh and paced a few steps in the hallway until Lavinia repeated her question. "How many did you copy off today?"

"Three. It was a good morning, actually. Do you want to come up and see?"

Lavinia turned and began to climb the stairs without further invitation. "Keep copying, now, don't stop," she said. "Oh, you'll soon have them done!"

"Heavens, Lavinia," said Mabel behind her, "you said there were over 500 poems in that box! Don't expect miracles!"

"Just finish the batch I brought you last week. Do you want me to try to count the poems in the box?"

They reached the room Mabel was using for her work. Lavinia looked around with appraising eyes at the writing table with its little Hammond typewriting machine, the shelves, the rocking chair, and the footstool with a shawl flung across it. "It's a good room. But your writing table is too small."

"Yes, it is rather small. I'd like to have a large, good looking desk there in its place. Maybe I can persuade David to let me look around in Boston the next time we're there."

"Let's speak to Austin about it," said Lavinia coolly. "He can buy us one and then you can organize Emily's poems better. Now show me what you finished."

"These." Mabel held out three typewritten poems.

"Is it hard to work these type machines?" asked Lavinia, squinting.

"Yes and no. Sometimes, I think it would be easier to copy them entirely by hand in fair copy. But David says the typing will come easier to me as I go."

"Look at this poem," cried Lavinia. "'I Lost a World' she says. I wonder what she meant. 'Row of stars'..."

"Oh find it—Sir—for me!" said Mabel, speaking the closing lines. "You see, I know some of them already by heart. What pleasure they've given me—despite the headaches I get from copying them."

But Lavinia hadn't listened. "I'll bring over a new batch tonight."

"No, not tonight," said Mabel, rubbing her brow. "I'm going to bed early."

"But we can't delay," said Lavinia, already on the stairs. "I could leave them with David then. Won't he be coming back late from the observatory?"

"No, he must go to Northampton early tomorrow morning. So don't bring anything over tonight, please, Vinnie."

"Well, tomorrow then. But we can't delay, we can't delay." Lavinia reached the bottom of the stairs and let herself out, while Mabel stood exasperated, holding on to the banister. In a moment, she climbed the stairs to her study, only to stand looking out the window across the roofs and the bare winter trees, her eyes unfocused. She stood that way a long time, expressionless, until at last, she turned from the window and reached for one of Emily's poems.

December 1887

~

A DESK? WHAT FOR? WHY MUST HE BUY you a fancy desk from Boston?" said David, raising his voice without warning. "No, I won't have it, it's the final straw. A man can't even outfit his own house with furniture, damn it!" He loosened his collar buttons roughly.

"David!" said Mabel, taken aback. "Shh, you'll wake Millicent."

"Bother Milicent!" He threw his collar buttons on the floor.

Mabel crossed her arms over her nightgown."What's wrong with my having a nice desk from Boston? You know I need something better than that old table to work on. I thought we had discussed it."

"I could have bought you a desk. Why didn't you ask me long ago?"

"But I did mention it, and you said we couldn't afford it..."

"You mentioned it, that was all," snapped David, his voice rising again. "Don't you trust my taste? Just because I don't come from royal Dickinson blood...."

Mabel got into bed. David finished undressing in silence. Then Mabel patted the space beside her. "Come here," she said. "This isn't about the desk, is it? It's about what we discussed earlier. The plan. The Experiment. Isn't it?"

David was still angry and huffy. "It's about a desk, as far as I'm concerned."

But Mabel persisted. "If you aren't reconciled to what we talked about a while ago, we have to discuss it again. We have to agree, that's what we said. And I thought you did agree. I thought you really could get used to it—if it happens."

"Well, if I said I could, what's the problem then?" David turned down the lamp and got into bed, but remained sitting up, looking straight ahead.

"I mean," said Mabel, "it's not as though it's something all three of us couldn't share. That's the beauty of it. And Millicent, too."

"It's Millicent that bothers me more than anything else," said David, folding his arms. "I still don't understand what we'd tell her."

"I can't quite believe it's Millicent who really bothers you, she's only a child. But anyway, we wouldn't have to tell her anything. Why would she assume the baby wasn't her brother or sister?"

David lay down without answering. Then, settling himself into the covers, he said curtly, "All right, there won't be any problem then."

When five minutes passed by in silence, Mabel lay down too, and then they both spoke at the same time. "What? Go ahead," said David.

"I was just going to say," said Mabel with forced patience, "that you told me you wanted another child, and that since I don't seem to be having one, I may as well do what we said."

"I know, I know. You don't have to remind me of everything I said. I do remember some things, you know. It's you who forget everything. You don't remember how upset you were when you had your only so-called 'interesting event' with Millicent, do you? You dragged around for weeks complaining and whining. You didn't want a baby, not at all."

"I did not whine, David, I did not!" said Mabel sharply.

David's voice was steady. "Oh, yes you did, Mabel, yes you did."

"Honestly!" Mabel turned huffily in bed. "That's neither here nor there. I want a child now, a brother for Millicent, if I had my wishes. And Austin would see that all his material needs were taken care of..."

David interrupted her. "I know all that. I trust Austin. Of course he'd do his best by any child of his."

"All right, then."

"All right," David echoed. "Let's go to sleep, for heaven's sake. Christ! How you love to complicate our lives!"

Mabel turned over.

After David had turned over too, and lay with his back to Mabel, he muttered, "Go ahead and get your desk. I don't really give a damn. I just like to cause trouble now and again so that you remember I'm around."

"Oh, David," said Mabel, turning to touch his shoulder, but he pulled away.

It was another two hours before Mabel slept, and although she felt weary the next morning, nothing could stop her shiver of pleasure every time she thought of the child she would carry for Austin.

CHAPTER 53

Early February 1888

Austin had picked up Mabel's note from Lavinia's dining room in haste, hoping he hadn't tracked in snow and mud. The snow storm had continued most of the day, and by now, Amherst village lay muffled and quiet, except for the wind and an occasional sound of someone splitting firewood. Lavinia was already in bed, feeling a cold coming on, but he had called up to her. "Everything all right, Vin?"

"Yes. Take your note, did you?"

"Yes."

He had read it on the spot. Wednesday, she wrote. Tomorrow. They would begin what they cautiously termed "The Experiment," the boldest proof of their love yet. If they were never to be husband and wife except in their own and God's eyes, they were entitled to some other testimony to their commitment.

But he could only half imagine it. A child. Theirs. If it could be another like Gilbert...He always associated his love for Gilbert with his love for Mabel. So maybe if it were a boy...But he still couldn't imagine it, and in addition, the idea of Mabel being pregnant, and then being busy with feeding and bathing and fussing over an infant...No, he did not like that idea. But Mabel's buoyant spirits, once she had thought of the plan, had carried him with her. She had fallen into depression so often during the past year that sometimes, he spent his time with her just holding her, wiping her tears with a sad hand. But now her energies had returned. He couldn't remember when she had last cried, and she often greeted him with playful laughter and lively stories.

But a child. To bring up in Amherst, cooly, as though nothing were out of the ordinary, when in truth, if anyone guessed, or if David slipped up somehow, couldn't handle the facts, told someone...The thought was too terrible to contemplate. Still, he consoled himself, David hadn't behaved erratically for a while, and his attentions had been distracted not only by his work, but also by a woman in Northampton, someone Mabel called, with a sniff, only "Miss Whatsit."

Before he entered the Dell Wednesday evening around 7:30, he took a minute to look up at the clear cold sky. Orion towered above, steady, bright, comforting. Emily had always loved to stare at Orion when they were young, and sledding or making snow angels, they had often stopped to gaze upwards. And the Pleiades, where were they? He searched a moment, then found them with a barely audible "ah." The seven sisters, daughters of Atlas. Emily had counted those among her favorites too. He must ask David more about the stars some day—the facts, the details.

He looked down and stepped across the rest of the snowy lawn to Mabel's door. Before he could turn the knob, the door opened and she was there, wearing a robe, her hair already let down, drawing him in for an embrace in the darkened hallway.

"I saw you out there," she said when they separated. "You were looking at the stars?" But she felt his hesitancy. "Are you afraid?" she asked, looking into his eyes. "If you are, I'll understand. Oh, your hands are so cold. Come close and let me warm them."

"David isn't apt to stop back in for something?" he whispered.

"No, no, he went to Northamptom after all. And while he's there, he'll probably see Miss Whatsit. No, we're quite alone. With Millicent in Washington, everything has worked out so well. Relax, my darling."

Austin still looked hesitant and unsure. Mabel took his hand and led him upstairs. "Come." He followed her up the stairs to the room they always used.

"Lie down," she commanded, pointing to the bed. "Lie down and we'll talk a while." She knelt above him, her hands on his chest soothing, caressing. From time to time as she talked, she bent to kiss his ears and neck.

"This is our moment, isn't it, oh my king? Our special wonderful moment. We planned it, we want it. This is our time, our sacred special time. What we have planned will be a consecration of our love, just as we said to each other. Won't it? I feel so sure we will succeed tonight." She stretched out to lie on top of him as he held her close, melting into her warmth.

"I love you," was all he said, and barring out all further thought, he joined with her in making love, the kind of love they had both long thought of as sacramental, so special that it set them apart from all other lovers. This night, the heaviness of the snow seemed to insulate them from the world outside and everyone in it—Sue, David, Millicent, Ned, Mattie. Their Rubicon had been crossed long ago. No turning back now. Whatever there was to fear doing had already been done, committed. As Mabel told him one day after reading Emily's poems, "Our love stands always at degreeless noon." When he looked at her blankly, she said, "I mean at a crisis of perfection. I got it from your Emily." And smiled as she reached for him.

Because she felt so sure she was carrying Austin's child, Mabel paid no attention later in the month to the nagging pain in her stomach and a familiar dragging sensation. But when the discomfort continued a second day, she could no longer concentrate on her work. The dull ache in her legs gave the final clue to the beginning of her monthly period.

Thus, when David arrived forty-five minutes later, Mabel was upstairs crying, her head bent over the blood-stained underwear which she rubbed viciously in the washbowl. Their bold experiment blasted. Why? Would they ever succeed? "We'll make it work, we will!" she told herself, even as the tears fell. It crossed her mind for an instant that she had never felt so depressed in her life. But as she heard David's approaching footsteps, she remembered that terrible night in Japan after the cruel failure of the eclipse expedition. "I hoped I'd never wake again," he had said. Had he felt as depressed as she did now?

When he came looking for her, she turned and held him, her head hidden so he could not see the tears. "Are you all right?" he asked.

"Yes, just tired of silly Amherst people," she said.

"You've seen Sue?" he said.

She let it go at that and withdrew from his arms. "Let's go downstairs." But the dull ache in her stomach did not let her forget anything, so that Phebe's chicken lost its flavor, and eating became just a tiresome chore.

After David left, she climbed the stairs wearily to her studio for a session with Emily's poems. Lines resonated in her head these days, and she had come to realize that she already knew many poems by heart just from copying them so carefully. Right now, in her head, she was not surprised to hear the lines, "There's a certain slant of light winter afternoons, that oppresses like the heft of cathedral tunes."

She reached for the top poem from Lavinia's hoard. Emily had sewn eleven poems into this little booklet, and Mabel was pleased to see that unlike the poem she had worked over yesterday, this next one contained no variant readings. Whenever Emily listed alternate words, Mabel was faced with difficult decisions. Lavinia was no help, of course, but strangely enough, David had been helpful, more so than she would have expected. And they would contact Emily's Mr. Higginson for more help when they were ready.

Mabel leaned back in her chair. This poem, although it contained two crossed out words, listed no word or line variants at all. And what a poem! Mabel read it eagerly.

"I like a look of Agony,/Because I know its' true—/Men do not sham Convulsion,/Nor....."

Mabel hesitated at the next word. It couldn't be "dimulate," of course, and since all the letters but the first one one were remarkably clear, the word had to be "simulate." She thought she had the vagaries of Emily's "s's" in hand now.

With a moment's hesitation, she made out the last word of the stanza to be "throe," wonderfully unexpected. "To simulate a throe." Mabel shifted her chair closer to the desk and smiled, pausing to wonder at the miracle of it. Why, how, had Emily known so much about agony and numbness and sharp joy? She, who had spent her hours in the solemn brick Homestead? But it didn't matter, really. All that mattered was the dazzle of it, the electric charges Emily passed into Mabel's mind and soul right now, here in the Dell, and the way they helped Mabel in the midst of her own pain.

Forgetting about herself, Mabel read the rest of the poem again, checked her reading three times until she was satisfied with her interpretation of the handwriting, and then began to copy the poem carefully onto a clean sheet of paper. She had stopped using the little type-writer; the laborious process of setting up its letters took far more time than writing by hand. It frightened her to think of all the poems waiting to be read and copied, some of them on torn scraps of paper, many with appallingly difficult handwriting. How often had Lavinia knocked on their back parlor door late at night carrying a basketful of poems in her large knotted hands, and pushing past David, dumped its contents on the floor in front of the fireplace. "There!" she would say. "And let's hurry!"

The "let's" never failed to amuse Mabel, for Lavinia rarely read the poems, yet referred to Mabel's labor as "our work" or even "my work." "What you don't know, Susan Gilbert Dickinson," Lavinia said one evening, standing back from the pile and rubbing her hands. "What you don't know."

Mabel added the newly copied poem to the pile in the box, which later, she hoped, David would check against the original. He had checked some that way already, unbidden, and although he was particularly busy now, she hoped they could settle into an editorial routine. He was already planning a trip to West Africa for a total solar eclipse next December. She did not want to go; she would not go, in fact. She had made up her mind and would stand firm this time.

The afternoon wore on, and Mabel added two more poems to the finished pile. Leaning back in her chair as the shadows crept across the room, she listened to the jangle of words and lines in her head. Then picking out the first poem of the afternoon, she read its lines again until she had them by memory.

"I love your brother, and I love you, Emily Dickinson," she said aloud softly. "I'm taking good care of him, you know." She did not light the lamps, but sat there a while longer in the late afternoon dusk, peaceful at last.

CHAPTER 54

March 1888

IT WAS LESS THAN A WEEK AFTER THE GREAT Blizzard, as they would all come to call it later, that Mrs. Jameson wrote to tell her son Frank all about it—and about the Palmer Block fire on Main Street, of course.

"As if there wasn't enough excitement with the blizzard," she wrote. "Poor Austin. How many years has he been in that office, I wonder?"

She looked out over the walls of snow still lining the street. The air itself had seemed gray Monday morning, March 12th, 1888, after a night of snow and more coming. It had snowed all night, thickly, relentlessly, muffling all sound so much that she and John overslept. She awoke with a peaceful warm glow from dreaming something about a sunny picnic in the Dickinson meadow, and was confused to see instead the gray heavy light outside the window. "What's going on?" she had asked John. And they had discovered the blizzard.

"I can't open the back door," John had called, and had begun shoveling from the back porch before breakfast even. But she liked the strange, tightly packed air, and the feeling of being barricaded inside with her tea kettle and her magazine stories.

"I guess you know this blizzard set a record in New York," she wrote Frank. "They had almost twenty inches! We are always better in the country than city people. People died, Frank, little children and old people, stranded, frozen."

Austin Dickinson had been in Boston, and she knew Sue must have worried about him. Ned certainly had, at least before the telegram came from Austin, saying he was all right. Ned had answered John's questions about his father as though he were very worried indeed. But a day later, in came Austin, having walked all the way from Northampton. Seven miles, in all that snow.

"But about the fire the night of the blizzard," continued Mrs. Jameson to her son. "A good part of Palmer's Block destroyed again, and Austin's office with it.

All those law books, can you imagine? I'm sure he's very depressed. He had enough on his mind before, what with people looking so critically at him these days. Even people who used to respect him completely. But Mrs. Todd takes the worst of it. I can't think why they don't come to their senses and behave properly. Life is too short to risk one's reputation, as your father and I have always taught you."

It was Mabel's idea, after the blizzard, to turn the Evergreens library into Austin's new office. It was far from ideal, naturally, but Austin's depression over the loss of his fine law books, valuable town records, and personal keepsakes, frightened her into practical action. Lavinia wrote Mabel in Washington, where she was visiting her parents, that he sat with his chin in his hand for a full hour one day, rocking in a chair he dragged into the frigid conservatory where Emily used to start her spring plants. The fire, the weather, Ned's recurring illness, the increasingly nasty gossip, and Sue's bitterness, had brought him to a standstill after the blizzard of March 13th.

Sue was horrified by the idea at first when Austin presented it to her—a law office in her home? People tramping in and out over her clean floors? Impossible. But it didn't take her long to see the advantages. Austin would be right there, under her eye. Fewer sly visits to Mabel. In fact, just knowing that Austin had put forth the idea at all gave her some hope. But she was afraid to hope. She had been through so much pain and seething anger that the anger itself almost pleased her.

"Your father will be staying at home more often," she told Mattie. Mattie, at twenty-two, had become her confidante, her ally, ready to spring to battle for every offense, real or imagined, from her father or anyone else.

"The house is an armed camp," Austin wrote to Mabel in Washington, where she was spending all of March. "I'm on the losing side. No, that's not true, I've already lost. But no one can figure out the terms of surrender."

CHAPTER 55

April 1888

W HEN AUSTIN ARRIVED AT THE DELL ONE
April evening for a reunion with Mabel and another attempt at The Experiment after her absence in Washington, the tables were turned: he was vigorous, sure; she was moody, uncertain. Not yet back in Amherst for a week, she already felt the small town gossip biting at her heels, already played the games of evasion and deception. Although David's frequent trips to work on the new observatory at Smith College left her free to welcome Austin, they also left her unprotected from the cold stares and deliberately penetrating glances of Amherst College wives.

Today had been particularly trying, yet it was the day she had set for their Experiment—the day she could most likely hope to conceive that month. Determined, she had packed Millicent off for an overnight stay at The Convent.

Once inside the Dell, Austin embraced Mabel, holding her so tight she could hardly breathe for an instant, but she broke away first. "I must fetch hot water," she said. "It's what I meant in my letter, you know, when I said I had learned some things to make everything a success." She started for the basement, Austin behind her. "I've got to bathe in it before—as long as I can—and as hot as I can stand it. It's supposed to make things more—receptive—or whatever." She tested the water on the stove. "Oh," she cried out exasperated, "it's so awful without Phebe to do things around here. Look how messy things are in this kitchen."

But her mood could not unnerve Austin this night. He had missed her too much while she was in Washington and had waited too long to be put off by anything. Amherst was complete again, now that Mabel had returned. Helping Mabel arrange her bath in his quiet way, he managed to relax her at last upstairs in the tub while he sat by her side and they chatted. After ten minutes, she allowed him to touch her—to caress her breasts gently and then to envelop her pubic mound with his cupped hand. But she still seemed moody and preoccupied in deciding when she could safely leave the almost tepid bath, and try to conceive.

"It's time," said Austin at last, straightening up. "Come, let me dry you."

She consented to stand and lean on him while he dried her back and held her hands as she stepped carefully out onto the braided rug in the glow of the lamp. She finished drying herself then while Austin went to their room to undress. He became aware of the clock ticking as he waited for her in bed, aroused and relaxed in the knowledge that no one had seen him cross the meadow and come to the Dell, and that no one could bother them now.

But Mabel seemed almost grim that night, placing a pillow under her hips and urging him to enter her quickly and abruptly before he imagined she was truly ready. "Push, take me, come!" she cried several times, and when he held back in his pleasure, she gasped hoarsely, "Stronger, harder!" When he finished, she clasped him in a vise-grip, holding him until his weight made her short of breath. She was not interested in reaching climax herself, even pushed his hand away.

Finally, they lay apart, silent for a moment. "I must lie quietly on my back now," said Mabel. "And with the pillow under my hips."

He turned sideways to look at her. "Are you so set on this? You won't be devastated if our plans don't work, will you?"

For answer, she gave a great gasp and choked out a deep long sob which came from low in her chest as though it had lain waiting there all evening. It threatened to choke her, and for a moment, she seemed to be gasping for air. Austin rose on his elbow to look at her, alarmed, then to bend over her murmuring, "No, no, it's all right, what is it, what is it? No, you musn't cry." Confused, he smoothed her hair and waited, hoping the deep sobs would stop so that she would talk to him, tell him what was wrong.

But she could not, did not want, in fact, to tell him how depressed she had been in the last months, how being in Washington had revitalized her so much that she almost didn't want to return to Amherst where her impossible situation blared its messages at her every day in the form of snubs, cold stares, and missed invitations. Every day, she had to arrange her activities to avoid meeting Sue or Mattie. Worse, she found herself impatient with Austin's appearance, at least, of accepting their dilemma—though she hardly knew what else he could do. Just when she felt like crying out, "Why don't you suffer like I do?," his pain would reveal itself to her in some unexpected way, and she would suffer instantly for him instead of herself.

But tonight, her inner resources had left her. She wished Austin would leave so that she could cry uninhibited all night—for to stop these sobs now seemed impossible. But one thought did, finally, stop her tears: the potential success of their Experiment. If she were to conceive, could this violent emotion, this heaving chest, interfere in some way? An article in a woman's magazine had suggested such a possibility.

She quieted her sobs then, to Austin's relief, and they lay side by side holding hands, she still on her back, her buttocks propped up by pillows to insure safe passage of the life fluids.

"I have some good news," he said, leaning over her. "In August, the whole family is going to Maine. Ask me for how long."

She didn't answer, but wiped her eyes and looked up at him.

"For a month, Mabel, four whole weeks."

"All of them? Ned, Sue, Mattie?"

"Yes," he said, "all of them."

"You're sure."

"I'm sure. And I'll stay here in my big lonely house, and come to visit you in your big house, and comfort you and love you. And maybe you'll even come visit me in my big lonely house." He held her close now.

"We'll take long drives," Mabel took up, "and sit on the piazza when it's all dark and the fireflies are out, and look at the paintings you promised to show me. And maybe go to Boston. Do you think we could manage a stay at the Parker House Hotel?" Mabel sat up, arranging her legs Indian style, and twisted her hair into an experimental bun.

"We'll go and pick Vinnie's wallpaper," said Austin.

"Oh no, is she still harping on that?" asked Mabel. "But when? As long as we're being realistic, who is busier, you or I? I've got several writing deadlines to meet for David's articles, plus the paintings I'm doing for my father's little book, and—oh, did you know Samuel Scudder is going to use my painting for his book on butterflies? The one with the milkweed, remember?"

"On my side, I think prospects are looking up for the Wildwood land purchase," said Austin. "I feel more optimistic—the town may buy that land yet."

Mabel's face fell. "Oh, Wildwood. Such beautiful acres; but I hate to think about it, somehow—all that land, a cemetery."

"But beautiful land just asking to be landscaped. And it's so needed, a new cemetery in Amherst, you know that. I'd like to be buried there, not at the family plot. I'd like to move Gib there."

"Then I want to be there too," said Mabel. "If you are there, I will be with you."

Austin turned up the lamp and looked at the time on his gold watch.

"You lie here, all warm and sleepy," he told Mabel. "Shall we plan for a ride this week?"

"Can't you come over again tomorrow night, to ensure The Experiment? Suppose tonight wasn't the right night?"

"I can't. Sue is having people in again for supper and games and music."

Mabel lay down and rolled into a ball. "She does it to torture me, you know." Austin made no answer.

"She loves to torture me," Mabel persisted. "If only we could have a child!"

Austin arose and began to dress quietly. Mabel lay and watched him.

"I'm so depressed tonight, I can't help what I say," she told him as he buttoned his shirt. You'll forgive me?" She reached out her arm to him. He took it and kissed her wrist.

"There's plenty to look forward to. Just knowing you are alive and loving me gives me hope to go on. Even if I couldn't hold you in my arms, I'd be happy. And yet I *can* hold you in my arms, and you live right here, in Amherst, close to me. We share the Sunderland fields and the Northampton Road meadows, and all the trees or creeks we've ever found and walked by together. Suppose we hadn't met at all? Suppose David forbade you to see me? But he doesn't. And Sue? She's here, and there's nothing we can do about that. It's what we have to live with. But she can't ever spoil everything—we said that to each other long ago—that *nothing* could ever spoil everything. So don't let it," he said, giving her arm a little shake between his stroking of it. "Don't let it."

For answer, Mabel lay and reached her hand to his face which she caressed gently. "My king, ever and always." He bent down to kiss her, and then stood again, his face solemn.

"I'll let you know by note as soon as we can find time again," he said, turning toward the door.

She waved sleepily at him and said, "Crickets."

"What?" he asked, at the door.

"Crickets. To look forward to."

He waved back at her and went downstairs to let himself out into an April night which smelled of damp new leaves.

Mabel turned on her back and lay dozing, being careful even in sleep to protect the life fluids she sometimes imagined she could feel working, multiplying, within her.

August 31, 1888

Millicent walked home via Main Street against her better judgment. But her friend Abbie had said they ought to make what she called a "mischief plan," to knock on Miss Lavinia Dickinson's door and then run away. Millicent wasn't at all sure she could do such a thing, but Abbie made her promise to look over the house and determine whether Maggie Maher, Miss Dickinson's servant, was home in the afternoon after school. They hoped she would not be. It was Miss Dickinson they wanted to see answer the door. "She's crazy, you know," said Abbie. "And be sure to see which bushes we could hide behind."

Millicent hoped Abbie meant the bushes around Mrs. Jameson's house. Or maybe at the edge of Henry Hills' property. Certainly not bushes on the Evergreens property. She couldn't imagine ever putting her toe on those grounds, and always eyed the place with a shudder.

She walked slowly up Main Street on the side opposite the Dickinson houses. Then she saw the carriage stopped in front of the Evergreens and the bustle of activity around it as the driver handed down Mrs. Dickinson and her daughter Mattie, while Ned—my he was old, someone told Millicent he was twenty-five!—held hat boxes and other parcels as the Dickinson's servant unloaded trunks from the carriage roof. Her heart sank. Her mother would not be glad to hear that the rest of the Dickinson family had returned after the month of August in Maine. There would be trouble: moodiness and headaches and long talks behind the study or the bedroom door. Mother hated Mrs. Dickinson. And Grandmother didn't want Mother to hate Mrs. Dickinson so much. Mother loved Squire Dickinson—that's what some old people in town called Mr. Dickinson. But Grandmother didn't want her to love him, and there seemed nothing anyone could do about this wrong loving and hating.

Millicent kept her head down as she walked closer and closer to Mr. Dickinson's house on her side of the street, for fear she would see him. He loomed tall in her mind, a dark mysterious figure, terrifying in the very mystery he evoked of his feelings for her mother. Kings in her story books were powerful men to be feared. She had overheard her mother call him "my king," in a strange voice, a voice she wished she had never heard. It was hard to put together the tall grim man with the funny thick hair who practically ran Amherst—that's what Mrs. Stearns said at school one time over tea to a friend—with the man who sat evenings right in their sitting room, who kept his brown velvet cap in their music case, and who often stayed late into the middle of the night. Many times Millicent had wakened and heard their voices on the stairs—worse, their laughter. She could not imagine Mr. Dickinson ever laughing, yet when he visited their house, he did laugh—though she never *saw* him laughing, only heard him. On that point, she could consider that she held a secret from everyone else in Amherst— "Austin wouldn't be caught dead laughing on Main Street," she heard her father say once. But it wasn't a secret that made her happy, or that made her feel any less afraid of Mr. Dickinson when he said gruffly to her, "Hello, child."

Millicent was opposite the carriage now, and even though she told herself not to look up, her head came up in spite of herself, and she saw Mrs. Dickinsnon, in a navy dress and navy gloves, pushing some bundles into her husband's arms. He looked older than she had ever seen him, his whiskers sticking out on either side of his lined face and his back slightly bowed over. While Mrs. Dickinson turned back to the carriage for another box, Mr. Dickinson's eye caught movement across the street and he saw her trying to walk home unnoticed. He stared at her without expression until his daughter Mattie followed his gaze. "Oh, it's that Millicent," she said to her mother, who looked too, and then went on searching for a box in the carriage. Finding it, she handed it to her husband and followed him up the stairs toward their front door. Mattie, with a final stare at Millicent over her shoulder, went toward the house too. Only Ned was left. Holding a valise and a tennis racket, he turned and waved to her. "H'lo Millicent," he said, and then turned to join the others.

Millicent began to run, without looking at bushes, as Abbie had instructed her, or anything else except the spot in the meadow where she would cross to her own house. She made her way through the prickly meadow, rustling with insect sounds, and around to the back of their house. Safely home, she lay down in the grass and looked up at the blue sky. A pale ghostly moon floated half way down the horizon, and she folded her arms while she thought about it. Her father's books contained many pictures of the moon, this moon. Some people said the pale lines on its surface were canals where people had once lived, or even lived now. Maybe dead people went to live there. Maybe Miss Emily Dickinson lived there now, where she could see all the stars and the sun much better than from earth. Millicent liked the idea of the moon as Miss Emily's house where everything would be peaceful and quiet. Surely Miss Emily never slammed doors or quarrelled with people. "Emily Dickinson was a very special person," her mother told her one evening when Millicent questioned her about all the papers Miss Lavinia brought over in box loads. "You've heard me read her poems to your father in the parlor—could you guess she was special? Yes, all those papers are poems."

Her parents had shown Millicent many wonderful things in the big telescope on the hill—Mars, the rings of Saturn, the strange canal-like things lining the moon. But earlier this month of August had come a special time when they had lain in the grass—her mother and father with her—to look at all the meteors. The Perseid Shower, her father called it. The word "shower" meant that meteors would fall a little like rain, her mother explained. The grass smelled special so late at night, way past her bedtime, and the quilts they lay on seemed especially cozy and warm. At first, Millicent had been disappointed—there wasn't anything like a rain shower of meteors. But there were plenty, if you counted them, and they tried. Her father wrote down the numbers.

She might have looked at the shower again the next night, but her mother said that two nights out late in a row was too much. Besides, Millicent knew her mother planned to watch the meteor shower with *him*—her king. Her father knew it too, but said he and Caro Andrews wouldn't worry about it at all when they were next together in Boston, and he laughed. Her mother had set down a box of poems extra heavily when she heard that. But she had said nothing.

"Millicent?" Her grandmother came to the door and called back over her shoulder, "She's here, Mabel, outside." Then to Millicent, "Time to come in, your mother wants you to pick out which books you want to take to Hampton."

"We're going to the sea already?" Millicent jumped up and ran into the house. "Will school start without me?"

Her grandmother seemed especially sober. "If we're not back in time, yes. It looks like you mother doesn't mind if school starts without you. A strange state of affairs; I should think we could postpone our trip a bit, but it's not up to me..."

Mabel entered the room, some tendrils of hair hanging damply over her forehead. "Mother, the weather is perfect for the trip right now, you can see that. Who knows how cold it will get in the next couple of weeks? Oh, I can't wait to get out of Amherst and everything in it." She wiped her forehead with a kitchen cloth and then threw it roughly down on the table.

"Well, dear," said Mabel's mother observing her, "you know what I told you about the Dickinsons long ago, but you didn't listen. We reap what we sow."

Mabel stamped her foot. "Millicent, go upstairs and lay out your books. Mother, for pity's sake, I'm not leaving because SHE's back in Amherst."

Mabel's Grandmother Wilder called from the hallway, "What's wrong, is anything wrong? I don't like raised voices."

"Now look," Mabel told her mother, "don't get her upset over nothing. I'm going to sit outside under the trees where the air is clearer." She took a few steps toward the door.

"Mabel, you're going to get yourself into deep trouble, there's no way around it."

Mabel went outside where she paced about, taking deep breaths.

Upstairs, Millicent knelt on the floor and looked slowly through her books. She would take the one about foreign lands that her father had brought her from New York. And she would take the story book her mother had brought her from Boston. She hoped she could take her paper dolls too, the whole family of them. They would miss her if she didn't line them up on the trunk in her room and kiss each one good night. In fact, she should take them out of their box now and tell them the good news: they were going to Hampton, New Hampshire, for a change of scene from the Dickinsons!

CHAPTER 57

November 1888

I CAN'T CONTINUE TO AVOID EVERY OTHER ladies tea just because of her, Mopsy," said Sue Dickinson, arranging a vase of dried fall leaves. "I'm going to this one; I've always liked Mary Stearns's teas. Let *her* stay at home. Besides, the world knows who is right and who is wrong."

"Then I have to go too—we need to make a united stand. But I can tell you, I feel too tired for it." Mattie Dickinson held up a page in the dress pattern book. "Do you like that one?"

"Too much ado in the shoulders, don't you think, dear?"

Mattie studied the shoulders. "Not really. I think it might look nice on me."

"The thing is," Sue continued, "I sense some changes. People who didn't see it before do now. Hilda Carson, for instance. On the way to Logtown Sunday School she said, 'Some people in this town who are nothing but show get all the credit, while people like you, who really do good deeds, are ignored. But that's changing, don't worry.' She knew she didn't have to use any names. And our persuading Cornelia to put a word in Professor Esty's ear about cancelling Mr. Todd's supper science lectures paid off. And it was so easy."

Sue gave a last look at her vase of leaves and carried it to the table by the window. "So you see, Mopsy," she said, "now is not the time to stay at home."

"I'll answer the R.S.V.P.," said Mattie, going at once for pen and paper.

"You don't seem quite yourself, Mabel," said Mary Stearns on the afternoon of her tea party. "Or is it just my imagination? It wasn't too much, asking you to pour tea when I know you're so busy with Emily's poems and everything else?"

"Of course it's not too much, and I'm fine. Being busy is what I like best, and it's an honor to pour at your teas." Mabel, in an azure dress trimned with cream lace and azure pendant earrings, smiled at Mary across a table laid with silver and china, then reached out to adjust a candlestick.

"The fire could be drawing better," said Mary. "It wants for Austin's touch, doesn't it? You didn't ask me yet," she continued in an undertone as they walked, "but I should tell you that Susan Dickinson and Mattie accepted my invitation. Or did you know all along?"

"I knew," Mabel said, without further explanation.

An hour later, both parlors, the dining room, and the entrance hall hummed with the sound of ladies' voices. Mabel presided over the tea urn at one end of the dining room table, Mrs. Emerson at the other end. Mary Stearns stood in the front foyer whenever possible, greeting the guests herself after one or another of her students had answered the door and a servant had taken their cloaks.

Mabel began to allow herself a small sigh of relief; perhaps Sue had decided not to come after all. Maybe the idea of a public stare-down didn't appeal to her or Mattie today. Or maybe Austin had said something; she wished that he *had* prevailed on her behalf for once.

She handed Mrs. Tuckerman a cup of tea with an especially bright smile and began to ask her about the weather for Thanksgiving, when a change in the noise level from the foyer drew her attention. The chattering and laughter dropped off strangely, while Mary Stearns's voice rang out: "How nice both you and your daughter could come, Mrs. Dickinson. It seems ages since I last saw you, Martha. You've been in New York so often."

From her position at the tea urn, Mabel saw the two, mother and daughter, walk past the dining room archway to greet other friends without a glance to either side. Sarah Tuckerman stared at the place where the two had crossed, cast a nervous glance at Mabel, and then moved away from the table so others could come forward to Mabel for their tea.

After a few minutes, Sue and Mattie, surrounded by a group of friends, entered the dining room. Sue was complaining in definite tones about the deterioration of street manners in Boston and New York City. "It's caused by immigration, too much immigration. When Mattie and I spent our theater week in New York, we hardly knew what country we were in every time we went shopping. Just a jabber of different languages, all sorts."

Leading the way, Sue stopped to greet those ladies being handed tea cups by Mrs. Emerson. Then she greeted Mrs. Emerson elaborately, and finally, those ladies standing at Mabel's end of the table. Pointedly ignoring Mabel, she picked up the thread of her earlier remarks. "Now Washington, there's a city with a different problem. The natives of Washington are already backwards and mannerless, we all have seen that!" She laughed, shifting slightly toward Mabel and then turning her back again.

Mabel, whose parents had recently arrived from Washington, but who were briefly out of town again, continued to hand out tea cups. It was well known she herself had been raised in the capital, and returned there often for long periods at a time.

But Sue wasn't finished. "We may be a simple New England village, but most of us can boast impeccable and sincere manners. Manners and morals go together, as far as I'm concerned. Outsiders might think they can change our village, but they can't. We stick together. We refuse to tolerate any slights to the life we are proud of. I feel sorry for anyone who tries to threaten us."

The room had grown quiet, since Sue's speech dominated the chatter which preceded it. After a pause, Mrs. Emerson said in a tremulous voice, "I'm glad you said that, Mrs. Dickinson. I do like to see the old-fashioned morality upheld."

Several women gathered toward Mrs. Emerson's end of the table, leaving the few by Mabel's side looking confused and awkward. Filling the silence, Mabel said to one of them, Mary Warner Crowell, whose husband was blind, "Tell me, what are you reading to your husband these days? I always like to keep up with whatever you and he are working on." After the others listened to the strangely isolated little conversation, they began to talk themselves, and the intensity of the moment seemed, at least, to diminish. But the group remained divided between those who talked to Mabel and those, a larger group, who clustered around Sue and Mattie Dickinson as they chatted both in the dining room and in the parlors. Sue had triumphed: her showdown had forced friends to show their colors, to support her in the village which had upheld and served her long before the thought of Amherst had ever crossed Mabel's mind. Sue was shrewd. Village manners and village propriety were so all-important that when she, one of the leading ladies, chose deliberately to defy tea party manners, her transgressions were accepted, for had she not reason? Mabel had come out the loser, and both of them knew it.

When Mary Stearns, who had not been present during Sue's speech but, sensing new tension in the air, entered the dining room, Mabel smiled at her as though nothing was wrong. But she clenched one hand in her lap while the pulse in her temples thundered. She looked out the window for a moment to maintain steadiness and saw the wintry sky of yet another impending Thanksgiving, another sky of dark bare branches. How many times had she felt the pain and irony of an Amherst Thanksgiving? Would nothing ever change?

Mary, seeing the way Sue stood with her back toward Mabel, and still sensing the tension in the air, stood by Mabel's chair. "Did I tell you, Mrs. Todd, how glad I am that you agreed to help preside over my table today? You and Mrs. Emerson make my teas special."

Mabel smiled and met Mary's hand with hers. But privately, she had begun to search her mind for calming words from Emily's poetry. To her pleasure, there appeared the first lines of a poem she had just recently skimmed: "What soft—cherubic creatures—/These gentlewomen are—/One would as soon assault a plush/Or violate a star—."

Mabel smiled, partly restored by Emily's humor, so appropriate for the occasion. Wouldn't Sue love to know that her sister-in-law and her arch enemy shared a secret joke just at that moment? She would look up that poem as soon as she got home and memorize it on the spot, for future need. And so when gentle Mary Crowell returned to Mabel's side, anxious for her, Mabel surprised her by saying, "Mary Stearns always gives such especially nice teas, doesn't she? I must be sure to find out how she made the orange muffins—they have just the right amount of tanginess. I so dislike extremely sweet muffins."

CHAPTER 58

March 1889

TELL HARRIET YOU DON'T NEED HER HELP
after all if she's such a miserable copyist!" said David a trifle roughly from his
chair in the parlor of the Dell one March evening. "But do something! All I
know is, I can't help you right now. You've overloaded yourself, face it, Mabel."

"Well, I can't send her away; she's hardly just arrived. I hired Harriet because I thought she would be such a help! But she makes so many mistakes
that she's turning out to be a hindrance, since I have to go over everything
anyway. I simply can't trust her as a copyist, much less as a reader of Emily's
handwriting. And besides, she seems to have no feeling at all for the poetry."

"Do it yourself by hand then. What's the rush?" said David, reaching for his
pocket calendar. "Can we discuss travel plans now?"

Mabel came to his side. "Yes, we can, but let me first tell you, David, the
rush is that we're within sight, at least, of submitting the poems for publication. I've finished about three hundred now. Three hundred, David! I want to
bundle them up and have them out of my hair. And have Lavinia out of my
hair, too, needless to say. It's time I thought about consulting Mr. Higginson.
Lavinia thinks she owns him, but I'd like to meet him myself, not have Lavinia
handle all the contacts with him. Who knows what he may think of her, really.
She's so odd sometimes that I worry about her ruining everything."

David opened his calendar. "First things first. I want to spend some time in
Washington making my case for the eclipse trip to Angola. If they consent
soon to appoint me chief of the expedition, we can begin to negotiate about
which Navy ship they will assign me. Unless they use a combat ship, there
shouldn't be any problem with your coming. And I want you to come." He
looked her straight in the eyes.

"Don't worry, I want to come too," Mabel said. "To leave Amherst far far
behind—yes, it's what I want. I've changed my mind about wanting to stay."

"All right, then. The eclipse falls on December 22nd. So we need to sail sometime in October to allow for travel, courtesy visits, and setting up equipment—and for whatever goes wrong—something always does. You spoke to Austin about pushing for my half salary while I'm on leave, by the way?"

"Not yet. I will though," said Mabel.

"Well, see that you do. I can't be pestering him too often. I'll leave that up to you. It's the least you can do, God knows."

"All right, David, all right," Mabel said, annoyed. "Enough said."

"Can you imagine?" he persisted. "I'll have you all to myself on this trip. No competiton. With your father along as historian or assistant or whatever he wants to be called, you'll be stuck, won't you? You'll have to behave yourself."

Mabel stood up to leave the room until David called her back. "Oh, come on, don't get all huffy. You've asked for it. I'm feeling low, that's all. It's not been easy lately, you know that."

"I don't like your affairs either," she returned. "I don't like the common women you seem to gravitate toward."

"Then maybe I'll see if the queen of Sweden is restless..." David said. "Would that suit you better?" He gave a snort of laughter.

"Oh, for God's sake," Mabel began, but David grabbed her wrist and pulled her down on his lap. "Common women, uncommon women, what's the difference? What does it matter to you? You've got Austin and me. At least, I assume you want to keep me."

He held her wrist until she said, "David, that hurts." But he gripped even tighter for a moment before releasing her wrist, white with the imprint of his fingers. "Last week," he said, "after you pushed me away, I wondered whether I'm still in the picture."

"Pushed you away?" began Mabel. "I never..." Then she remembered. "Oh. That." A silence hung between them. "But I had to," she said. "I thought you understood from the start. It has to be that way for a while. You agreed, you *did*, that if we were going to try The Experiment, Austin and I, that we had to do it right. So I had no choice but to push you away in time to make sure nothing got in me."

"Well I don't like it. I'm reconsidering the whole thing. We don't need another baby, God damn it. It's entirely crazy!"

"No, no, don't talk like that!"

"Will you never give the whole thing up? I mean, give him up? You don't see the results of your actions. You even try to make me believe that Sue doesn't know you and Lavinia are planning to have the poems published. Frankly, I don't see how she can *not* know, the way you two run back and forth between houses with bundles of papers in your hands.!"

"Lavinia hardly ever sees Sue these days. Anyway, Sue isn't likely to mention the poems—she's just not interested in them, thank heavens."

"Aren't you lucky?" David said. "Sue leaves you her husband and her sister-in-law's poems as well. Quite a lot to play with, isn't it?"

"David," said Mabel, raising her voice. "I'm not in the mood for satirical remarks. If you persist, I'm going upstairs."

"Don't I even get any thanks for helping with the poems?" asked David. "I spent two hours sorting them last week, to say nothing of the proofing."

"And I do appreciate it, more than you know. I love you for it."

David stood. "I have to make a short trip to the observatory. Want to come?"

"But it's so cold..."

"Oh, come on, Mabs, come to the observatory with me. If you're willing to trek to Africa, you can make it to the college observatory."

"Well, I prefer walking out at night anyway—no chance of social insults. The Great Black Mogul won't be out there to hound me for a change."

"Well then, a look at the sky will distract you. You used to love to sit up there with me when we first moved here. Remember?"

The brisk walk under a clear starry sky refreshed Mabel. Overhead, she found the Big Dipper, then Capella, and not far off, Castor and Pollux. Orion was slipping toward the western horizon and would be lost behind the hills as the spring advanced. Jupiter stood brilliant, brighter than Sirius. One of Emily's poems came to mind, and she quoted aloud to David: "I lost a World—the other day!/Has Anybody found?/You'll know it by the Row of Stars/Around its forehead bound./A Rich man—might not notice it—/Yet—to my frugal Eye,/Of more Esteem than Ducats—/Oh find it—Sir—for me!"

"I remember reading that one," he said. "I wonder how often she came out to look at the stars?"

"I have no idea," said Mabel. "I'll ask Vinnie. We should take Millicent out more often, you know. She's ready to learn more."

David unlocked the door of the little observatory. The familiar odor of wood and damp air enveloped them as David lit the lamps and went to his desk.

"You're not using the telescope tonight?" she asked, her voice echoing in the spaces above their heads.

"No, I just need to gather up some calculations and pack some lenses."

"But I want to look." She began to climb the ladder. "Can you open the roof for me?" She climbed higher, loving the feeling of coming closer to the ceiling and further from everything below.

David set about activating the mechanism to open the roof and joined her at the top of the platform. "What do you want to see tonight?"

"How about the Beehive Cluster? M44."

David seated himself and manipulated the telescope. After a while, he turned to her. "There you are, Praesepe, the Beehive Cluster. And I must go down now."

The sound of his footsteps echoed as he receded, leaving the skies to Mabel. She pulled her cape around her and stared at the many stars in the cluster, some burning orange, some white, some with a reddish hue, and some actually multiple star systems. Who could know what it all meant, these burning balls of matter deep within space, yet visible from the iron globe she occupied for however many years left to her? Who could ever know? The mysteries of creation. The mysteries of love. Both beautiful to the point of pain.

Seeing the stars so far off strengthed her resolve to accompany David to West Africa—to ignore distance and time and to breathe without Austin—for distance and time would be nothing when measured against the profundity of the stars. She must learn more, experience more, and surrender what only appeared to be obligations at home, including Millicent. Her mother could perfectly well take care of Millie as she had always done, leaving Mabel free to see a continent she could barely imagine.

She began to think about ways to calm the fragmented state of mind which plagued her daily. She would manage to finish preparing the poems so that Lavinia's Mr. Higginson could look at them, and she would go to Africa with a clear conscience. Africa! She hadn't forgotten Japan—the way it smelled and tasted, the way people led lives so different from hers. Africa would give her a whole set of new impressions to savor. She would write about it all when she returned and give talks to the ladies of Amherst and Northampton, Springfield and Washington. "Mabel Todd, such an amazing person!" she could imagine people saying, as they did after her lectures on climbing Mt. Fuji. What a pity that Susan Dickinson had to miss all her talks.

CHAPTER 59

July 1889

THE ATTACK NED SUFFERED THE FIRST WEEK in July was severe, just when Austin had hoped the episodes might be diminishing. The familiar piercing cries heralding an attack had sounded from his bedroom, arousing Austin instantly from his and Sue's room where he had been sleeping again for the past few weeks, and into his son's room, where Ned lay tense, with his hands clenched and his eyeballs rolled upward. But no sooner had Austin reached his side than Ned's arms and legs began to twitch and globs of spittle appeared around his mouth, followed by vomit. Austin turned him quickly on his side and lowered his head over the bed to prevent him from swallowing his vomit while he continued to twitch silently. Like a bizarre wrestling match, the scene played itself out much as it always did. Austin's arms ached and his knuckles showed white from holding his son half on and off the bed, until eventually the jerking subsided and Ned fell limp.

Austin supported the head back onto the pillows knowing Ned would sleep now, and hung his own head for a moment in exhaustion before he began the work of clean-up. His feet and body were freezing—he wore no slippers or robe. A movement behind him let him know Sue had arisen. She stood in the half opened doorway, barely visible in the gloom. "A bad one?" she whispered.

"Yes. I'll clean up, go back to bed."

"I'll light the lamp and get fresh linen then," she answered.

In a moment, the hallway lamp revealed the shocking sight of blood on the floor and on Ned's pajamas, along with a pool of urine in the bed.

Together, they worked silently to clean up the mess, hoping that Mattie would sleep through it all. Austin finished by sponge bathing Ned and dressing him in fresh night clothes while Sue left the room carrying the soiled laundry.

They met again in the upstairs hallway outside Ned's room. "How you are shivering," Sue told him. "Get back in bed and try to sleep. You've got a busy day if you're going to Boston tomorrow."

"I don't know if I can sleep," said Austin. "Maybe I'll go to the spare room."

"Please don't," said Sue. "Just please don't."

Wordlessly, he went into their bedroom and pulled back the comforter, noting with disgust the bits of vomit on his feet. With a sigh, he got up again and wiped them off. When Sue returned, Austin lay with his back to her. "When will it ever end?" he said tonelessly.

She did not answer, and although both of them lay awake for the better part of an hour, they slept at last, back to back.

Mabel read with pain the despondent letter Austin wrote to her the next day from Boston where he had gone on business, drawn and depressed. He mourned Gilbert anew and found himself missing his father as well, as he often did when he felt depressed. "I'll talk to Emily," he thought for the flash of a moment. Then that light vanished too.

Being away from Mabel that day seemed intolerable, but being near her in Amherst only to watch her suffer the insults of a gossiping village was equally difficult. He was trying to get used to the prospect of her being in Africa for months, but he had so far found no way to adjust to such a long separation.

Mabel slipped Austin's letter into her journal. She had been busier than ever since her return from Washington and the confirmation of David's eclipse expedition in Africa. Their ship would be the *Pensacola*, a combat vessel, but David felt sure he could manage to change the rule barring women from its decks. He was so optimistic and set on her accompanying him that he had already made inquiries about loading a piano on board for her.

If they sailed in October, not returning until spring at the earliest, Mabel knew she ought to finish copying the rest of Emily's poems, making some 700 in all, before they left. If all went well, she and Lavinia would contact Mr. Higginson and set the process of publication into motion before she sailed.

All the work of reading and copying poems pulled her to Amherst just when David expected her to shuffle back and forth with him to Washington. He had helped her before with the poems, but now his patience wore thin as he labored to bring his expedition off. When she had protested, saying, "I'm trying to make a real contribution here, David," he had shot back, "*You're* trying to make a contribution? What about me? If my automatic photography works during the eclipse, we astronomers will be able to produce pictures of the corona recording the exact moment they were taken. And not just *some* pictures, many many pictures! Mabel, I could extend our ability to study totality as never before."

Austin also seemed too preoccupied to give much attention to her work with Emily's poems, though of course their time together was so limited as to make talk about anything but themselves and their predicament unlikely. But she herself continued to revel in the sharp beauty of the poems, turning over page after page in the little booklets Emily had painstakingly sewed together.

Since even Lavinia seemed unable to focus on the poems themselves enough to study and enjoy them, Mabel spent one afternoon sharing them with Mary Stearns. But some of the poems troubled Mary. "Did she ever doubt the Christian view of God?" she asked, looking up from the poem beginning with the line "Apparently with No Surprise." Others simply bewildered her: "I can't see what she means, 'Oh last communion in the haze,' it makes no sense to me." Mabel's attempts at explanation left her blank. She nodded politely and reached for the next poem.

So Mabel did her editing and her thinking about the poems alone for the most part, and in the end, she preferred it that way. The hours she spent alone with the poems gave her great satisfaction, as well as freedom from the pressures of life in claustrophobic Amherst. If no one else in her circle understood the genius of the poems, the way was all the more open for her to present them to the world, and the sooner the better. Her head ached sometimes from the close work, and when she closed her eyes, lines of spidery writing danced in space, but she persisted. The goal was close. Lavinia would soon be able to cease her frantic visits to the Dell.

CHAPTER 60

August-October 1889

AUGUST BROUGHT A WINDFALL FOR AUSTIN and Mabel. With both their families out of town—David in Washington most of the time planning for the expedition, Sue on vacation with Ned and Mattie, and Millicent at the New Hampshire seashore—the sense of pressure lifted dramatically.

"It's just like last August, remember?" sighed Mabel ecstatically one soft early evening, lying back in Austin's arms in the bedroom they used at the the Dell. The muslin curtains blew drowsily toward their bed, and Austin raised the sheet to cover Mabel's shoulders.

His voice was husky with feeling: "You make me so happy."

For answer, Mabel turned and held him tightly, closing her eyes against his shoulder. Then she turned and held up the back of one hand. "I love wearing the ring—when I can."

He put his palm against hers and touched the gold wedding band on her finger, the band he had given her that spring. She wore it when they were alone together, or when she herself was alone. "I consider you to be my wife in every way," he said simply. "And I adore you."

"And I consider you to be my husband in every way."

Austin wiped his tear-brimmed eyes. "A week ago I felt so depressed. Now I'm so happy. These moments together make it all worthwhile."

Mabel sat up. "You must see something wonderful. A poem Emily wrote. It might have been written just for us. I'll get it, just stay there, all cozy." In a minute she returned, carrying a folder of poems. "I'll read it to you."

There came a Day at Summer's full,
Entirely for me—
I thought that such were for the Saints,
Where Resurrections—be—

The Sun, as common, went abroad,
The flowers, accustomed, blew,
As if no soul the solstice passed
That maketh all things new—

The time was scarce profaned, by speech—
The symbol of a word
Was needless, as at Sacrament,
The Wardrobe—of our Lord—

Each was to each The Sealed Church,
Permitted to commune this—time—
Lest we too awkward show
At Supper of the Lamb.

The hours slid fast—as Hours will,
Clutched tight, by greedy hands—
So faces on two Decks, look back,
Bound to opposing lands—

And so when all the time had leaked,
Without eternal sound
Each bound the Other's Crucifix—
We gave no other Bond—

Sufficient troth, that we shall rise—
Deposed—at length, the Grave—
To that new Marriage,
Justified—through Calvaries of Love—

They were both silent a moment. Then Austin said, "Read the last part again about 'that new marriage'." Mabel read him the last stanza and then handed the paper to him. "Here, look at it yourself a minute."

"Amazing," he said finally.

"It's almost our poem," said Mabel. "But where do you suppose she found the inspiration for such a poem? Who did she love in that way—like we do?"

"I have no idea," said Austin. "I think she probably cared for Otis Lord very much, but not in the way of this poem. And this poem seems so specific— 'There came a day at summer's full'—Do you have the original handwriting?"

"Just a minute." Mabel scampered off to return with the original.

"Her handwriting changed as she got older," he said, studying the page. "This looks like early handwriting."

"I thought so too," said Mabel.

"It's a mystery to me," said Austin, putting both copies of the poem aside. "I have no idea how she came to write that. But there was no one in her life she could have felt so passionate about. I would have known."

"Are you so sure?" said Mabel.

But Austin was adamant. "I'm sure," he said. "But it's a beautiful poem. 'Calvaries of love': that's us."

In the remaining days of their time together unhampered by family, they found sequestered hours alone at the Evergreens when Mary, the household servant, wasn't there. The heightened sense of risk and the effrontery to convention intensified their moments together, lengthening and shaping each hour into something measureless, exotic. But there was also the homespun beauty of prosaic conversation, chatter over village events or household problems. During one simple evening meal together, Austin had set them both to laughter as he described a village character. Mabel had made them a cake and was just cutting Austin's piece when a rattle at the front door froze them, followed immediately by the sound of someone pushing open the door. "It couldn't be Vinnie, not at the front door," whispered Austin, half rising, as he stared at Mabel. But it was Vinnie, who rushed in, all excitement.

"I had to warn you," she gasped. "Reverend Dickerman is heading this way. Maggie met him on the street outside his study door, and he told her some urgent parish business required that he speak with you right now. She rushed ahead of him to tell me while he went back inside for his keys, and here I am."

Austin stood up. "Mabel, you go next door with Vinnie."

"Yes, that's the best thing," said Mabel.

In a moment the sharp rap of the door knocker made them jump. Without a word, Mabel and Lavinia slipped into the kitchen and out the back door. When they were almost to the Homestead, Austin went to the front door to let in Reverend Dickerman, who was full of apologies for not making an appointment ahead of time. "But I may need your signature on this petition," he said.

"It's no matter," said Austin. "I was just relaxing. Come join me for a piece of cake. My wife left it for me."

In New York during August and September, David scuttled about supervising the shipment and storage of equipment for the trip to Africa in October. He worked under considerable pressure: the logistics of the trip loomed immense before him. The polar axis alone required twenty-four different instruments to be mounted. The driving-clock of the photoheliograph which would move the polar axis had been a particular problem. He would also be shipping two reflecting telescopes, four clock telescopes, and a pneumatic commutator to open camera shutters and shift the sensitive plates. All the equipment would have to be meticulously packed to ensure absolutely dry conditions during the passage across the ocean and especially during rough surf landing.

He felt tense, but it was a kind of tension he liked. Each eclipse expedition was a huge gamble, a game of roulette to be played out during a few crucial moments on a given day. There was absolutely no way to predict the success of any expedition; all an astronomer could do was make his plans and remain calm. He and Mabel's father, Eben Loomis, kept in regular touch, along with Captain Yates of the *Pensacola*, Mr. Preston of the geodetic survey team, and other members of the U.S. Nautical Almanac Office.

Some days in New York, he was far too busy to eat proper meals, and brought food from the immigrants' stands to consume in the parks: spicy sausages, hot potatoes, sauerkraut and fried fish. Despite his busy schedule, however, David made time to walk across the Brooklyn Bridge, standing in the middle to gaze below where the *Pensacola* would steam down the river to the sea on October 16th. The wind whipped his clothing frantically this way and that as he let his mind wander over projects he found himself dreaming of lately: a hot air balloon expedition; a campaign to raise funds for an observatory built to withstand high altitudes in Japan or South America; a conference about life on Mars. His colleagues at Amherst were not interested in these projects; instead, they carried out their teaching duties with what he considered stultifying regularity, and devoted the rest of their time to church or reading the *Springfield Republican*.

Meanwhile, he looked forward to having Mabel accompany him to Africa. For one thing, he needed her help in writing up data. But more important, he noticed she no longer talked about having Austin's child. In fact, she talked less and less to him about Austin during their evenings together, but centered her efforts instead on helping David's career when she wasn't working on Emily's poems. She managed to do it all—not without the steep price of exhaustion and ragged nerves—but she did it all nevertheless. David allowed himself one last hope that with an eight month absence from Austin, Mabel might be led to discontinue the affair. After all, Austin was growing old. He was sixty now, and looked it, in David's opinion. He worked too hard, he walked more slowly, he often looked preoccupied. Old men lose their sexual prowess, thought David, and Austin will lose his, if he hasn't already. Mabel will tire of him.

"Mrs. Dickinson's carriage has arrived," Phebe told Mabel one afternoon in early September as the crickets droned their rising, plaintive song. Thus ended the August interlude Austin and Mabel had savored, day by peaceful day. Mabel closed the front door of her house and walked briskly upstairs, ready to concentrate all her attention now on copying the last of Emily's poems.

By October, she had managed to copy all the poems. "You must have a glass of wine!" said Lavinia, clasping her hands in joy at the Homestead when Mabel told her the good news. "Go sit in the parlor and let me wait on you. You deserve your rest."

But Mabel, torn in all directions, shook her head. There were David's trunks to fill, as well as her own and Millicent's. There were college matters David had asked her to handle for him while he continued to make other last minute arrangements. There were final plans for Millicent, who would stay with Mabel's mother and grandmother. And there must be time set aside for her and Austin before the trip.

On October 12th, a rainy evening, tons of equipment were loaded on the train cars in Washington to be hauled out the next day to the Brooklyn Navy yard and onto the *Pensacola*. Mr. Loomis boarded the same train. Official permission for Mabel to sail on the all male combat vessel had not yet come through. But David told her, "I'll have it for you. Pack and come." On October 14th, Mabel arrived in New York alone, only to discover that permission had been categorically denied. There was no other recourse but for Mabel to give up the trip. On October 15th, David left Mabel at the Albemarle Hotel while he rushed about attending to last minute preparations. "I'll come back this evening to say goodbye before I have to board," he told her. "We sail at 7 a.m."

But last minute chores and loading procedures made his return impossible, and the ship cast anchor as scheduled, lowering its top masts as it sailed under the Brooklyn Bridge in rough waters. Mabel, waiting in their cramped hotel room, let the tears fall as she looked out across the busy New York streets. Now all plans would have to be rearranged. She and Millicent, along with her mother and grandmother, would have to spend the winter in Boston, far enough from Amherst to spare her the ugly glances and cold eyes, but close enough to allow her to visit every few weeks or for Austin to visit her. On the bright side, she would be able to resume music lessons at the New England Conservatory, take in lectures and concerts, and enjoy the sophisticated city environment. Things could be worse, she realized, but for the moment, not having been able to say goodbye to David left her with an eerie feeling. Was he not going to the dark continent? Who knew what diseases or accidents he or her father could succumb to?

She pulled a chair to the window where she sat staring into the street. It wasn't until hours later that a knock on the door brought her a short goodbye note from David written just before the ship sailed. Suddenly she could hardly stay awake, even though it wasn't yet dark outside. Holding David's letter and one from Austin, she lay on the hard mattress and slept dreamlessly until morning.

CHAPTER 61

November 1889

Y<small>ES, MR. HIGGINSON IS AN IMPORTANT MAN,</small>
but a very pleasant one besides, judging from my first meeting with him,"
Mabel told Millicent on November 6th in Boston, less than a month after
David had sailed to Africa. "You can stay and listen to us talk since your cold
is so much better. Besides, you've heard so much about Miss Emily's poems
that I imagine you're as curious as I am to find out what Mr. Higginson says
about them. He's had them long enough to examine them pretty thoroughly, I
should imagine."

"I hope he likes them," said Millicent, "because I certainly do."

Mabel smiled and adjusted the ribbon in her daughter's hair. "We're experts, aren't we?" she said.

When the landlady of their rooms in Boylston Street showed Mr. Higginson
to their door, it was Millicent he saw first, staring up at him in a navy blue
pinafore with a matching blue ribbon in her hair. His face lit up in a grin which
crinkled the many lines around his eyes and raised the tips of his gray moustache. "Why hello, girl, nobody told me there was a young Miss Todd here! I
would have brought my own Margaret along. What is your name, then?"

Millicent smiled shyly and looked at Mr. Higginson with renewed interest.
"I'm Millicent Todd," she said. "Please come in."

Mabel stepped forward smiling. "Mr. Higginson, thank you so much for
coming. I am most anxious to know you better and to work on these remarkable poems I've become guardian of. Make yourself comfortable."

"Good afternoon, Mrs. Todd. It is indeed a pleasure. Millicent," said Mr.
Higginson with laughing eyes, "I see you aren't in school. Are you playing
hookey so you can talk with us?"

"Oh no sir," began Millicent seriously when Mabel intervened. "Millicent
has been suffering from a cold, so I thought it best that she should rest a few
days before going to her new school."

"Perfectly right," said Mr. Higginson. "Do you cycle, by any chance, Millicent?"

"No, sir, I don't."

"You must learn. I love to cycle myself, and my daughter Margaret rides behind me. She may be a little younger than you, but not much, judging from the looks of you. Maybe you'll meet her while you are in Boston."

"I didn't know you had a daughter," said Mabel, when they were seated. "Have you other children too?"

"No, just my Margaret. My first wife died some time ago, but I remarried and Margaret is our child. She has become our pride and joy. Quite a lively thing, full of stuff and character, I always tell people. She can climb a tree and roll her hoop, but she sits still to play the piano and to draw beautifully, too. But to our business, or I'll spend the whole time talking about Margaret." He winked at Millicent, who sat on a footstool not far from Mr. Higginson.

"Mrs. Todd, I haven't been well lately—I'm sixty-six now, and when a cold or fever lodges in my lungs, it seems to stay there. Don't let that happen to you, young lady," he said to Millicent with a twinkle in his eye. "These poems deserve our attention, though I hardly need tell you that. You have spent hours and hours with them. And I take it that the Dickinson family which has entrusted you with these poems has pressed you somewhat...?"

"Miss Lavinia Dickinson has pressed my mother," said Millicent boldly from her footstool.

"Millicent, shh," said Mabel, but Mr. Higginson slapped his knee and laughed. "Miss Lavinia Dickinson is interesting, shall we say? But then so was her dear sister, in an altogether different way. You wrote that you did not meet Emily, Mrs. Todd?"

"No, I never did," began Mabel, but Millicent couldn't contain herself. "I saw Miss Emily one time," she said, "just one time. She stood by the door and smiled."

"Millicent was only about six when Emily died," said Mabel. Her memories are a little vague."

"Well," said Mr. Higginson, "my memories are not vague in any sense of the word. She was a most unusual and striking person. And so too are her poems." He tapped the satchel he carried containing the poems Mabel had given him. "But I must confess, Mrs. Todd, to feeling some lingering doubts about actually undertaking to publish these poems. They are so highly irregular in almost every way—I can't think that the public will take to them very easily."

"With all respect," returned Mabel, "I think the public will be greatly impressed with the power of these poems. Their very force and irregularity set them apart from what has become almost humdrum these days in the world of poetry. I wonder if people aren't ready to see something different. And as to their irregularity, it is possible to make minor alterations occasionally."

"I do understand that since you have spent such long hours with the poems, copying each one..."

"And there are more, many more," said Mabel, leaning forward. "I've copied something like three times what you've seen, and Lavinia has still more."

"Amazing indeed," said Mr. Higginson. "But let me play devil's advocate for a moment. After all, being as closely involved as you are, it's easy to forget how others less familiar with the work may be apt to view it. Several years ago, when Mrs. Dickinson spoke to me about her sister-in-law's writing, I discouraged her without having seen but a handful of poems. Now I admit I was wrong, and I am glad Mrs. Dickinson has renewed her interest through you—I take it that she and Lavinia have enlisted your help? You are distantly related?"

"Not at all," said Mabel hastily, "I am not related to Mrs. Dickinson. I have worked only with Lavinia, who is a friend of mine, as is her brother, Mr. Austin Dickinson."

"Ah, then you surely know Mrs. Dickinson as well and have no doubt been a guest in her lovely home," said Mr. Higginson. "She is a remarkable hostess."

"Remarkable," said Mabel shortly. "But to the poems. Could you not submit them to your publishers with some explanation? Your word alone might launch them."

"All 200 of them? Definitely not. No, Mrs. Todd, having played devil's advocate, here is my proposal. Since you know the poems best and since you are young and healthy, not an old man like me"—and here he winked at Millicent again—"I advise you to divide the poems into categories so we can better deal with them. For instance, I thought one group might include what you think are the very best poems. I imagine some of your favorites would fall here. Then a second group might contain the poems with striking ideas marred by too many irregularities of the sort we discussed the last time I saw you. And the third group would include those poems which are particularly obscure or irregular—the ones the public would most likely not find appealing. I could look the groups over as soon as you finished them and decide how to approach a publisher. In a nutshell, that's my idea."

Mabel took a deep breath. "How soon would you want them?"

"As soon as you can arrange them. But you know best your schedule."

"I'm very busy, but I feel strongly that the faster we work, the better. How about ten days to two weeks?"

Mr. Higginson smiled. "Fine. I hope you understand that with my own schedule and my health problems, I don't see my way clear to sorting the poems myself, and naturally you know the poems better anyway."

"I understand perfectly," said Mabel.

"I've been meaning to ask you," continued Mr. Higginson, "should we title the poems?"

"Title them?" said Mabel, thinking the idea over. "Well, the idea has crossed my mind. Some almost defy being contained in titles though."

"But how else to present them?" persisted Mr. Higginson. "People expect titles. So do publishers. Though how to title one of my favorites, I can't imagine—that wonderful one beginning 'I know some lonely houses off the road.'"

"Yes, isn't that one wonderful?" exclaimed Mabel. "Tell me, have you considered more what we talked about last time—altering some of the words to rhyme where it seems feasible? Because often enough, I've gone ahead and done it."

"For various reasons," said Mr. Higginson, "I'm somewhat less enthusiastic about that idea than I was. The power of the off-rhyme becomes more appealing. Have you discussed this issue with Mrs. Dickinson? She seemed to have good literary judgement when I met her those several years ago."

"No, I have not," said Mabel, "and not with Lavinia either. Her only thought is 'Hurry, publish!' I'm not sure she understands what the poems are about."

Mr. Higginson laughed. "In some instances, I'm not either." He placed his hands on his knees. "Well, Mrs. Todd, I have some other calls to make here in Boston before I return to Cambridge. Would you think me very rude if I left after such a short time?"

Mabel rose. "I understand your situation, and I am only glad that we have been able to meet again so soon. I'll begin work immediately on the poems and try to send you the lot within two weeks, as I said. In the meanwhile, I'll have made a visit to Amherst. I continue to give music and painting lessons there every two weeks."

"A charming little town," said Mr. Higginson, rising. "Never more beautiful than it was the spring day of Emily Dickinson's funeral. I was honored to attend. Mrs. Todd, thank you for your tireless work. I hope it will pay off. Between us, we may conquer the odds and launch this unusual cargo of poems."

"It is my goal," said Mabel as she and Millicent accompanied him to the door.

"Miss Millicent Todd, I have found you charming company, and I shall inform Margaret to that effect this very night. May I take your hand?"

Millicent extended her hand, and smiling, watched him bow with another wink over it. When the door closed behind Mr. Higginson, Millicent decided her cold had quite gone away, and asked her mother to recite the poem about the lonely houses off the road.

"I know only parts of that one," said Mabel, "but we'll look it up later." To herself, half under her breath, she said, "Two weeks. I am tired, tired. And imagine his thinking I was related to Mrs. Susan Dickinson! To the Great Black Mogul? Horrors! Wait until I tell Austin!"

CHAPTER 62

November, December, 1889

~

IN THE NEXT TWELVE DAYS, MABEL WORKED
to divide the poems into three categories, arranging at the same time to take
voice lessons at the New England Conservatory and to practice the piano there
as well. Meanwhile, by the first week in November, David's eclipse expedition
had dropped anchor for the first time in the Portuguese Azores where his team
checked their magnetic instruments and set up a small press where David
could issue instructions.

After Mabel finished dividing the poems into sections and sending them to
Mr. Higginson, she turned her attention to the purchase of a new hat for the
Boston Symphony concert. During the same time in November, David, her
father, and Captain Yates had arrived at the Gold Coast where they called on
Quanco Andoh, an Ashanti King who stood six feet four inches tall, and who
seated his foreign delegation under a lithograph of George Washington while
his body servant lay in front of him, holding the king's bare feet expression-
lessly. They learned to try corn beer, to shake insects from their shoes, to look
for leopard tracks, and to view the ship as home. On December 2nd, they
crossed the equator.

By the second week of December, Mr. Higginson continued to be amazed
at the power and form of the poems he now read more carefully than before,
including the group he had never seen. And in the semi-arid terrain of Cape
Ledo, Angola, David and his team busied themselves setting up tents for everyone, including those for marines to guard the camp against theft. Watching
the turbulent surf carefully from both ship and camp, they prepared to land
the delicate equipment during a lull.

The days of December 1889 sped by faster and faster. Lavinia fretted that
the poems could not be published at once, but Mabel enjoyed a welcome
respite while Mr. Higginson continued to read and evaluate them. In Angola,

thousands of miles from Boston, David labored without pause to make all preparations for solar eclipse day, December 22nd. He felt the mood swings he always experienced on eclipse expeditions—the thrill of thinking and planning for every obstacle, along with the dragging fear of failure.

Eclipse day, Sunday December 22nd, began with rain in Boston. Mabel, feeling shivery, sat before the fire in her dressing gown and wrote to Austin while her mother and grandmother attended church with Millicent. Since they had both moved in with her and Millicent, her days semed full of even more obligations—requests for this and that, sessions with the dressmaker, special items to buy at the market—so that a Sunday morning spent alone came as an esteemed prize. Since the Dell was closed up and since Mabel's activities were regarded with such suspicion in Amherst when she returned there every two weeks to give lessons, she had no choice but to stay with Henry Hills and his wife, a guest in the town where she and David owned their own home. But of course, she and Austin managed to snatch brief hours alone in the Dell anyway, feeling even more secure since all the shades were drawn. They also continued to risk meeting at the Evergreens occasionally if Sue was away.

Before the fire on this particular dreary Sunday, Mabel could expect, at most, a telegram from David about eclipse day; or at the least, a letter, which would take days to arrive. She stood by the window and looked out at the street, trying to imagine what Angolan skies might look like at this same moment.

She was to hear the details of eclipse day later from both her father and David. But now, it was impossible to imagine that the skies over Angola were partially clear at first, allowing David to hope for success, in spite of his better judgment. But at 1:15, clouds rolled in. The start of the eclipse was thus obscured until at 1:35, a rift in the clouds showed the sun with the moon's bite well into its disk. Some members of the team let out cheers, but others pushed unsmilingly ahead with their experiments. Those who cheered, groaned when at 2:07 the clouds rolled in again, hiding the sun entirely. And yet the progress of the eclipse in the next fifty minutes could be sensed by the ominous light, the magical disappearance from the sea's horizon of a ship with white sails, and the silence of the birds. At 2:55, the blue-black shadow of the moon appeared on the sea, after which pale lemon-yellow light first leaked slowly in the southwest and then swept, flood-like, over the sky. The instruments worked perfectly and David took more and better pictures than ever before. But the corona and its spectrum had remained obscured through the eclipse. Then, as if to mock the team, the clouds disappeared a half hour after totality, leaving a clear, bare sky.

Mr. Loomis sat on his canvas chair under the sun at that and held his head in his hands. But David kept on working stoically. "Nothing to do but accept it," he called over. "No choice, is there?"

By December 25th in Boston, Mabel had developed a case of flu marked by headache, fever, dizziness, and cough. To make matters worse, she had quarrelled with her mother Christmas afternoon over her obvious interest in the prestigious General Francis Walker, president of M.I.T. and acquaintance of David's whom she had met at a reception in November.

"I'm sorry, Mabel, but I think it's highly inappropriate for you to even consider letting him call on you here. It can only lead to misconstrued assumptions."

"But he knows David, Mother, you know he does. Oh, what nonsense! I don't care at all what people think and that's all there is to it. We happen to share common interests, including Amherst College. He went there, you know."

"You *do* care what people think, Mabel. Have you not learned your lesson in Amherst?" Mrs. Loomis tightened her lips and left the room.

Millicent, arranging the furniture in her new doll house, winced as her mother flounced to the day bed and lay with her hand over her eyes. There had been no mail from Austin for four days and Mabel felt angry at him, at David for being in Africa, at her mother—at the world in general. Her anger needed venting. Wrapped in a blanket, she labored dramatically over to the desk to fetch her writing case, kicking aside a doll chair that lay in her path. Imagining Austin sitting in his warm parlor by the fire, having been fed a hearty meal by Sue, perhaps entertaining the Hills, the Seelyes, or some other family friend, inflamed her anger even more. Here she lay, sick, away from home in rented rooms, apart from her husband and her lover, without sexual outlet, chained to an endless round of dreary responsibilities, and yet her mother wished to deprive her of even this simple contact with General Walker. Maybe some people could survive on the monotony of church, newspaper, and dinner menus, but Mabel was not one of those people.

To add to her malaise, it struck her that the people she knew best demanded too much of her. There had been Vinnie, clamoring after her to copy all those poems, and then David, expecting her to leave Amherst and help him prepare for his trip. Now she found herself responsible for the welfare of three dependent people—her mother, her grandmother, and Millicent. Surely she could be allowed the luxury of venting her feelings. Because Austin had apparently not taken the time to write her in four days, he would be the recipient of her anger. She put pen to paper.

When Austin came to Boston four days later, Mabel was penitent. Despite her cough and runny nose, he held her close in the parlor of friends who pressed him to conduct his legal affairs from their home while they were away for the day. They had little time together—Mrs. Loomis and her mother had also contracted bad cases of the flu which was making the rounds in Boston, and Mabel was nursing them both. But she still told him about General Walker.

"He has told me to call him Francis now, what do you think of that?" she asked. "I think he's used to having his way. He's a big man and looks me straight in the eye."

"His wife wasn't present, I take it, at this meeting?" asked Austin.

"No."

"You know best how to deal with such situations," said Austin briefly, turning to other matters. "I wanted to tell you—Professor Mather has been very ill. He looks so thin and pale. We're all quite concerned. I've had to put aside some things in order to visit him."

"But you're overworked already, Austin. You can barely find time to write me!"

"But it's Richard Mather I'm talking about. He's been our friend and neighbor and professor at the college for years. I simply have to make time for him. That's religion, you know, in a sense, anyway, isn't it?"

Mabel did not answer.

When Austin returned to Amherst, she continued to inform him of General Walker's attentions which had increased when he came to Boston without his family. They met often at social gatherings, but twice, he had called at Mabel's lodgings while Mabel's mother and grandmother were still recovering from the flu upstairs. It became clear to Mabel that he wished to push the relationship beyond the bounds of propriety—and being tempted, at least, she could not help but hint at the truth in her letters to Austin. One side of her wanted to torture Austin, living with a wife he claimed not to love yet remaining unable to make any changes in his situation. Another side of her asked to be deterred from temptation. What Austin knew about, he could protest. She needed his protests, for Francis Walker's physical presence pervaded her senses with the kind of raw appeal neither David nor Austin had ever held. He wasn't afraid to stare at her, and handing her into a carriage, let his hand slide insolently from her waist toward her bodice. He was in no way an introspective man; he had seen what he wanted and he was simply ready to take it.

A few days before Francis Walker proposed to call on Mabel to "talk about something special," Mabel received letters from both David and Austin. David wrote his from Cape Town after two weeks at sea, projecting that the *Pensacola* would call at St. Helena in another two weeks. Thus, Mabel realized, he was probably there now. "St. Helena," he wrote, "land of exile. A suitable place for me, the way I feel right now."

Austin's letter took the position that General Walker's intentions were an assault on her womanhood, an assault which he would support her in overthrowing. But Mabel knew better: her letters to Austin about Francis Walker's impending visit had hurt him but he was presenting an unruffled appearance. His quiet calm in the face of her calculated teasing chastened Mabel. She put on the wedding ring he had given her and sat in her room thinking quietly. When Francis Walker arrived a few days later, her demeanor told him all he needed to know.

Mabel remembered David's words about "the land of exile." They were both in a kind of exile—only she hoped it would end for both of them when David returned in June and they could take up residence in the Dell again.

But while David and Mr. Loomis explored St. Helena, they found their imminent return to American village streets and trolley cars and apple cider impossibly hard to imagine. David discovered himself deeply affected by the island's isolated atmosphere, its twisted pines, its lava, and its claustrophobic sense of history. Reminders of Napoleon lay everywhere. They visited The Briars where Napoleon had lived while his permanent residence, Longwood, was built, and then visited Longwood as well. They walked the windy ridge Napoleon walked, leading to the deep valley, "Devil's Punch Bowl," where he must have stared out, his head filled with images of the past and the prison of the future. They knelt and drank from a clear gushing spring where Napoleon had also drunk, lonely and brooding during his exile. At Napoleon's tomb, Mr. Loomis was unnerved and confused to see that David stood weeping. He looked away, then asked, "Anything wrong, David? Or is it just this place?"

But before David could answer, an old black man limped up to them. In broken English, he told them he remembered Napoleon. David became visibly excited. Learning that Napoleon had conceived a scheme to escape in a hot air balloon, his spirits revived considerably.

"With some more help, he could have escaped in a balloon. Stranger things have happened!"

"But David, 2,000 miles from South America and 1,200 from Africa? Hardly likely."

"Don't be so skeptical," was David's firm answer.

CHAPTER 63

March 1890

Austin paused in his walk over the Wildwood acres he had succeeded in acquiring for a town cemetery and lifted his face to the breeze of a bright blue March day. His forehead had begun to throb that morning, a return of the malarial headaches he continued to suffer occasionally, especially when he was tired. It was probably good that Mabel was in Chicago now visiting one of her cousins. Besides, there remained so much for him to do at the college for President Seelye, who was often ill these days. It was time Julius Seelye retired. Austin wondered how long he himself could shoulder the added responsibilities of Amherst College for the president.

He leaned on his walking stick and looked around him with a critical eye. If he and Mabel could be buried together here—though how that might come about, he couldn't imagine—which spot would they choose? Over there in the middle of that grove of hemlocks, maybe. Or closer to the hillside, perhaps, where more sun shone through. He walked toward the hillside and surveyed the area more closely, imagining a single stone bearing both their names. Or their names with the letters intertwined, as they sometimes spelled them out for each other: AMUASBTEILN. Would anyone ever understand the heroic depths of their love? Bostonians fluttered over Wagner's tragic lovers, Tristan and Isolde, yet he and Mabel viewed their own love, played out quietly in an obscure New England village, as equally heroic and tragic.

He thought again about resuming their Experiment—their efforts to have a child. If Mabel had their child, he told himself, they would manage somehow to bring it up together to understand what their love was—so that he, if it were a son, would see to it that he and Mabel were laid side by side in this cemetery and would write about them someday. After all, there would be no one to speak in their behalf one day when they were gone—though he had been returning the letters Mabel had sent him over the years so she could keep all their correspondence.

He took a last look around him and then headed along the back path through the trees and blueberry bushes toward the Evergreens for noon dinner, leaning on his walking stick from time to time. He entered his house to find Sue and Mattie by the fire passing some papers back and forth.

"I'd forgotten about this one," Sue was saying to Mattie. "She sent that to me way back in the '60's. You weren't even born."

Austin sat down by Sue. "What do you have?" he asked.

"Some letters and poems from Emily, ages old. I got to thinking about them last night and dug them out. I wanted Mattie to see them. Not every girl has an aunt as talented as yours was, Mattie. I think I might try again submitting a couple of these poems to a magazine—*Scribner's* maybe. Of course, Lavinia still has that huge box of poems. If I had time I could ask her to let me see them again and pick a few—she's too scattered to have done anything with them. Austin, maybe sometime you could bring back a bunch for Mattie and me. Lavinia doesn't need all those poems over there cluttering up her house. She's not doing anything with them, is she? I knew she would never have even the faintest notion about how to begin getting them published anywhere."

Austin remained silent looking at the fire and picturing uncomfortably Emily's poems divided right now between Mabel's rooms in Boston and Mr. Higginson's study in Cambridge.

"Austin?" persisted Sue.

"I don't see the point in dragging them back here now," he said. "Can't you use the poems you already have? Let's keep things simple."

"I suppose you're right," said Sue.

Austin closed his eyes in quiet relief. A moment later, they heard the front door open and footsteps cross the hallway. "There's Ned," said Sue. "We ought to eat so he can be back at the college library desk by 2 o'clock."

Mattie continued the conversation where it had left off. "Let's look in the latest edition of *Mrs. Logan's Home Magazine* to see what kinds of poems they're publishing. I might submit some of my own, you know."

"That's an excellent idea, Mattie," said Sue, rising. "Let's go in. We're having boiled tongue. Austin, you look pale. Are you having another headache?"

He arose and followed her to the dining room. "I'm afraid so."

Ned moved toward the dining room, but Mattie lingered in the parlor, turning the pages of the magazine quickly before she joined them for dinner, but now, she let out a strange cry of disgust.

"What is it?" called Sue from the dining room.

Ned came back to see what his sister had found in the pages of the magazine, for she had tossed it on the floor and sat staring at it.

"What is it, Mopsy?"

She groaned, then hissed, "Shhh," and handed over the magazine while pointing to the top of one page. Ned read the caption from the book review section, "Bright Bits from Bright Books," and then the name below: Mabel Loomis Todd.

"We can't escape her, can we?" whispered Mattie. "She might leave Amherst, but she pesters us by reviewing books and forcing her way again into our home. Don't tell Mother she's writing for her favorite magazine!"

"Too late, here she comes," hissed Ned, just as Sue entered the parlor again.

"Mattie? What are you two looking at?"

It was too late to hide the magazine which Ned still held open. Sue reached for it, scanned both pages, and found the name. "Time to eat," she said, moving them toward the dining room, but as she followed them, they heard the thud as the magazine hit the floor.

"Shall I say the grace?" asked Austin, who had missed the scene. "Don't bother," said Sue, reaching for her knife.

After dinner, a painful hour during which Ned and Austin said almost nothing, Sue relented. Austin, she could see, wasn't feeling well, and it was pointless to punish him for the series of book reviews Mabel Todd had evidently begun from Boston. No, the point to be thankful for was that Mabel Todd was indeed in Boston and had been, for the most part, since mid-October. Clearly, Boston agreed with her—she had doubtless seen to it that she met Boston's important people. Good. Maybe she would decide to stay in Boston, whether or not her silly little husband stayed in Amherst. But many of the Amherst College faculty were not pleased with David Todd, not at all. More important, neither was President Seelye. He found him negligent in his duties, Austin reported after a meeting with Julius Seelye, and erratic as well. Sue had questioned him about that last—"Erratic? How, erratic?" Erratic in the sense that David often strayed from the main point into talk of his own schemes and plans, schemes which struck most people as decidedly odd. Erratic in the sense that he sometimes talked to himself, loud enough that others could hear, or that he seized other faculty members without warning to hold forth in sudden fits of animated conversation. He praised his own work often and without provocation.

Had losing his wife to another man made David unbalanced? Would she herself become unbalanced? Certainly not, she knew how to guard against that. David's case was surely unrelated to his private affairs. In fact, the more "erratic" David became, the better for her family. If the college asked him to leave, Mabel couldn't possibly return to Amherst, and the way would be clear to put the Dickinson family back together again. But in the meantime, there was nothing for it but to face Mabel's eventual return this spring or summer.

Austin lay on the day bed in the downstairs "sick room" nursing his headache. Sue stood in the doorway unobserved, staring at him for a minute.

"Austin? I have to know. When are the Todds coming back to Amherst?"

"Probably May."

"May? I thought it would be later."

"My understanding is May."

"And they'll come straight here?"

"As far as I know."

She had thought about holding her hand gently over his forehead—she had imagined it carefully as she stood in the doorway—but she could not do it, after all. She could not even stay in the room any longer, but simply turned and left. March was almost over. That left only April before her freedom would again be destroyed, her ability to move comfortably around her own village ruined.

The house was quiet. Ned had returned to his job at the college library front desk, and Mattie sat at the piano preparing to practice. "I think I'll just sit quietly and listen, if it's all right with you, Mopsy," Sue told her, sitting down and propping her feet on a footstool. After the second repetition of a Bach prelude and fugue, Sue kicked aside the magazine she had thrown down before and reached for the little sheaf of Emily's poems. A few minutes later, she got up for her writing materials and prepared to copy the poem beginning, "There came a day at summer's full." She hoped very much to see it in print. In the sick room, Austin snored gently, freed from his headache for the time being.

CHAPTER 64

April 1890

~

In April some weeks later, Lavinia lay dozing on the parlor sofa with a calico cat on her legs when a sharp voice calling her name penetrated her consciousness. There was no time to dislodge the cat or collect her wits before she saw Sue Dickinson, dressed in black, filling the hall doorway and staring at her. Lavinia started visibly.

"Well I did knock and call out several times, Vinnie, I'm sorry," said Sue. "I came over to borrow your large tureen. Mary just put a crack in ours, and I'm getting ready to send corn chowder over to Mrs. Mather. Don't bother, I'll get it. Is it still in the dining room cabinet?"

Lavinia sat up, tucking tendrils of hair behind her ears. "Yes," she said, still confused with sleep and the unusual sight of Sue Dickinson in her parlor.

Sue went into the dining room. She was gone longer than Lavinia thought necessary, but although she stood up and folded her blanket, she remained in the parlor, listening. When Sue returned, Lavinia asked her, "You telegraphed Austin about Mr. Mather's death?"

"Yes, and he says he'll try to be back from Boston on the 7:30 train tonight. Mrs. Mather is asking for him constantly. 'Where is Austin, where is Austin?' We may as well wait to make all arrangements until he returns—she won't have anyone else help her anyway, so there's no use in trying."

"Today is Austin's birthday," remarked Lavinia.

"Sue put the tureen in a canvas bag. "By the way," she said, advancing toward Lavinia in the parlor, "you might be interested to know that *Scribner's Magazine* has just accepted one of Emily's poems for publication later on this summer."

"What?" said Lavinia loudly. "How can that be?"

"How can that be? I sent a few in, that's how. I have some of my own, you know, poems Emily sent me over the years which Mattie and I have kept. You thought I'd never do anything, didn't you? But you see, I did, and I was successful. They're even going to pay me. Maybe now you wish you'd left that box full of poems with me. You have to face up to the fact, Lavinia, that you can't do anything with all those poems yourself. It's too hard a job to convince anyone to look at them, all in a muddle as they are."

She set her bag down in the hallway, took a few steps into the parlor, and glanced openly about her, while Lavinia stepped backwards. "It's been ages since I was over here," Sue said. "I hardly remember the last time. You're to blame too, because you open your doors to that woman in defiance of me and my family. I have no wish to be visiting here if she and I might—" she paused, searching for the word—"intercept each other. But while I'm here, I might as well tell you that I'm prepared to take drastic steps for changes."

She returned to the hallway to pick up her bag, and with the tureen rattling inside, made her way to the back door. "I'll send the tureen back with Mary," she called over her shoulder, "or," and she laughed, "come again myself."

Lavinia waited for the sound of the back door closing. Then she bustled over to the parlor desk to take out pen and paper, talking out loud all the while. "Mabel, you'll be amazed to hear this. It's awful—she beat us to it! But no, nothing will matter when we finish our work. Still, when she finds out what we've done"—she grimaced. "She can't know about you and the poems, no, she can't. She'd kill me! You can't have your name on the poems, no, not anywhere. Just Emily's name and maybe Mr. Higginson's. Then it'll be all right. Please, Mabel."

She began to write to Mabel, then realizing that Mabel was now in Chicago visiting cousins, said "Damn!" and tore up the paper. "I'll tell Austin," she said after some thought. "He'll straighten it all out."

The back door opened again and Maggie called out, "Miss Vinnie, I'm here!"

"Oh, Maggie," said Lavinia, hastening toward the kitchen, "I can hardly wait for the Boston train tonight—I've got to speak to Austin as soon as he gets in!"

CHAPTER 65

May 1890

MILLICENT RAN DOWN THE BACK STAIRS TO see Maggie Maher right away so she could escape her mother's restlessness and the strange smile she had worn for the last half hour on the train from Boston. Suppose Mr. Dickinson stood, all dark and sober, in the back parlor to greet them? She would detour the parlor and run down the back stairs.

"Maggie will be there to cook us supper our first night back," Mabel had told Millicent. "Phebe is with her sister again. Do you think Maggie will notice that you've grown during all this time that your father has been in Africa?"

Millicent did not usually like to be hugged, but she submitted to Maggie's embrace now in the warm kitchen smelling of roast pork, apples and blossoms from the cherry tree outside. "You've grown," said Maggie. "Your father will be amazed. He hasn't seen you since October, and here it is May already, seven months, and you ten years old! He probably looks as tanned as a pirate by now, or as dark as those Negroes who live over there in Africa. When is your father coming back, Millie?"

"In a week," said Millicent, wandering around the kitchen looking for tidbits. "Do you have something for me to eat?" she asked.

"Sure and I do, sweet child," said Maggie. "Here's some ginger cookies just baked. Have one."

Millicent sat in a white kitchen chair to eat her cookie, swinging her boots and licking the sprinkled sugar off first. When she finished, she made no move to leave but watched Maggie work. After a few minutes, Maggie asked her, "Won't your mother want you upstairs to help unpack?"

Millicent pretended to ignore her question, gazing around the kitchen instead and spotting an egg beater, which she arose to toy with, spinning the handle.

Maggie looked at her a moment, then said softly to herself, "Maybe the poor thing isn't wanted upstairs after all. Three's a crowd? Something in that line, I imagine. "Miss Millie," she said, "take off your coat and break me some eggs into the green bowl. Then you can put that beater to good use."

Thus Millicent was spared the sight of her mother in Austin's arms as they stood by the parlor fire, and the sound of their murmured voices and muffled laughter. She did not have to see their reflection in the little painted mirror or the way Austin settled Mabel in a chair and knelt by her side, holding both her hands with both of his and gazing at her with an expression never to be seen by anyone else outside this house. She did not have to shrink at the strange pervasive hush Mr. Dickinson brought to the house each time he visited.

When her mother called her from the stairs an hour later, Mr. Dickinson was gone—she sensed that right away—and the parlor fire was crackling cheerfully while Steven, a handyman borrowed from the Evergreens household, finished carrying the last trunk upstairs.

"Only a week, just think, Millicent, and we'll be a family again," said Mabel. "It may take us some getting used to, having your father around again," she laughed. "But won't we be glad, after all!"

David's return in May was anticipated by a flurry of marketing and some rearrangement of furniture as Mabel bustled about the rooms in the Dell which had been closed up for so long. Sometimes she called to Maggie, who still managed to help out both at their house and at the Homestead, "Maggie, I'm dying to get out. You don't think I'd run into her now, do you?" She filled vases with spring flowers, touched up the paint on her parlor screen, arranged decorative urns by the hearth and on the mantlepiece, and laid down a new hearth rug from Boston. The Dell never looked more light and airy, like the Queen Anne cottage it was meant to be.

One night before her father returned, Millicent was awakened by the muffled but frightening sounds from upstairs she had heard sometimes before they went to Boston, the sounds connected with Mr. Dickinson's strange night visits after she was in bed. Whether her mother was crying or laughing, she did not know, but she held the pillow over her head to muffle the sounds.

The next morning, Maggie Maher walked over from the Homestead to finish cleaning the pantry. "Mrs. Dickinson has just set out for Springfield," she told Mabel. "Did you say you wanted to walk about in the village?"

When Mabel and Millicent set out a half hour later to do errands, they saw Mr. Dickinson across the Common talking to his law partner. When they passed him, he raised his hat and smiled politely, but they did not stop and chat. In fact, Millicent could tell that her mother wished to hurry on, even though Mr. Dickinson had laughed with her upstairs the night before. The sensation of something shameful and embarrassing overwhelmed her as never before, so much so that she walked a little distance away from her mother while they completed the rest of their errands.

A few days later, Millicent and Mabel went to the depot to meet David. He was the first passenger off, a slim and tanned smiling figure who held out his arms and embraced them so roughly that his buttons bruised Millicent's cheek. "Massachusetts seems like a foreign country," he laughed as they walked down the platform toward the hack. "Millicent, you look so much older. How did that happen? Here, carry this package so I can get an arm around my beautiful wife."

After supper, he brought out all sorts of presents: a strange carved pipe from King Andah, a necklace made of dark brown nut shells, special coffee, a fragrant sachet containing crushed flowers, a doll with dark skin, and more. While Millicent took her treasures to a corner of the parlor, her parents lingered at the table, then carried their tea cups into the parlor to talk. Bits of their animated conversation caught her attention: "Yes, it was worth it, scientifically, despite the failure during totality," David was saying. "I made contributions. Now I have to have the results published in as many places as possible."

Millicent glanced over to see her mother reach out to touch David's hair. "What a funny haircut," she said tenderly. "Did my father cut it for you?"

"No, a fellow in New York cut it the morning we anchored."

Mabel ran her finger behind his ear. "You look all sweet and funny."

"Tell me more about it later upstairs," he said in a low voice.

"I will," said Mabel, "I will."

"What about the poems?" he asked in a moment. "I gather Mr. Higginson's flu set you back quite a bit. I am sure Vinnie was fit to be tied. In fact, speakng of Lavinia, it's a wonder she hasn't banged on the door yet."

"She's a bit under the weather, but she'll find you tomorrow, I'm sure. She's slowed down some—she's grown more arthritic. But the poems are in good shape. I'm going to run down to Cambridge at the end of the month and meet with Mr. Higginson for what I hope is his final selection of the lot. Then I'm prepared to take them myself to Mr. Niles—it's faster that way. Mr. Higginson is rather slow."

"But you'll have time to work with me on the scientific articles?" David said.

"Certainly," Mabel said. "Maybe I can give some talks on the expedition later, what do you think? I told you about the one I gave in Chicago on climbing Mt. Fuji. I was such a success! I wonder if I have a potential career on my hands. If these poems do well, I could talk about them and Emily."

"We're a good team, whatever else we are," said David. He sighed and narrowed his eyes over his cup. "How's the other member of our team?"

"Busier than ever. Tired. Still hounded by the Great Black Mogul, damn her. You should see her, sailing up Main Street with that dreadful glowering look she has. Sort of like a great battleship with the cannons raised and pointed."

"For God's sake, she can't be that bad!"

"But she is, David. I can hardly venture out!"

"Wouldn't you look the same way if someone had taken your husband? Anyway, I'll probably see Austin tomorrow. I want to find out what obligations they've given me for the fall. Plenty, I imagine. They're so demanding at the College, as though every time I go off on a trip it's some kind of vacation. It was no vacation. I'm lucky I didn't come back with some disease, and our living conditions were pretty rough. It'll be a while before I go away for so long again. In fact, never. I didn't lose my place here, did I?"

"Shhh." Mabel turned her head in Millicent's direction. "You'll soon get the answers to your question upstairs." In a louder voice, she called over to Millicent, "Time to put things away and think about getting ready for bed."

CHAPTER 66

July 1890

By mid July, when the Dickinson meadow hummed with bees, and butterflies alighted on Millicent's arms as she played there, Mabel and Lavinia rested triumphant: Roberts Brothers in Boston had agreed to publish 116 poems if Lavinia would pay for the plates.

"We've done it! Mabel told Lavinia. "I toast you with a bon-bon!"

"But what comes next," persisted Lavinia, twisting a button on her dress with gnarled fingers. "Are you finished with your work?"

"Oh, no, certainly not," said Mabel. "They'll make up proofs and send them to us first to check over. Then there's the frontspiece to decide on, and a preface by Mr. Higginson. He wants to write an article in *Century Magazine* too before the book comes out, to prepare the public, you know. Then if all goes well, they should publish sometime in November."

"He wants to write an article?" said Lavinia falteringly. "But Sue will see that."

"Well," said Mabel, "what of it? Did you think she would somehow never see the published poems? Of course she'll see it, and them too. She'll have to live with the whole idea."

Lavinia stood up and moved toward the door.

"You're not leaving?" asked Mabel.

"Yes, I must go," said Lavinia, and left abruptly.

"She seems stranger every day," said Mabel smiling to herself, sinking into a chair and picking up a magazine to read, a welcome change from the close editing she had done for so long.

But she was not smiling when she met David at the door one afternoon soon afterwards, waving a letter from Mr. Higginson. "I'm in total shock, David. How could Vinnie be so treacherous? How could she? After all the work I did? The work she *begged* me to do."

"*Now* what's happened?" said David, setting his leather case down. "If it isn't one Dickinson, it's another disrupting our lives."

"Well, I can't help it," said Mabel in an irritated voice. "And I found out about this by accident. Look, Mr. Higginson sent me a letter he had from Vinnie asking that my name not be included on the poems anywhere. I should be "sub rosa" is how she so delicately put it. Poor Mr. Higginson couldn't read her writing and missed the whole point, so he sent the wretched thing to me to interpret. She asks that my name not be mentioned on the poems I myself copied by hand— that I be just cut out of the whole project. No recognition at all."

She paced the floor, nearly bumping into David as he held out his hand for the letter. "Oh, Lavinia will hear a thing or two, you can be sure of that." David read both Lavinia's and Mr. Higginson's letters before sitting down. "He must think we're all crazy. Did she do this because she's afraid of Sue?"

"It looks that way. I knew she was afraid, but good Lord, she must be terrified."

"Well, Mabs, are you going to fight for your name?"

"I certainly am! Damn her, anyway, letting her fear of Sue control her like that. She thinks she can make *me* pay the price for what she asked me to do behind Sue's back. Well, I won't. I deserve full credit for discovering Emily. I'll just write Mr. Higginson and tell him to ignore all this. He'll listen to me—he already knows Lavinia is strange."

David picked up the rest of the day's mail from the hall table and sat down in the parlor to read it. "It's strange to think the College will have a new president in a few months. This Merrill Gates is too religious for me. He looks as though he wants to cut you down and then say a prayer over you after-wards. I don't know how poor Charles Garman in philosophy will fare with him. His methods of teaching are too unorthodox for the likes of Gates." He held up a letter. "One for you from Mr. Howells. Did you see it?"

Mabel reached for it. "Yes, but I didn't have the energy to read anything else after that firecracker from Mr. Higginson. William Dean Howells—how lovely! I told him so much in Boston about Emily's poems that I wanted him to know right away about approximate publication dates. If he could review her favor-ably he could do us so much good."

She opened the letter. "Look, he always asks about Millicent first off. He and his wife fell in love with her while you were away, David, I wish you could have seen it. He played croquet with her, read to her, and his wife asked to brush her hair. They miss their little girl so much—I don't know how they have borne her death—but they always had love to give Millicent."

"Did she like them back though?" asked David.

"Of course. She's playing upstairs right now with the puzzle they gave her."

"I just wondered," said David, slitting open an envelope, "because the way she edges around Austin is pathetic—and she's been awfully standoffish with me, too, since I've come back from Africa. Of course, the way Austin talks to her is so stilted—I don't think he has any idea of how to talk to a young girl."

"That's not fair David," said Mabel. "Millicent is so shy and awkward around him..."

Without warning, David tossed down his mail. "What I really mean to ask is, have you dropped that tom-fool idea of getting pregnant—by your king, of course?"

Mabel turned, stunned. Then she shot back, "Why did you bring that up now? We were having a perfectly nice conversation. Why did you ruin it like this?" Her face contorted suddenly and she choked out, "Oh, not you too, hacking away at me? Not you too." She ran from the room and up the stairs.

David sat shuffling the mail in his hands for a few minutes, smiling at times, at other times groaning slightly. Finally, he rose slowly to his feet and climbed the two flights of stairs to the third floor where he knew Mabel would be. He would make things right. He knew he could. Meanwhile, he thought he felt oddly better for having provoked this quarrel. He would apologize, yes, but he felt better. Decidedly better.

CHAPTER 67

September 1890

Austin received Mabel's brief note at the Homestead when he stopped to check on Lavinia at noon on a brisk September day. "It's something about Mr. Higginson's article on the poems," Lavinia told him. "She was in a hurry, but she said, 'Get ready for trouble.' Oh, I tried to make withhold her name on those poems for my sake, but now I'm stuck. I wish you'd have tried to help more."

Austin pocketed Mabel's note. "I can't keep track of everything, Vinnie, there are some things you and Mabel must settle between you. Is she coming back for an answer?"

"Yes, in an hour."

"Then tell her the usual place—I can get away."

The sky clouded over as the afternoon wore on, and the wind blew up sharp and cold, causing Austin to look anxiously out the window from his trustee meeting at the college. The new president, Dr. Merrill Gates, followed his anxious glance with a raised eyebrow. "A little storm won't trouble us, will it?"

When at last Austin was free and turned the carriage out Pleasant Street, he spotted Mabel's familiar figure among the trees. She held her hat on with one arm and warded off the wind with the other. "At last," she said, climbing quickly into the carriage. "But I needed to tell you right away—Mr. Higginson's article about Emily's poems has come out already! He gave me the impression it wouldn't be until October, but to my horror, Mr. Niles mentioned in a letter I received this morning that I could read the article myself tonight in the *Christian Union*. Drive, before anyone comes bumbling along." She tied her hat ribbons firmly under her chin and reached for her handkerchief. "On top of all this, I think I'm getting a cold."

Austin flicked the reins, but reached over to squeeze Mabel's hand. There was silence between them a moment as they held hands, their faces bent into the wind and the eddies of falling leaves.

"Well, you know what this means, don't you?" Mabel asked him. "You've either got to prepare Sue or let her hear about it from someone else. I told you you ought to break it to her but I suppose you never said a word, did you? Between you and Vinnie, I don't know...I never saw two people so afraid of someone." She glanced at him. "But I do understand why, my love. Don't be thrown by my mood this afternoon. I suppose I'm dreading it as much as you."

"I'll pull over to the old barn so we can talk," said Austin, and spoke no further until he reached an abandoned property they often used for shelter and privacy. Placing the carriage out of sight behind a grove of trees, he turned to her and held out his arms.

"But I've got a sore throat," she said.

"No matter. Come." He opened his arms wider and she submitted, nestling against his chest and sighing, "Oh dear God, it feels wonderful to be near you at last. I've had such a hectic day. I spent all morning going over the plate proofs and the table of contents. I sent them back to Boston just an hour ago. And now I'm so worried about what will happen when your "power" hears about Mr. Higginson's article in the *Christian Union*. What do you think she'll do?"

"Probably just what you imagine. But I can honestly tell her I had nothing to do with yours and Vinnie's plans. It's you and Vinnie she will attack more than me. So I will try to defend you both. Beyond that, I'm afraid we must all just weather it. Remember that nothing else matters but the fact that we have each other. Let me kiss you."

Mabel kept her head down but Austin said, "Please. I must."

When she raised her head he kissed her long and deliberately until she clung to him with a little cry. "It's been ages, oh, so long," she said between kisses, and then as he reached for their blankets and prepared to step from the carriage, "I wasn't prepared..."

"No matter," Austin said, as he left the carriage and held his arm out for her to descend. They entered a corner of the barn and spread their blankets to make love. "I've desired you all afternoon," was the last thing he whispered before Mabel's cries made words superfluous.

"Drive anywhere, I don't care," said Mattie to Ned the next afternoon. "Just keep moving. And don't look to right or left—I don't want to talk to anyone."

"Was Mother still crying when I picked you up?"

"I think so, but she wants to be alone now. She's in her room by the fire. I don't see how she can sort it all out, but she's trying. Who would have dreamed that Aunt Vinnie could have given those poems to Mrs. Todd? I just can't take it in, can you?"

Ned turned to wave at Mrs. Stearns who stood across the street from the observatory, but Mattie kept her head down. "No," he said. "No, I can't. It's as though she had planned to trick us in the most calculated way. And yet, I do remember hearing Aunt Vinnie asking Mother to help with the poems and Mother said she wasn't interested."

"But that doesn't give her the right to take the poems to someone else! They belong to the family!" protested Mattie. "It would be bad enough if she'd taken them to Henry Hills or Mrs. Mather or—or the grocer. But to Mrs. Todd—no, I can never forgive Aunt Vinnie, or Father either. But not forgiving father goes without saying."

They drove along the Northampton road, the trees resplendent in fall oranges and reds. Dark clouds blew overhead in the cold north wind, a hawk balanced in the drafts, and the goldenrod swayed low. Mattie tied the ribbons of her hat firmly under her chin, but Ned took his hat off and tucked it under the carriage robe.

"What will the Jenkins family say when they read about Aunt Emily's poems?" said Mattie. "They take the *Christian Union* don't they?"

"They'll congratulate us," said Ned. "I hope they don't have even a hint about Father and Mrs. Todd anyway. Why would they, unless some gossip from home has written to them?"

"But that's just what I think someone must have done by now, Ned," said Mattie. "Mrs. Jenkins writes to so many people here from the old days when he was the minister—I can't believe that someone hasn't mentioned it. I'm always so uncomfortable when we go to visit them I can hardly stand it, imagining what they know, worrying that they pity us and Mother. Oh, I could just die!" She dropped her head into her cupped hands and wept while Ned glanced at her helplessly.

When she stopped crying, she said in a muffled voice, "Do you ever think you might not want to be married?"

"I don't know. I'm not sure anyone would have me anyway."

"Don't be silly. And anyway, I don't mean that, I mean, doesn't it seem grim, being married? And risky? So often, nothing good at all comes out of it. Quite honestly, I'm not sure I would like it. Maggie's cousin died after her very first baby, and she was only seventeen. And Mary from Miss Porter's—her husband won't let her go anywhere."

They rode in silence for a few moments. Then Mattie spoke again. "But I know there *can* be value in marriage. I'd like to make a good marriage, of course, but can you imagine how hard it would be to find someone from Amherst to marry? That's why you should travel with Mother and me as much as you can. New York, Geneva, Boston—we'll be sure to meet people of good social standing there. I'm certainly not interested in anyone from this provincial town and you shouldn't be either. I want to marry someone who knows nothing about all the gossip, either. I intend to rise above it, and when I do, I'll take Mother to live with me and my husband so she can rise above it too."

"I'm afraid my being sick so much will affect my chances," said Ned. "Father is so steady with me when I'm sick—I can never forget that. He thinks I don't remember those times in the night, but I do; at least, I think I do, some of them. Do you?" He turned to look at her.

"No. Well, yes, some, to be honest."

"Why haven't you ever mentioned it?" Ned swallowed. "Are they so terrible that you can't bear to mention them? What's it all about, anyway?"

"I don't know. Mother always said not to mention them. She thought it would disturb you to talk about it."

"Disturb me? Me? I'm already disturbed enough when I'm sick. How could it be worse to mention being sick? I hate mysteries. What exactly is supposed to be wrong with me, then? That's what I can't figure out."

"I don't know, Ned. Something like the falling sickness, I presume."

"I presumed something like that too. Like Julius Caesar?"

"I just don't know, Ned."

"I wonder what causes the falling sickness. Maybe something horrible in the family past. But we don't have anything horrible in our family past."

"No," said Mattie, "only in our family present, and her name is Mrs. Todd. Look, Neddie, I don't know if you have what they call the falling sickness, and even if you did, I can't imagine it came from anything horrible in the past, as you say. Why don't you ask Mother about it, right out?"

"No, not now, anyway. She's got enough to worry about. I just wondered about it because I figured maybe someday I'd need to mention it to any lady I consider marrying—if I ever meet such a person. After all, I'm twenty-seven now. I'd like to be married and on my own soon. Trouble is, I don't know what I'd like to do—to earn a living, you know. It worries me a lot."

"Marry a rich woman if you can," said Mattie.

"Oh, be serious," said Ned.

"I am serious, marry a rich woman," Mattie repeated. "There's nothing wrong with that, not a thing in the world. That's why you should spend as much time as you can in Boston and New York or the vacation hotels. You'll meet eligible women there. I'd like to live in New York or Boston in the winter and travel in Europe in the summer. You could do the same."

Ned shook his head. "I can't quite imagine living anywhere but Amherst."

Mattie cut him off. "Well I certainly can! I dream of it, of getting away from that house and that street and the small-minded people. The Evergreens can go up in flames, as far as I'm concerned! I shouldn't tell you, but sometimes I imagine it burning."

"Mattie!" said Ned. "Don't! Should we turn around and go back soon?"

"But I don't want to go back. What will we do at home, anyway? Sit and listen to Mother cry? Wait for Father to come home and then ignore him? Go next door and tell Aunt Vinnie what we think of her? You tell me!"

"We can't drive around forever, Mattie Let's go back and play checkers by the fire. Maybe Mother will be glad we're nearby."

"All right," said Mattie, "turn around. But I'm not speaking to anyone I see, I'm tired of everyone and everybody." She folded her arms across her chest and looked stonily ahead as the horses turned toward Amherst. "Not only that, I'm going to plan some way to punish Mrs. Todd for what she has done, trying to grab all the credit for *our* aunt's poems. Those belong to *us*. The very thought of her touching them, even reading them, makes me sick."

"But Mopsy," said Ned, "despite everything, I'm curious to see what this book of poems will look like. Imagine, reading Aunt Emily's poems in print. I always liked what Aunt Emily wrote, though it never occurred to me that people outside the family would read the poems. But now that it has happened, I'm glad in an odd way. Especially if it's what Aunt Emily would have wanted. Who paid to publish them?"

"Aunt Vinnie did. I heard Father tell Mother that."

"November 12th, you say, is the publication date?"

"Yes," said Mattie.

"Then we should be prepared to answer questions. Let's decide on the answers with Mother. Will Mrs. Todd's name be in the book somewhere?"

"Oh no, I didn't think of that!" said Mattie, covering her eyes. "I'm sure it will. Everyone in Amherst will see Mrs. Todd's name linked with Aunt Emily's.

How terrible, oh, poor Mother, poor us, what will we do, Ned?" She crossed her arms against her chest and rocked back and forth.

"Mopsy, calm down! It isn't as terrible as you're making it."

She raised her head and said with gritted teeth, "We'll decide how you and Mother and I will handle this, and we'll never waver. We'll hold our heads high and act as though nothing has bothered us. Meanwhile, I intend to make Mrs. Todd suffer for this."

"Let's still have a game of checkers by the fire."

"Yes, we'll have a game of checkers until Mother comes down. Then we must take care of her and protect her. Do you agree?"

"I agree," said Ned. "We'll make a fence and keep everyone out but us— you, me, and Mother."

CHAPTER 68

September 1890

N O, MY DEAR, SUSAN HASN'T SAID A WORD about you in connection with the poems. Only about Lavinia." Mrs. Stearns accepted a teacup from Mabel's hand in the Dell parlor. "But she held forth most forcefully on the subject of Lavinia's treachery, I'm sorry to tell you."

"She didn't waste any time. Mr. Higginson's article about the poems has only been out for a week and a half. What was her argument then?" asked Mabel.

"She claimed that the poems had been given to her by Emily, and that she owned them."

"She *owned* them?" exclaimed Mabel.

"Yes, that's exactly what she said. That she owned them, and that Lavinia had borrowed them and then deceived everyone by publishing them. She said the whole family was embarrassed by it all, but allowances had to be made for Lavinia, who doesn't understand the ways of the world."

"Well, that last part is true, anyway. Lavinia surely doesn't understand the ways of the world. I found that out vividly. So did Mr. Higginson. I told you, didn't I, about her asking him to leave my name off the poems? Austin and I finally made her change her mind. But who is to say how one should deal with Lavinia? Somehow David knows that best."

Mabel held out the cake tray. "Have a slice of pound cake. I've saved the letters Emily sent me, you know. Have you had letters from her?"

"Yes indeed. I save any interesting correspondence, or correspondence from people I care about, and Emily fitted both those descriptions. She was a caring person, and ferociously intelligent. Everyone knows how quick our Emily was." Mrs. Stearns bit into Mabel's pound cake. "Marvelous cake, Mabel, so moist."

"It did turn out rather well. But oh yes, Emily thought quite a lot of me, I could tell. I feel sure she wanted very much to meet me face to face, but couldn't make any exceptions in her decision not to mingle with people. It's too bad—we would have had much to tell each other. I know she admired me. I had a letter from her when I was in Europe signed 'America.' Such a clever touch. She admired my talents. Austin often talked with her about me." She shook her head. "Mary, you can't imagine what a relief it is to have one friend who knows something of the way I feel about Austin and how much I've tried to make his life happier. You stand back without judging—that's rare. Ever since we talked last year I've felt so much better."

"But don't tell me more than I need to know, Mabel. I know enough to make me uncomfortable already. I hope this spotlight on Emily's forthcoming poems won't exert too much additional pressure on Susan and Austin."

With no answer forthcoming, both sat silently until Mrs. Stearns changed the subject. "Do you still correspond with Mr. Howells? I love to hear about him from you, admiring his books as I do."

"Oh," said Mabel, "he wrote two weeks ago to say he'll be sending me the proofs of his review of Emily's poems soon. He wants me to check it over for accuracy before he sends it to *Harper's*."

"Really! I'm so glad, my dear. I love to hear about all your activities—you're so much in the thick of things."

"Yes, I am, and I love it. But I think I'd give it all up to live peacefully in this town without the nastiness—you know full well what I mean—to live in this town in peace. I won't say a word more, but I know you understand. Having your loyal friendship has meant so much to me, Mary, I'll say it again." She reached briefly for Mrs. Stearns's hand and then arose. "Please excuse me while I check on Millicent upstairs."

While Mabel was upstairs, Mrs. Stearns leaned back comfortably in her chair and enjoyed the warmth of the fire while she gazed at the mantel decorations—the framed family portraits, the urns from Switzerland, the fans from Japan, the dried flowers from the Dickinson meadow, all displayed artistically. The airiness of Mabel's parlor contrasted with her own, which was crowded with heavy furniture and draperies. She found Mabel's parlor fascinating—another atmosphere from hers altogether, modern, breezy, assured. But she preferred the solid tradition of her own in the long run.

She raised her teacup to drink when a sharp tap at the parlor window made her start violently, spilling some tea. Turning, she saw a flash of blue as someone moved from the window. She stood, puzzled, until another sharp rap, only this time at the front door, caused Mabel to appear at the top of the stairs.

"Someone is at the front door," said Mrs. Stearns. "Shall I go?"

"Please," Mabel called down. "Phebe is off and I need to wash my hands from this sticky cough medicine. It's probably Vinnie—I know her knock."

But there was no need for Mrs. Stearns to open the door, since Lavinia opened it herself, calling out, "It's me. Who's in here? Oh, it's you, Mary Stearns. Have you heard about Emily's poems? They will be published on November 12th, thanks to me. Now the whole world will learn about my sister. I can hardly sit down ever since I heard the good news." She paced about the entrance hallway hugging her checked shawl. "Where is Mabel?"

"She's upstairs tending to Millicent. Why don't you sit by the fire with me?"

"Oh, I doubt I could sit for very long," said Lavinia, advancing to a chair by the parlor fire even as she spoke. "My mind has been going every which way. I wake up every hour during the night, thinking and thinking. You know that the poems will be published in early November?"

"Yes, you said..." began Mrs. Stearns.

"Aha! Let me be the first to tell you. Emily's poems will be published the first or second week of November, and there may be the very devil to pay. But don't worry your head about that, no, you wouldn't be expected to understand that." She took a turn around the room, pausing to look out the window a moment. "Mabel should get Austin to put in another tree right there, that space of lawn is bare as Buddha's belly."

To Mrs. Stearns's relief, she heard Mabel descending the stairs. "Is everything all right, Vinnie?" Mabel asked her as she entered the parlor.

"Yes, yes, I just wondered if you'd thought any more about what the royalties might be, and whether someone we know still has an active tongue."

"Sit down, Vinnie, rest yourself. I wish you wouldn't think about royalties now—we don't even know whether the poems will sell yet. It's always wise to be cautious in the publishing business. That's why you signed the contract agreeing to pay for the printing plates."

"But what *could* royalties amount to, that's all I wondered," persisted Lavinia.

"Impossible to say. You mustn't even think about it now. Just be happy we brought Emily's poems to light so everyone can enjoy them. I'm optimistic, but we still have to wait. I'm tired, Vinnie. We deserve a rest!" Mabel caught Mrs. Stearns's eye and smiled. "Eat some cake, Vinnie."

"I'll take a piece home. I'd prefer to eat it after supper alone." She reached for the cake plate, took a piece in her hand, and turned toward the door.

"Wait, let me put it on a plate and cover it for you," said Mabel. Lavinia followed Mabel to the pantry and the house became suddenly quiet. Mrs. Stearns suspected Lavinia was whispering to Mabel, probably discussing something she had held back when she discovered Mabel wasn't alone.

In five minutes, Mabel emerged alone and rejoined Mrs. Stearns by the fire. "That was vintage Lavinia," she said, shaking her head. "She left by the back door clutching her cake and telling me she would ask David about royalties. I tell you Mary, I may have published one book by one Dickinson, but I could write another one myself about the lot of them."

"Lavinia has a good heart though, doesn't she?" said Mrs. Stearns.

"She does. I don't think she would ever cause me intentional pain. No, I have nothing to fear from poor Lavinia Dickinson."

Both women sighed in pleasant relaxation before the fire while the afternoon shadows lengthened on the lawn and the Pelham hills, and the late afternoon train whistle hooted two miles out from the Amherst depot.

November 1890

~

S TAY LONGER," SAID MILLICENT'S FRIEND
Alison. "We can start putting together the new puzzle your grandmother sent
since you brought it along."

"All right," said Millicent, following along into her friend's play corner. "It
shows George Washington's home in Mount Vernon. I've been there. Twice."

"Twice?" Alison said, opening the puzzle box and dumping the pieces onto
a low table. "I've never been. Who took you, your mother and father?"

"My grandmother took me once and my parents the other time," said
Millicent, sitting down at the table and spreading the puzzle pieces out.

"Do you have two fathers?" asked Alison abruptly.

"Two fathers? Of course not. How could I have two fathers?"

"Oh look," said Alison, "I found a corner piece already!"

"Save it," said Millicent. "Shall we try to find all four corners right away?"

"All right," said Alison.

"What do you mean, about two fathers?" Millicent rolled up her sleeves.

"I heard my mother talking with someone. Mother said it was too bad all
women couldn't have two husbands like your mother does, and how convenient it must be. She said your mother knew how to play her cards right, and
so did Mr. Dickinson. So I thought maybe you had another father in Washington, since you go there so often."

"Of course I don't," said Millicent. "I have only one father and you know his
name. Professor David Todd."

"Well, that does make more sense. I wondered..." Alison said. "But my
mother says your family goes by different rules. Hey. Move your hand, there's
the second corner piece, right there." She reached around Millicent's fingers
and set the piece aside.

Millicent moved her chair back from the table and frowned.

"You're not mad, are you, about what I just told you?" Alison said, looking over. "Don't be mad, I was only asking. You never know about things unless you ask."

"No, I'm not mad. But I think I should go," said Millicent. "It's too late in the afternoon to start this puzzle. I think I should go home and practice for the recitations next week. Do you know your poems yet?"

"One of them. I have to learn the other two. Don't you hate it? I can't bear to learn poems by heart."

"I like it," said Millicent. "My mother knows lots of Miss Emily Dickinson's poems by heart and I know some too. If you want to see what the poems look like in a book, I'll show you soon. I told you that my mother made Miss Dickinson's poems into a book."

"All right," said Alison. "Can I work on this puzzle while you're gone?"

"Yes, it doesn't make any difference to me," said Millicent. "I may be too busy tomorrow to work any more on it because my father will be taking me with him to Northampton. Put in all the pieces you want. It's all right."

She pulled on her coat and walked quickly out into the fall afternoon air, slowing her steps as soon as she reached the Common so that she could think—and she had much to think about. Sometimes it struck her that she hardly had one father, let alone two. Did Alison's mother mean the other father was Mr. Dickinson? She shuddered. What did it mean, anyway? Was it a joke or something with truth in it? Mr. Dickisnon could not be her father—she had been born before her family moved to Amherst. Relief swept over her. Although she understood something about how babies came into the world, much of the process remained a mystery. However, Alison's mother had given her some ideas she had to think about again. Could it be that when Mr. Dickinsnon stayed late into the night, he was trying to give her mother a baby? But if that were true, why had not a baby come? If what she had heard from her friends were right, when a man lay down with a woman and did what Millicent found to be unimaginable, a baby was always the result. But there was no baby. So Mr. Dickinson could not have lain down with her mother after all. Instead, it must be that they laughed some of the time and talked very seriously some of the time.

Still, it was not right or proper that Mr. Dickinson should spend so much time with her mother in their home or on carriage rides or in their upstairs guest room. Millicent was more and more aware of that fact from conversations she overheard and from her own common sense. A woman should have one husband only, and he and their child should be the center of her world.

Millicent cut across some lawns and onto College Street. After a few more shortcuts, she reached her house and entered from the rear porch steps. Her mother sat in the back parlor with an opened parcel beside her containing some books with white covers, all alike. She held one of these books in her lap and turned the pages, smiling.

"Look, Millie, here are the poems, all finished. I'm getting to see them before almost anyone else. Come here, look. Isn't it exciting?"

But Millicent did not enter the parlor. Her heart thumping as she carried out a deliberate snub, she went to her room upstairs without answering. She hoped her mother would call her back. She would still not go, and then maybe her mother would be sorry and ask her what the matter was. She wouldn't tell, but later, she would sit beside her mother, resting her head on her lap if she could manage it. But although Millicent stood still halfway up the stairs to listen, her mother did not call her back. Her mother was completely absorbed in the new book of poems. If she hadn't been angry, Millicent would have liked to see what her mother's name looked like in print inside the book, along with Mr. Higginson's, and of course, Miss Dickinson's. But she would not go back into the parlor now. She would go to her room even though it was cold there, and stay as long as she could stand it. And if anyone ever asked her about having two fathers, she would have a very definite answer ready for them. She opened the door of her room and knelt by the window. After a few minutes, she wrapped her quilt around her and returned to the window to watch the trees sway and the smoke rise from the neighbors' chimneys, including Mr. Dickinson's chimney on Main Street. She hated Mr. Dickinson's house and everyone in it, for that matter.

When her mother finally called her, her knees were stiff and her hands were cold. But her mother acted as though nothing was wrong. "Are you hungry, Millie? Come down and let me hear your recitations while we set the table."

Thus David found his wife and daughter in apparent harmony when he came home from college a half hour later, and he even listened while Millicent recited a poem about the rainbow's colors. But as always, her parents settled themselves in the back parlor and brought out the endless papers they were always reading and correcting. "I want you to rework your explanation of figures here," her mother said, handing a paper over to her father. "It seems rather labored to me—do you really want all those semicolons?"

"Fix it," her father said amiably.

Thus her parents worked companionably while Millicent wrote lessons in her geography notebook and then assembled a paperdoll family in her doll house. "Time for bed, Millie?" her mother said, looking up.

Millicent put her papers away without protest and stood up, preparing to carry out a plan she had concocted while she played. "Good night, Daddy," she said, giving him a kiss on the cheek. She bypassed her mother without a word and went shakily upstairs, amazed at her own snub.

"What was that all about?" asked David. "Is she trying to rub your nose in something?"

"I have no idea," said Mabel. "Whatever it is, I'm sure she'll get over it quickly enough." She handed him another page. "I think a paragraph is missing here. The section on the corona ends before you finish explaining the temperatures."

Upstairs, Millicent got ready for bed and lay down to think, fixing her eyes on the faint square of light from her window. Her thoughts roamed. Imagine having Mr. Dickinson for a father. She turned toward the wall with a grimace and was soon asleep.

January 1891

W<small>HY IS GOD CRUEL? WHY IS GOD DEAF?</small>" Mabel groaned to herself, sinking into her studio rocking chair and holding her cramping abdomen. "Why is it that Sue set herself against bearing children, yet had three, and I can have none from him?"

She leaned back and rocked quietly, looking out the third floor window at the wintry landscape, listening to the sleet falling on the hard snowy lawn. She had plenty to do, yet for the moment, she felt unable to move. She ought to be jubilant, with the poems into yet another edition and the reviews positive. She and Mr. Higginson already had plans for a second volume of poetry, and she had accepted several speaking engagements about the poems, much to Sue's disgust, she knew. The events and successes of the past days had been among her finest.

Yet when others could casually enjoy the company of those they loved, she wasn't even able to stroll on Main Street with the person she esteemed above all others in the world. She wondered more and more: was loving Austin worth this pain and suffering? Could she endure it for years and years? Should she ask him again about relocating in the Midwest? True, she could not imagine it, leaving David and going to some other town with Austin, but then she would have been unable to imagine feeling married to two men, either, until she fell in love with Austin. All things were possible. She must not give up hope. Not about a child, either, for a child might be the convincing element, the event that would force Austin to make a move.

The thought of a child reminded her again sharply of her cramping abdomen and her renewed disappointment this month. But they had not been together many times in the past few months—it was always hard to find time and privacy in the winter. In spring and summer, things would be different. Meanwhile, she must focus on her busy schedule. "No matter the ugly gossip,

I am more admired and respected than gossiped about," she told herself. "I was meant to be a leader, to share my talents, and so I will, starting with my two latest projects besides Emily's letters: chairing a committee to form an Amherst Faculty Club and beginning my 'Mondays at home'."

Inviting her friends in to see her would go a long way to reducing the stress she suffered from snubs at other people's social functions. Having her own regular "at homes" would draw together those who respected her, effectively filtering out all the others.

A movement outside caught her eye—Austin, head bent low against the sleet, crossing into her lawn from the back. They had made no plans to meet; could something be wrong? Or maybe—and she smiled—surprisingly right?

She went to the door and squinting against the sleet, leaned out over the stairs they had built for just such occasions—unobtrusive entrances into the Dell. Austin, with a quick glance up at her, climbed the stairs. She held the door open until he stamped his feet on the top steps and entered the warm hallway. Quickly and wordlessly, she brushed the sleet from his overcoat, opened it, and put her arms around his warm body. They stood in this embrace quietly for a moment until she broke away, her cheek wet with sleet from his collar. "A wonderful surprise! Everything all right?"

"Yes, I just found some unexpected free moments. Mr. Parker canceled his appointment and Sue went to Northampton with Mattie this morning, despite the weather, while she rehearses for a recital next week."

"Come sit in my cozy studio, my love. Let's make the best of our time."

She shook his coat in the lavatory over the tub and then joined him by the fire. "Piano and cello, is it, for this recital?"

"Yes, with one of Mrs. Lacey's pupils."

He leaned back and stretched his feet toward the fire. "Are you still going ahead with the plans to collect Emily's letters?" he asked.

"Yes," said Mabel sitting down and reaching for Austin's hand. "Mr. Higginson is still as enthusiastic as I am. Why?"

"I still have some reservations, but I'm willing to let them go. It's just that I have something I've kept for five years now. I thought it was time I showed you." He reached into his breast pocket and pulled out a large envelope. Mabel reached out her hand but he held the crackling envelope back a moment. "Vin gave them to me soon after Emily died. She burned so much, you know, but these she felt bound to save, at least until she showed them to me."

"But what are they?" asked Mabel, again reaching out her hand.

"Her letters to Otis Lord—Judge Lord, you remember? Not many, but they're decidedly strong. They leave no doubt but that they loved each other. I thought you ought to see them and we could decide together what to do with them."

This time when she reached her hand to him, he gave her the envelope. "And you had them all this time? You didn't show me? Why?"

"I don't know—they took me by surprise, I think. I had no idea she felt this strongly about him. I thought I should respect her privacy."

"You didn't throw any away?"

"No, none."

"But these look like rough drafts. How do we know she actually sent them?"

"You'll see—she answers questions from his last letters, things like that."

"Where are his to her?" asked Mabel.

"I suppose Vin burned them without looking at them. She says she doesn't remember."

Mabel groaned. "I think these should be published along with everything else we can collect. Why not?"

"But they are so private—she was so private."

"Not anymore. All that's changed now."

Her eye was drawn back to the pages she held in her hand, and for a few minutes, she concentrated, her face reflecting what she read. Sometimes she laughed—"Jumbo Lord?" How wonderfully funny and sweet. Imagine, calling herself Jumbo, did you know that, darling?" Sometimes she shook her head in wonderment—"'Incarcerate me in yourself—rosy penalty,' oh Austin, how powerful!"

Her expression changed suddenly as a thought crossed her mind. "Does SHE know about these?"

"No, she doesn't."

Mabel sighed. "Good. I wouldn't want her to know before I knew." She leaned back in her chair, suddenly weary, the letters in her lap. "I forgot to tell you my news. Another monthly came today. Another failure. I'm so depressed."

"Don't be," Austin said. "We weren't together enough, for one thing. Let's not worry over it. Remember, we'll have hours and hours of time in August. She'll be in Maine again. Don't make our Experiment a burden."

"No, no, I won't," said Mabel a trifle impatiently. "May I keep the letters?"

"Yes, keep them. No one better. If anyone had to see them, I think Emily would have chosen us."

The room had darkened as the afternoon shadows drew in, even though the sleet had stopped. "Have you declined the Faculty Club dinner invitation as we agreed?" asked Mabel. "Because if you go with her, then David and I will have to stay home."

"Yes, I declined it. An overnight appointment in Boston came in handy and solved the dilemma. So go, by all means, you and David."

"I am rather looking forward to it. I know people will want to ask me about the poems and how I managed it all. It will be a good chance to ask for letters, too. Do you think it would be appropriate?"

"I don't see why not." He stood. "I imagine she and Mattie are nearly back by now. I should go." He held out his arms and they embraced. Mabel retrieved his coat and after another embrace, Austin walked carefully down the icy steps and crossed along the side of the house to College Street, where he walked toward campus until he connected with the Common and then struck out for Main Street in the direction of his house. He just missed David Todd who, coming home early from his office, strode quickly along College Street blowing his nose with a large handkerchief. His cold had worsened but he looked forward to the back parlor fire and maybe a warm whisky punch.

In her third floor studio, Mabel read Emily's letters to Judge Lord of Salem for the fourth time. "I wish I could show you my special letters too," Mabel said softly. "I wish I could."

March 1891

IN MARCH, SUE RECEIVED WORD FROM William Ward of *The Independent* that he would publish two poems she had sent him by Emily Dickinson. When she told Austin in his study, he objected on the grounds that Lavinia held the copyright.

"I'm tired of hearing about it, Sue. I don't want anything to do with it."

Sue advanced to the doorway. "That's just too bad, because you *have* plenty to do with it, and you know it. You sit there and pretend you wash your hands of the whole issue when you knew long ago that Vinnie and Mabel were going to publish the poems. How could you dare hide that from me? And now, when I manage to have two poems published in the paper, just two, all havoc breaks out. Mr. Ward writes to Mabel, Vinnie writes to Mr. Ward, on and on. Yet you say you don't want anything to do with it. My dear dishonest Austin, you have everything in the world to do with it!"

"Leave it alone, leave it alone," said Austin from his desk, not raising his voice. "Don't try to publish any more poems or you'll have Vin on both our backs again. She's adamant about this, and she does hold copyright. You can't get around that."

Sue stood in the doorway, rigid, clenching her fists and speechless in her anger, until her frustration gave way and she seized Austin's walking stick from the corner, throwing it as hard as she could toward him. It glanced off the edge of his desk, knocking his pen stand and a small photograph of Gilbert to the floor. Austin had shielded his face with his elbow, but hearing the tinkling of glass, he let his head fall into his hands. The picture frame lay shattered, releasing Sue's anger even further, as though Austin had knocked it down himself. She picked up the walking stick and advanced with it to whack the front of the desk several times, drawing air over her clenched teeth. As Austin half stood in alarm, she threw down the stick and backed off, shouting, "And we used to love each other so much, Emily and I. We did, we did. 'What do you suppose marriage is like?' she asked me. I couldn't tell her. And to imagine that you and I would be fighting over the poems, Emily's beautiful poems. I think I'm going to be sick!" and she rushed from the room, retching, passing Ned who stood hunched at the foot of the stairs, holding his ears.

Austin rose without a word and closed the door of his study where shaking, he stood with his eyes closed for a full three minutes before kneeling to pick up Gilbert's picture and the broken glass around it. A silence fell over the house. Sue had run outside, and stood now, trying to control her nausea. Ned had tiptoed upstairs to the stair landing with a racing heart where he paused and then headed for the door leading to the back bedrooms, that portion of the house unused since Gilbert's death. Closing the door from the main corridor behind him, he stopped at Gilbert's room on the left. He could see the familiar objects through the little window opening onto the hallway, the same window his mother had used to check on all of them when they were young. There was the tricycle, the rocking horse with its coat of gray felt, the brass bed, the low cupboards. He entered Gilbert's room with the same sense of hush and refuge he always felt. Here, surrounded by Gilbert's toys and furniture, he could be alone and give way to melancholy. Sitting on a rocking chair by the tall windows, he embraced his shoulders with both crossed arms and looked with unseeing eyes over the wintry March trees and Main Street. He was still there when his father left the Evergreens by the front door a half hour later and strode up the street toward the college, and he was still there when Mattie came home from an afternoon tea party, all unsuspecting of the recent turmoil inside. He resolved not to speak to her or anyone else, for that matter. He would stay in Gib's noiseless room until he felt sleepy, despite the cold. He reached for an old quilt. If necessary, he would sleep away the afternoon up here, away from everything and everybody. He had long grown used to the painful sight of Gib's tricycle. He settled himself more comfortably by the window and began his patient wait.

CHAPTER 72

March 1891

D AVID TODD UNLOCKED THE DOOR TO ROOM
number 35 of his New York hotel, ushered in Mrs. Myrna Roberts, saleslady in
Macy's lingerie department, and kissed her full on the lips while she was still
reaching up to take out her hat pins. "And more to come, Missy," he said.

"I wish my rascal of a husband could see me now," said Myrna. "Wherever
he run off to, it would still give him a turn to see me doing what I'm doing."
She winked at David. "And you a professor, no less. My my, just proves you
never know what's about to happen next."

"Well, I know what I would like to happen next," said David. "Just like the
last time we met here. You had no complaints then, did you?"

Myrna rolled her eyes as giggling, she made her way into the bedroom and
sat on a chair while David knelt by her feet to unbutton her shoes.

When they had made love with groans and giggles and lay quiet finally
amid the tangled bedclothes, Myrna pulled the sheet up over them both and
ran a finger around David's sideburns. "You're pretty nice, you know?" she
said. "I never thought professors and the like could be as nice as you."

"They aren't all so nice," said David. "A bunch of in-grown snobs, most of
'em. Never have an original idea, sit around judging other people."

"You poor thing, it must be tiresome, being surrounded with a lot like that.
And then all that trouble with your wife, running around."

"No matter, I have you now." David put his arms behind his head and
stared at the ceiling. You're lots of fun. A person has to have some fun in life."

Myrna snuggled up to his side. "I just wish I could see more of you, but I
understand how things are. Don't worry. I won't make any trouble for you."

"I don't see how you could ever make any trouble," said David with a little
snort. "Not when you consider the trouble she has made for me."

"He must be an odd fellow, this one she sticks with. Does he go to church
and all that sort of thing? I mean, does he act as respectable as you say?"

"Oh, he's Big Wig in his church. Has a pew, sits there with his sister. His wife doesn't go with him anymore since the trouble began."

"He sounds awful!" said Myrna. "I've heard of rich fellows like him, strut about and preach one thing but do another. He ought to be taken down a peg if you ask me, and soon!"

"But it's not like that," said David. "It's hard to explain. He's my friend... No, he really is," he went on as she snorted. "He's a quiet serious man, you know, sort of the Lincoln type."

"You're joking!" said Myrna, "I can't figure this one out at all."

"I've known him a long time now, since 1881. That's ten years now. He has ruined my life, but he's my friend."

"You're a deep one, you are then." Myrna yawned. "I think I'm going to fall asleep now. What do you say we take a nap before dinner? Then I'll show you that restaurant I told you about. Beautiful chops they serve up and coconut pie you won't find anywhere else."

David slapped her rump as she lay curled for sleep and listened to the trolleys in the street below while he thought about Austin Dickinson and whether his own life had really been ruined. Now that he had spoken the words aloud, they seemed true, and he wanted to consider them.

He still loved Mabel—that stood without question. He loved her, needed her, and admired her. The Myras and Caros of the world didn't come close to Mabel, even though he needed them to enjoy his life and to establish his own sexual self respect. If Mabel had fallen in love with someone his own age, he might feel angrier, more threatened. But Austin—Austin was like a father figure in many ways. Reliable, even-tempered. Not like David's own father, of course. That was just the point. Since his parents had separated, David rarely saw either of them, and left the management of his mother's erratic moods to his sister, Naomi. Austin was more like Eben Loomis, only wiser. "Austin Dickinson is exactly your father's age, do you realize that?" David had told Mabel years ago when he returned from the Transit of Venus expedition and discovered that she was in love. And now, even while he saw his own life ruined by this strange triangle, he also saw her love for Austin as logical. He loved Austin too, and some of his happiest moments in Amherst had been when the three of them sat by the fire together in the Dell, ate cozy suppers after long fall carriage rides, or sat on the Evergreens piazza summer evenings while Sue and the children vacationed out of town. But of course, his life had changed entirely, would never be the same again since the day he had realized

Mabel's attraction to Austin was more than an infatuation. A disturbing sense of futility lay at the back of his thoughts no matter what he was doing— traveling, planning an observatory, doing calculations.

Some small release came in his enjoyment of Mabel's jealousy over his affairs once he discovered how much they irritated her. In early days, after they fought about the women she called "common," she often wanted to make love, as though having him then would make him forget about everyone but her. But now, she remained irritated, not amorous, and refused to talk with him for hours at a time. If they were in the middle of a writing project together, he held off teasing her with his affairs until their work was over, their deadlines met. Then he tormented her, taunting her with her inconsistency.

The course of his married life might well be determined by the success or failure of Mabel's scheme to have a child by Austin. He had given up arguing with her about it, even keeping track of her monthly times. What would be would be. A year or so from now might find him alone in the Dell, and Austin, Mabel, Millicent, and a baby in Milwaukee or Chicago or Lincoln. If he lost his mind after that, as his mother apparently had, he would be fulfilling his family destiny.

He studied the leafy pattern of the wallpaper, the way it repeated every third square. He saw no answers for the tangle his life had become, none but this one in hotels and borrowed rooms. He had five days remaining to him in New York while he consulted with the makers of some new telescopic equipment. He would work hard and after work, enjoy Myrna's uncomplicated and pleasant company. He was glad to be far away from the stodgy Amherst College faculty who looked at him so strangely, or laughed when he mentioned his ideas about travel to Mars in the next century. His stomach growled. Mabel was probably preparing cucumber sandwiches for her Mondays evenings at home, but he was ready for pork chops and pie washed down with a glass of heavy ale.

CHAPTER 73

April 1891

MABEL WENT STRAIGHT TO LAVINIA'S HOUSE from the depot and waited impatiently for someone to answer the door. She stood listening for a few minutes in the cold slant of the late afternoon shadows, and hearing nothing from within, tried the door. It opened and she entered the hallway quickly. Two cats stalked by the stairs, while two more emerged from the library.

"Vinnie?" she called. There was no answer. She advanced into the hallway and went to the kitchen. In a moment, she heard Lavinia at the back door with the ash can. "Vinnie, it's me, Mabel. I just got back from giving a talk in Springfield to the Woman's Club and wanted to leave a message for Austin."

David would be staying a day later in New York. She hoped Austin could manage to come to the Dell later in the evening since Millicent was staying overnight at The Convent. She was tired and out of sorts, but this was her propitious time of the month. It couldn't be wasted.

"Where did you talk in Springfield?" asked Vinnie.

"At Mrs. Holland's on Maple Street. There were at least sixty women there, and they loved me. I told them several anecdotes about Emily, like the gingerbread for the children and her opinion of your cats."

"You mentioned my cats and Emily?"

"Yes, and they laughed a good bit about it, too."

"Well, you don't need to tell them personal things. I think you ought to ask me for permission first," said Lavinia in an irritated tone.

"Oh, for heavens' sake, Vinnie, give me some credit! I'd never say anything inappropriate, you know that. I'm just trying to let people know about your sister, that's all, and to have more people buy the poems."

"Did they pay you?" asked Lavinia, looking up narrowly.

"Yes, they did," said Mabel coldly.

"How much?"

"Ten dollars and expenses. Does that bother you?"

"I guess it's all right. But I am true owner of the poems, that's all," said Lavinia, rinsing ashes off her hands.

Mabel reached abruptly for her purse. "Then please, take half. I certainly wouldn't want to cheat you. Here's five dollars."

Lavinia shook her head. "I don't want it, I just wanted to remind you that I am the owner of the poems. People come up to you and gush on about Emily's poetry, when they should come up to me. She is *my* sister. But I don't want your money."

Mabel put the money back in her purse with tight lips and bent her head to Austin's note. When she finished writing, she sealed it in an envelope and set it against a small cracked pitcher. "I'm going home now. Maybe tomorrow we can go over some more of the letters and talk about your cousins, Loo and Fanny. We need to figure a strategy to get them to let us see their letters." She left, closing the front door sharply.

Lavinia sat at the table waching Boxer, her youngest cat, while he played with a pine cone on the floor. In a minute, he was joined by Granny, while Higgie, named for Mr. Higginson, jumped on the table. "No one could say I couldn't use five dollars," she muttered to herself. "Wouldn't take it, though. Do you think it's quite fair? I'm the sister, after all. The other Dickinson sister. Mabel can't say that. Isn't that right, Higgie? Boxer? Dinner time, boys and girls, time for dinner."

About an hour later, Austin entered the kitchen without knocking. Lavinia sat at the table reading the newspaper. "Do you want me to empty the ashbucket?" he asked, without preliminaries, and picked up Mabel's note.

"She left about an hour ago," said Lavinia. "I told her to wait but she was in too much of a hurry. Too puffed up from giving that speech in Springfield."

Austin was reading his note, his back to Lavinia.

"David is still in New York," said Lavinia.

"Yes, much to the annoyance of President Gates. David forgot to arrange for his classes again. I tell you, he needs to be careful. Just today, I sat in a trustee meeting and heard Gates hold forth about poor Charles Garman."

"What for?"

"He thinks he's not religious enough. Doesn't teach what he should. He even went so far as to suggest that we ought to determine whether he's a heretic."

"Wouldn't Emily laugh!" said Lavinia.

"She would. I would too if it didn't irritate me so. Anyway, David needs to watch his step."

"Sit down. Or are you waiting for supper next door?"

"I'm not hungry. I told them to eat without me."

"Try some of my rice pudding," said Lavinia, indicating a bowl on the table.

"No, I'm all right."

"Yes, try some," said Lavinia, getting up for a clean spoon. "It's still warm."

He sat down and put his spoon obediently into the pudding.

"You should see Dr. Cooper if your appetite doesn't soon return, Austin. How are your bowels?"

Austin shook his head. "Let's not talk about my constitution right now. Do you have any chores for me this evening?"

"You could help me sort through Emily's letters."

"Anything but that. You can do that sort of thing with Mabel."

"Sometimes I have the impression she thinks she owns the poems. Have you noticed that?" asked Lavinia watching Austin finish his rice pudding.

"No, I haven't. She's just involved with them, that's all. You know yourself how many weeks it took to copy them. What would you have done without her?"

"She got paid for speaking in Springfield today," said Lavinia.

"Well, why not?"

Lavinia didn't answer.

"Why not?" repeated Austin.

"No reason," said Lavinia, standing to take away his dish.

"Well, then, that's that. I think I'll read the paper for a while and go over to the Dell later."

"Good. Stay here, it's your other home." She handed him a copy of the *Springfield Republican* and picked up the Amherst paper for herself. They read companionably thus at the kitchen table, sharing bits of news now and then, until Lavinia went into the dining room for her sewing basket and Austin climbed the stairs slowly to clean up before going over to Mabel's. As the clock struck eight, he left by the front door and crossed the remaining meadow land for the lights of the Dell.

He found Mabel in the back parlor rearranging a spray of pussy willows.

The room was chilly and damp though, and only one lamp burned low. "You've had no fire?" he asked her after their embrace.

"I let it go out; it didn't seem worth the trouble—I've only been back from Springfield a few hours and besides, we'll be going upstairs. I lit the fire up there. I could feel spring in the air today, though, couldn't you?"

"Yes, I could. We should visit our special spot in Sunderland..."

"Oh bother these pussy willows," Mabel interrupted impatiently, pushing the arrangement aside. "They need something to go with them. Let's go upstairs—we don't have much time this evening. I suppose you want to get back soon, even though I don't see why we couldn't throw propriety to the winds and have you stay here. Ridiculous, running out into the night leaving me all alone here."

Austin followed her up the back stairs and into the room they considered theirs. She pulled back the quilts on the bed while Austin sat in the rocking chair and took off his shoes, but his motions were slow. "I've hardly said hello yet," he said. "How was Springfield? How are you?" He reached up and took her hands.

"Springfield was fine. I was a big success, luckily, because I put a lot of valuable time into that talk. Lavinia seems to think my talks aren't worth much."

"Why do you say that?" said Austin.

Mabel dropped his hands. "Oh, just that look she gave me earlier when I told her I earned money from the talk. It's the second time she's hinted that she thinks I oughtn't to be paid. Sometimes your Lavinia defies my understanding."

"Oh, don't mind Vin. She has no understanding of the world and its ways and she's too forthright. Those two things make her seem worse than she is."

Mabel sat on the bed. "It's my fertile time, my good time. Did you remember?"

"I wasn't sure," said Austin from his chair.

"Come, come," she said, patting the place beside her. "If we have such short times together, we have to make use of them. We should have been together last night too, but you said you couldn't get away."

She threw off her dressing gown and lay down, watching in the dim light while he took off his clothes and joined her. She kissed him first, lifting his hand to touch her breast. But their kisses, their movements, remained forced, and when, a few moments later, she reached down to touch him, she drew away sharply. "You're not interested in me tonight, not at all!"

"I'm sorry. I don't think I can. I'm tired and you seem in such a hurry..." He lay on his back and stared at the ceiling. "Can't we just relax and be together?"

Mabel turned too and lay on her back. "It's my fault. I know, I'm rushing. I'm no more ready than you. Somehow I thought we could manage it. I feel so—so much in a foul mood tonight. All I can see are the things in my life that are wrong. Wrong, wrong wrong! Lavinia was the final straw, acting as though I didn't deserve to be paid. After I stopped everything to get those poems copied and published! Sometimes I think the poems are all I have that's true in my life. Bringing them out is my accomplishment in the world—well, one of them. I intend to be recognized, you know."

"Please try to forget Vin right now. Don't take her so seriously."

"I suppose it isn't really Vinnie anyway. It's wanting to be with you and not being able to, and having to avoid Sue and Mattie all day long, and having David away and then you don't come over—and oh, just the whole awful mess. Everything is hopeless. And now we can't manage to have a child together."

Neither spoke for a few minutes. Then Austin said softly, "Would it depress you more if we forgot about our Experiment for a while? Sometimes I think it's put us apart from each other. It's always there, as though we *ought* to love each other for some ulterior motive. But I don't need any ulterior motive, Mabel, you know that. I've told you from the start: I love you and I am always going to love you with all my soul, whatever happens. We knew it wouldn't be easy and we have to live with that now. We have to face it every day and it drains us; it even threatens to destroy us. But we agreed: we would withstand those pressures and triumph over them. We have loved each other without a child and we will continue to do so."

Mabel turned to nestle into him, burying her face in his chest. "All right," she said in a muffled voice. "Let's forget about propitious times and all of that. You're right, as usual, and I love you for it. But I still feel defeated and trapped here."

Austin held her close and stroked her back. "If you're trapped here, it's with *me*. Don't forget that. With me, and I love you. You have made my life worth while. Didn't we always say how lucky we are to have the Pelham hills and Mount Toby and groves of beautiful trees and the crickets, all ours to enjoy? Remember the smell in the air when we went by the gate, our Rubicon night? Nothing could make me regret those things and the fact that we met."

Mabel lay quietly in his arms. "I've cast my lot, I know it, but lately it's been so hard, harder than ever. And when I see Sue in the street, I feel murderous sometimes, absolutely murderous! But I never felt that way until I knew she could strangle me in an instant."

"No, no, don't talk that way."

"It's true, Austin, she could strangle me in the street. I feel her malevolence all around me when I see her."

"Maybe you feel some of your own too, don't you think?"

"My malevolence? No, I do not! It's all hers! I have no malevolence."

Austin didn't try to contradict her. "Shall we go to Boston soon? We could be together all night then. I will probably have to go next month."

"I think I'll be speaking at the Boston College Alumni Club next month. Maybe we can work things out around that. Mr. Higginson wants us to share the podium together. He just needs to determine the date with their president."

"Maybe I could come hear you."

"Would you?" She looked up at him. "You've never heard me give a talk."

"I wouldn't make you nervous?"

"No, of course not. Only proud," said Mabel, becoming more animated at the prospect of days together in Boston. "I hope they pay me a fortune and then I'll rush back to count it in front of Lavinia."

"You and Lavinia..." began Austin. He kissed her. "Time to go."

Mabel let herself become perceptibly heavier in his arms. "Tell Sue I hate her."

"All right," said Austin aimiably, refusing to defer to her moodiness again. "She'll return the compliment."

But walking across the dark meadow to his house, Austin wondered whether in lifting Mabel's depression he had not reawakened his own. She was indeed imprisoned in a town, many of whose citizens did visibly reject her, yet there was nowhere else to go, no possibility for change that he could see. Yes, Sue would indeed return the compliment of hating Mabel. And he was doomed to stand in the middle.

CHAPTER 74

August 1891

LAVINIA MARCHED ALONG THE PATH BETWEEN her house and the Evergreens and walked in the back door without knocking. Since Sue, Ned, and Mattie had been away for the month of August, she had gone over brazenly five or six times, usually to speak to Austin, but sometimes to borrow something she needed, and once, to look in the attic store room for one of the old rocking chairs that had belonged to Emily but which Emily had given to Sue when Ned was born. "I just want to see it again," she told Austin when she came down. "Can you bring it over later to put in Emily's room?"

Another time David and Lavinia joined Austin and Mabel at the Evergreens for a simple supper cooked by Mabel—potato soup made from Austin's potatoes, lettuce and tomatoes also from the meadow vegetable garden, and Mabel's applesauce and soda bread. The atmosphere was unusually lighthearted, mostly because of Mabel, who talked animatedly, laughed often, and smiled enigmatically to herself while others were talking. At dusk, they sat on the piazza to enjoy the cool evening air while the buzz of the cicadas rose and fell in undulating waves about them.

"How are the proofs of the new poems coming along?" Lavinia asked Mabel.

"I only received them yesterday," said Mabel. "David has promised to help me since I've been so busy with the inventory of the unpublished poems."

David groaned comically. "Alphabetized by first lines, no less. I wish the woman had titled her poems, damn her!"

"But I think I can make the deadline for a November publication," Mabel continued "I finished the preface already for Mr. Higginson to look over."

"I think my name should be on the title page along with Mabel's and Mr. Higginson's and Emily's," said David. "Lord knows I've put in my share of work."

"And my name too," said Lavinia.

"I hear you got a check," David told her. "How much? $179.51? You're a rich lady, Vinnie, a rich lady."

Lavinia let out a satisfied chuckle. "Now I can spend it all on some mahogony furniture."

"I am so glad Mr. Higginson didn't give in to worry and hold back that wonderful poem," said Mabel, "the one that begins 'Wild Nights.' He told me he was worried about reactions from the ministerial crowd and the old lady set."

"Did he put it that way?" asked Austin. "Ministerial crowd and old lady set?"

"No, those are my words," said Mabel. "And he wasn't terribly worried anyway. He thinks the poem is too powerful to worry about reactions, thank heavens."

"Well, knock me over," said David, "because I'm surprised. That poem is a real sex poem. Maybe he doesn't understand it."

"It is *not* a sex poem," said Lavinia. "My sister did not write s-e-x poems."

"David, are you going up to Mary Stearns's to walk Millicent back?" asked Mabel. "Their little play practice should be well over by now."

"Why don't you go instead? I've just settled in. Besides, the racket of those crickets or cicadas or whatever you call them is driving me crazy. You know what we need, Austin? Some brandy. Wouldn't that just set us up for a gentleman's summer evening? Have you got any?"

"I know there's some in the house; Sue often takes some before bed."

Mabel gave a rude snort. "*Some*? I thought I heard differently."

"Mabel, that was uncalled for," said David from the shadows.

"I'll go find some brandy," said Lavinia getting up, leaving the other three suddenly quiet in their chairs.

"There are a lot of bats out tonight," said David, looking at the gas light.

A silence fell among them as they watched the bats and fireflies and enjoyed the gentle summer evening. After a few minutes, the wicker chair creaked as Mabel arose, and patting Austin's knee, went to the steps. "I'm going to fetch Millie," she said. "But nothing will persuade her to come back here and sit on the porch with us, so I suppose I'll have to go home with her."

Austin got up. "You can't go unescorted. I'll walk you part way and then come back alone."

They stepped onto the lawn and started up the street. "I know we shouldn't walk out like this," said Mabel, "but I just had to say something since I won't see you for a few days while I'm so busy with the proofs. But guess what? I'm really late. No special monthly friend and no sign of it. And I feel different somehow, I don't know, just different. So it's possible...it's at least possible. I wasn't even going to tell you, but I've been bursting with it." She took his arm impulsively and hugged it to her. "Oh, let's pray that it can be so."

Austin squeezed her back. "Did you tell David?"

"No, of course not! And I won't unless I'm absolutely positive. You should turn back here. We're bound to meet someone from here on."

They separated after a quick clasp of hands, and Austin hurried back to the Evergreens. Mabel found Mary Stearns's porch aglow and several other parents calling goodnight as they picked up their daughters. Behind them stood Millicent and two other girls who giggled conspiratorially. Seeing her this way from a distance, before she herself was seen, Mabel was struck by how different Millicent looked with her friends, how relaxed and light-hearted, and how much older, at nearly twelve, than she looked at home. "Maybe she's not going to be a somber child after all," thought Mabel. As she stepped up to the door and Millicent caught sight of her mother, her expression changed. Her look wasn't surprise, or fear either, but it was a combination of the two. Or was it wariness? Mabel couldn't tell, but for a moment, she felt like an outsider, a woman coming to pick up someone else's daughter.

"Thank you very much, Madame Stearns," said Millicent in her company voice, preparing to leave. "Good evening."

"You're welcome, Miss Millie. I'll see you Monday, Mabel, for your 'at home'."

"Yes, I'm counting on you. Good night."

They walked along together. "Do you want to sit on the piazza with us for a few minutes since you can sleep late tomorrow? Miss Dickinson has some cake in a tin she'd love to open up for you. Or you could catch fireflies."

"Oh, Mother, I'm too old for that now. I want to go home."

They walked in silence the rest of the way to the Dell where Mabel lit the lamps and saw Millicent walk upstairs to her room. Neither said a word until Mabel called up, "Do you have a light in your room now?"

"Yes," came down the answer.

"Then I'm leaving now to get your father."

With a sigh, she returned to the Evergreens. From across the street, she was glad to see that the vines around the piazza made it almost impossible to see that anyone was there. Only up close did the one candle they had carried out shine through the leaves.

Everyone held a brandy glass now. David sat with his feet up on a wicker stool, Lavinia held a cat in her lap, and Austin was standing, looking out for her. He went to the steps and extended a hand.

"Millicent refused to come?" asked David from the shadows.

"Naturally."

"That girl isn't like me," said David. "Always hangs back. Not like me."

Mabel sat down beside Austin who handed her a glass and caught her eye briefly in the candle's glow before she looked away. "A child?" he was thinking. "Another child, eleven years younger than Millicent." It was not a comforting thought. But there was nothing to say and both of them sat quietly watching the evening while David chatted about the latest faculty meeting and Lavinia asked the company at large what to do about ear mites in cats.

By the time Sue and Ned returned from their vacation in Maine, Mabel and Millicent had gone to the town of Wyoming, New York to visit Mabel's Cousin Lydia. Later in the week, David joined them and found Mabel strangely ebullient during the first few days—animated and good-humored, yet complaining of headaches at the same time. The spacious house, full of talkative, laughing relatives, the long tables where they ate, someone always getting up or down to attend to the children who ate on the lawn, energized David, and as one of the few men there, he captivated everyone by his stories and jokes, and by his enthusiasm about astronomy. He taught the children a few magic tricks, though he noticed Millicent hung back from these sessions, and regaled the adults with news about the improved telephones being developed, the new automatic switchboard, the uses electricity could be put to in every home, the changes in photography, and the delicious cans of pineapple he had bought in Manhattan. On several clear evenings, at least half of the household took quilts outside and lay on the lawn to star-gaze, the children saying "Where, where?" at every turn, the adults trying to map the sky for them. David held forth with information about stars, planets, distances between this and that, with Mabel quiet at his side, listening.

"You were wonderful," she said to him in their room that night. "I'm so glad you came."

He came to embrace her, but she drew back. "I've got a surprise monthly, a troublesome one, for some reason. It's come off schedule."

"Is this connected with your headaches then?" he asked.

"I assume so," she said, going to the open window in her nightgown and looking out at the dark lawn where an hour ago, they had looked at the sky. "The bleeding is different—all clotted and thick." She kept her back to him. "In fact, I've been wondering if I've had a miscarriage."

"A miscarriage? But you—you're not pregnant." He stopped. "Did you think you were pregnant?"

"Maybe." She turned the rocking chair toward the window and sat down.

David began to undress slowly. Finally, he sat on the bed and asked what he had to: "Was this the pregnancy you wanted? The one you intended?"

"If I was pregnant, I believe it was the one I intended, if you want to put it that way. But it doesn't matter now, because I must not be pregnant anymore, not with this blood, and I don't think I'm going to try again. That's all over." Her head went into her hands, but David did not go to her, and when she looked up, he saw she hadn't cried at all. Her features remained perfectly composed as she rose from the chair and joined him in bed without another word on the subject.

"Do you think you can stand to help me some more on the proofs?" she asked him as she pulled up the covers, as though the matter of pregnancy were inconsequential. "The proofs Mr. Higginson sent arrived safely yesterday and I'd like to finish them off to ensure a November publication. People are already anticipating the second series of poems."

"I'll help," said David, moving close to her so that they snuggled together.

"You know what?" said Mabel. "I think I'm glad I'm not pregnant. I feel tired all over. But good tired. And I'm so glad you came here to be with me."

For answer, he kissed her ear softly. "I think we can both rest here. No one will believe me when I tell them, but Amherst is a tiring place."

CHAPTER 75

Fall to Spring 1891-1892

I F WE PUBLISH THE LETTERS, I DON'T WANT
Sue's name printed," said Austin one October evening in the back parlor of the
Dell. "I don't want her involved in any way."

"But I don't see how we can avoid using Sue's name, and if *I* say that, of all
people—"

"Yes, but I don't want her involved. I don't think she was patient enough
with Emily's sensitivities. It doesn't bear going into, Mabel, let's drop it. But if
I find letters I don't like, I reserve the right to destroy them."

"Destroy them? Oh, Austin, you'd do that?"

"I already have. I burnt one from Sue some months ago long before we ever
thought about collecting letters. Vinnie found it in Emily's sewing basket, long
forgotten. After I read it, I took it from the table where Vin left it and burnt it
one night. I didn't like its tone. In fact, I've burned several."

Mabel took in this news. The idea of burning letters had always been re-
pugnant to her, but in this case, involving Sue, the matter was clouded.

"Couldn't we use selected early letters from Sue..." Mabel began, but Austin
stood up and poked at the fire. "I don't think so. Let's not talk about Sue."

"You so rarely do. At any length, at least."

"I should think that would please you."

"It does, mostly," said Mabel. "Let's talk about David for a minute. The odd
things he does worry me more these days."

"What has he done lately?"

"Well, for one example, he showed me a letter he wrote to Thomas Edison—
who may not even remember him from their meeting in Newark."

"When was that?" asked Austin.

"In '76. Mr. Edison actually offered David a job. David says he put it forcefully—he really wanted David to work with him. He was on the rise then, and
if David had accepted that offer, he would have risen along with Mr. Edison."

"But you would have lived in Newark."

"Yes," said Mabel, "so we won't cry over David's decision to stay with astronomy. Anyway, David's recent letter to Mr. Edison proposed a collaboration, very elaborate, some kind of light signal to reach Mars and determine once and for all whether there is life there."

Austin looked sharply at Mabel. "A light to reach Mars? What was his thinking behind that?"

"Oh, don't ask me," said Mabel. "It's obviously no flash of genius, it's the kind of craziness that pops up just when I least expect it."

"Did Mr. Edison answer the letter?"

"Not yet, and I hope he doesn't. It's too embarrassing. What *can* David have been thinking of? He can be so clever and inventive, and yet sometimes his ideas run amok. It seems to happen more and more often these days. Imagine, incandescent lights to reach all the way to Mars!"

"Maybe it's the nature of the inventive mind. Seemingly crazy ideas come before realistic ones. I imagine people thought Mr. Edison was crazy too."

"No, I can't pass it off that easily. David's mother is so mentally unstable that I think it must run in that family. And the whole thing concerns me especially when you say President Gates has it in for David. I never know what David might do next, after he asked Mrs. Gates at the inauguration reception if the decor on her hat was a snake!"

"Well, " said Austin, "don't forget that you have me in the center of decisions at the college. I won't hesitate to use my authority where David is concerned."

"You can't imagine how often I've thought of that and felt relieved," said Mabel. "Enough. Do I have your official permission then to continue collecting Emily's letters for publication? As long as I show you which ones I have?"

"Yes, you do."

Mabel rubbed her hands together in delight. "Oh, I can hardly wait to tell Vinnie. I love going collecting! I think we should stop to celebrate the Second Series of poems though on November 9th, the day of publication. Where shall we celebrate, here or at Vin's?"

"I wish I could whisk you off to Boston alone and celebrate there," said Austin.

"Ah," said Mabel, "but that would be a celebration of something else altogether."

CHAPTER 76

August 1892

THE FIRST WEEK OF AUGUST, EVERYONE TALKED of nothing but Lizzie Borden and the grisly murders in Fall River, Massachusetts. "Oh, Maggie, how exciting!" Lavinia had said one day. "What's your theory? Why do you think she would have hacked her father and her stepmother to death?"

"Saints, either Miss Lizzie was the most evil woman in the world or else those two treated her cruelly. Some people can be cruel in hidden ways, and the anger builds up. Then"— she struck her hand on the table—"Boom!"

"So you think Lizzie did it then?"

"Who else?" said Maggie, putting potatoes into steaming water on the stove. "From what I read, she was the only one in the house. No, that Lizzie Borden was pent up to the boiling point about something, that's my theory."

"Oh, I love a good murder," said Lavinia.

When Sue, Ned, and Mattie went on vacation the second week of August, Mabel began to spend late afternoons and evenings at the Evergreens, even some nights. Austin, who had a nasty summer cold, frequently napped before supper. From the Evergreens' topmost windows one late afternoon in August, Mabel watched wires of white lightning fracture the sky, felt the tremor of thunder claps, and gazed at the dense rainy gusts swirling the evergreen trees below.

She raised her eyes to the ceiling of the cupola, as she called it, though it wasn't technically a cupola, and clasped her arms, smiling. If Austin weren't sick, how she would make love to him right now on the downstairs bed, flinging back the counterpane and pointing: "Let me have you! Now!"

The rare and precious forbidden hours she dared to live as Mrs. Dickinson of the Evergreens when Sue and her children were away thrilled her more than she dared admit, yet at the same time suffusing her with a sense of peace and fulfillment along with a sharp sexual urge she never had anywhere else, even at the Dell with Austin. "Don't we just live for August?" she had said to Austin earlier that morning.

"Don't we just," he answered hoarsely, smiling despite his sore throat.

She had fixed him clear soup and cool pudding, had felt his forehead for fever, fetched him his law briefs, watched him doze, and had read to him, first an article from the newspaper about the Lizzie Borden case and then a chapter from one of Mr. Howells' books, *Their Wedding Journey*, which Austin said he wanted to read again. This afternoon, his throat had improved but he still felt feverish, and lay dozing, despite having protested vigorously that he was not sleepy. Since the storm had not interfered with his rest, Mabel took the chance to slip into the upper storage attic, the cupola, in search of letters from Emily.

"I saved them, I'm fairly sure," Austin had said a few days earlier. "There must be quite a bundle from my Harvard days—she wrote often to me while I was there, and I packed them all up when I left."

Moving aside items like the picnic basket, a perambulator, and some decorative urns, she looked over the assortment of boxes, crates, and baskets filled with family items. Squinting in the gloom as the sky darkened and the thunder began to rumble, she bent over to read the crayoned letters on one box. "Austin: Miscell." it read in an unknown hand. Austin's mother's? She pulled the box out from its place and tugged at the string. She would need a knife or scissors. Holding up her skirts and running downstairs two flights, she flipped open Sue's sewing basket and took out the tortoise shell scissors. Before running upstairs again, she glanced in at Austin. Still sleeping. Good.

Back in the attic, she cut the string and opened the box, turning over some old books, a badly framed little watercolor signed only "J.S.," a carefully wrapped, but cracked, teapot and matching cups, and finally, packets of letters, each tied with blue ribbon.

Rain began to beat on the roof as she untied the first bundle and saw instantly the envelopes filled with Emily's famliar writing. Laughing aloud, she grabbed the rest of the bundles and stood up, leaving Austin's box open and the boxes around it disarranged. The scissors fell unnoticed to the floor. Running down the steps again she looked into Austin's room once more, approaching the bed with the letters in her hand. He opened his eyes partly and muttered, "So sleepy."

"Good, sweet King," she answered. "Keep sleeping. But I found Emily's letters!" She waved them in his line of vision, set them by his bedside, and, rushed back to the little attic room with the double windows on each side, eight windows in all, to enjoy the storm. "And no one has any idea I'm here!" she laughed to herself as the thunder rolled ever closer and the wires in the sky flashed their iridescence over the meadow across the street. Mabel pushed a dressmaker's bust aside and knelt by the window nearest Main Street as the first drops of rain pattered on the roof with the wind, then smashed against, pelted, the glass. "Oh, wonderful!" Mabel breathed. "Freedom! I could stay here forever!"

The next shimmering crack in the sky, this time over the train depot, was followed almost instantly by a detonation of thunder. At the same time, she thought she saw a flash of movement below along the path, but no, it must be the bending trees. Despite the rain, it was hot in the little room from hours of the summer sun, and she wiped her brow with her handkerchief, moving to another window and kneeling again after pushing stored items aside.

In the lull, she tried to resist the torture of imagining herself as Mrs. Dickinson of the Evergreens, with Austin for her true and legal husband. Mrs. Austin Dickinson, with Monday afternoons at home, evening musicales every month, the best carriage in town at her disposal, a Dickinson pew in First Church, and the blessing of God and the village on their union.

A ripping green light with a mighty explosive discharge shook the windows and thumped the floorboards, causing Mabel to cover her face with a cry. The thought flashed across her mind, "So this is how they will find me, struck dead here." But she was not dead. Something else must certainly have been struck, though. Her thoughts flashed to Austin who was surely wide awake now.

Her handkerchief fell to the floor as she arose in the clatter of the rain and eased her way down the first little flight of stairs, then ran down the rest to the first floor. Austin stood at the door to his room looking disheveled and confused in the gloom.

"I'm here," called Mabel coming to him. "A terrible storm, that's all. I think something nearby must have been hit. That's what you heard." She took his arm. "Here, go back to bed. This house has a lightning rod, doesn't it?"

"Yes, it does. Maybe the lightning struck it, in fact. Or a tree. I couldn't tell if the sound came from the front or the back."

"I couldn't either." She gripped his arm as another flash quivered and thunder followed. "I love it! But I hope it didn't hit one of your favorite trees."

"I'll get dressed and look."

"Austin! Don't be ridiculous! I wouldn't let you go out there now even if you weren't sick. I'll go to the back and look out the door, will that satisfy you?"

They both froze as the sky lit up again, but this time, the thunder sounded farther off. Mabel gave Austin a quick kiss. "Husband, go lie down," she said.

"My beloved wife, I will," he replied, kissing her hand and turning to his bed. "I feel so wonderful when we're here together like this, even when I'm sick."

"Yes, yes," she smiled at him. "I'll take a look outside and then if you want, I'll read some more. I told Mr. Howells and Elinor we were reading his book. She says so much of it is based on their own wedding journey."

"Shall we try reading from George Washington Cable's periodical next, now that he's one of your acquaintances too, and so close by, in Northampton?"

"Yes, or one of his novels. I like him—I like reformers. He has the right idea about the problems in the South."

"Just don't read me stories about the South in dialect. That dialect repels me. In fact, the South repels me too."

"My dearest love, what a closed mind you have. Just because you had such a miserable time on your trip to the South in '87 doesn't mean the whole South is horrible."

"Doesn't it?"

"Oh, shoo," Mabel laughed back at him as she left the room. Another clap of thunder made the teapot lid tremble in the cupboard as she made her way through the hall into the kitchen and pantry area and finally, to the back door. She opened it for a moment against the wind and let the rain hit her face as she stooped to peer up into the trees around the yard. She saw no branches dangling, no scars splitting the tree trunks, only smaller branches scattered on the ground and littering the barn roof. Murky clouds hung low in the dark sky. She closed the door and withdrew into the kitchen where she stood by a window.

A sense of coziness comforted her, as she thought of the quiet evening ahead of them in the darkened Evergreens with the door locked. They would eat supper close together at one end of the dining room table. Then she would read aloud until Austin began to nod, when she would tuck him into his side of the bed and cozy up beside him. She would sleep by his side peacefully and joyfully, the wedding ring he had given her on her finger. With David away and Millicent staying with her friend Hannah on Pleasant Street, the house seemed truly theirs.

In the midst of all these comforting thoughts, the dark, discheveled and hooded face that suddenly met hers at the rain-drenched window jolted her with all the power of another thunder clap. A soft scream escaped her lips as she pushed against the door to keep the demon or whatever it was from entering, but an instant later, she made out the face: Lavinia's. Trembling in fear mixed with anger, Mabel held her head briefly in one hand, then opened the door.

"Vinnie! You scared me to death! Never surprise me like that again!"

Lavinia stepped inside and threw back the old coat she had arranged over her head. "Well, I'm sorry, but what else could I do? I found Millicent at my doorstep a while ago looking as strange as I do now, and I had no choice but to come over here. I nearly got mangled by tree branches on my way!"

"Millicent is over there? She's supposed to be sleeping over at Hannah's house."

"Well, she isn't. She told me something about Hannah's aunt dying in Springfield and the whole family rushing off this afternoon. She must have told them she'd come straight home, but of course she didn't, did she? I don't know where she was all afternoon. Lonely, hanging about the Dell porch, I guess, but when the storm blew up, she finally came to my back door, only from the looks of her, she must have sat in the barn a while."

"Oh, good God," said Mabel. "What is in that child's mind? Why didn't she come here right away? Is she in your house now?"

"Yes. She's at the kitchen table drinking hot beef broth. I don't see how she could have had any supper, but I'll let you ask her about that."

"She didn't think I was at your house, did she?" asked Mabel.

"I don't know what she thought," said Lavinia, sitting down at the kitchen table, "but I know one thing: she's terrified of *this* house. She wouldn't come over here, even with me. Absolutely refused."

"Now I either have to tramp over there," said Mabel crossly, "and take her home with me and ruin my evening—or leave her there with you." She sat down facing Lavinia. "Vinnie: Do you suppose you could keep her there overnight? Just this one night, of course? Austin has such a cold and I think I should stay with him. He needs me. Millie would never stay in this house with us anyway, at least not without putting up a horrible fuss, and I'm not in the mood for horrible fusses. I'll come over with you now, of course, and settle her down. What do you think? Would it bother you too awfully much?"

"Oh, I don't think so. In fact, it might be nice, having a girl around the house like the old days when Mattie was little and sweet."

"Then I'll come over with you right now after I see if Austin is still asleep, and we'll settle Millie down. I ought to give her a good scolding, but I won't."

"I wouldn't, if I were you," said Lavinia. "I think being out in the storm alone scared her pretty much."

"You don't mean she was out alone during those huge lightning strikes, do you?" said Mabel, standing up.

"Oh yes. She banged on the door after one or two, but I thought it was tree branches falling. She was safe in my kitchen though when that great loud crack split open. It sounded like it hit something nearby. I half expected a ball of fire in my chimney."

"Poor Millicent, what a silly thing she is, not to come to me all this time."

"Well, would you have, in her place?" said Lavinia. "Would you, if your mother was with a big whiskered man not your father, and in a half dark house besides on a stormy night? Sometimes, Mabel, sometimes you miss the obvious, if you don't mind my saying so."

Mabel held her head rigid and left without a word to check on Austin. But she muttered to herself as she went down the hallway, "The nerve, the very nerve."

Pursing her lips, she turned to complete her irksome tasks as fast as possible so that she would not lose any more time than necessary from her precious hours as Mrs. Austin Dickinson of the Evergreens.

CHAPTER 77

September 1892

~

SUE WAS SECRETLY RELIEVED THAT AUSTIN had not returned from an appointment in Boston when she arrived in Amherst from vacation. She and her children could feel comfortable in the house for a few days, anyway. Mattie was set on retrieving Emily's letters from the attic ever since some Amherst friends had written to her mentioning Mabel's and Lavinia's plans for publication. "You're sure we have those letters?" she had asked.

"Yes, I'm positive, dearie. I put the box up there myself after your grandmother asked Austin to collect some of his things. He brought boxes over but never got around to looking through them, so I went through the contents hurriedly, but not so hurriedly that I didn't see what was there. There were letters from Emily, I'm sure, because I remember asking Austin how often she wrote to him—she was writing to me too at the same time."

So it was that one afternoon after Austin had returned from Boston but was attending a town commission meeting and Mattie had gone to Salem, leaving Ned at loose ends about the house, Sue set out to retrieve the box containing Emily's letters. But the moment she reached the topmost flight of stairs, the crumpled handkerchief with its unfamiliar lavender-embroidered "M.L.T." caught her eye, as shocking a sight as a dead bird, or a pool of blood.

"No," Sue whispered to herself, "No. Not here too? My God, not here too?"

She made her way up the remaining stairs and emerged to see the disarranged boxes, one of them with its lid standing open, and then finally, the scissors lying in a spider web, her favorite tortoise-shelled sewing scissors, which her sister Martha had given her for her eighteenth birthday. Clapping one hand over her mouth and the other on her stomach, she stood stock still in the dim light. Sounds reached her ears with peculiar clarity: a squirrel running across the roof, wind in the branches, Mrs. Jameson's voice from across the street. Still holding one hand over her mouth, Sue bent over to look more closely at the boxes before her, but a glance was all it took to locate the theft, even though she knelt and ruffled savagely through the contents of the box she knew had contained Emily's letters.

"Gone," she whispered. "My property stolen, my privacy..." she searched with incongruous precision for the word..."deflowered. Defiled." She took her hand from her mouth, lifted her head toward the ceiling, and screamed, jolting herself with the surprise of it, the force of her own voice and the short flat echo which followed.

The scream released her full anger. Seizing the scissors from the floor, the dust balls and spider webs entangled in it, she rushed to the stairs and hurried down, hardly lifting her skirts as she went, stumbling and elbowing the wall, wondering what it would feel like to fall into the pointed end of the scissors. But she did not fall. She lurched, heart pounding, onto the upstairs landing, where she heard Ned from below call up, "Mother?" She did not answer, but descended the last flight of stairs like a javelin thrower now, straight with purpose, her eyes slightly narrowed and her arm above her to take aim.

In a swish of skirts she burst into the library with a cry and brought the scissors down onto the first sheaf of papers she saw on Austin's desk. Throwing aside his pen, she dragged the scissor points across the blotter, then turned to drag them across the spines of books in the nearest shelf. She turned to see Ned staring at her from the hallway, and then rushed past him toward the piazza doors, which she opened with a jerk and passed through.

Ned sprang into action. "Mother? Mother! Where are you going?" He caught up with her as she began to cross Main Street, headed like an arrow to the Dell, the scissors still in her hand. "Come back!" At the edge of the meadow he reached for her arm, squinting in the sun at the scissors. "I need to talk to you. Let's go back home and talk."

Sue stopped suddenly and looked at Ned, then at the scissors. "Take them," she said. And then, looking around her: "Edward Dickinson's meadow. What's left of it." She turned and walked briskly home, Ned following her with the scissors. Inside the house, she sat in the parlor as though nothing had happened, despite her shaking hands, and picked up some sewing from the basket. Ned looked into Austin's study and was picking up the pen when he heard her calling him through her laughter. "Ned? I need my scissors. No, it's safe now, I'm just going to cut some thread." She extended her hand for the scissors, cut a thread, and laughed some more, wiping her eyes finally with a handkerchief and lapsing into silence.

Ned hovered awkwardly near her in the parlor, pretending to read a magazine, looking out the window, and stealing glances at her. "I don't need to talk, dear," she said. "I'm fine now. Run along and do whatever you were doing before. No cause for alarm."

"You're sure?"

"Yes, I'm sure. Go do whatever you were doing, please."

In the end, Ned sat in the barn for a while, then went next door to look over Lavinia's garden, and finally, returned to the barn where he watched Stephen polishing the carriage. Inside, Sue continued to sew, first darning socks, then turning the frayed cuffs of Austin's and Ned's shirts. Once she gave a short laugh and then immediately groaned and held her head. "Lizzie Borden," she whispered. When her eyes tired and when the thought of supper didn't revolt her, she put away her work and laid the tortoise shell scissors carefully into the basket, closing the lid gently. But she did not straighten Austin's library, nor did he mention the damage in his study when he returned that evening from the Amherst depot.

December 1892

MABEL AND DAVID WENT TO WASHINGTON
for Thanksgiving despite Lavinia's protests that not a moment could be spared
from copying Emily's letters. "I suppose you'll be lecturing and socializing all
week when you could be working here," Lavinia had told Mabel in the
Homestead hallway.

"You may suppose it. I shall be having a well deserved rest," Mabel had
replied, closing the door behind her with a jerk as she left.

While Mabel spoke about Japan to a select gathering at Mrs. Hilliard's home
in Washington, David met Myrna for a midday meal near the street where she
was visiting her sister. "Oh, and how I've always wanted to eat in this hotel
dining room," she told him in the lounge where he arose as soon as he saw her.
She looked older than he had remembered, and the skin on her face was
reddened and rough in the cold early December wind. "Have you been here
long?" she said, taking his arm.

He held his arm at a stiff angle and glanced around him, reaassuring himself that no one he knew was nearby. "No, not long," he answered, and they
stepped into the dining room.

Over the meal, he told her about his plans for the upcoming summer at the
Chicago Fair. "An Amherst College booth, focusing on my work in astronomy,
of course. A clever idea, don't you think? It will call attention to my projects.
Who knows, I might turn up an exciting job from some other university, or
from an inventor like Thomas Edison. Or maybe a partner to help me with the
plans no one else but me believes in."

"I wish I could come," said Myrna. "Aren't these fried apples delicious?"

"So I have to plan everything well in advance," continued David. "Mabel
and I will go in July."

"Oh." Myrna's face fell. "She's going with you, then?"

"She prefers to travel as much as possible these days. Things have become so unpleasant in Amherst for her. The gossip and all that, you know."

"Why doesn't the bloke marry her, for God's sake?" said Myrna irritably.

David laid his fork down wearily. "Let's not go over all that again," he said. "And he's not exactly a bloke. I told you."

"Well then," said Myrna, "don't bring it up."

"Good. I won't."

There was an uncomfortable silence. David looked around the room while Myrna watched him. When he picked up his fork again, she asked, "What is it you're up to, these days, then?"

"Studying Mars, among other things. To discover once and for all whether there is life there."

"Now which star is Mars?" asked Myrna, smiling at the waiter who filled her water glass.

"Which star? Oh for God's sake, haven't you got that straight yet? It's a planet, a planet Myrna, the red one, named after the god of war. Mars, you know, in mythology."

Myrna shrank, then took the offensive. "Well, I can't keep all this straight, what do you expect? You study this planet business and all the rest of it day and night. Some of us have other things to do, as well. I've got to earn a living, you know."

"And you don't think what I do is earning a living?"

"No, I didn't mean that. But you act like what you do is the only thing in the world. The most important thing, anyway."

"You're right, I apologize," said David. "Let's drop the subject."

They ate in silence for a few minutes, then tried to make small talk for the rest of the meal. When they had finished eating they stood once again in the dim little lobby. "Care to sit a while?" David asked her.

"You don't have time for anything else?"

"No, I have an appointment. I hope you don't mind. I didn't know what you expected..."

"I didn't expect anything," Myrna said, standing up. "I need to go too. I'm going to mind my sister's children while she has a lie-down."

"You're sure you don't mind."

"Perfectly sure," said Myrna with stiff dignity.

"Then we'll meet some other time."

"I'm not sure if I can get away easily for a while though," she said. "We'll just have to see."

"That's right, we'll just have to see," repeated David. "It probably won't be this trip. Might have to be in New York as usual."

She nooded. "Goodbye then," and left without thanking him for the meal.

That evening when he and Mabel shared a light cold supper with Mabel's father, David told them, "Can you imagine? Some people don't even know the difference between a star and a planet."

"Amazing," said Eben Loomis.

"Not at all amazing," contradicted Mabel. "Most people aren't half as well educated as we are, or as curious, either."

Seeing his son-in-law wink at Mabel across the table, Eben smiled. He would tell Molly how well "the children" were getting along these days when he wrote her in Boston this week. His wife worried too much.

CHAPTER 79

July 1893

WHILE MABEL TOOK TEA WITH HER COUSIN
Lydia Coonley at her grand new Chicago home, and Millicent played croquet
in the garden with her second cousins, David left the Amherst College exhibit
at the glittering Columbian Exposition long enough to meet Austin at the busy
modern train station. He scanned the disembarking passengers restlessly—
some of his materials had fared badly on their trip across the country, and he
had much to do to set the astronomy section of the exhibit to rights. He was
shocked at first to see Austin's lined and scraggy face at the door of the fifth
car; he looked worn and quite out of place. "Is he ill?" David wondered immediately. And then, "How old he is. Mabel will see that, at last."

But once Austin saw David, his blank expression changed, causing his face
to lose some of that impression of ill health, and the two men shook hands
vigorously. "You'll be glad you came," David told him as he took one of his
bags. "The exposition is first rate—impossible to see it all. There is something
for everyone, but wait until you see Little Egypt!"

"The dancing girl I keep reading about?" asked Austin.

"Dancing woman is more like it. When she moves...well, let's say she gives
an anatomy lesson. Don't be a prude, come see her with me. Nothing like her
in Amherst! I want you to ride on the hot air balloons too—they're going to be
the latest thing in travel by the next century, I'm sure of it. And did Mabel tell
you—Mr. Edison is here with exhibits."

But Austin was already distracted by the crowds and the effort to make sure
his bags were in order on the platform that bore no resemblance to the little
Amherst depot.

In the end, Austin and Mabel met on the Midway Plaisance in the midst of
the crowds thronging over "The White City": men pushing sedan chairs for
elderly ladies, children watching the fountains with their parents, vendors
selling food and souvenirs, and women on club tours clustering together.

"The trip wasn't too tiring?" she asked him, looking anxiously at his tired face. And before he could answer, "Imagine, no one knows us here. Isn't it wonderful? You're mine, mine to talk to in front of them all," and she gestured at the crowds around them. "Are your rooms all right?"

"They are fine, but lonely, of course. I hope you can visit them."

"I can and I will. I'll just need to find out Lydia's exact schedule for me after today—she's planned all sorts of things." She smiled brightly at him, but found herself snatching critical looks at his face when he wasn't looking—he seemed so out of place at the bustling Columbian Exposition, the grandest show on earth, with its acres of white buildings, its gondolas, its Parisian fashions on wax models, its parfumerie, its wild animals, and its weapons display.

Though they settled themselves at a comfortable outdoor restaurant to catch up on news and enjoy a leisurely midday meal, the atmosphere around them made talk of Amherst seem pale, extraneous. Mabel did not ask about Sue, only whether the Dell attic had been leaking and whether he had brought her mail. Mostly, she talked about the whirl of activity at her cousin's fine new house. "I expect to meet Frances Willard and Julia Ward Howe, thanks to Lydia," she told Austin, passing him the rolls. They will both be speaking here—at the Women's Building. And Lydia has arranged a special tour of it for the Women's Club chapter here. It was a woman who designed the building—you knew that, didn't you? And there will be concerts by female composers. And you must see the model kitchen. You can't imagine all the modern gadgets!"

After seeing some of the exhibits, they met David for late afternoon coffee, and though he longed for a nap, Austin agreed reluctantly to ride the spectacular Ferris Wheel. It seemed that everywhere he looked, it loomed on the skyline—a 264-foot high bicycle wheel looking like the rotund sister of the Eiffel Tower. But once they negotiated the crowds and stood wearily in the shadows of its huge cars, they discovered a line of people snaking along the pavement waiting to ride. Mabel told David, "No, David, another day. Can't you see he's tired? He only just got here."

"That thing might make me dizzy, anyway," said Austin, staring up.

"Then a brief stop for Little Egypt, come on now," insisted David. "You can wait outside for us."

"David, how impossibly common you are! He isn't interested. And I'm certainly not!" But even as she spoke, David drew them helplessly with him through the crowd which pulsed in the direction of the dancers' tent. "David!" Mabel shouted, "Wait!"

Her grip on Austin's hand was broken by a fat man smoking a cigar who pushed between them, so she had no choice but to keep Austin's head and shoulders in sight as he was carried along with the crowd. Under the sign reading "Little Egypt: Fahreda Mahzar direct from Cairo!" she caught up with him. "Where's David?" she asked, gripping his hand.

"He must have paid his admission and entered. I don't see him anywhere."

"I hate it here, it's vulgar and pushy, and contrary to everything the Women's Building stands for," said Mabel. "Do you see what David expects me to tolerate? Let's go to your rooms in the city."

"But I gathered you weren't free for long. And what about David? Won't he be alarmed if he can't find us?"

"Don't be silly—he went too fast to allow you to follow him, and surely he didn't expect you to leave me out here alone in this awful crowd. It's dangerous! There are thieves everywhere and all sorts of unsavory elements. Come on."

Thus when David emerged from the tent, his ears full of jingling bells and drums, his eyes vivid from bright red scarves, full bosoms, sequins, and lips redder than any he'd ever seen, Austin and Mabel were nowhere in sight.

"Six thousand acres to be lost in," he thought to himself as he returned to the Amherst exhibition on astronomy, eating a cup of ice cream as he walked. "Good riddance."

Austin was indeed tired, and although they undressed and made love as soon as they arrived at his rooms, Mabel almost wished they hadn't. In fact, both of them had been pushed almost to the limit by the city's pace and the novelty of the Fair. Austin's rattling cough worried Mabel, and she studied his pale chest and flaccid skin critically when she thought he wasn't looking. But he caught her: "What's wrong?" he asked. "Don't I look all right to you?"

She smiled and pulled the sheet tidily around them both. "I'm sorry. I'm not staring. I think you look tired, that's all."

"It's just the trip out here plus the cold I had."

"You should be slowing down."

"Well, I can't. Everything I do is important, in my opinion, and I'm certainly not going to give *you* up, unless of course you want me to."

Mabel smiled, but he did not. Seeing his face, she turned away slightly and said, "Well I didn't intend to be a drain on you."

Austin reached for her. "You know that isn't what I meant. I just wish I had your energy and your enthusiasm—you can get away from everything and be rejuvenated. It seems I can't be."

Mabel's shoulder was stiff. "You're here, aren't you? You're away from everything in Amherst. And yet so far, you complain more than you enjoy."

Austin sat up and leaned on his elbow. "I've said all the wrong things. I don't know how I can be so callous when I am so happy to be with you. You're right about my being so tired—can you chalk it all up to that?"

Mabel stroked his arm. "I'll try. Just so you don't imagine that I ever forget what I'm trying to escape when I travel all over the place. I do enjoy travel, that's true, and I love meeting so many important people, but I'd much rather be your wife back in Amherst making a happy home for you. I hate it when you sound jealous of me."

"Please forgive me."

"You're forgiven. Oh, I love you so much. Let's just be happy. Once you get a good rest you'll perk up. Isn't David a trial though, trying to drag you to the belly dancing? I'm constantly afraid he'll embarrass me at Lydia's. He told one of the Women's Club representatives to Chicago that she ought to be at home with her husband. She stood up for herself and then asked him whether he was one of the baboons who didn't think women should vote."

"Baboons?" said Austin, laughing. "She said that?"

"She did indeed. I must say, I had to laugh, which probably saved the day because David never had to answer. We ladies moved the conversation to other topics, having made our point. And don't let me hear you say a word against women's suffrage or I'm going to call you a baboon too."

Austin chose to change the subject as the ladies at Lydia's dinner had done. "Will we dine together tonight as you hoped?"

"Yes, just the two of us. Millicent is having a good time her cousins, I needn't worry about her. I want you to nap right now, and then we'll stroll about a little while—there's a lovely park nearby, and for another day, there's the Arboretum."

Austin's eyes brightened.

"I thought that might interest you, my darling king," said Mabel leaning over him. "Rest now. You're not in Amherst. You've nothing to do but be my husband this week."

A day later, Mabel insisted that Austin visit her at her cousin Lydia's for tea. "I just want you to," she insisted. "I want to be with you in front of people. This is practically our only chance. I'll introduce you as a good friend visiting the Fair from Amherst. Be there at 4 o'clock. Take the number 5 trolley."

But neither of them was comfortable from the start. Although Mabel's pulse jumped to hear his voice in the hallway, he seemed strained when he appeared in the parlor. His clothes looked provincial, and Mabel made a mental note to take him to the tailors when they were next in Boston.

To make the situation more uncomfortable, one of the guests, a Mr. Harrison of Fall River, Mass., had cousins who had once lived in Amherst and had heard of the Dickinsons. "Your wife is Susan Gilbert?" he asked. "My cousin knew her back in the '60's. A lovely woman. So talented and active in Amherst society. How is she?"

Conversation was distracted from Sue, however, as soon as Mr. Harrison had let it be known he was from Fall River, where the trial of Lizzie Borden had ended and she had been acquitted.

The next day, listening to the splashing of water in front of the MacMonmies Fountain, Austin told her, "Let's not do that again. It was painful."

"I'm sorry, my love. I thought it would be a good idea but it wasn't."

"I have to admit, I thought you would have more free time," Austin said.

She glanced at him. "But we've had time together. What did you imagine, then?"

"Oh, I don't know," he said, staring at the statuary, the rowing maidens in the fountain. "Just more time. I didn't think the same hectic pace we lead in Amherst would continue here."

"But Austin, that's not fair," Mabel protested. "How can you claim we are leading a hectic pace? This is all different—seeing sights, going places—we did come to see the Fair, after all. We didn't come here *entirely* to see each other." Her face fell after a moment. "You did come entirely to see me, didn't you?"

"Well, of course," he began.

"But I thought you'd enjoy all this too, the excitement and the change of pace. It's simply the biggest Fair ever. People will be talking about it for years, and we will have been here. Together."

The fountains stopped playing suddenly, and Mabel's last words jutted into the comparative silence.

"It's just that I'm not a good traveller or a good sightseer. You are. You thrive on it. I want to be back in familiar surroundings. I like to know where I am and what I'm supposed to do. I like to be with familiar people. I knew as much on that terrible trip through the South. I should have known I can't take the country out of this country lawyer."

Mabel frowned and sighed. "But you're not having a positively awful time?"

"No, I'm not, don't fret over it. I just want you all to myself, without the crowds and the noise. I wish you were coming back with me."

"I wish I could say so too, but honestly, I can't. I'm sick unto death of the gossip and the pressure—oh, don't let us start! Please, Austin, think about what we said a while back—about a house of our own in Amherst, or about writing to your friend in Omaha to see what things are like there. If you don't consider a new start now, you never will." She lowered her voice. "It needn't involve divorce, you know. We could just go. Sue would get along fine without you and David would get along fine without me."

"I don't believe that for a minute," said Austin, also lowering his voice. "And there's Millicent."

"She'd come with us, of course."

Austin waved one hand in front of his face. "This is enough for now. I'll have lots of time to think on the train. You wanted me to see the Great Pyramid?"

Wearily they got to their feet as the fountains jetted into the air once more. Austin took Mabel's arm and began to thumb through his Fair guidebook as they strolled along looking like any other tourist couple.

The last leg of Austin's train trip home, from Boston to Amherst, brought him as close to happiness as was possible these days without Mabel by his side. The familiar Massachusetts towns winding by the windows, the fields rich with peach-colored grain in the late sun, the celadon hills alive with gently fanning trees in the lucid air, seemed to nourish him palpably. Chicago and the crowds at the Fair struck him now as demonic—he could hardly wait to sit quietly on his own piazza, to chat with the people of Amherst he had known and loved for years. Sue and Mattie would still be visiting Brooklyn friends when he returned, and Ned was at Pittsfield for three more days, so he felt no need to brace himself for conflict.

A shadow crossed his thoughts when he remembered his promise to write to Arthur in Omaha about the prospects of practicing law there. "Why would you want to leave Amherst when you're doing so well?" Arthur would write back politely before answering his questions. "Is it Mrs. Dickinson who wants to relocate?" An unpleasant chore. But he would write a letter anyway. It had to be done. He wanted to be able to tell himself and Mabel that he had tried, at least.

The train reached Amherst station just as the sun set behind the hills. Austin stepped onto the platform and filled his chest with the air redolent of his youth, his roots, his life. Faces he recognized surrounded him, a sweet smelling evening was nearly upon them, and he was hungry for the supper he would share with his sister.

"Welcome back, Mr. Dickinson," said Charles Kelley in his Irish accent.

"Thank you, Charles," said Austin. "I won't be leaving again for some time."

August, September 1893

❦

THROUGHOUT AUGUST, PREPARATION OF EMILY'S letters inched slowly forward. Mabel bent over her desk for hours each day, working her way through the set from Emily to Austin, then those to the Clark family, the Norcross cousins, and Maria Whitney. Sometimes she arose at sunrise to work, enjoying her tea in the pellucid light.

One particular day, she expected a visit from George Washington Cable, the Louisiana writer who had settled in Northampton and for whose periodical she had recently submitted a piece. He almost always arrived on a bicycle, his blue eyes alive, his mouth smiling above his neatly trimmed and pointed beard as he dismounted and walked to the front porch. "No reason why you couldn't ride a bicycle too, Mrs. Todd," he told her. "You're an independent woman, why don't you set a trend? Healthiest thing in the world! You too, Miss Millicent!" he said, catching sight of her.

Millicent spent time reading her geography books quietly the third week of August—she was experiencing her second menstruation. She had waited for it and it had come, right on time, a private little miracle. It comforted her to cherish this secret from all but her mother and two close friends. She supposed her mother had told her father, but she hoped not, and cast her eyes down when David looked closely at her one evening. "You're quiet this evening, Millie," he said. "Not wanting to start school again?"

"I like school," said Millicent. "Especially geography."

"Just so you don't have fleas," said David, winking at Mabel and laughing.

"Oh for heavens sake, David, don't be disgusting! That's the most common expression in the world! Imagine, asking a lady to say she has fleas when it's her monthly time. All I can think of is Lizzie Borden when I hear that—it's what she said!"

Millicent left the room hurriedly. "Now see what you've done, David," said Mabel. "She's sensitive about it, can't you understand that?"

Just as Mabel began to settle into the routine of work in Amherst and to hope for the resumption of meetings with Austin, a telegram from her mother interrupted everything: "Grandma W. died 2 p.m. Funeral Lynn, Mass. Aug. 25."

Mabel walked into her parlor holding the telegram and stood by the window. Grandma Wilder was ninety-two and her death not unexpected, but a sense of loss and shock gripped Mabel nonetheless with surprising force. She would have to tell Millicent as soon as she came home this afternoon. The party of young people she was invited to join at the Crawfords before school opened would have to be canceled, and of course, mourning clothes brought down from storage.

Millicent did not cry at the funeral, but took frequent walks back in Amherst afterwards, holding Mrs. Loomis's hand or arm and sitting close by her in the parlor each evening. The two of them became familiar figures to the neighbors as they strolled amid the falling leaves.

With her mother staying in Amherst until October, Mabel's freedom was curtailed. She longed to escape the house and lost no time upon her return from the funeral to arrange a visit to the Homestead with both Austin and Lavinia.

"You look so haggard in black," said Lavinia staring openly at Mabel. "And older, too."

"Well thanks for the kind words, Lavinia," said Mabel shortly, eyeing the gravy stain on Lavinia's worn blue flannel dress. She sighed and held out a jar of canned pears. "From my relatives in Lynn."

Lavinia took the pears. "Thank you. Bring me up to date on the letters."

"There's nothing particular to tell since I last talked to you—all remains as I said. Mr. Niles wants us to delay publication until well into the new year, and we should respect his judgment. Austin is coming, isn't he? I was afraid he didn't get my note in all the flurry."

"I thought he'd be here by now," said Lavinia. "He's just coming down from another college finance meeting—although those things drag on forever."

"Oh, for heavens' sake," began Mabel, standing at the window.

But Lavinia changed the subject. "Sue is harassing me. She sent that horrible dog of hers over here to chase my cats and tear up the garden—you can't imagine the mess! I saw it all from upstairs. Whippers barely made it to the apple tree in time and George scuttled under the porch. I came rushing down and nearly had a heart attack chasing the monster off with a broom but he tore through the garden and trampled the last of the marigolds. Now go sit for tea."

They both heard the front door open. Austin reached Mabel in swift steps and held her quietly in the parlor while Lavinia went back to the kitchen in the shuffling gait she had developed as her arthritis worsened. They said nothing at first, but just held each other in the joy and relief of being together.

"It's strange to see you in mourning," he said finally, close into her ear.

She leaned her head back to look at him. "How I've missed you. Is everything all right? Oh, I wish we were alone."

"We will be. Patience. How long is your mother staying then?"

"Until October."

He sighed.

"I know. We'll have to be creative for a while. But we'll manage to get away together. We have to or I'll go mad." She kissed him quickly. "Your sister says I look awful and she's ordered us to the dining room for tea. Come on. Maybe she'll leave us alone for a while if we drink up our tea."

They could hear Lavinia singing to herself as she shuffled along the hallway carrying a large tray filled with cups, saucers, and the teapot. "Austin," she called out, "Fetch down the dessert plates for me."

In the dining room, Austin opened the cupboard doors and brought out three of the blue china plates. "There's a dead fly on this one," he said.

"It's probably been there for ages," said Lavinia. "Just brush it off."

"No, these plates should be washed. They're all so dusty—I doubt they've been used in months."

"More like years," said Lavinia as she set out the cups and saucers. "Here, give me the plate that had the fly. I'll use it."

"No, no, wash them all," said Austin.

A crash from the kitchen sent Lavinia flying back, and they both heard a "damn!"

"Probably the cat knocked something over," said Austin.

"Now," Lavinia said, returning and giving them each a damp plate. "You can have your cake. Lemon sponge on this side of the plate and Boston brown bread on this. And I have something to show both of you. Wait a minute." She left the table and walked slowly into the parlor. In a moment she returned with her green plaid knitting bag. Bending her arthritic knees painfully, she eased herself into her chair and fumbled in the bag, turning over skeins of wool mixed with pencils, several recipes, a broken necklace, and even a mouldly lemon which she removed with a laugh. At last, her knotted fingers produced a small bundle of letters which she held up and shook slightly before their eyes.

"What are those? New letters?" asked Mabel.

"Yes and no," said Lavinia. "I found them a long while ago and then lost them, and when I found them again, I wasn't sure what to do with them. I almost burned them. But I decided Austin ought to see them."

"And me too, I hope," said Mabel. "Certainly if they're Emily's letters."

"But these are very strange," said Lavinia. "I meant to show them to you first alone, Austin, but at this point, it doesn't matter. I don't know if Emily ever sent these letters, because they look like rough drafts, but the thing is, I can't figure out who they were for. There are only three, and two of them are for someone she calls 'Master'."

"Let's see." Mabel held out her hand.

"No, let Austin see first." Lavinia handed the packet across Mabel, who folded her arms across her chest in annoyance, to Austin, who opened the top letter, written in ink, and read it all without a word before handing it to Mabel and opening the next one, which was written in pencil.

As Mabel read the first one without interference from Lavinia, she sat up taller and taller, absorbed in the words. "What a letter!" she said, accepting the second one from Austin and laying her left hand on her throat for a moment. While reading the second letter, she had to stop a moment and raise her eyes to the ceiling, blowing air gently through her lips. "What could..." she began, but didn't finish her sentence as her eyes were drawn urgently back to the page. Then, "Daisy," she breathed. "She calls herself 'Daisy'." Turning to Lavinia, she said, "What does it mean, Vinnie? Who was she writing to?"

Lavinia said nothing, watching them, her knotted hands moving gently back and forth on the tablecloth.

Austin was finishing the third letter, the last one. "You don't know anything about the circumstances of these, Vin? She said nothing to you?"

Lavinia shook her head.

"Do you know when they might have been written?"

Lavinia shrugged her shoulders.

"It's early handwriting," said Mabel, "that much I can see. Oh—" and she looked up from the letter again. "Did you see this? 'You send the water over the dam in my brown eyes'—sweet lovely Emily. Someone hurt her? Someone loved her and hurt her? What's it all about? Who could it be? Vinnie, you kept these so long? How could you stand it?"

"Don't you have any idea who she's writing to, Vin?" asked Austin.

"None."

"But that's impossible. Surely we can figure out something."

"It makes no sense to me," said Lavinia. "She must have been hiding something from us. There must have been someone we knew nothing about."

"I can't believe that," said Austin. "Surely not. We knew her better than that. I just don't understand. Did she correspond secretly with someone? Could it be a literary person? Like Mr. Higginson?"

"Impossible," said Mabel. "Don't even suggest it. He doesn't fit this at all."

"I know. But who does? Who could?" said Austin.

"You see why they puzzled me," said Lavinia. "They surprised me so much I didn't want to think about them for a while."

"Otis Lord!" said Austin suddenly. "Could it be?"

"Too early," said Mabel. "I know that handwriting—it's pre-war, I'd say. Anyway, Judge Lord was married then. So it couldn't be him."

An uncomfortable silence followed her remark as all three of them saw the irony in her reasoning.

"Well anyway, it's not Otis Lord, I feel sure of that," said Lavinia finally, breaking the silence. "More cake?"

Austin held out his plate.

"Of course," said Lavinia, "we won't publish these. Should we burn them?"

"Burn them, did you say burn them? No, no," said Mabel. "Of course not. We'll keep them. We must keep everything Emily wrote."

"I think we should consider carefully what to do with them," said Austin. "Where to keep them, for example."

"They're so beautiful!" said Mabel looking up from the last one. "So beautiful, even if they are strange and hard to understand. Look how she's labored over them, too. She's crossed out words, searching for the right one. She didn't seem to be satisfied with any version. They're certainly not finished, but I'd still like to publish some of these..."

"No," said Lavinia and Austin in unison.

"Too delicate a subject, too shocking to her friends," said Lavinia. "I won't have people speculating about her and who she may or may not have loved. They do entirely too much speculating about that already. We can't publish and I think maybe we should burn them."

Mabel seized the letters to her breast. "Never. How can you even imagine it? Even if we do nothing with them, they must be saved. Maybe one day, we'll understand them. Then we can consider bringing them to light."

"I'll be dead before I understand these," said Lavinia bluntly.

"It doesn't matter," said Mabel. "Even if you and Austin and I never figure them out, we have to pass them on to someone for safe keeping. Millicent can take over from us." Seeing Lavinia's smile, Mabel said, "Yes, Millicent. Don't be so sceptical. She's hardly left her childhood yet, I know, but time flies and she will be a woman before we know it. More to the point, she cares about the letters and has helped David and me along the way. She knows all about our Emily. And you've said a hundred times you don't want Mattie involved in any way. May I take them to copy, Vinnie, and in the meantime, we can all think some more about what to do?"

"Maybe Sue could shed some light..." began Lavinia, but Mabel said, thumping the table with her knuckles, "No! How can you, of all people, suggest showing them to Sue? You don't really mean it, do you?"

"No, I guess I don't. But way back when, those two were so close. Maybe..."

But Austin interrupted her. "Be sensible. We do not want Sue involved in any way."

All three sat silently a moment.

"Then can I copy these three letters?" asked Mabel finally.

"Yes, if you copy them here."

"Oh please, let me take them."

But Lavinia was adamant. "No, here, now. I don't want them to leave this house." She leaned back and sighed. "Ah, I feel so much better, having shown you those letters. Austin, don't bother her. Will you look over my bank book while you're here? I'm sure I made a big mistake somewhere—I can't remember to write down all my checks." She pushed back her chair and rose slowly, taking some of the plates with her to the kitchen, then reaching for her sunbonnet on the nail and going outside to the garden.

At the table, Mabel pushed aside the rest of the cups and plates and held out her hand to Austin, wiggling her fingers. "Paper and pencil, quickly! I thought I was tired when I came here, but no more. What a treasure trove! That Lavinia—keeping these priceless letters to herself all this time!"

While Austin fetched her the pencil and paper, Mabel leaned forward and studied the first letter carefully. When he returned, the newspaper under his arm as well, she began to copy eagerly, a curl slipping over her forehead as she bent her head to the paper. Austin settled back at his place and opened the *Springfield Republican*, but he did not read with much concentration. Instead, his eyes returned to Mabel's face again and again. Looking at her, being with her, would restore his strength for yet another tedious meeting this evening concerning town zoning. He would not worry about these strange new letters.

He had found the idea disturbing that Emily might have loved someone with the intensity he could now imagine only in himself and Mabel, but looking at Mabel's placid face as she copied, he lost his uneasiness. Emily could not have loved as he and Mabel now did. Impossible.

"'Master' she calls him," said Mabel looking up. "And I call you 'king.' We have something else in common, Emily and I."

CHAPTER 81

October 1893

IN LATE OCTOBER, AFTER MRS. LOOMIS returned to Washington with Eben Loomis, Austin and Mabel made plans to take a carriage ride. They had not been alone together all month except for short periods at Lavinia's. "I can pick you up at the usual spot Monday at 10," his note read. "Say yes or no."

Mabel left her "yes" with Lavinia that evening, and all seemed set. Monday was fair, and Mabel stationed herself near the grove of trees far out on Pleasant Street to await Austin's carriage. At 10:15 she began to grow impatient. By 10:30, she felt chilly and worried, and by 10:45 she was angry and worried at the same time, pacing past the sunflowers and looking continually up and down the road. At 11, she hurried home, turning over in her mind all the frightening possibilities which could have detained him.

Just as she reached Main Street in the center of town and prepared to cross the street and hurry up to Lavinia's, the carriage she knew so well passed in front of her. Looking up, she saw Austin himself driving, an inscrutable expression on his face as he flicked the reins. Sue sat next to him looking deliberately ahead, a slight smile on her face, while Mattie sat in the back making a pretense of adjusting her bonnet. All three were dressed in Sunday clothes. No one said a word. The carriage passed on, going the opposite way from Mabel as she turned and strode up Main Street, so stunned that her vision seemed blurred. As the scene replayed itself in her mind with all its sudden meanness and confusion, a bitter taste rushed to her mouth, and she stumbled on a stone, steadying herself on a hitching post and saying "damn." By the time she reached Lavinia's house, her confusion had turned to such fury that she marched up the front steps and entered without knocking.

"Lavinia!" she said loudly in the front hall. "Lavinia, I need to talk to you!"

Not just Lavinia, but also Ned, dressed in riding clothes, appeared.

Mabel stared blankly at Ned, who had successfully avoided her for so long, and who now stood blinking in startled confusion. Looking at his thin young face with the carefully groomed moustache, the strained mouth with its awkward chin, not at all like Austin's, the careful part in the middle of his slicked down hair, and the worried transparent eyes, she remembered all in a rush the times they had spent together when she first came to Amherst—the way he had stared at her, confided his worries to her, tried to impress her with gestures he imagined to be manly, and finally, the times his gaze went from her eyes to her mouth, back and forth, until he kissed her full on the lips and she did not stop him.

Overwhelmed with all that had happened in the last ten minutes, Mabel reached her hand to the entrance table to steady herself. "Please," she breathed, "I'm sorry I came in without knocking. Something upset me but it's all right now."

"Don't mind Neddie being here," said Lavinia. "Just come in and sit down before you fall down. I never saw you act this way, but I think I have an idea about what's going on. They went to Northampton for Mattie's concert. That's it, isn't it? You had other plans, I imagine. He didn't have time to let you know. Sorry, Neddie, we can't avoid saying something about it to her, can we?"

"It doesn't matter," said Ned, "I'm going anyway." But he returned to the parlor along with Mabel and Lavinia and stood by the window, one thumb slipped into his jodhpurs pockets. He looked at Lavinia first as he spoke. "They went to Mattie's concert in Northampton. Father thought it was next week but it wasn't." He looked directly at Mabel now. "It was this week."

Mabel sank into a chair and looked back at him. Without warning, she smiled directly at him. Caught off guard, he smiled back, then shifted his feet and frowned, pretending to look out the window. "You're looking well," said Mabel. "I see you've been riding. Your costume becomes you."

Ned frowned again and nodded at the same time, moving toward a chair, the one farthest away from her. He had not been in the same room with Mabel Todd for months and months. Instead, he had seen her from afar—had stared at her from afar, both hating her and remembering how he had loved her. She would always be the first woman he had kissed—really kissed. And the first woman he had lost—really lost.

He had almost forgotten how she looked at close range. There were the familiar dimples at the edge of the perfectly shaped lips. The brown eyes. The full bosom he had always wanted to touch but never had, never would. She had cared for him during a short bountiful time, and right now, even the vivid reminder of it brought him a strange happiness, even in the face of everything else—his anger, the silences in his family, and the endless accusations.

"You didn't plan to hear your sister play?" Mabel asked.

"I have an engagement tonight," he said. "At the college. A dance."

"You're escorting Sylvia Warner, aren't you?" said Lavinia. She turned to Mabel. "Mattie arranged it through one of her friends."

A frown crossed Ned's face. "I asked her, Aunt Vinnie, not Mattie."

"Have a wonderful time," said Mabel. "And now I must be off."

Ned rose. "I'm sorry that I can't see you home."

"Ned," broke in Lavinia, "the whole family is gone, clean gone, to Northampton. If you want to walk Mabel Todd home, you can. I would like you two to be friends."

"I am always Ned's friend," said Mabel, "but I wouldn't want him to think he has to walk me home." She got up and went into the hallway. "'Bye, Vinnie. We'll have tea soon." Outside, she drew on her gloves, but as she began to descend, she heard the door open. Ned joined her swiftly on the steps. "I don't hate you," he said. "I wanted you to know." And he was off, following the path toward the Evergreens, holding his riding crop under his arm as he walked.

"Do you want to talk a little?" Mabel called after him quickly.

He turned. "No," he said. Then "Maybe," even as he took a few steps backwards towards the Evergreens.

"Come," she said. "We can walk through the meadow. Or maybe out to the stream you showed me once so long ago. It isn't so far."

With a glance around him, Ned met her on the sidewalk. "I don't want anyone to see us and anyway, that's too far."

"Well, never mind then," began Mabel, but Ned interrupted her.

"We'll walk over to the graveyard, you know, behind Mt. Pleasant."

"Shall we walk on Triangle Street?" asked Mabel, "or is that too public?"

"Triangle Street is fine," said Ned. He made a point of angling around Mabel so as to be on the curb side, stumbling slightly as he did so.

"Tell me about this dance," Mabel said as they began to walk. "Do you often put into practice all those steps we used to do together, remember?"

"Not so very often," he said, and then, "Well yes, fairly often I guess."

"And you still like your job at the college library?"

"It's all right. But I'm ready for a change. I might like to leave Amherst one of these days."

"I don't blame you, so would I."

"You would? I can't imagine that you would want to leave Amherst."

"Can't you?" she asked in a low voice. "You well know there are plenty of reasons." When he did not answer, she added, "I never planned all that happened. It just happened. I hope you understand that."

"I can't talk about it," he answered, his face reddening. "Please don't ask me to talk about it. I'll have to turn around if you do."

"Of course not, no, shh, shh," said Mabel. "Please forgive me. But I've always regretted that I have never been able to speak to you anymore over these years. It's been since Gilbert died that we last talked in any real way, hasn't it? But I've wanted to speak to you. Believe that. I have."

Ned said nothing for a moment. Then, as they passed the corner of Lessey Street, he said, clearing his throat, "Why?"

"Because I didn't want to stop being your friend..."

Ned laughed a little under his breath.

"And because I wanted to defend myself," she continued. "Although now, I realize that is probably not possible."

"I don't want to talk about those bad things," Ned said. "I told you."

"All right, we won't. We'll talk about other things and we'll look at the gravestones."

Together they turned into the group of evergreen trees at the entrance to the graveyard. "Not a soul about," she said, gesturing to a log bench. "Shall we sit?"

He sat obediently next to her in the dim light under the trees, stretching his feet out in front of him purposefully, the better for Mabel to admire his legs, made longer and thinner by the jodhpurs.

"Have you missed me, just a little?" asked Mabel, turning to look at him. "I did enjoy your company, you know."

Ned did not answer, but his heart pounded in confusion, remembering the times he had hated her with all his heart, all the time knowing that he could never forget how she had flirted with him, deliberately and unremittingly, as none of the girls he knew had ever done, and how he had kissed her. Just sitting beside her excited him now, exactly as it had done all those years before everything had changed. But at this moment, both because of and in spite of the unspeakable truth ringing in his ears—that this woman had lain naked with his father— that she was a woman who had passed on the other side of that curtain, that strange curtain of marriage—a woman who had experienced the ultimate act with two men and yet still spoke to him softly, still—could it be?—found his company interesting, his youth attractive—he wanted to seize her, to stretch his length upon her, weep against her breast and be encircled by her. But he said nothing. Only looked straight ahead into the rows of white gravestones.

"If you left Amherst, where would you like to go?" asked Mabel, holding her bonnet in her lap and smoothing a bluebird feather between her fingers.

"New York, maybe. Or possibly Geneva because of my mother's family connections there. But I don't know yet what I would like to do. I don't seem to be suited for anything."

"You'll find something," said Mabel.

"And my health is still uncertain," he finished.

"I believe you have lost some weight," said Mabel. "You should try to gain it back. But otherwise, you look fine to me. I like your moustache," she added. "You have no need of sideburns, as I see you have discovered. A clean-shaven look becomes you."

"Thank you."

A breeze blew up, tossing tendrils of Mabel's hair along with the feather in her bonnet. Suddenly, Mabel turned to face him, bumping her knees with his for an instant. "Ned, listen. We may never sit like this and talk again, who knows. In case we never do, I want to thank you for walking with me now and for not acting as though I were some kind of fiend, someone who premeditated everything that has happened. I did not plan it and I can't help what happened. We are all going to have to live with things as they are. But in the meanwhile, I will tell you that I like you, and nothing will change that. I'll always be ready to listen to whatever you have to say, despite the difficult position we find ourselves in. I wish your sister could feel the same way, but she's not like you, Ned, not at all. I see you are as sweet as you always were. That's why I liked you when I first met you, and why I still do. Can you stand to look at me?" she asked, to break his eyes from their gazing into the distance. "Can you?"

For a moment, he turned his head away from her and stared into the trees. Then he turned his face to hers at last. He could never remember afterwards whether it was she who clasped his hand first or he who reached for hers. But their hands met, followed by their lips in a brief kiss that he was to replay in his mind dozens of times over. Then they were both on their feet, looking at each other as though their meeting had just begun. But Mabel backed a few steps toward the path. "I should probably go back first," she said. "There will be more people in Triangle Street now. Remember what I said, Ned."

With a firm touch on his arm, she left him standing by the bench under a hemlock tree, the present already turning into the past, his longing turned toward the future. He hardly had time to watch her recede, she walked so fast, and suddenly he was staring at trees, a barn roof, and a patch of sky. He turned, already feeling and analyzing his pain, and walked without thinking toward his grandparents' graves, where he stood with unseeing eyes until he knew Mabel had reached her house and closed the door behind her. Only then did he turn and walk slowly, slowly, home.

CHAPTER 82

October 1893

At Smith College in Northampton, Austin sat beside Sue in the little recital hall with its creaking wooden floors and stared ahead while Mattie played the piano. He could not stop reviewing the agonizing scene in Amherst: Mabel's sweet familiarity on the corner before him and he, unable to respond. The cruelty of it seared his nerves and cramped his stomach.

As the piece Mattie had called "Autumn Song" ended, Austin clapped along with the rest of the little audience. But as soon as she began to play again, his mind went to work on ways to salvage the rest of the evening. If the reception for Mattie didn't last long, he could escort her and Sue to Clark Seelye's house well before dusk where they were to have dinner and spend the night. But he had already found his excuse: since one of his cases in the Northampton court had been postponed two days, he pleaded the very real need for client consultation early the next morning in Amherst.

Mattie was now playing a piece she called "The Indian Maiden." Austin continued to plan. If he left Northampton by 4:30, surely he could manage to return in time to find Mabel and explain the unfortunate episode that morning. He tapped his foot in impatience, aching to leave and be on the road again.

When the concert ended, he found himself caught among the members of the audience, including old friends from Northampton and some from Amherst. By the time he had shaken hands and chatted with a dozen people, it was nearly 4 and there was the reception still ahead of them at the Seelyes— more shaking of hands, more chatting. He found himself wishing he had not dismissed the utility of the new telephone apparatus so casually. By the time he had carried Mattie's last bag to the Seelye's upstairs bedroom and exchanged the last small talk in the hallway with their guests, it was after 6. The maid pressed a basket of food into his hands and he was off at last, from

Round Hill Drive, past the summer house and the hemlocks, and onto the Northampton road.

It was dark by the time he arrived in Amherst and drove on dusky streets past closed shops. In his haste to reach Mabel, he considered driving directly to her house, but restrained himself with difficulty, and drove the carriage into his own drive and back to the barn door, where he climbed wearily down, his knees stiff and one of his arms half asleep and tingling from holding the reins.

Stopping quickly only to wash his hands and drink some water, Austin left by the front door and stepped across the street and into the meadow where he inhaled the cool damp air which rose upwards, redolent of earth and hay. The plaintive crickets' song rose around him, a reminder that summer was over. He made a mental note to remind Lavinia about the meadow land he wished Mabel to have when he was no longer alive. Lately he worried more and more that Lavinia would not be strong enough to insist, in case Sue decided to contest his wishes, even though she cared nothing about the land. The frequency of Lavinia's petty quarrels with Mabel concerned him—he did not understand what motive lay behind them, unless it was only jealousy and possessiveness of Emily's poems and her memory. Already, she had begun to insist that Mabel's name should not appear on the frontspiece of the Letters.

He walked toward the light in the Todds' back parlor and knocked. Hearing the rustle of skirts as the door began to open, he stepped excitedly forward, only to find himself face to face with Millicent who stood in the lamplight holding a book at her side, her fingers marking her place. Her face conveyed no warmth, but for once, she did not look away as she usually did. "My mother's not home," she said. "She went walking with my father."

"I'd like to wait for them. May I?"

Millicent let him enter. He stood a moment, surveying the evidence of Mabel's work on the letters. By the looks of the parlor, she must have worked most of the afternoon and evening, for papers lay in piles on both tables and on the arms of two chairs. Someone had spilled ink on the carpet, and two empty teacups sat on a tray.

"Please sit down. My mother will be back soon."

To his relief, she left the room. He stretched out his aching legs, and picking up the sheaf of copied letters closest to him, discovered he held the letters Emily had written to her cousins, Fanny and Loo Norcross. Mabel had labored long and hard over these, he knew, frustrated because the cousins refused to let her see the originals, only censored versions copied in their own hands instead. "They are the most exasperating creatures!" Mabel had told him the last time they had discussed the letters.

Weariness began to overtake him; he wanted more than anything to stretch out on the sofa and give in to sleep. But he sat alert when he heard the distinct sound of Mabel's laughter and David's voice at the front of the house. They were on the porch one minute, both talking at once, and then inside the house. The front door shut. Austin sprang to his feet. He had stood up too fast, and his ears hummed for a moment as he grabbed a table edge for support.

Unable to decide whether to stay where he was, call out, or advance, Austin stared at the parlor doorway, listening to David finish a story for Mabel as they hung up their coats. "...So he claimed he failed the last test because the mice in his rooms left turds on his papers and his roommate threw them out. Did you ever hear such a contrived excuse?"

Mabel's laugh rang out freely, as though she hadn't a care in the world. "Oh, Davey, I do believe you are going to have to flunk that boy after all."

She entered the parlor smiling and saw Austin, gripping the edge of the table and staring at her. Her smile faded instantly and she stood still. "Are you all right?" she whispered.

"Yes, I'm all right, I didn't mean to take you by surprise, I..."

"Did Millicent let you in?"

"Yes."

"You probably gave her a shock, but not as much of a shock as you gave me."

"I'm sorry, I decided..."

But she interrupted him. "No, no, I don't mean now. I meant before."

"I'm sorry. It was horrible. But I completely forgot about Mattie's concert, and there was nothing I could do. I had to go. But I managed to get Ned to run over to Vinnie's and let her know, at least, where I was going. Did you see her?"

"I not only saw her, I saw Ned. We had a little chat. Don't worry, it was quite pleasant. Sit down."

"Is that Austin in there?" David called out.

"Yes," Mabel called back. She sat down and looked critically at his face.

"I couldn't concentrate on anyone or anything after what happened," said Austin. "All I could think of was your expression, standing there on Main Street. Please forgive me."

Mabel put her arms around him and held him tightly. "It was the same with me. All I could think about was *your* expression. So—so alien, I thought. Not you." Her voice was muffled against his chest. "I admit that I was angry. I marched like a demon up to Lavinia's."

"What are you doing here?" said David, entering the room. "I wasn't aware of any plans for tonight. For once, Austin, I feel like telling you to leave Mabel to me in my own parlor."

"David!" said Mabel. "Please, none of that. Austin just got in from Northampton to explain a confusion we had this afternoon."

"Don't tell me you've had a quarrel?" said David, laughing without smiling.

"Nothing of the kind," said Mabel.

Austin stood up. "You have every right to be annoyed, David. I'm going now, and you will have Mabel to yourself. I'm very tired too."

Mabel stood up too, but instead of following Austin to the door, she remained by the sofa. David moved behind her and clasped her shoulders. Averting his head, Austin turned and left without another word, sick at heart, and trudged homeward across the meadow.

In Boston a few weeks later, trolleys rumbled up and down the tracks in the dark street below room number 25 in the Parker House Hotel. Austin groaned and turned on his back. "Again. Let's give it up for now. I'm sorry."

Mabel sighed gently, lying on her back too and looking at the ceiling. This was Austin's second failure in two weeks.

"Nothing is turning out right these days," he said. "It seems we have less and less time together. I want you so much and yet when we are here together, all alone for once..." Mabel sighed again but to snuggled against his shoulder.

"Don't give up on me," he said. "I love you so much."

"Things will come right," she said. "We've been under so much pressure."

Austin drew her close. "I would do anything for you."

"Then will you leave Sue?" Mabel asked with sudden cruelty.

He relaxed his hold but said nothing. In a moment, Mabel gently disengaged herself and lay by his side, so that only their shoulders barely touched. They watched the shadows play across the ceiling, listened to the sound of running water in the next room, and felt the October air from the open window. Neither spoke, lying still and breathing open-mouthed, no longer willing to risk speech. Just as Mabel debated whether to punish Austin more by turning over without a word, or to apologize and turn with civility for sleep, she heard the gentle sound of his snores. In disgust, she raised herself on an elbow to look at him. But seeing his tired and lined face in repose, his weathered forehead, the sun line where his shirt lay against his neck, and the pallor of his pale chest with its gray hairs, her harsh thoughts melted in a rush. Tears flooded her eyes as she turned from him and lay facing the pale square of light at the window. She felt wide awake, yet in what seemed like the space of only a few minutes, she found herself dreaming something about Mr. Niles and Mr. Higginson who stood in Wildwood Cemetery arguing about what to do with a box of Emily's letters. "Put them on my headstone," she heard herself tell them. Later, waking again in the night, she found it hard to believe she had slept at all, but the next time she woke, the light at the window was distinctly brighter. When at last she heard the first bird sing, Austin turned and reached for her hand. Nestled against him, she slept again until the rumble of trolleys woke her and Austin leaned over her and smiled. "I dreamed I was building a new house for us," he said. "When you asked me how many windows we should have, I said fifty. When I woke, I was just starting to cut out the first one."

"Fifty windows, imagine!" said Mabel. "What do you suppose all those windows would look out onto?"

"Meadows," said Austin. "Fifty meadows."

CHAPTER 83

Christmas 1893

MOTHER, THERE IS NO GIFT AT FATHER'S place," said Ned, inspecting the breakfast table Christmas morning, 1893. Each plate except Austin's was brightened by a small beribboned bundle wrapped in tissue paper.

"I ran out of favors," said Sue, with no further explanation. "Put an orange at his place if you wish. Or split the contents of Lavinia's little basket with your father's. I'd have had enough to go around if she weren't coming. Maybe she'll change her mind at the last minute. I had no idea she'd actually accept the invitation when I sent you over there last week with it."

Sue's elderly friend, Mrs. Althea Wilkins, whom she had met in their Berkshires hotel, was visiting for a week. Her husband had died long ago yet she still wore black. Her own health was precarious. "I have had a weak heart for some years," she told Sue. "I must avoid all excitement."

"We must bring some joy to her life," Sue had told Ned and Mattie. "She has lost her husband. She needs to feel part of a home."

Mattie avoided Ned's eye at that, but both of them had dutifully remained in the parlor for music and conversation each evening. Mrs. Wilkins was not much of a conversationalist, however, and often gazed pensively into the fire, her embroidery untouched in her lap.

When the aroma of fresh rolls began to fill the house and to mingle with the scent of coffee, ham, eggs, cinnamon, and bayberry, Sue told Ned, "Go next door and fetch Lavinia. If she doesn't come on time, she needn't bother to come at all."

He found his aunt standing at the top of the stairs struggling with her dress buttons. The combs from her hair had fallen on the top step where one of the cats was playing with them, and a cameo pin lay precariously on the curve of the banister.

"Oh, Neddie, I don't think I'll go after all. I can't even get dressed, and Sue will be so cross with me. Does she really want me to come?"

"We all want you to come, Aunt Vinnie," said Ned, ascending the stairs and retrieving the combs and the cameo. "Come back in your bedroom and sit down. I'll do up these buttons for you. I thought Maggie would be here to help you."

"Poor Maggie, she has to have time off for Christmas too. Oh bother, I think I'll give it up."

"No, I want you to come see us," said Ned, working on the buttons. "It's been so long since you've stayed for a meal. I know things aren't always easy at home, but don't forget, Father will be there, and anyway, we need you to liven things up. Mrs. Wilkins is rather a serious creature, and quite fragile besides, although I think she enjoys being fragile. Mattie and I are bored, if you want to know the truth."

"Your mother frightens me," said Lavinia, reaching up to replace the combs in her hair.

"It's only the Gilbert family temper," said Ned, not believing what he said.

"Have you been feeling all right these days, Ned?" asked Lavinia, looking fondly at him. "Are you stronger than last winter?"

On the path between the houses, Lavinia looked up at the sky. "A mackerel sky," she said, "my favorite. Emily's too. Remember, Neddie, how Aunt Emily used to run out to look at a mackerel sky?"

Inside the Evergreens, Lavinia stared around the hallway and the parlor, both festooned with evergreens, holly, and aromatic pomanders which Sue and Mattie had made themselves. Bayberry candles had been placed on tables and in the candle brackets on the parlor walls, where they burned steadily and blended their aroma with the rich mix throughout the house. Lavinia stood confused by all the sights and smells until Austin had to lead her into the parlor to meet Mrs. Wilkins.

"My sister, Lavinia Dickinson," he said. "May I present Mrs. Althea Wilkins."

"I am glad to meet you at last," said Mrs. Wilkins. I understand you live next door but rarely visit, is that right?"

"You've got me confused with my sister Emily. Don't tell me you've heard some of the stories people make up? They irritate me so, nobody knows how much. Do you find people like to make up stories about the dead? I see you're wearing black—did you lose a sister too?"

"My husband," said Mrs. Wilkins quietly, "I lost my husband."

"Oh, that's different then," said Lavinia. "I doubt I could have been as close to a husband as I was to my sister Emily. Tell her, Austin. Tell her how close we three children were over the years. Some people can't understand it."

Austin smiled reassuringly at Mrs. Wilkins and steered Lavinia toward a chair. "We're not going to talk about death or the Dickinsons today, Vin. It's Christmas. Let's talk about other things."

Sue came into the room along with Mattie. "Ah, you have met my sister-in-law," she said to Mrs. Wilkins. "You see how convenient it is that we all live so close together. Village life is the only life for us. And we're not removed from the larger world, not at all. Did you know that I entertained Ralph Waldo Emerson right here in this parlor?"

"She knows about Emily's poems, doesn't she?" asked Lavinia from her chair. "She knows we have a poet in the family?"

"Sue mentioned it," said Mrs. Wilkins, "and I think it's wonderful. But I don't follow poetry very much. It's a failing, I am sure, but there you are."

No one said anything for a minute. Sue broke the silence by gesturing toward the dining room. "Our Christmas breakfast is ready. Austin, will you take dear Althea in to the dining room? Ned, please escort your aunt."

As the others advanced into the hallway, Sue hung back to whisper in Mattie's ear. "Did you manage to make two baskets from Lavinia's favors?"

"Yes," Mattie hissed back. "Both baskets are awfully small, but they won't notice. Mrs. Wilkins has the largest and that's what counts. Father and Aunt Vinnie can easily do with less."

"That's what I thought, too," said Sue, and the two of them joined the others at the table.

Around 4 o'clock, Mabel and David left President Gates's Christmas open house and walked home. The snow of two weeks ago had melted and the air felt unusually warm for late December. The starlings put up a racket in the maple tree nearest them. "I'm stopping in on Lavinia right now," Mabel told David. "I have a present for her—I'm sure she's expecting one."

"I'm going home to take a nap; all this Christmas entertainment has worn me out. I hate being on good behavior around President and Mrs. Gates. They're so infernally proper!"

"We'll have a light supper tonight," said Mabel. "But don't wait for me in case I'm late."

"Oh, so it's one of those meetings with Lavinia—you're going to see him aren't you?"

"David, I haven't seen him for several weeks! Poor dear, he's been run ragged with everything Sue has asked him to do before Christmas."

"Several weeks? He came over to the house two weeks ago while I was gone—the poor dear. Don't deny it. I pried it out of Millient."

"Well, I'm going, and that's all there is to be said about it." Without a backward glance, Mabel cut abruptly over to Main Street and quickened her pace. She picked her way through some puddles around to the back of the house in order to avoid being seen by someone in a carriage coming up Main Street, and let herself into the Homestead after two sharp knocks on the back door.

"Lavinia?" she called.

She advanced into the hallway and stood still, listening. Nothing. She tiptoed through the library and peered into the dining room, taking off her hat and coat as she walked but holding on to her string bag, and then returning to the hallway. "Lavinia?" she called again, only more softly. In the parlor, the double layer of shawls over the sofa revealed the turn of Lavinia's hunched shoulders as she lay with her gnarled hands nestled under her chin. Still tiptoeing, Mabel reached for the remaining free blanket on the sofa's arm. Moving quicky now, she took it with her into the dining room and then returned to the hallway where she stood and thought a moment. Then once again, she tiptoed into the parlor.

Lavinia raised her head. "Mabel? Is that you? What time is it?"

"It's about 4, Lavinia, I'm sorry if I woke you, but I thought I had told you I was coming this afternoon." She laid her hat and coat on a chair.

"It's all right, you did tell me. I just fell asleep. All that rich food next door and the effort of entertaining that insipid Mrs. Wilkins tired me out." She threw off her covers and sat up, smoothing the wrinkled skin under her eyes and focusing on the bag in Mabel's hand. "What's in your bag?" she asked.

"A present for you. A Christmas present, of course."

"Then sit down and let me open it," said Lavinia, patting the space beside her. "Very kind of you, my dear."

She tore off the wrappings to reveal a lavender wool shawl and a rose pomander. "I made the pomander myself," said Mabel.

"Quite lovely. Thank you so much. Oh, I love the scent of roses!" She examined the shawl and threw it around her shoulders. "Far too good to wear, far too good. I will have to store it away in tissue paper. It would make a nice gift for Mattie one day."

"I didn't buy it for Mattie, I bought it for you," said Mabel. "Please don't give it to her—I will be quite annoyed to see her wearing it."

"We'll see, we'll see," said Lavinia. "Now you wait here a minute. I think I can put my hands on something for you." Gathering the shawl around her shoulders, she hobbled slowly across the parlor in her stockings.

Mabel sat and waited, twiddling her thumbs in impatience and wondering whether Austin would be able to get away and join her. Her physical desire for him was sharp, and she had thought about him all morning.

From the dining room came the sound of crockery being moved. Then the clink of silverware rubbing together. After a bit, Mabel heard Lavinia say sharply, "Get down!" Finally, there was the sound of her footsteps returning as she muttered to herself or to the cats.

"Here." Still wearing the lavender shawl, she handed Mabel a broken china plate.

"What's this?"

"Your Christmas gift. It's from our china set— surely you recognize it, you've used it here with me often enough."

"But it's broken. Shouldn't you have it mended and keep it with the set?"

"Have David mend it, and then you can use it. Yes, you keep it. Mind you don't cut yourself on that jagged edge."

"Lavinia, how can David mend it when you haven't given me the broken piece?"

"Oh, yes, I forgot. Wait right there and I'll get it. Be patient now."

Lavinia tossed the shawl on a table and hobbled off again, leaving Mabel in her chair holding the broken plate and shaking her head in exasperation. "What else should I expect?" she muttered to herself, putting the plate down on a table. "After an hour of looking for the right shawl for her in Boston..."

A movement outside caught her eye: Austin, his auburn hair blown in tufts by the wind, his face pale in the late afternoon light, strode across the front lawn. Mabel rushed to the door and stood behind it, holding the heavy gold knob at the ready until she should hear his steps at the entrance. When his boot touched the first step, she flung open the door, still standing behind it, and leaped to embrace him the moment he was inside, kicking the door closed with her foot. His arms wrapped about her without question; his lips bent to her forehead as he said in a muffled voice, "I thought I would die until I could see you!"

"Well, can I come out now?" said Lavinia from the dining room door.

"I'm sorry, Lavinia," said Mabel, "I've missed him so much. You've seen him nearly every day. But I've been starved!"

"Just don't gobble him all up," said Lavinia. "Leave some of him for the rest of us. Shall we all have some sherry? I'm certainly not hungry after that big breakfast next door and the strain of trying to talk to that woman, whatever her name is."

"Vinnie," said Austin, hanging up his coat, "Mabel and I need some time alone. You understand. We'll join you later for sherry. Would you mind if we had the dining room to ourselves? This is the only chance we've had for weeks to talk quietly together."

"Oh, go ahead, go ahead," said Lavinia. "Who worries about me these days except Maggie? But you'll freeze in there."

Austin was already steering Mabel through the library toward the dining room, where he turned to close the door behind them and to tell Lavinia, "I'll close the other side too. We won't be long—just give us a chance to chat. You understand."

"You said that," Lavinia muttered to herself, going through the front hallway toward the kitchen. "They don't even care if there's no heat in there. Lucky it's a warm December."

Behind the dining room doors, Mabel had already unbuttoned the top of her bodice, loosened her stays, and brought Austin's hand to one breast, watching while he bent to kiss the other breast. Breathing heavily, she ran her hands down his body until she found the confirmation of his desire she longed for. "Love me, love me, love me," she whispered. "I don't care about anything else. The whole world has to stop for us now. I'm dying for you."

"I love it when you touch me," gasped Austin. "You're the only one, ever and always, the only one."

"There's no chance to make things very comfortable but I don't care, my king, my darling, let's make each other happy now, no hesitation. Now!"

Together, they sank to the couch, making the blanket into a pillow for Mabel, all the while kissing deeply, desperately. Entering her, Austin reached his climax quickly, leaving Mabel writhing to press against him. He had withdrawn when they both heard a loud knock at the front door and the sound of Lavinia walking into the hallway from the pantry.

"Hold your horses, hold your horses," she was calling out.

Frozen, Austin and Mabel listened long enough to recognize Ned's voice asking, "Is father here? There's been..." but they could not understand the rest.

"But touch me again," whispered Mabel, "please again, before you go. I have to have..."

But Austin was already obeying her wish, breathing excitedly with her as she whimpered softly, high in her throat. Lavinia's voice sounded out somewhere in the library and moved closer to the other side of the dining room door. "Austin?" she called.

"Quickly, pull yourself together," whispered Austin, getting clumsily to his knees and rearranging his clothes with shaking hands. "Stay here. Do not leave this room. I'll go into the kitchen and come out from the hallway. Will you be all right? I love you."

"Yes, yes," said Mabel. "How I know it. Go. But I can hardly bear it."

She moved in slow motion to avoid making even the slightest sound after Austin opened the back dining room door and tiptoed out. Lavinia's voice came even nearer to the dining room door. "Austin? Where are you? Neddie's here. There's been an emergency with Mrs. Wilkins next door."

"Vin," called out Austin softly from the hallway outside the kitchen now, "I hear you. Don't mention that Mabel is here."

"Of course not," Lavinia hissed. "What kind of a ninny do you think I am? Come on, Ned's waiting."

"What is it, what's happened?" Austin said, meeting Ned in the front hallway, his knees still shaky and his hair askew.

Ned's eyes ran up and down his father's figure without expresion. "Mrs. Wilkins fainted when she tried to go upstairs a few minutes ago. Fortunately, she caught herself and just sank down, but she's terribly weak now, and she says her heart seems to skip beats. We got her onto the downstairs bed. Mary's too lame to run after Doctor Cooper. Mother wants you to fetch him."

"I'll try to find him. But on Christmas day, of all days..."

"I thought you came over to help Aunt Vinnie," said Ned. "I really thought you had."

"I did. Let me be on my way then..."

"I saw her coat the minute I stepped into the hallway. Her coat and her ostrich-feathered hat. On Christmas day, of all days..."

"Ned!" said Austin sharply, and left the house.

Ned stood in the hallway a few moments looking down at the floor, his hands in his pockets. Finally he said to Lavinia when she appeared in the hallway, "Well, I'll leave you two together. She must be tired of hiding now. Merry Christmas, Aunt Vinnie."

"Merry Christmas, Neddie," said Lavinia. "But don't be so sensitive. I have learned not to be. You can too. Everything will come out right in the end."

But Ned had already gone out the front door just as Lavinia had begun her last sentence.

The sky was dark now over Amherst, and Austin cringed at the scene he had just endured, but as he walked to fetch Dr. Cooper, his blood beat with the fullness of satisfied desire and his heart sang out that he was loved by the woman he cherished more than anything else in his life.

~

PART FIVE

LAST COMMUNION IN THE HAZE

~

1894-1895

April 1894

A UNT VINNIE? IS THIS A GOOD TIME TO visit?" called Mattie, entering the Homestead kitchen one April morning.

"Hello, Mattie. I thought you were still in Pittsfield." Lavinia sat at the table peeling potatoes while a pot of water hissed on the stove.

"I came back early."

"Sit down and visit."

"I'd rather sit in the parlor."

"I rather expect the fire has gone out..."

"Get Maggie to fix it and we can sit there. I don't see why we should huddle in the kitchen. Besides, I came to visit you, not Maggie."

Lavinia put down her potato and knife and heaved herself slowly up. "My knees will soon be as arthritic as my fingers," she said, "and then what will I do? Just look at these fingers!" She held out both hands, damp and dirty from the potatoes, and let Mattie inspect with distaste the swollen knuckles.

"Go wash your hands, Aunt Vinnie. Your fingernails have dirt under them."

"Well, of course, I've been potting plants and peeling potatoes. Come see, in the conservatory. More hyacinths are out and of course all the herbs."

Maggie followed her aunt into the conservatory, where she loved to remember quiet chats with her Aunt Emily among the red clay pots, the delft bowls, and the delicate aroma of hyacinths in the chilly air.

"See?" said Lavinia, pointing to rows of plants on trays facing the sun.

Mattie held her hands to the sun and smiled.

Lavinia studied her. "You have a lovely smile," she told her.

The smile faded. "I do?"

"Of course. Lovely. Now tell me what you are doing these days. Do you have any new beaux?"

"None that please me," began Mattie.

Lavinia slapped her thigh. "None that please you? Oh, child. That sounds as though you have a veritable string of them!"

"No, no, I don't. But I do let John Williams write to me from Brooklyn—you might remember him."

"What ever happened to Thurston what's-his-name, the one who took you to so many sleighing parties in December. Didn't he belong to First Church?"

"Thurston, he's so dull and plain, Aunt Vinnie! He has pock marks all over his face. I can't stand looking at him."

"Poor Thurston. I suppose you don't want me to speak to his mother..."

"Aunt Vinnie! Of course not! How can you even think of such a thing!" She reached for the smallest hyacinth in its pot and looked critically at it.

"Oh, courtship and marriage," said Lavinia. "What a difficult business. Your Dickinson grandparents kept their courtship letters. I should let you see them some day. Would you be interested?"

"Oh, I don't know, maybe some time." She continued to turn the little plant around in her hands.

"They aren't terribly interesting," Lavinia went on. "Well, what is interesting is the way my mother held my father off for so long. She refused to visit Amherst and she kept on postponing the wedding date."

"She did? Why?"

"I have no idea. I never asked her. But then I never read the letters until after she died, and I haven't read them all even now. They make me feel peculiar."

"Grandmother never said much about...well, about herself and Grandfather. Or anything beyond the usual daily talk. Was she always like that, or just when she got old?"

"She was always like that," said Lavinia simply. "Here, Mattie, help me repot a couple of these."

"Right now? I hate to get all dirty..."

"Oh bother. You have to stop worrying about dirtying your hands sometime. Who cares if your fingernails get dirty? You can always wash them, can't you? Put this old towel over your dress."

"But don't you have gloves?"

"Gloves, gloves. All right, let me find them." Lavinia rummaged through an old basket behind her and produced mismatched gloves. "Two left hands." She tossed them aside. "You'll have to risk your nails."

"No, I can wear them. I just won't use my thumb on the right hand."

"You are serious about your hands, aren't you?"

"Well, I'm going to a social tonight and I'd rather not spend a half hour cleaning my fingernails."

"Remember when you fell in the refuse hole on our lawn? You were so small. Four? Five? Maybe that's why you hate dirt so much now."

"It was horrible. But you laughed at me."

"Well, you did look funny. Here, I think this plant can stand being moved now."

"Aunt Emily didn't laugh at me," said Mattie, accepting the plant.

"She was always a better person than I was."

"Ned says Aunt Emily is the cream of the Dickinson crop. He says the Dickinson name is in jeopardy, too, but I don't believe that, of course."

"What on earth does he mean? A little more soil in that one."

"For one thing, he means that if he doesn't get married, he won't be doing his duty in carrying on the family name—you know, since Gilbert... Ned's already thirty-one. He's too shy. Mother tries to help him, but Father hasn't helped at all. You know very well what I mean. But you can stick close to home and ignore all the embarrassing gossip and the poisonous atmosphere, whereas Ned and I can't do that, we have to go out and about. We have to try to make our way through it all."

"Well, we all do, dear, in our fashion. I have had to make my way too, what with some of the things I have to put up with, or the things I am sometimes asked to do. I don't like to talk about wills, though, I must say. I'd like to close my ears when your father brings up the subject of his will and what I'm supposed to do. After all, if the extra things aren't written down, how am I supposed to do them?"

Mattie froze in the act of pulling off one glove. "Father's will? What do you mean, what has he asked you do to?"

Lavinia clapped her hand over her mouth. "Oh Lord, now I've gone and done it!" She bit the ends of her fingers. "It's nothing. Now don't get the wrong impression. It's just some things your father asked me to do one day, small things. It needn't concern you."

"Then why are you so upset? Something that would go against Mama?"

"No, no, nothing like that. Just some little matters he wanted me to look after. It doesn't even matter, Mattie, because I'm going to die first, I'm sure of that. Let's forget the whole thing. I just wish he wouldn't ask me to take care of his affairs for him, that's all." She brushed the soil off her skirt and laid down her trowel. "I have to see how Maggie is doing in the kitchen and I need the potty chair too, if you must know. You won't run off now, will you?"

But Mattie held her aunt's arm. "Wait a minute. Just tell me what you mean, that if Father dies before you, you have to do something for him."

"No, I won't talk about it anymore because it's nothing that will ever happen, and anyway, it's nothing that would affect you—you have no interest in land. Land isn't as important as it's cracked up to be. Let me go, my bladder is bursting."

When Lavinia came downstairs some ten minutes later, Mattie was no longer in the conservatory. "Mattie?" she called, walking slowly back to the kitchen.

"I must go, Aunt Vinnie," said Mattie at the back door.

"All right dear, if you must. Just promise me you won't dwell on that silly thing I said. It's of no consequence."

But Mattie had already closed the door and was hurrying toward the path between the Homestead and the Evergreens.

Sue studied Austin's face that evening at supper. Since Ned was still in Pittsfield with his friend Mac Jenkins and Mattie had excused herself from supper altogether because of a headache, they sat at the table alone. She had felt appalled, so much so that her hands trembled whenever she thought about what Mattie had told her that morning. She had never imagined her husband as her enemy—a person who conspired actively against her best interests. She viewed him as stubborn and selfish, yes. A man who was nothing like the man she thought she had married. But as someone who might deprive her and her children of property or goods in favor of another woman? For what else could Lavinia have meant? What else? Austin intended to see to it that Mabel got something from the Dickinson estate. What, exactly, she did not know. She had spent the day trying to imagine that, distressing herself more and more as her imagination embraced never-ending unpleasant possibilities. But she always came back to the same conclusion: her husband must be viewed as her enemy now. Could there be any other way? When the man you have raised your children with conspires behind your back to deprive you of money or property, items which his lover could acquire instead, then he is your enemy.

"I put the new well cover in place," said Austin, looking up from his roasted potatoes.

"Good," Sue replied, pulling her dish of applesauce toward her. It was soft—it would slide past the thickness in her throat. She ate a few spoonfuls and stared at him again as he cut himself a slice of bread and buttered it. The thought struck her that his character had at last completed the long transformation begun some years ago, even long before he met Mabel Todd: the transformation from being a responsible man, a Dickinson, after all, to this inward, inscrutable person who withheld his emotions and needs completely from her, who lived in the airless oblong of his own bell jar, and then suddenly gave her to understand he could lift the bell jar, could love a woman other than herself with unrestrained passion. This was immorality. The kind of immorality she had never met before first-hand, let alone in her own family. Though she had learned about Austin's shortcomings during their marriage, she had never, until now, failed to count on his moral character, sustained like his father's before him. Lavinia had once showed her a few of Edward's courtship letters to Mrs. Dickinson. Although Lavinia hooted at some of the little lectures Edward wrote to Emily Norcross, she, Sue, found the letters admirable—full of a sense of duty, responsibility and character. It was these qualities that she had looked for in Austin Dickinson and had found, at first.

Austin had put down his piece of bread and reached to unloosen his top shirt buttons. Suddenly, he put both hands on the table, palms down, and looked straight ahead with unseeing eyes.

"What?" she said. "What?"

"I'm dizzy," he said. "Very dizzy. Hold on, hold on..." He froze in position, his hands still flat on the table. She waited, ready to reach for him if necessary.

"Better?" she asked.

He did not answer for a full minute while she stared. Then he closed his eyes. "Yes, some. It's going away I think." He relaxed his hands and then lifted one palm to his chest, staring again with those unseeing eyes. "This is the second spell I've had today."

"Shall I call Dr. Cooper?"

"No. If they get worse in the next few days, then maybe. But what can he do about them, anyway?" He folded his napkin and began to push his chair back.

"Shouldn't you wait a few minutes before you try to get up?"

He said nothing but sat still.

"I'm afraid the parlor fire has gone out," she told him.

"Can you start it up?"

Sue went, alarmed now, into the parlor and added kindling to the fireplace. When had she last built a fire while Austin was in the house? When he had that terrible flu in '74, the year his father died. Any other time? She couldn't remember any. She packed in the small twigs, added a couple of large logs, and lit them. Returning to the dining room, she found Austin sitting in the same position.

"Ready to move?"

"Yes, I think so. But this dizziness—it turns my stomach."

"We'll try some mint tea later. Lean on my arm. If you go down, I'll never get you up. Oh, I wish Ned were coming back tonight."

"I'll be all right," said Austin. "It's just the work overload. I can't do what I used to when I was young. I'll try to cut back on something. These spells give me the chance to say 'no' to those requests I shouldn't be answering in the first place."

"You're not a young man," Sue said. "Why won't you realize that?"

They made their way slowly into the parlor where Austin headed toward an armchair. "Where's my book?" he asked.

"Which one?"

The short stories by George Washington Cable."

"Oh. I was reading them. Here they are. I suppose he'll be bicycling into town again now that the winter is over. I can't think all that pedaling is very healthy for a man of his age—or very dignified. I think he looks ridiculous." She watched while Austin sat slowly down. "Are you all right?"

"Yes, fine."

Sue returned to the dining room. Mattie had said Lavinia went on and on about how she would die before Austin, and that she would never carry out whatever Austin had asked her to. But nothing ever turned out as one expected.

She carried a tray loaded with dishes into the kitchen. Mary Moynihan was visitng her ailing sister in Holyoke but Maggie had promised to come over as soon as she could. Actually, with Austin in the parlor, Sue preferred to stay in the kitchen now, where she could think and plan. Her heartbeat seemed to thrum in her temples, and she felt dramatically alert. She would need a strategy, an effective one, to deal with Lavinia, and the sooner the better. In fact, if she talked to Lavinia now, tonight, she might get a sense of things.

Maggie rapped on the door and came in. "Sorry I'm late, Mrs. Dickinson, but I got held up, between Miss Lavinia and Mrs. Todd's chores. There's a dinner party planned at the Dell."

"Maggie," said Sue, "Mr. Dickinson had one of his dizzy spells a while ago. He feels much better now—he's by the parlor fire at the moment. But I need to go next door and talk to Lavinia for a while. Something rather urgent has come up. Will you keep an ear out for Mr. Dickinson?"

"Of course, but Miss Lavinia was talking about retiring early when I left."

"Then I'll leave right now and be sure to catch her. I won't stay long."

Sue pulled her old green shawl from its hook, stepped out into the sweet-smelling April evening, and set out to the path between the two houses. She veered toward the lights at the front of the house—the kitchen was dark—and stumbling once or twice in her detour, found herself at the front door. She knocked loudly three times, then opened the door, the force of her anger venting itself on her husband's family home.

"Lavinia? Where are you? I want to have a word."

There was no answer. Sue advanced through the library toward the light in the dining room where she saw Lavinia dozing in a chair by the table, wrapped in a red shawl, her head limp on her chest. Various papers lay in her lap, while more had fallen by her side.

"Lavinia?"

With a start and a stifled cry, Lavinia jerked awake and stared, wide-eyed. "Help!" she called. "Help!"

"Lavinia, it's Sue! Don't be so silly! Who did you think I was?"

"Oh my." Lavinia covered her trembling lips with one hand and stared.

"Well, I'm sorry, I didn't think I'd disturb you so much—Maggie said you were still up. I thought I ought to tell you that Austin just had a terrible dizzy spell."

"What? What? Oh dear Lord, Austin!" Lavinia began to wail as she struggled to her feet, clumsily gathering the shawl around her. "What did Dr. Cooper say? Let's run over and ask him what to do." She shuffled a few steps forward.

"Stop, Lavinia. Dr. Cooper isn't there."

"He left already?"

"I never sent for him."

"What? Then let's find him, we'll run over and ask Maggie to fetch him."

"Austin doesn't need a doctor now. Don't you think I would have sent for Dr. Cooper if things were serious?"

"But you said he had a terrible spell."

"Nobody likes to have a spell, but I imagine we all must endure a spell or two once in a while. Austin is sitting in a chair by the fire and he told me *not* to fetch the doctor. He knows best, don't you think? No, I want to ask you about some other things. Mattie told me a frightening thing today—I can hardly grasp it. She says you told her this morning that Austin has asked you to do something about his will—something behind my back, I gather, since he never told me anything."

Lavinia groaned before Sue finished her sentence.

"Why do you groan? Is my mentioning this so onerous? How do you think I felt today when I heard this piece of news? You listen to me, Miss Lavinia Dickinson, my husband's will affects me and my children, so anything you know about it or are hiding from me should be brought into the open and made clear. So tell me and tell me right now: did Austin ask you to do something for Mabel Todd that he didn't dare put in his will? Something that I wouldn't like?"

Lavinia groaned and began to move toward the parlor, but Sue prevented her. "Stop! Stay right here and answer me. I mean it, Lavinia. I'm fighting for my children. I'll find it out, so you may as well tell me."

"But I don't know anything," said Lavinia in a whining voice. "I don't understand these legal things."

"You understood well enough to make a promise. How much, Lavinia, how much are the Todds going to get?"

"Nothing, nothing, it was just talk about some gifts, that's all, some gifts he wanted made."

"Why didn't he make them, then, right now?"

"Because you..." Lavinia stopped and groaned again.

"Just tell me and stop beating around the bush. What does Austin want to give Mabel Todd?"

"I don't know, I didn't understand it. I couldn't follow it."

"I repeat, what does Austin want to give Mabel Todd?"

"It could have been a little piece of land, but I don't think so, no, that couldn't be it. She wouldn't want that anyway. But it wasn't money, I'm sure it wasn't money."

"Land? Land? Your brother would give land to that woman instead of to his own children? And you were a part of this whole plan?"

"No, no, I wasn't. It could have been my land. I didn't understand it. He just thought about these things and he told me some of it, but I'm sure he's changed his mind, and anyway, I never did understand it, I told you that. I'm not having anything to do with it. I told him I wouldn't outlive him anyway and I won't."

"Lavinia, sit down in that chair and stop wandering around. We have to have this conversation and you know it. What were you supposed to do?"

"Nothing. I was just supposed to tell anyone who asked me what Austin said about some land. But I don't understand it, so I can't tell anyone, and besides, I'm going to die first. I told Austin I would and I will."

"Lavinia Dickinson, if your brother dies tomorrow and you are a party to conveying to that woman what rightfully belongs to me, you'll be so sorry you won't believe it. You can't imagine how sorry you will be. No one will stand up for you, either. Not Mattie, not Ned. You'll be alone. So very alone in this huge empty house without even Austin to come check on you."

Lavinia's jaw had been trembling, but now her teeth began to chatter. "I told you, I don't understand any of this legal talk. I wouldn't take land from Ned and Mattie, you know I wouldn't. I want to go to bed now but I don't think I'll be able to sleep." She wiped one eye with a trembling hand and pulled the shawl closer around her.

Sue backed up a few steps and stood looking at Lavinia in her chair. "Will you promise to keep Ned's and Mattie's best interests at heart in the future? And mine, of course. But especially theirs. You should know what a hard time they've had of it in the past few years—or maybe you aren't able to think about it—that Dickinson short-sightedness. Austin has it, naturally, but you do too. You want what you want, period. Even Emily wanted far too much from me— I couldn't give it."

"I'm going to bed," said Lavinia, getting up suddenly. "I won't sit here and listen to you talk unkindly about Emily. Good night." She picked up the kerosene lamp, walked into the hallway, and began to climb the stairs without another word or a backward look, leaving Sue in shadows below her.

Sue sighed in exasperation and picked her way to the door. She had not thought to bring a light, and now the night seemed so much darker. Opening the front door, she looked up at the sky where ghostly clouds scuttled in front of a dim half moon. Main Street lay quiet. No lights shone in the Hills's house up the street or at the Jameson house, but their own gas light in front of the Evergreens shone as always.

Sue hoped she had frightened Lavinia. "She does whatever the last person tells her to do, the fool," she muttered to herself as she bent against the chilly breeze and walked toward the Evergreens.

Inside, she found Austin still by the fire.

"Where did you go just now?"

"Next door. I had a few things to clear up with your sister. You might know what they are, but we'll not bother to discuss them now. Go to bed for now. I'll tend to the fire."

Austin got up slowly. "I feel so weak. Will you make sure I'm awake by 6 tomorrow? I have to be in Northampton for a hearing."

"Yes, certainly I will. I'll be keeping a close eye on you these days," she told him, breaking up the fire roughly with the poker and watching the sparks fly, her face red with the heat and the exertion of hacking the glowing logs apart. "There. No more fire. Go to bed."

CHAPTER 85

Late Spring 1894

Spring freshened into a May of two balmy weeks followed by a period of chilly rain. Mabel spoke in Brooklyn several times about Emily's poetry, finished her article for *The Century* about Emily's difficult handwriting, and began two new articles on eclipses.

"I wasn't going to tell you," said Austin one evening, "but maybe I should—apparently Lavinia let something slip to Mattie about the meadow land I want you to have."

"What? She *told* her about it?"

"I'm not quite sure what she told her. But enough to set up an alarm, because I took Sue's gunfire a few weeks ago, a little while after those dizzy spells I told you about. I told her Lavinia had things all mixed up, but that I had considered giving you and David some of the meadow land—I didnt say *all* of it. I told her it was mine to give, after all—it's father's land left to me."

"And how did she react to that?"

"She told me I could not leave you the land and that was that. She left the room and we haven't referred to the matter since."

"That Lavinia! She's like a crumbling old building!"

"I'll have a talk with her when things quiet down and when I feel better."

"I thought you said you felt so much better."

"I do. I'm just being careful."

"Come, Austin, put those papers away. I must hold you close," said Mabel. She put her arm around his shoulder and bent her head to kiss his lips deliberately. He kissed her back until they breathed heavily together and Austin gripped her tightly.

"Millicent is away for the weekend, just as I told you," Mabel said softly, kissing his neck. "Do you want to?"

"And David?" asked Austin.

"The usual. A late night at the observatory. He'll recognize my signal and won't bother us. Come on." She stood up, pressing his hand to her breast, then turning around to lead him from the room by the hand, lowering the lamp as she passed the table. "We have time. I want you so much. It seems ages since we were together this way. I feel strangely—good—young—tonight."

She led the way upstairs. "I'll light a lamp," Mabel told him. "I want you to see me and I want to see you, please. Let's not turn it out tonight. I want it to be like it was in Childress meadow that time, remember, the summer of '87?"

"July of '88," said Austin, "because Sue had missed the train in Geneva and telegraphed to say she would be delayed a day."

"Yes, you're right. July of '88. Her telegram sent us to that meadow. Oh, Austin, the way we looked at each other in the sun that afternoon. The way you let me look at *you*! So free, so beautiful, in all those sunny leaves."

"I'm sorry if I disappoint you sometimes—it goes against my nature to enjoy myself as much as we did that afternoon," said Austin, his arms around her. "But you know the depth of my love for you."

"Let's not talk," said Mabel. "I need you, so very very much—if you'd known my thoughts in the last week you might have blushed! Let's go slowly—and then fast!" she breathed.

She took off her garments, piece by piece, and then pressed against him. "It's your turn now—you must take everything off. No hiding from me tonight. I won't let you cheat now!" She tugged on one shirt sleeve and loosened both cuff buttons.

When Austin was completely undressed, she insisted they embrace in the lamplight, standing up, before getting into bed. "Like lovers in the South Sea islands," she said. "I've read about it, how natural they are, how they view pleasure as healthy. Wouldn't that be a wonderful way to live?"

"It's the way I feel when I'm with you," said Austin, "even though I can't throw off all my outward habits. I'll never be a South Sea islander but I'll let you bring me as close as you can."

They fell upon the bed, Mabel taking the lead in their lovemaking. She kissed his chest, inching her way down his stomach until he flinched and raised his head. "Let me kiss you there, please let me," she whispered. "Relax, trust me." Austin lay rigid and silent with his eyes closed but groaned in pleasure when she stopped and lay her head beside his once more. In the end, she straddled Austin, riding him up and down until he gasped and shouted, and she herself threw back her head before slumping over him, damp with sweat but smiling in the lamp's glow. "We'll forget them all," she said between breaths. "President Gates and the Parish Committee and the woman who thinks she is your wife." She laughed a low chuckle. "They would think *this* was a scene from hell. But no." She collapsed against him, then lay the length of his body and kissed his lips. "No, it's heaven. Pure heaven. And you are my God."

They lay quietly a few moments. Then she felt his face move and raised her head to look at him. "You're laughing?" she asked. "What's the joke?"

"I'm not really laughing. But I'm very pleased with myself right now," Austin said as he smiled up at her and caressed her hair from her temples. "I was afraid things might go wrong tonight. But they didn't and I'm so happy. I feel young, can you imagine? And not at all like a Dickinson."

"Let's lock the door and stay here all night. We'll get Maggie to tell everyone we went away, but all the time, we'll be right here in this room, naked! Naked while the sermons roll from First Church and while Mrs. Tyler calls her silly little dog and while Merrill Gates adds more sins to the faculty list of 'thou shalt not's'. Austin? Are you dozing?"

"No. But it could easily happen."

"I'm going to keep you here all night. David can tell Sue that you took the train to Boston on the devil's business."

"A sweet wish. My love, I must get up. David could be along any moment."

"So what? He knows what he knows. Tonight I don't care about appearances. For him, anyway. He doesn't worry much about appearances when he decides to have his fun, does he?"

"Well, I'm getting up," mumbled Austin sleepily, but he lay quietly while Mabel pulled the quilt around his shoulders. In a few moments, they both slept, so they did not hear David's footsteps outside on the porch or the sound of the back door opening. It took David but a moment to notice Austin's coat and walking stick in the back parlor.

"Horse manure!" he said, picking up the coat and then tossing it roughly down. "I'm sick of it. Who lives here, him or me, damn him!"

He looked at his pocket watch, saw that it was only 8:30, and went out again, crossing his lot and then the meadow until he reached Main Street where lights shone in Lavinia's downstairs windows. He walked across the grass and knocked softly at the back door. "Lavinia? It's David."

In a moment, Lavinia, a blue towel wrapped around her head, came to the door carrying one of her cats. "What's the matter, got company at your house again? He doesn't come here much anymore. Prefers your house."

"You look like a sultan! What's that towel for? I thought I'd mend your pantry shelf before it falls down entirely. I finished my articles now, I've got time."

"I washed my hair, what do you think? Maggie told me I smelled. How do you like that, the proverbial smelly Irish telling me such a thing. I took her words to heart, D.P. Todd. Well, hurry in before I freeze, I'm drying my hair in front of the dining room fire." She clicked a loose false tooth.

David followed her through the dark library to the dining room where the fire cast quivering shadows on the walls. "It's damned hot in here," he said.

"Don't complain, or I'll make you go straight to work. I haven't talked to a soul all day today, except Maggie, and she told me I stank, so I won't count her, the dear fat thing. Well, tell me what you've been up to these days. What's happening with the heavens or with the Amherst College faculty, if you prefer." She took the towel off her head and picked up a brush thick with her long coarse hair.

"Don't make me talk about that stodgy faculty," said David, pulling a chair back from the fire. "If I had the money, I'd leave this place in a minute and set myself up as an independent researcher. I can't do my work here—Seelye always loaded me up with too many classes and now Gates is doing the same. Between teaching at Smith and here, writing articles and traveling, I'm a frazzle. And they seem surprised when I skip a class here and there. To top it all off, when I come home from the observatory, Mabel's got company."

"Oh, that. Well, Mabel thinks she owns my sister, and now she thinks she owns my brother." Lavinia set her arthritic fingers to the brush with one hand and tried to untangle her long auburn hair with the other trembling hand.

"Ouch!" She winced as her fingers met a snarl.

"Well, she *does* own Austin," said David. "He does whatever she wants, you know that." He moved his chair further back from the fire. "Lavinia, the rung of this chair is hanging loose."

"Yes, you can fix that too," said Lavinia. "This hair! I can't untangle it. Can you get this piece, dear David?"

David stood up and looked at the hank of damp hair she held out to him. "I'll try." He took the brush and began to work it and his fingers alternately until slowly, the strands of hair began to come free. "Good God it's tangled!" he said. "What do you usually do?"

"I try to avoid washing my hair."

David worked on in silence until finally he could brush the section of hair freely from top to bottom. "What about the rest?"

"Would you, dear boy? You're so sweet. Have you noticed I have no gray in my beautiful auburn hair? Tell me about your latest schemes. I love to listen to you talk. Are you still going to signal Mars?"

"Certainly." David began to section off another length of Lavinia's hair.

"You still think Mars supports life?"

"Didn't I show you those pictures of the canals? Imagine how immense they must be if we can see them through our telescopes from earth! Those creatures, whoever they are, must have developed an extensive and sophisticated civilization there by now. Probably sophisticated enough to communicate with other life in the universe, including us. We just don't know how to receive their messages yet. I want to make my name by being the first to do that."

"Ouch!" said Lavinia as David pulled on a tangle. "But how can you communicate with them?"

"That's what I'm working on now. Since it doesn't look as though anyone can build an observing station on Fuji, I want to investigate building one in the Andes. Chimborazo, that's the place."

"Chimborazo? Where they climbed in the '60's? Emily used to love to read about those expeditions. She thought Frederic Church's painting of Chimborazo was wonderful."

"Well, I want to go there. If I see the terrain, I can decide whether an observatory could be built there. Did I pull too hard that time?"

"No. How could you possibly put an observatory on top of a mountain in the Andes? No one could carry all that equipment, much less build it."

"The Egyptians made the pyramids, didn't they? And there's Stonehenge, put together hundreds of years ago. We'll figure a way if we have to tunnel. I think it could be done. I've always been a good engineer, and once I get the germ of the idea, I could hire the best in the field and see it through. I'd be famous, there's no question. And of course, we could finally communicate with another form of intelligence in the universe, which is worth any obstacles. I tell you, Vinnie, it's schemes like this that keep me going when I get discouraged with Mabel."

"You poor dear, I understand. It's as though she has abandoned you."

"She'd come back if I were famous. I'd be in the history books: the first man to discover and communicate with extra-human life." He put down the brush. "Your hair is pretty much unsnarled now."

Lavinia reached up for the brush and combed unsteadily through her hair. "It feels wonderful. Would you like some brandy as a reward?"

"Brandy? Yes, just the thing. Do you have anything good and strong? Not that peachy stuff."

"I have good brandy I use for the Christmas fruit cake and for Emily's black cake recipe." She stood up slowly, dropping the towel from her lap as she shuffled off to the pantry. "Get two glasses from the cabinet," she called as she went off. "I'll have a nip."

David leaned down and retrieved the towel, then went to fetch two liqueur glasses, the tinted red ones. He was beginning to relax. Thinking about his plans invigorated him, and Lavinia was a good audience, albeit a strange one. Austin never had time to listen to his schemes, and Mabel was no longer a fresh audience. He could see her attention wander every time he talked to her about the Andes plan. She had questioned him closely about it when he first began to bring it up, but now she listened absently.

"Here's your brandy," said Lavinia. "What shall we talk about next? I wish everyone were as interesting as you. Austin has become very boring in his old age. All he wants to talk about is tomatoes or business."

"I suppose he spent some time with you going over the land business—the land he wants to leave Mabel and me," said David, tilting back his head and drinking his brandy in one gulp.

Lavinia shuddered and waved her hands in the air. "Oh, that horrible business! The trouble it's caused me! He's put me in the middle of a huge—" she gestured with her hands—"what do you call those things? A vise, with him on one side and Sue on the other. Why don't you tell him to stop, David! Tell him you don't care about that silly land. If something happened to Austin and I had to try to make Sue give up that land...Well, I just couldn't. But Austin can't understand that. He doesn't realize what a position he puts me in."

"But if Austin wants us to have that land, we should have it," said David. "He thinks Mabel deserves some payment for all the work she's done on Emily's poems and I agree..."

"Bat bullets!" said Lavinia. "Just bat bullets. I am so tired of hearing about all the work Mabel has done. What about me? There wouldn't be any poetry to work on, or any letters either, if it weren't for me! More brandy?" She handed David the bottle and he filled his glass, reaching over to fill hers as well.

"Do what you can and forget the rest," said David, stretching out his feet to the fire. "Besides, you're getting ahead of yourself. You may never have to do anything. Worse things could have happened by now and didn't."

"Like what?"

"Like Mabel and your brother producing a son. Or a daughter."

Lavinia stared at the fire.

"Did I shock you?"

She raised her hand stiffly to her mouth. "Yes. I can't believe we're talking about such things. What would Father and Mother say?" She held her brandy glass to the light of the fire with a shaky hand and stared at the amber glow. "But to be honest, the thought used to cross my mind sometimes in the middle of the night. Once I raised it with Emily in a roundabout way, but she didn't seem to be worried. So I didn't worry either."

"Well, it didn't happen and I don't believe it will, even though the intention might have been there at one time. You're looking awfully odd—have I embarrassed you too much?"

"I'm just not used to such conversations."

"Imagine what I've had to put up with."

"Can we ever break them up?"

"Don't be silly. My wife and your brother are a fact of life. We go on from here, that's all. We take it day by day. How *do* you do, this brandy goes down well. I'll bet you haven't sat here and drunk it before the fire in ages. We should do this more often." He poured himself more, spilling some when one of the cats jumped on his arm which held the glass. "Scat!" He slid down into his chair.

"I'm getting sleepy," said Lavinia. "Do you mind if I go to bed? Stay here as long as you like. Stay here all night, I don't care, right here on the dining room couch. You know where the blankets are."

"I just might do that," said David, his words slightly slurred. "I just might."

"Good. You're a dear boy. Consider this always your home." She picked up a cat and struggled to her feet. "Goodnight."

"Goodnight." David reached sleepily for Lavinia's hand and squeezed it as she walked by.

After she left, David raised his glass to the lamp as Lavinia had done and stared through the brandy at the fire. Then he poured more brandy, spilling some, and drank it down at a gulp. He leaned back and half dozed for a few minutes and then carefully stood up, reaching unsteadily for the lamp. The fire burned low, and he remembered to pull the screen across it before he made his way over to the couch. "I like it here, it's private," he mumbled happily to himself before he fell asleep.

He did not know that while he had settled on the couch, Austin had walked stealthily to his own house, still weak from getting out of bed and dressing so fast in the cold air. He had worried about meeting David on his way back from the observatory, and now expected to meet someone in his own household.

But he met no one, and sank thankfully into his downstairs bed, still recalling the sensations he had experienced a few hours before and the sight of Mabel bending her head over him, assuring him that nothing could be wrong between them. He remembered the night he had come to this bed after the first time they had consummated their love. He had prayed then in happy thanks. Now, he nestled into the covers and rejoiced that another spring had come in his life with Mabel.

Outside an owl hooted. The house creaked. He did not have any court cases the next day—maybe he could make time to take a carriage ride with Mabel into the woods looking for trees to transplant. His thoughts grew hazy and blurred as he drifted into sleep. "I'll take Gilbert with us," he thought. "It's been a long time since we went tree-hunting with Gilbert."

CHAPTER 86

August 1894

Ⅰ N August, Fanny Norcross arrrived at last to visit Lavinia and discuss the issue of sharing her letters from Emily. "It doesn't always strike me as the right thing to do, publishing the precious letters Emily sent Loo and me over the years," she told Lavinia.

"Mabel will have apoplexy if you keep your letters back now, and so will I," said Lavinia.

In the end, Fanny agreed to let Mabel use copies of the letters, or edited portions of them, Fanny and Loo keeping the originals. Mabel fumed privately at this arrangement, but had no choice but to cooperate.

Several afternoons later, Mabel looked up from Emily's letters to see Lavinia at the back door in her blue flannel dress and white cotton stockings. "You usually appear after sundown," Mabel said, letting her in.

"I wanted to ask you how things went with Fanny."

"Well, since you ask, she tried my patience sorely. She even considered withdrawing her letters. She wouldn't even let me *look* at them, except for a glimpse to check the handwriting style."

"Be careful what you say, Mabel," said Lavinia. "She is one of my favorite cousins, and she was so close to Emily."

"Then don't ask me again how things went," said Mabel coldly. "If I can't give an honest answer, I won't answer at all. Anything else on your mind?"

"Yes, the contract for the letters," said Lavinia.

Mabel resisted the temptation to hold her head in exasperation, but said instead, "Sit down then. Let's try to clear up that matter once and for all. Did you talk to Austin?"

"Yes, and he wants it specified in the contract that you will get half of whatever income we get from the letters."

"Yes?" said Mabel. "And?"

"And I'll pay for the plates, as we discussed. But I don't want it in writing that you'll receive half the income—it doesn't seem good business to say that, in case anything changed in the future."

"Anything changed? What could change, Vinnie? What could keep me from deserving my share of income from these letters I've worked so hard on?"

"But you wouldn't even have the letters if it weren't for me."

"You believe that? You honestly believe that? Who wrote to all those correspondents and asked for letters? Who went out and gathered them? It was me, Vinnie, me."

"Well, some of them..."

"*Some* of them? Oh, you know better than that. But I refuse to sit here and argue now. All I can say is that you should listen to your brother. He says you should sign the contract as he discussed it with you and Mr. Hardy, and besides, how could it be good business practice not to write something down? If you refuse to put it in writing that I will get income, how can I trust that you will give it to me?"

"You don't trust me? After all the time we've known each other?"

"I think I should be asking you that question. You don't trust me!"

"I never said I didn't trust you. And don't use Austin against me. Remember, he's not writing down what he wants done with that meadow land or those paintings you're to have, and he's a lawyer."

"That's different. You know very well why he can't write it all out. Please, Lavinia, sign the contract as Austin advised you. It's August. We hope to go to press by late October or early November, but we'll never make that deadline if you don't cooperate. If you don't sign something, you'll be postponing the whole project, and dear God, I don't think I can stand that. I have so much work staring me in the face—writing projects of my own, work for David— the list goes on and on, and yet we stand here, stalled by this contract. You respect your brother, don't you? Sign. Sign."

"All right," said Lavinia to Mabel's surprise. "Don't be so nervous. Everything will work out. It's just that I have to watch out for my rights." She turned and left without another word.

Mabel breathed a great sigh and moved to stretch one hand behind her head, knocking over the ink bottle from her lap board as she did so. "Damn!" she shouted. The ink puddled on her skirt, the chair arm, and on one of the laboriously copied letters. Furiously, she put the writing materials and lap board aside and made her way to the kitchen, holding her skirt carefully out in front of her but muttering all the way. She felt as though she never wanted to see Lavinia Dickinson again. Once she had changed her skirt and labored to clean the chair arm and the lap board, she set herself again to the task, for there was the index yet to do and the preface. She pulled the curtains closely together across both the windows and the door so that if Lavinia reappeared, she would not be able to see into the room. Sighing and rubbing her tired eyes, she bent her head to her work and did not move again until the clock struck midnight.

CHAPTER 87

October 1894

Mr. Fletcher, you're wonderful," said Mabel to Amherst College's librarian, who was spending yet another evening at the Dell going over the final details for the index to the Letters. He smiled, adjusting his cuffs in embarrassed pleasure. David, and Millicent were also helping.

"Lavinia Dickinson has been giving us some problems with this project," said Mabel. "But now, she's forced us into a corner on the preface. She insists it should read that *she* collected the letters, rather than I. She's going to have her way, too. I'm too tired to argue. The proof went in yesterday as she wants it."

David, turning pages as he proofread, asked Mabel, "There shouldn't be an asterisk on page ten, should there?"

Mabel thumbed ahead. "No, there should be no asterisk. Delete it."

"And how do you spell 'condolence'? With an 'a' or an 'e'?"

"With an 'e'."

A gentle knock sounded at the back door. "It must be Austin," said Mabel, getting up. "Lavinia either doesn't knock at all or bruises her knuckles."

She let Austin in, her face softened as she returned quietly to her place.

"Good evening, Mr. Fletcher," said Austin. "I understand this might be the last late night on this proofing."

"It could be," said Mr. Fletcher, putting down his pen and stretching his fingers. "It's been hard work, but I've enjoyed it. It's always an honor to work with material of this quality."

"Well, don't forget to bill us as soon as you total up the hours you spent," said Austin. "Vinnie hasn't been here this evening, has she?" he asked Mabel.

"No, thank heavens. She's won her day in court so to speak, so she's staying out of my hair for a while."

"What do you mean, what's the latest problem?"

"It's the preface," said David, leaning back and yawning. "She made Mabel change it. She won't let Mabel say she was asked to prepare the letters. It has to read that *she*, Lavinia, gathered the letters."

"Don't tell me you sent the preface in that way, as she wanted it?"

"I felt I had to," said Mabel.

"Why didn't you ask me first, so I could reason with her?"

"My dear," Mabel began, before catching herself and glancing quickly at Mr. Fletcher, "it's not always that easy to find you."

"But I can't stand by and see the preface printed that way because it's not truthful. It doesn't do you credit for all the hours and hours of work. I'll wire Mr. Hardy in the morning and tell him to print the first version..."

"Austin, it won't be worth the trouble..."

"No matter. If she wants to behave like a child, then I'm going to treat her like one. I'll ask Mr. Hardy to print a small number of copies her way and all the rest your way. She can content herself with those few copies and never know about the others."

Millicent glanced nervously at Austin from her chair in the corner. David slapped his knee and gave a hoot of laughter. "Oh, poor Lavinia!"

William Fletcher, however, looked from one face to the other, dismay and concern wrinkling his brow. "How...irregular," he said.

"Austin has shocked you," said Mabel.

"No, not so much as...well, perhaps a little, yes," he smiled timidly.

"I shouldn't have spoken," said Austin. "But you have no idea what we three have gone through with my sister over the preparation of these letters. I don't know how our hard-working Mabel keeps on going."

Millicent suddenly stood up and walked toward the hallway door. Standing next to the tapestry her mother had recently acquired, she said soberly, looking at a spot in the ceiling, "Madame Stearns taught us at school not to practice deception." Then she turned and left the room.

After a pause, David turned to smile at Mabel. "She told *you*, didn't she?"

Mr. Fletcher gathered up his pencils and eraser and stacked the papers nearest him into two piles. "I must go now." He turned to Mabel and gave a slight bow. "Once again, it has been a pleasure working with you and your husband." He turned to Austin. "Good night to you—I'll see you at the College tomorrow no doubt."

"I'll see you to the door, Mr. Fletcher," said David.

While they were gone, Austin paced in front of the fireplace a moment. "What makes Vinnie this way, so suspicious and stubborn?"

"I wish I knew, dearest," said Mabel. "Now you understand a small part of what I suffer with her."

Austin looked out the window. A bright half moon lay in the sky above the cherry tree whose nearly bare branches stood firm against the October breeze. "Would you approve if I sent Mr. Hardy a telegram first thing tomorrow morning telling him to print ten copies of the preface worded as Vin wants it and all the rest as it should rightly be?"

Behind him, David had returned to the room and was listening. "Whoever heard of such a thing!" he said. "I'd be surprised if he went along with that scheme. It bothers me to see Lavinia deceived by the pair of you and in particular by you, Austin, her own brother. Is it really necessary?"

"I think it *is* necessary in this case," said Austin. Lavinia knows nothing about the business world or the publishing world, yet she persists in embarrassing me. Her position is grossly unfair to Mabel.And furthermore, I don't intend to have Emily's memory insulted by all this bickering. If I let Vinnie run us about on this matter, I'm only doing a disservice to Emily. It's one sister or the other."

"The either/or fallacy," observed David dryly. "Do what you want, of course. It's just the deception that bothers me. There's too much of it. At least we three are"—he paused—"reasonably honest with each other. And now I'm off to the observatory."

"I'll walk out with you. I'm turning in early tonight." Austin reached for Mabel's hand and went into the hallway with David.

Alone in the parlor, Mabel sat down in the chair closest to the fire and stared into the flames. After a few minutes, she reached wearily for her lap board and the proof sheets she had been working on earlier. Millicent slipped quietly into the room and resumed her position at another pile of papers. She had tied her hair back with a ribbon, rolled up her sleeves, and put on an apron to protect herself from ink spills. They worked in silence for a half hour or so except for remarks relating to their corrections, but when the clock struck ten, Mabel leaned back and said, "One day you'll be glad you were part of all this."

Millicent laid a corrected sheet on the finished pile and reached for another. She said nothing, but allowed herself an enigmatic smile in Mabel's direction.

"Are you tired?" Mabel asked. "You're usually in bed by now."

"I want to stay up tonight. It's one thing I especially like when we work on Emily's things. As though I'm grown up."

"You are grown up, Millicent, in many ways. It's fine. Just fine."

"I feel sorry for Lavinia Dickinson though," said Millicent, dipping her pen in the ink. "I believe in what Madame Stearns has told us so many times: practicing deception is always wrong."

"Madame Stearns is a wonderful woman but she doesn't know everything and certainly not everything about this situation. Letting Lavinia think she has had her way will solve our problems for the time being, anyway, and everyone will be happy. I wish you wouldn't imply that I'm dishonest in my dealings with her. It's she who has been the more dishonest with me." She drew her shawl around her and stood up to poke at the fire. "I'm going to bed. No more work, no more talk."

Millicent stood up obediently and the two of them lowered the lamps and went upstairs, Mabel going straight to her room and closing the door. Millicent hesitated in the hallway a moment. Then she called, "You didn't say goodnight."

"Goodnight," called Mabel a trifle roughly from behind the door.

Even though she knew she would not be awakened by any sounds from Mr. Dickinson climbing their stairs this night, Millicent still had trouble falling asleep. A vague sense of uneasiness troubled her, and she wondered if grown-up Mattie Dickinson ever had trouble sleeping in her fine bedroom at the Evergreens. As she drifted off to sleep at last, the image of her mother's hand floated in her mind—the hand with the other gold band on it, the band that appeared and disappeared from week to week, even hour to hour, but which remained on her hand whenever she was with Mr. Dickinson. Once, as he and her mother sat by the parlor fire, she saw Mr. Dickinson raise her mother's hand and touch the gold band, smiling a secret smile. They thought she did not notice; they never realized she noticed their every movement without even trying when she sat quietly in their presence.

As she drifted further into sleep, the wedding band dangled in her mind's eye, and various figures jumped through it as though it were a hoop—her grandmother, Mattie, sad-faced Ned, and First Church's minister, Reverend Goodspeed. Millicent imagined she was raising her hand to touch the ring, but sleep overcame her and her hand lay inert by her side. The gold band vanished and all was darkness.

CHAPTER 88

November 1894

THERE'S A BIG PACKAGE COME FOR YOU, M'AM," said Mabel's new servant girl. "I pushed it to the back of the hallway."

"Oh—could it be?..." Mabel ran to find the long-awaited copies of Emily Dickinson's Letters, six complimentary sets. Dragging the boxes back to the kitchen, she seized a knife, pulled off her gloves, and slit one box open. There, nestled in packing paper, lay the prize: her hard labor, her infinite toil, now boxed and bound in light green buckram, pale emerald bullion to Mabel's eyes. She bent to sniff the binding, then raised the set to eye level before holding it to her chest. "Oh, the joy of it!" she called out.

Picking two sets from the packing boxes, she rushed through the door and set out for Lavinia's, but in a moment, she hurried back to her front porch. Opening the first volume of the set she had unpacked, she turned hastily to the preface. A quick glance reassured her. "Mr. Hardy did it right! Oh, how clever we are." Keeping a lookout for activity at the Evergreens, she set out again, but no one was stirring there as she approached the Homestead's back door, and in a moment, Maggie let her in. "Maggie, my darling, I carry a long-awaited treasure! Look what our Emily has produced for us all!"

"The letters, yes, the letters!" said Maggie. "I knew the day was close. Let me touch them. Saints, I can't imagine any human writing so much. It seems impossible! Won't Miss Lavinia be excited!"

"She'd better be," said Mabel. "Where is she?"

"Fussing over them kittens, scared to death Sue Dickinson's dog will get them. Now what do we need with a litter of kittens, I ask you?"

Mabel started toward the front of the house but paused when she heard a man's voice. "Is Mr. Dickinson here?" she asked Maggie.

"No, it's Ned, come to visit a bit. He comes more often, now that his sister doesn't set foot here anymore. Not talking to her aunt, the little tyrant. I think Ned is trying to make up for it."

Mabel smoothed the curls around her face. "Ned, is it?" Still carrying the two boxed sets, she went into the kitchen and found Ned and Lavinia kneeling in the pantry by the box of squirming kittens. Laughing in boyish pleasure at the kittens' antics, Ned's smile turned to a look of alarm as he saw Mabel. He began to rise but Mabel, setting down her boxes and entering the pantry in a few fluid steps, put out her hand to stop him and knelt too. "How lovely to find you all here playing with kittens!" she said.

"What did you set down with such a thump over there?" asked Lavinia. "Is it the ship I've been waiting for so long? Has my ship come in?"

"Your ship docked this morning and sits in berth waiting for you to examine it," said Mabel. "Aren't you happy?"

"Hooray and hooray!" shouted Lavinia, struggling to her feet. "Help me, Neddie, I can't get up." Suppporting both her arms, Ned helped his aunt up and then stood uncertainly between the pantry and the kitchen.

"Stay here," said Mabel softly. "Let her look at her prize alone for a minute. Then it will be your turn. Help me watch these darling kittens and say hello to me. I haven't seen you for so long."

Ned returned to Mabel's side and after a moment's hesitation, knelt down again and stretched his hand into the box along with hers as they fondled the kittens, sometimes touching each other's hands as they did so. "You look well," Mabel told him. Has it been a good autumn? I've seen you only off in the distance and at the library, of course, and here it is almost Thanksgiving."

"Oh, it's been all right, I suppose."

"Your sister seems to have written off her aunt, or at least, that's what I've been told—she hardly speaks to Lavinia anymore. I don't blame Mattie for punishing me, but it's too bad to punish Lavinia too. Thank heavens you don't try the same tactics." She handed him an especially active gray kitten and smiled into his eyes, letting her hands rest on his cupped ones below hers for a moment. "I often wonder how you are."

Lavinia called from the kitchen where she was examining the books at arms' length without her glasses. "The preface is perfect," she said, "and the painting of Emily came out beautifully. I don't see any mistakes so far. A thousand copies, and all just as beautiful as this one!"

"Nine hundred and ninety copies," Mabel said softly to herself, ignoring Ned.

"She can't see a thing without her glasses," said Ned.

"I heard that," said Lavinia. "I can see more than you think and don't you forget it."

"I was only joking, Aunt Vin," said Ned.

"Where's my check, Mabel?"

"Check? There won't be a check for a while," said Mabel. "The early royalties are being withheld to pay for the plates, remember?"

"Well, I want you to find me some more furniture in Boston as soon as the checks start coming in. I'll have more than two copies, won't I? I want you to send one to Loo and Fanny right away."

Mabel gently blew the fur of a black kitten with white feet. "Lavinia, I think I've paid these kittens their due, cute as they are. May I play something for you and Ned on the piano to honor Emily's second entry into the literary scene?"

"Yes, go ahead. I'll join you in a moment, but I have to see where Nippers is. Her kittens will be cold if she doesn't hurry back. Oh, Neddie, do tell your mother to keep that awful dog away from here."

"Ned must come in the parlor with me now while I play the piano," said Mabel. As Ned stood and followed Mabel, Lavinia frowned in their direction, but went outside. The parlor was cold and damp, and Mabel shivered.

"Aunt Vinnie is trying to save wood—this house is far too big for her. She probably doesn't want me to light a fire."

"No matter," said Mabel. "I'll put her shawl around my shoulders and play a few minutes. Here, you take this lap robe." She shook out a plaid green and yellow lap robe and stood close to drape it around his shoulders, standing back to laugh at the effect. Then she took his hand, pulling him to the piano. "Sit with me at the piano and we'll sing, come on."

"I don't know," said Ned. "I'm not sure I'm in a mood to sing..."

"Well, try anyway, I insist," said Mabel, patting the chair beside her stool. "I feel so good, seeing those letters in print. Sing for your famous Aunt Emily, anyway. Oh, how I wish she were upstairs listening to us the way she always did! How about 'The Sweetest Story Ever Told'?" She began to play the introduction. But the sound of a barking dog and Lavinia's shouts outside toward the front of the house interrupted her.

"Our dog must be chasing one of the cats again," said Ned. "She thinks Mother sets the dog after the cats just to annoy her."

"Well never mind. I'll give you a piano lesson. It'll be fun. Everything and everybody has been so serious lately I can hardly stand it. I'll teach you a song in the key of G. If you learn to play the melody, I'll play the accompaniment. Let's see. What about 'After the Ball is Over'?"

"Yes. I don't think that's too hard."

Mabel began to play the melody for him, and when he joined in on the piano an octave higher, missing notes frequently, she laughed as he rushed to make corrections. They practiced the melody a few times, the covers slipping from their shoulders as they played and leaned closer together.

"Are you ready for my accompaniment?" said Mabel.

"Well wait," said Ned laughing. "Let me get your shawl first. You'll freeze in this damp old place."

"Has anyone ever described the great Mansion as a 'damp old place'?" said Mabel, pretending to be shocked. "What fun."

"Here," said Ned, "I'll tuck you in so that you can still keep your arms out to play." Mabel sat still while he went through an elaborate procedure of tucking the shawl around and under each arm, until she suddenly burst out laughing. "You're tickling me!" she said.

"Oh. In that case..." He sat back. "Let's play."

"Let's not play this piece seriously," said Mabel. "Let's play it the way it might be played in a saloon or someplace like that. It suits my silly mood. I'll sing and then you play your part, Ned!" She nudged him with her elbow to begin, and together, they began, she playing the harmonies and singing loudly, Ned playing the melody with one finger. When Mabel forgot the words they both stopped and laughed and sometimes substituted silly words.

"Oh Ned Dickinson," said Mabel finally, "it's fun being with you."

Ned sat looking down at the keyboard. "I'm in a difficult position, of course," he said.

"Yes, yes, don't let's think about it."

"I've always felt I would stand by you, if you were in danger," he continued, still looking at the keyboard. "If I could do so without my mother knowing, I mean. I mean, if it ever came to that."

Mabel shrugged one arm out of her shawl and reached for his arm, which she squeezed, touching his hand finally. "You'll never know what that means to me. How very very happy and warm it makes me feel, your saying that."

Ned shrugged his shoulders awkwardly but let her take his hand and sat very still, looking down at the piano keys.

"I feel I want to tell you something," said Mabel. "Maybe it's the right time, if there ever is a right time. But I'd hate so much to upset you..."

"I can take it, whatever it is," said Ned, still holding her hand.

"Oh, it's nothing terrible. It's just awkward. It has to do with something your father wants me to have if anything should ever happen to him. Something very small, and I bring it up only because I had felt sure that his wishes would never be respected—until now. Until what you just told me, that you'd stand by me."

"What is it? What does he want you to have?"

"Just some art work he bought that he knows I've admired—to remember him by one day, that's all—the oil by Johann Gottfried Pulian and the engraving of the lions at Persepolis. Your mother had nothing to do with their purchase or I'd not even mention it. But he wants me to have them someday. He's not very realistic. How does he imagine I could get them? But if *you* were to respect his wishes..."

"Not land? He doesn't want you to have land?" asked Ned, looking up suddenly and meeting Mabel's eyes.

"Land? Oh—no. No, not land." Mabel disengaged her hand from his gently and struck middle C so softly that it did not sound. "Why should you think that?"

"Just something Aunt Vinnie told Mattie."

"You know Lavinia gets things confused."

"Yes," said Ned. "My father hasn't been well lately," said Ned. "Are you afraid something will happen to him?"

"Well, sometimes. But he's got a strong constitution, ten times stronger than most. People ask too much of him, and he can't say no."

"But *you* don't ask too much from him..." said Ned.

"Oh, Ned, don't even imagine it. Never! Just tell me you'd do your best by me if you had to."

"All right, I will. I'm telling you."

Mabel took his hand again and smiled into his eyes. Then she leaned forward to hug him, her head on his shoulder, but he pulled back and kissed her swiftly on the lips as though he'd planned it all the time. When she drew back, he kissed her again although he trembled, until she opened her mouth to him and he made a whimpering sound in response, breathing so heavily she pitied him. When they turned their faces aside and his chest continued to heave, she held him close, but in a moment, she understood that he was crying.

"Sweet Ned," she told him. "My sweet Ned. It's all right. Everything will be all right. And I do care for you. So special, you are. Sometimes I wish...Oh, never mind. Dear Ned."

They sat awkwardly thus at the piano, holding each other quietly, Ned sniffing occasionally. When they heard Lavinia opening the kitchen door and starting into the back hallway, they separated, and Ned reached for his handkerchief as he stood with his back to Mabel, wiping his eyes and blowing his nose.

"Where is everyone?" Lavinia called. "Not still sitting in that freezing parlor, are you?"

"We were just coming out," called Mabel, closing the piano lid and squeezing Ned's elbow as she went to meet Lavinia. "I must go home now. I may have finished one book, but David wants me to work on his *Stars and Telescopes* tonight, can you imagine? We've got another deadline."

"You mean *we* have finished one book—it was a joint effort, don't forget," said Lavinia, wagging her finger and narrowing her eyes in her wrinkled face.

"It was a triad," said Mabel coolly. "There was Emily, remember?" She softened her voice. "Ned? Take care. And thanks."

After she left, Lavinia sniffed. "Now that's typical! Did you hear that?" Imitating Mabel's voice, she repeated, "'There was Emily, remember?' Sometimes that woman exasperates me with her ego. Ned, you'd better to attend to that sniffle. You're not taking cold, are you?"

"I'm fine. I'll come by again tomorrow when I have more time to look at Aunt Emily's book. Mattie says she won't look at it in deference to Mother, but I want to see it."

"Don't forget to tell your father to come over here and attend to me!"

Lavinia stood at the parlor window a moment watching Ned cross the property. Then she went into the library and stood by that window, looking for signs of activity on the street. Seeing nothing of interest, she picked up the *Springfield Republican*, hoisted her calico cat, Gumbo, into her lap, and dozed off before she had finished the obituary page.

CHAPTER 89

Thanksgiving to December 1894

THE DAY AFTER THANKSGIVING, AUSTIN DROPPED
by the Dell, his coat and whiskers whitened by sleet and his face pale against
the sunless air. "I can't stay long," he said, as Mabel shook out his coat for him
and scrutinized his face, "but I wanted to get a rough draft of this deed to you.
I'll feel better if I know it's in your hands. All it needs are the exact measurements of the strip of meadow land. Keep it in a safe place."

He took a large envelope from his coat pocket, opened it, and spread the
document on the table. "All you really need to know is that it would convey to
you, upon Lavinia's signature, the strip of land adjacent to this house at the
western end of the meadow. I measured that strip when we built this house.
It's fifty-three feet wide. But you know that."

"Yes. And does Lavinia know you're going to leave the deed with me?"

"I'll tell her again. Let's just hope she remembers."

"She remembers what she wants to remember."

"There's no point in trying to explain too much to her. I've told her to
respect my wishes, no questions asked."

"Does Ned know about this land? That you want to give it to me?"

"Ned? Why do you ask?"

"Because he asked *me* about it the other day."

"He did? You've been talking to Ned?"

"Just briefly, at Lavinia's."

"What did you tell him?"

"Oh, I don't remember. What *does* he know, Austin?"

"He may know about it. When Mattie got something out of Lavinia, she
undoubtedly told Ned too."

"And HER, too, of course. With your household against me, there'll be no
hope. You may as well tear up that deed! Go ahead, just tear it up!"

"My love," said Austin, reaching for her hand. "Don't talk that way. You shall have this land because I want you to have it."

"But I don't want to think about it anymore, because if you're gone, I won't care about anything at all. God hates me, do you know that? He does, he hates me more with every passing month because he tortures me, just the way you're doing now."

"Steady, steady," said Austin. It pains me to think that you view what I'm trying to accomplish for you now as torture. Neither God nor I wants to torture you."

"But that's exactly what you're doing. You say you love me more than anything, yet you return each day to the woman who makes your life and mine miserable. You talk about resettling elsewhere yet you stay here. You hold out to me the land we both love so much, and yet make it all dependent on a half-deranged woman. That's torture! Tell me it isn't!" She stood with her back to him now. "It's killing me to talk to you this way, but I can't help it. My stomach is aching, I have a headache every time I steel myself to face the snubs out there on the street, and my own daughter even gives me the silent treatment from time to time because of you."

Austin sat in miserable silence, looking down and rubbing his hands slowly back and forth. When Mabel began to cry, Austin did not go to her, but continued to sit miserably, only now he held his head in his hands. "Has it not been worth it, then?" he asked, finally. Is that what you think? Please say no."

After an interval during which Mabel blew her nose and paced about the room, she said in a muffled voice, "At this moment, it's hard to imagine that it's been worth it, but of course it has. We both know that. It has." And with the last words, her voice broke and she began to sob again, only more loudly than before. She paced the room, shaking her fist with the crumpled handkerchief in it from time to time and kicking aside a book in her path. Austin, his own head throbbng, arose, and putting one arm around her, paced in tandem with her until she slowed down and finally stopped. With a last blow of her nose and a wipe of her red and swollen eyes, she smiled, taking him by surprise. "Look at us," she said. "As crazy as Lavinia or David. All right, my fit is over for now. We'll sit down and drink some tea and get on with life. I'm sorry for the way I acted—but only because it has upset you. Just because I have begun to wish I were dead is no reason for me to drag you down with me."

"Now you're torturing *me*," he said.

She ignored his remark. "When you've made a fair copy, we'll lock it away for...for the future." Her face contorted for a second but she controlled herself by looking straight ahead.

Austin stood up. "We'll start with a fresh slate the next time we see each other. We're both so tense."

"Yes, maybe that's best," she said, rising to get his coat.

The sleet had turned to snow. Maybe enough would fall to keep her indoors for a week. Feeling feverish and drained, she trudged slowly downstairs, not bothering to bathe her swollen eyes.

Mabel managed to make a Thanksgiving centerpiece for the Women's Club, to work on corrections for a second edition of the Letters, and to give an informal talk on Emily in Northumberland, all despite her strange physical fatigue and an insidious feeling of malaise. But in early December, when it became an effort even to sharpen her pencils and the sight of the manuscript for *Stars and Telescopes* choked her, she took to her bed. Millicent came home from school each afternoon to find the little back parlor empty, the manuscripts untouched, and the curtains drawn.

"I'll be up and around soon," she told Millicent after a few days, half sitting up in bed and shading her eyes to squint at her daughter. "No, don't let in the light, it hurts my eyes. The thermometer shows no fever, but I feel sure I have one. If I could just sleep some more..."

David often took noon dinner at Frank P. Woods's restaurant on North Pleasant and Amity Streets, while he and Millicent shared uncomfortably quiet suppers cooked up by their servant and served in the dining room. After a week, David carried the newspaper to the table and read unabashedly, making no further pretense at conversation, lingering there over desserts which Millicent declined so that she could escape to the parlor and do her homework in peace.

During the second week of Mabel's stay upstairs, after laboring over her mail, she set Millicent to work writing to the publisher about ways to increase sales of the Letters. "I'll dictate, you copy," she told Millicent, sitting up with a thick shawl around her shoulders, her hair unarranged. "I'm sorry, I simply can't write yet. I'm utterly exhausted. So if Mr. Hardy wants an answer, it'll have to be this way. You checked Lavinia's for messages today? Or did I ask you that already..."

By the end of the second week, she no longer asked Millicent or David to check with Lavinia for messages. Sometimes when Millicent tiptoed into the room, she saw that her mother had been crying. Her books lay unread on the table. David, who had been sleeping in the spare room, brought on a flood of tears one morning when he dropped in before going to his first class. "You've got a bunch of gray hair over your right temple," he said, peering at her in the sunlight that leaked through a gap in the curtains. "Oh Lord, don't start crying. You're only thirty-eight, for God's sake."

At the beginning of Mabel's third week upstairs, Millicent herself began to cry one afternoon as she took instructions from her mother about errands to be done that day. "It will soon be Christmas, Mother, and you'll be in bed! What will we do, how will we manage? Will you make me do all the decorating? And won't you be getting a present for me? I'm going to get you one. Everybody is having fun out there except me. They have parents to do things with, but I have no one except Madame Stearns who really cares about me."

"You silly goose, you know that's not true. You're just feeling sorry for yourself. Can't I even be sick in peace?" Mabel shifted position, and Millicent heard the crackle of paper under the pillow from the notes she knew Austin had sent her mother the first week.

"Mama, you're not really sick and you've had your rest. Why don't you get up?"

But Mabel ignored everyone's complaints and accepted no one's visits outside the family except those of Mary Stearns, who dropped by twice to bring food and to chat briefly.

"You've run out of fight for a while, my dear," she told Mabel, patting her hand. "Your body has told you to retreat. Don't you think that might be the trouble?"

Mabel turned her face away but nodded after a moment.

"Well, don't fight then, just give in for a while. Restore your strength, just as you are doing, and when the time is right for you to come out again, you'll know it. You'll just sense it."

"I suppose Sue is crowing like a rooster out there..." Mabel said.

"Come to think of it, I *have* seen more of her than I usually do," said Mary, "but I've seen decidedly less of Austin. He seems to be as fatigued as you are. But I'm glad to see you have the curtains and the blinds open today. Can you see that lovely bright cold blue sky from your bed?"

Mabel smiled. "At least I can stand to look at it now. Poor Millicent. I've given her a horrible time. She's had to do Christmas things practically by herself. Thank you so much for making the wreath with her!"

"She's such a pleasure. One of my favorite girls, as you well know."

"And thanks for helping me order the Christmas gifts from Boston. You'll have made Millicent very happy, come Christmas day."

On December 25th, Mabel dressed slowly, fixed her hair attentively, and accompanied by a smiling Millicent, came downstairs to sit in the parlor with a robe tucked around her. She ate a hearty Christmas breakfast, produced gifts for David and Millicent, and opened her own gifts with appropriate expressions of pleasure. In the late afternoon, she asked for the papers she had been working on before her confinement to be handed to her—the plans for an Emily Dickinson yearbook she had been considering with the publishers. She answered several letters, including one from Mr. Higginson confirming his plans to visit Amherst on December 29th. She also ate turkey and plum pudding, and sent David over to Lavinia's with a small gift for her and a note for Austin.

"Well, Millicent, you have a mother again," said David at the door, buttoning his collar against the windy village streets of Amherst.

CHAPTER 90

January 1895

~

GEORGE WASHINGTON CABLE LEANED BACK in his chair while Mabel filled his coffee cup. "You can see why I like living so close to Amherst, Mr. Higginson. With Mabel Todd to serve me perfect dinners, it's a wonder I persist in living as far away as Northampton!"

"Our Mrs. Todd is a gem in every way," Mr. Higginson replied, smiling at Mabel. "It's good to see you back on your feet after you illness. You had me worried. You mustn't lose any more weight."

Mabel, wearing a forest green velvet skirt and a cream bodice accented by an emerald pendant and emerald earrings, passed a plate of pound cake to Mr. Higginson. "I needed a rest and I got one at last. My poor family had to be patient." She smiled at Millicent who sat next to Mr. Cable and who wore a pair of her mother's cameo earrings for the occasion.

"You're looking so grown-up these days," Mr. Cable told Millicent. "How old are you, if you don't mind my asking?"

"I'll be fifteen next month—February 5th is my birthday."

"Then I'll stop by in a month and three days and wish you a happy birthday."

"You were still a slip of a girl when I first met you," said Mr. Higginson. "You and my Margaret—you're both growing up all too fast. Can you believe we are only five years away from the turn of the century?" He turned to Mabel. "It pleases me so much to know you're ready to take up active lecturing again. I've had an enormous number of requests. Tomorrow before I leave, we can settle which ones you care to honor. Just don't take on too much again."

"Oh, Mabel is tough," said David, reaching across for another piece of pound cake. "Besides, she's had to cut back on some of her other activities, which frees up her schedule a bit."

"Civic responsibilities, no doubt?" Mr. Cable asked politely.

"You could call it that, in a way," said David laughing, "since it involves work with a civic leader."

Mabel coughed and hastily rolled her napkin, inserting it into her silver napkin ring, while the others, sensing a source of tension, followed suit.

"And that reminds me," said David, "I thought Austin was dropping by."

"I expect Mr. Dickinson will be by soon enough," said Mabel. "He particularly wanted to see both of you gentlemen. I expect a client has held him up. He does his legal work from his own home now, even during evening hours sometimes."

"Probably Sue has held him up," said David. "By the heels."

"Is there any chance she will be dropping by too?" asked Mr. Higginson, who had not heard David's last remark. "Sometimes I feel as though Lavinia and Mabel have been hiding her from me." He laughed, despite his sense that he'd gone too far, judging from the silences or non-committal answers with which Mabel always met his inquiries about Susan Dickinson.

"Susan Dickinson and Mabel do not see eye to eye," said David.

"Let's adjourn to the parlor," said Mabel. "I imagine Mr. Dickinson will join us for some coffee soon." She rang for Pearl and led the way. Millicent excused herself and set off to change her clothes and join some of her friends for a sleigh ride, to be followed by hot punch at the Hills's home.

Mabel glanced at the French clock from time to time when she thought no one was looking, but when Austin had not arrived by 8:30, she realized he would not be coming. His failure to arrive did not bother her as much as it might have a month ago. Although she had regained much of her physical strength since her strange illness, she had emerged with a considerably more sober view of her predicament and of the next five or ten years of her life if nothing changed from its present course. While she lay in bed, she had come at last to accept the chilling truth of Austin's inability to relieve her suffering or to make any significant changes in the stalemate of their relationship. He could not and would not leave Sue. And he would not defy convention and sit by her side or acknowledge her as more than a distant friend on the frequent occasions they met in public. Instead, they would turn away from each other across the room in deference to propriety, tradition, and to Sue, whose presence drew an imaginary line between her half and Mabel's half of any room she and Mabel inhabited together. Nothing would ever change. Prayer was as futile as were entreaties to Austin—for God and Austin often seemed to be one and the same to Mabel, and she had found herself capable of reviling them both, at the same time as she regretted it.

And so although Mabel knew she could never stop loving Austin, she would try to make an even fuller and richer life for herself away from him and from

Amherst than she already had. She planned to travel as often as possible, to speak wherever she was asked, to help David as often as she could, and to immerse herself in writing and preparing Emily's remaining poems for publication. If she did nothing else but work on the poems, she would have spent years, but their publication would bring her more recognition than anything else she might do. If she could not have Austin entirely, she wanted full and total recognition for her talents—now and after she was gone.

However, when Austin did not stop by or leave a note the next day, Mabel sent Millicent over to Lavinia's to inquire about him. "Good Lord, child, he's very ill, very ill," Lavinia told her, holding the front door ajar and clicking her false teeth. "But do I dare go over and see myself how he is? Not with the lion guarding the door. Tell your mother he's bad though." And she closed the door on the white puffs from Millicent's breath in the cold air.

Millicent gave her mother the news and left her downstairs staring out the back parlor windows as the sun sank and the shadows drew in. "Shadows hold their breath," Mabel whispered to herself. She did not allow herself to finish the lines of the poem, but with heavy steps, set about writing Austin a note which she would take to Lavinia herself first thing tomorrow morning to be delivered to the Evergreens by Maggie.

When she herself had been ill, she had hoped to punish him by not sending any word about her health for days at a time. David had been Austin's only source of information most of the time—and a decidedly second-hand source at that. "She's still just lying there. Doesn't want to get up, that's all."

Now she felt guilty about making Austin suffer and about her resolution to remain at least partly disengaged from him, even as she knew she must if she were to save her health and sanity. She felt unable to work the rest of the day and into the next, and took long brisk walks in the clear cold sunny air, dreaming of the time the meadow would sing again with crickets and grasshoppers, and the clover would stipple the ground with bumblebees.

On Friday, Lavinia put her out of her misery by delivering a note in the morning. "Here," she said, shifting her market basket from one arm to the other and holding out an envelope. "I took it from him myself a half hour ago. Sue was there but dressing upstairs. She's hired a nurse from New York. And Dr. Cooper was just arriving."

"But what is it, Lavinia, what's wrong? Please, please tell me!"

"Pneumonia. I thought you knew that much. He can't breathe lying down and must half sit and half lie there, even though sitting up brings on nausea. He looks awful—as white as can be—and I wish someone would trim his whiskers."

"Oh, if only I could!" Mabel wrung her hands. "Pneumonia, you say?"

But Lavinia hastened off in her peculiar gait, leaving Mabel to hold her head and give a little scream of frustration before she tore open Austin's note.

The lightly pencilled script covered barely half a page and broke off in mid-sentence, although he had managed to sign a large, scrawled "A" before he was interrupted. He reassured her that Dr. Cooper was optimistic about a hasty recovery but was insisting on total rest, and he reminded her of the two times of the day when they tried to think about each other. "Be with me at 5 today!"

She pressed the note to her chest and then loosened her bodice to insert it under her clothing near her heart. Thus reminded of the way she used to carry notes to Austin on a regular basis, she rushed to her desk and wrote a note for him. She would go to the Homestead while Lavinia was on Pleasant Street shopping, and see if Maggie was there. If she was, surely she would take pity on Mabel and run next door to slip the note to Mary Moynihan or even to Ned.

She threw on her coat and crossed the stubbly meadow over to Main Street. Fixing her eyes insistently on the silent Evergreens windows, she saw that all the front shades were pulled down. A loose shutter blew gently in the wind. Dr. Cooper's carriage stood in the driveway.

Mabel made for the back of the Homestead, taking the long way around through the bare, chilly garden, so as to avoid notice by anyone next door. Although she knocked, she did not wait for anyone to answer, but pushed hastily into the mud room and then into the kitchen itself. "Maggie?" she called to the woman with her back to Mabel bending over to pick something up. "Maggie, can you do me a big favor and right now?"

As soon as she uttered the words, the tinny taste of fear and horror permeated her mouth. The unthinkable had happened at last: she and Sue Dickinson were face to face, alone, on Dickinson property.

January 1895

Y

OU," SAID SUE IN A LOW VOICE, STRAIGHT-
ening up and turning around, holding something which she had retrieved
from the floor. And then louder, "You!"

"I came for Maggie..." began Mabel

"I don't care what you came for! I want you out of here! This instant! I had
prayed I'd never see you again! Never!"

"And don't you think I haven't prayed for the same thing?" But Mabel's head
trembled and her mouth was dry with the shock.

"You've made him sick," said Sue, staring at Mabel—her eyes, her clothes,
her figure— with a glittering intensity. "If he dies, it will be your fault. You've
run him around and around and up and down, a man of his age—what an
embarrassment for him and all of us! What a disgrace! You're going to pay for
what you've done, too." Something in her hand clinked dully. "You're going to
pay long and hard!"

"I won't stand here and listen to you," said Mabel, "when you're the one
who has worn him down."

Sue advanced on Mabel, holding what Mabel now saw to be a ceramic
mortar and pestle for grinding medicines. "How dare you tell me that! Austin
and I are husband and wife in the eyes of God, and you dare tell me I've worn
him down? Get out of here!" she said, shaking the pestle in Mabel's direction.
"You'll pay for what you've done, and sooner rather than later. You and Lavinia,
you'll both pay, and for years to come!" She raised her arm menacingly.

Mabel turned and reached for the door, rushing out as though in a dream.
Rounding the corner blindly, she heard Sue's voice again. "Do you think I
don't know how often you've been in my house? If I weren't a Christian, I'd—"
She paused, then half growled, half shouted, as though fighting to maintain
shreds of control—"tear you to bits."

In her confusion, Mabel turned the wrong way as she exited the Homestead, and instead of entering Emily and Lavinia's garden, she found herself on the Evergreens side. Stumbling on pine cones hidden in patches of snow, she began to make her way toward the pavement with as much dignity as she could muster, dismayed to see that Dwight Hills was walking toward the village.

"How do you do, Mrs. Todd," he said, lifting his hat. "Isn't it a lovely day?"

"Lovely," said Mabel, tripping on a root just as she reached the pavement.

"Dear me," said Mr. Hills, holding out his hand. "Watch your footing."

Refusing his hand, Mabel waved and crossed the street, leaving him to shake his head ever so slightly after her before resuming his walk.

Although the scene she had just endured was one she had dreaded nearly every day, Mabel grew strangely calm as she walked home. Her trembling abated, she was able to notice that the sky was clouding, and it occurred to her that she ought to stop at the market for eggs if she planned to make a pound cake for tomorrow's Culture Club. Had the worst happened? Sue had met her, reviled her, threatened her, but she had not thrown the mortar and pestle at her, not humiliated her in front of anyone, and most of all, had not taken one iota of Austin's love away from her. Yes, it had been a terrible scene, but if Mabel were a novelist, she might use just such a scene for comic effect: a large, severe woman waving a ceramic mortar and pestle.

"I have paid my dues," thought Mabel. "No more." It had taken weeks in bed, depressed and exhausted, to figure a path through the wreckage, but now that she had done so, she would not be brought down. Detachment would not be easy—she would often fail to achieve it. But if she achieved it ten percent of the time, she would have made an improvement from last month.

On the strength of those thoughts and in order to calm her nerves still further, she dropped in at the market for eggs. On the Common, she met Lavinia.

"I didn't expect to see you," Lavinia told her.

"The morning has been full of surprises," said Mabel. And now I must be off." She waved and stepped lightly across the grass.

CHAPTER 92

February 1895

Lavinia did not visit Austin again, but kept herself apprised of his condition through Ned, who dropped by every other day, and through Maggie, who remained in daily touch with Mary in the Evergreens kitchen. Within a week, she was relieved to learn that Austin had left his bed, although he remained at home reading, taking naps, and catching up on paperwork. In happy relief, Mabel resumed her speaking schedule, traveling first to Worcester, where she spoke to 200 women on the quest for Emily Dickinson's letters.

The Dickinson household soon returned to its normal routine as well once Austin resumed college duties and his obligations to regular clients. But Austin's face looked different somehow since his last illness, and people found themselves trying to pinpoint the reason even as they talked with him about trees on the Common or the condition of the town reservoir. "Something strange about the color of his face," Dwight Hills told his housekeeper, Frances Seelye. "Or the look of his eyes, I don't know. Both, I guess."

By the first week in February, after giving several talks in Boston, Mabel returned by the early afternoon train on Millicent's birthday, as she had promised. Wearing a new cobalt hat, her arms full of packages, she raved about the success of her talks to Millicent, who had walked to meet her at the depot.

"Your father is coming in on the 4:30 train—he was detained."

"We'll still have my birthday dinner?"

"Of course, I'm counting on it."

A cold wind began to bluster by supper time. As it turned out, David's train was late and he didn't arrive in Amherst until 8:30. By the time they heard the clatter of his valise on the porch, dinner was over and Clara and Amy,

Millicent's friends, were on their way home. Millicent did not go to the door.

"You're just in time for the birthday gifts," Mabel said, going to meet him.

"Whose birthday?" Millicent heard her father ask.

"Millicent's, of course! Oh David, for heaven's sake! I hope she didn't hear you!"

"Well, I didn't know! I've got a lot of things on my mind," David said crossly. "Damn near lost my hat in that wind out there." But he entered the parlor with a hearty smile for Millicent. "How is my abandoned daughter? Is that cake you're eating?"

"It's my birthday cake."

When David had settled down with his cake and tea, Mabel brought out the presents: a handsome edition of Robert Louis Stevenson's *Catriona*, a sapphire brooch set aside for her by Great-Grandmother Wilder, a box of handkerchiefs from Boston, and a decorated wooden box containing fancy lavender soaps.

"Everything is beautiful, Mama," said Millicent, examining her gifts again, smelling the soap and running her finger across the silky lavender surfaces, inhaling the fragrant aroma of the leather book covers, and watching the sapphire catch the firelight. "I like being fifteen years old."

There was a gentle knock at the door. "Austin," said Mabel, going to the door. "Don't run away, Millie. He just might have a gift for you."

Millicent sat back and folded her hands in her lap while her father drained his cup, wiped his mouth with the back of his hand, and reached for the teapot. They both heard the door being opened and muffled voices for a moment. Then silence. The fire popped, David rattled the lid on the teapot, and Millicent looked at the floor. The muffled voices resumed, and then Mabel appeared with a tousled looking Austin. He carried self-consciously under one arm a package wrapped in tissue paper.

"By God," said David, "it must be windy out there. You look all blown around. Sit down, rest your weary feet and all that. What's that you have in your hand?"

"It's for Millicent. A birthday present." He handed it to Millicent on the sofa, then sat down on the other side of the room and stared at the fire.

"That was sweet of you," said Mabel. "I can't wait to see what it is. Open it, Millicent. Go ahead!"

Millicent carefully removed the tissue paper, examined the rectangular box inside, and felt for the clasp to the lid. Looking at all of them as though for permission, she slowly opened the lid and discovered a graceful leather-bound cylinder nestled inside on satin.

"You see what it is, don't you, Millicent?" said Mabel going over to her. "Hold it up to the light."

Millicent turned toward the lamp nearest her and raised the splendidly crafted kaleidoscope. They watched as she peered with one eye at the brilliantly tinted clicking and falling bits of glass. In a moment, she turned the instrument toward the fire and they turned their heads with her. After a moment of listening to the tiny clicks, David said impatiently, "Well? Say something!"

"It's beautiful," said Millicent, lowering the kaleidoscope and handing it to her father.

"Let me see," said Mabel, taking the kaleidoscope herself and aiming at the fire. "It's really quite spectacular. Have a look, Austin."

"You snatched it from me and now you hand it to him," said David peevishly.

"Take it, of course, it's your turn," said Austin.

"Well, Millicent," said Mabel, "what do you say?"

"Thank you very much, Mr. Dickinson. It's a beautiful kaleidoscope."

"Would you like some of Millicent's birthday cake?" Mabel went on.

"I believe I could take a small slice, yes."

"Cut him a piece, Millie, would you? And some tea, of course."

Millicent did as she was told and then remained standing. "I believe I'll take my presents upstairs now and then get ready for bed, Mother. So goodnight, and thank you all for the presents."

"Goodnight, dear," said Mabel. David, who appeared to be immersed in deep thought as he stared at the fire, said nothing.

Millicent gathered up all her presents except the kaleidoscope and left the room. Upstairs, she put her handkerchiefs away, laid the book on the bed, put the brooch on her bureau, and then knelt to unwrap one of her dolls from its tissue paper in the drawer where it had lain for months. She couldn't remember when she had last played with it, but tonight, she felt a strong urge to take out Melissa from her storage.

"How is my child? Did you think I had forgotten you?" She put on her nightgown and took the doll to bed with her, turning down the lamp. "Did you think that because I am fifteen that I don't want you anymore?"

April 1895

~

ON APRIL 19TH, AUSTIN APPEARED ON THE Dell lawn before noon with stakes, ribbons and a mallet to mark the boundaries of the meadow he talked more and more about, this part of his father's patrimony which he wanted to add to what he had already given David and Mabel. Mabel, kneeling in the garden, waved a hand laden with daffodils at him.

"Shall we walk off the lines now?" he asked.

"You aren't worried who might come by at this hour?"

"No," he said simply, and headed toward the boundaries he knew so well. Using measuring tapes and consulting his notes now and then, he located the spots to be marked. "Here's an old marker," he remarked, kicking his boot against one worn wooden stake sunk low in the ground.

"Is this another?" Mabel asked from the front of the property, pointing down.

"Yes. Father put that one in."

Mabel knelt and touched the marker. "I wish I could have met him. Oh—" She reached into the grass and carefully pulled out something. "A four-leaf clover, my love." She crossed the lawn and handed it to him just as Mr. Cable rode into view on his bicycle, his book satchel thumping behind him.

"Now I know spring is here if you're out riding again," said Mabel. "I suppose you came all the way from Northampton..."

"Of course. Nothing in the world like a bicycle ride in spring. Mrs. Todd, you really should try to set a trend for Amherst women and make it lady-like to ride. You're already a trend-setter—anyone who has climbed Mt. Fuji..." He raised his hat to Austin. "And how are you this morning, Mr. Todd? Oh, I do beg your pardon—I meant to say Mr. Dickinson."

"I am quite well, thank you."

"Hallo, hallo!" called David, home from the College for the noon meal.

Mabel took David's arm. "Mr. Cable, we are almost ready to eat. Please join us."

"How kind, my dear Mrs. Todd, but I am invited by the Clarks." He stepped back and looked at David and Mabel linking arms in the sunlight. "You two, you young two, remind me of an open air tableau, the way you're standing on the grass framed against the sky—something timeless and lovely about your faces this morning. The beauty of matrimony, perhaps. Do you see it, Mr. Dickinson?"

"I'm not quite sure what you mean," Austin said, bending down to pull away the grass from one of his father's old stakes."

"Something in their young faces—the beauty of husband and wife—"

He released the kickstand on his bicycle, bowed to them all, and with a running bound, was off.

"He talks balderdash," said David. "What's for dinner?"

"Escalloped oysters," said Mabel huffily, leading the way inside. "I'll turn Austin over to you so you can ask him anything your heart desires about your funding. Just don't tire him out."

"You presume to caution me about that, Mabs? Ha! Come on, Austin, let's talk budget first, and second, how to assassinate President Gates. I can't stand the man!"

"Well," said David that evening, "I'm going to go out there and dig a few holes. Didn't he mark off the spots for plantings?"

"Yes, yesterday morning while I was out. But it's too dark to plant."

"Oh, I can see enough to dig some holes. It's the least I can do. Austin stood up for me today again about my office hours. Austin told Gates I didn't have to keep them as regularly as the others because of observatory work. I'd be in a pickle without Austin around the college to put in a word for me. Let's keep Austin healthy."

"You sound so callous..."

David's voice was gentle. "But I'm not. I love the man. Despite everything, he's my friend. My true friend."

Mabel came to embrace him quietly. They stood together in the dark hallway for a few moments in an attitude of childlike weariness until Millicent came from the kitchen and they separated.

Later, after David went outside, the sound of digging—shovel hitting rock, dirt spraying bucket—reached their ears as they read in the parlor.

"Why...?" began Millicent.

"Mr. Dickinson wants to put in some trees and shrubs for us to mark the land he plans to deed us. Your father doesn't think he's strong enough to be digging."

"Oh. Plantings to remember him by?"

Mabel looked at her daughter. "Well, I wouldn't put it that way. He will enjoy it all with us, of course."

They lowered their heads to their work, while the sound of digging persisted in the spring night air. Now and then, they heard the thud of a rock hitting the wheelbarrow and David's grunts. After a while, Mabel sighed and got up to close one of the windows.

"Father's digging bothers you?"

"Of course not. It's getting chilly in here, that's all."

Millicent laid down her papers and arose to fetch the vase of blue hyacinths from the front parlor. "Mmmm," she said, setting it down in front of her. "Spring!"

They worked on, and though the sound of David's spade still reached their ears, they did not speak again until he came in, flushed with exertion, and stood by the window drinking a glass of beer and looking over the dark meadow.

The next day Maggie brought a note from Austin. "He had the old breathing problem again yesterday," she said. Dr. Cooper says he's been exerting himself far too much given his condition."

Mabel opened the note. "He's better and intends to come over tomorrow morning. That's good news. How's Lavinia?"

"She's busy washing and re-labeling all them jars of preserves she put by last year—the cats messed on them down in the fruit cellar."

"How disgusting!"

"It tries my patience, I can tell you that. Must be over twelve cats about the place now. I can't bear to count!"

"I'm going to dash him off a note right now. You'll see that he gets it, won't you Maggie?"

"I'll take it over to Mary. It's doubtful Miss Lavinia will set foot in that place, as fearful as she is of Mrs. Dickinson. It's a mercy Mr. and Mrs. Edward Dickinson aren't alive to see the quarreling going on between the two houses. I'll be off, then, Mrs. Todd."

CHAPTER 94

May 1895

❧

IN LATE MAY, MABEL LECTURED IN SUNDER-
land one afternoon. Her talk was followed by a tea and the usual questions about Emily and her writing, but for once, Mabel was not energized by the interest of her audience. She had the nagging impression that something was amiss, yet when she examined this idea, she could find no reason for it beyond her usual concerns about Austin and her current irritation with David's disorganized working habits.

This afternoon, the countryside in Sunderland seemed even more achingly beautiful than the familiar Amherst landscape. As the tea ended and the afternoon light began to wane with warm hues, presaging a colorful sunset, Mabel knew suddenly what would temper her uneasiness: a visit to the familiar Sunderland picnic grove and the spot by the farmer's field where she and Austin had stood so many years ago in the setting sun and first touched hands. She had returned there before, but not for a few years now, and not with this same vague sense of urgency. She must go, she must lean on that same fence and look westward while she let her thoughts unravel. Once she had made up her mind, she could hardly wait to leave. Seeking out Elizabeth Donaldson, whose husband had taken them in his carriage from Amherst to Sunderland, she pressed her arm. "I think I have time for a sentimental walk since your husband isn't yet here with the carriage. Could you meet me at the picnic grove whenever you're ready?"

"Of course."

Flocks of red winged blackbirds arose and alighted about her, jangling their busy calls as she made her way to the picnic grove. Daffodils and jonquils dotted the grounds, along with violets, trillium and mayflower. The clouds in the west had already begun to turn salmon and pink as the sun sank, and a sudden cool breeze carried a new floral scent mixed with a mossy, fungus-like odor, redolent of evening. Damp earth sticking to her shoes, Mabel crossed the picnic grove with her eyes fixed firmly on the field ahead of her in the distance. Was the fence still there? Yes, she could see it was. The cows were gone though. If only the Donaldsons wouldn't come just yet. If she could stand by that fence and think, uninterrupted, recalling the sweet excitement of that day so long ago, the hopes she was too naive to discard, the charge of youth that had electrified her body without a care for the future.

The field was looming larger and larger, stretching across the scope of her vision. The fence began to stand out in the sunset, even the exact place where she knew she and Austin had stood that afternoon—that "mitered afternoon," as Emily had written. Her hands remembered how the rough wood was going to feel against her skin—some smooth places here, a deep split there, insect holes cratered all about. And with a last rush of steps, she was there, reaching out with both ungloved hands for the gnarled fence which took all her weight, let her lean her mind and body against it, let her stare at the comfort of a western sky and inhale the weary confusion of loving Austin Dickinson.

The blackbirds landed in the bushes nearest her, the red patches in their wings appearing and disappearing as they congregated, flexed their hoarse voices, and rode green tendrils up and down. The setting sun behind the nearest farm began to darken the barn, silo and house, and to silhouette them along with the surrounding tall oaks and hemlocks. Behind Mabel, the sky remained blue with a three quarter moon the color of Indian pipe.

She felt, vaguely, the way she did before the long trips to Japan or Africa or Europe: aware of the central reason for the costly and tiring expeditions but distracted by the details necessary for departure. She measured the descent of the sun by the barn roof in the distance. "This is why we did it," she whispered, not knowing herself exactly what she meant. "It was for all this. And it's not over yet. No, it's not over."

"Yoohoo!" called Rev. Donaldson. "Yoohoo!"

Mabel turned and waved her handkerchief before gripping the fence once more and facing the field, the sinking sun, and the salmon sky mixed with touches of hyacinth and swatches of blood. "But could I bear to start it again?" she whispered. "The answer should be clear."

Then she turned. "I'm coming, I'm coming."

CHAPTER 95

July 1895

~

ᴮECAUSE THE SUMMER OF 1895 WAS excessively humid and sultry, the gardens flourished, even as Amherst residents languished on their porches or fanned themselves by open parlor windows. "Your hollyhocks, Mabel!" exclaimed Mary Stearns one particularly heavy day when she came up the front path for luncheon. "I've never seen them so tall! And in this strange light, they look almost luminescent. Surely it's going to rain soon and clear this air. Oh, I hope so!"

Indeed, as David, Mabel, Millicent and Mary Stearns adjourned after dinner to the parlor for strawberry ice and hot coffee, despite the heat, the sky turned a greenish tint, casting a peculiar patina throughout the parlor and across their faces. David went to the window. "Here it comes," he said. "Look at it, an absolute wall of green rain across the meadow."

They could all hear it sweep with a hundred hisses over the streets, the meadow, and the lawn as it raced to bombard their roof with water pellets which richocheted furiously. Millicent held her ears. Mabel ran to the window to see whether the hollyhocks would withstand the battering, while David went to check on a leak in the pantry. Steam seemed to fill the air.

Lying in bed atop his quilt at the Evergreens, Austin awoke reluctantly from his nap. It had taken him a long time to find sleep through this recurrence of labored breathing. He hoped the rain would cleanse the heavy air. He could hear footsteps rushing all over the house closing windows—Mary and Sue, probably. He propped himself on one elbow, gathering strength to close his own windows, but someone rushed in and attended to it; Mattie, he saw, as she forced one down with a bang and went to the second without looking at him. When it too had been forced down with a resonance that made him flinch, she left the room without a word.

He released his elbow and let his torso down heavily, breathing with opened mouth and listening to the torrents of rain batter the glass and drum on the roof. As long as it didn't rain tomorrow, he would direct his laborers to cut the summer hay in the meadow. Haying time in the meadow—always something to look forward to. He dozed, remembering how often he and Gilbert used to walk together in the sweet-smelling meadow after mowing. Thoughts, images, of the meadow had occupied much of his waking hours for the last month, along with memories of his father, part of whose land he wanted Mabel to own.

Meanwhile, as the rain pelted down, Mary Stearns and Mabel settled themselves again in the parlor, fanning their faces slowly with old church fans. Millicent had excused herself and gone upstairs.

"What's the news on Austin?" said Mabel. "Now that he's confined to bed so often, I can't keep in touch, what with Sue guarding the door half the time against Lavinia's visits."

"Sue has sent for Dr. Bigelow—Dr. Cooper is out of town, but I think she had been ready to send for a specialist anyway."

"Well it's about time. Austin should have a specialist in attendance, shouldn't he, David?" said Mabel glancing up at David who had just come back from the attic. "Why has she waited so long?"

"I don't have much faith in medicine," said David. "How long has he been seeing one doctor or another, including that throat specialist in Boston, with no improvement? In my opinion, it's the state of mind which controls the state of the body. Modern medicine goes about things the wrong way. Don't send me to a doctor if I get sick. I'll find my own way."

"But maybe doctors are God's way of helping us..." began Mary Stearns.

"I don't believe in God," said David, picking at a hangnail.

Mary Stearns fingered her cameo pin and looked out the window while Mabel frowned and shook her head at David.

"Austin needs one of those faith healers," David went on.

"Oh dear," began Mrs. Stearns, while Mabel said, "That's the third time you've mentioned this notion, and I don't even dare ask where you got it..."

"Laugh if you want," said David, "but that's my opinion. You yourself insist that Austin's trouble comes mostly from nervous exhaustion. Well, how can a doctor cure that? You said yourself he doesn't have time to rest long enough to start healing. What's left? A faith healer, that's what. And Betty, my—Betty—knows a good one in Boston."

"Let's drop the topic for now," said Mabel, covering her eyes with one hand.

"I can hardly bear it, watching him get worse like this."

"Well, then, why are you so..." began David, but Mabel cut him off.

"Let's drop it, I said!"

While the rain pounded down, Mrs. Stearns and Mabel began to fan themselves again slowly in the greenish light.

CHAPTER 96

July 1895

The rainstorm cleared the air partially and lowered the temperature for a few days. But the interlude was not to last. As Mabel turned her attention each day to chapters for the astronomy textbook she and David were writing together, she found it necessary to roll up her sleeves and carry her work to a the west window in the morning while the sun blasted the meadow on the other side of the house and roasted the stubble into brown stinging needles.

One morning, she began writing a section on the aurora, setting off in her mind the flash and sparks of Emily's lines, "Of bronze—and Blaze—the—North—Tonight—," lines which reverberated in her head all that day and into the evening. Another afternoon, she wrote about comets, and on yet another, Saturn's rings. The celestial objects she explained in her reserved authorial voice took on a lurid, fantastical quality in her mind as she labored in the oppressive earthly heat amid the rising panic of her fears for Austin's health. She could imagine that even while Austin's heart labored to push his blood, Saturn, the gargantuan gas planet, spun in black space with its eerie rings. While Austin swallowed beef broth against his nausea, a black cinder of a comet streaked toward the sun somewhere. The minutes, yes, even the seconds, that comprised Austin's life, took on cosmological significance as massive as gravity, as pervasive as Doppler's law. Although their hearts did not beat side by side, both Austin and Mabel faced a mutual struggle for existence—a struggle to postpone their final physical separation.

For Austin was not improving. The doctor who visited Tuesday provided no diagnosis for the increasing weakness, the labored breathing, and the nausea. That afternoon, Austin managed to write Mabel a note which he sent via Mary to Maggie, who hand-delivered it within the hour at the Dell. He insisted he could recover enough strength to walk out and see her the next day, and enclosed a return envelope for her reply, which he received that very evening via Maggie again.

"I'm going to stay in all day tomorrow," Mabel told David, "so that Austin can come whenever he's able."

The next day, Thursday, another sweltering, hazy day when even the dust seemed to shimmer in the roads and the sparrows drank from the puddles of cleaning water the housewives threw out, Mabel paced the floor as the hours dragged by with no note, no message of any kind from Austin. Unable to eat, she imagined horrors which drove her to tears, and felt a constriction in her chest like none she had ever felt before, along with a sense of helplessness which made her scream aloud until she remembered David's endorsement of faith healers.

With shaking hands, she stooped to lace up her boots more tightly for a walk to David's office. "If I got the name now..." she whispered. "Why didn't I do it before? If I run..." She hastened to scribble a note for Austin and left it on the back door.

Rushing out, she nearly collided with Lavinia who was raising her hand to knock. "Lavinia!" Mabel pulled her in with both hands and kicked the door shut behind her. "What's going on, please tell me. Do you realize I've been pacing the floor since breakfast?"

"He's in my parlor right now waiting for you."

"What?" Sweat trickled down her neck. "What?" She stared at Lavinia, who was mopping her forehead with one sleeve. Then she looked skyward and inhaled deeply. "Thank you, God, thank you. Oh, Lavinia, tell me he's better."

"He claims he is. But oh, I'm so afraid!"

"Let's go to him instantly," said Mabel. "And as soon as I come back, I'm going to send for a specialist my cousin knows in Boston, Dr. Knight. And then maybe another kind of specialist, a faith—oh, never mind, I'll find someone. We must try everything, we musn't stop to analyze and question. We will try everything until we find what works. Come on."

At the Homestead, Mabel rushed from the back door through the front parlor, its curtains and shades drawn against heat and light, to the back parlor, where she found Austin in the wing chair, resting his head to one side, his collar open. Running to him with a gasp, she fell to embrace him, half kneeling, half sitting at his feet while he bent forward to receive her. They stayed thus, holding each other silently, until Austin's cough and a movement from Lavinia behind them in the front parlor separated them.

"I suppose you want to be alone?" Lavinia said. "But I need to spend some time with you too, Austin."

"And we *will* spend some time," said Austin. "But Mabel and I will talk first alone, if you don't mind. You understand..."

For answer, Lavinia closed the parlor doors.

Mabel rested her head on Austin's knees. "My love, my life! I'm dying without you and I'm torn apart because I can't do all the things for you I long to do. *She* gets to take care of you. I want to read to you—she doesn't take the time to do that, does she?"

Austin didn't answer, but stroked her neck. "Does she, then?" Mabel asked, her voice muffled from his knees.

"Only sometimes. What does it matter? Don't torture yourself."

"No, no, I won't. I'm glad she reads to you if you like it. But oh, it does torture me!" She looked up at him. "I'd like to find a specialist for you myself in Boston. If I found one, could you make it seem your idea and send for him?"

"But we have Dr. Bigelow now, and he's excellent." Austin ran his hand gently under her chin and around the back of her neck.

"I must try someone new anyway. David has suggested we try a faith healer."

"A faith healer? Please don't."

"But when the mind and spirit are afflicted, as yours and mine have been for years, the mind and spirit need treating as much as the body. A faith healer can give you mental strength to fight any obstacles to your health. I never thought about it before, but now I see the idea has merit. You wouldn't want to leave any method untried, would you? I can't believe you would be so sceptical as to endanger our lives, because what affects your life affects mine, too."

"Come, let's sit together on the sofa now," said Austin. "Please forget about a faith healer." The movement of standing brought on a rumble in his chest followed by a bout of coughing which left him holding the wing of the chair. On the sofa, Mabel put a pillow behind his head and a footstool under his feet.

She held out her hand. "You see? I'm wearing the ring you gave me. I've worn it all week, every minute."

He smiled. "I'm glad."

"And my notes to you this week," she said. "You destroyed them?"

"Yes."

"I feel so vulnerable..."

"But I want you to have faith now in what we've meant to each other all these years," said Austin, "so that even when I can't get letters to you or your letters can't reach me, we won't lose heart. You'll always know I'm thinking of you and I'll always know you're thinking of me. I never doubt it for a minute. How do you think I survived all those weeks you were in Africa or Europe or Japan?"

"Of course, you're right. Now is the time to keep our resolve. Let's say our special words."

Looking into each other's eyes, they repeated the litany they had devised for difficult times: "For my beloved is mine and I am his. What..."

But Austin broke off to cough, and when he spoke again, he said,"You have taken good care of that deed?"

"Yes, of course."

"Maybe Vin can sign it tomorrow. After church, if she goes."

Mabel was quiet a moment. Then she said, "Tomorrow is Friday, my love, not Sunday. You've been in bed too long."

"But I thought Vinnie said something about putting flowers in the pew just a while ago."

"I don't know what she was talking about, but tomorrow isn't Sunday."

"Well then, I seem to have lost a few days."

He began to cough again, dropping Mabel's hand and bending over his knees. When he was finally quiet, he leaned back and rested against her, breathing rapidly, while she slipped a forefinger over his wrist and felt his racing pulse. "It's always high after I cough," he said. "It will go down."

"Stay still," she said.

Lavinia's voice broke in suddenly and insistently. "I want to come in! I can't sit out here alone anymore. I have rights too. I want to see my brother!"

Mabel squeezed Austin's arm and called, "Come in, then."

Lavinia opened the parlor doors and hastened in, followed by two cats.

"Don't let those cats climb all over Austin," said Mabel. "They'll start him coughing again."

"Oh, don't worry so much. There are plenty of other things to worry about," snapped Lavinia. "Like where is Sue, that she let you come tramping over here in this heat?"

"She thought I was so much better that she went off to do an errand with Mattie. But I still can't stay long—I admit that I tire whenever I get up, and I don't want her to guess I was over here or she'll quarrel with me. I don't have the energy for a quarrel."

"Of course you don't," said Mabel. "I'm going to insist you go back soon so that you'll get better faster. Then we can spend real time together."

Austin smiled at her. "Her cheeks look so healthy and pink, don't they,

Vinnie? It's a pleasure for me to see a beautiful, healthy woman who isn't dressed in nurse whites. I wouldn't be surprised to look out my sick bed window one afternoon and see you, Mabel, riding by on a bicycle to set a new trend. Wouldn't the elderly church ladies sputter over that! But to my eyes— a lovely sight."

"What a sweet thing to say," said Mabel. "But you ought to be realistic, my love. I think I'd shock even you just a bit if I sailed down the Common on a bicycle or pedaled coolly in front of Walker Hall."

"Never," said Austin taking her hand. "I love you for your daring, you know that."

"Unless I take to the streets with the Suffragettes," said Mabel, pulling his ear lobe. "Confess."

But Austin began to cough again. Unable to stop, he gagged into his hand-kerchief until he gained control and leaned forward, concentrating on breathing. Sweat beaded his forehead; his face remained flushed.

"You must go back to your bed as soon as you're up to it," said Mabel, alarmed. "No more talking." She loosened his cuffs and unbuttoned several buttons on his shirt. "It's no wonder you can't breathe in this heat."

"You send me home like this, half buttoned, for Sue to speculate about?" Austin managed to say, smiling.

"You're a dear," said Mabel. "But I'm going now. You visit with your sister a while and then I expect you to tuck yourself back into bed."

"Then I'll plan to see you in a few days. I'll try to have Mary post notes through the mail, but failing that, I'll get something to you through Maggie or Vin. Don't worry if you don't hear from me at first. And say hello to David for me. I miss seeing him. I hope his plans for the eclipse expedition are going well."

"He wants to see you too. I'm sure you can make it over to the house soon. But no going out until this cough is better too and your pulse is down. Why don't we ask Ned to come help you back home?"

Austin shook his head. Looking helplessly at him, Mabel stood up, and Austin struggled up too, although she tried to restrain him. She turned to Lavinia. "Lavinia, I'm going to hold him once more even though I know you Dickinsons don't like to see other people hug." They embraced wordlessly. Mabel was quick enough, upon release, to hide her tear-filled eyes from Austin, but Lavinia saw and quickly stared at the floor.

"Goodbye," Mabel called from the doorway by the hall.

Austin took a breath to call "goodbye" but coughing prevented him, and Mabel did not see his hand lifted to her in a gesture of farewell.

July 1895

News from the Evergreens the rest of July was sporadic. Twice Lavinia came to the back parlor in the late evening, having either seen Austin briefly or having learned news of him through Ned. She brought Mabel three notes in all from Austin written in a shaky hand, with an occasional sentence unfinished.

Each day dawned hot with no promise of change, although the sky turned from hazy to clear blue some afternoons and the roses shook gently in a tentative breeze. Mabel and David turned their energies to work, David out of pressure and the deadlines for his eclipse expedition plans, Mabel out of sheer nervous agitation. They plodded through the chapters of David's astronomy textbook, a pitcher of iced tea between them.

Millicent helped check copy of Emily's poems, a familiar process, but she also spent much of her days with a group of friends from The Convent. Not once in July or August did her mother ask her to run over to the Homestead for news, and although her parents talked more and more about Mr. Dickinson in hushed voices, Millicent thought about him less and less since he did not visit.

In the last week of July, Maggie told Mabel that another nurse had been engaged but that Sue herself was in constant attendance on Austin. Soon after, a short note from Austin arrived on July 27th through the mails. Mabel ran upstairs to her studio and read it with one hand on her beating throat. He talked about how his chief nurse —whom Mabel understood to be Sue— watched him closely to prevent him from writing and kept Mabel's notes from reaching him. Worse, he spoke of being moved to a "new climate" as early as the next week.

When David came home that afternoon, he found Mabel lying in her chemise across the bed on the top floor, a cold cloth on her head. "What are you doing up here?" he said in the doorway, mopping his brow, the shirt sleeves under his arms stained with sweat. "This is the hottest damn place in the house. Don't tell me you're going to take to your bed again like you did at Christmas! Or has there been some change...?"

"They're going to take him away somewhere soon—I don't even know where. As if he's fit to travel! I can't bear it!"

"Well, you have to bear it. Lying up here under the eaves won't help your state of mind anyway." He looked at her. "What have you got there, anyway, stashed under the pillow? Your love letters? I can see them sticking out, you needn't bother to hide them."

"Just leave me alone up here for a while," Mabel said. "I'm thinking."

"Good, think all you want. I'm going to read the paper and eat something. Someone has to have a normal life around here."

On July 30th, Maggie told Lavinia, "They've sent for a heart specialist."

"It's Dr. Knight," said Ned, when he dropped by his aunt's that evening. He'll be here tomorrow."

After Dr. Knight left the next day, Lavinia hastened along the path to hear his report. She knocked loudly three times on the front door, then entered. She found the house in confusion: Mattie stood in the hallway arguing with the nurse about whether it was time for the new medicine; Mary was leaving Austin's bedroom with a pile of dirty linen; while at the same time from the kitchen, Sue was calling Mary and Ned was trying to give Mary a list of items to be purchased from the apothecary.

When Mattie saw Lavinia, she raised her hand. "Don't go in his room, we're changing the linens and bed clothing."

"It's not Lavinia already, is it?" said Sue, coming into the hallway. "Ned? Can you bring her up to date?"

And so Lavinia was out of the house and on the path back home under the evergreen trees without ever seeing Austin. A mere half hour later, Mabel stood in the Homestead kitchen to find out the news.

"It's the heart—the outer walls," said Lavinia. "Something about them being so thin that the blood can't get around. That's why the lungs are so weak— they don't have enough blood. Or air. I can't keep it straight. It's a madhouse over there, everybody running this way and that. I didn't even see Austin."

"They didn't let you see him? You, his own sister?"

"Well, they wanted me out of there as fast as they could get me out. If it weren't for Ned, I don't think anyone would have talked to me.

Mabel groaned. "It's time to try what I should have long ago. Why did I let Austin dissuade me? We shall have a faith healer."

When the train from Amherst to Boston set out ten minutes late that same afternoon, Mabel turned the pages of a book without reading a word until they reached Palmer. Then she let the tears seep slowly from her eyes until the next stop, when the car filled up and a young woman with a child sat across from her. But her nose and eyes remained reddened, and the young woman glanced at her curiously from time to time. When she got off with her child at the third stop, she said, "I hope you feel better," which only made Mabel's tears flow more freely.

Rain had spattered the soiled train windows intermittently, but now it stopped, and from time to time, light seemed to be struggling through the clouds in the west behind the cars. Ahead, the clouds darkened to a bruised hue, and from time to time, Mabel could see brown curtains of rain falling from them. As the train slowed and rounded a sharp curve, shuddering as it went, Mabel saw a vivid sword of golden light cut into the west, and then suddenly, the whole sun itself, free of clouds above the swaying foliage. Ahead, the sky grew even darker in contrast. Squeaking, the train labored out of its curve at last and pointed straight toward the east, carrying Mabel directly into the miraculous and sudden arc of a rainbow over Boston.

Letting her book fall to the floor, Mabel clasped her hands in a gesture of prayer. "See the rainbow?" people were exclaiming.

But Mabel was thanking God for what she believed to be a sign. Austin would not only live, but she would have saved him by her quest for a faith healer. She could devote her life to the good and the infinite, because nothing else mattered if Austin might live and breathe and love her. She would never complain, never cry again, but hold her head high in Amherst.

She prayed again, pressed the wedding ring on her left finger, wiped her eyes, and when the train reached Boston, was the first to descend.

CHAPTER 98

August 1895

∼

Some Amherst villagers were tempted to go out of their way to walk past the Evergreens that next week. It wasn't that they expected to witness tangible proof of the incipient disaster behind the Italianate windows and the arbor on the west piazza—but they expected to see some sign, some indication of the downward spiral. Sometimes they found themselves on the pavement trailing behind visitors to the Dickinson household, those friends who left the pavement to climb the Evergreen steps carrying flowers in their hands, or covered dishes tucked into baskets. If the door opened to these friends while the curious slowed their steps on the pavement, they looked into the hallway as far as they could, straining to see something, something they could not name.

But mostly, there was less activity at the Evergreens rather than more, unless an observer saw the nurses changing shifts, for of course, no clients climbed the steps to confer with Mr. Dickinson, nor did the Dickinson children venture out for the social occasions they used to be so fond of. One or another doctor visited, of course, but only once a day. The figure everyone wanted to see was just the figure they could not see. And so they were forced to conjure up another image of him apart from the one they already knew so well: a new death bed image of his worn and pale face against Sue's embroidered pillow cases. Such an image stood in bleak contrast to the way the villagers wanted to remember him, striding out in his black hat to stroll in the meadow, crossing the Common on a busy Saturday and leaning on his walking stick to chat with those he met there, or planting a tree.

"I can't imagine Amherst without Austin Dickinson," said Mrs. Jameson to her husband, "but then I can't imagine the twentieth century either, and yet I see us being dragged toward it and forced to live in it."

"Well, that's one way of putting it," said her husband, glancing at her curiously for her way of viewing the inevitable turn of the century.

The humidity broke the second week in August. As the haze lifted, Mabel inhaled breaths of hot but clear air redolent of roses. In the evenings, she sat on her porch alone or with Millicent and listened to the crickets, leaning her head back against the wicker chair and thinking of Austin, loving Austin, looking through the trees at the stars, and then letting her eyes range over the meadow where they had walked so many times amid the resonance of bees and grasshoppers.

There had been no news about Austin on the morning of the 15th, and the news the day before from Lavinia, who seemed more and more confused, had been vague and inconclusive. Thus Mabel was grateful for David's invitation from the Academy in New Salem to represent Amherst College for their hundredth anniversary celebration. "Austin's grandfather taught there," she told David. "I'm going to send Austin a note through Maggie and tell him about our invitation."

Because, then, she passed the morning on the way to New Salem, she knew nothing about the way Austin began to struggle for breath. Because she ate luncheon with the teachers of the academy and copied a recipe for lemon cake, she knew nothing about his inability that day to swallow anything but a few sips of water. Because she was walking in the maple grove at New Salem listening to speeches and a band, she knew nothing about the fact that Austin did not receive her note and probably could not have read it if he had.

But he survived the night and thought about her, sensing her presence, even though his thoughts were hazy and shifting. Sometimes he thought he stood in the meadow with Gilbert. Another time, he thought he took his father aside in the parlor next door and began to explain something important. "The land—you'd approve of my plans if you could see the whole situation," he was telling him. Edward Dickinson leaned forward in his chair and listened, stroking his chin with a frown. "Ask Emily," he told his father.

And then the crickets set up their song throughout the night, both in the meadow across the street and in his memory, while his family stared at his impassive face.

Mabel and David Todd, returning from New Salem the next evening, reached the hushed Amherst streets at 7:20 just as Austin struggled for his last breath and exhaled it quietly. A new era had begun.

CHAPTER 99

August 1895

~

AMHERST WAS IN MOURNING. STORES, THE bank, and many offices remained closed for the funeral. A crowd attended the service at the Evergreens conducted by Reverend Jonathan Jenkins of Pittsfield, Austin's friend, whose step was slower than when he had officiated at Emily's funeral nine years before, and whose eyes swam when he gave the final prayer.

Neither Mabel nor David attended the funeral. Mabel lay much of the day in the darkened guest room at the Dell, David huddled in a wicker chair on the back porch, and Millicent tried to read a book in the parlor, wanting to move the kaleidoscope Mr. Dickinson had given her from her line of vision on the table. But at noon, before the funeral at 3 o'clock, Mabel descended the stairs dressed in black and carrying a small bag, her hair neatly done, and went out. Millicent saw her grip David's wrist hard before she opened the door, and when she returned shortly afterwards, she spoke to no one, but climbed the stairs to the top floor and did not come down again until that evening.

After the funeral, Ned escorted his shaky and confused Aunt Lavinia back home. As soon as they were safely inside the kitchen, she asked him the question she had wanted to for several hours: "Did you manage to do what she asked, then? Let her in to see him today, lying there?"

"Yes."

"I didn't think you would. Or could." She took her handkerchief from her sleeve and sank trembling into a chair. "You're a good boy, Neddie. When did you take her in?"

"While you were all at the dinner table. You didn't hear anything, did you? I brought her safely through the porch door to the library. She let herself out, so I don't know how long she stayed, but she had enough time to say goodbye to him alone."

"But did *we*, Neddie, did we?"

Ned did not answer, but stood looking quietly out the window. After a few minutes, he said, "I think I'll walk around the garden a bit."

Lavinia remained at the kitchen table stroking a cat in her lap with her gnarled hand and staring into space. Outside, Ned wandered up and down the dry flower beds in his Aunt Emily's garden trying not to think, not to think about anything at all.

The Daily Own of Love

THE OCTOBER BREEZES WHISTLED THROUGH THE balsam fir and spruce around Mabel Todd's summer home at Hog Island, Maine, and blew pine needles over the front steps while the surf hummed, but neither she nor her husband was there to hear it. Mabel Todd had been laid to rest a week past in Amherst's Wildwood Cemetery, not many yards from where Austin Dickinson and his family lay. Her husband, David Todd, aged seventy-seven, shuffled through the corridors of an institution far away, talking to himself about "vital engineering," his current plan to extend life indefinitely.

By 1932, the suffocating vacuum bell of Austin Dickinson's influence, as Millicent viewed it privately, had lifted enough so that mother and daughter could talk at length about early Amherst days. But it was only Emily Dickinson, their common focus and infatuation, who made that cautious talk possible.

The priceless contents of Mabel's Chinese camphorwood chest—Emily's uncopied letters and poems—had safely passed into Millicent Todd Bingham's steady hands, she who stood ready at last to finish what her mother had begun so long ago in 1887. Nothing would stand in the way anymore of bringing Emily Dickinson's remaining poems and letters to light. Millicent and her mother had agreed on this at last over the past few months, and had begun once again to sort through the pages of strange bold handwriting, each resolved to muffle the unique, respective pains which the manuscripts evoked. But at her winter home in Coconut Grove, Florida, death had overtaken Mabel Todd.

The summer island cabin was losing heat that October afternoon of 1932, but Millicent's husband had already gone outside to bring in more wood for the fire. Indeed, before they returned to Washington, D.C., their permament home, the two of them would stay by the fire mornings and evenings while they sorted the clothes, books, and papers Mabel had left there.

"Time for a break, Walter?" Millicent called as he came inside with logs.

"I should think so, it's nearly 4 o'clock. Any of that date bread left we brought with us from Amherst?"

"Yes, just enough to go with some tea. Let's slow down for a while, I'm tired."

"No wonder. You were tired *before* your mother died. From what you wrote me, you two must have talked more than ever before in those last weeks."

"You know, I think we did. And I'm so thankful. How could we have known those would be our best talks—and our last ones." She touched his hand briefly and arose to heat water for tea.

"It helped some, then, the talking?" he asked. "To heal some wounds?"

"At times I thought I felt worse, but I don't think so now. I feel more at peace. It helped, hearing Mother tell me something, at least, of what she felt about Austin Dickinson and the atmosphere of Amherst. We were able to make some long-deferred decisions. Somehow I knew she would have to return to the poems and letters, despite the trial and what Lavinia Dickinson did to her—at least if she wanted to be at peace with herself and Austin. She *had* to do it, partly for Austin's sake. And in turn, I feel at peace because Mother and I agreed on Emily's work being our top priority."

He watched her while she cut the bread Amherst friends had given them after the funeral. "But can Emily's work still be top priority now for you?" he asked. "How can you struggle with those poems and letters and keep up your own lectures and research as well? Your work in geography means so much to you."

"That's where I've done some thinking over the past few days here on the island. I don't know how many walks I've taken on that dear winding path that goes down by the shore and then past the marsh—I wouldn't try to count them all. And I see something new on each walk too—I must show you that patch of pincushion moss covered with spruce cones tomorrow. But Walter, I've decided I must give up everything else and concentrate on getting Emily's work published. All of it. Including the letters to Judge Lord."

"Those too? Would she want people to read letters to a man she loved?" Millicent arranged the buttered slices of bread on a hand-hewn wooden tray and set out two cups and spoons. "I don't know if she would or if she wouldn't, but it doesn't matter now. That might seem callous, but Emily Dickinson isn't just anyone. Besides, you don't think twice reading Keats's letters to Fanny, do you?"

"No. I see your point."

"And anyway, there's nothing improper in them, what few of them we have. She had a right to care for him and he for her. And Austin and Lavinia knew all about them. It wouldn't be like deciding to publish Mother's and Mr. Dickinson's love letters."

"Will we read *those* someday? Could you bring yourself to it?"

"No. Maybe I can't come to terms with all those years after all. But still, do you know another reason why I feel a strange kind of peace now?"

"Why?"

She attended to the boiling water. "Because I don't have to feel so jealous anymore. Jealous of Mr. Dickinson. In the end, finally, Mother and I had each other and Emily Dickinson. The ghost of Austin stood back at last and let Mother and me touch each other through Emily." She smiled. "I think Emily would like knowing that."

They settled down before the fire. "It seems so dark. Time to light some lamps?" Walter asked.

"Oh, let's wait a bit and just look at the fire."

"You never finished about giving up everything else to edit that mass of material—all those pieces of paper—in that camphorwood chest. It looked full to the brim last time I saw it in Florida. Do know what you're getting into?"

"Of course I do. Remember, Mother spent years transcribing the earlier poems and letters and I used to help, along with Father. I used to wonder how she could stand it, poring over that inscrutable handwriting on all those scraps of paper. Lavinia used to bring over the poems in bushel baskets which she overturned on the floor in front of the fireplace. The back parlor was always overflowing with Emily's old papers and Mother's fair copies—I quit going in there to read my books because there was nowhere to sit safely. But the editing job can be done, Mother proved that. And oh, the poems are so special! They are worth almost any sacrifice. It will be a sacrifice, too. When we return to the city, I'll have to start immediately clearing the way for all this work. There will be plenty of people to see all right, and plenty of loose ends to tie up. But luckily, my lecturing contract is almost up. And some of my geographical articles are so far underway that I can finish them with no problem and satisfy the journals."

"You seem to have given it a lot of thought, haven't you?"

"Death always makes people think a lot."

"Did you think a lot when Austin died way back in ...what year was it?"

"It was August, 1895. I was fifteen, and I'll never forget that awful day. Mother crying, Father crying, Ned running over to the house with a smuggled message about his father's last moments. And of course, Mother wearing mourning in public for the whole town to see. Sue Dickinson and Mattie were furious! Mattie wasn't at all like her brother Ned— when she was angry, she let everyone know it. And I was so embarrassed because Mother's decision to wear mourning clothes was something I couldn't pretend to ignore. I even overheard conversations about it in the stores and post office. But Mother just walked right down the streets in her black dress—when she wasn't at home crying."

"Poor Millicent. Who kept the house together?"

"Pearl worked for us then. She was a valiant girl if ever I saw one, and for a few weeks, she virtually took over the house. Mother used to tell Father she wished she were dead too, along with Austin. How scared I was!"

"Did your mother take comfort at all in religion in those days?"

"Austin was her religion, I think. Only Austin. Oh, in times of emergency she tried to pull out some faith to suit her needs, like the time shortly before his death when she travelled to see a faith healer in Boston, praying for his recovery all the way, and then saw a rainbow soon afterwards. She claimed God had spoken to her."

The wind rattled the windows suddenly, and pine cones hit the roof.

"You know, I just remembered something else about that awful week after Austin died. Something very strange. It unnerved me."

"What was that?"

"Well, the morning right after Austin died, a handsome red bicycle was delivered to the house. I went to the door because Mother was still in her bedroom and Father was on the back porch, I guess. It was a Saturday, and I didn't think to ask who had sent the bike. It wasn't for me—its label had Mother's name on it. When I told her about it, she came walking downstairs, still dressed in her robe, slowly at first, with the oddest expression, and then she was on the run through the hallway and outside. She stared at the bicycle leaning against the porch, and then walked over and began to caress it—the handlebars, the seat, the back wheel. 'It's from him,' she whispered.

"And then she tried clumsily to ride it, her robe trailing in the grass on one side and sticking in the spokes of the wheel on the other. I was so unnerved that I ran behind the house to find Father. Then I left the two of them standing there, staring at the bicycle. I didn't want to have anything to do with it— because I guessed right away that she thought Austin had somehow sent her the bike. Why she thought he would have sent her a bike, I don't know. I'm sure now that her friend George Washington Cable must have sent it anonymously, because he had been pedaling to Amherst often that summer from Northampton to collect material from Mother for the periodical he was editing. He was like that—he loved surprises, and he admired Mother very much. But I never got a chance to ask him about the bicycle."

"Did she keep the bike?" Walter stood to poke the fire.

"Did she keep the bike?" Millicent laughed. "And how! She struggled to ride that wretched thing for days until she learned. I can still see her, wobbling about the paths, and later the streets nearby. Come to think of it, I assume the bike is still at the Coconut Grove house. Probably all rusted by now in the salt air. We'll have to look when we next go down to Florida. Had enough tea?"

"Yes. Shall we do a little more sorting of your mother's things before supper?"

"Yes, let's. You're sweet, my love. What would I do without you to listen to my tales about the past? You help ease the pain of it all. I still feel compelled to write myself notes about Mother and Austin and Amherst and Dickinsons. But it's different when I talk to you—I come up with new perspectives."

"You will tell me more later and you'll feel even better. Never forget, whatever you endured because of your mother's love for Austin has been compensated for a hundred times over by the chance to uncover the rest of *her* work—Emily's. Nothing can touch that, can it?"

"No, nothing can ever touch that. Or the fact that if it hadn't been for Mother, the poems and letters would never have been published." Millicent stood up and turned to the pile of clothes behind her. "What will I do with all of these? I can't bear to give them away and I can't bear to keep them."

"Why don't you save these dresses with her hand-painted panels and cuffs for the Amherst Historical Society. After all, she helped start the Society." He picked up one summer dress. "Here, look at this one. I never saw flowers like these on a dress. And you say she painted these herself?"

"Oh, yes. I think Mama painted flowers on anything and everything! But I'm surprised she brought this dress up here on the island. She didn't wear it anymore of course; it's quite out of fashion. Millicent held the dress high. "She's wearing this in one of the photographs in our album."

"I wonder if anyone saved Emily's clothes. Do you remember much about them?"

"No, except for a brown silk net she wore to keep her hair in place. I was fascinated by the silk tassels which hung from each side, and used to try for the same effect at home with pieces of ribbon or string from Mother's sewing box. I only saw Emily briefly when I went to play around the Homestead and glimpsed her from one of the windows. She always waved to any children she saw, but the older children had known her better than I. I came on the scene too late, when she was getting old and her friends and relatives were dying all around her. And she herself died when I was only about six."

"But Lavinia liked to have you around?"

Millicent chuckled. "Not especially, I don't think, and I didn't especially like to be around, as far as that goes. I *did* like to collect handouts when I was little, though, and sometimes Mother asked me to fetch and carry things for her in addition to all the messages I carried. But if Lavinia gave me an apple, I had to be careful how I ate it— she couldn't stand certain sounds, especially chewing or crunching sounds. I used to eat my apple behind a door."

Walter whistled between his teeth. "Good heavens."

"And you couldn't rustle your newspaper while you read it. That's what Mama told me. And yet Lavinia didn't mind Austin and Mother meeting there to be together. Neither did Emily. But then they went upstairs and ignored everything while Mother and Austin were visiting. Much later, I wondered how they really felt, because I hated it when Mother shut herself up with him upstairs. It was unspeakable, I can hardly talk about it, even now." Her voice had begun to rise, and she picked up a dress and tossed it roughly down on the pile again.

"I don't want you to be upset again, Millie, the way you used to be sometimes before you visited your mother."

Millicent had begun to pace about the room in her gentle way, always pausing to look out over the screened porch and Muscongus Bay. "Oh, it's just that I hear myself claiming that everything turned out for the best, but something deep inside me isn't convinced. If I look at the present logically, things did turn out for the best. But why don't I *feel* as though they did? Why? Oh, is it too late for another walk? I can't sit still."

"Come here, come here." She crossed to him over the pile of boxes and clothes, and he pulled her down onto the arm of his chair. "Here's what we'll do: We'll either decide to close the subject of the past for now, in which case, I'll tell you about my latest research— after all, psychology always distracts you pretty well. Or, we'll agree on a time limit for you to tell me what most bothers you about those old days. And when the time limit is up, we'll absolutely stop talking about Amherst. What do you say?"

"I'll take the second choice. I like your idea of a time limit. Can you bear it?"

"I can bear it, let it fly. What will the time limit be? When the porch thermometer drops a degree?"

"I'll be even more specific. In fifteen minutes. Are you wearing your watch?"

He took it from his pocket and laid it on the side table. "There you are. We'll stop at three minutes after 5. Go."

She smiled, tucking in wisps of hair. Then she moved to the other armchair and stared at the fire. "There's an image that symbolizes it all, in a way. An image that haunts me. It's the two sets of rings Mama owned as long as I can remember, and often wore together, a wedding and diamond engagement ring on each hand. And that's not the worst. Papa's ring was on the right hand. Austin's was on the left. The left hand, Walter, can you imagine?" She bent over, as though her stomach ached. "Oh, it hurts me, it pains me so."

"Why is that image almost the worst for you?"

"I don't know, I don't know," she wailed softly, rocking back and forth. Then she sat up and thought, clear-eyed, for a minute. "I think it's because I felt—how was it—alone? No, it was more. I felt...disinherited. As though what brought me into the world, the union between my parents, held little significance for anyone. Especially her. Mother. Yes, that's it. I felt disinherited. Second place. A stepchild to my own parents."

"And having Austin around so much didn't dispel that feeling!" said Walter.

"Austin! Much as I tried to ignore him, he was in a way the terrible center of our universe. I never passed his house without crossing the street first and looking the other way. I never willingly stayed in a room where he was, I never willingly spoke his name to anyone, and yet he was always there, the crux of the scheme of things. I can see him now, sitting by the fire with Mother in our house when I came home after school. Any fire he sat by became *his* fire, by the way. No one was allowed to tinker with the logs or kindling. This was just taken for granted."

"But he was never unpleasant to you, was he?"

"No, because he hardly ever spoke to me or acknowledged my presence."

"Are you sure? Remember, you were just a child."

"But that's how I remember it. And that's what galls me now, that they didn't think I noticed anything. But I noticed everything. Every single thing. How when they had to take me on carriage rides, sitting between them, they leaned behind me and whispered. How Mama called him "My King" when she thought I couldn't hear. How I always found myself facing locked doors. Especially the locked door upstairs where they stayed together by the hour. How could they do it, how could they?"

"They loved each other. I don't think they could do anything else, judging from what you've told me."

"But it wasn't fair, it wasn't fair! They tore me to pieces with it."

"Your mother put you in the intolerable position of loving her, yet hating her. And of disapproving of them yet wanting to defend and protect them. Am I right, that you wanted to defend them too?"

She was crying now. "Yes, I wanted to protect my mother from outsiders. I even wanted to protect Austin, even somber, solemn, scary, terrible Austin Dickinson. But not my father. No, not him, because he let it all happen. He clapped Austin on the shoulders, shook his hand at the depot, and shared Mother with him. I used to hear him whistling on his way home from the observatory as his hint to the two of them that it was time to break it up. For years I thought I would never want to marry."

"But your mother stayed with your father and supported him, didn't she? She learned to survive without Austin?"

"At first, I wasn't sure if she would. Eventually she did, yes, but she was never the same after he died. Never. Her inner light was gone."

"The clock is ticking away. Do I get a few words now?"

"Yes, please."

"You may as well stop trying to understand it completely, because you never will. And I'm sure you don't want to carry heavy grudges for the rest of your life."

"No, never."

"Well, there's a bright side to the whole affair, besides your coming to work with Emily's poetry. And that bright side is love. Whatever you yourself thought of Austin, your mother loved him, so much that she was willing to risk her reputation and even her happiness for him. Because while of course he made her happy in many ways, they made each other miserable in others. They could never have things just as they wanted them. And yet, your mother clearly loved your father too. You showed me the letters they wrote, remember? And you are witness to the fact that they rarely quarreled, given the pressures on them, and that they supported each other grandly in their work. Think of all the writing she did for him, all the support she gave him on those astronomy expeditions abroad! So though your father may have let her love Austin, as you say, what real choice did he have? The best he could do was love her in his own way and stick by her, too. Most husbands would have walked out. But he didn't want to, nor did she really want him to. Could that be the way it was? So you did suffer and your mother made mistakes. But she loved you and you survived. Here you are, overall mentally healthy and strong, productive, and loving. I'm the lucky beneficiary of that. And that's my view of the bright side. Come on, let's get some air on the porch and look at the bay. Did I cut too much into your time?"

Millicent tossed a heavy shawl around her and they walked together toward the porch door and the sound of the ocean. "Not at all. In fact, guess what? I'm finished. And before my time limit, too."

"But honestly now. Do you feel better?"

"Yes, I'm all right. I can't guarantee I won't have other upsets, especially when we visit Father in the Home, but I'm all right. Love is a strange beast, isn't it?"

"Nothing else but."

They stood on the wooden porch looking over the trees toward the bay and watching the last small boats scuttling in to shore, their lights twinkling in the dusk. Gulls and terns cried overhead.

"The island is full of birds this year. How smart Mother was to buy the island and save it from the loggers and hunters. Our Hog Island may be only two miles long, but it's a safe little haven for us and for wild things. That makes me happy. Sometimes I wonder though, what will become of the island after you and I aren't around to protect it as Mother did. After all, we have no children to pass it on to. I doubt we'll be able to spend much time here anyway."

"There are still plenty of options."

"I just had an idea, something to think about, anyway. Why don't we consider giving the island to the National Audubon Society one of these days? That way, it'll be safe, and we'll be continuing the work Mother began in the Everglades with the Audubon Society."

"Your mother would love that idea. And she would love you for thinking of it."

They slipped their arms around each other's waists and watched the bay begin to turn dark while birds streamed on to the island to roost.

List of Works Consulted

Allen, Mary Adele. *Around a Village Green: Sketches of Life in Amherst,* Northampton, Mass., 1939.

Bianchi, Martha Dickinson. *The Cathedral and Other Poems.* Charles Scribner and Sons, 1901.

Bianchi, Martha Dickinson. *Emily Dickinson Face to Face: Unpublished Letters with Notes and Reminiscences.* Boston and New York, Houghton Mifflin, 1932. Reprinted, Hamden, Conn., Archon Books, 1970.

Bingham, Millicent Todd. *Ancestors' Brocades: The Literary Debut of Emily Dickinson.* New York and London: Harper Brothers, 1945.

Bingham, Millicent Todd. *Emily Dickinson's Home: Letters of Edward Dickinson and His Family.* New York, Harper, 1955.

Bingham, Millicent Todd. *Mabel Loomis Todd: Her Contributions to the Town of Amherst.* New York, George Grody Press, 1935.

Brown, Arnold, R. *Lizzie Borden: the Legend, the Truth, the Final Chapter.* Nashville, Rutledge Hill Press, 1991.

Burgess, John William. *Reminiscences of an American Scholar.* Columbia University, New York, 1934.

Cable, Mary. *The Blizzard of '88.* New York, Atheneum, 1988.

Cody, John. *After Great Pain: The Inner Life of Emily Dickinson.* Cambridge, Mass. The Belknap Press of Harvard University Press, 1971.

Dedmon, Emmet. *Fabulous Chicago: A Great City's History and People.* Atheneum, New York, 1981.

Dickinson, Emily. *The Letters of Emily Dickinson.* Ed. Thomas Johnson. 3 vols. Cambridge, Mass., Harvard University Press, 1951, 1955.

Dickinson, Emily. *The Poems of Emily Dickinson.* Ed. Thomas Johnson. Little, Brown, & Co., Boston and Toronto, 1960.

Dickinson, Susan Gilbert. "Annals of the Evergreens," published as "Magnetic Visitors," *Amherst College Alumni Magazine,* Vol. 33, no. 4 (Spring, 1981).

Edelstein, Tilden S. *Strange Enthusiasm: A Life of Thomas Wentworth Higginson.* New Haven and London, Yale University Press, 1968.

Emily Dickinson: Letter to the World. On the Occasion of the Emily Dickinson Centenary Conference and Exhibition. The Folger Shakespeare Library, 1986.

Farr, Judith. *The Passion of Emily Dickinson.* Harvard University Press, Cambridge, Massachusetts, London, England, 1992.

Franklin, Ralph W., ed. *The Manuscript Books of Emily Dickinson.* 2 vols. Cambridge, Mass, The Belknap Press of Harvard University Press, 1981.

Franklin, Ralph W. *The Editing of Emily Dickisnon: A Reconsideration.* Madison, University of Wisconsin Press, 1967.

Hammond, William Gardner. *Remembrance of Amherst: An Undergraduate's Diary, 1846-1848.* Ed. George Frisbie Whicher. New York, Columbia University Press.

Hampshire County, *Records of the Superior Court and of the Supreme Judicial Court of the Commonwealth of Massachusetts,* Hampshire County Court House, Northampton, Mass., 1896-98.

Jenkins, MacGregor. *Emily Dickinson, Friend and Neighbor.* Bobbs-Merrill Co., Indianapolis, 1930.

King, Stanley. *The Consecrated Eminence: The Story of the Campus and Buildings of Amherst College,* Amherst College Press, 1971.

LeDuc, Thomas. *Piety and Intellect at Amherst College 1865-1912.* Arno Press and the *New York Times,* 1969.

Leyda, Jay. *The Years and Hours of Emily Dickinson.* 2 vols. New Haven, Yale University Press, 1960.

Longstreet, Stephen. *Chicago: An Intimate Portrait of People, Pleasures, and Power: 1860-1919.* David McKay Co., Inc., New York, 1973.

Longsworth, Polly. *Austin and Mabel: The Amherst Affair and Love Letters of Austin Dickinson and Mabel Loomis Todd.* Farrar, Straus, Giroux, New York, 1984.

Longsworth, Polly. *The World of Emily Dickinson.* W.W. Norton and Co., 1990.

Lombardo, Daniel. *Tales of Amherst: A Look Back.* The Jones Library, Inc. Amherst, Mass., 1986.

Loomis, Eben Jenks. *An Eclipse Party in Africa.* Boston, Roberts Brothers, 1896.

Patton, Phil. "The Great Chicago Fair, a Wonder of Wonders." *Smithsonian,* Vol. 24, no. 3 (June 1993) 38-51.

Pollack, Vivian, ed. *A Poet's Parents: The Courtship Letters of Emily Norcross and Edward Dickinson*. The University of North Carolina Press, Chapel Hill and London, 1988.

Reunion of the Dickinson Family at Amherst, Massachusetts, August 8th and 9th, 1883. Binghamton New York, Binghamton Press, 1884.

St. Armand, Barton Levi. *Emily Dickinson and Her Culture: The Soul's Society*. London, Cambridge University Press, 1984.

Sewall, Richard B. "In Search of Emily Dickinson." *Extraordinary Lives*. Ed. William Zinsser. American Heritage, New York, 1985.

Sewall, Richard B. *The Life of Emily Dickinson*. 2 vols. New York, Farrar, Strauss and Giroux, 1974.

Sewall, Richard B. *The Lyman Letters: New Light on Emily Dickinson and Her Family*. Amherst, Mass., University of Massachusetts Press, 1965.

Smith, Martha Nell. *Rowing in Eden: Rereading Emily Dickinson*. University of Texas Press, Austin, 1992.

Stearns, Alfred E. *An Amherst Boyhood*. Amherst, Mass., Amherst College Press, 1946.

Todd, David Peck. *A New Astronomy*. New York, American Book Co., 1897.

Todd, Mabel Loomis. "An Ascent of Fuji the Peerless," *Century*, (August, 1891).

Todd, Mabel Loomis. "The Eclipse Expedition to Japan." *The Nation* (September 1, 1887).

Todd, Millicent. *Mary H. Stearns*. Riverside Press, Cambridge, Mass., 1909.

Tyler, William S., *History of Amherst College During its First Half Century, 1821-1871*. Springfield, Mass., 1873. A new edition extending the history appeared in 1895, published in New York.

Walsh, John Evangelist. *The Hidden Life of Emily Dickinson*. New York, Simon and Schuster, 1971.

Walsh, John Evangelist. *This Brief Tragedy: Unravelling the Todd-Dickinson Affair*. Grove Weidenfeld, New York, 1991.

Warner, Charles Forbes. *Representative Families of Northampton*. Northampton, Picturesque Publishing Co., 1917.

Wolff, Cynthia Griffin. *Emily Dickinson*. Alfred A. Knopf, New York, 1986.

250 Years at First Church in Amherst: 1739-1989. The First Congregational Church in Amherst, Amherst, Massachusetts, 1990.